Jim Henson's
FRAGGLE ROCK™
OMNIBUS

Published by
ARCHAIA™

J-GN
FRAGGLE ROCK
463-6398

Designer **Scott Newman**
Original Series Editors **Tim Beedle, Joe LeFavi, Paul Morrissey**
Collection Editors **Sierra Hahn** & **Cameron Chittock**

Special thanks to **Brian Henson, Lisa Henson, Jim Formanek,
Nicole Goldman, Maryanne Pittman, Carla DellaVedova,
Justin Hilden, Karen Falk, Stephen Christy**, and the entire
Jim Henson Company team

Ross Richie CEO & Founder
Matt Gagnon Editor-in-Chief
Filip Sablik President of Publishing & Marketing
Stephen Christy President of Development
Lance Kreiter VP of Licensing & Merchandising
Phil Barbaro VP of Finance
Arune Singh VP of Marketing
Bryce Carlson Managing Editor
Mel Caylo Marketing Manager
Scott Newman Production Design Manager
Kate Henning Operations Manager
Sierra Hahn Senior Editor
Dafna Pleban Editor, Talent Development
Shannon Watters Editor
Eric Harburn Editor
Whitney Leopard Editor
Cameron Chittock Editor
Chris Rosa Associate Editor
Matthew Levine Associate Editor
Sophie Philips-Roberts Assistant Editor
Amanda LaFranco Executive Assistant
Katalina Holland Editorial Administrative Assistant
Jillian Crab Production Designer
Michelle Ankley Production Designer
Kara Leopard Production Designer
Marie Krupina Production Designer
Grace Park Production Design Assistant
Chelsea Roberts Production Design Assistant
Elizabeth Loughridge Accounting Coordinator
Stephanie Hocutt Social Media Coordinator
José Meza Event Coordinator
Holly Aitchison Operations Coordinator
Megan Christopher Operations Assistant
Rodrigo Hernandez Mailroom Assistant
Morgan Perry Direct Market Representative
Cat O'Grady Marketing Assistant
Liz Almendarez Accounting Administrative Assistant
Cornelia Tzana Administrative Assistant

ARCHAIA™

Jim Henson
THE JIM HENSON COMPANY™

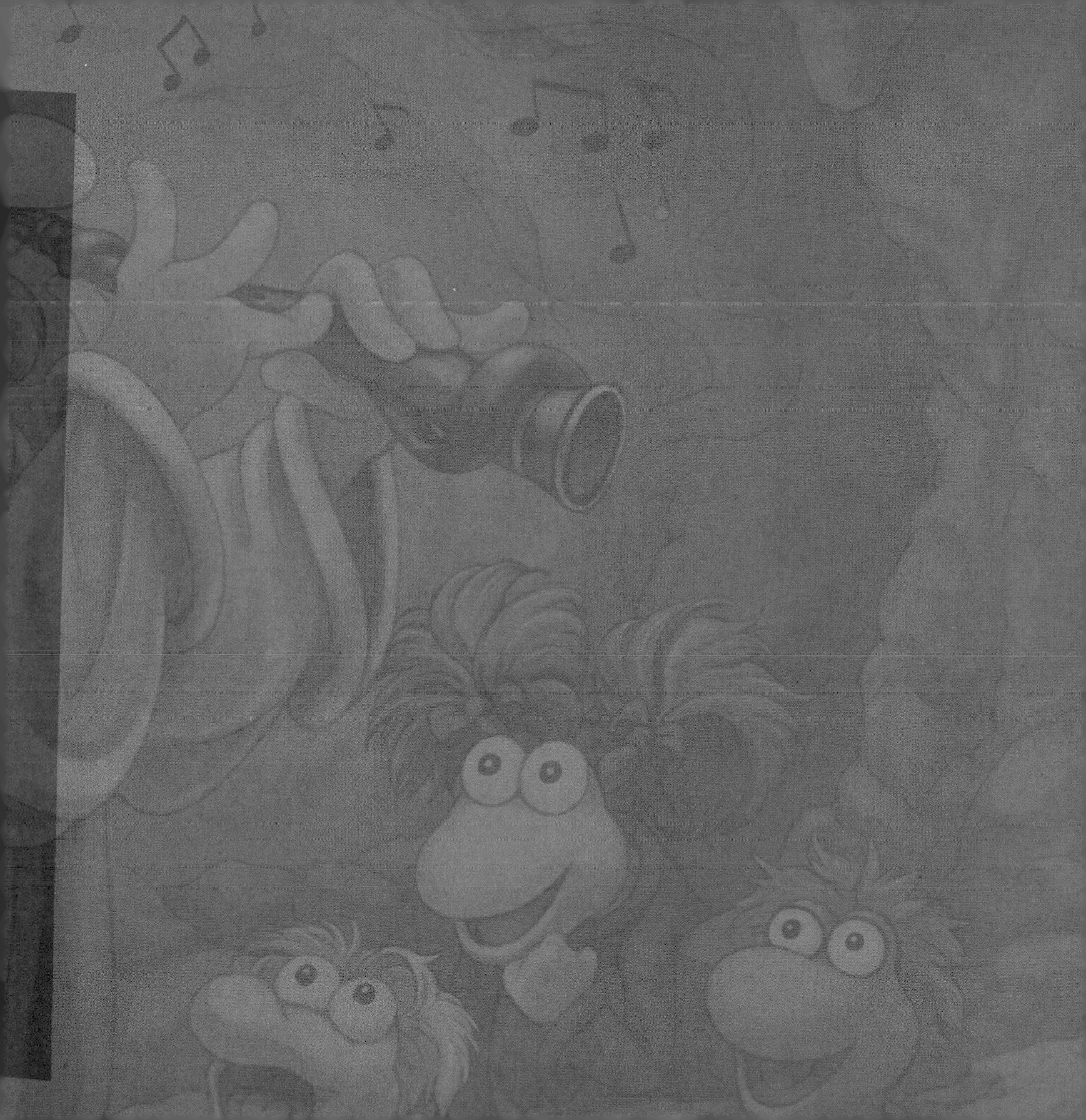

TABLE OF CONTENTS

WHERE HAVE ALL
THE DOOZERS GONE?
Story by **Adrianne Ambrose**
Art by **Joanna Estep**

BOOBER THE DOOZER
Story by **Nichol Ashworth**
Art by **Jake Myler**

TO CATCH A FWAGGLE
Story by **Bryce P. Coleman**
Art by **Michael DiMotta**

WEMBLEY AND THE
GREAT DREAM-CAPADE
Story by **Grace Randolph**
Art by **Caravan Studio**
Pencils and Inks by **Chris Lie**
Colors by **Hendry Iwanaga**
and **Fandy Soegiarto**

THE FRAGGLE
WHO CRIED MONSTER
Story by **Jason M. Burns**
Art by **Chandra Free**

SHOPPING WITH
SILLY CREATURES
Story by **Katie Strickland**
Art by **Lindsay Cibos**

MY GIFT IS MY SONG
Story and Art by **Katie Cook**
Colors by **Joanna Estep**

BRAVE SIR WEMBLEY
Story by **Joe LeFavi**
Art by **Cory Godbey**

RED'S CHOMP-A-THON
Story by **Paul Morrissey**
Art by **Nichol Ashworth**

THE MEANING OF LIFE
Story by **Joe LeFavi**
Art by **Heidi Arnhold**

BOOBER AND
THE GHASTLY STAIN
Story by **Jake T. Forbes**
Art by **Mark Simmons**

THE PERFECT WORDS
Story by **Tim Beedle**
Art by **Ross Campbell**
Colors by **Lizzy John**

FRAGGLE ROCK ACTIVITY PAGES
By **Katie Cook**

Letters by **Deron Bennett**, **Dave Lanphear**

Cover by **Jeff Stokely**
with colors by **Lizzy John**

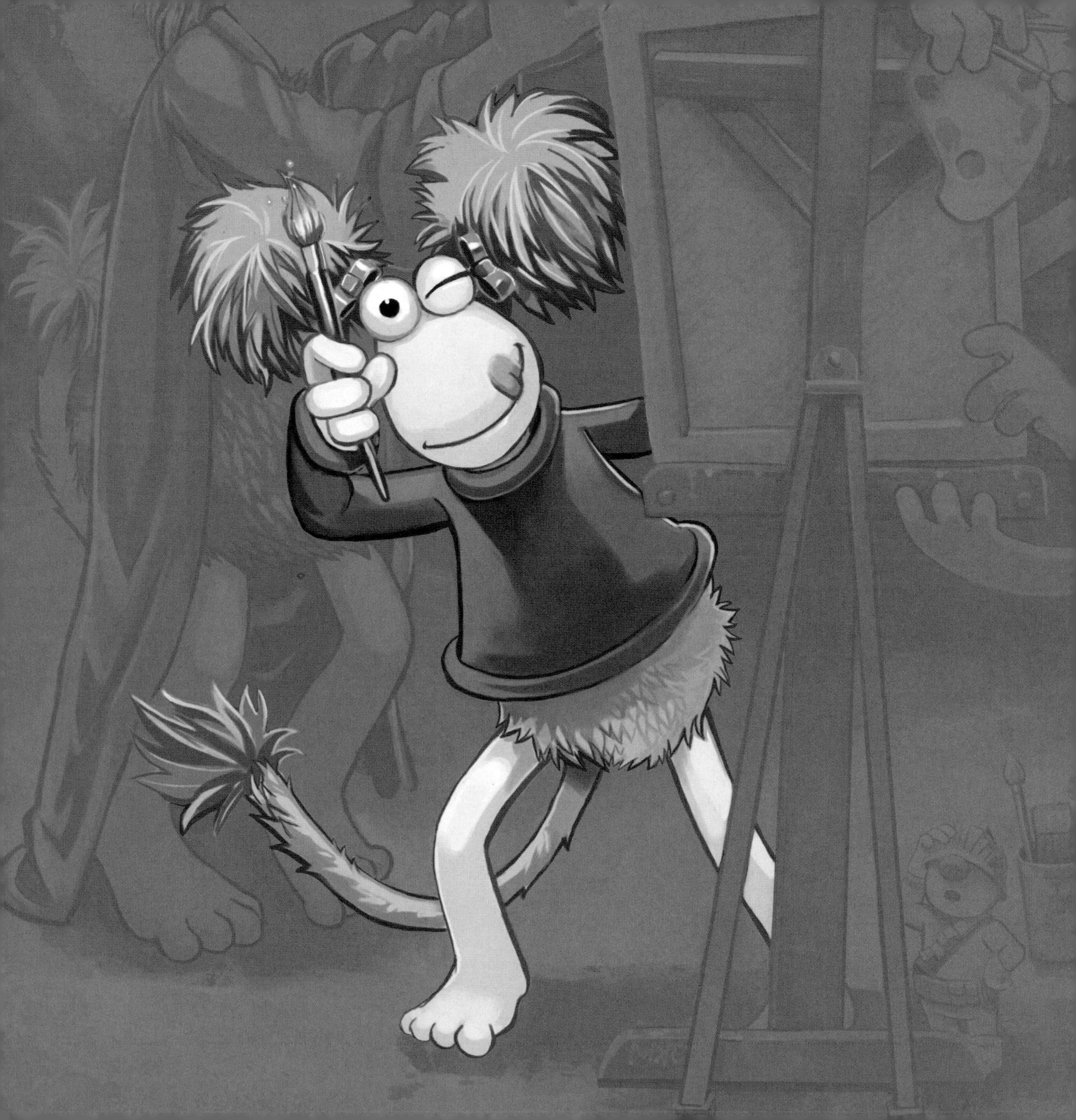

FOREWORD

Hey Silly Creatures and Fraggle fans,

I am honored to write this introduction for the first *Fraggle Rock* graphic novel. I, and it seems everyone who had the precious opportunity to work with Jim Henson on the original *Fraggle Rock* television series, continue to be awed by the show's power to inspire. And curiously, at the same time, I haven't been particularly surprised by this either, in a "Well, of course, what else would you expect?" Marjory-the-All-Knowing-Trash-Heap, stating-the-obvious kind of way.

The ongoing enthusiasm about *Fraggle Rock* is, at its essence, a continuation of the deep, positive force we all felt working on the show. We didn't create that force. It was—and is—a collection of ideals about healthy, responsible, joyful humanity that have been around as long as humans (known to the Fraggles as Silly Creatures) have been around: Explore. Dance. Sing. Laugh. Question. Care. Find strength. Give hope. Take personal responsibility. Dare to truly feel. Appreciate. Share. Use common sense. Empathize. Look past your differences with others and embrace your literal and figurative connections. Don't take yourself so seriously. Think. Love. Have fun. Those ideals—along with the understanding that they can be surprisingly difficult to achieve—resonated with everyone who worked on *Fraggle Rock*. We simply used the series as a way to wrap those timeless ideals in a new joy that resonated with a new generation.

Many people who were not much bigger than Fraggles when the show first aired are now at an age when they can pass those joyfully wrapped ideals on to their children or anyone else who will find them entertaining and thought-provoking. As an artist and writer as well as a puppeteer, I can appreciate the challenge of gathering up the boisterous energy of the Fraggles and getting them to hold still and lie down flat so that their stories can be passed on in comic book form. A big, thankful "Whoopee!!!" is in order for the artists, writers and the team at Archaia and The Jim Henson Company for their hard work creating these new Fraggle stories. And of course, even bigger thanks are due to Jim Henson, Jerry Juhl, Jocelyn Stevenson, Michael Frith and Duncan Kenworthy, who originally envisioned the world of the Fraggles, and the artists, cast and crew who brought their first stories to life.

I'm writing these thoughts just a short time after the twenty-year anniversary of Jim Henson's passing and the memorial that took place a few days later at the Cathedral of St. John the Devine in New York City. At Jim's request, there was music, color and laughter. At emotional moments in the ceremony, the cavernous hall spontaneously filled with a sea of fluttering rod puppet butterflies that had been given to attendees. Puppeteers, writers, producers, directors, musicians, puppet builders and designers from *Fraggle Rock*, which had finished production just four years earlier, were there. Jocelyn Stevenson, who was one of the show's head writers, talked about each of us who had worked with Jim as being "Jim seeds," to take what we gained from that experience and pass it on, each in our own way. I feel that those who are inspired by *Fraggle Rock* are also "Jim seeds." Whether you grew up with the show or are discovering it for the first time, whether you are a comic book creator or a comic book enthusiast, if the ideals so joyfully presented by the stories, music and characters of *Fraggle Rock* resonate with you, take that seed and, as the Fraggles sang, "Pass It On."

Thank you, Fraggle fans. You rock!

And now, since this introduction has almost certainly violated the Fraggle ideal of not taking oneself so seriously, I will have to remedy that in a most Fragglish way by signing off and balancing a pickle on my nose.

Karen Prell
Puppeteer of Red Fraggle
May 2010

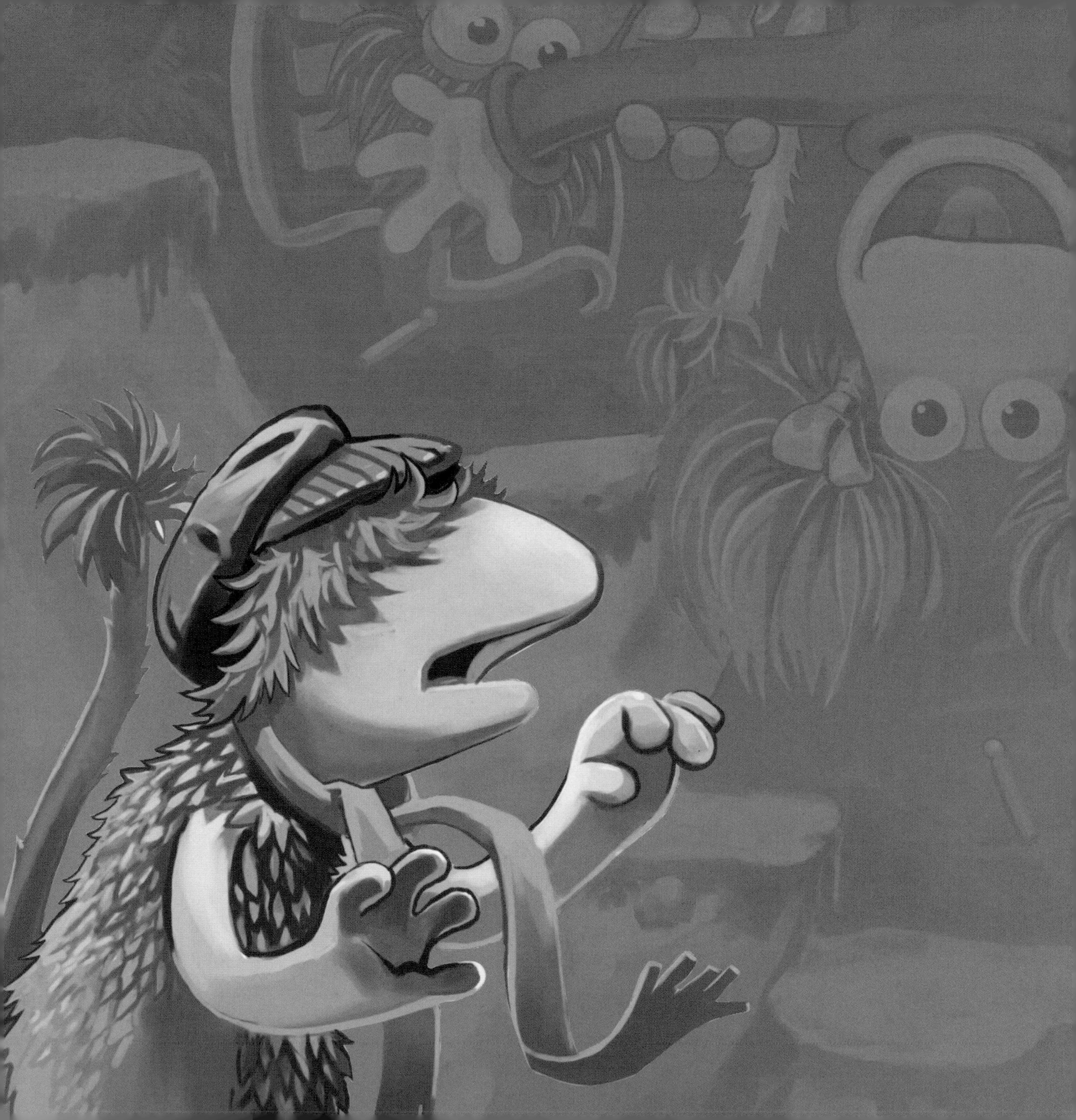

INTRODUCTION

"I'd like to do a show that stops war."

It was a weekend in 1981; Jim Henson, in the midst of shooting *The Dark Crystal*, had called a group of his creative team together to discuss an idea for a new television series aimed at 7 to 12 year-olds. Of course, Jim was not so naive as to think a television series could really stop war. But he thought we should try. We would do a television series that was great fun, but beneath all the singing, parties and adventures would be the theme of harmony. The stories would revolve around conflicts between characters, species and the environment. The Fraggles would find ways to resolve these conflicts, all the while having the time of their lives. They would be forces for good.

When I was about 10, our family went camping and I made friends with the other kids in the campground. We went exploring and discovered a "cave" made from giant boulders that had fallen against each other, leaving irregular spaces in between. We slithered through the crevices "deep underground"… okay, maybe it was only a few feet, but the wonder of our "cave" adventure has never left me. Fraggle Rock is a vast series of magical underground caverns. A backdrop for endless adventures of the body, mind and heart.

We performed the Fraggles as ageless; each is a mixture of child and adult. I think we carry our history within us, like rings in a tree. The most hard-boiled executive has a child buried deep within, and the most innocent child has flickers of great wisdom. That's what our work is about: we're miners in the cavern of the heart. We try to unearth the child within the adult and the adult within the child.

Those of us who worked on *Fraggle Rock* consider it one of our favorite projects. It changed our lives; in my case it led to having children. When they started school, I noticed that raising children brought out the best in the parents. We tried to show our kids how to respect others and our environment. We became our best selves.

It was my great good fortune to work with Jim Henson for 17 years. Under his playful, gentle guidance, everyone grew. He respected all opinions and encouraged everyone in the room to contribute ideas—then he used what he felt would work best. Our producer, Larry Mirkin, expressed this most elegantly: he said, "We are all working in service of the best idea." It was creative utopia.

I am thrilled that The Jim Henson Company remains the custodian of *Fraggle Rock*, for the Henson family understands what *Fraggle Rock* means. In the pages of this book you will find even more Fraggle adventures to share with your children. So put in a load of laundry, curl up with your child, grab some Doozer sticks, and enjoy the magical world of *Fraggle Rock*. Maybe war won't disappear, but learning about harmony will only make the world better.

Dave Goelz
Puppeteer of Boober, Travelling Matt, Philo,
The World's Oldest Fraggle & Large Marvin

THE RESIDENTS OF FRAGGLE ROCK

GOBO

Gobo is the natural leader of the Fraggle Five. He is an explorer, spending his days charting the unexplored (and explored-but-forgotten) regions of Fraggle Rock. He is highly respected by other Fraggles, although they occasionally find him a little pompous. He is also somewhat egocentric, which can make it hard for him to admit mistakes. As a leader, Gobo often provides his friends with direction, although, since he's a Fraggle, it's sometimes a fairly silly one.

RED

Red Fraggle is a nonstop whirligig of activity. To her fellow Fraggles, Red is often seen as a flash of crimson racing to her next athletic pursuit. She is Fraggle Rock champion in Tug-of-War, Diving while Singing Backwards, the Blindfolded One-Legged Radish Relay, and a number of other traditional Fraggle sports. She is outgoing, enthusiastic, and athletic, but take note--her impetuosity can get her into real trouble.

BOOBER

According to Boober Fraggle, there are only two things certain in this world: death and laundry. Boober is terrified by the former and fascinated by the latter. He is also paranoid and superstitious. According to Boober, anything that can go wrong surely will, and when it does, it will inevitably happen to him. But Boober's negative attitude has a big plus--he can see real trouble coming a mile away, a useful attribute in a land of eternal optimists!

WEMBLEY

Wembley is indecision personified. He only owns two shirts, and both have a banana-tree motif. If he had any other clothes, he'd never be able to get dressed in the morning! Wembley has an uncanny ability to find merit on both sides of any issue. He is steadfast in his admiration for his best friend and roommate, Gobo. It was Gobo who encouraged Wembley to apply for his job with the Fraggle Rock Volunteer Fire Department. Wembley is the siren.

MOKEY

Mokey is an artist, poet and philosopher. She seems to be in touch with some sort of higher Fraggle consciousness. Mokey is fascinated by the beauty and intricacy of the world around her, and is always seeking new ways to share this feeling with others. Mokey may have her head in the clouds, but she's also very courageous and resourceful. Her job is to brave the Gorg garden to gather the radishes the Fraggles eat.

UNCLE TRAVELLING MATT

Gobo's Uncle Travelling Matt is the greatest living Fraggle explorer--the Fraggle equivalent of an astronaut. After completing his exploration of Fraggle Rock, he ventured forth into our world, a place the Fraggles call "Outer Space." He sends his observations back to Gobo on postcards in care of Doc.

DOC & SPROCKET

Doc, the man who inhabits the workshop that contains the hole that leads to Fraggle Rock, is an inventor and a tinkerer. If it's a wee bit odd, Doc has probably already invented it. Doc doesn't know about Fraggles. Sprocket is Doc's extremely intelligent and expressive dog. Sprocket knows that the Fraggles exist. He's seen them lots of times...but he just doesn't have the words to tell Doc about them. This drives Sprocket crazy!

MARJORY THE TRASH HEAP

A matronly, sentient pile of compost who acts as an oracle for the Fraggles. She sees all and knows all, but at times her offerings of wisdom go awry in the hands of the Fraggles. Nevertheless, Marjory's advice is usually beneficial. She likes to encourage the Fraggles not just to find temporary solutions to their problems, but to become more self-reliant and work to live in harmony with the other species around them.

JUNIOR GORG

Sweet, loveable, galumphing Junior is the apple of his mother's eye and the bane of the Fraggles' existence! All he wants to do is "get those Fwaggles." The Fraggles raid the Gorg garden for radishes, and the garden is Junior's pride and joy. But the Fraggles are never really in any danger. Junior isn't very bright or coordinated, and really wouldn't hurt a fly.

THE DOOZERS

Totally unlike the Fraggles, Doozers spend their lives working. The greatest joy in a Doozer's life is to get up, put on a hard hat and take a place on the Doozer work crew. Doozers mine radishes from the Gorg garden and make Doozer sticks with them, with which they build elaborate crystalline Doozer constructions throughout Fraggle Rock--which the Fraggles then eat with relish. This pleases the Doozers immensely, since it allows them more room to build.

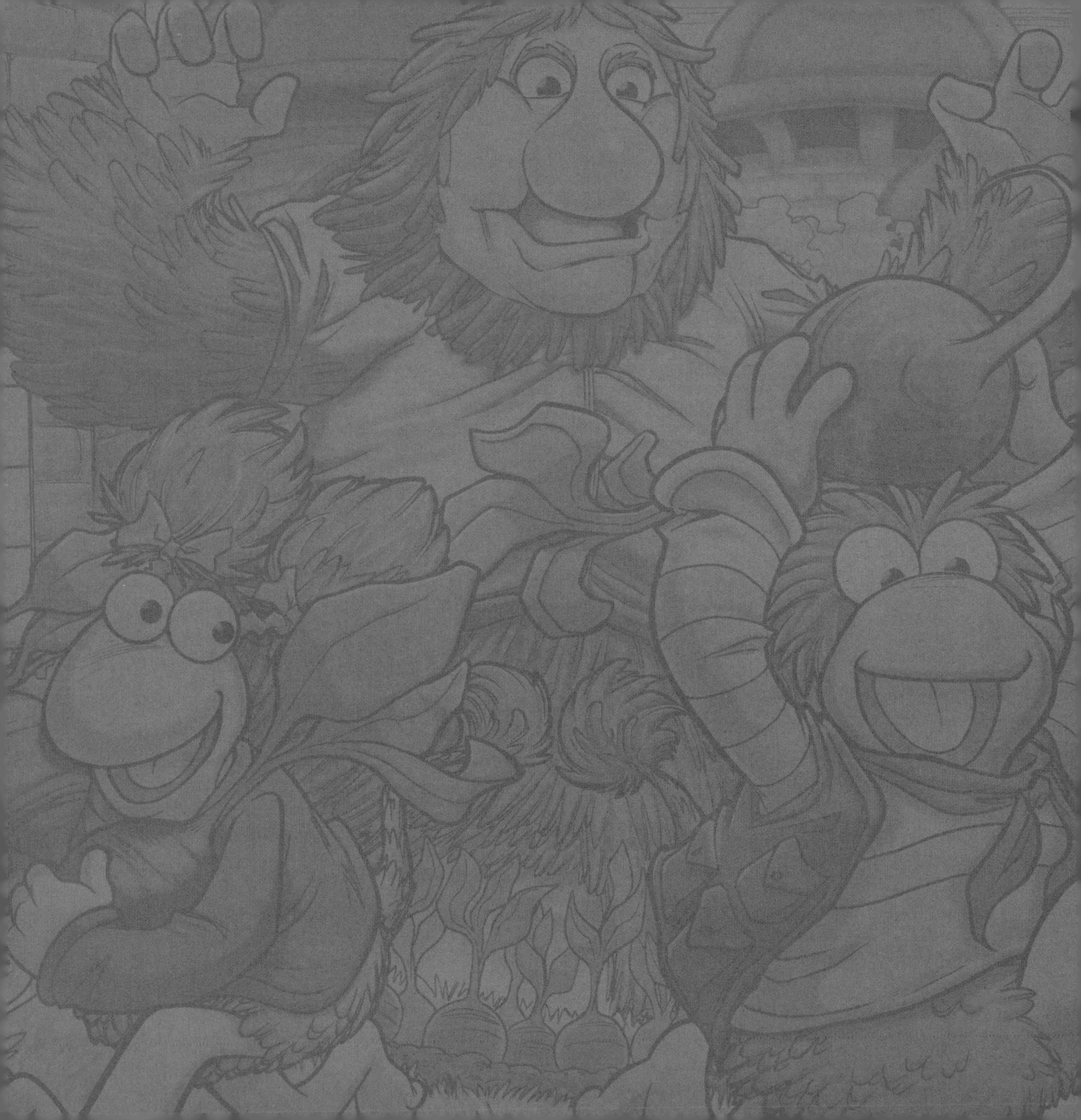

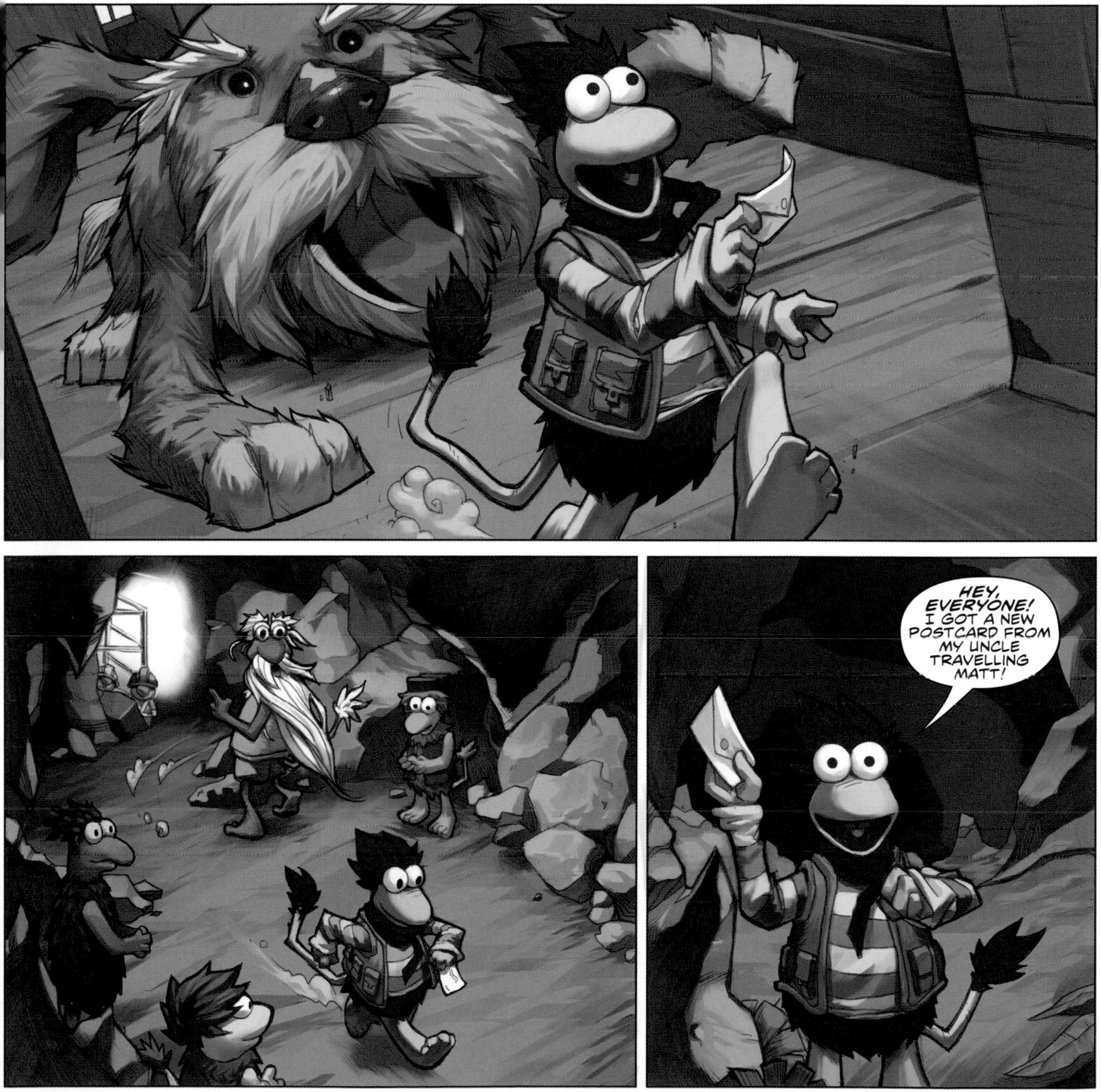
HEY, EVERYONE! I GOT A NEW POSTCARD FROM MY UNCLE TRAVELLING MATT!

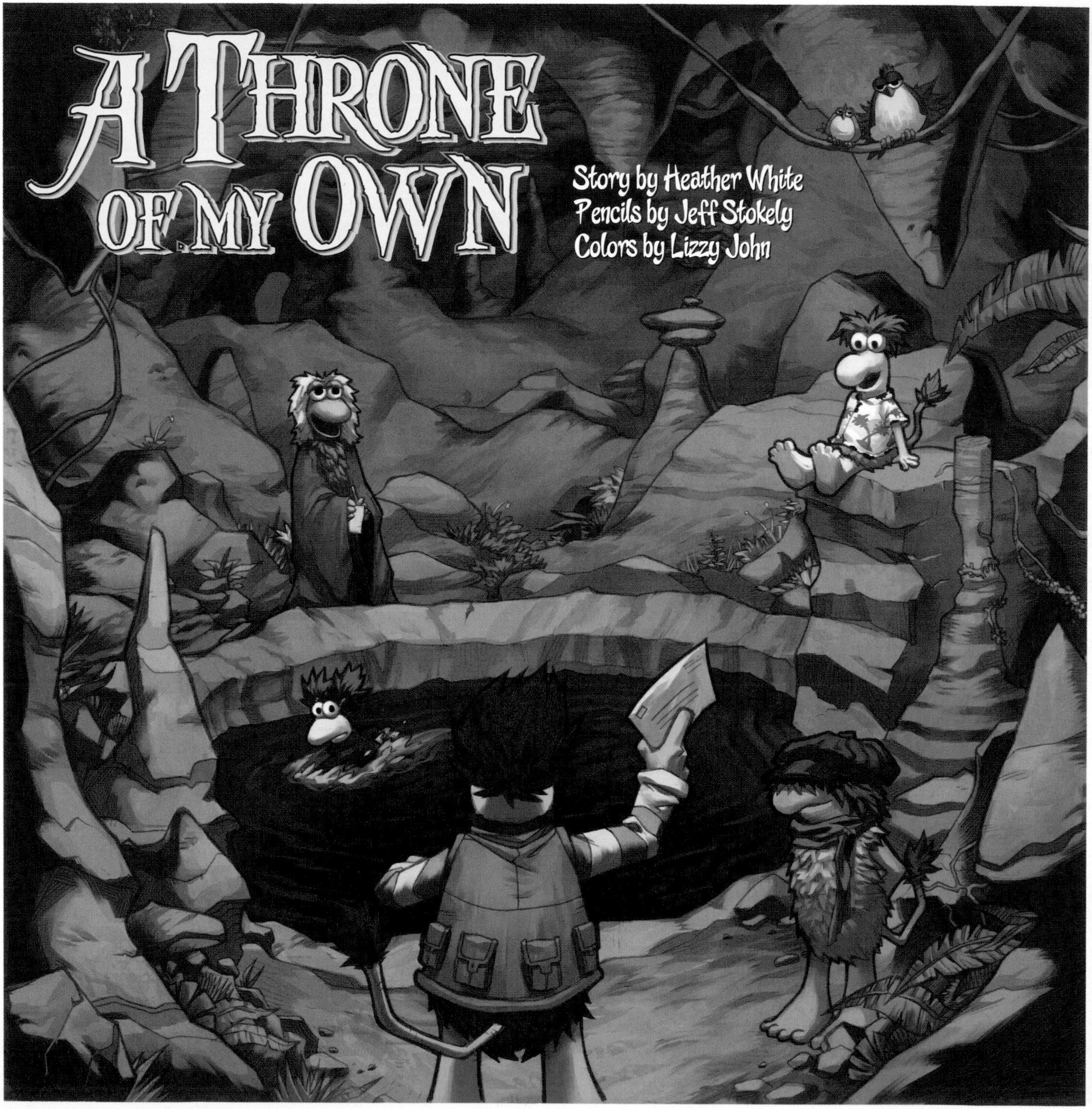
A THRONE OF MY OWN
Story by Heather White
Pencils by Jeff Stokely
Colors by Lizzy John

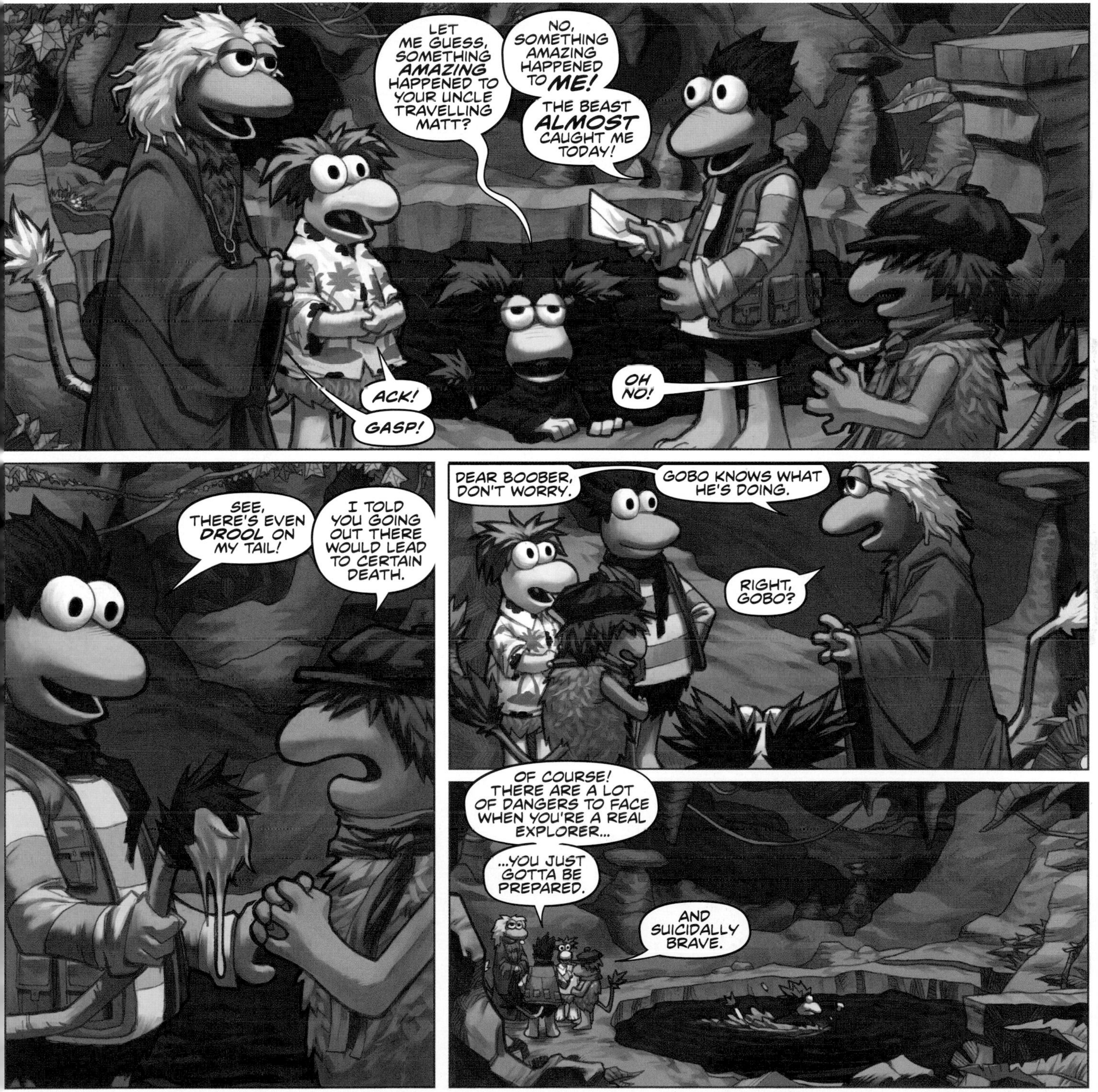
LET ME GUESS, SOMETHING AMAZING HAPPENED TO YOUR UNCLE TRAVELLING MATT?
NO, SOMETHING AMAZING HAPPENED TO ME!
THE BEAST ALMOST CAUGHT ME TODAY!
ACK!
GASP!
OH NO!
SEE, THERE'S EVEN DROOL ON MY TAIL!
I TOLD YOU GOING OUT THERE WOULD LEAD TO CERTAIN DEATH.
DEAR BOOBER, DON'T WORRY.
GOBO KNOWS WHAT HE'S DOING.
RIGHT, GOBO?
OF COURSE! THERE ARE A LOT OF DANGERS TO FACE WHEN YOU'RE A REAL EXPLORER...
...YOU JUST GOTTA BE PREPARED.
AND SUICIDALLY BRAVE.

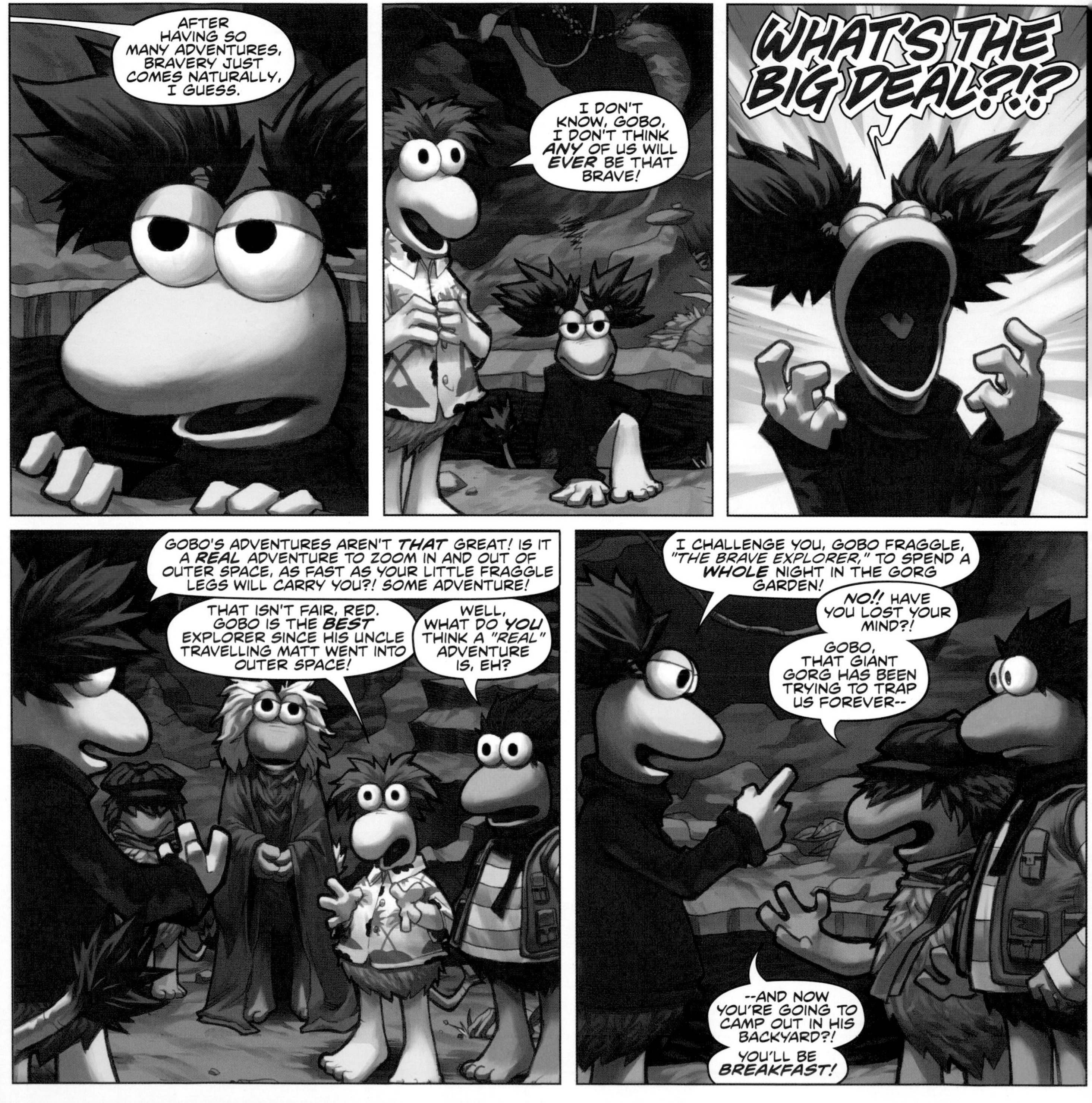
AFTER HAVING SO MANY ADVENTURES, BRAVERY JUST COMES NATURALLY, I GUESS.
I DON'T KNOW, GOBO, I DON'T THINK ANY OF US WILL EVER BE THAT BRAVE!
WHAT'S THE BIG DEAL?!?
GOBO'S ADVENTURES AREN'T THAT GREAT! IS IT A REAL ADVENTURE TO ZOOM IN AND OUT OF OUTER SPACE, AS FAST AS YOUR LITTLE FRAGGLE LEGS WILL CARRY YOU?! SOME ADVENTURE!
THAT ISN'T FAIR, RED. GOBO IS THE BEST EXPLORER SINCE HIS UNCLE TRAVELLING MATT WENT INTO OUTER SPACE!
WELL, WHAT DO YOU THINK A "REAL" ADVENTURE IS, EH?
I CHALLENGE YOU, GOBO FRAGGLE, "THE BRAVE EXPLORER," TO SPEND A WHOLE NIGHT IN THE GORG GARDEN!
NO!! HAVE YOU LOST YOUR MIND?!
GOBO, THAT GIANT GORG HAS BEEN TRYING TO TRAP US FOREVER--
--AND NOW YOU'RE GOING TO CAMP OUT IN HIS BACKYARD?!
YOU'LL BE BREAKFAST!

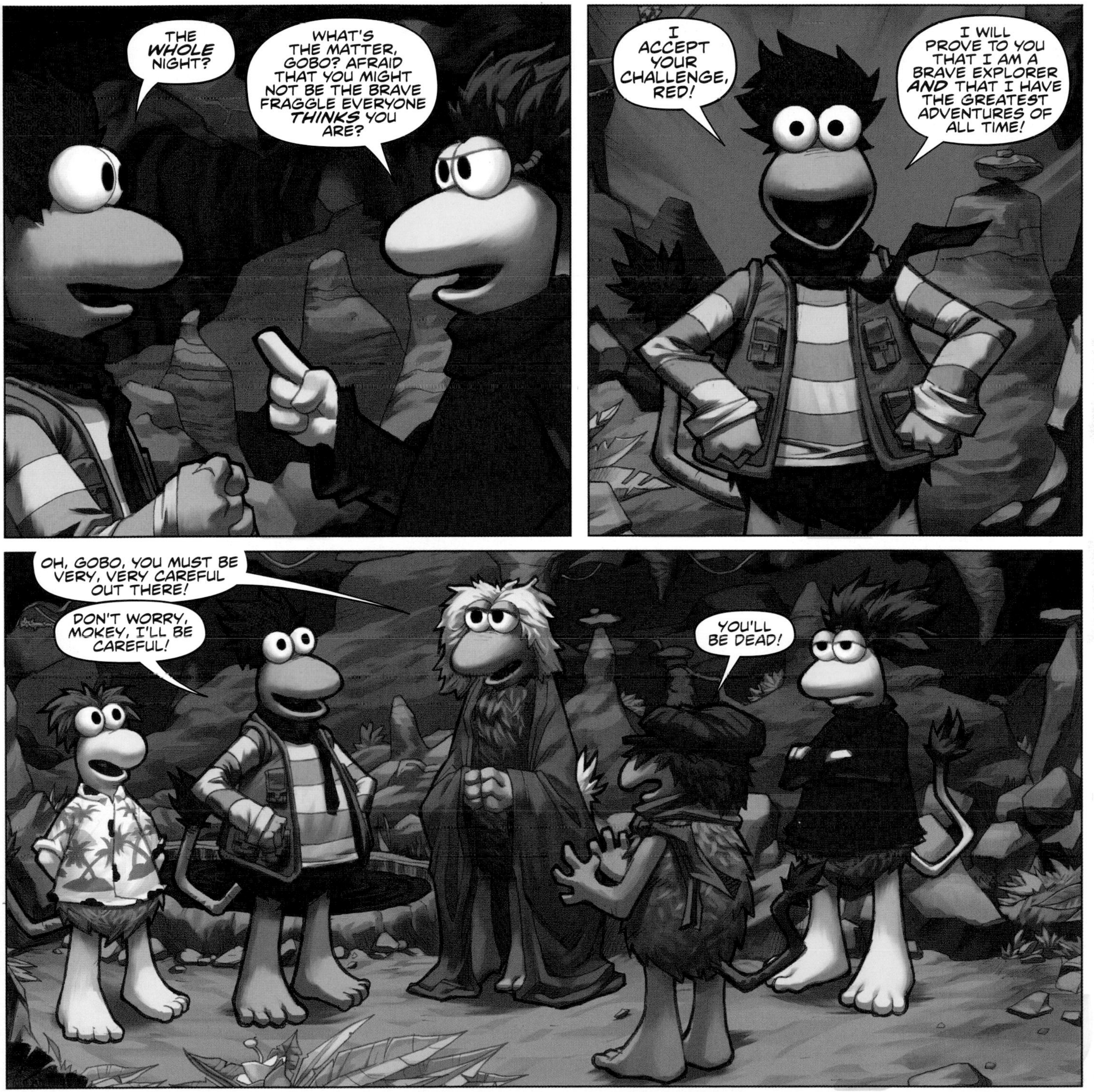

THE *WHOLE* NIGHT?
WHAT'S THE MATTER, GOBO? AFRAID THAT YOU MIGHT NOT BE THE BRAVE FRAGGLE EVERYONE *THINKS* YOU ARE?
I ACCEPT YOUR CHALLENGE, RED!
I WILL PROVE TO YOU THAT I AM A BRAVE EXPLORER *AND* THAT I HAVE THE GREATEST ADVENTURES OF ALL TIME!
OH, GOBO, YOU MUST BE VERY, VERY CAREFUL OUT THERE!
DON'T WORRY, MOKEY, I'LL BE CAREFUL!
YOU'LL BE DEAD!

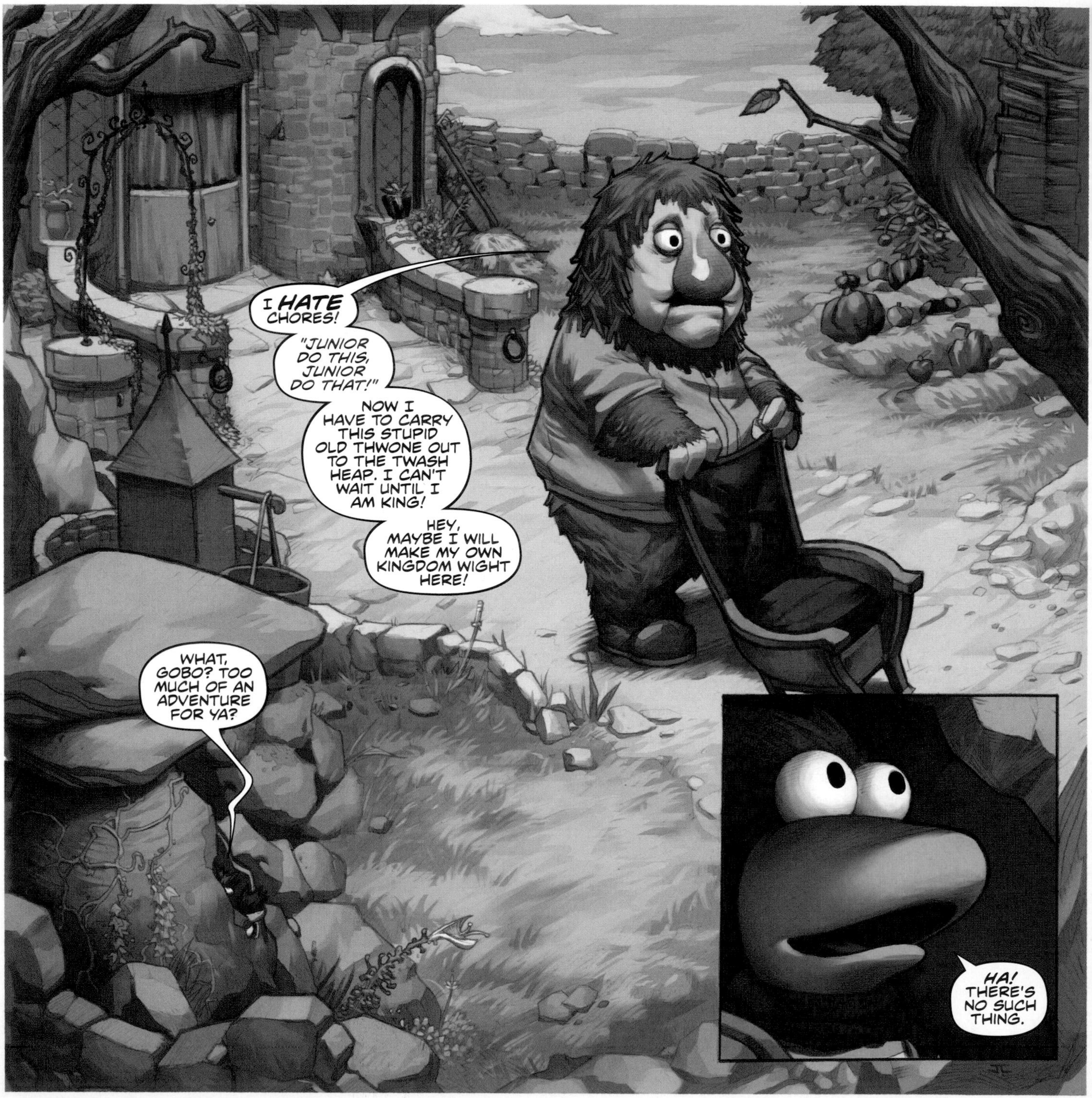
I HATE CHORES!
"JUNIOR DO THIS, JUNIOR DO THAT!"
NOW I HAVE TO CARRY THIS STUPID OLD THWONE OUT TO THE TWASH HEAP. I CAN'T WAIT UNTIL I AM KING!
HEY, MAYBE I WILL MAKE MY OWN KINGDOM WIGHT HERE!
WHAT, GOBO? TOO MUCH OF AN ADVENTURE FOR YA?
HA! THERE'S NO SUCH THING.

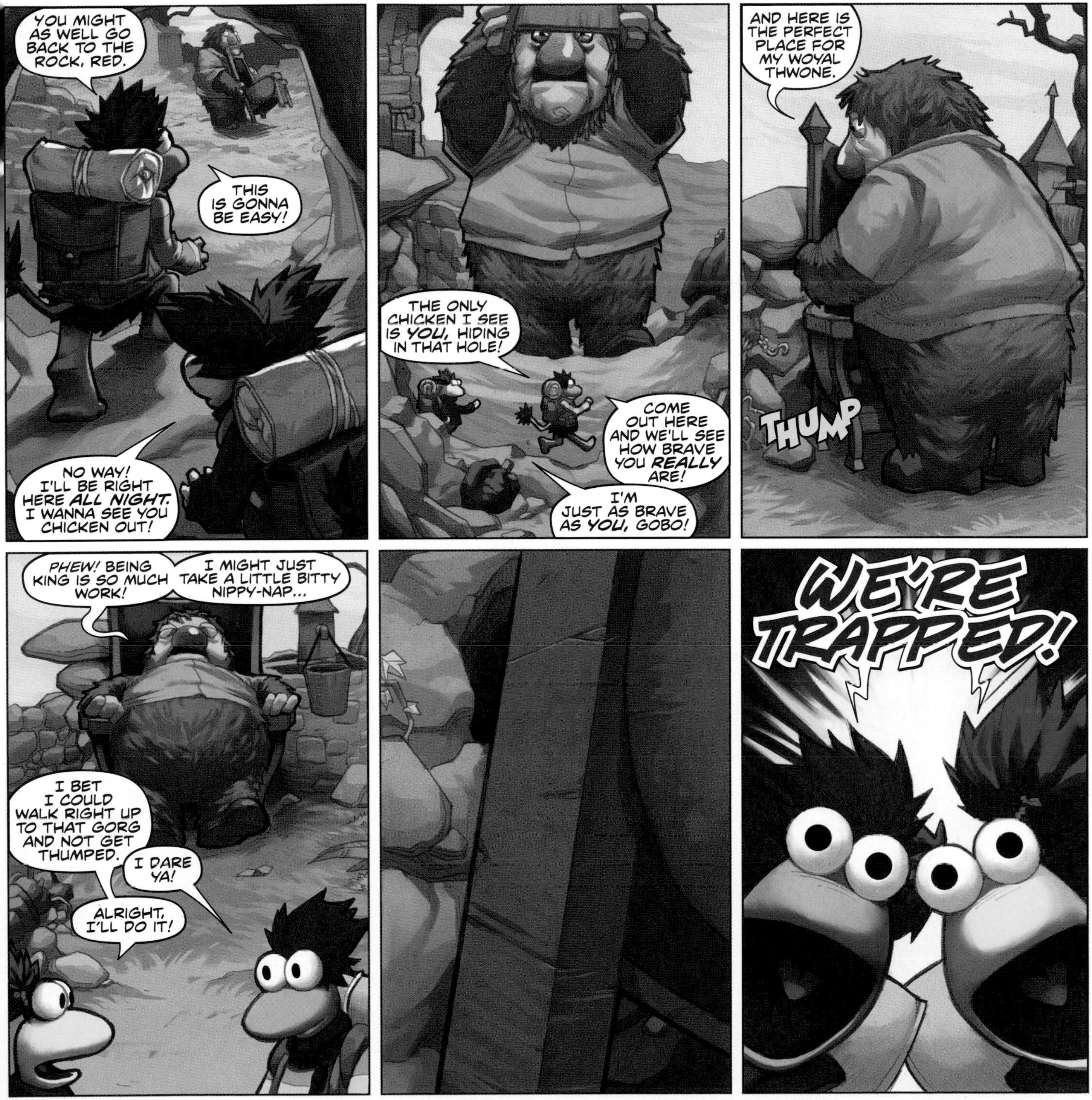
YOU MIGHT AS WELL GO BACK TO THE ROCK, RED.
THIS IS GONNA BE EASY!
NO WAY! I'LL BE RIGHT HERE ALL NIGHT. I WANNA SEE YOU CHICKEN OUT!
THE ONLY CHICKEN I SEE IS YOU, HIDING IN THAT HOLE!
COME OUT HERE AND WE'LL SEE HOW BRAVE YOU REALLY ARE!
I'M JUST AS BRAVE AS YOU, GOBO!
AND HERE IS THE PERFECT PLACE FOR MY WOYAL THWONE.
THUMP
PHEW! BEING KING IS SO MUCH WORK!
I MIGHT JUST TAKE A LITTLE BITTY NIPPY-NAP...
I BET I COULD WALK RIGHT UP TO THAT GORG AND NOT GET THUMPED.
I DARE YA!
ALRIGHT, I'LL DO IT!
WE'RE TRAPPED!

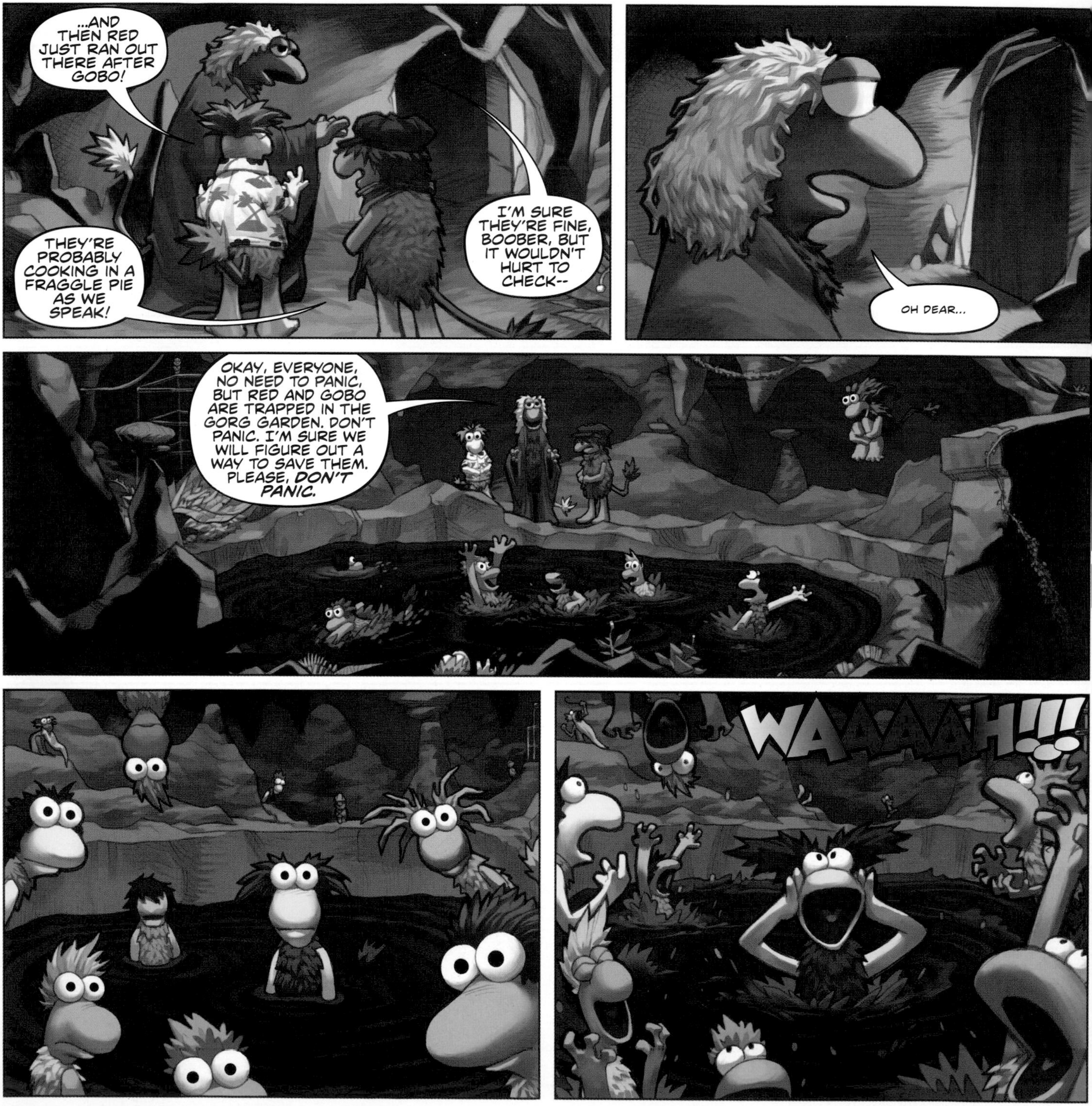
...AND THEN RED JUST RAN OUT THERE AFTER GOBO!
THEY'RE PROBABLY COOKING IN A FRAGGLE PIE AS WE SPEAK!
I'M SURE THEY'RE FINE, BOOBER, BUT IT WOULDN'T HURT TO CHECK--
OH DEAR...
OKAY, EVERYONE, NO NEED TO PANIC, BUT RED AND GOBO ARE TRAPPED IN THE GORG GARDEN. DON'T PANIC. I'M SURE WE WILL FIGURE OUT A WAY TO SAVE THEM. PLEASE, DON'T PANIC.
WAAAAH!!!

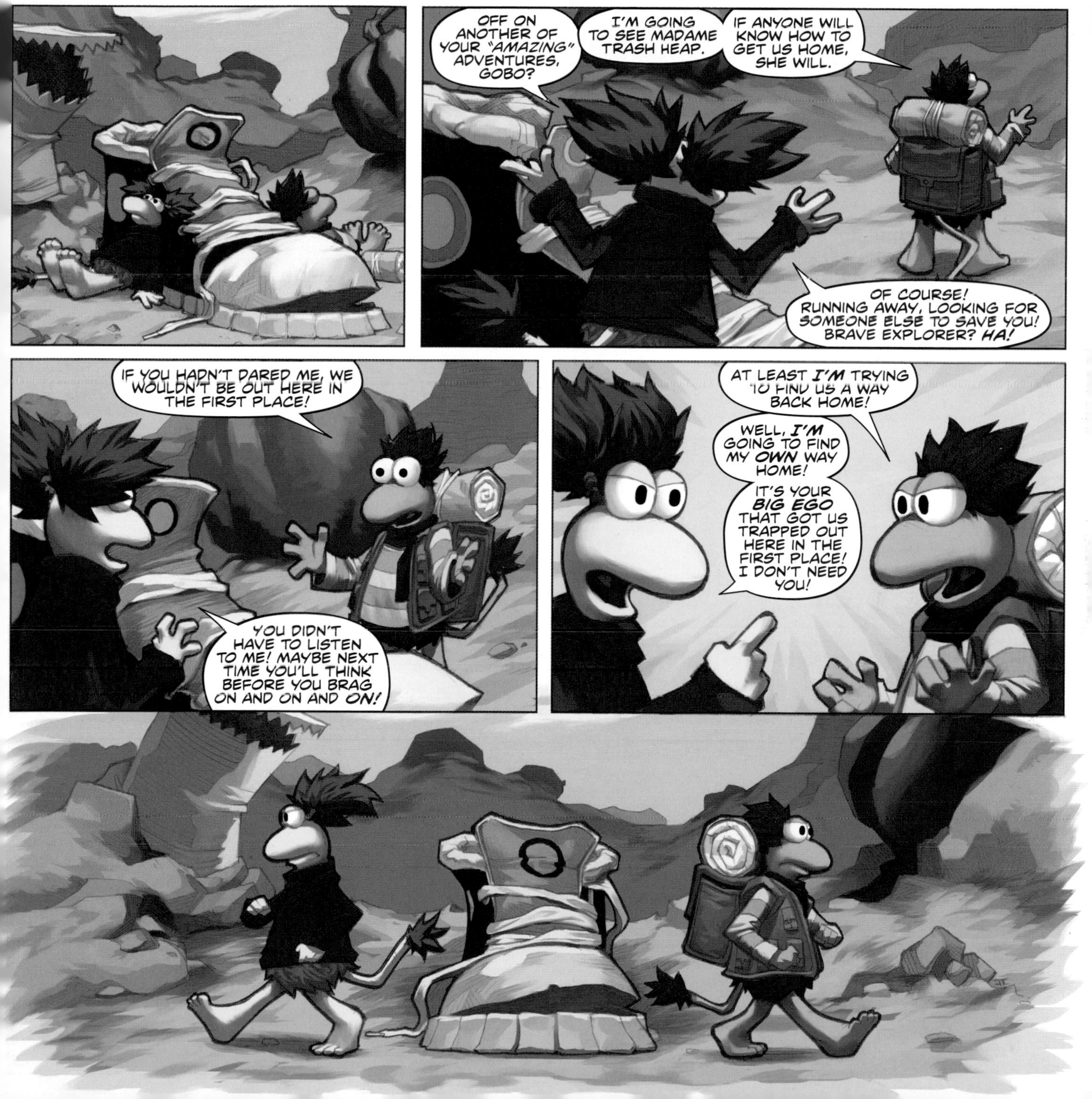
OFF ON ANOTHER OF YOUR "AMAZING" ADVENTURES, GOBO?
I'M GOING TO SEE MADAME TRASH HEAP.
IF ANYONE WILL KNOW HOW TO GET US HOME, SHE WILL.
OF COURSE! RUNNING AWAY, LOOKING FOR SOMEONE ELSE TO SAVE YOU! BRAVE EXPLORER? *HA!*
IF YOU HADN'T DARED ME, WE WOULDN'T BE OUT HERE IN THE FIRST PLACE!
YOU DIDN'T HAVE TO LISTEN TO ME! MAYBE NEXT TIME YOU'LL THINK BEFORE YOU BRAG ON AND ON AND *ON!*
AT LEAST *I'M* TRYING TO FIND US A WAY BACK HOME!
WELL, *I'M* GOING TO FIND MY *OWN* WAY HOME!
IT'S YOUR *BIG EGO* THAT GOT US TRAPPED OUT HERE IN THE FIRST PLACE! I DON'T NEED YOU!

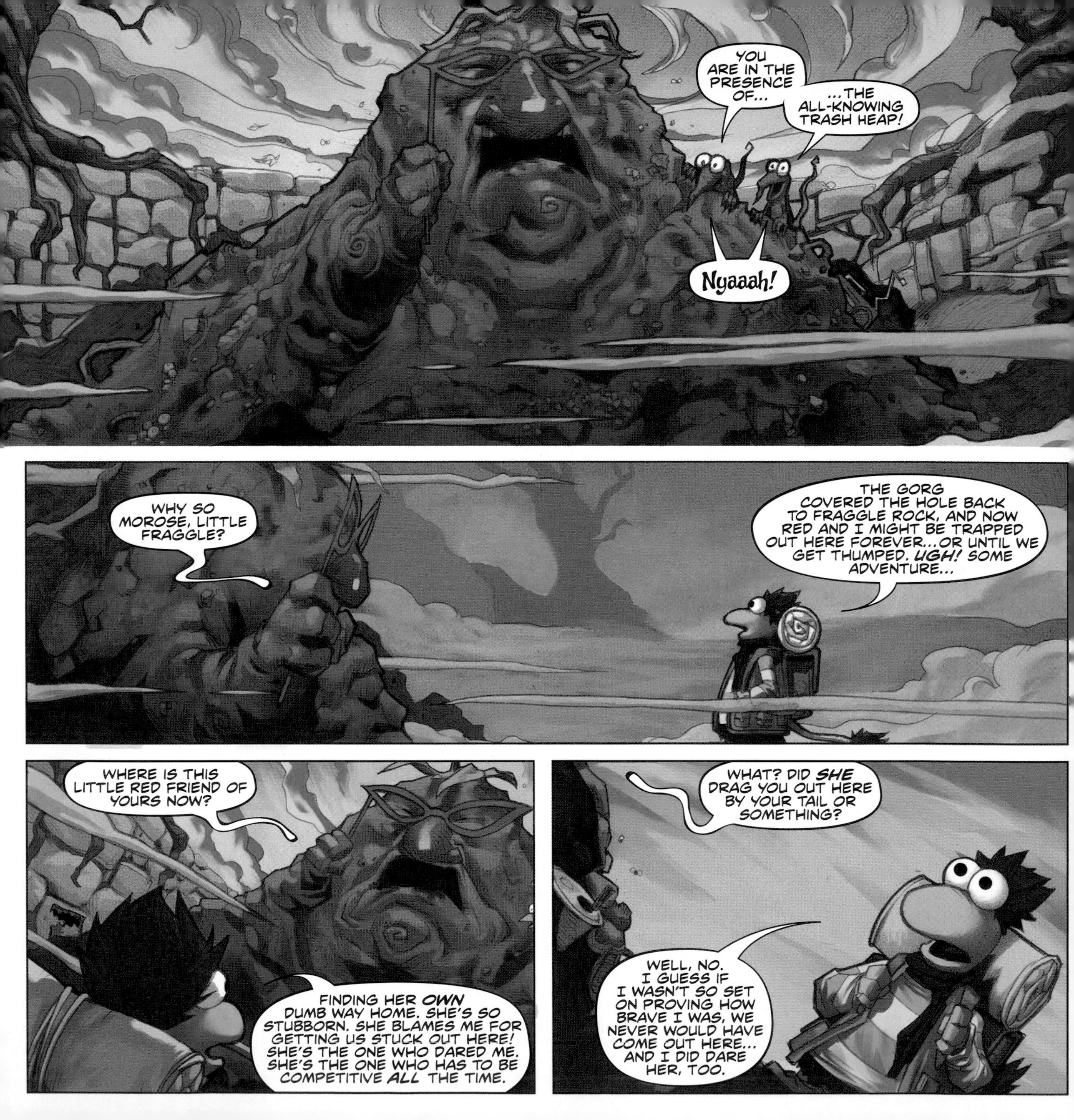

YOU ARE IN THE PRESENCE OF...
...THE ALL-KNOWING TRASH HEAP!
Nyaaah!
WHY SO MOROSE, LITTLE FRAGGLE?
THE GORG COVERED THE HOLE BACK TO FRAGGLE ROCK, AND NOW RED AND I MIGHT BE TRAPPED OUT HERE FOREVER...OR UNTIL WE GET THUMPED. UGH! SOME ADVENTURE...
WHERE IS THIS LITTLE RED FRIEND OF YOURS NOW?
FINDING HER OWN DUMB WAY HOME. SHE'S SO STUBBORN. SHE BLAMES ME FOR GETTING US STUCK OUT HERE! SHE'S THE ONE WHO DARED ME. SHE'S THE ONE WHO HAS TO BE COMPETITIVE ALL THE TIME.
WHAT? DID SHE DRAG YOU OUT HERE BY YOUR TAIL OR SOMETHING?
WELL, NO. I GUESS IF I WASN'T SO SET ON PROVING HOW BRAVE I WAS, WE NEVER WOULD HAVE COME OUT HERE... AND I DID DARE HER, TOO.

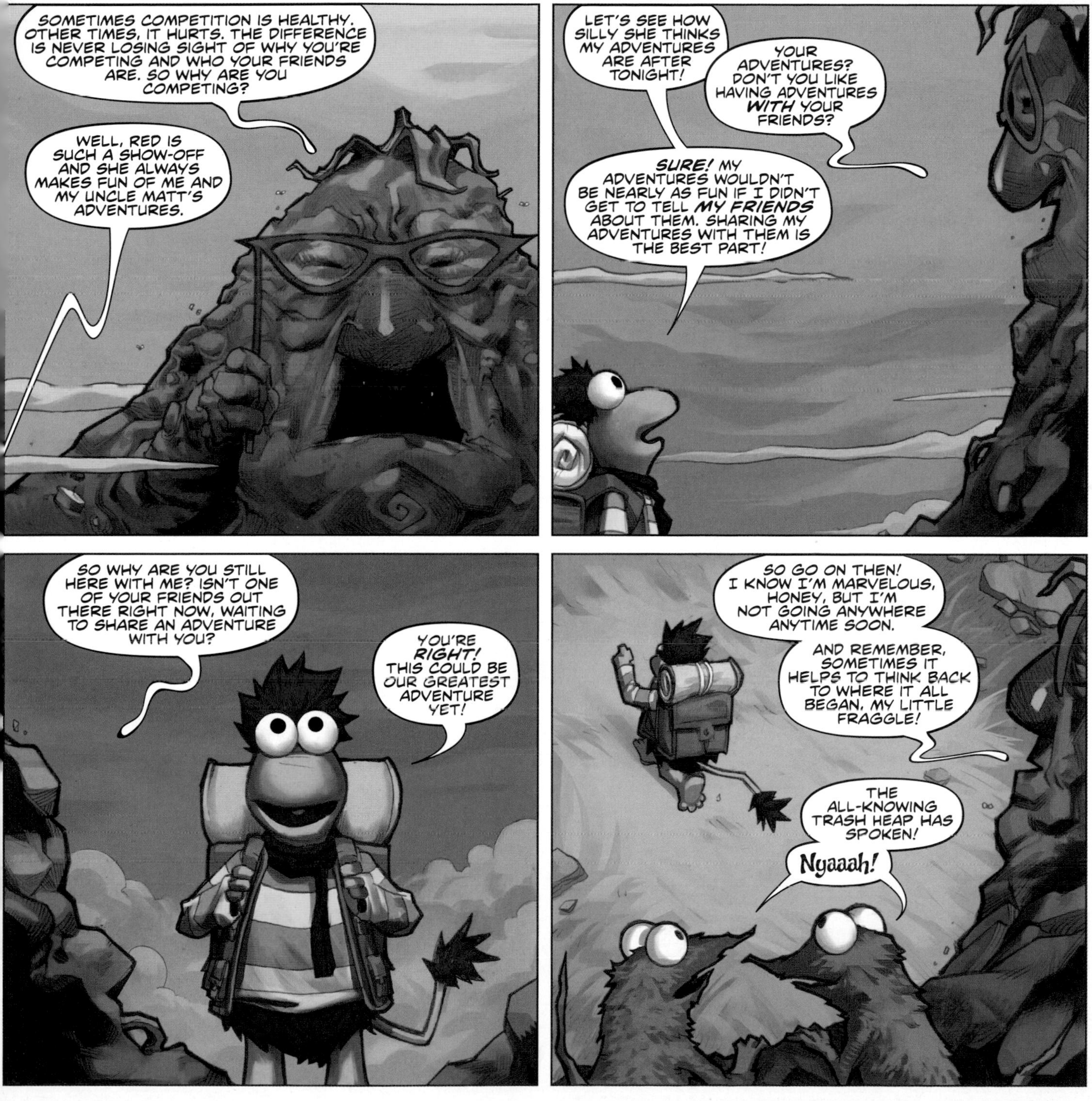
SOMETIMES COMPETITION IS HEALTHY. OTHER TIMES, IT HURTS. THE DIFFERENCE IS NEVER LOSING SIGHT OF WHY YOU'RE COMPETING AND WHO YOUR FRIENDS ARE. SO WHY ARE YOU COMPETING?
WELL, RED IS SUCH A SHOW-OFF AND SHE ALWAYS MAKES FUN OF ME AND MY UNCLE MATT'S ADVENTURES.
LET'S SEE HOW SILLY SHE THINKS MY ADVENTURES ARE AFTER TONIGHT!
YOUR ADVENTURES? DON'T YOU LIKE HAVING ADVENTURES *WITH* YOUR FRIENDS?
SURE! MY ADVENTURES WOULDN'T BE NEARLY AS FUN IF I DIDN'T GET TO TELL *MY FRIENDS* ABOUT THEM. SHARING MY ADVENTURES WITH THEM IS THE BEST PART!
SO WHY ARE YOU STILL HERE WITH ME? ISN'T ONE OF YOUR FRIENDS OUT THERE RIGHT NOW, WAITING TO SHARE AN ADVENTURE WITH YOU?
YOU'RE *RIGHT!* THIS COULD BE OUR GREATEST ADVENTURE YET!
SO GO ON THEN! I KNOW I'M MARVELOUS, HONEY, BUT I'M NOT GOING ANYWHERE ANYTIME SOON.
AND REMEMBER, SOMETIMES IT HELPS TO THINK BACK TO WHERE IT ALL BEGAN, MY LITTLE FRAGGLE!
THE ALL-KNOWING TRASH HEAP HAS SPOKEN!
Nyaaah!

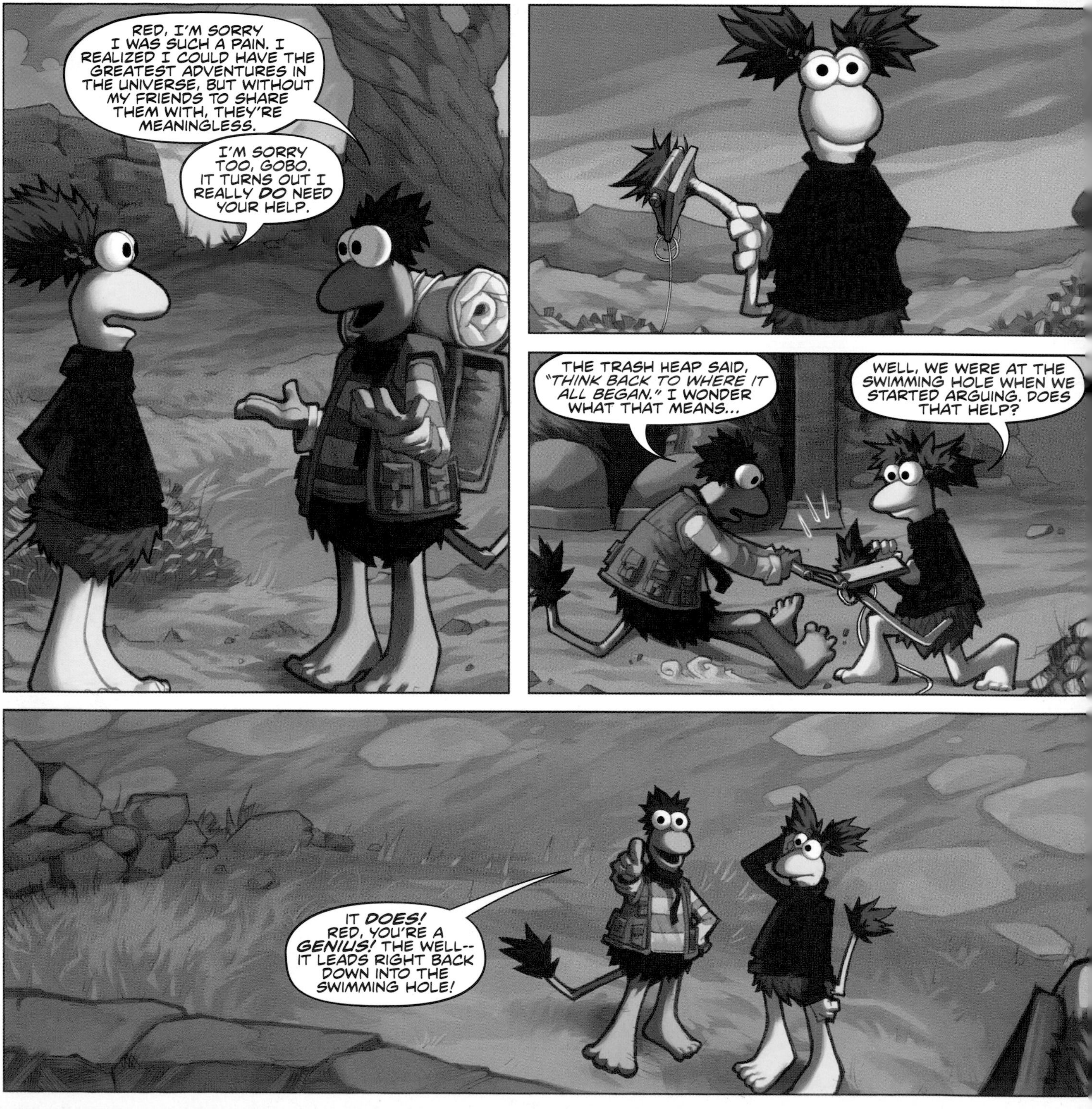
RED, I'M SORRY I WAS SUCH A PAIN. I REALIZED I COULD HAVE THE GREATEST ADVENTURES IN THE UNIVERSE, BUT WITHOUT MY FRIENDS TO SHARE THEM WITH, THEY'RE MEANINGLESS.
I'M SORRY TOO, GOBO. IT TURNS OUT I REALLY *DO* NEED YOUR HELP.
THE TRASH HEAP SAID, "*THINK BACK TO WHERE IT ALL BEGAN.*" I WONDER WHAT THAT MEANS...
WELL, WE WERE AT THE SWIMMING HOLE WHEN WE STARTED ARGUING. DOES THAT HELP?
IT ***DOES!*** RED, YOU'RE A ***GENIUS!*** THE WELL-- IT LEADS RIGHT BACK DOWN INTO THE SWIMMING HOLE!

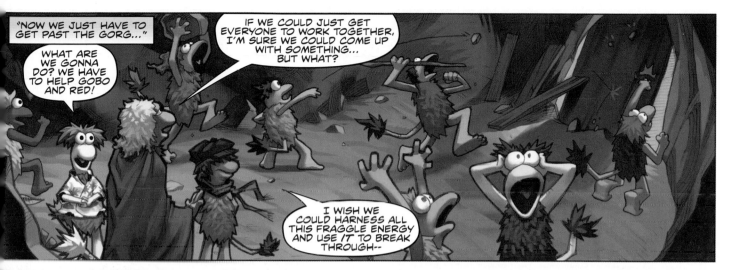

"NOW WE JUST HAVE TO GET PAST THE GORG..."

WHAT ARE WE GONNA DO? WE HAVE TO HELP GOBO AND RED!

IF WE COULD JUST GET EVERYONE TO WORK TOGETHER, I'M SURE WE COULD COME UP WITH SOMETHING... BUT WHAT?

I WISH WE COULD HARNESS ALL THIS FRAGGLE ENERGY AND USE *IT* TO BREAK THROUGH--

THAT'S IT!!

HEY, EVERYBODY!

HEY, EVERYBODDDDDYYYY!!!!

I...UM... I THINK MOKEY, BOOBER AND I HAVE A PLAN!

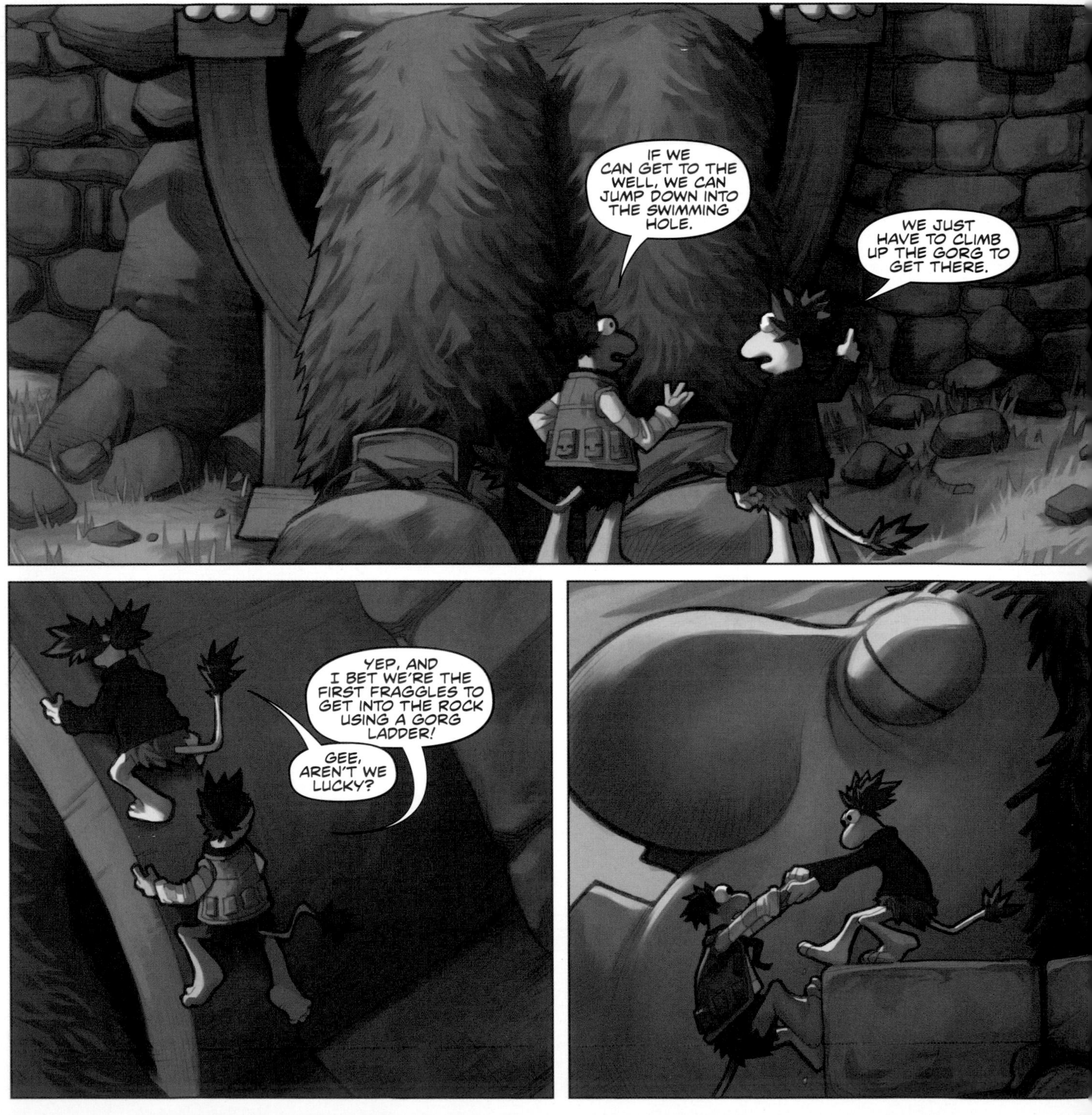
IF WE CAN GET TO THE WELL, WE CAN JUMP DOWN INTO THE SWIMMING HOLE.
WE JUST HAVE TO CLIMB UP THE GORG TO GET THERE.
YEP, AND I BET WE'RE THE FIRST FRAGGLES TO GET INTO THE ROCK USING A GORG LADDER!
GEE, AREN'T WE LUCKY?

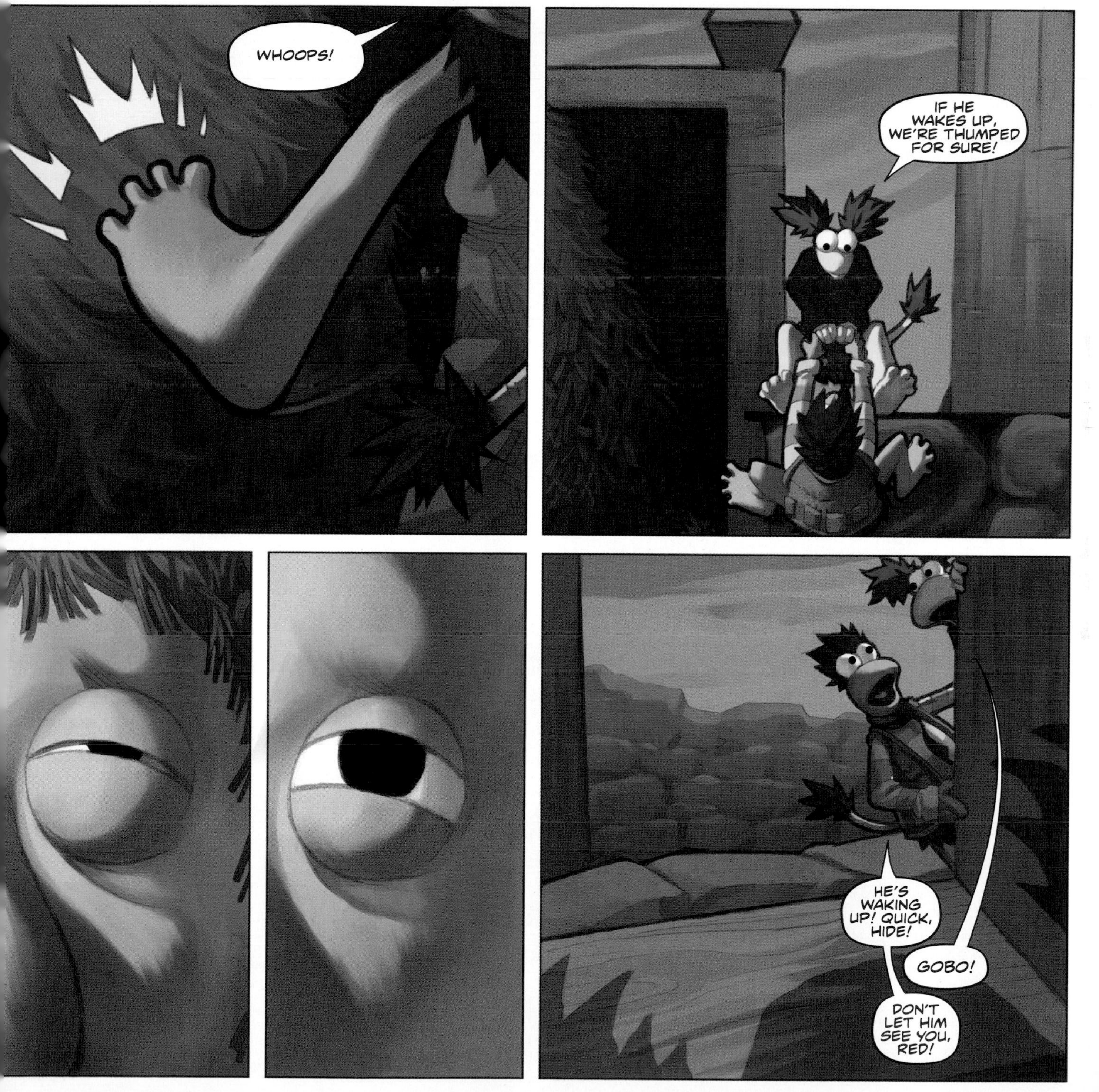
WHOOPS!
IF HE WAKES UP, WE'RE THUMPED FOR SURE!
HE'S WAKING UP! QUICK, HIDE!
GOBO!
DON'T LET HIM SEE YOU, RED!

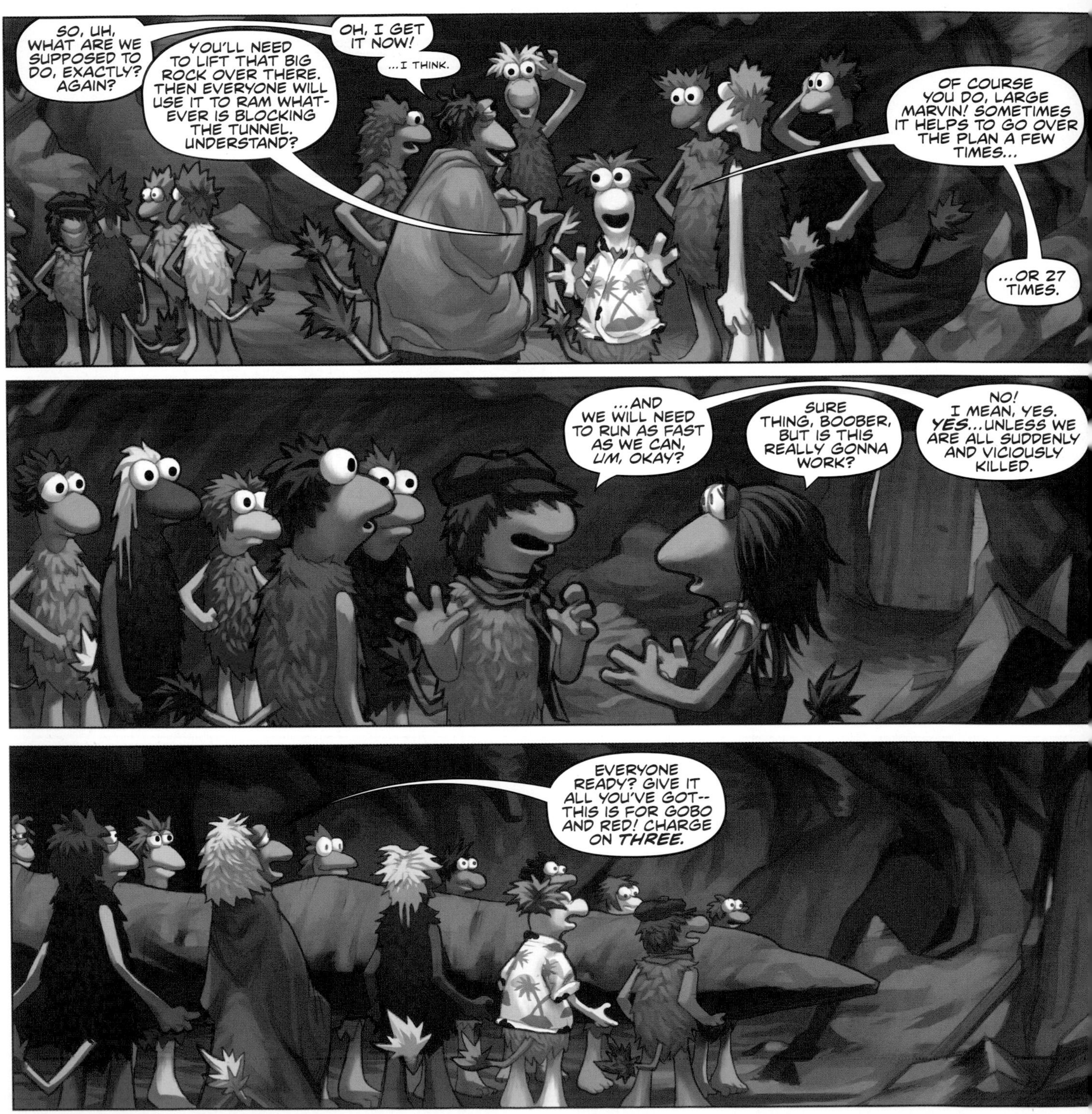
SO, UH, WHAT ARE WE SUPPOSED TO DO, EXACTLY? AGAIN?
YOU'LL NEED TO LIFT THAT BIG ROCK OVER THERE. THEN EVERYONE WILL USE IT TO RAM WHATEVER IS BLOCKING THE TUNNEL. UNDERSTAND?
OH, I GET IT NOW!
...I THINK.
OF COURSE YOU DO, LARGE MARVIN! SOMETIMES IT HELPS TO GO OVER THE PLAN A FEW TIMES...
...OR 27 TIMES.
...AND WE WILL NEED TO RUN AS FAST AS WE CAN, UM, OKAY?
SURE THING, BOOBER, BUT IS THIS REALLY GONNA WORK?
NO! I MEAN, YES. *YES*...UNLESS WE ARE ALL SUDDENLY AND VICIOUSLY KILLED.
EVERYONE READY? GIVE IT ALL YOU'VE GOT-- THIS IS FOR GOBO AND RED! CHARGE ON *THREE*.

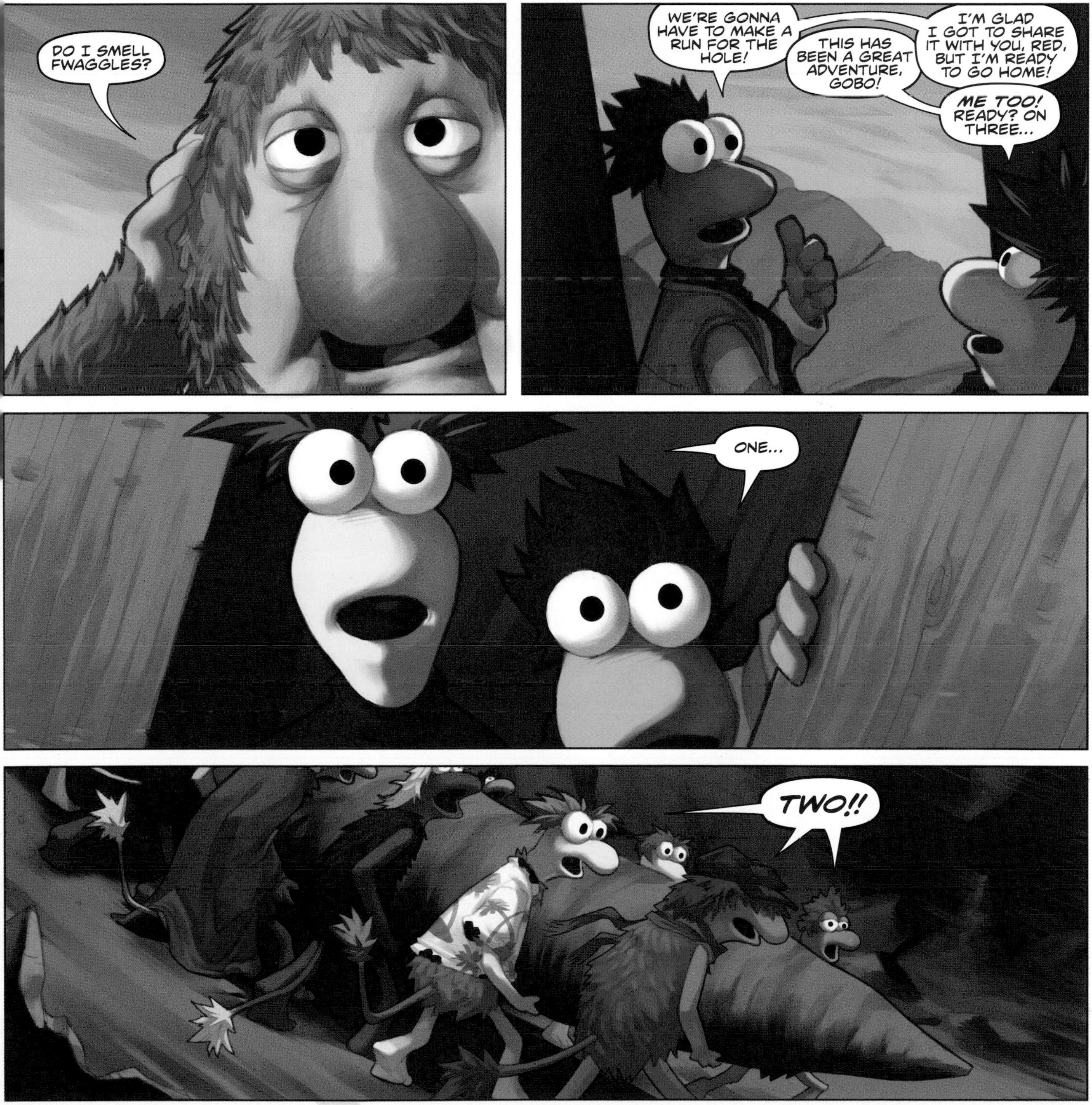
DO I SMELL FWAGGLES?
WE'RE GONNA HAVE TO MAKE A RUN FOR THE HOLE!
I'M GLAD I GOT TO SHARE IT WITH YOU, RED, BUT I'M READY TO GO HOME!
THIS HAS BEEN A GREAT ADVENTURE, GOBO!
ME TOO! READY? ON THREE...
ONE...
TWO!!

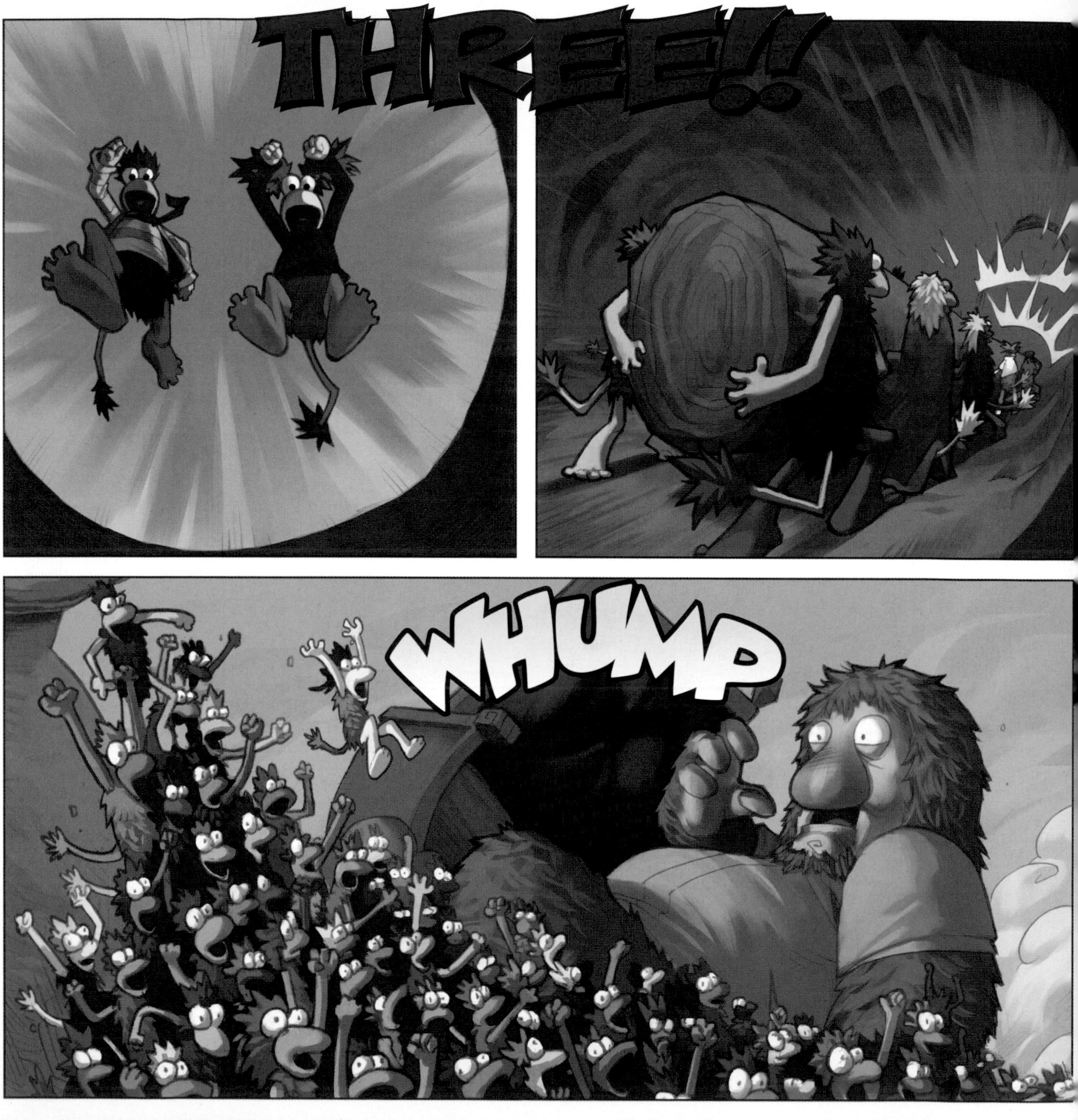
THREE!!
WHUMP

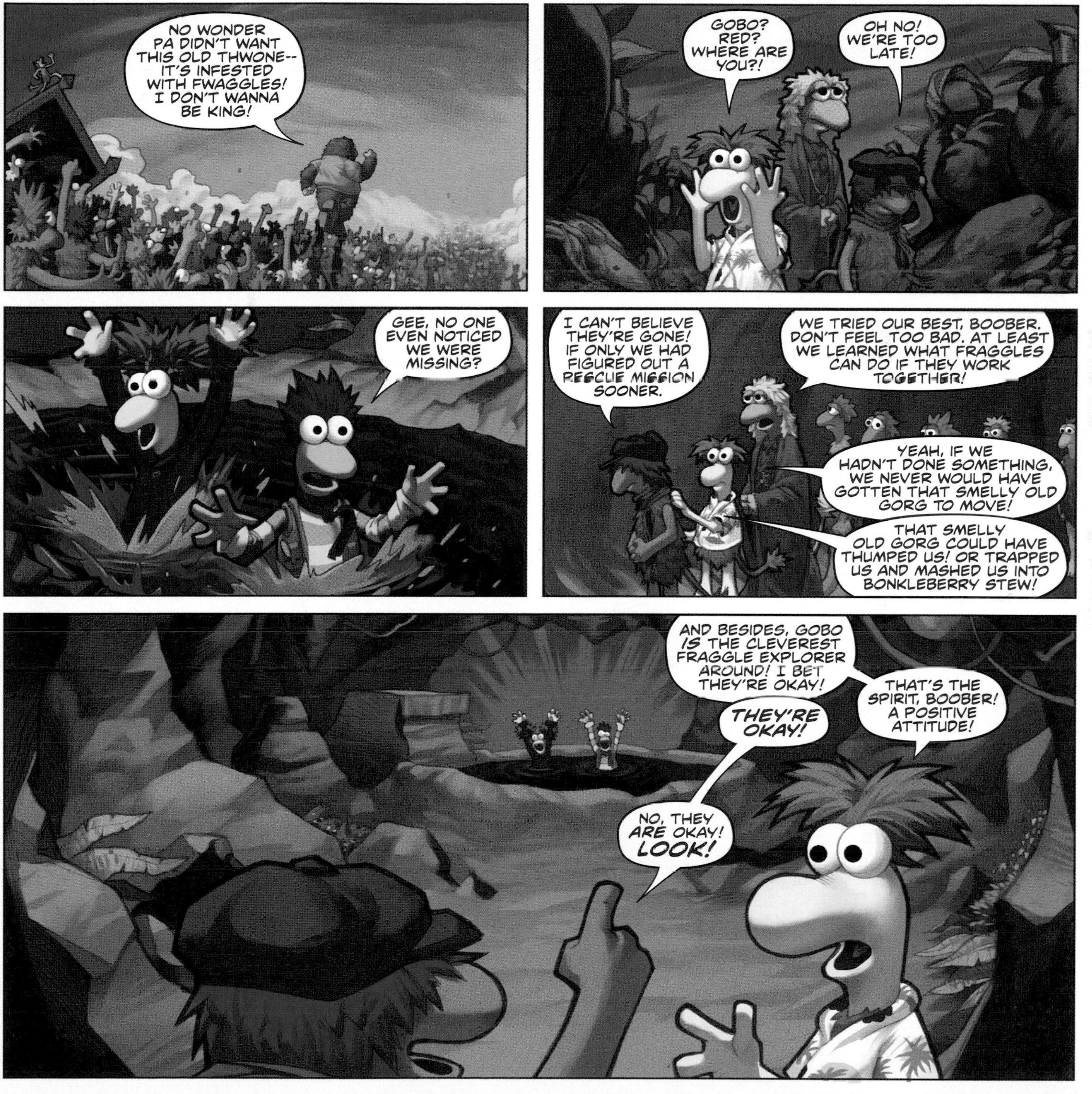
NO WONDER PA DIDN'T WANT THIS OLD THWONE-- IT'S INFESTED WITH FWAGGLES! I DON'T WANNA BE KING!
GOBO? RED? WHERE ARE YOU?!
OH NO! WE'RE TOO LATE!
GEE, NO ONE EVEN NOTICED WE WERE MISSING?
I CAN'T BELIEVE THEY'RE GONE! IF ONLY WE HAD FIGURED OUT A RESCUE MISSION SOONER.
WE TRIED OUR BEST, BOOBER. DON'T FEEL TOO BAD. AT LEAST WE LEARNED WHAT FRAGGLES CAN DO IF THEY WORK TOGETHER!
YEAH, IF WE HADN'T DONE SOMETHING, WE NEVER WOULD HAVE GOTTEN THAT SMELLY OLD GORG TO MOVE!
THAT SMELLY OLD GORG COULD HAVE THUMPED US! OR TRAPPED US AND MASHED US INTO BONKLEBERRY STEW!
AND BESIDES, GOBO *IS* THE CLEVEREST FRAGGLE EXPLORER AROUND! I BET THEY'RE OKAY!
THAT'S THE SPIRIT, BOOBER! A POSITIVE ATTITUDE!
THEY'RE OKAY!
NO, THEY *ARE* OKAY! *LOOK!*

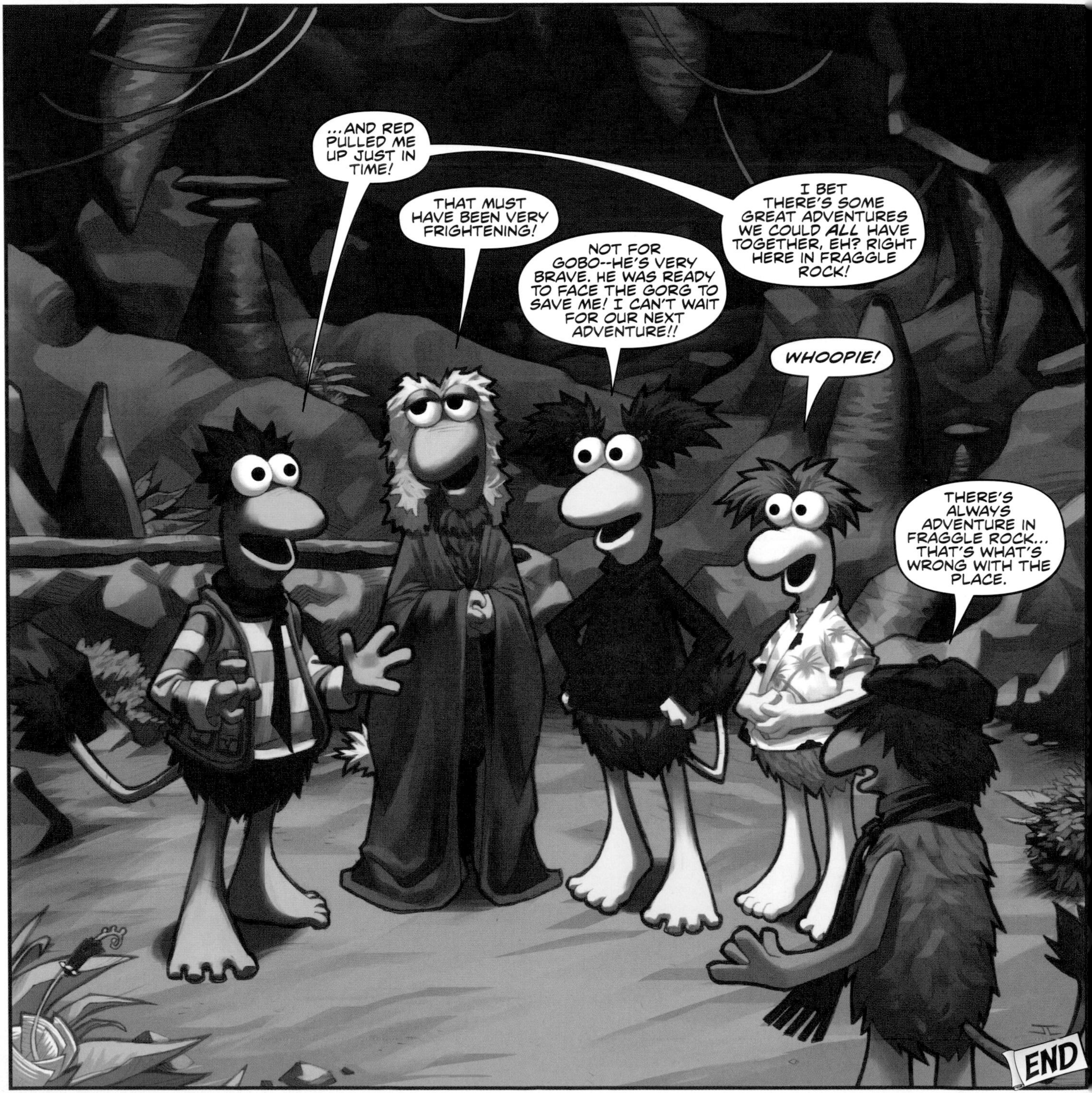
...AND RED PULLED ME UP JUST IN TIME!
THAT MUST HAVE BEEN VERY FRIGHTENING!
NOT FOR GOBO--HE'S VERY BRAVE. HE WAS READY TO FACE THE GORG TO SAVE ME! I CAN'T WAIT FOR OUR NEXT ADVENTURE!!
I BET THERE'S SOME GREAT ADVENTURES WE COULD *ALL* HAVE TOGETHER, EH? RIGHT HERE IN FRAGGLE ROCK!
WHOOPIE!
THERE'S ALWAYS ADVENTURE IN FRAGGLE ROCK... THAT'S WHAT'S WRONG WITH THE PLACE.
END

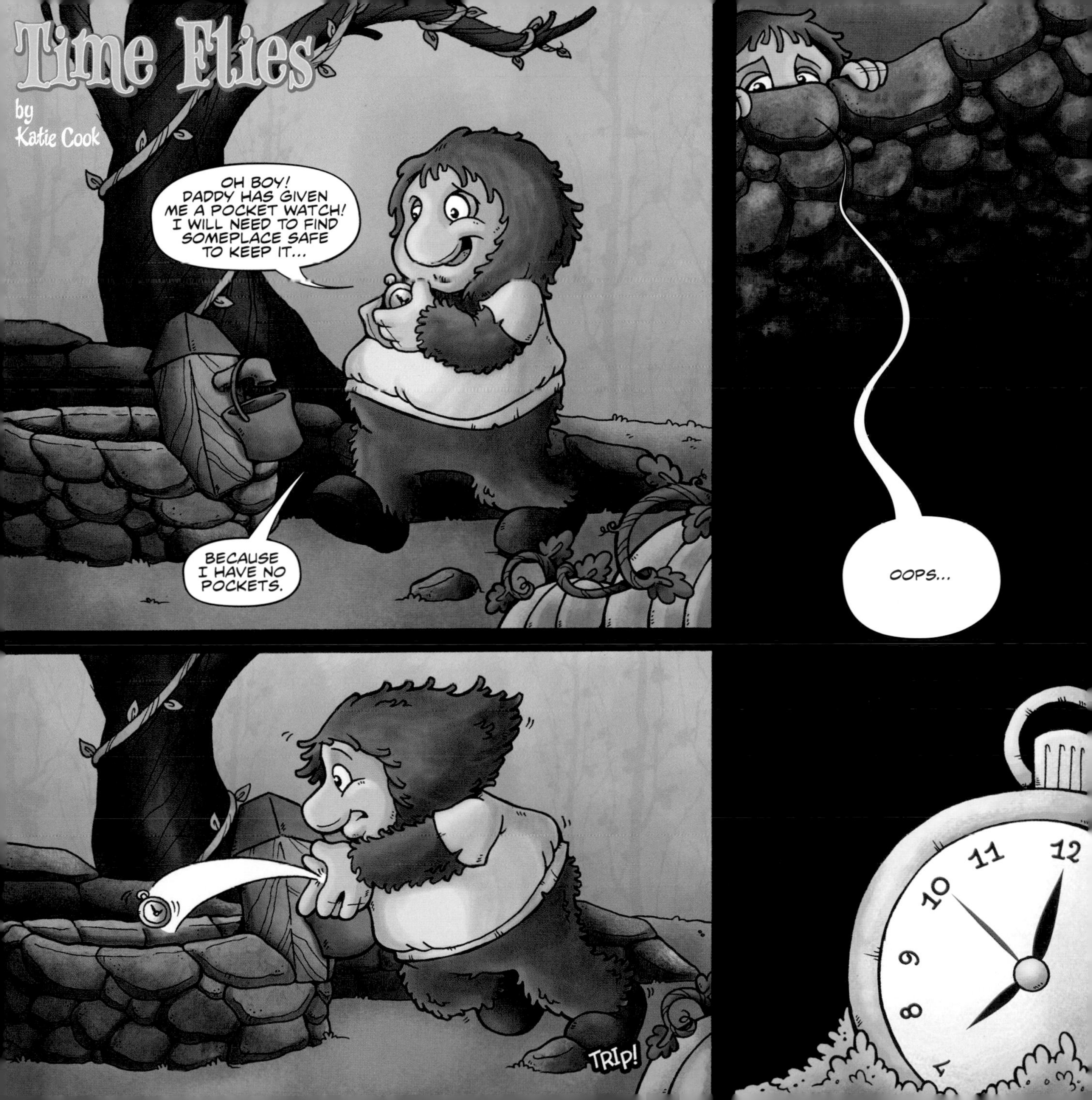
Time Flies
by
Katie Cook
OH BOY! DADDY HAS GIVEN ME A POCKET WATCH! I WILL NEED TO FIND SOMEPLACE SAFE TO KEEP IT...
BECAUSE I HAVE NO POCKETS.
TRIP!
OOPS...
11
12
10
9
8
7

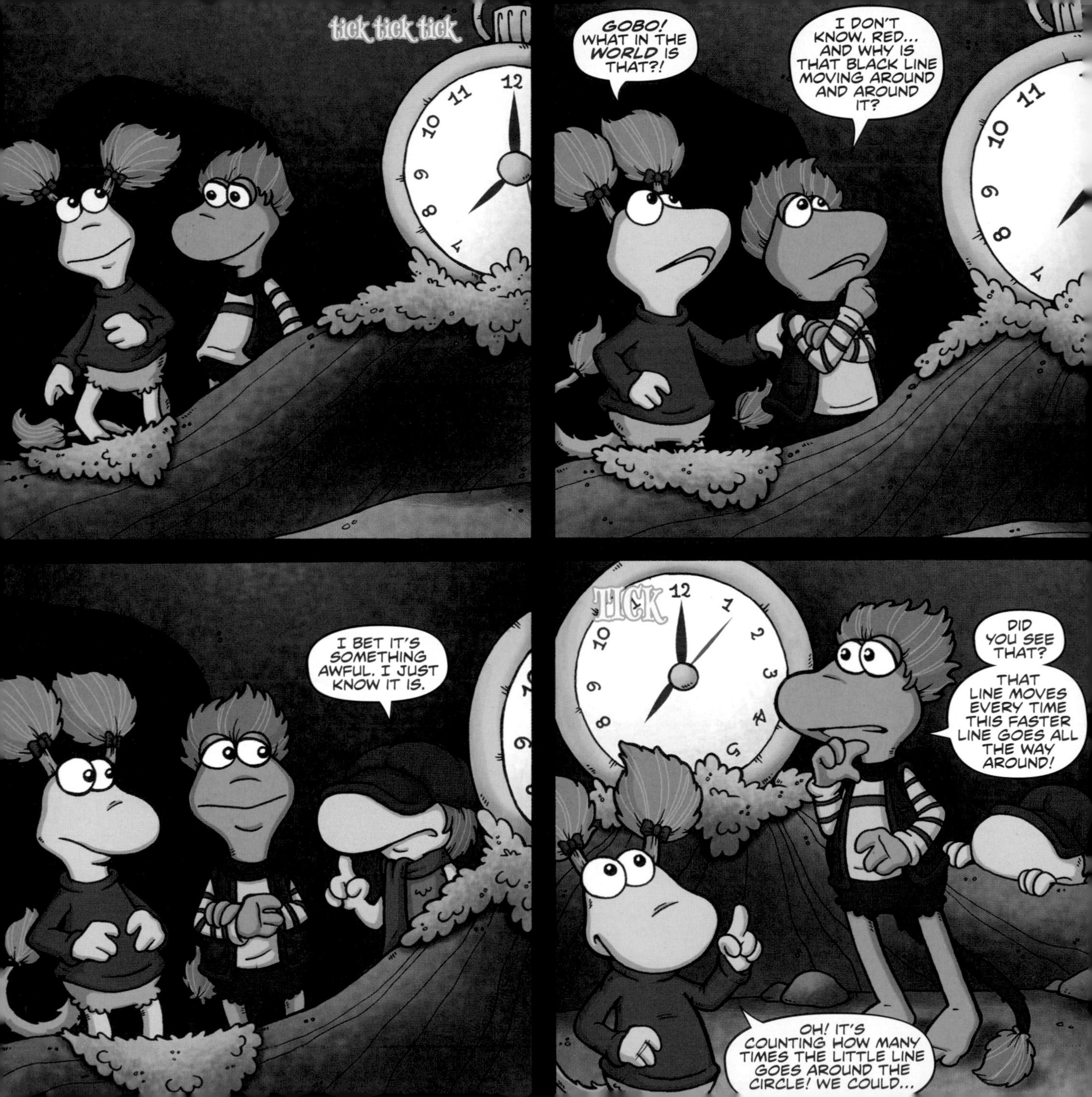
tick tick tick
GOBO! WHAT IN THE WORLD IS THAT?!
I DON'T KNOW, RED... AND WHY IS THAT BLACK LINE MOVING AROUND AND AROUND IT?
I BET IT'S SOMETHING AWFUL. I JUST KNOW IT IS.
TICK
DID YOU SEE THAT?
THAT LINE MOVES EVERY TIME THIS FASTER LINE GOES ALL THE WAY AROUND!
OH! IT'S COUNTING HOW MANY TIMES THE LITTLE LINE GOES AROUND THE CIRCLE! WE COULD...

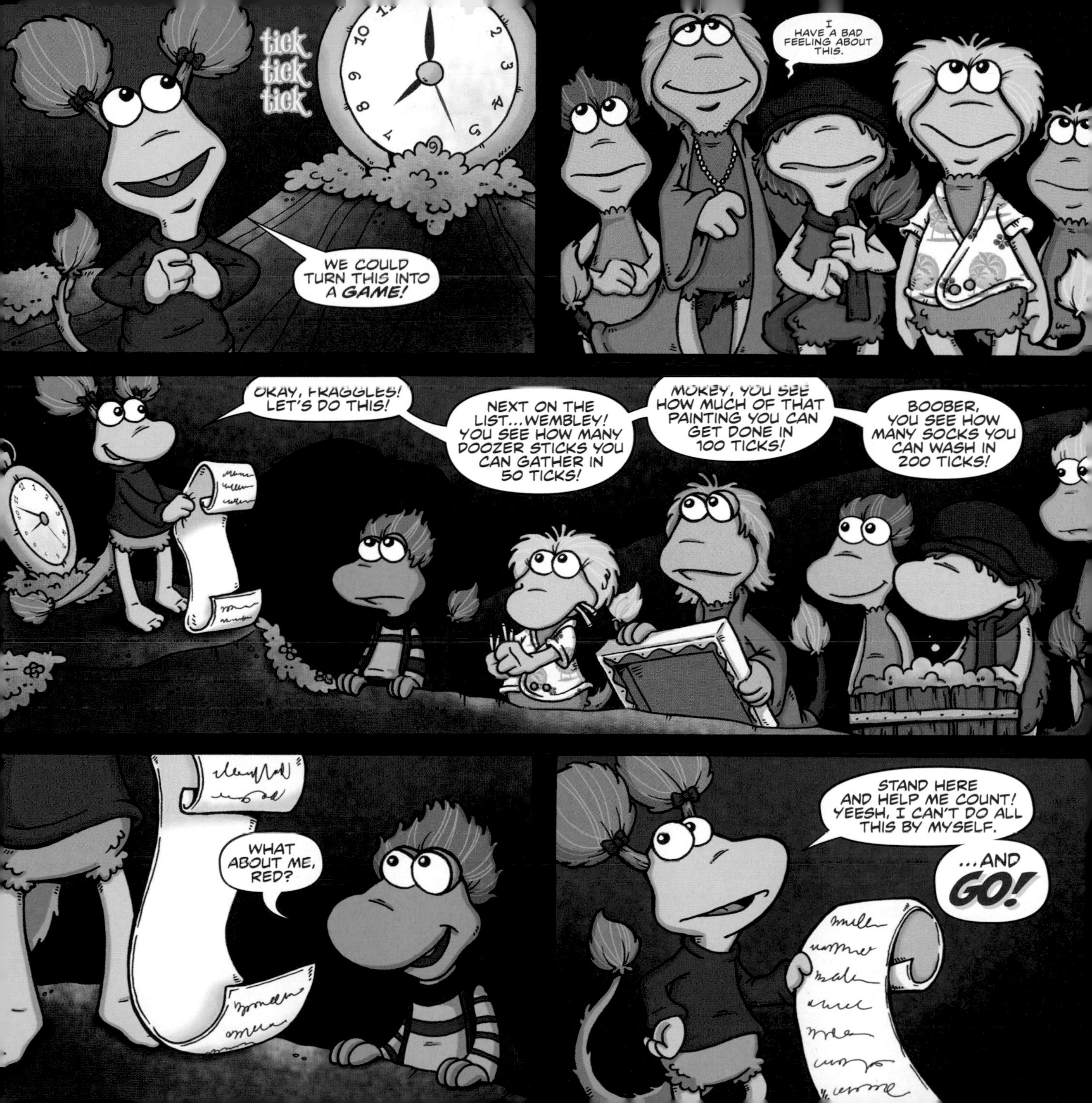
tick
tick
tick
WE COULD TURN THIS INTO A GAME!
I HAVE A BAD FEELING ABOUT THIS.
OKAY, FRAGGLES! LET'S DO THIS!
NEXT ON THE LIST...WEMBLEY! YOU SEE HOW MANY DOOZER STICKS YOU CAN GATHER IN 50 TICKS!
MOKEY, YOU SEE HOW MUCH OF THAT PAINTING YOU CAN GET DONE IN 100 TICKS!
BOOBER, YOU SEE HOW MANY SOCKS YOU CAN WASH IN 200 TICKS!
WHAT ABOUT ME, RED?
STAND HERE AND HELP ME COUNT! YEESH, I CAN'T DO ALL THIS BY MYSELF.
...AND GO!

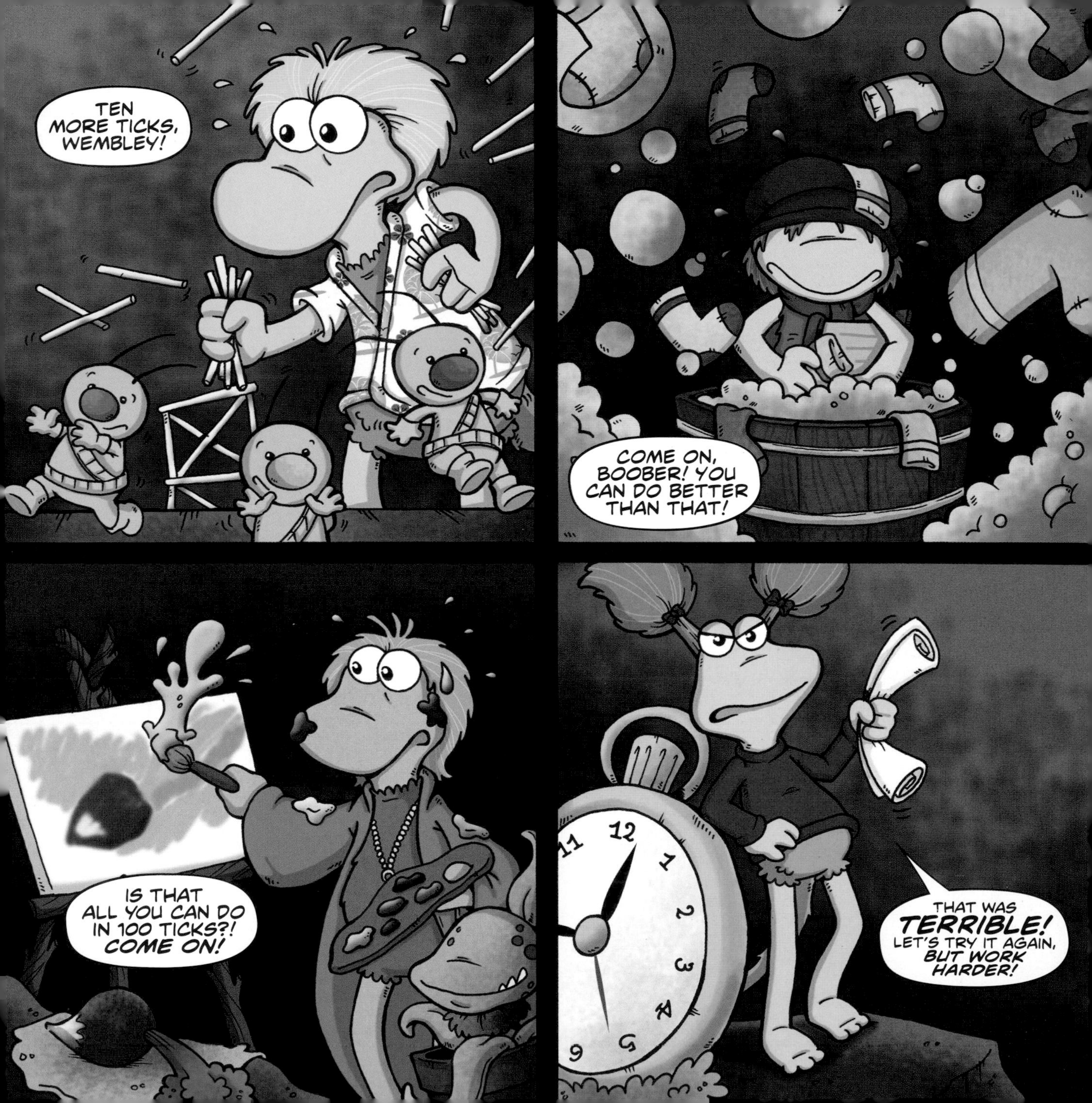
TEN MORE TICKS, WEMBLEY!
COME ON, BOOBER! YOU CAN DO BETTER THAN THAT!
IS THAT ALL YOU CAN DO IN 100 TICKS?! COME ON!
12
1
2
3
4
5
6
11
THAT WAS TERRIBLE! LET'S TRY IT AGAIN, BUT WORK HARDER!

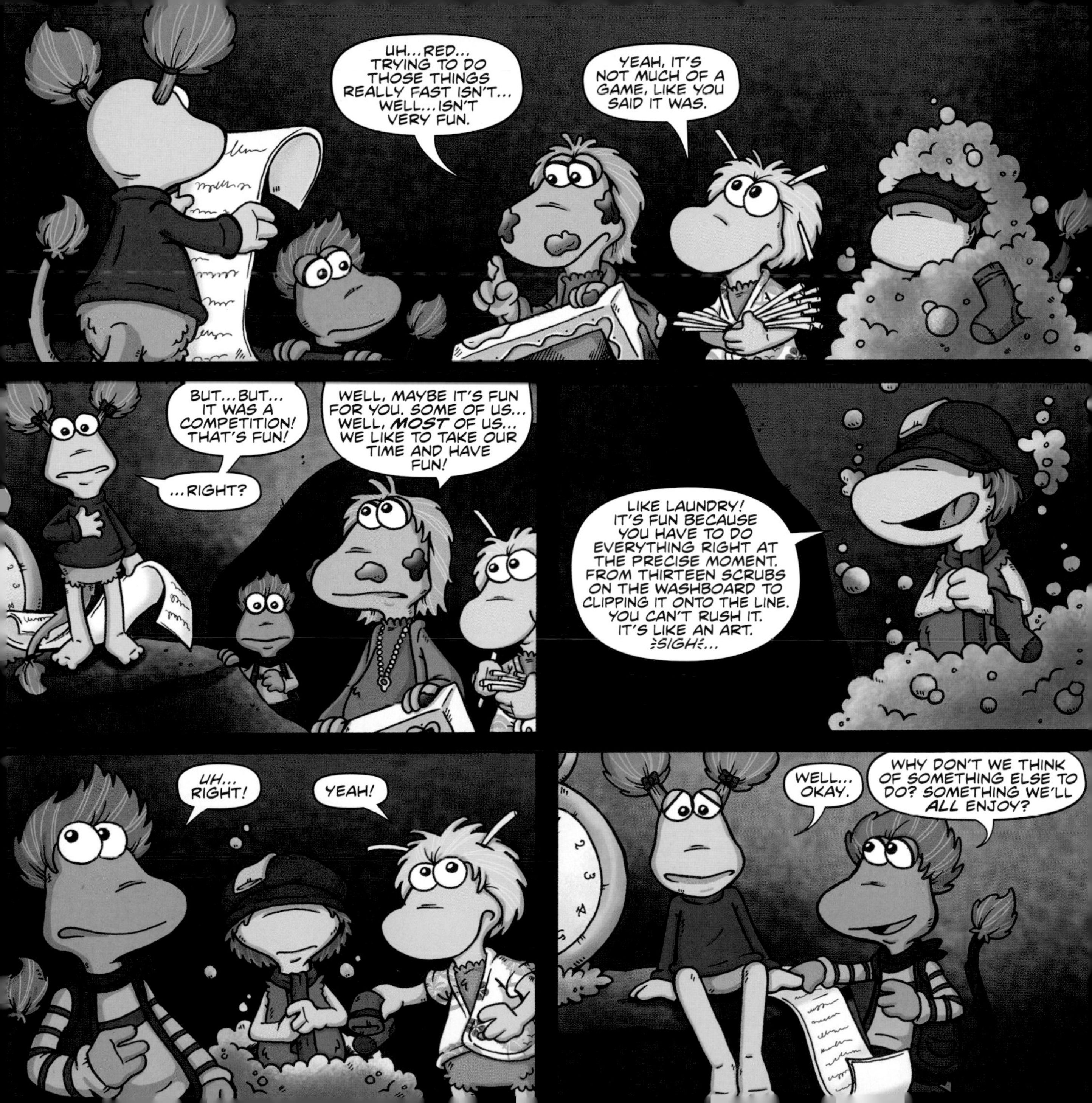
UH...RED... TRYING TO DO THOSE THINGS REALLY FAST ISN'T... WELL...ISN'T VERY FUN.
YEAH, IT'S NOT MUCH OF A GAME, LIKE YOU SAID IT WAS.
BUT...BUT... IT WAS A COMPETITION! THAT'S FUN!
...RIGHT?
WELL, MAYBE IT'S FUN FOR YOU. SOME OF US... WELL, MOST OF US... WE LIKE TO TAKE OUR TIME AND HAVE FUN!
LIKE LAUNDRY! IT'S FUN BECAUSE YOU HAVE TO DO EVERYTHING RIGHT AT THE PRECISE MOMENT. FROM THIRTEEN SCRUBS ON THE WASHBOARD TO CLIPPING IT ONTO THE LINE. YOU CAN'T RUSH IT. IT'S LIKE AN ART. *SIGH*...
UH... RIGHT!
YEAH!
WELL... OKAY.
WHY DON'T WE THINK OF SOMETHING ELSE TO DO? SOMETHING WE'LL ALL ENJOY?

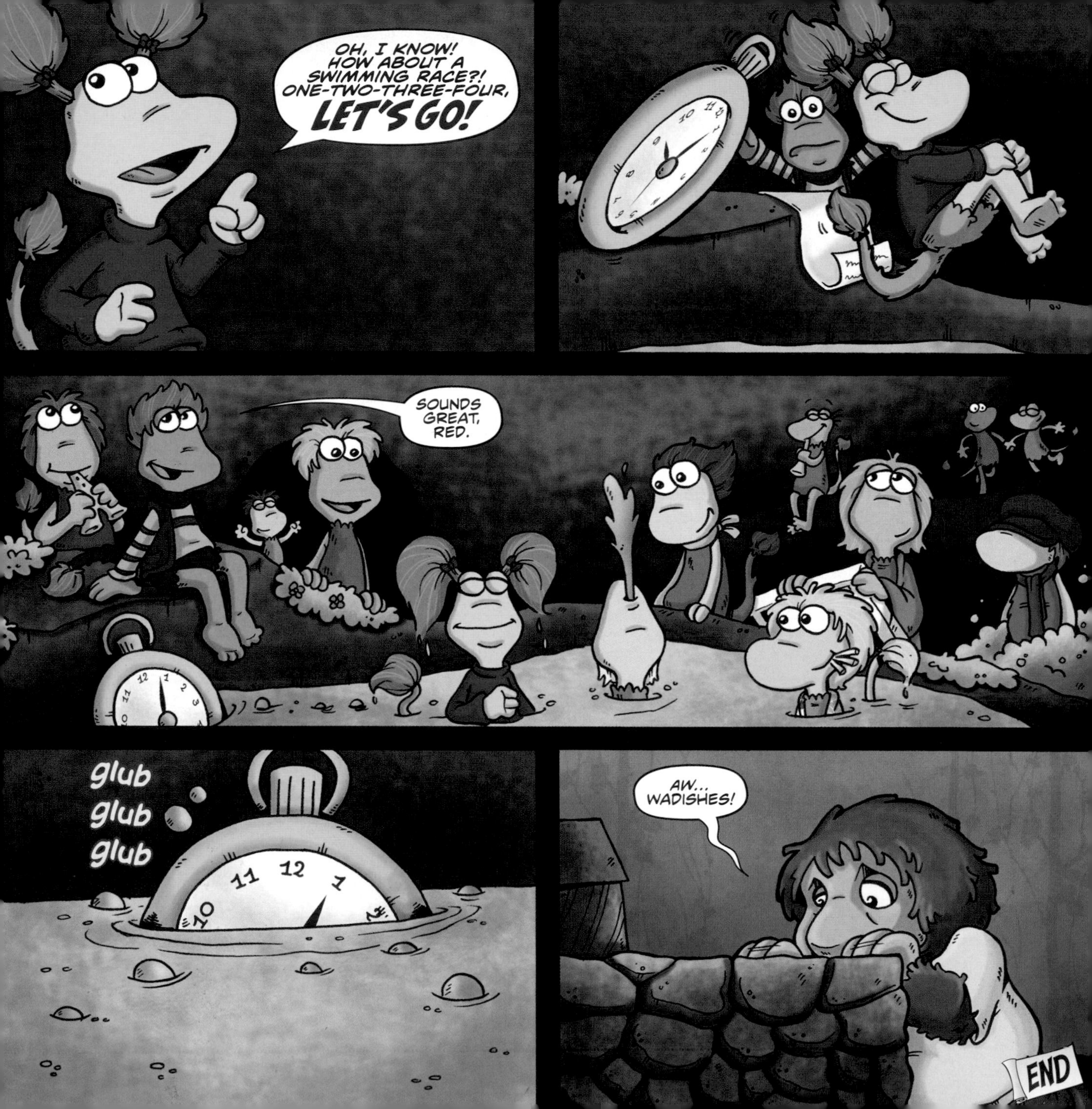
OH, I KNOW! HOW ABOUT A SWIMMING RACE?! ONE-TWO-THREE-FOUR, LET'S GO!
SOUNDS GREAT, RED.
glub
glub
glub
AW... WADISHES!
END

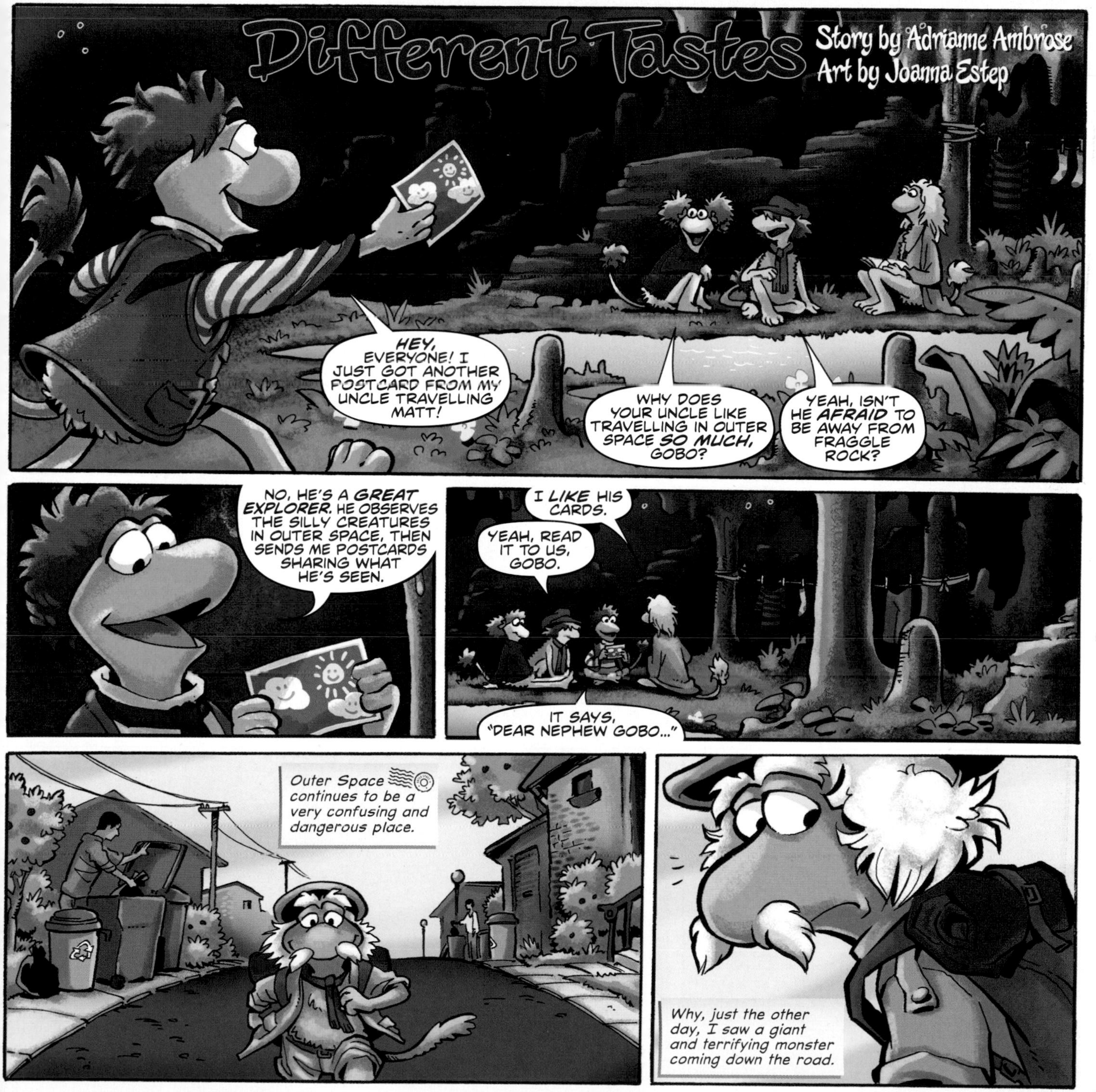

Different Tastes
Story by Adrianne Ambrose
Art by Joanna Estep
HEY, EVERYONE! I JUST GOT ANOTHER POSTCARD FROM MY UNCLE TRAVELLING MATT!
WHY DOES YOUR UNCLE LIKE TRAVELLING IN OUTER SPACE SO MUCH, GOBO?
YEAH, ISN'T HE AFRAID TO BE AWAY FROM FRAGGLE ROCK?
NO, HE'S A GREAT EXPLORER. HE OBSERVES THE SILLY CREATURES IN OUTER SPACE, THEN SENDS ME POSTCARDS SHARING WHAT HE'S SEEN.
I LIKE HIS CARDS.
YEAH, READ IT TO US, GOBO.
IT SAYS, "DEAR NEPHEW GOBO..."
Outer Space continues to be a very confusing and dangerous place.
Why, just the other day, I saw a giant and terrifying monster coming down the road.

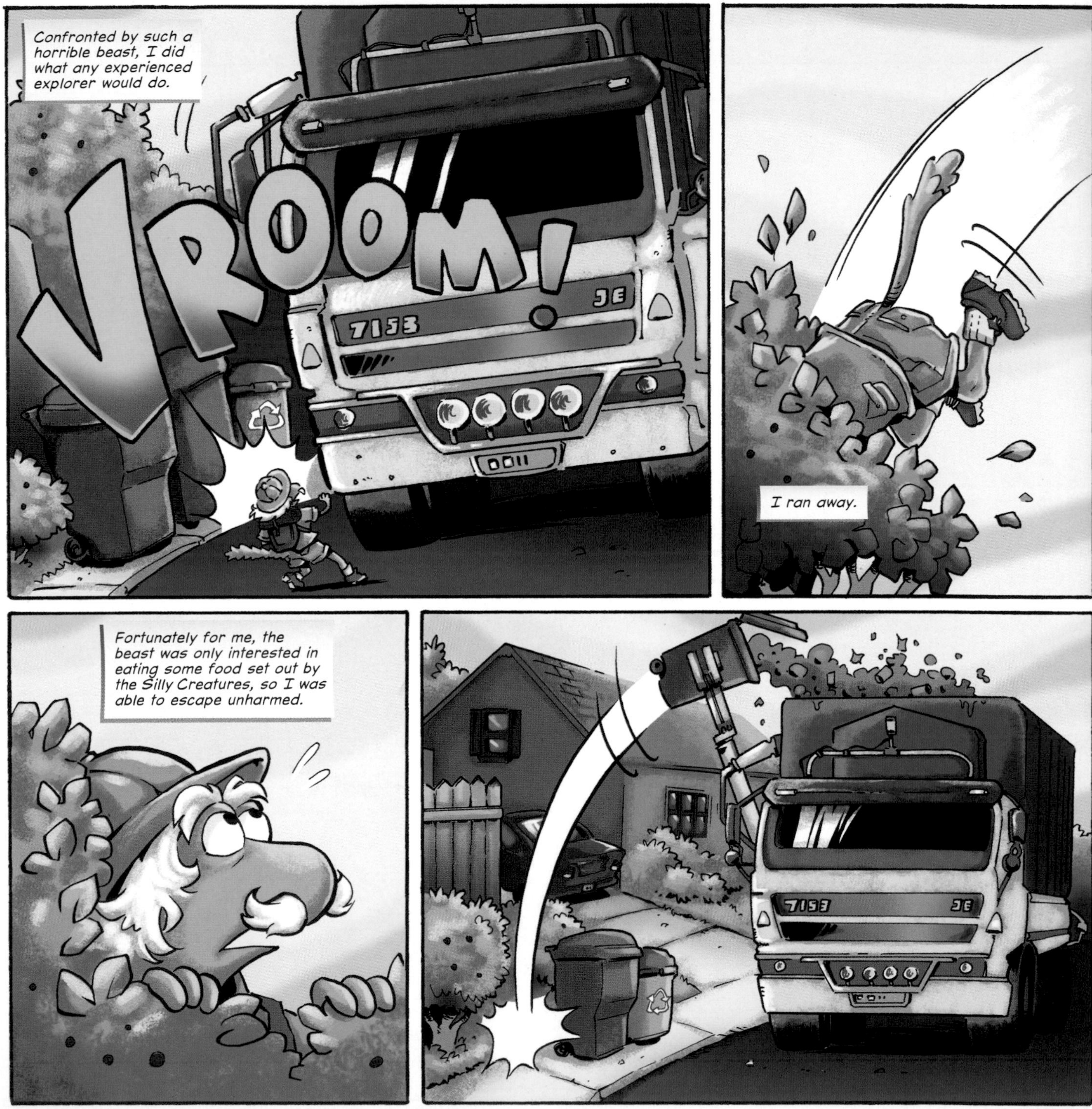
Confronted by such a horrible beast, I did what any experienced explorer would do.
VROOM!
7153
JE
I ran away.
Fortunately for me, the beast was only interested in eating some food set out by the Silly Creatures, so I was able to escape unharmed.
7153
JE

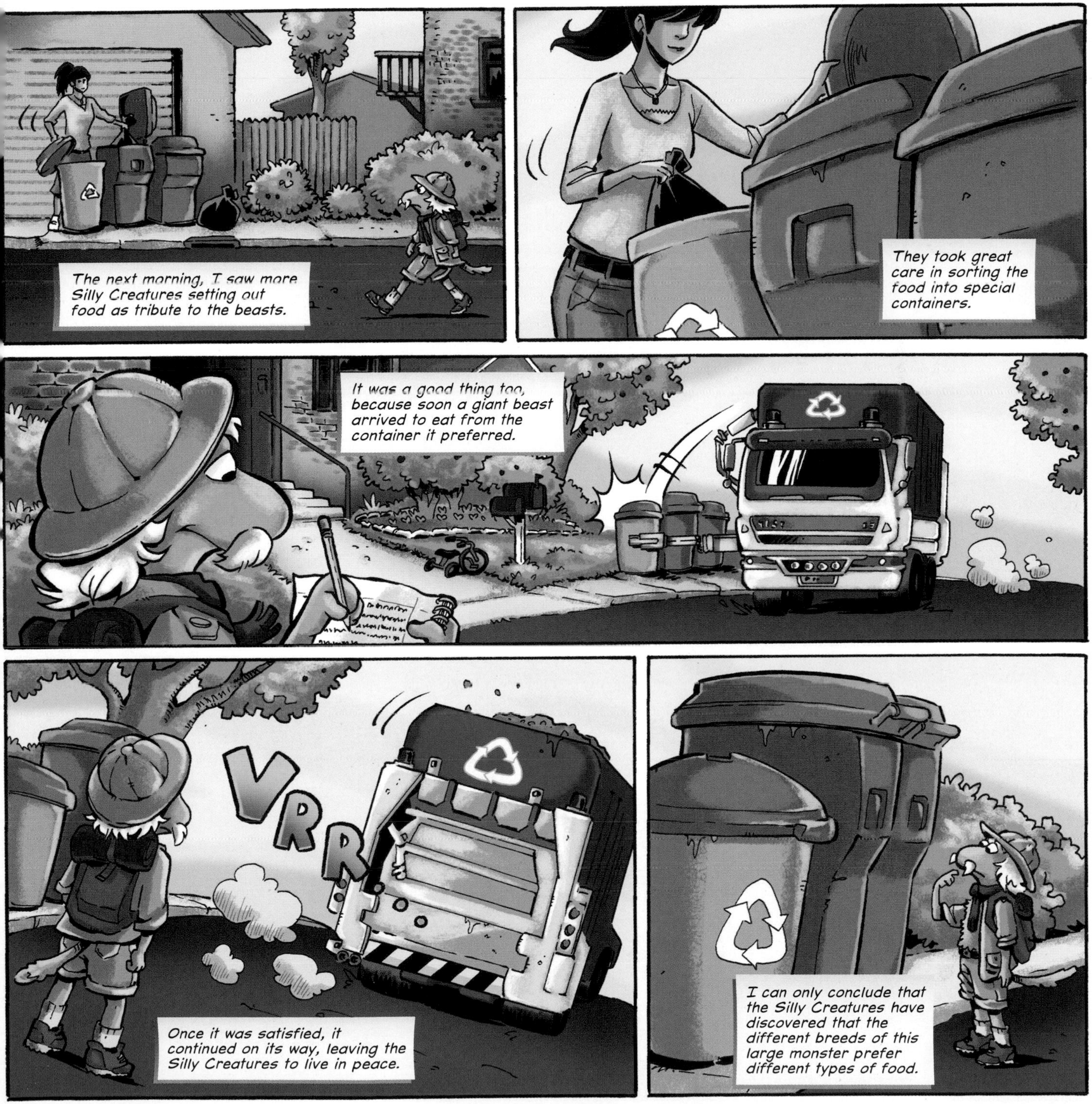
The next morning, I saw more Silly Creatures setting out food as tribute to the beasts.
They took great care in sorting the food into special containers.
It was a good thing too, because soon a giant beast arrived to eat from the container it preferred.
VRR
Once it was satisfied, it continued on its way, leaving the Silly Creatures to live in peace.
I can only conclude that the Silly Creatures have discovered that the different breeds of this large monster prefer different types of food.

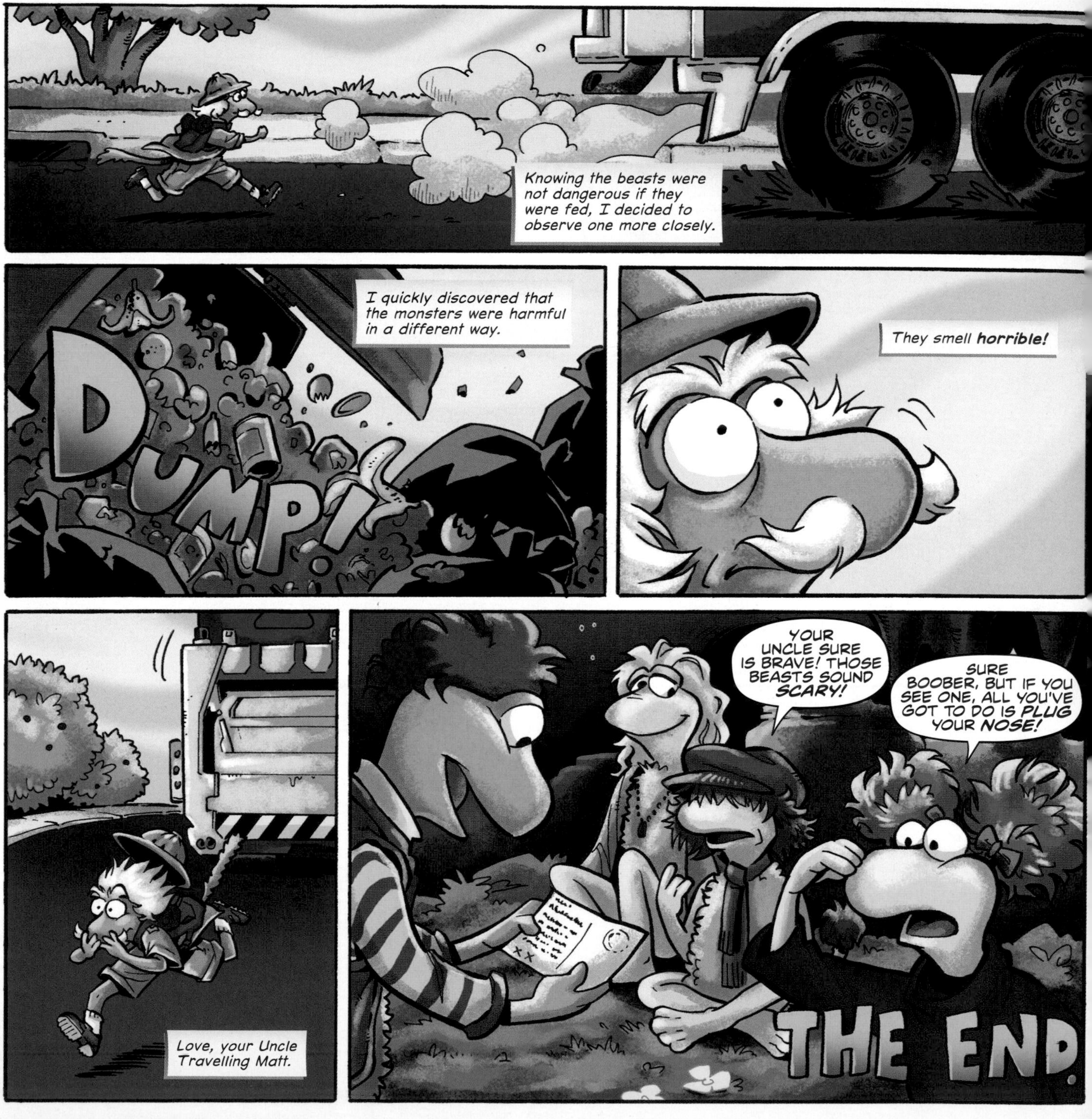

Knowing the beasts were not dangerous if they were fed, I decided to observe one more closely.
I quickly discovered that the monsters were harmful in a different way.
DUMP!
They smell **horrible!**
Love, your Uncle Travelling Matt.
YOUR UNCLE SURE IS BRAVE! THOSE BEASTS SOUND *SCARY!*
SURE BOOBER, BUT IF YOU SEE ONE, ALL YOU'VE GOT TO DO IS *PLUG* YOUR *NOSE!*
THE END.

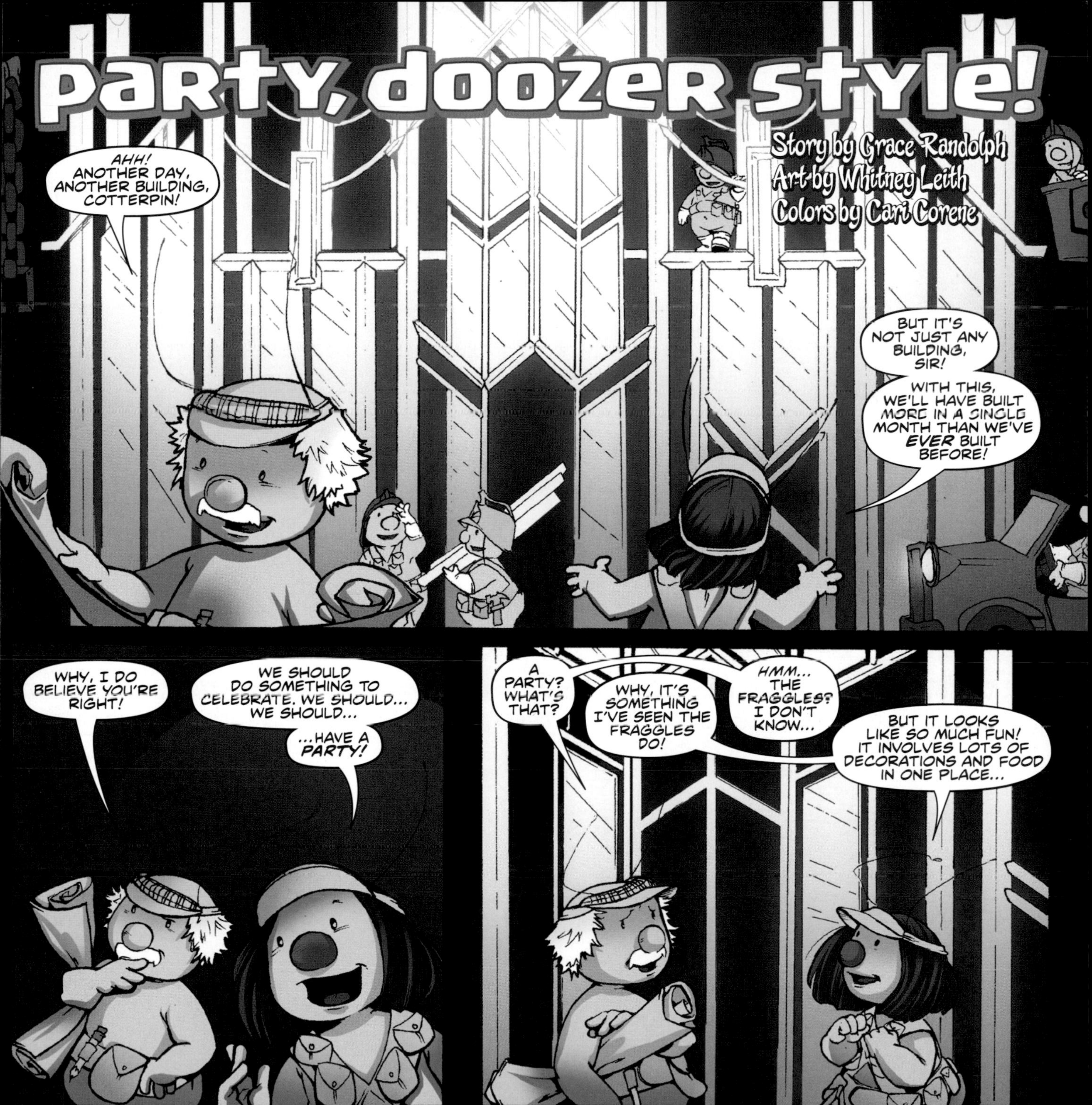
PARTY, DOOZER STYLE!
Story by Grace Randolph
Art by Whitney Leith
Colors by Cari Corene
AHH! ANOTHER DAY, ANOTHER BUILDING, COTTERPIN!
BUT IT'S NOT JUST ANY BUILDING, SIR!
WITH THIS, WE'LL HAVE BUILT MORE IN A SINGLE MONTH THAN WE'VE EVER BUILT BEFORE!
WHY, I DO BELIEVE YOU'RE RIGHT!
WE SHOULD DO SOMETHING TO CELEBRATE. WE SHOULD... WE SHOULD...
...HAVE A PARTY!
A PARTY? WHAT'S THAT?
WHY, IT'S SOMETHING I'VE SEEN THE FRAGGLES DO!
HMM... THE FRAGGLES? I DON'T KNOW...
BUT IT LOOKS LIKE SO MUCH FUN! IT INVOLVES LOTS OF DECORATIONS AND FOOD IN ONE PLACE...

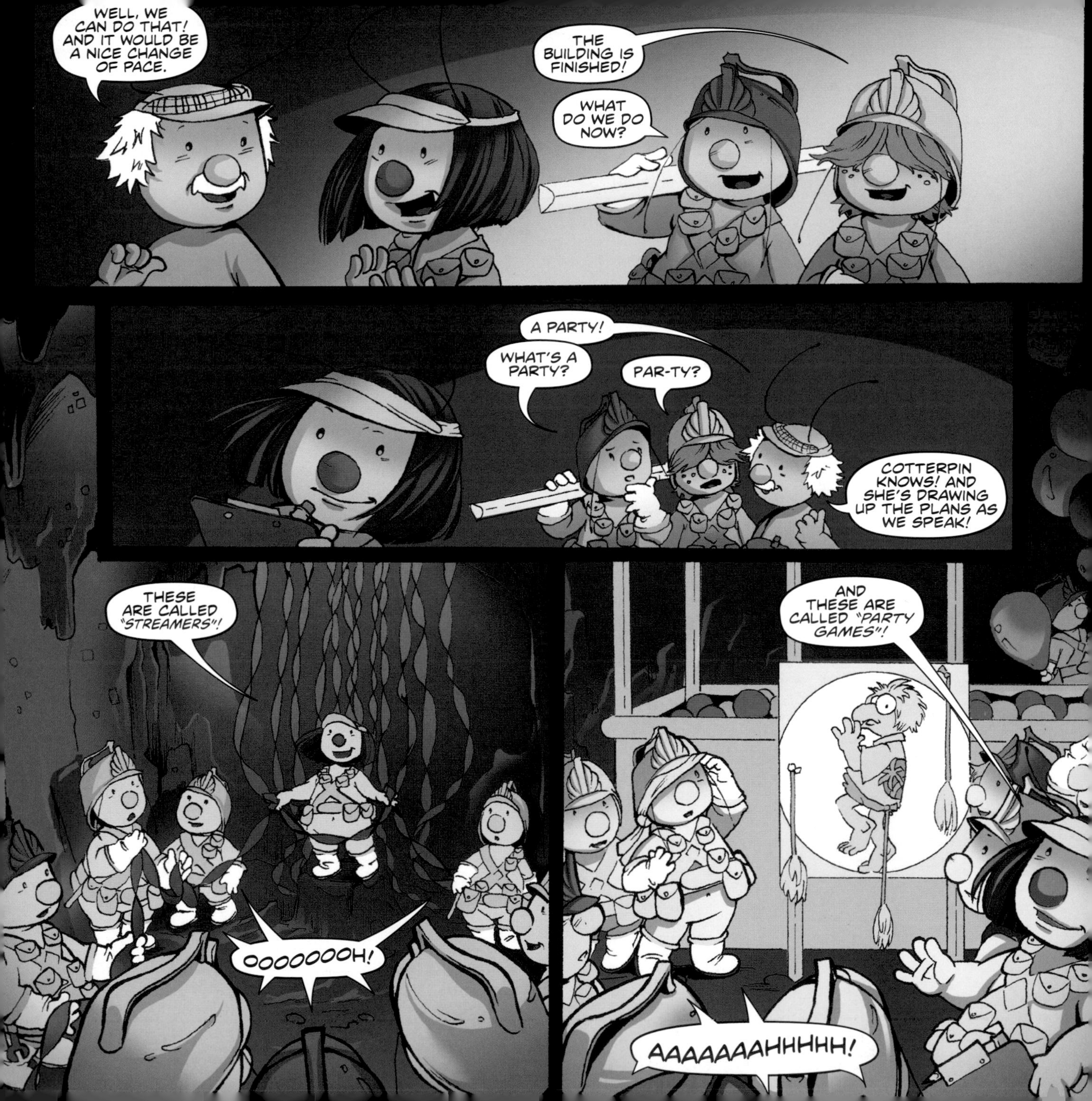
WELL, WE CAN DO THAT! AND IT WOULD BE A NICE CHANGE OF PACE.
THE BUILDING IS FINISHED!
WHAT DO WE DO NOW?
A PARTY!
WHAT'S A PARTY?
PAR-TY?
COTTERPIN KNOWS! AND SHE'S DRAWING UP THE PLANS AS WE SPEAK!
THESE ARE CALLED "STREAMERS"!
OOOOOOOH!
AND THESE ARE CALLED "PARTY GAMES"!
AAAAAAAHHHHH!

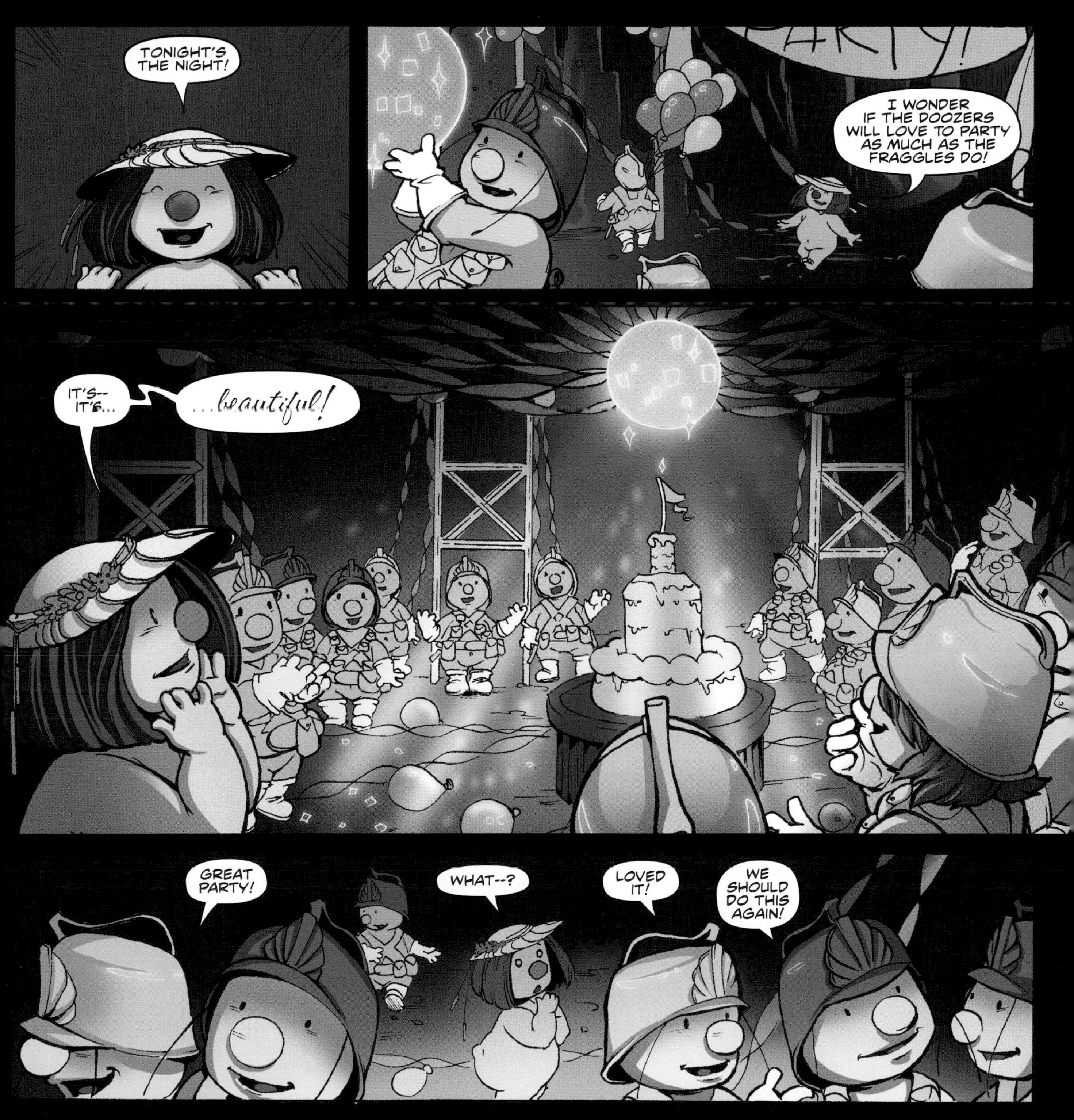
TONIGHT'S THE NIGHT!
I WONDER IF THE DOOZERS WILL LOVE TO PARTY AS MUCH AS THE FRAGGLES DO!
IT'S-- IT'S...
...beautiful!
GREAT PARTY!
WHAT--?
LOVED IT!
WE SHOULD DO THIS AGAIN!

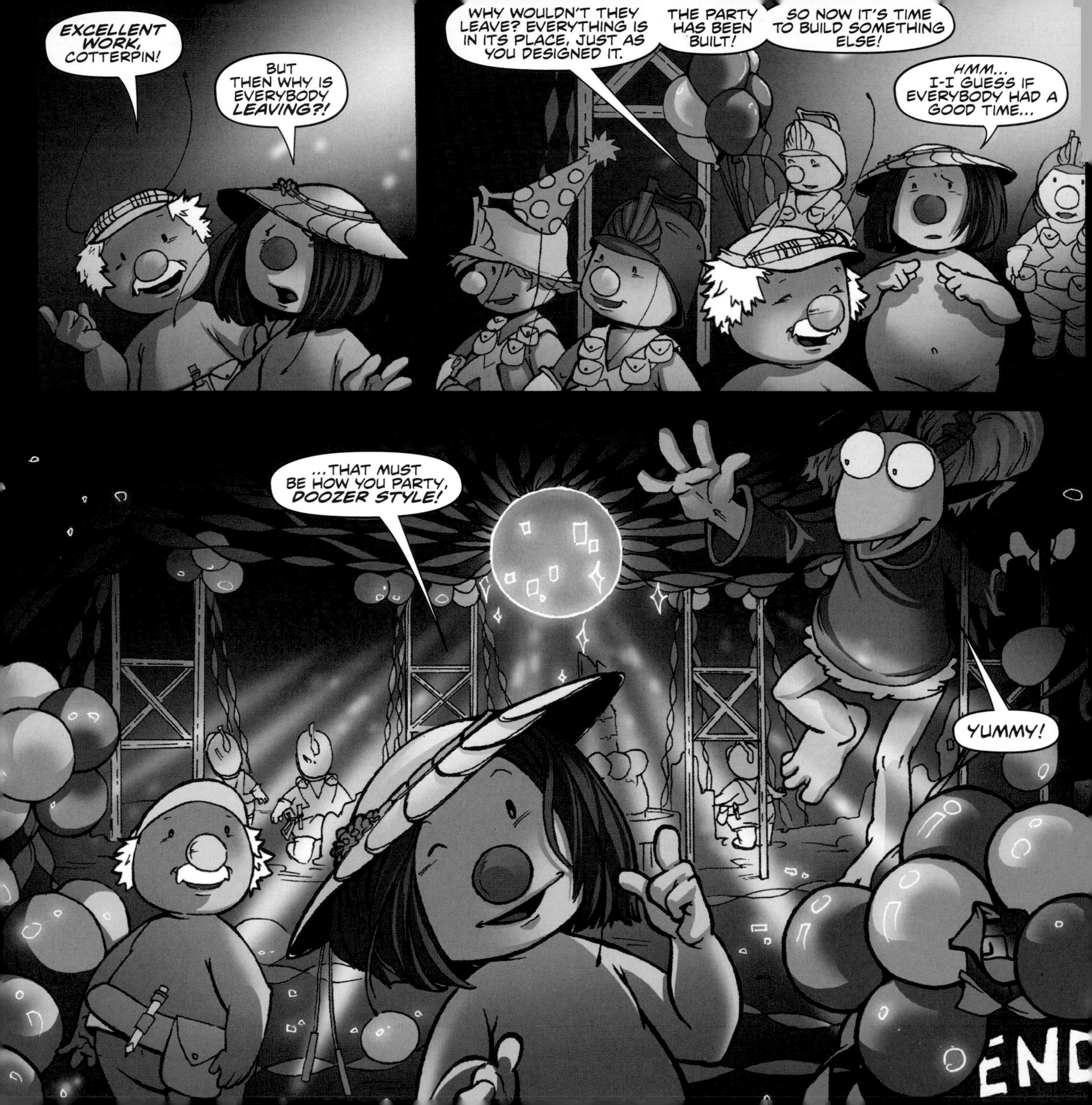
EXCELLENT WORK, COTTERPIN!
BUT THEN WHY IS EVERYBODY LEAVING?!
WHY WOULDN'T THEY LEAVE? EVERYTHING IS IN ITS PLACE, JUST AS YOU DESIGNED IT.
THE PARTY HAS BEEN BUILT!
SO NOW IT'S TIME TO BUILD SOMETHING ELSE!
HMM... I-I GUESS IF EVERYBODY HAD A GOOD TIME...
...THAT MUST BE HOW YOU PARTY, DOOZER STYLE!
YUMMY!
END

A Visitor from Outer Space

Story by Leigh Dragoon Art by Jake Myler

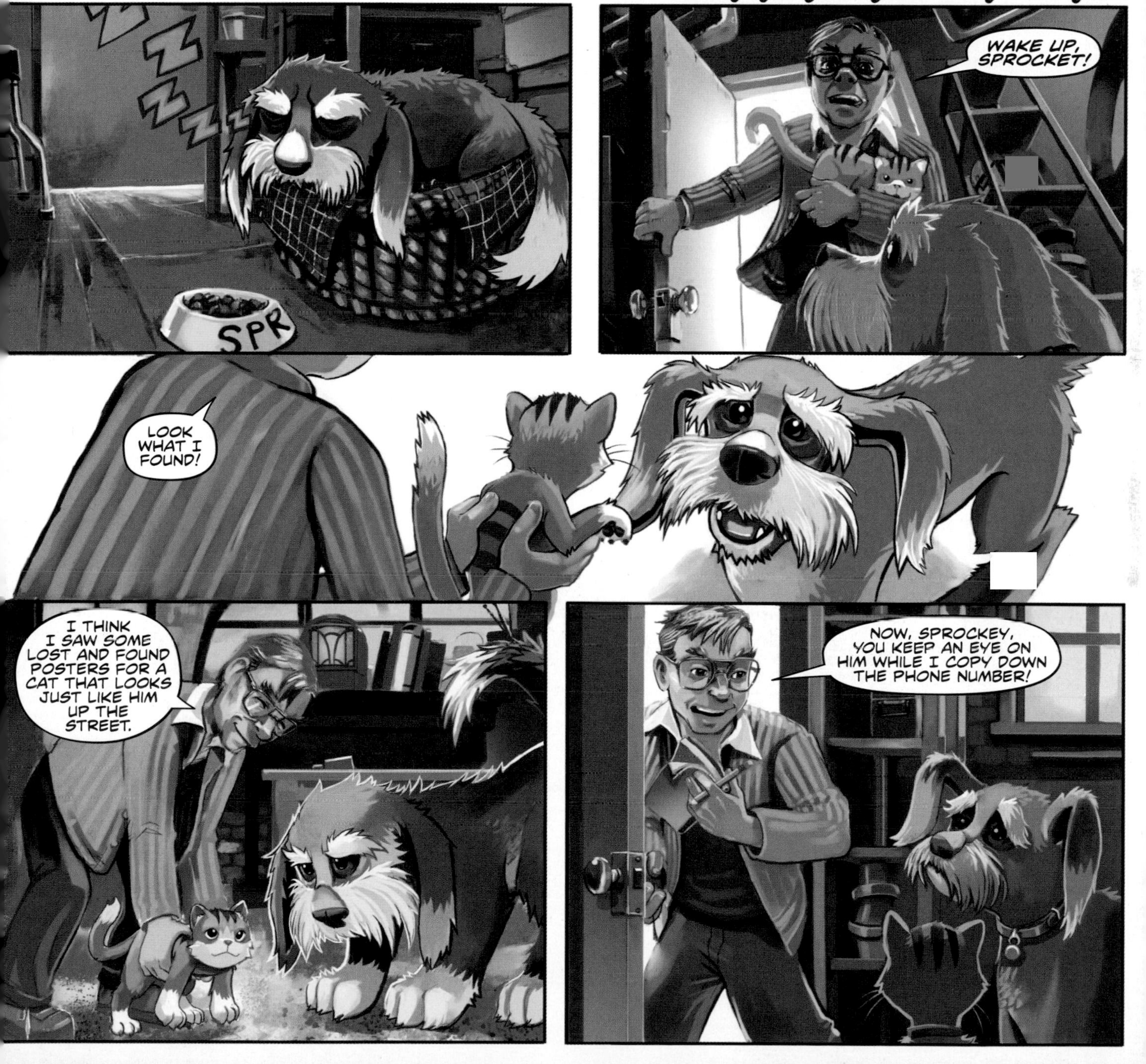

SPR
WAKE UP, SPROCKET!
LOOK WHAT I FOUND!
I THINK I SAW SOME LOST AND FOUND POSTERS FOR A CAT THAT LOOKS JUST LIKE HIM UP THE STREET.
NOW, SPROCKEY, YOU KEEP AN EYE ON HIM WHILE I COPY DOWN THE PHONE NUMBER!

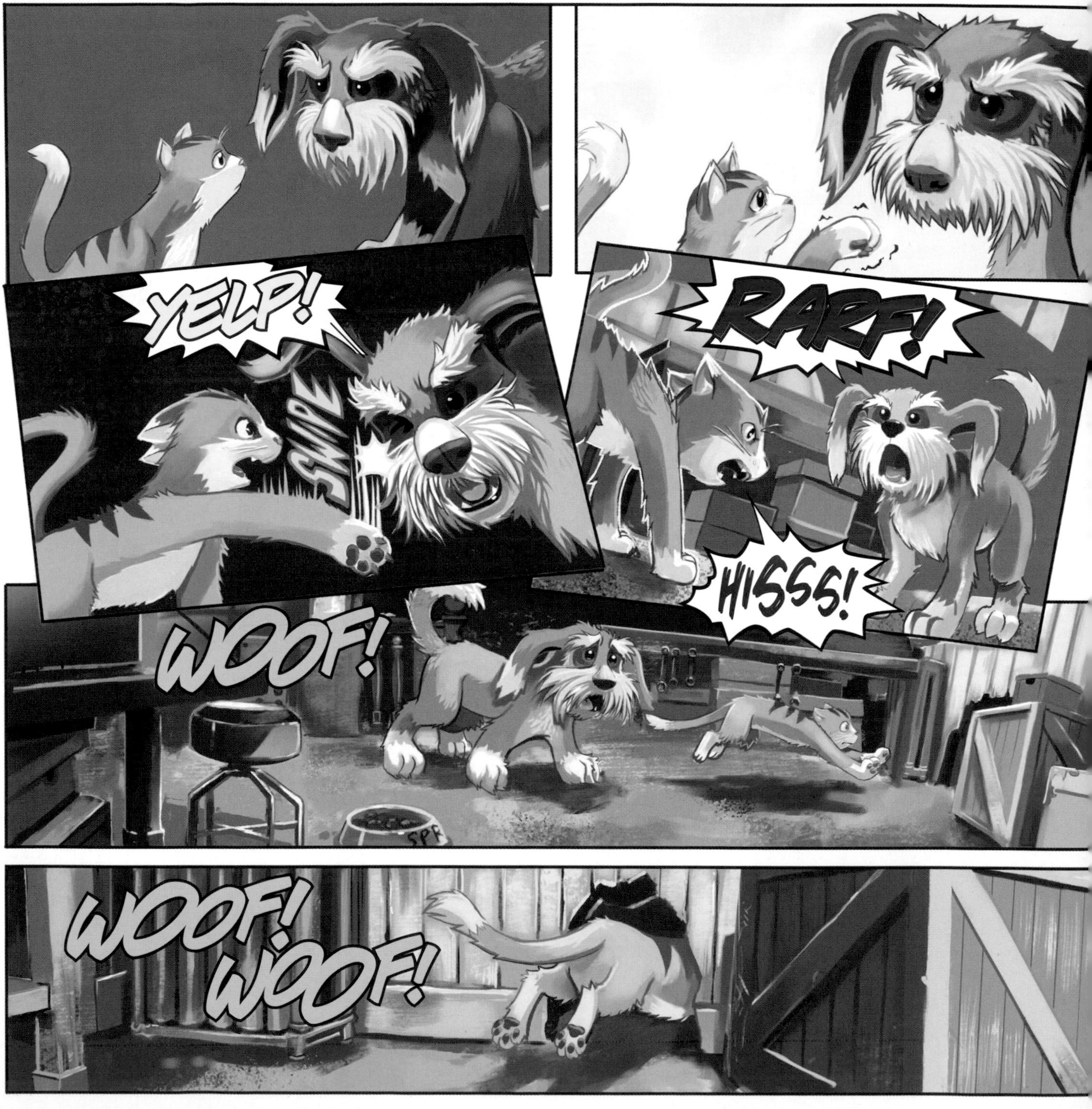
YELP!
SWIPE
RARF!
HISSS!
WOOF!
SPF
WOOF!
WOOF!

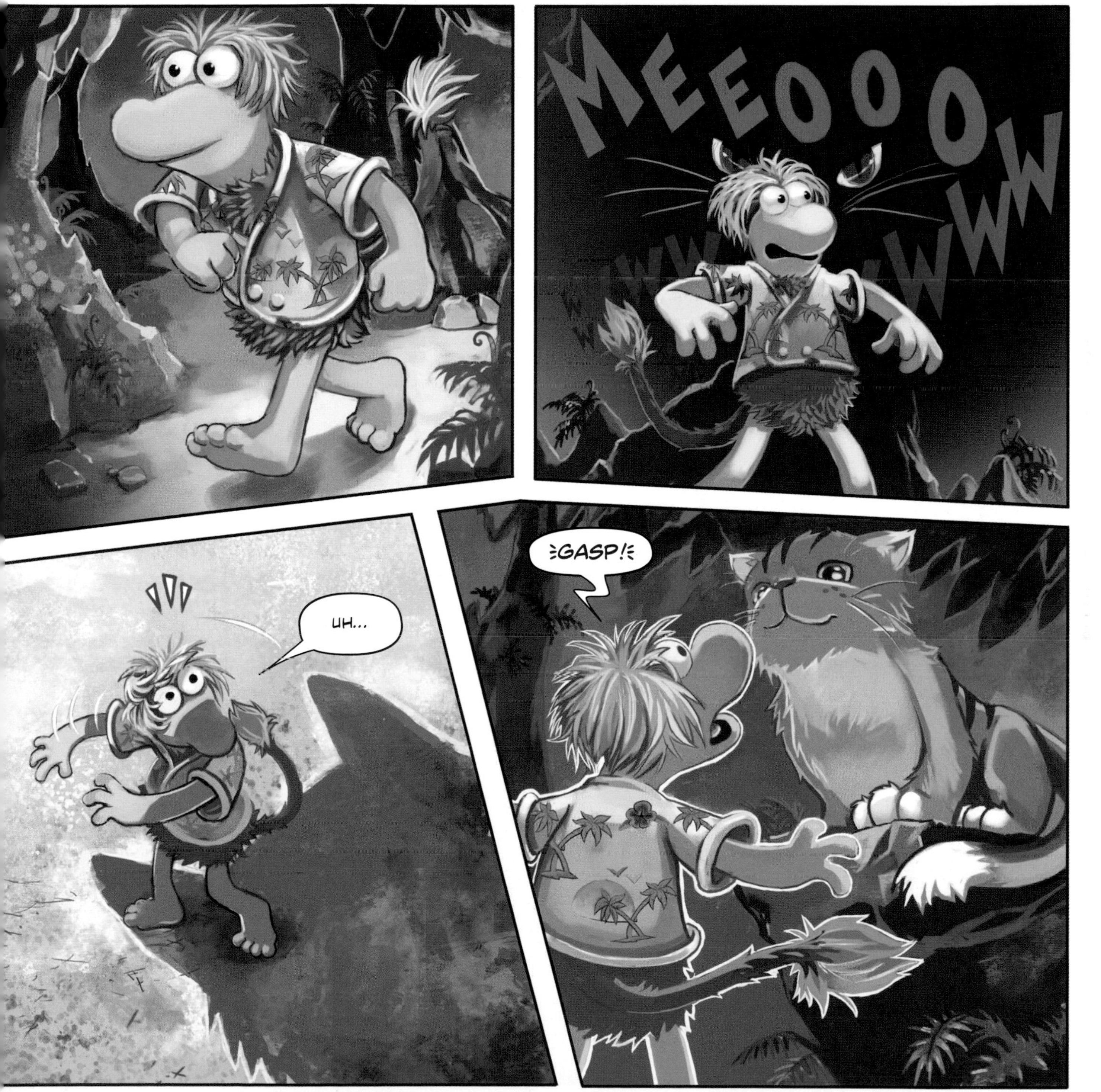
MEEOOOWWWWWWWWW
UH...
GASP!

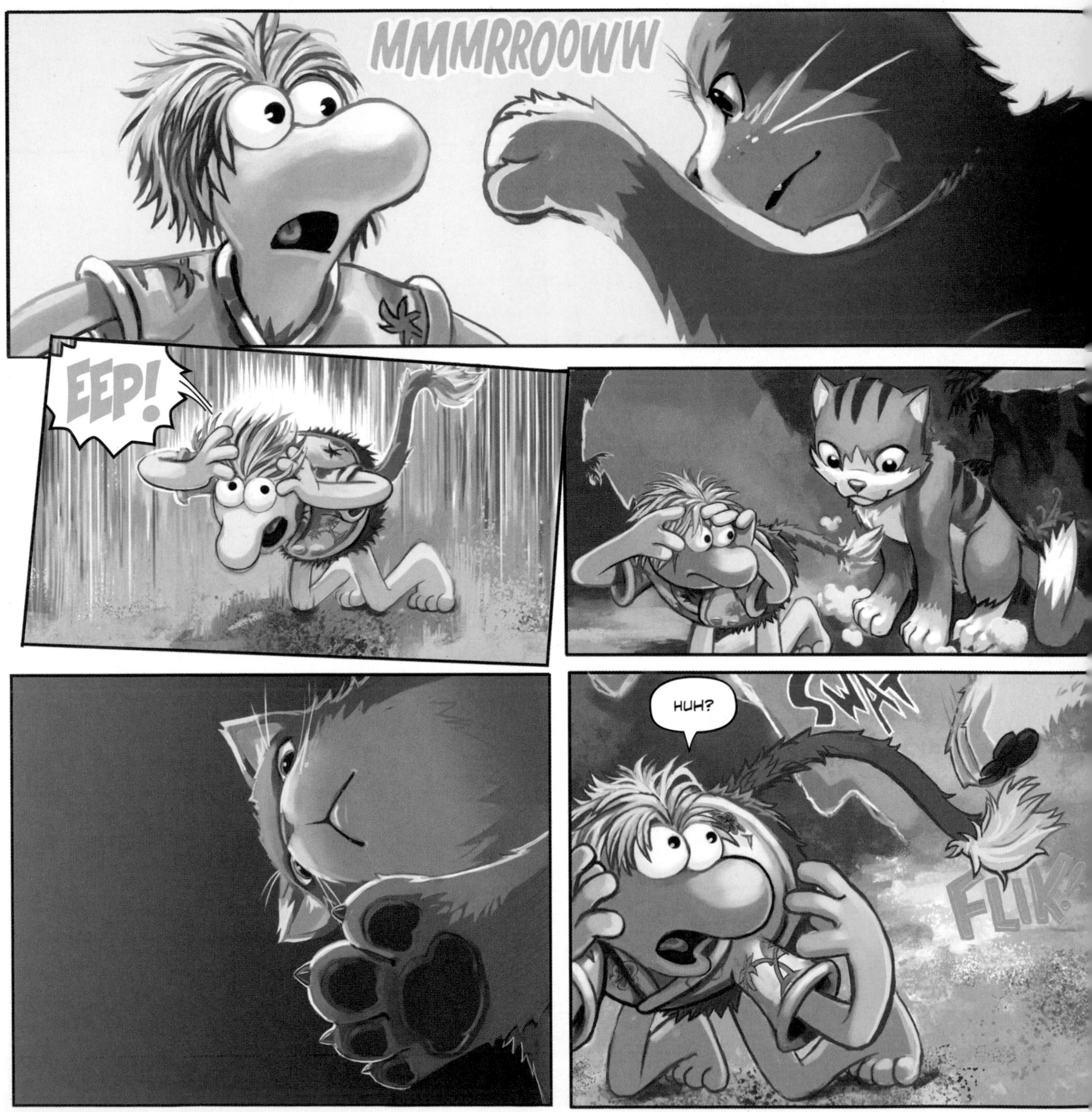
MMMRROOWW
EEP!
HUH?
SWAT
FLIK!

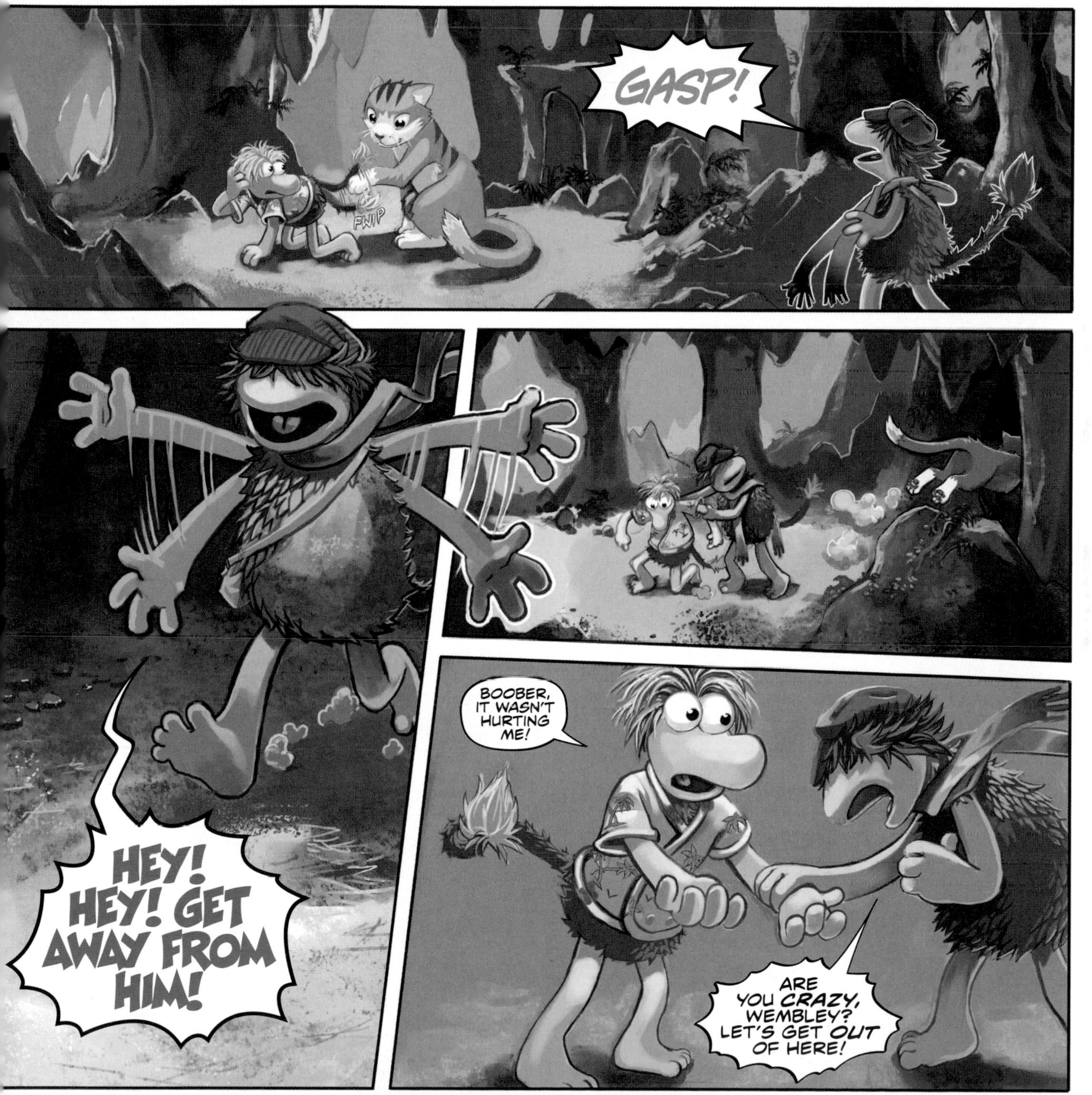
FWIP
GASP!
HEY! HEY! GET AWAY FROM HIM!
BOOBER, IT WASN'T HURTING ME!
ARE YOU CRAZY, WEMBLEY? LET'S GET OUT OF HERE!

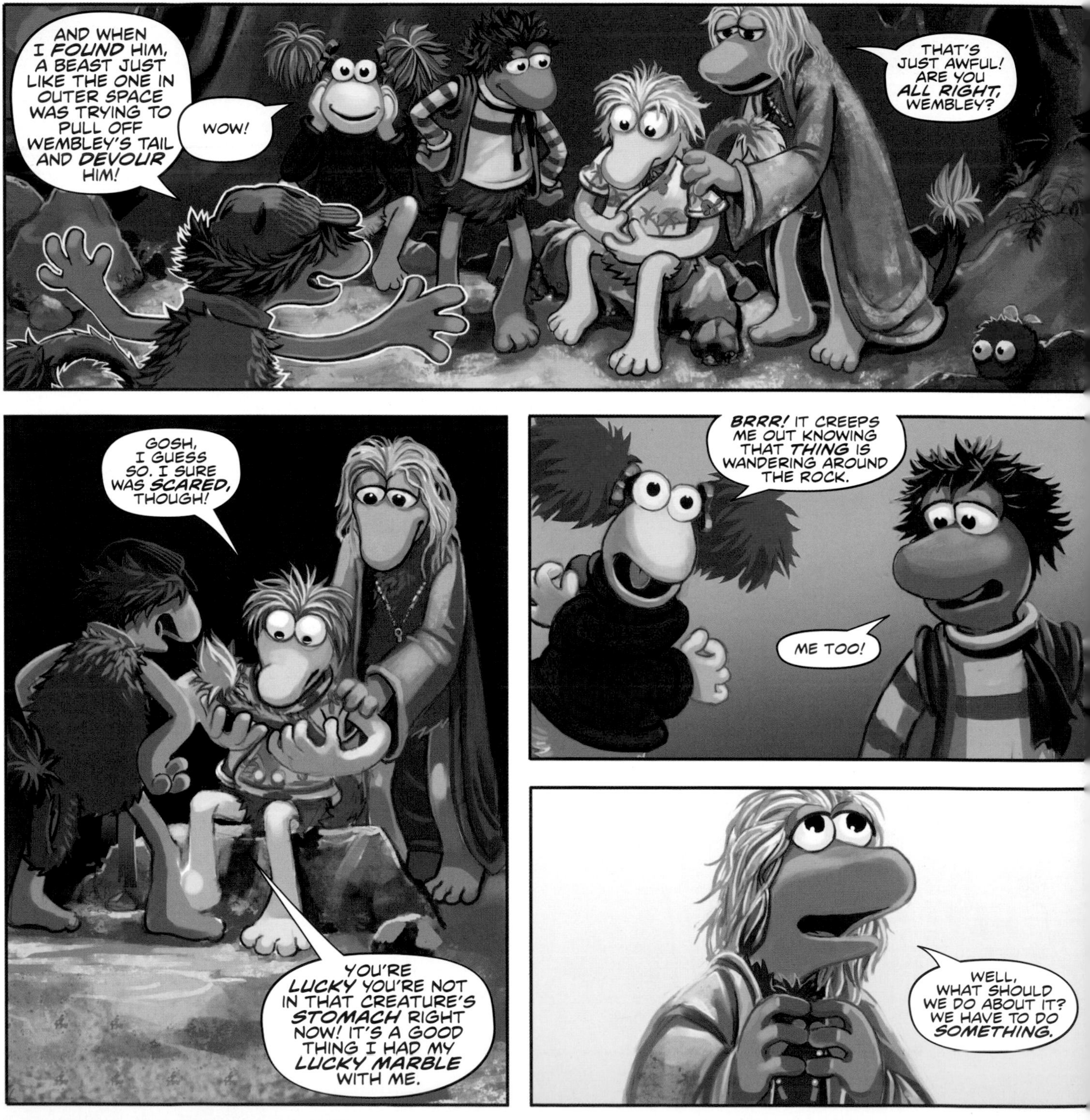
AND WHEN I FOUND HIM, A BEAST JUST LIKE THE ONE IN OUTER SPACE WAS TRYING TO PULL OFF WEMBLEY'S TAIL AND DEVOUR HIM!
WOW!
THAT'S JUST AWFUL! ARE YOU ALL RIGHT, WEMBLEY?
GOSH, I GUESS SO. I SURE WAS SCARED, THOUGH!
YOU'RE LUCKY YOU'RE NOT IN THAT CREATURE'S STOMACH RIGHT NOW! IT'S A GOOD THING I HAD MY LUCKY MARBLE WITH ME.
BRRR! IT CREEPS ME OUT KNOWING THAT THING IS WANDERING AROUND THE ROCK.
ME TOO!
WELL, WHAT SHOULD WE DO ABOUT IT? WE HAVE TO DO SOMETHING.

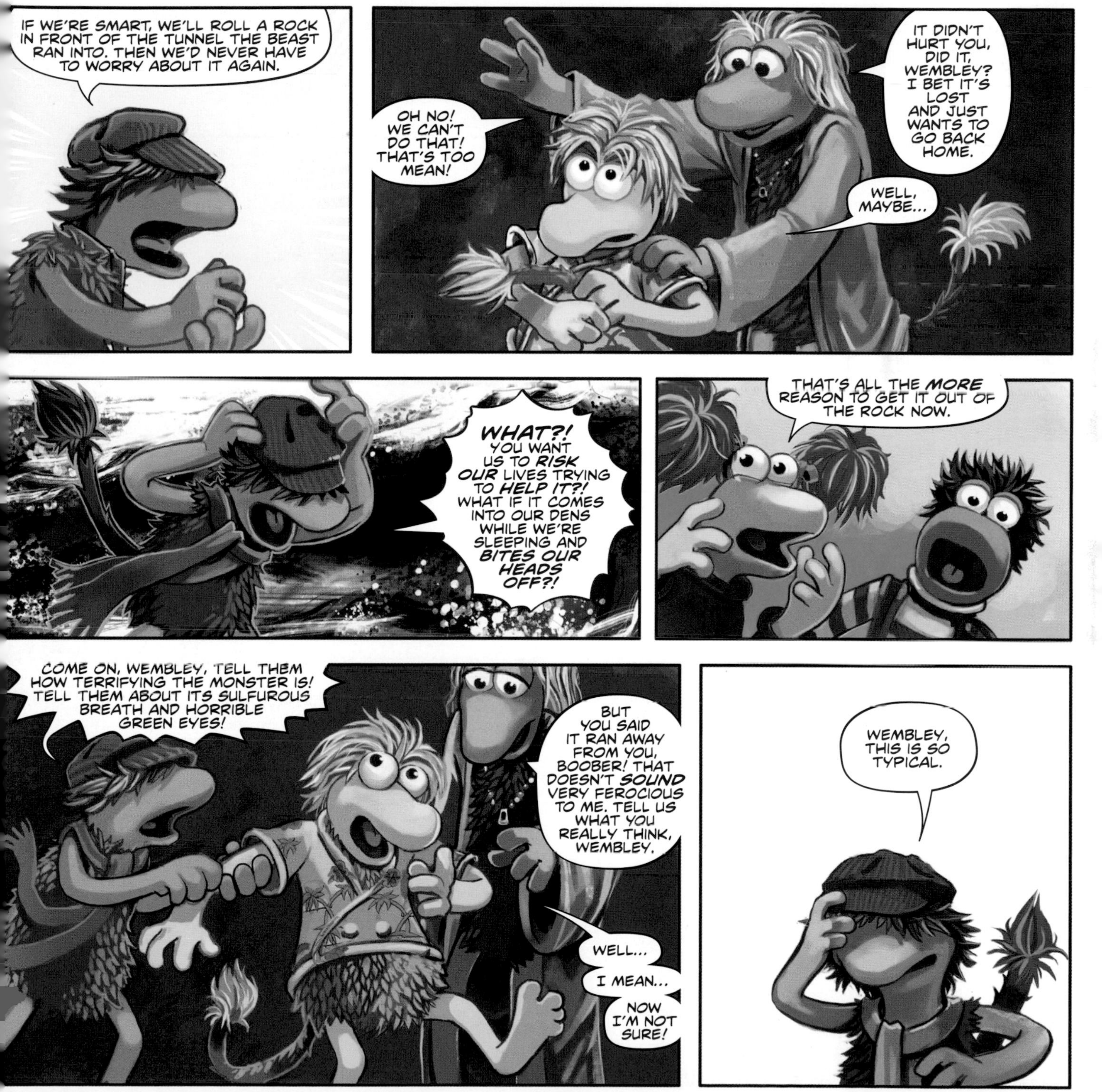
IF WE'RE SMART, WE'LL ROLL A ROCK IN FRONT OF THE TUNNEL THE BEAST RAN INTO. THEN WE'D NEVER HAVE TO WORRY ABOUT IT AGAIN.
OH NO! WE CAN'T DO THAT! THAT'S TOO MEAN!
IT DIDN'T HURT YOU, DID IT, WEMBLEY? I BET IT'S LOST AND JUST WANTS TO GO BACK HOME.
WELL, MAYBE...
WHAT?! YOU WANT US TO RISK OUR LIVES TRYING TO HELP IT?! WHAT IF IT COMES INTO OUR DENS WHILE WE'RE SLEEPING AND BITES OUR HEADS OFF?!
THAT'S ALL THE MORE REASON TO GET IT OUT OF THE ROCK NOW.
COME ON, WEMBLEY, TELL THEM HOW TERRIFYING THE MONSTER IS! TELL THEM ABOUT ITS SULFUROUS BREATH AND HORRIBLE GREEN EYES!
BUT YOU SAID IT RAN AWAY FROM YOU, BOOBER! THAT DOESN'T SOUND VERY FEROCIOUS TO ME. TELL US WHAT YOU REALLY THINK, WEMBLEY.
WELL...
I MEAN...
NOW I'M NOT SURE!
WEMBLEY, THIS IS SO TYPICAL.

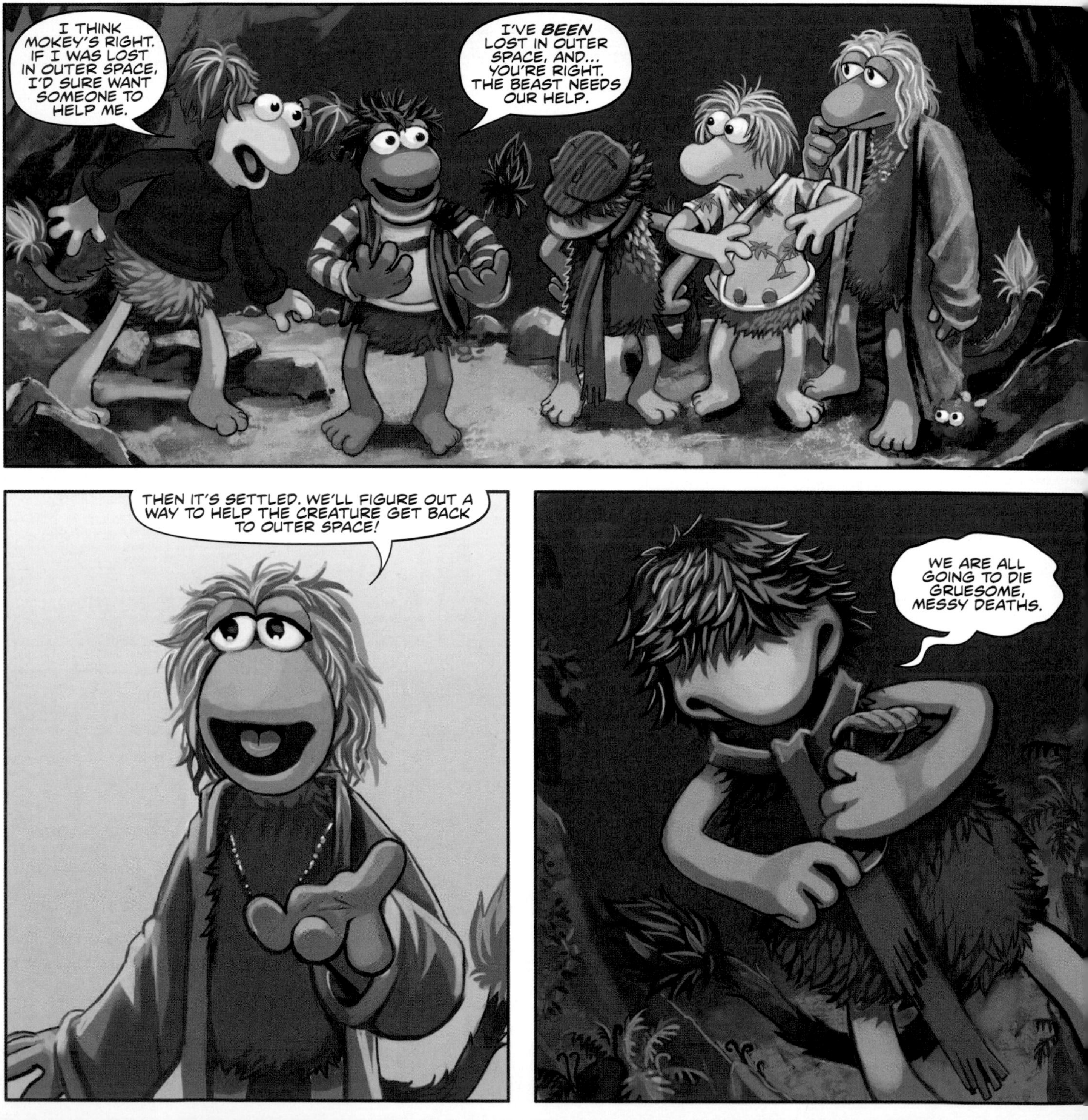
I THINK MOKEY'S RIGHT. IF I WAS LOST IN OUTER SPACE, I'D SURE WANT SOMEONE TO HELP ME.
I'VE BEEN LOST IN OUTER SPACE, AND... YOU'RE RIGHT. THE BEAST NEEDS OUR HELP.
THEN IT'S SETTLED. WE'LL FIGURE OUT A WAY TO HELP THE CREATURE GET BACK TO OUTER SPACE!
WE ARE ALL GOING TO DIE GRUESOME, MESSY DEATHS.

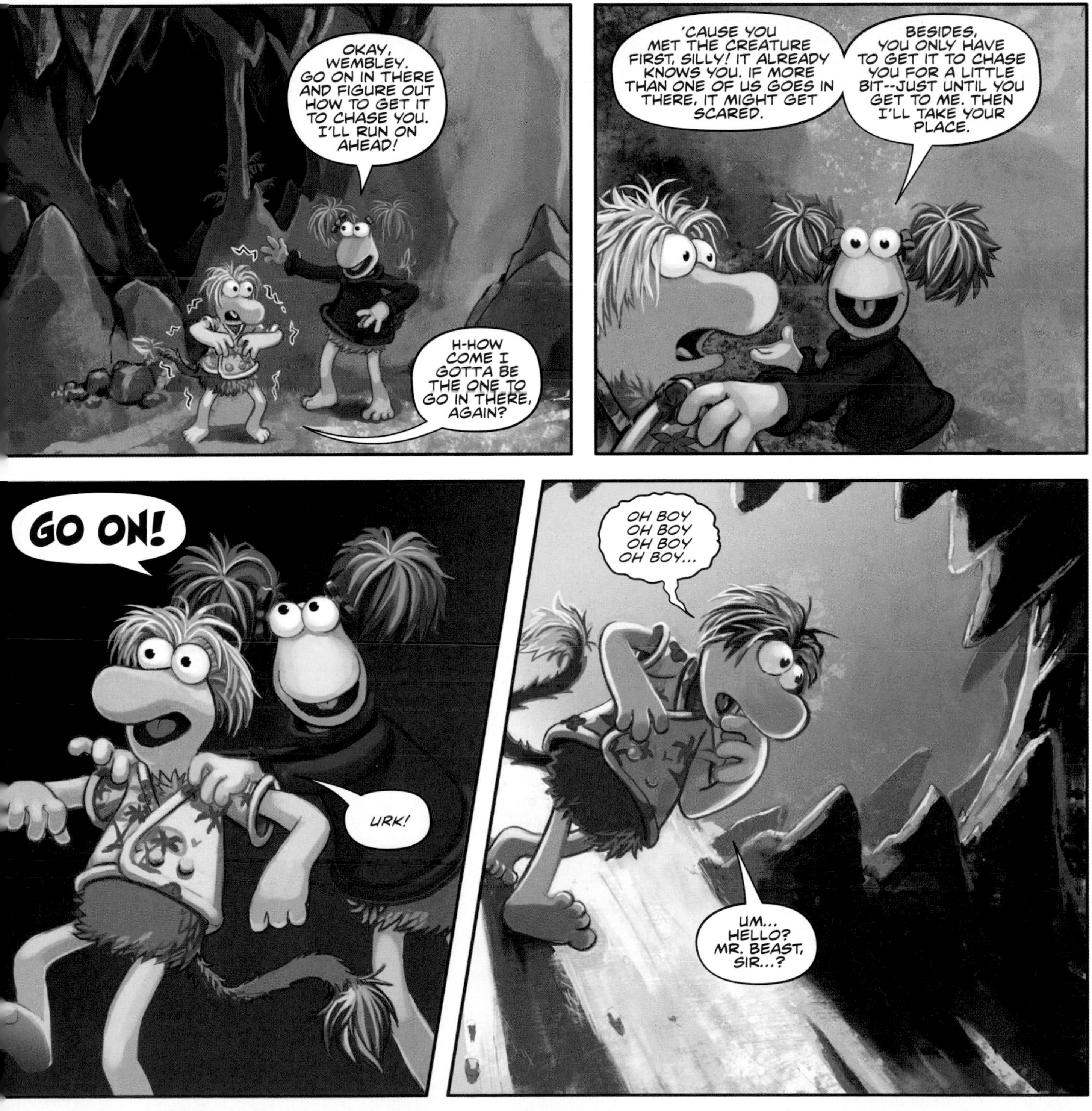
OKAY, WEMBLEY. GO ON IN THERE AND FIGURE OUT HOW TO GET IT TO CHASE YOU. I'LL RUN ON AHEAD!
H-HOW COME I GOTTA BE THE ONE TO GO IN THERE, AGAIN?
'CAUSE YOU MET THE CREATURE FIRST, SILLY! IT ALREADY KNOWS YOU. IF MORE THAN ONE OF US GOES IN THERE, IT MIGHT GET SCARED.
BESIDES, YOU ONLY HAVE TO GET IT TO CHASE YOU FOR A LITTLE BIT--JUST UNTIL YOU GET TO ME. THEN I'LL TAKE YOUR PLACE.
GO ON!
URK!
OH BOY OH BOY OH BOY OH BOY...
UM... HELLO? MR. BEAST, SIR...?

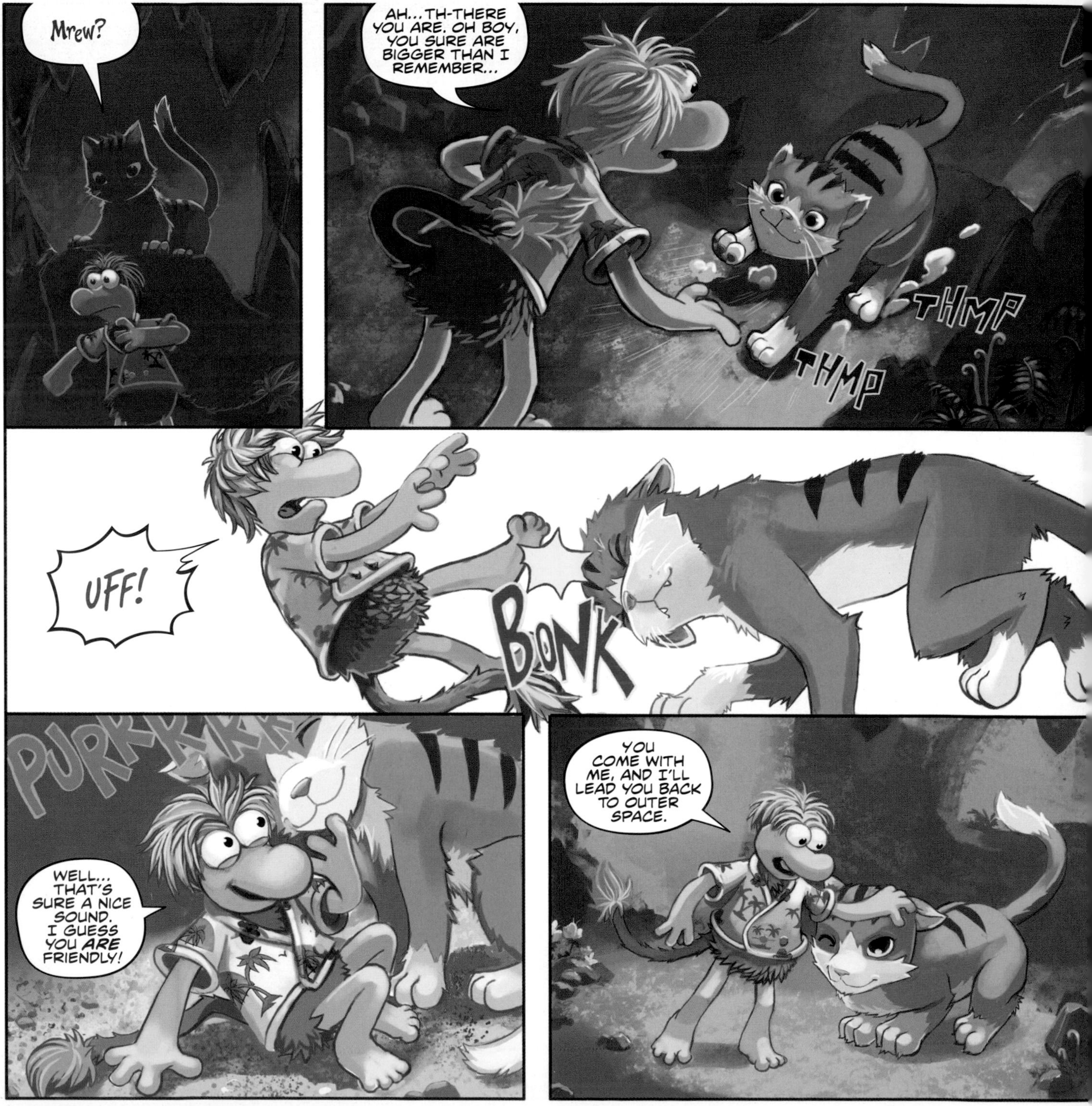
Mrew?
AH...TH-THERE YOU ARE. OH BOY, YOU SURE ARE BIGGER THAN I REMEMBER...
THMP
THMP
UFF!
BONK
PURRRRR
WELL... THAT'S SURE A NICE SOUND. I GUESS YOU ARE FRIENDLY!
YOU COME WITH ME, AND I'LL LEAD YOU BACK TO OUTER SPACE.

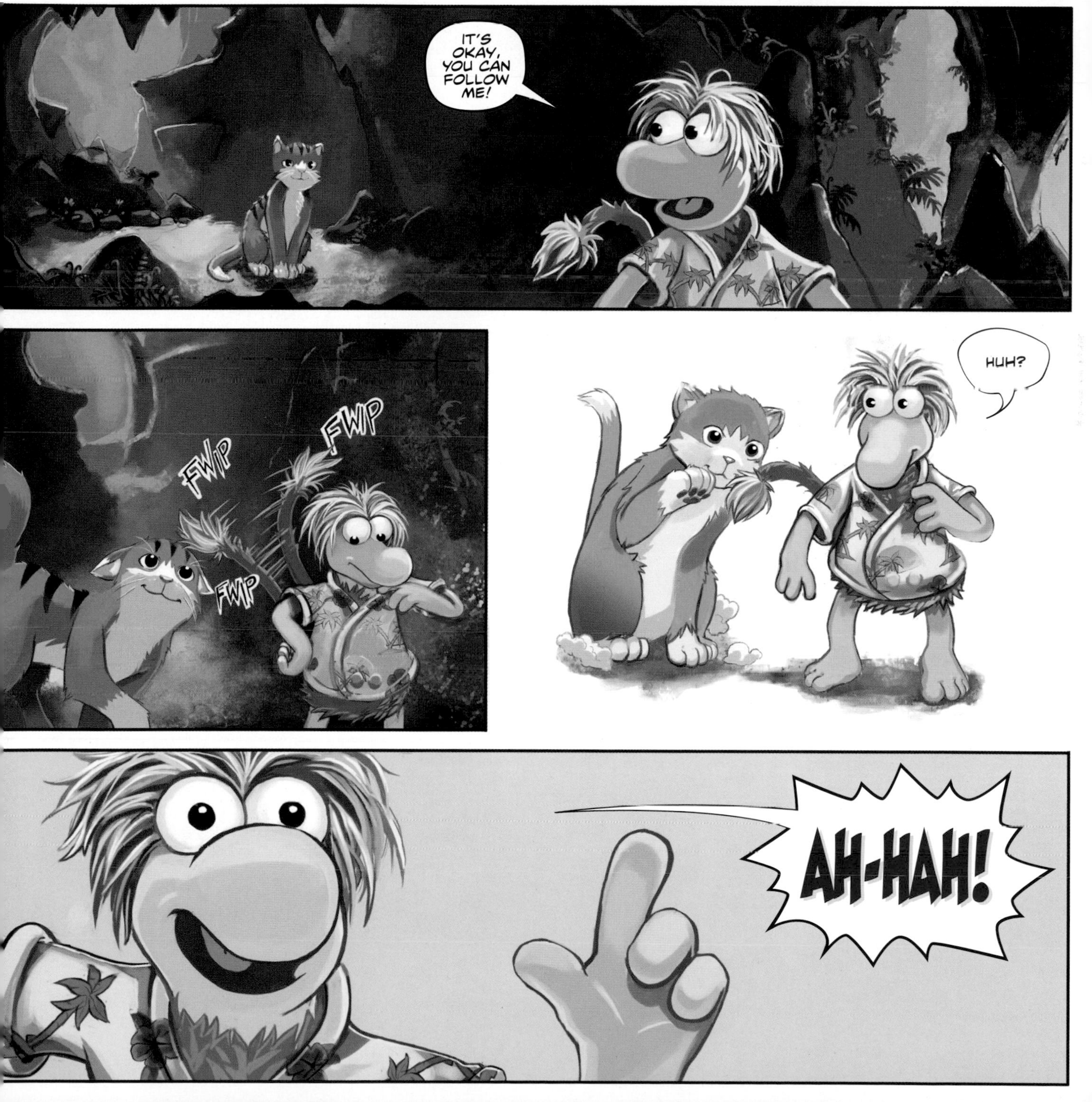
IT'S OKAY, YOU CAN FOLLOW ME!
FWIP
FWIP
FWIP
HUH?
AH-HAH!

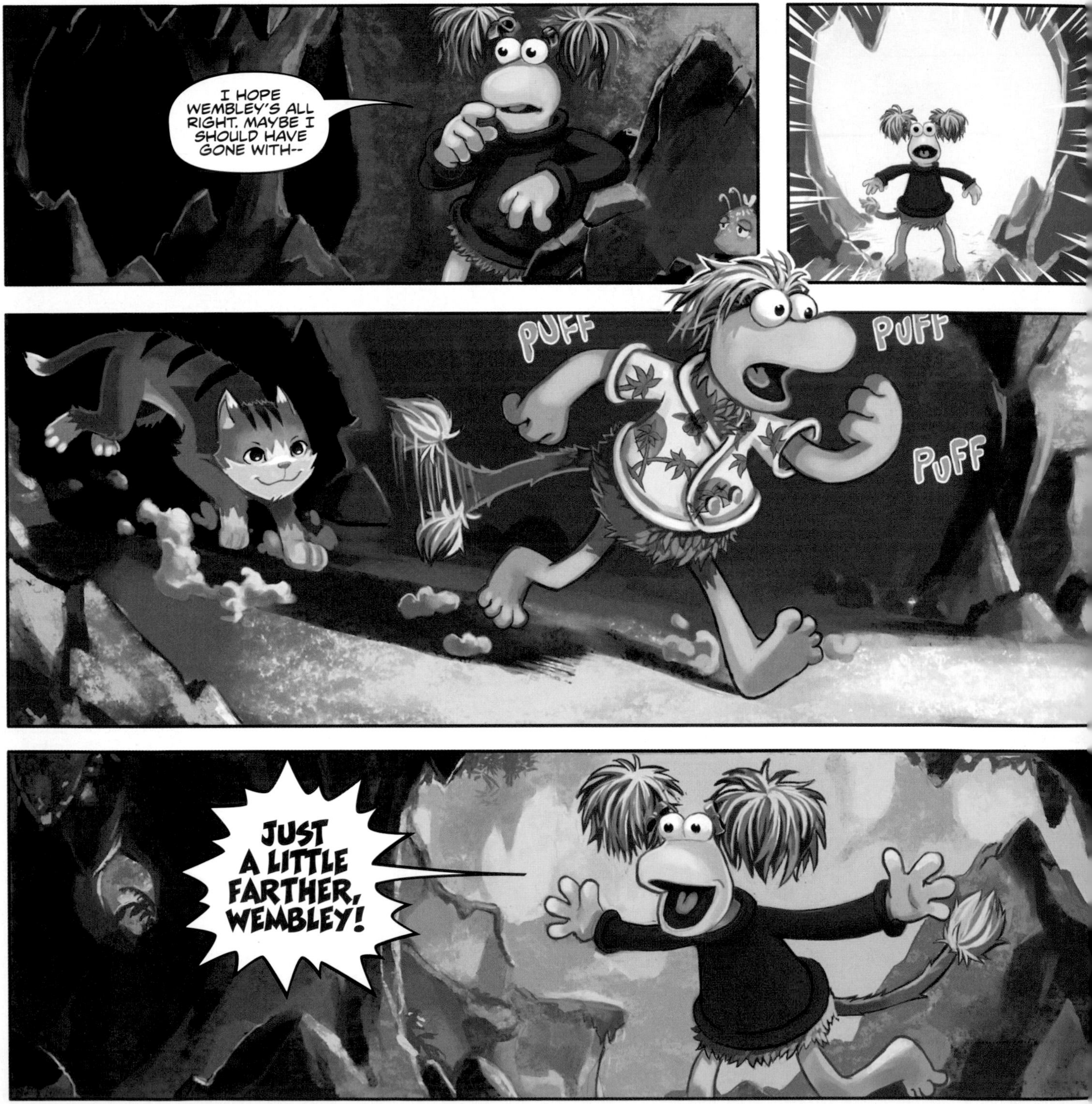
I HOPE WEMBLEY'S ALL RIGHT. MAYBE I SHOULD HAVE GONE WITH--
PUFF
PUFF
PUFF
JUST A LITTLE FARTHER, WEMBLEY!

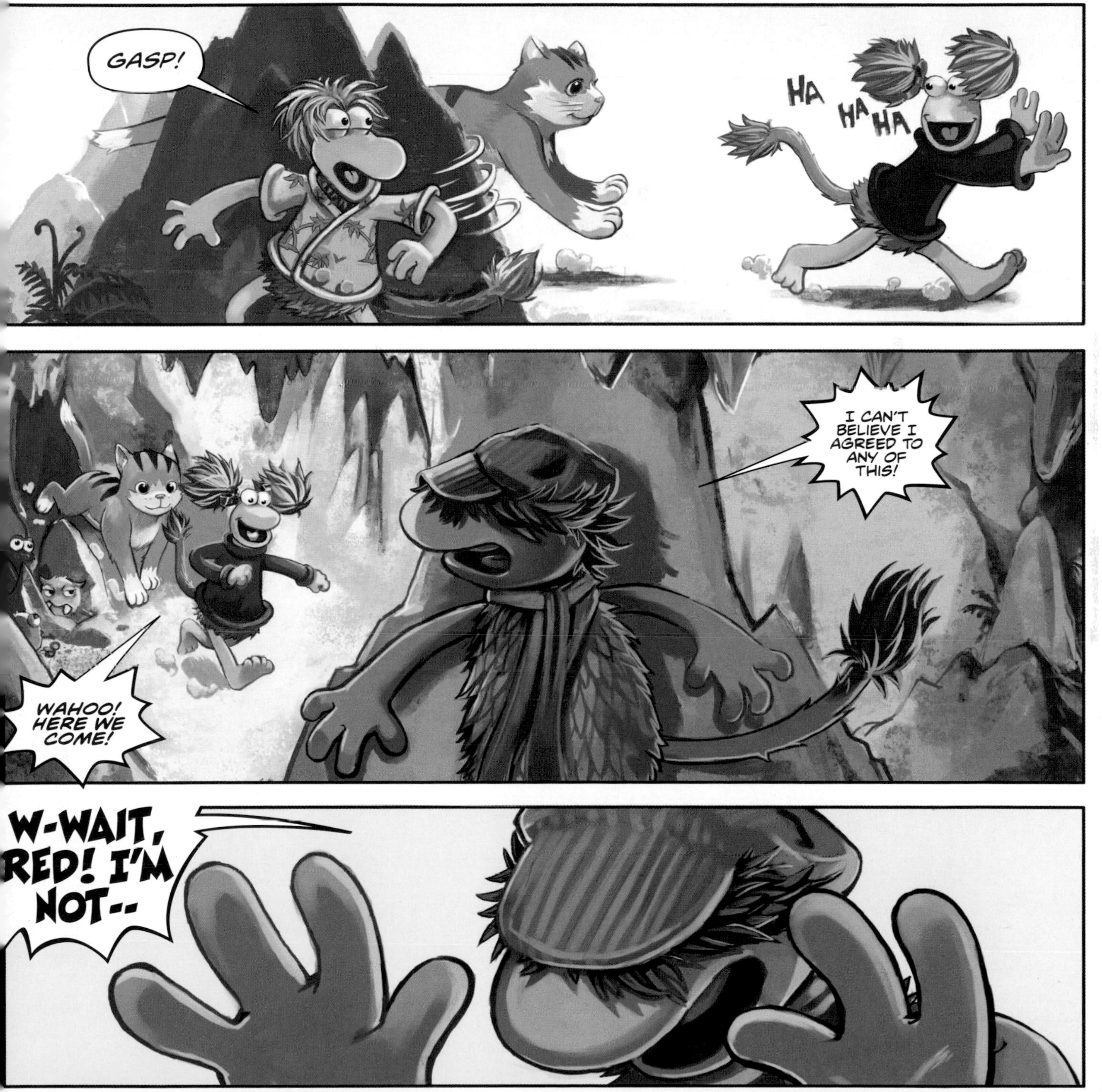
GASP!
HA HA HA
I CAN'T BELIEVE I AGREED TO ANY OF THIS!
WAHOO! HERE WE COME!
W-WAIT, RED! I'M NOT--

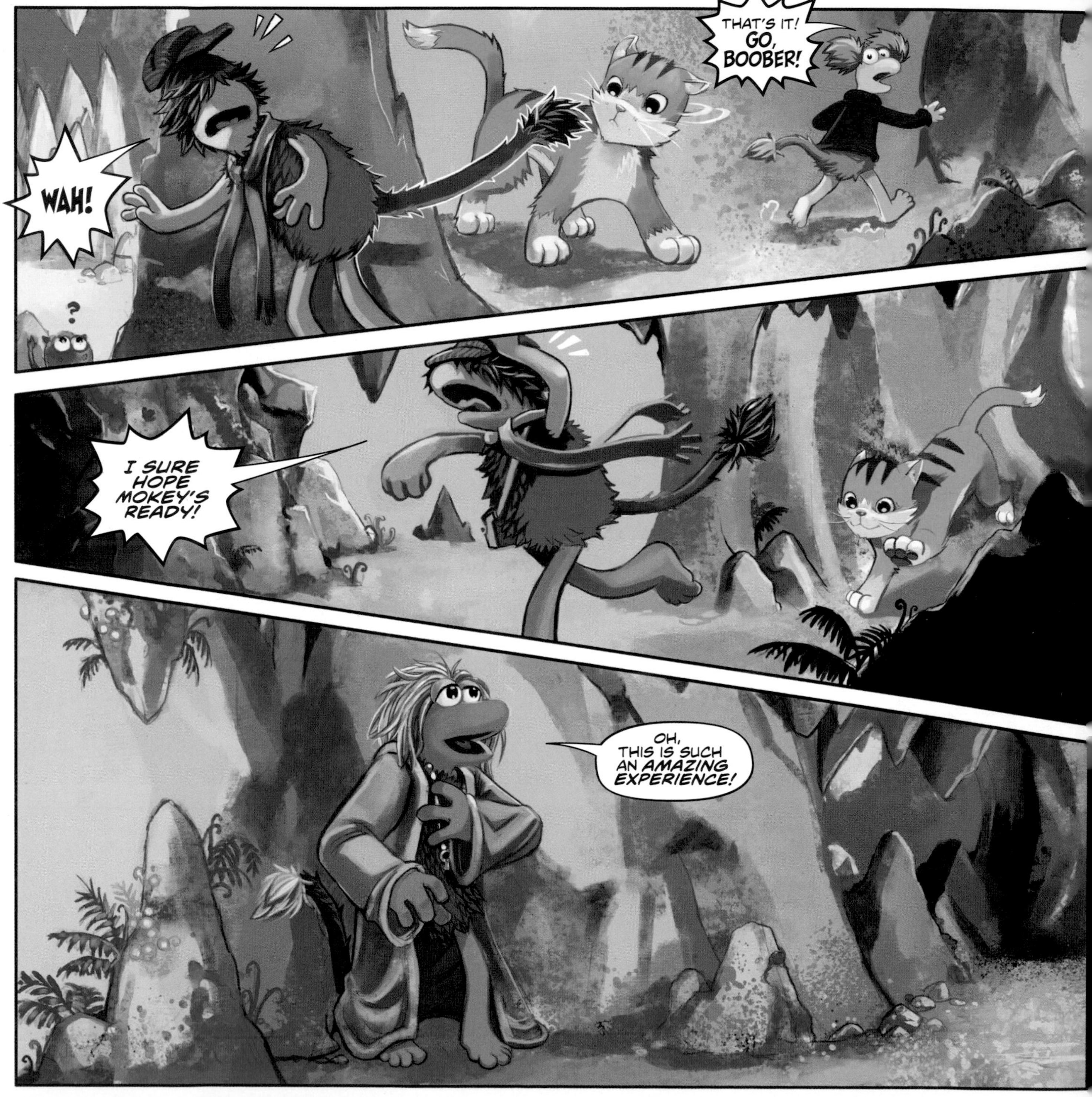

THAT'S IT! GO, BOOBER!
WAH!
?
I SURE HOPE MOKEY'S READY!
OH, THIS IS SUCH AN AMAZING EXPERIENCE!

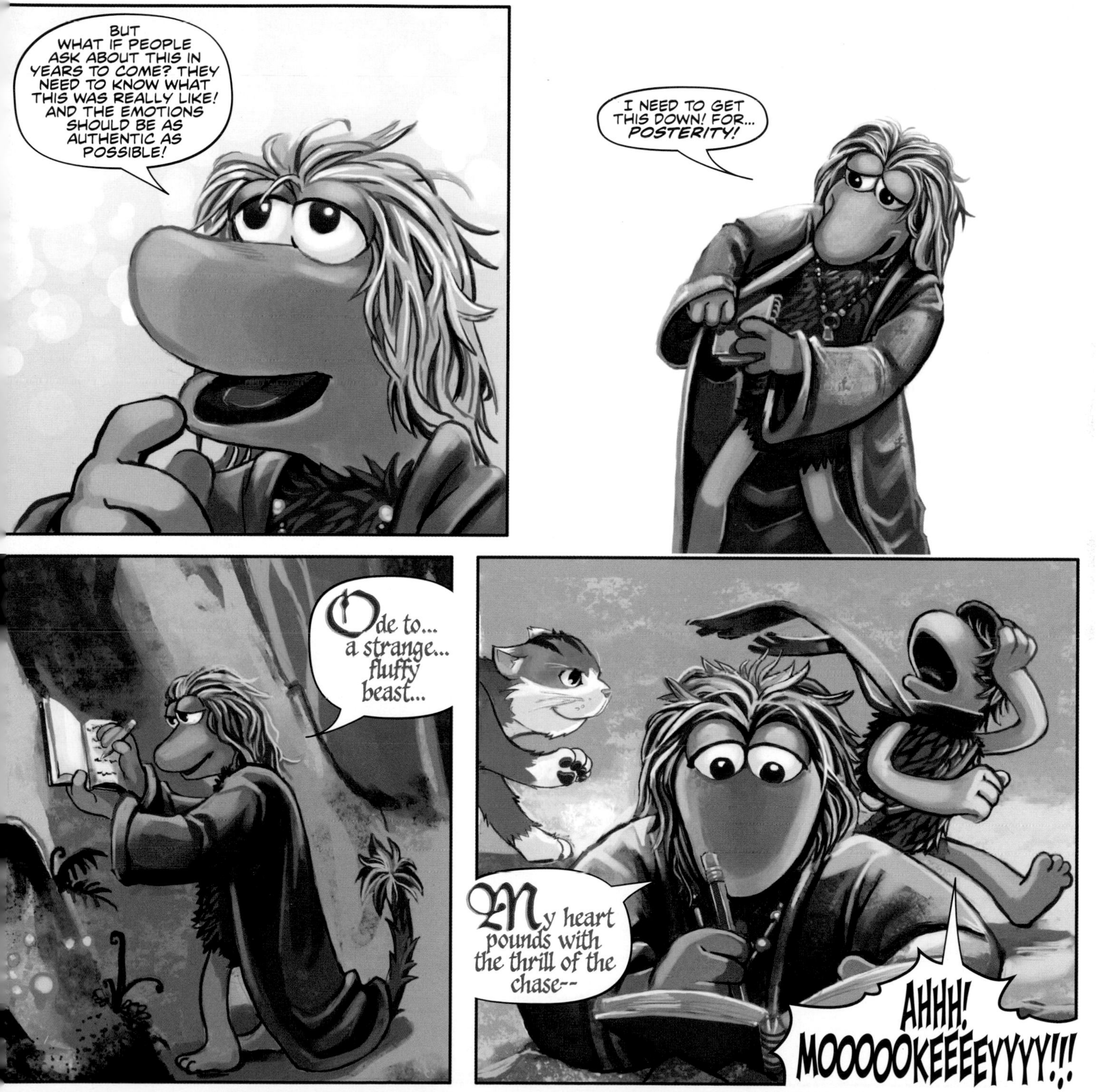

BUT WHAT IF PEOPLE ASK ABOUT THIS IN YEARS TO COME? THEY NEED TO KNOW WHAT THIS WAS REALLY LIKE! AND THE EMOTIONS SHOULD BE AS AUTHENTIC AS POSSIBLE!
I NEED TO GET THIS DOWN! FOR... *POSTERITY!*
Ode to... a strange... fluffy beast...
My heart pounds with the thrill of the chase--
AHHH! MOOOOOKEEEEYYYY!!!

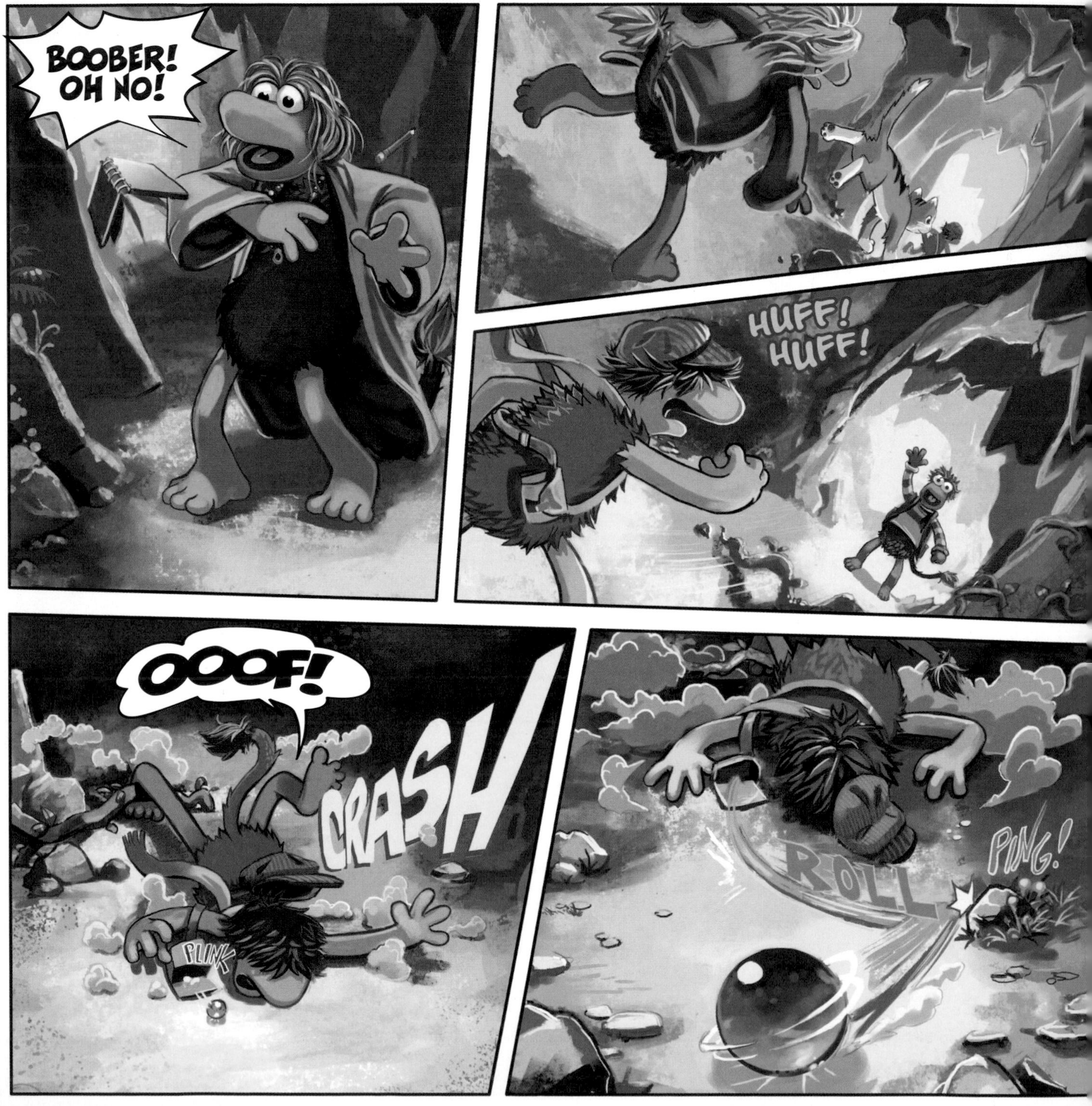
BOOBER! OH NO!
HUFF! HUFF!
OOOF!
CRASH
PLINK
ROLL
PING!

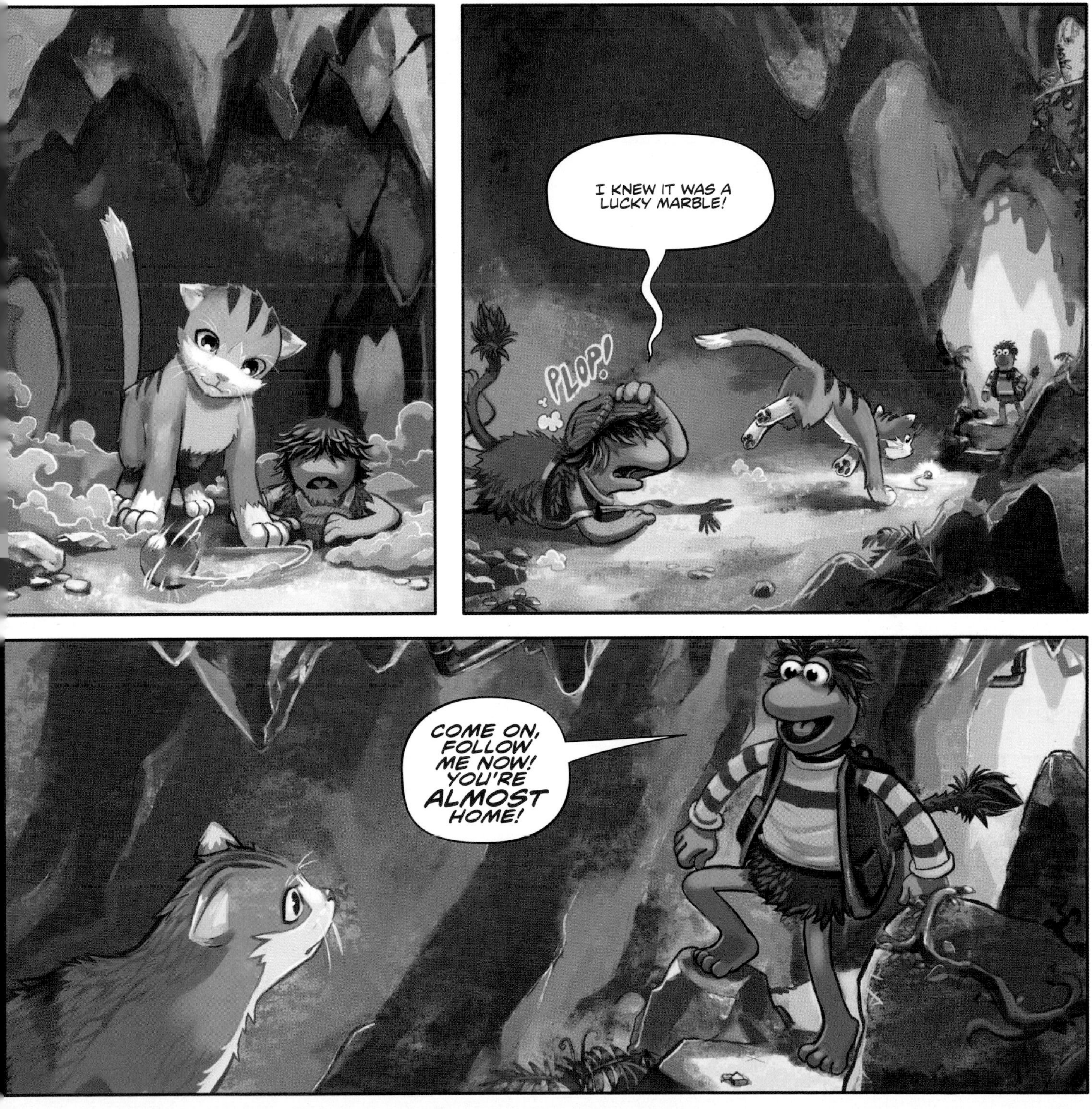
I KNEW IT WAS A LUCKY MARBLE!
PLOP!
COME ON, FOLLOW ME NOW! YOU'RE ALMOST HOME!

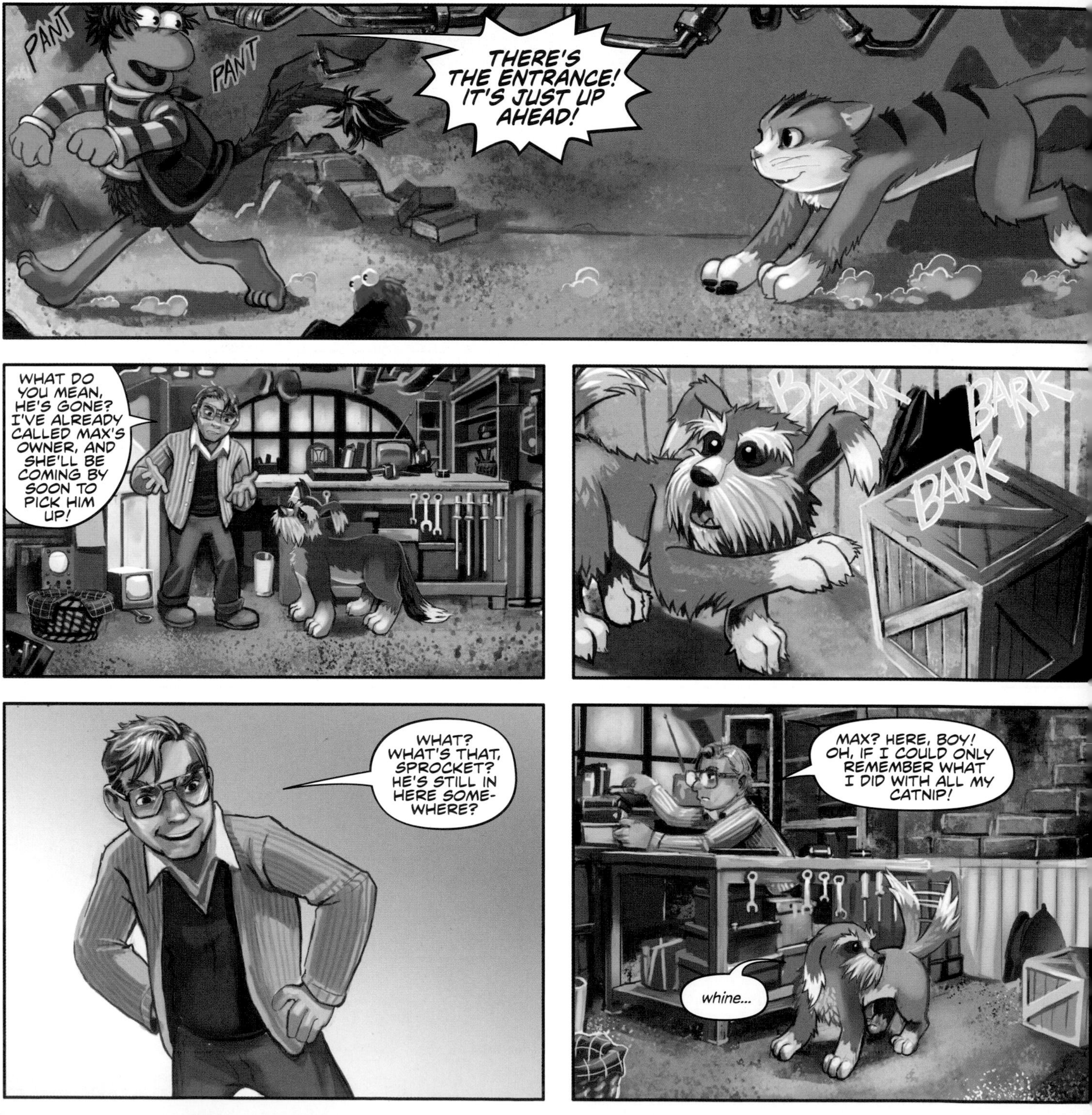
PANT
PANT
THERE'S THE ENTRANCE! IT'S JUST UP AHEAD!
WHAT DO YOU MEAN, HE'S GONE? I'VE ALREADY CALLED MAX'S OWNER, AND SHE'LL BE COMING BY SOON TO PICK HIM UP!
BARK
BARK
BARK
WHAT? WHAT'S THAT, SPROCKET? HE'S STILL IN HERE SOME-WHERE?
MAX? HERE, BOY! OH, IF I COULD ONLY REMEMBER WHAT I DID WITH ALL MY CATNIP!
whine...

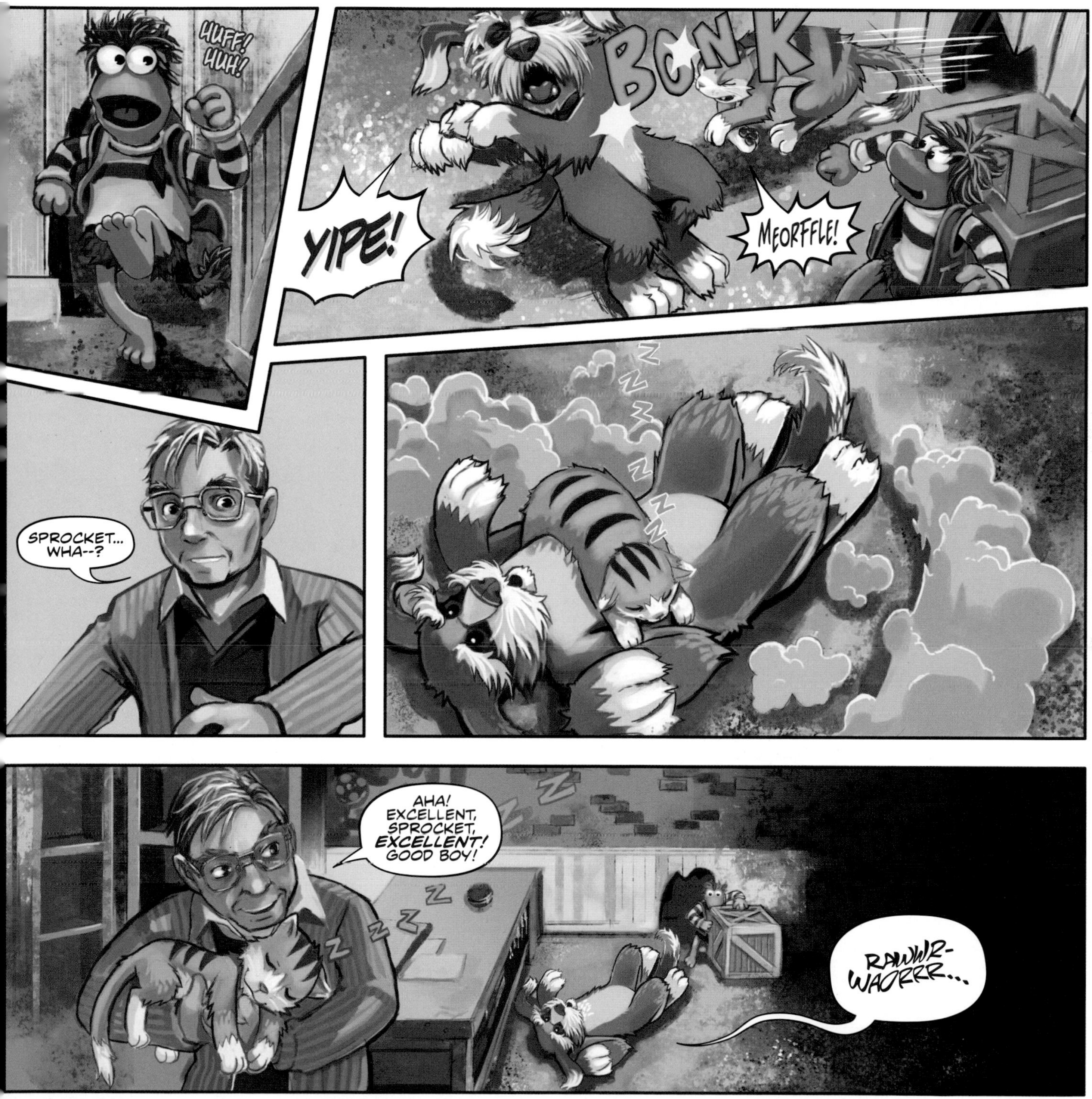
HUFF! HUH!
BONK!
YIPE!
MEORFFLE!
SPROCKET... WHA--?
AHA! EXCELLENT, SPROCKET, *EXCELLENT!* GOOD BOY!
RAWWR-WAORRR...

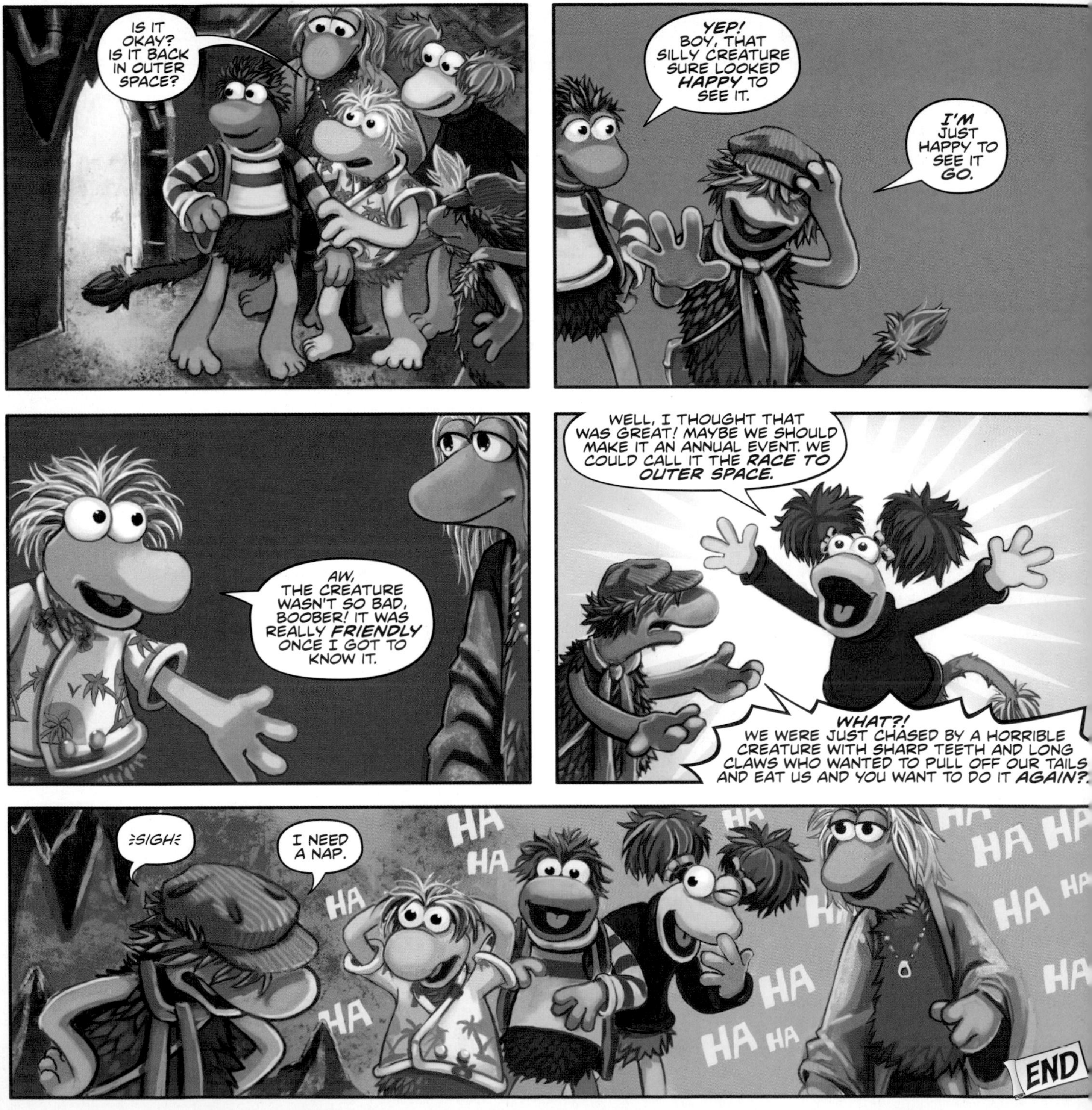
IS IT OKAY? IS IT BACK IN OUTER SPACE?
YEP! BOY, THAT SILLY CREATURE SURE LOOKED HAPPY TO SEE IT.
I'M JUST HAPPY TO SEE IT GO.
AW, THE CREATURE WASN'T SO BAD, BOOBER! IT WAS REALLY FRIENDLY ONCE I GOT TO KNOW IT.
WELL, I THOUGHT THAT WAS GREAT! MAYBE WE SHOULD MAKE IT AN ANNUAL EVENT. WE COULD CALL IT THE RACE TO OUTER SPACE.
WHAT?! WE WERE JUST CHASED BY A HORRIBLE CREATURE WITH SHARP TEETH AND LONG CLAWS WHO WANTED TO PULL OFF OUR TAILS AND EAT US AND YOU WANT TO DO IT AGAIN?!
SIGH
I NEED A NAP.
HA HA HA HA HA HA HA HA HA HA HA HA HA
END

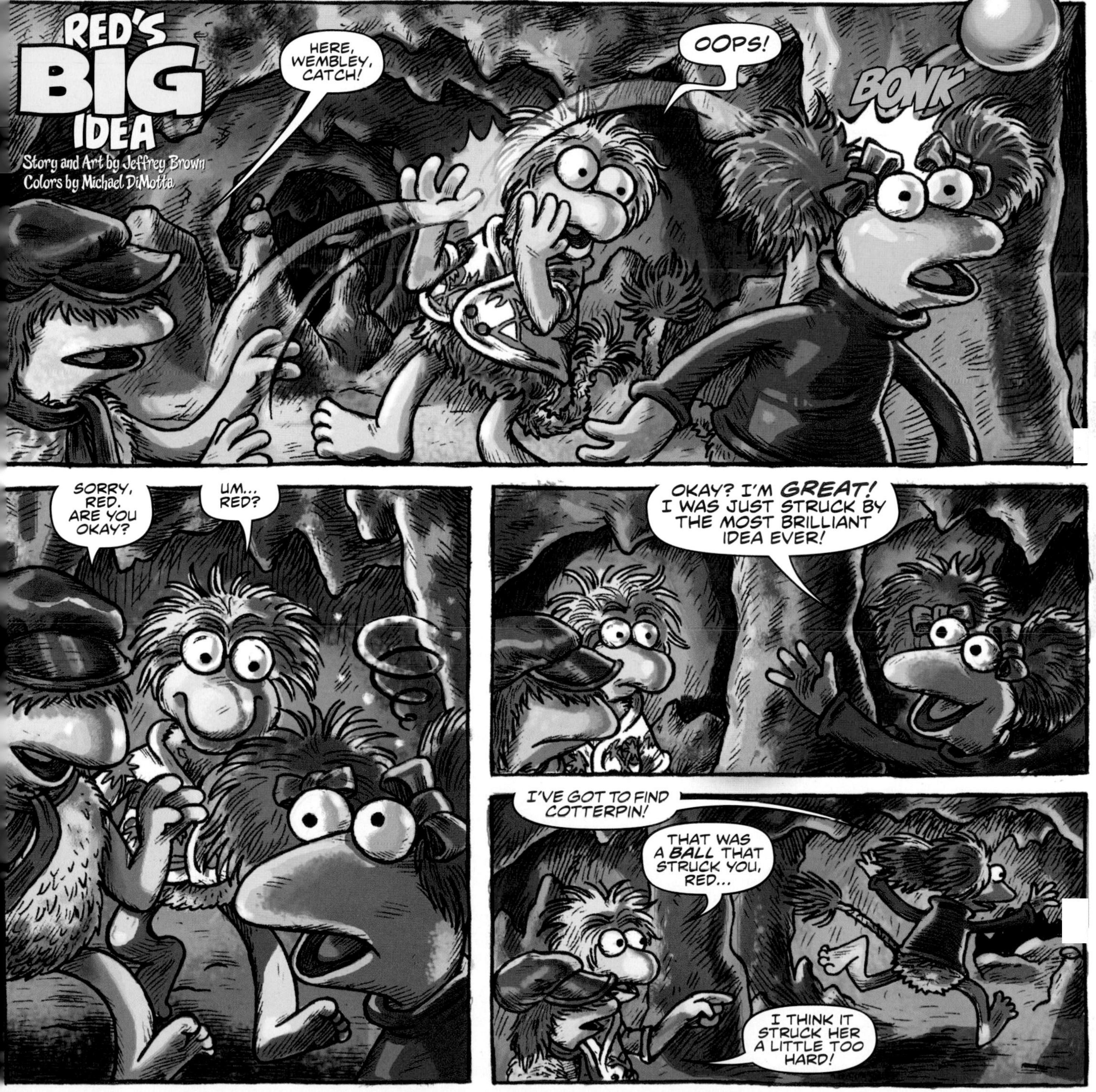
RED'S BIG IDEA
Story and Art by Jeffrey Brown
Colors by Michael DiMotta
HERE, WEMBLEY, CATCH!
OOPS!
BONK
SORRY, RED. ARE YOU OKAY?
UM... RED?
OKAY? I'M GREAT! I WAS JUST STRUCK BY THE MOST BRILLIANT IDEA EVER!
I'VE GOT TO FIND COTTERPIN!
THAT WAS A BALL THAT STRUCK YOU, RED...
I THINK IT STRUCK HER A LITTLE TOO HARD!

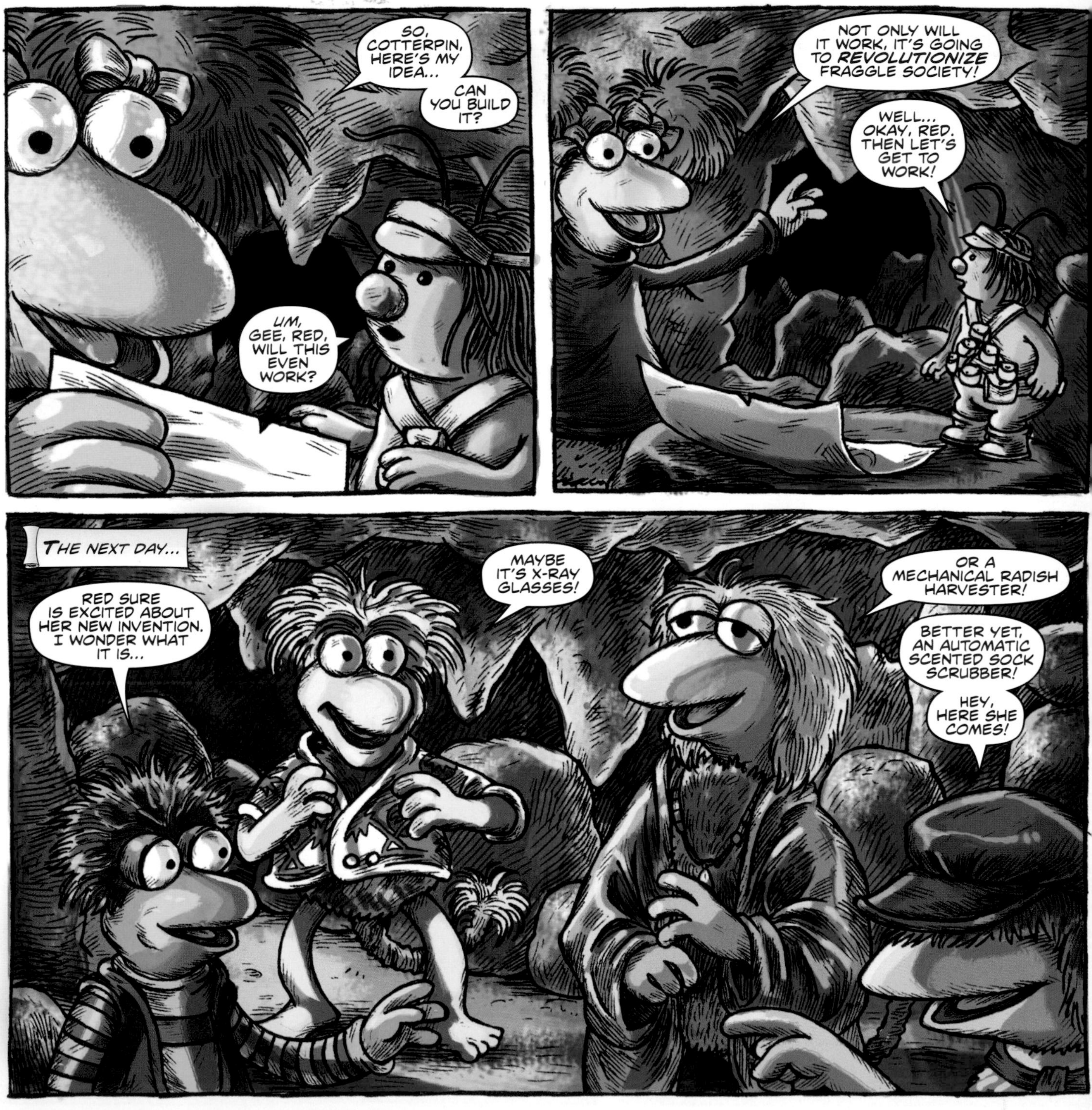
SO, COTTERPIN, HERE'S MY IDEA...
CAN YOU BUILD IT?
UM, GEE, RED, WILL THIS EVEN WORK?
NOT ONLY WILL IT WORK, IT'S GOING TO REVOLUTIONIZE FRAGGLE SOCIETY!
WELL... OKAY, RED. THEN LET'S GET TO WORK!
THE NEXT DAY...
RED SURE IS EXCITED ABOUT HER NEW INVENTION. I WONDER WHAT IT IS...
MAYBE IT'S X-RAY GLASSES!
OR A MECHANICAL RADISH HARVESTER!
BETTER YET, AN AUTOMATIC SCENTED SOCK SCRUBBER!
HEY, HERE SHE COMES!

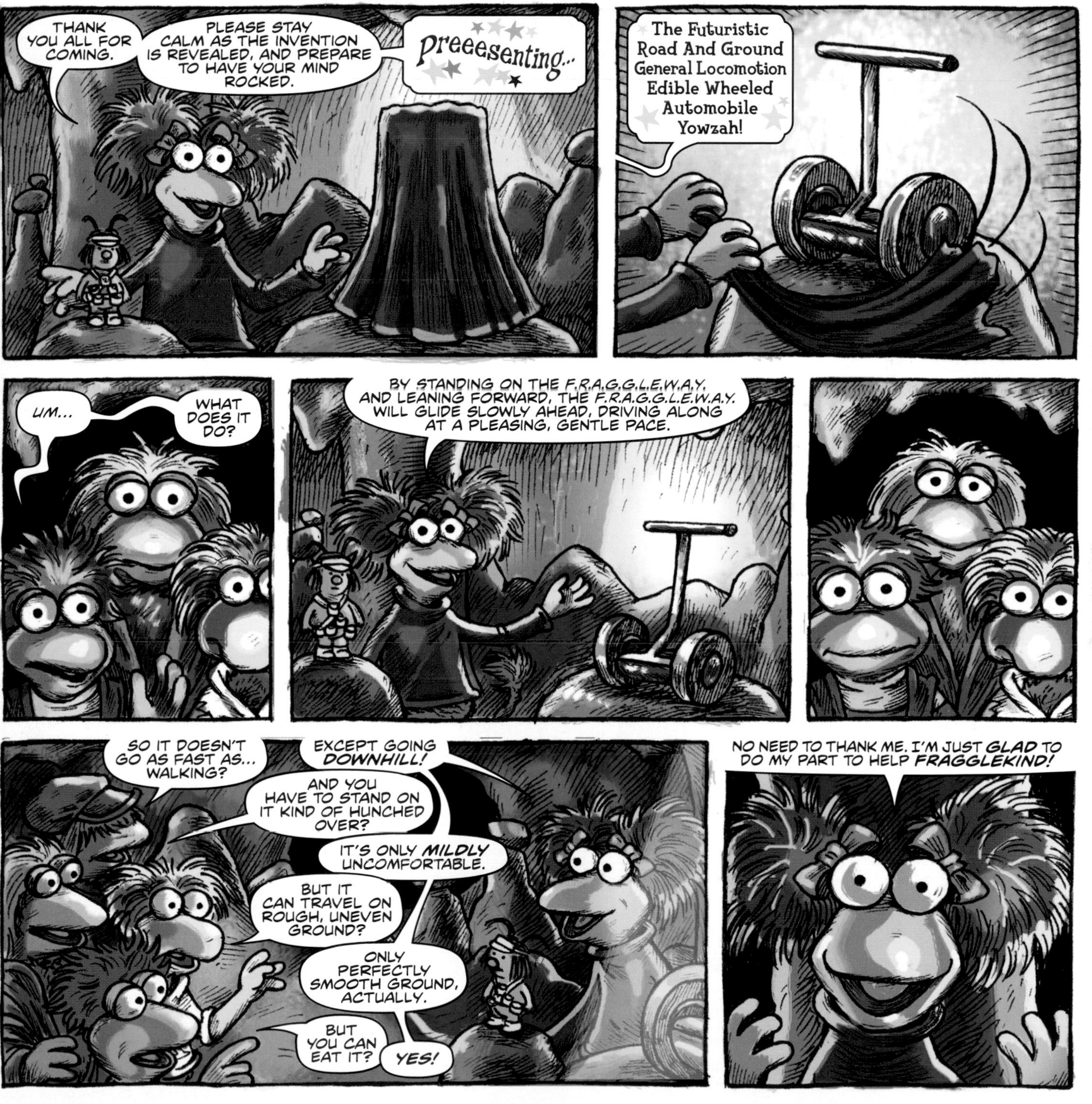
THANK YOU ALL FOR COMING.
PLEASE STAY CALM AS THE INVENTION IS REVEALED, AND PREPARE TO HAVE YOUR MIND ROCKED.
Preeeesenting...
The Futuristic Road And Ground General Locomotion Edible Wheeled Automobile Yowzah!
UM...
WHAT DOES IT DO?
BY STANDING ON THE F.R.A.G.G.L.E.W.A.Y. AND LEANING FORWARD, THE F.R.A.G.G.L.E.W.A.Y. WILL GLIDE SLOWLY AHEAD, DRIVING ALONG AT A PLEASING, GENTLE PACE.
SO IT DOESN'T GO AS FAST AS... WALKING?
EXCEPT GOING *DOWNHILL!*
AND YOU HAVE TO STAND ON IT KIND OF HUNCHED OVER?
IT'S ONLY *MILDLY* UNCOMFORTABLE.
BUT IT CAN TRAVEL ON ROUGH, UNEVEN GROUND?
ONLY PERFECTLY SMOOTH GROUND, ACTUALLY.
BUT YOU CAN EAT IT?
YES!
NO NEED TO THANK ME. I'M JUST *GLAD* TO DO MY PART TO HELP *FRAGGLEKIND!*

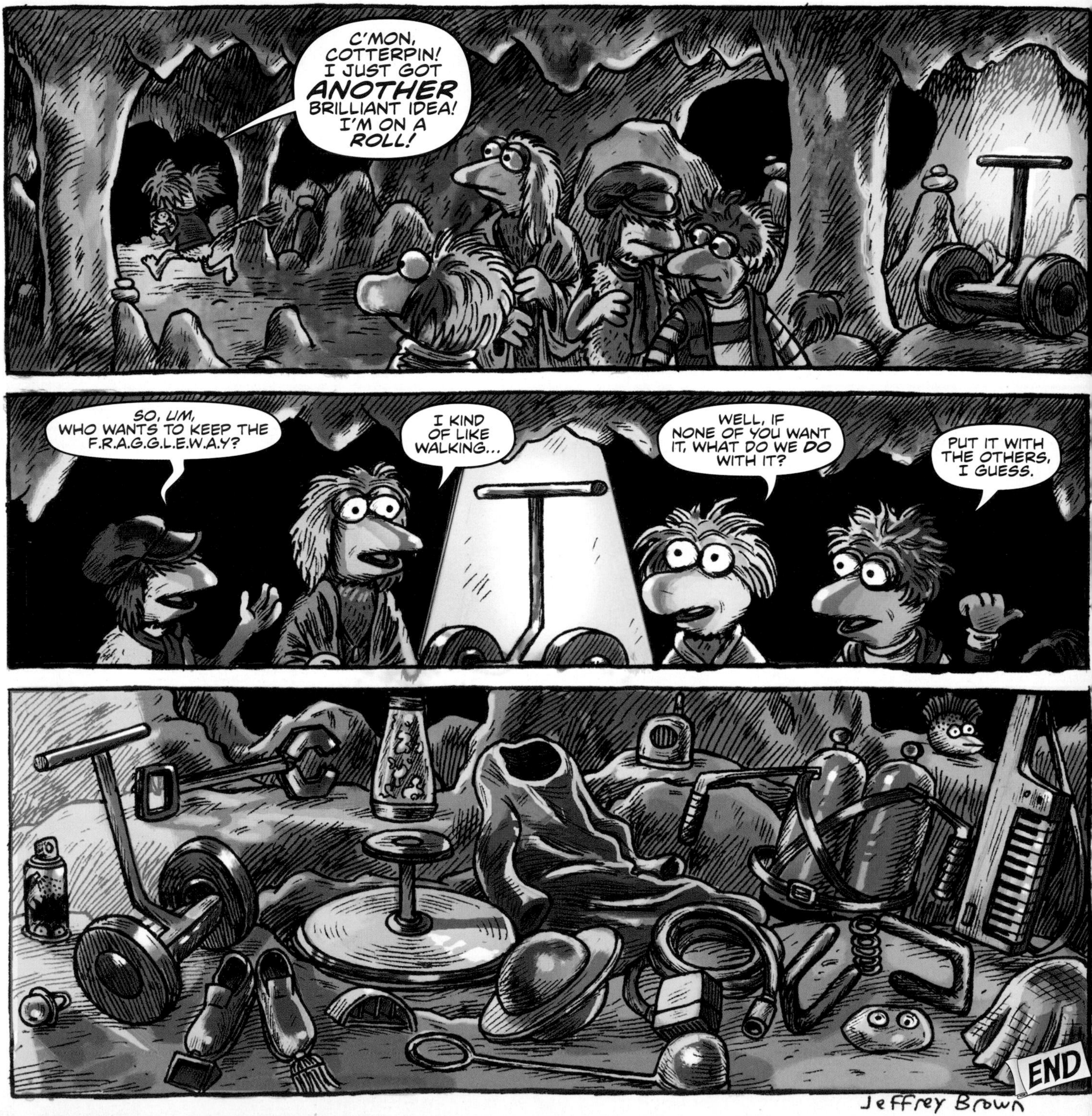
C'MON, COTTERPIN! I JUST GOT ANOTHER BRILLIANT IDEA! I'M ON A ROLL!
SO, UM, WHO WANTS TO KEEP THE F.R.A.G.G.L.E.W.A.Y?
I KIND OF LIKE WALKING...
WELL, IF NONE OF YOU WANT IT, WHAT DO WE DO WITH IT?
PUT IT WITH THE OTHERS, I GUESS.
END
Jeffrey Brown

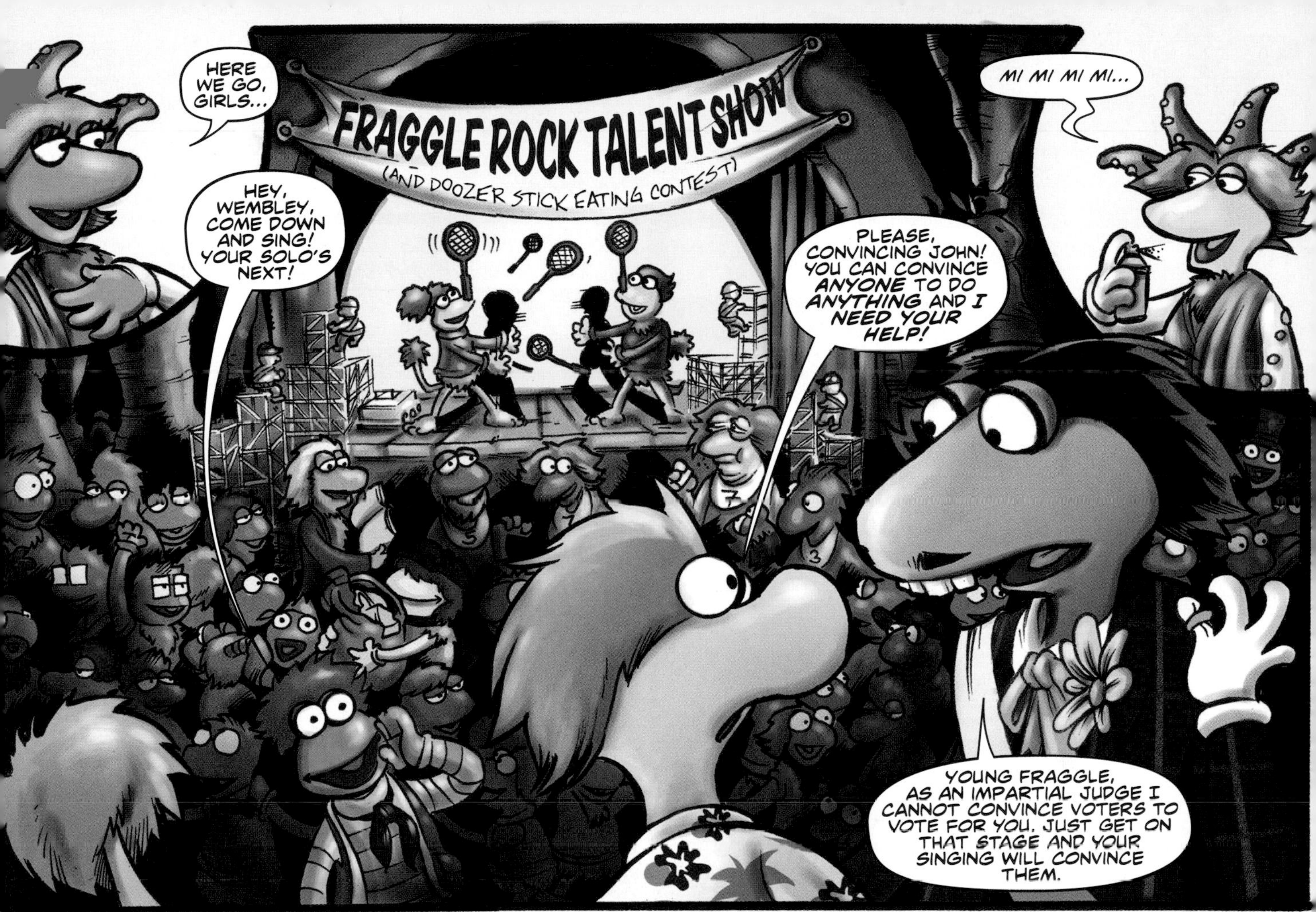
HERE WE GO, GIRLS...
FRAGGLE ROCK TALENT SHOW
(AND DOOZER STICK EATING CONTEST)
HEY, WEMBLEY, COME DOWN AND SING! YOUR SOLO'S NEXT!
MI MI MI MI...
PLEASE, CONVINCING JOHN! YOU CAN CONVINCE *ANYONE* TO DO *ANYTHING* AND I *NEED YOUR HELP!*
YOUNG FRAGGLE, AS AN IMPARTIAL JUDGE I CANNOT CONVINCE VOTERS TO VOTE FOR YOU. JUST GET ON THAT STAGE AND YOUR SINGING WILL CONVINCE THEM.

THE CONVINCING OF CONVINCING JOHN

Convincing Lyrics by Neil Kleid   Motivational Artwork by Fernando Pinto

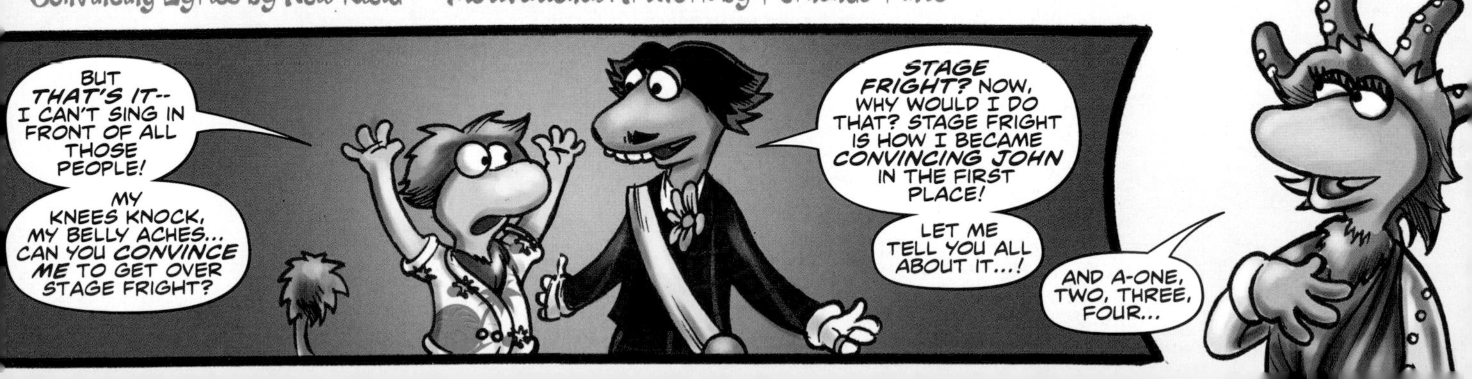
BUT *THAT'S IT*-- I CAN'T SING IN FRONT OF ALL THOSE PEOPLE!
MY KNEES KNOCK, MY BELLY ACHES... CAN YOU *CONVINCE ME* TO GET OVER STAGE FRIGHT?
STAGE FRIGHT? NOW, WHY WOULD I DO THAT? STAGE FRIGHT IS HOW I BECAME *CONVINCING JOHN* IN THE FIRST PLACE!
LET ME TELL YOU ALL ABOUT IT...!
AND A-ONE, TWO, THREE, FOUR...

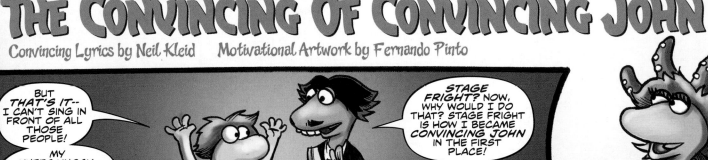

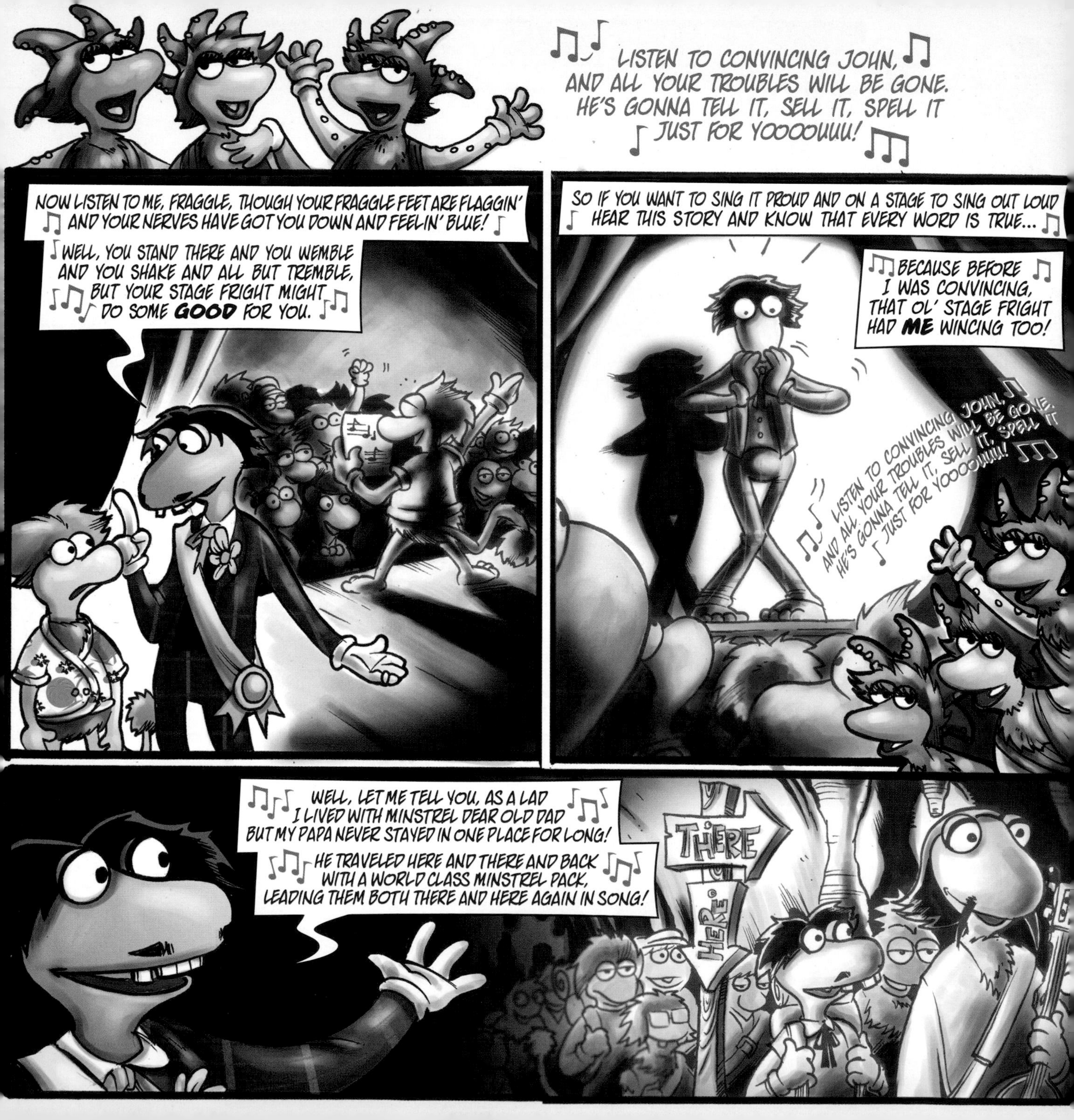
LISTEN TO CONVINCING JOHN, AND ALL YOUR TROUBLES WILL BE GONE. HE'S GONNA TELL IT, SELL IT, SPELL IT JUST FOR YOOOOUUU!
NOW LISTEN TO ME, FRAGGLE, THOUGH YOUR FRAGGLE FEET ARE FLAGGIN' AND YOUR NERVES HAVE GOT YOU DOWN AND FEELIN' BLUE!
WELL, YOU STAND THERE AND YOU WEMBLE AND YOU SHAKE AND ALL BUT TREMBLE, BUT YOUR STAGE FRIGHT MIGHT DO SOME **GOOD** FOR YOU.
SO IF YOU WANT TO SING IT PROUD AND ON A STAGE TO SING OUT LOUD HEAR THIS STORY AND KNOW THAT EVERY WORD IS TRUE...
BECAUSE BEFORE I WAS CONVINCING, THAT OL' STAGE FRIGHT HAD **ME** WINCING TOO!
LISTEN TO CONVINCING JOHN, AND ALL YOUR TROUBLES WILL BE GONE. HE'S GONNA TELL IT, SELL IT, SPELL IT JUST FOR YOOOOUUU!
WELL, LET ME TELL YOU, AS A LAD I LIVED WITH MINSTREL DEAR OLD DAD BUT MY PAPA NEVER STAYED IN ONE PLACE FOR LONG!
HE TRAVELED HERE AND THERE AND BACK WITH A WORLD CLASS MINSTREL PACK, LEADING THEM BOTH THERE AND HERE AGAIN IN SONG!
THERE
HERE

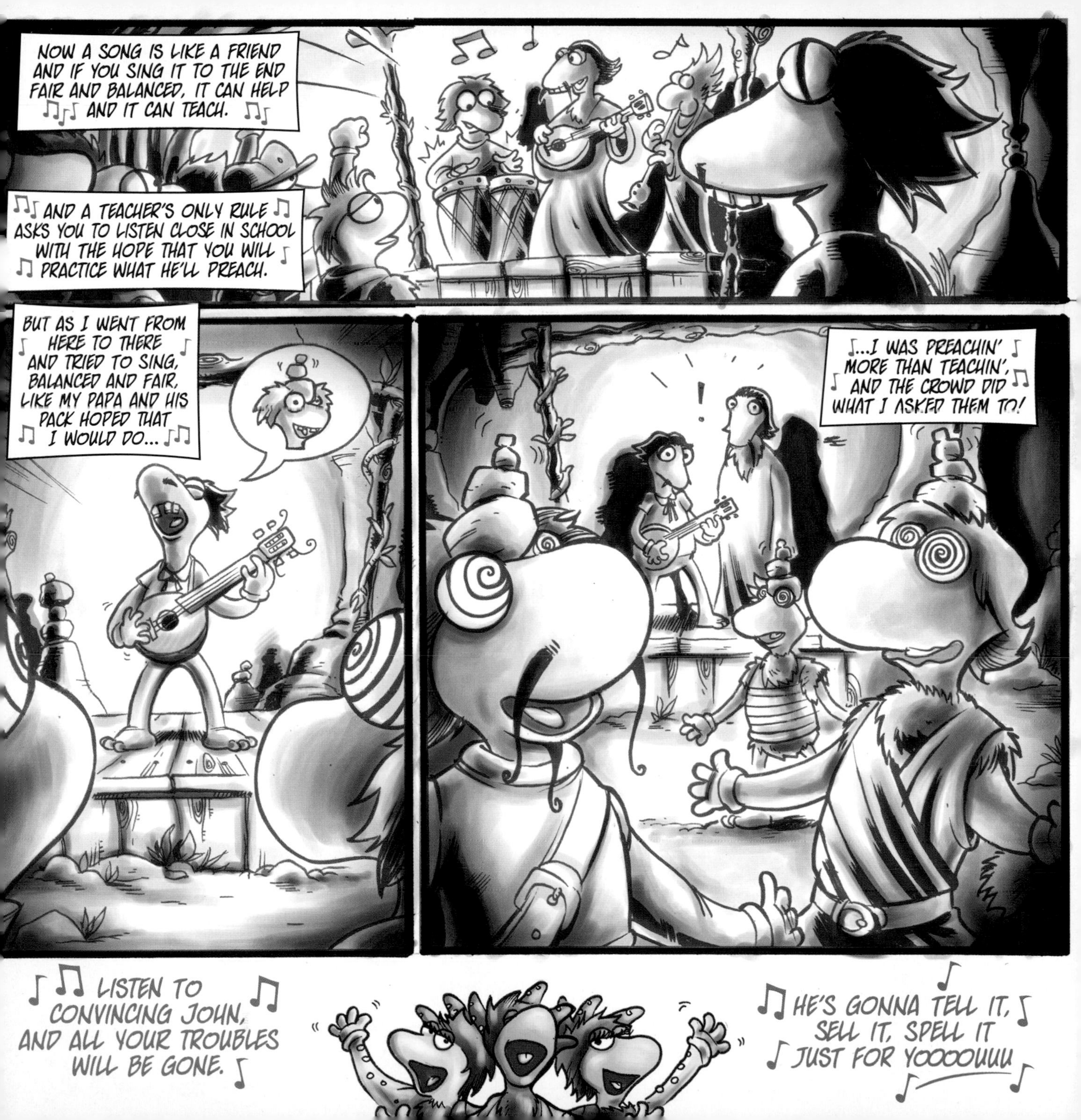
NOW A SONG IS LIKE A FRIEND AND IF YOU SING IT TO THE END FAIR AND BALANCED, IT CAN HELP AND IT CAN TEACH.
AND A TEACHER'S ONLY RULE ASKS YOU TO LISTEN CLOSE IN SCHOOL WITH THE HOPE THAT YOU WILL PRACTICE WHAT HE'LL PREACH.
BUT AS I WENT FROM HERE TO THERE AND TRIED TO SING, BALANCED AND FAIR, LIKE MY PAPA AND HIS PACK HOPED THAT I WOULD DO...
...I WAS PREACHIN' MORE THAN TEACHIN', AND THE CROWD DID WHAT I ASKED THEM TO!
!
LISTEN TO CONVINCING JOHN, AND ALL YOUR TROUBLES WILL BE GONE.
HE'S GONNA TELL IT, SELL IT, SPELL IT JUST FOR YOOOOUUU

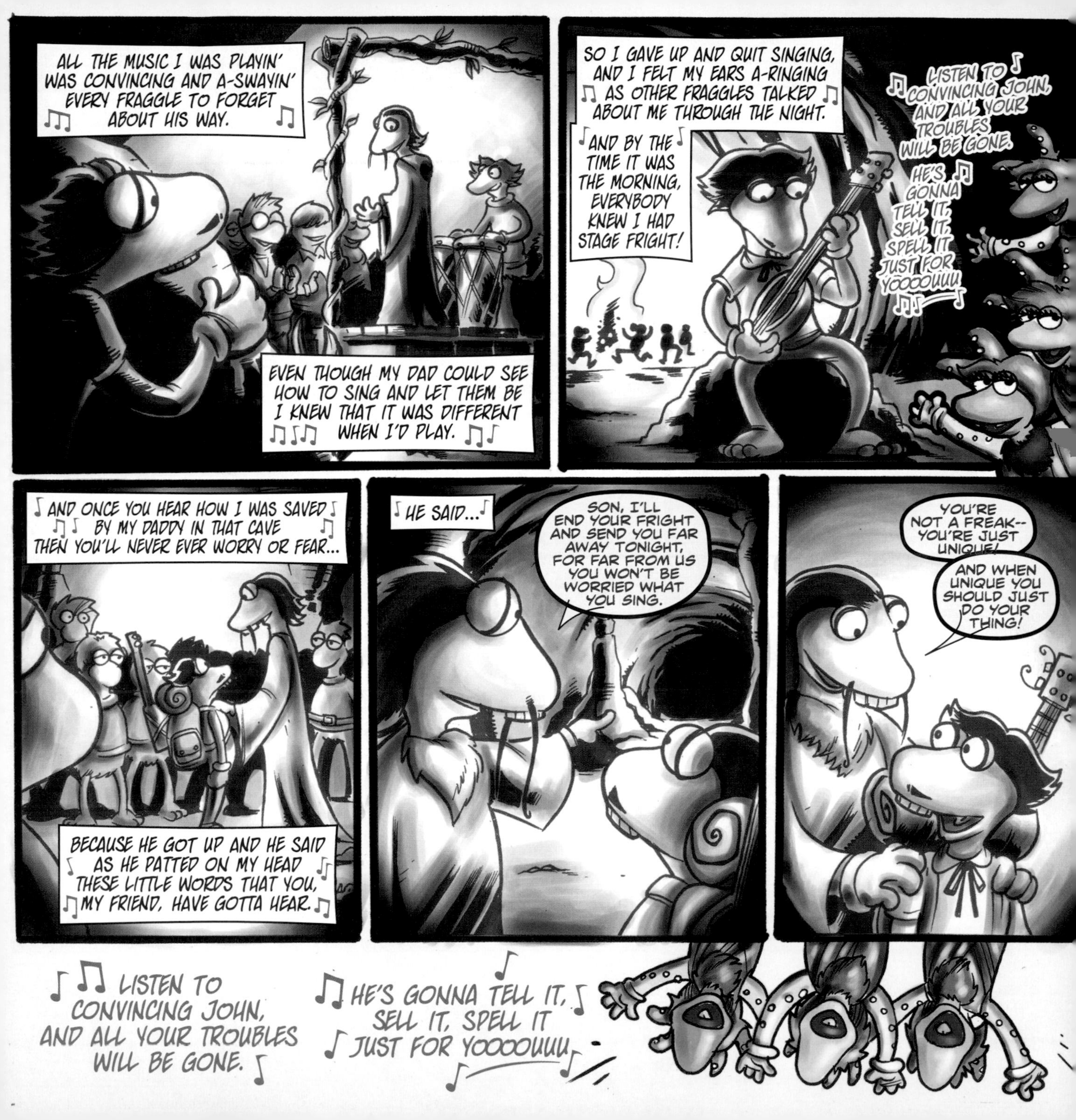
ALL THE MUSIC I WAS PLAYIN' WAS CONVINCING AND A-SWAYIN' EVERY FRAGGLE TO FORGET ABOUT HIS WAY.
EVEN THOUGH MY DAD COULD SEE HOW TO SING AND LET THEM BE I KNEW THAT IT WAS DIFFERENT WHEN I'D PLAY.
SO I GAVE UP AND QUIT SINGING, AND I FELT MY EARS A-RINGING AS OTHER FRAGGLES TALKED ABOUT ME THROUGH THE NIGHT.
AND BY THE TIME IT WAS THE MORNING, EVERYBODY KNEW I HAD STAGE FRIGHT!
LISTEN TO CONVINCING JOHN, AND ALL YOUR TROUBLES WILL BE GONE.
HE'S GONNA TELL IT, SELL IT, SPELL IT JUST FOR YOOOOUUU
AND ONCE YOU HEAR HOW I WAS SAVED BY MY DADDY IN THAT CAVE THEN YOU'LL NEVER EVER WORRY OR FEAR...
BECAUSE HE GOT UP AND HE SAID AS HE PATTED ON MY HEAD THESE LITTLE WORDS THAT YOU, MY FRIEND, HAVE GOTTA HEAR.
HE SAID...
SON, I'LL END YOUR FRIGHT AND SEND YOU FAR AWAY TONIGHT, FOR FAR FROM US YOU WON'T BE WORRIED WHAT YOU SING.
YOU'RE NOT A FREAK-- YOU'RE JUST UNIQUE!
AND WHEN UNIQUE YOU SHOULD JUST DO YOUR THING!
LISTEN TO CONVINCING JOHN, AND ALL YOUR TROUBLES WILL BE GONE.
HE'S GONNA TELL IT, SELL IT, SPELL IT JUST FOR YOOOOUUU

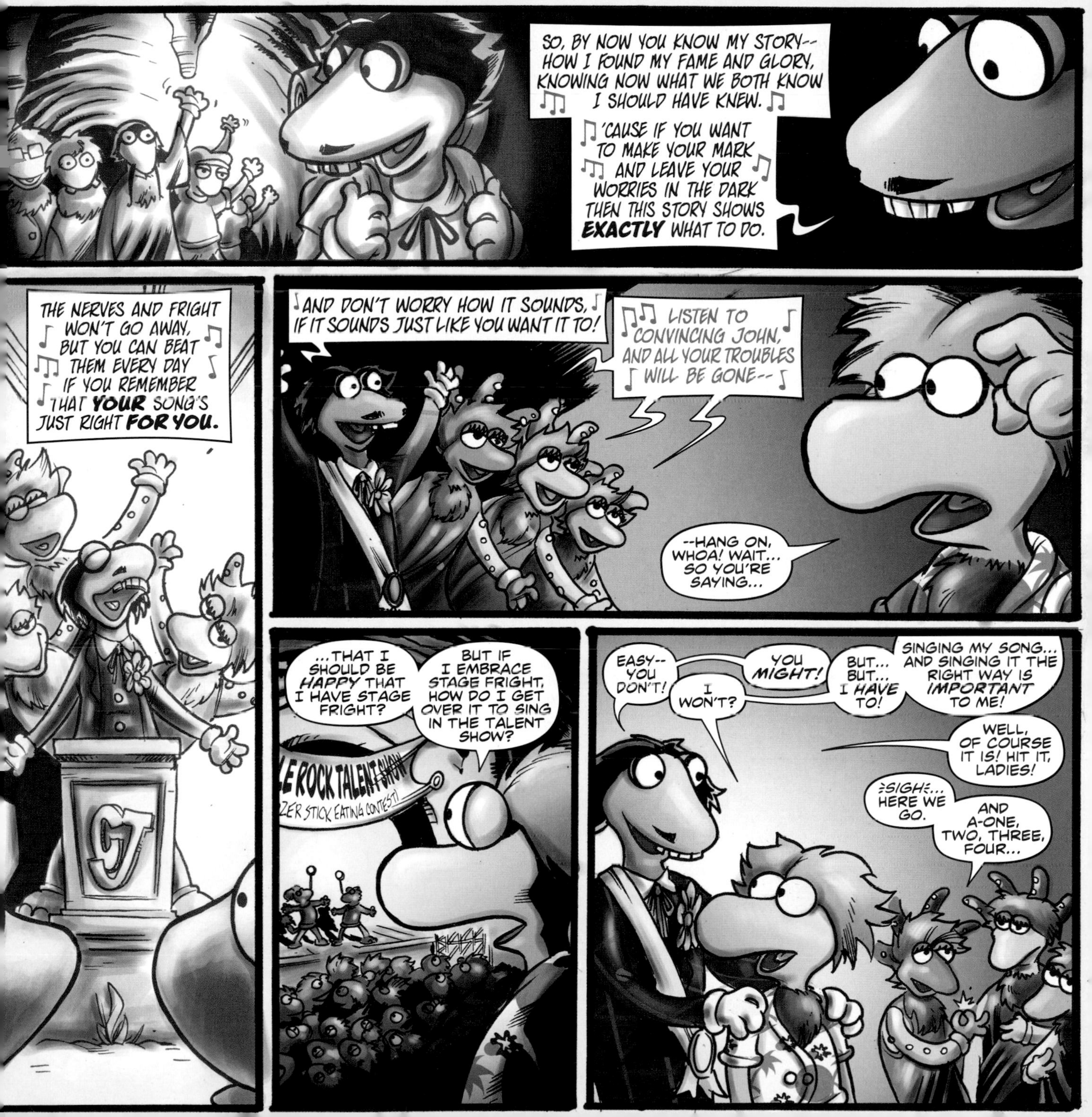

SO, BY NOW YOU KNOW MY STORY-- HOW I FOUND MY FAME AND GLORY, KNOWING NOW WHAT WE BOTH KNOW I SHOULD HAVE KNEW.
'CAUSE IF YOU WANT TO MAKE YOUR MARK AND LEAVE YOUR WORRIES IN THE DARK THEN THIS STORY SHOWS **EXACTLY** WHAT TO DO.
THE NERVES AND FRIGHT WON'T GO AWAY, BUT YOU CAN BEAT THEM EVERY DAY IF YOU REMEMBER THAT **YOUR** SONG'S JUST RIGHT **FOR YOU.**
AND DON'T WORRY HOW IT SOUNDS, IF IT SOUNDS JUST LIKE YOU WANT IT TO!
LISTEN TO CONVINCING JOHN, AND ALL YOUR TROUBLES WILL BE GONE--
--HANG ON, WHOA! WAIT... SO YOU'RE SAYING...
...THAT I SHOULD BE *HAPPY* THAT I HAVE STAGE FRIGHT?
BUT IF I EMBRACE STAGE FRIGHT, HOW DO I GET OVER IT TO SING IN THE TALENT SHOW?
LE ROCK TALENT SHOW
ZER STICK EATING CONTEST!
EASY-- YOU DON'T!
I WON'T?
YOU *MIGHT!*
BUT... BUT... I *HAVE* TO!
SINGING MY SONG... AND SINGING IT THE RIGHT WAY IS *IMPORTANT* TO ME!
WELL, OF COURSE IT IS! HIT IT, LADIES!
SIGH... HERE WE GO.
AND A-ONE, TWO, THREE, FOUR...

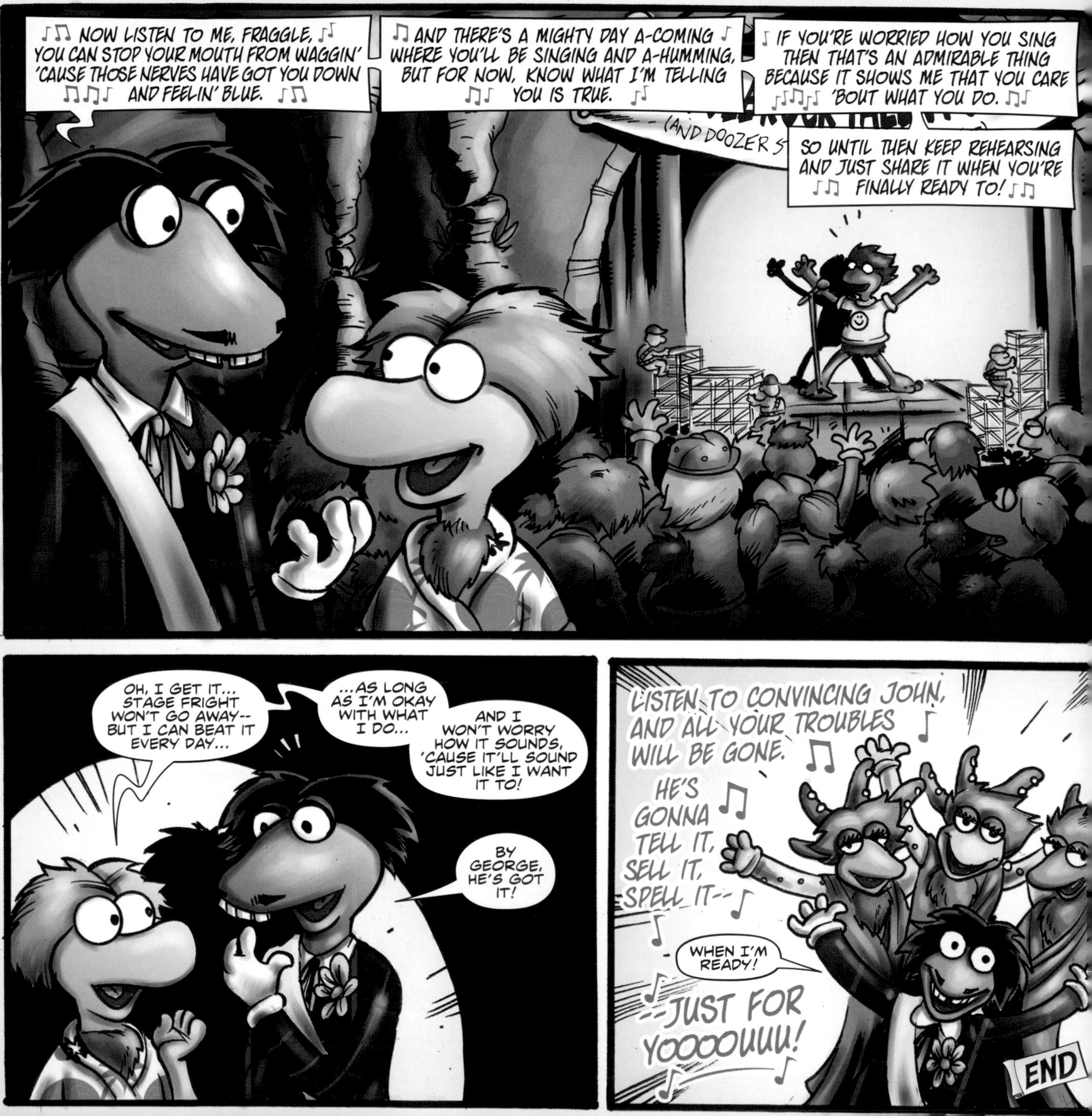
NOW LISTEN TO ME, FRAGGLE, YOU CAN STOP YOUR MOUTH FROM WAGGIN' 'CAUSE THOSE NERVES HAVE GOT YOU DOWN AND FEELIN' BLUE.
AND THERE'S A MIGHTY DAY A-COMING WHERE YOU'LL BE SINGING AND A-HUMMING, BUT FOR NOW, KNOW WHAT I'M TELLING YOU IS TRUE.
IF YOU'RE WORRIED HOW YOU SING THEN THAT'S AN ADMIRABLE THING BECAUSE IT SHOWS ME THAT YOU CARE 'BOUT WHAT YOU DO.
SO UNTIL THEN KEEP REHEARSING AND JUST SHARE IT WHEN YOU'RE FINALLY READY TO!
OH, I GET IT... STAGE FRIGHT WON'T GO AWAY-- BUT I CAN BEAT IT EVERY DAY...
...AS LONG AS I'M OKAY WITH WHAT I DO...
AND I WON'T WORRY HOW IT SOUNDS, 'CAUSE IT'LL SOUND JUST LIKE I WANT IT TO!
BY GEORGE, HE'S GOT IT!
LISTEN TO CONVINCING JOHN, AND ALL YOUR TROUBLES WILL BE GONE.
HE'S GONNA TELL IT, SELL IT, SPELL IT--
WHEN I'M READY!
--JUST FOR YOOOOUUU!
END

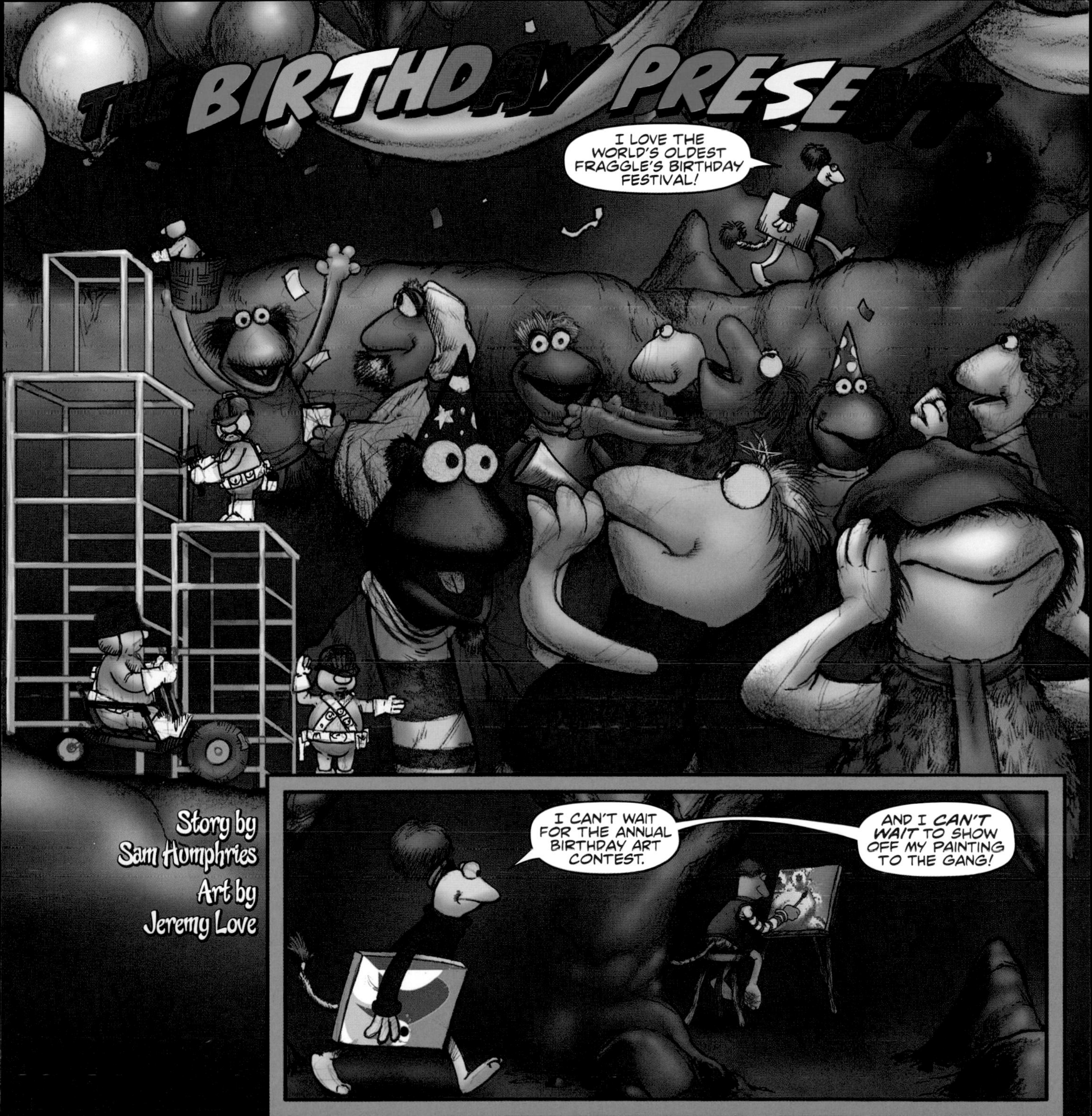
THE BIRTHDAY PRESENT
I LOVE THE WORLD'S OLDEST FRAGGLE'S BIRTHDAY FESTIVAL!
Story by Sam Humphries
Art by Jeremy Love
I CAN'T WAIT FOR THE ANNUAL BIRTHDAY ART CONTEST.
AND I *CAN'T WAIT* TO SHOW OFF MY PAINTING TO THE GANG!

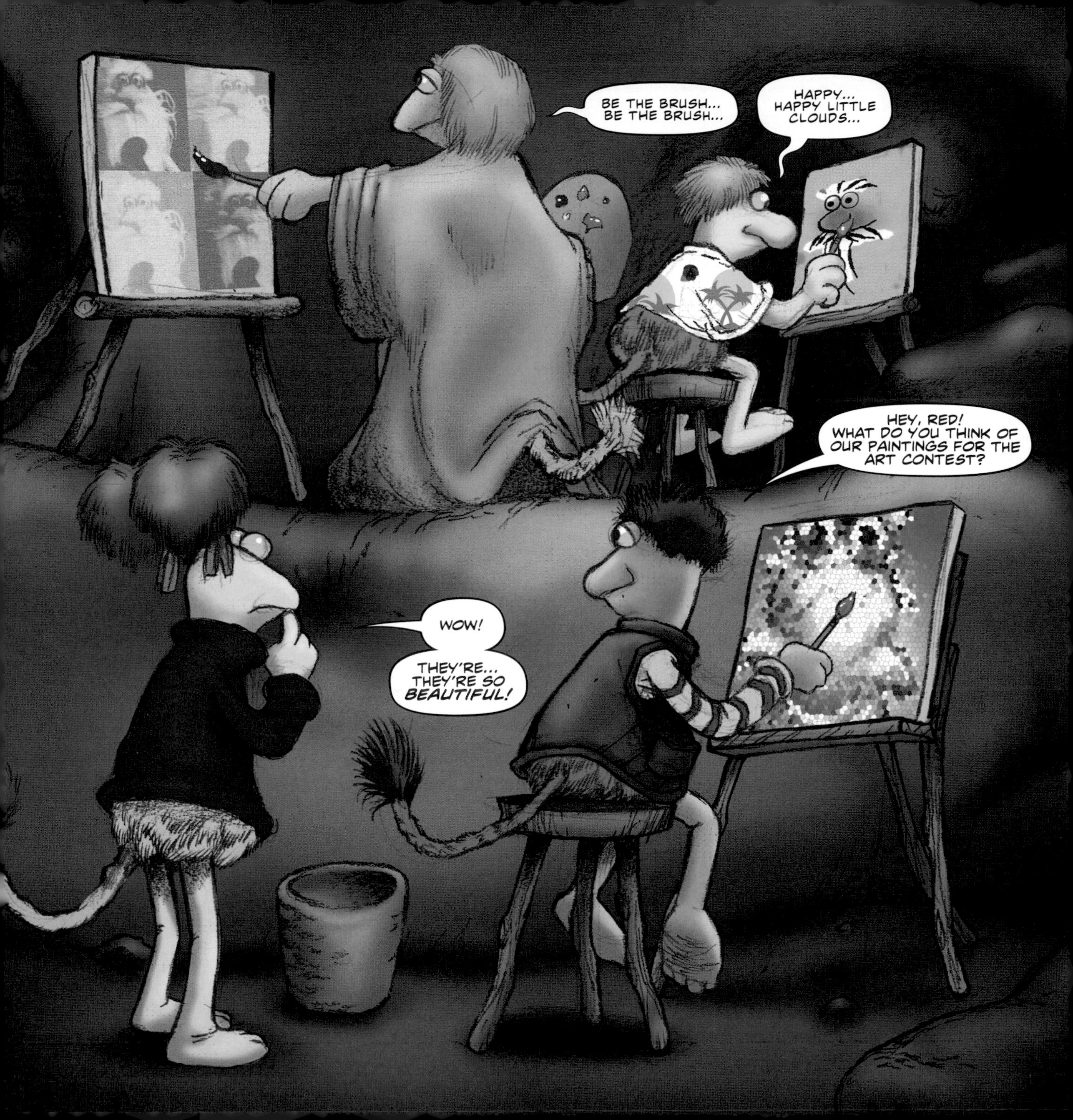
BE THE BRUSH... BE THE BRUSH...
HAPPY... HAPPY LITTLE CLOUDS...
HEY, RED! WHAT DO YOU THINK OF OUR PAINTINGS FOR THE ART CONTEST?
WOW!
THEY'RE... THEY'RE SO BEAUTIFUL!

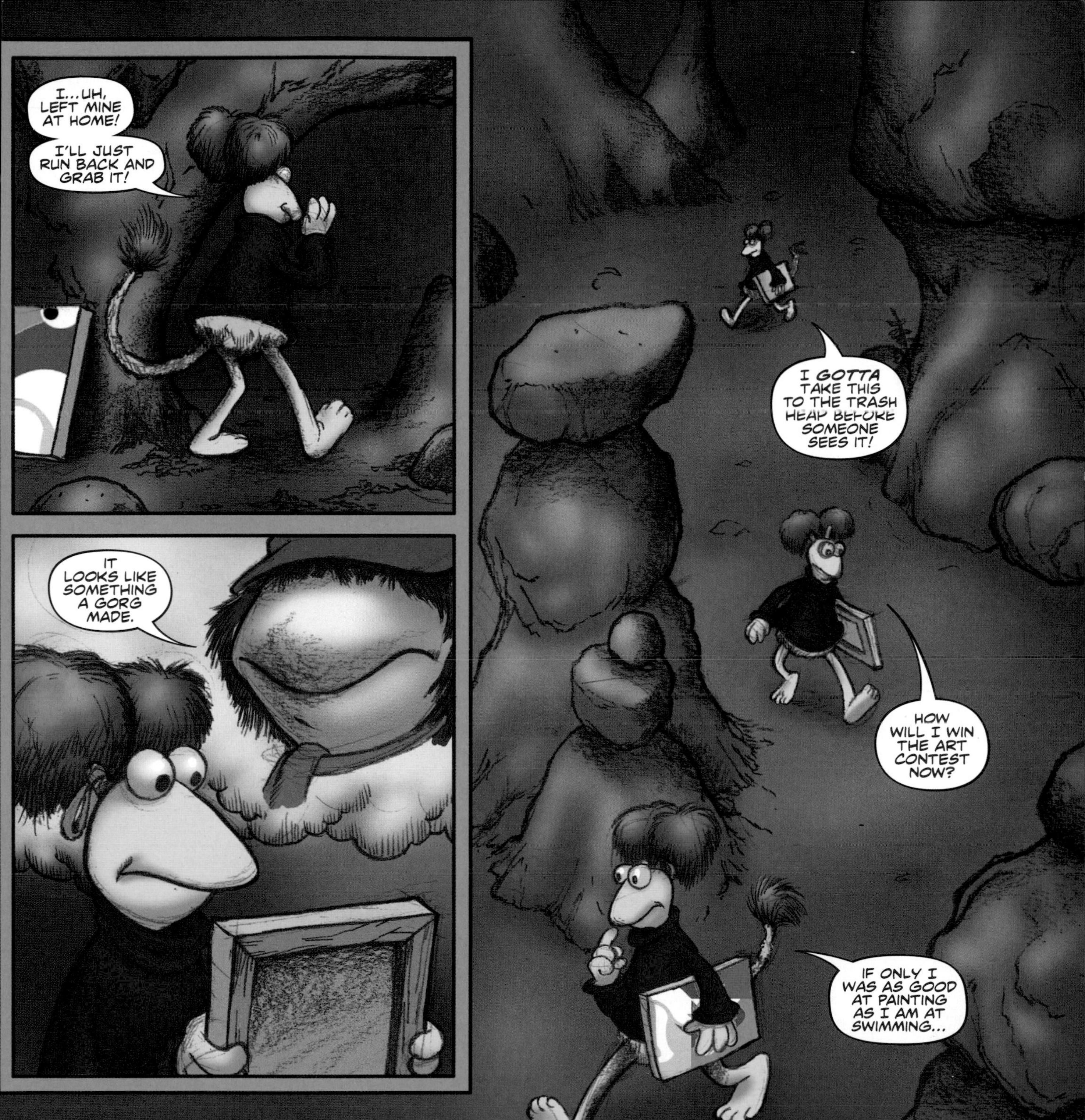
I...UH, LEFT MINE AT HOME!
I'LL JUST RUN BACK AND GRAB IT!
IT LOOKS LIKE SOMETHING A GORG MADE.
I GOTTA TAKE THIS TO THE TRASH HEAP BEFORE SOMEONE SEES IT!
HOW WILL I WIN THE ART CONTEST NOW?
IF ONLY I WAS AS GOOD AT PAINTING AS I AM AT SWIMMING...

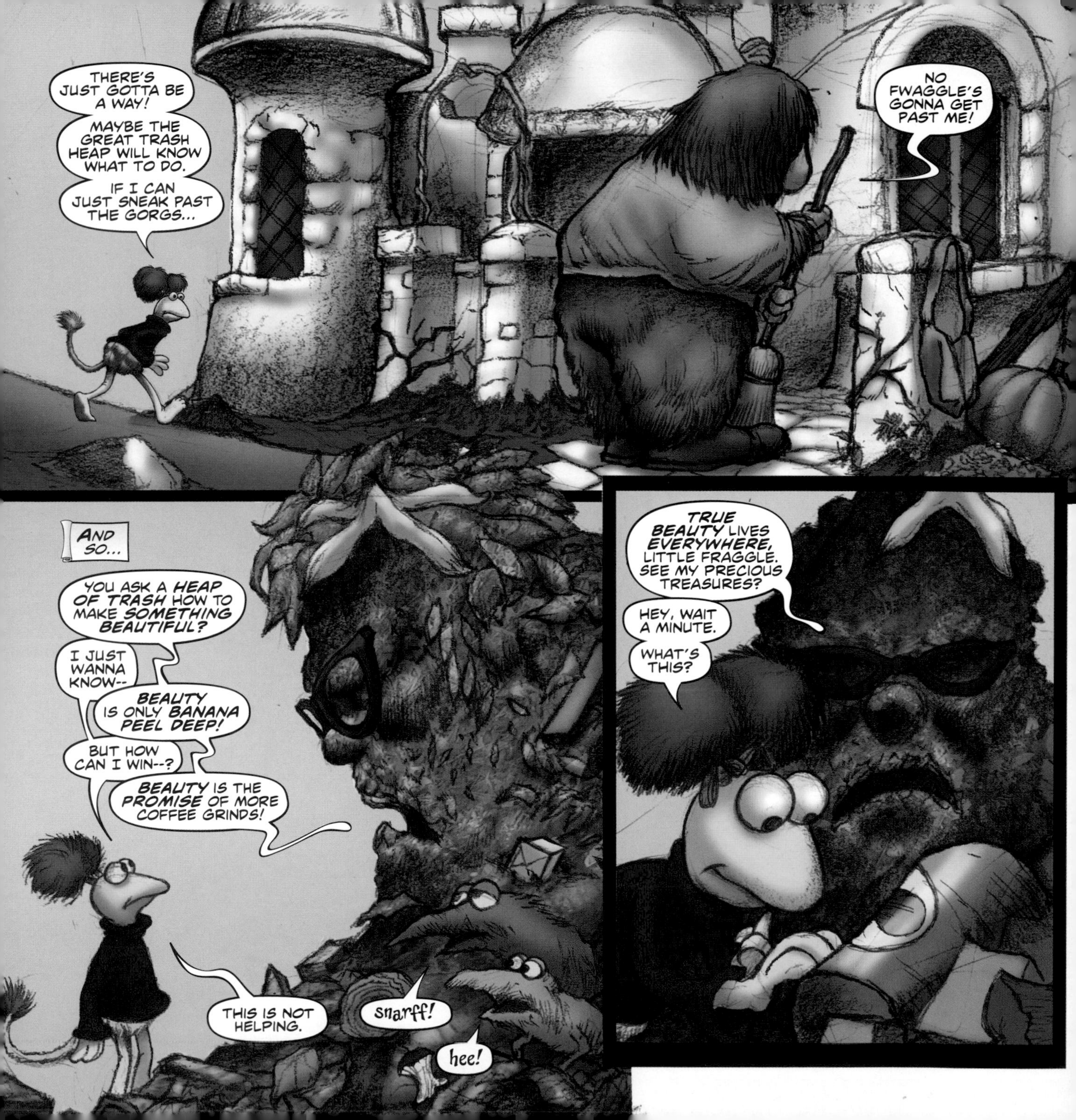
THERE'S JUST GOTTA BE A WAY!
MAYBE THE GREAT TRASH HEAP WILL KNOW WHAT TO DO.
IF I CAN JUST SNEAK PAST THE GORGS...
NO FWAGGLE'S GONNA GET PAST ME!
AND SO...
YOU ASK A HEAP OF TRASH HOW TO MAKE SOMETHING BEAUTIFUL?
I JUST WANNA KNOW--
BEAUTY IS ONLY BANANA PEEL DEEP!
BUT HOW CAN I WIN--?
BEAUTY IS THE PROMISE OF MORE COFFEE GRINDS!
THIS IS NOT HELPING.
snarff!
hee!
TRUE BEAUTY LIVES EVERYWHERE, LITTLE FRAGGLE. SEE MY PRECIOUS TREASURES?
HEY, WAIT A MINUTE.
WHAT'S THIS?

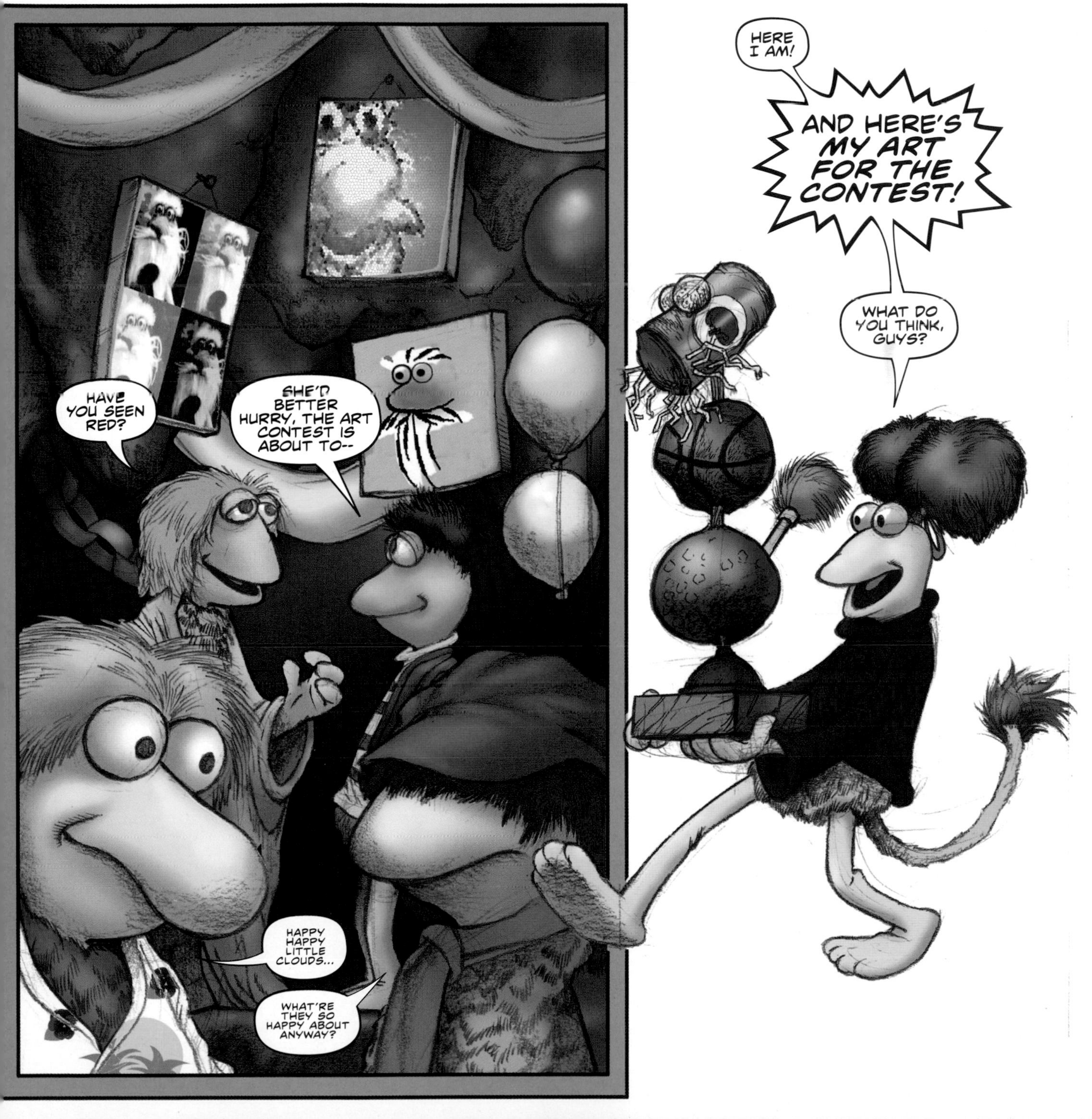
HAVE YOU SEEN RED?
SHE'D BETTER HURRY, THE ART CONTEST IS ABOUT TO--
HERE I AM!
AND HERE'S MY ART FOR THE CONTEST!
WHAT DO YOU THINK, GUYS?
HAPPY HAPPY LITTLE CLOUDS...
WHAT'RE THEY SO HAPPY ABOUT ANYWAY?

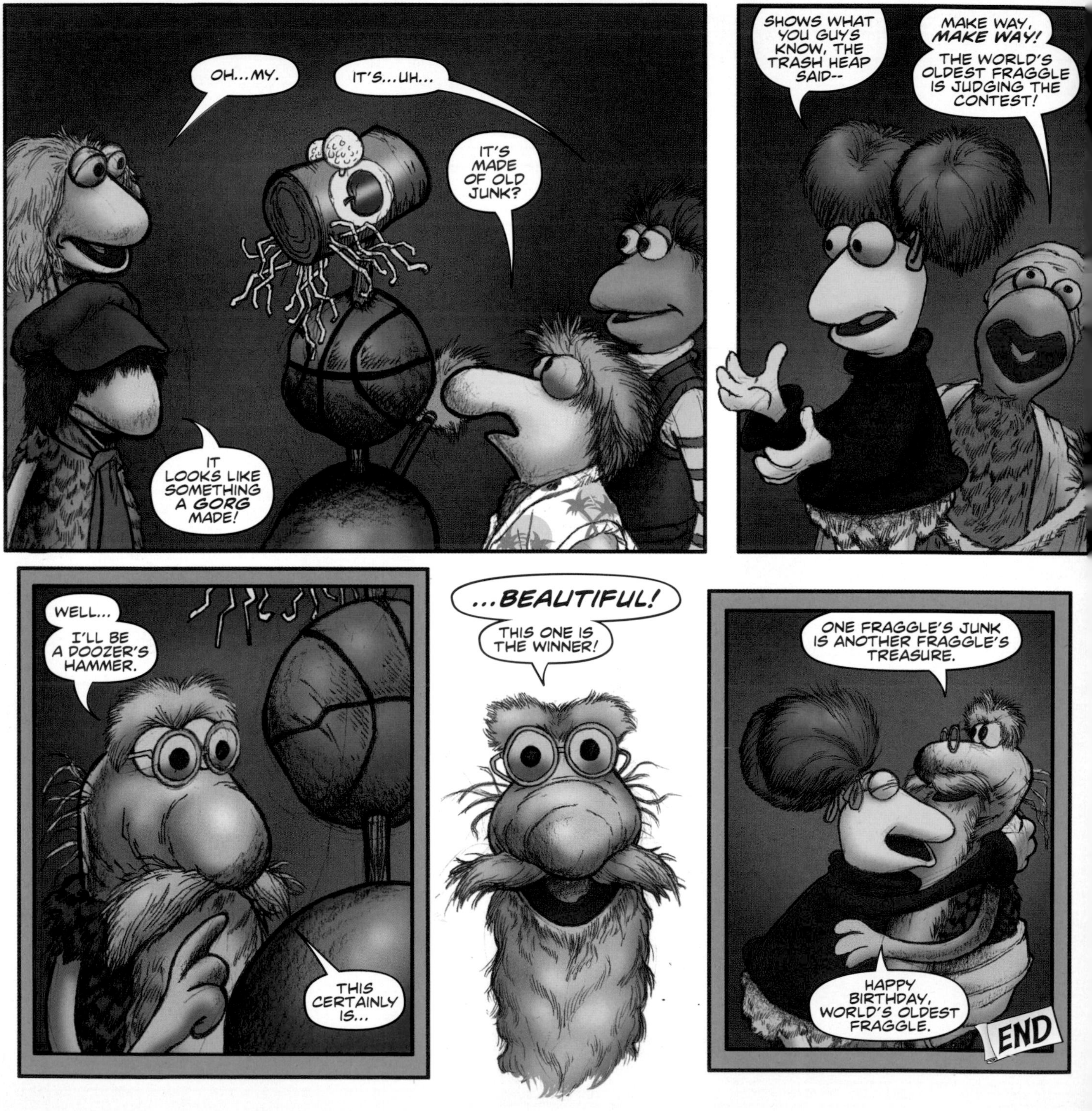
OH...MY.
IT'S...UH...
IT'S MADE OF OLD JUNK?
IT LOOKS LIKE SOMETHING A *GORG* MADE!
SHOWS WHAT YOU GUYS KNOW, THE TRASH HEAP SAID--
MAKE WAY, ***MAKE WAY!***
THE WORLD'S OLDEST FRAGGLE IS JUDGING THE CONTEST!
WELL...
I'LL BE A DOOZER'S HAMMER.
THIS CERTAINLY IS...
...BEAUTIFUL!
THIS ONE IS THE WINNER!
ONE FRAGGLE'S JUNK IS ANOTHER FRAGGLE'S TREASURE.
HAPPY BIRTHDAY, WORLD'S OLDEST FRAGGLE.
END

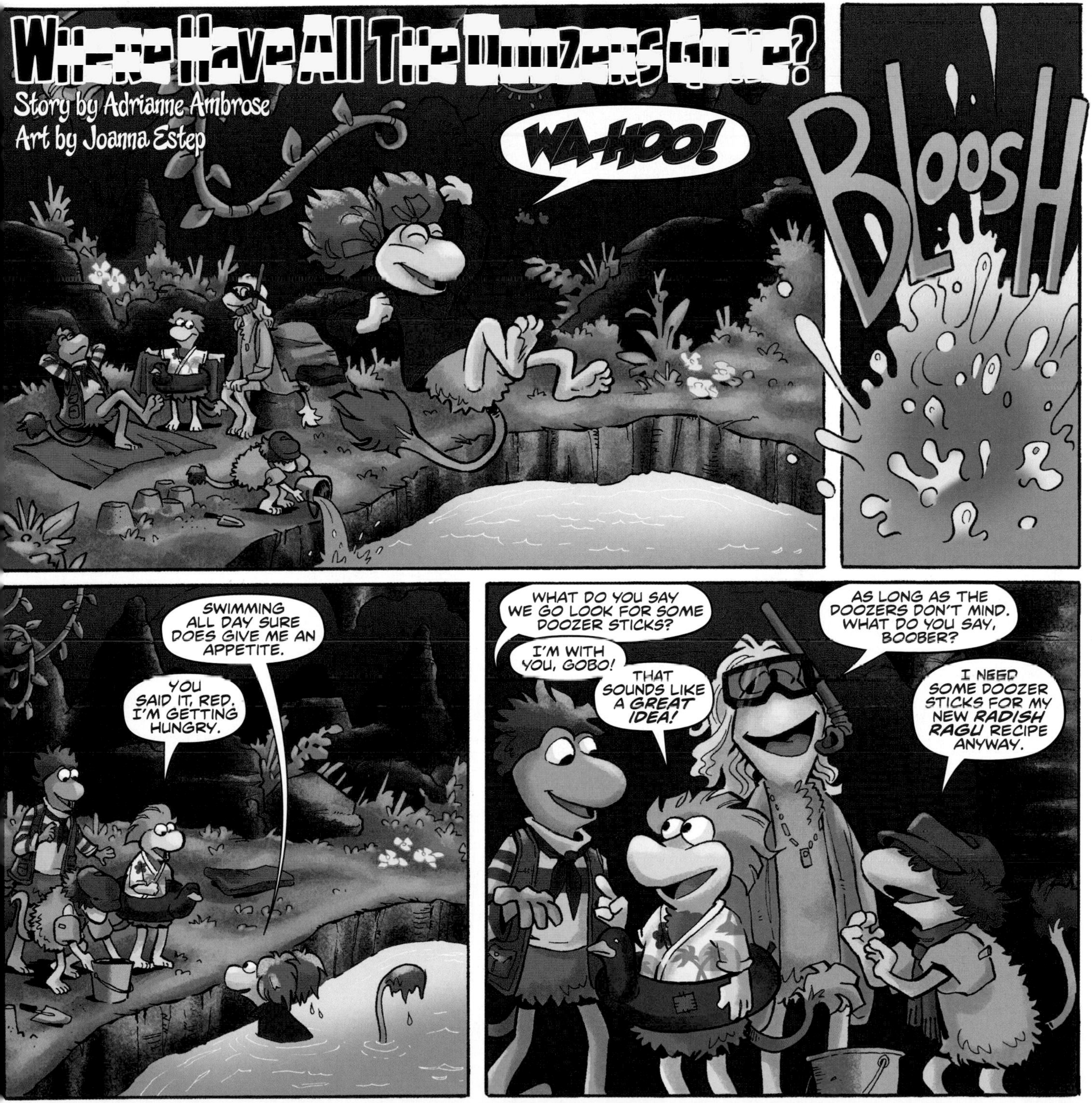

Where Have All The Doozers Gone?
Story by Adrianne Ambrose
Art by Joanna Estep
WA-HOO!
BLOOSH
SWIMMING ALL DAY SURE DOES GIVE ME AN APPETITE.
YOU SAID IT, RED. I'M GETTING HUNGRY.
WHAT DO YOU SAY WE GO LOOK FOR SOME DOOZER STICKS?
I'M WITH YOU, GOBO!
THAT SOUNDS LIKE A *GREAT IDEA!*
AS LONG AS THE DOOZERS DON'T MIND. WHAT DO YOU SAY, BOOBER?
I NEED SOME DOOZER STICKS FOR MY NEW *RADISH RAGU* RECIPE ANYWAY.

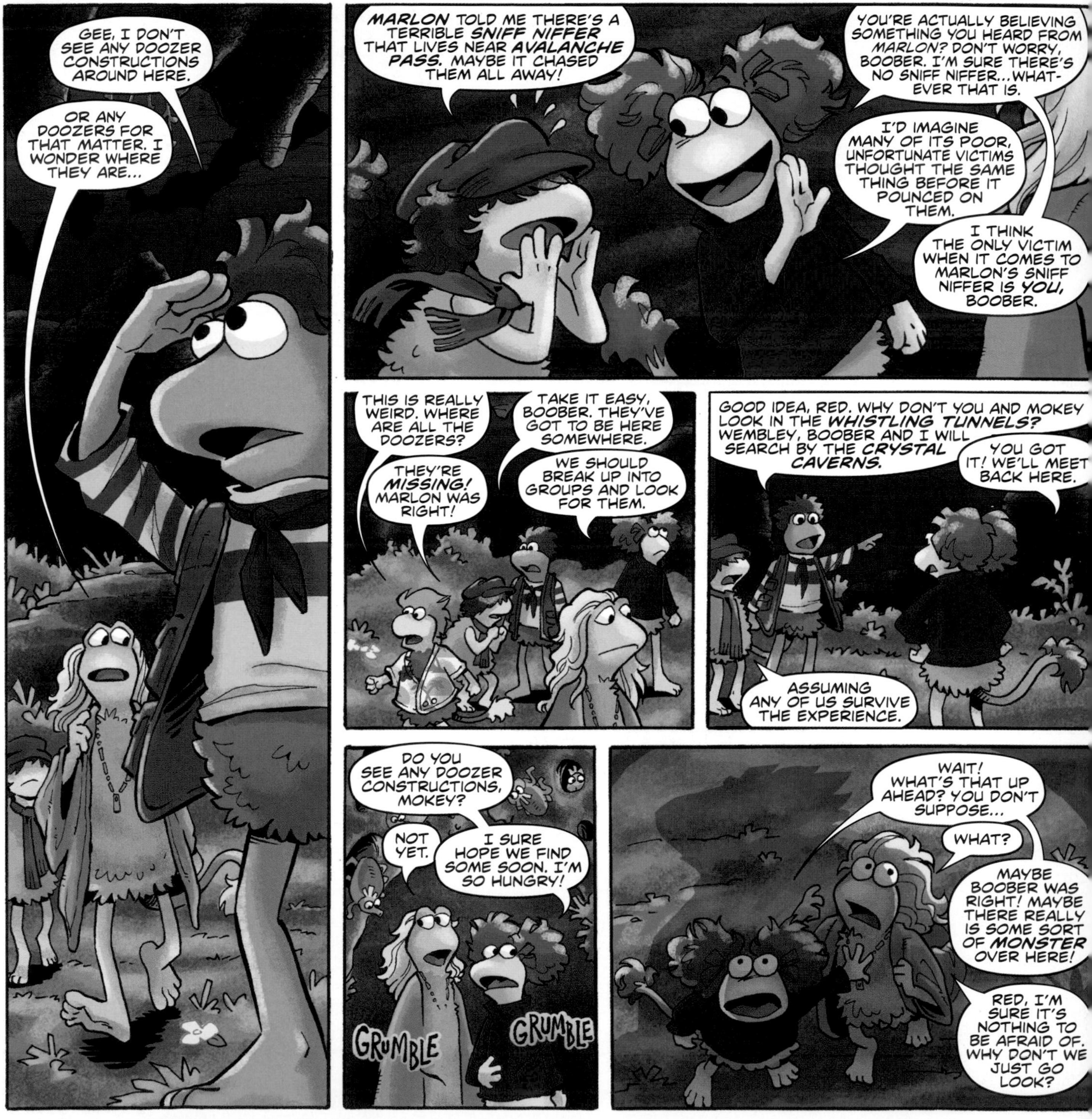
GEE, I DON'T SEE ANY DOOZER CONSTRUCTIONS AROUND HERE.
OR ANY DOOZERS FOR THAT MATTER. I WONDER WHERE THEY ARE...
MARLON TOLD ME THERE'S A TERRIBLE SNIFF NIFFER THAT LIVES NEAR AVALANCHE PASS. MAYBE IT CHASED THEM ALL AWAY!
YOU'RE ACTUALLY BELIEVING SOMETHING YOU HEARD FROM MARLON? DON'T WORRY, BOOBER. I'M SURE THERE'S NO SNIFF NIFFER...WHAT-EVER THAT IS.
I'D IMAGINE MANY OF ITS POOR, UNFORTUNATE VICTIMS THOUGHT THE SAME THING BEFORE IT POUNCED ON THEM.
I THINK THE ONLY VICTIM WHEN IT COMES TO MARLON'S SNIFF NIFFER IS YOU, BOOBER.
THIS IS REALLY WEIRD. WHERE ARE ALL THE DOOZERS?
THEY'RE MISSING! MARLON WAS RIGHT!
TAKE IT EASY, BOOBER. THEY'VE GOT TO BE HERE SOMEWHERE.
WE SHOULD BREAK UP INTO GROUPS AND LOOK FOR THEM.
GOOD IDEA, RED. WHY DON'T YOU AND MOKEY LOOK IN THE WHISTLING TUNNELS? WEMBLEY, BOOBER AND I WILL SEARCH BY THE CRYSTAL CAVERNS.
YOU GOT IT! WE'LL MEET BACK HERE.
ASSUMING ANY OF US SURVIVE THE EXPERIENCE.
DO YOU SEE ANY DOOZER CONSTRUCTIONS, MOKEY?
NOT YET.
I SURE HOPE WE FIND SOME SOON. I'M SO HUNGRY!
GRUMBLE
GRUMBLE
WAIT! WHAT'S THAT UP AHEAD? YOU DON'T SUPPOSE...
WHAT?
MAYBE BOOBER WAS RIGHT! MAYBE THERE REALLY IS SOME SORT OF MONSTER OVER HERE!
RED, I'M SURE IT'S NOTHING TO BE AFRAID OF. WHY DON'T WE JUST GO LOOK?

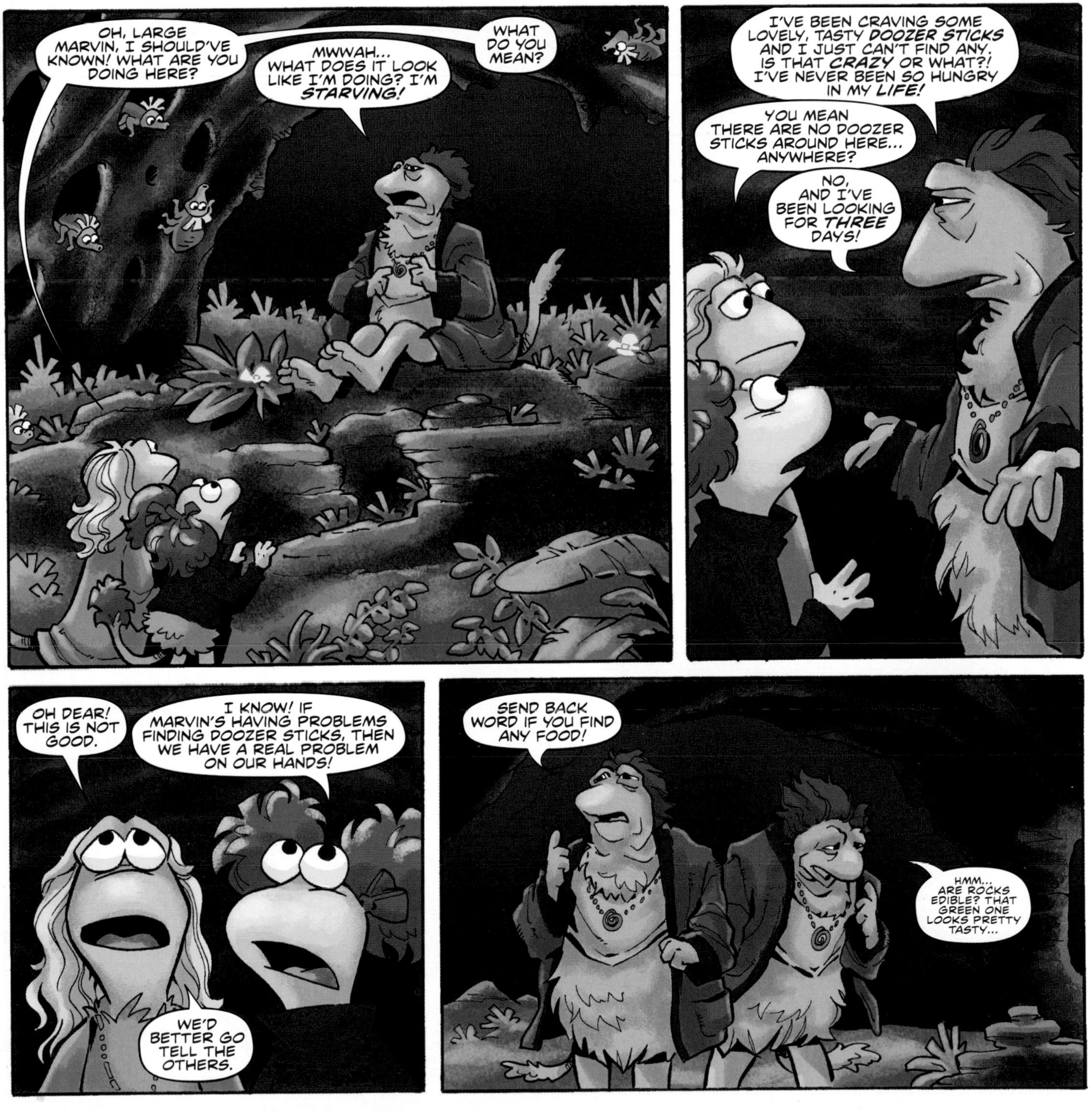

OH, LARGE MARVIN, I SHOULD'VE KNOWN! WHAT ARE YOU DOING HERE?
MWWAH... WHAT DOES IT LOOK LIKE I'M DOING? I'M STARVING!
WHAT DO YOU MEAN?
I'VE BEEN CRAVING SOME LOVELY, TASTY DOOZER STICKS AND I JUST CAN'T FIND ANY. IS THAT CRAZY OR WHAT?! I'VE NEVER BEEN SO HUNGRY IN MY LIFE!
YOU MEAN THERE ARE NO DOOZER STICKS AROUND HERE... ANYWHERE?
NO, AND I'VE BEEN LOOKING FOR THREE DAYS!
OH DEAR! THIS IS NOT GOOD.
I KNOW! IF MARVIN'S HAVING PROBLEMS FINDING DOOZER STICKS, THEN WE HAVE A REAL PROBLEM ON OUR HANDS!
WE'D BETTER GO TELL THE OTHERS.
SEND BACK WORD IF YOU FIND ANY FOOD!
HMM... ARE ROCKS EDIBLE? THAT GREEN ONE LOOKS PRETTY TASTY...

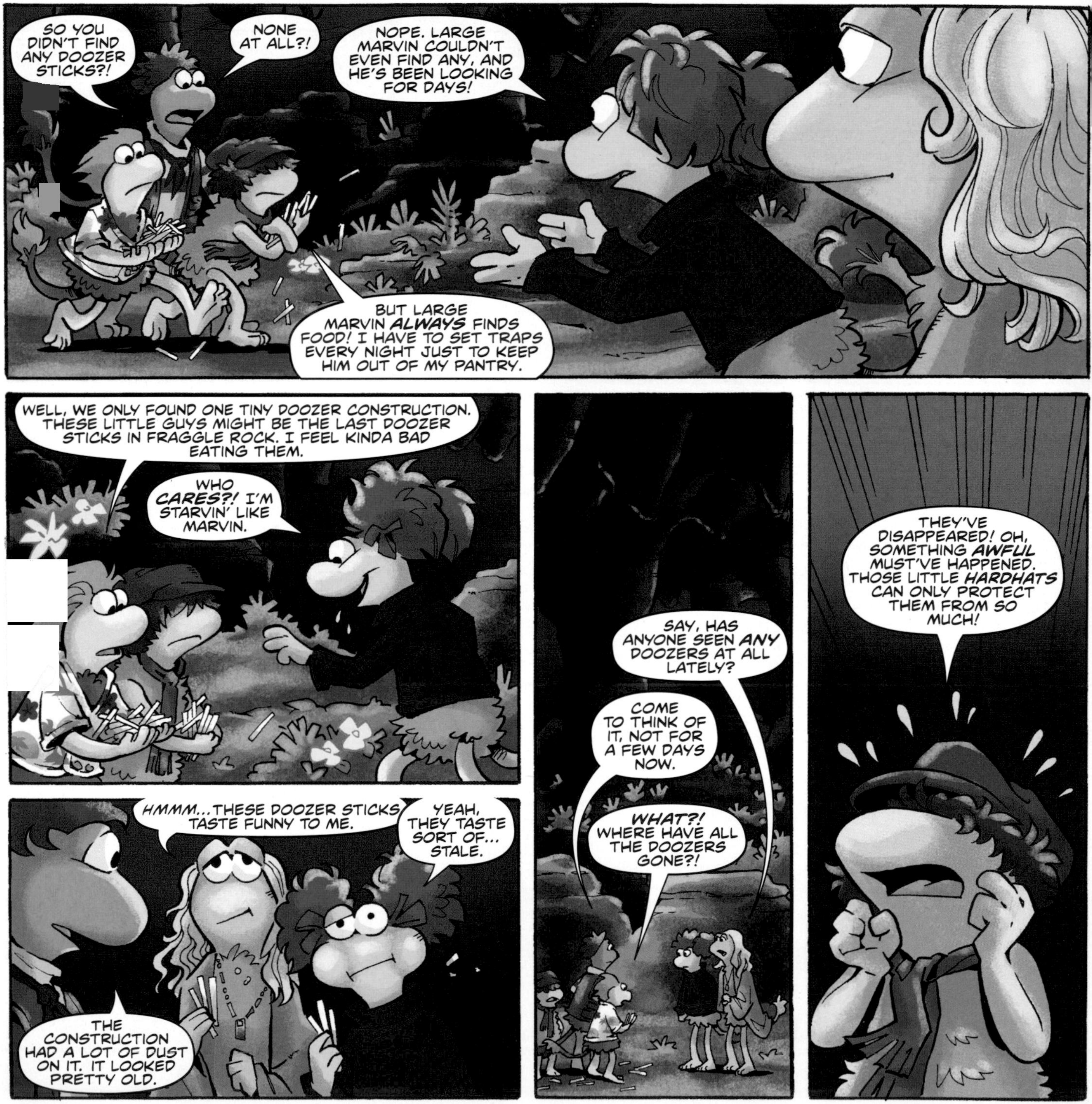
SO YOU DIDN'T FIND ANY DOOZER STICKS?!
NONE AT ALL?!
NOPE. LARGE MARVIN COULDN'T EVEN FIND ANY, AND HE'S BEEN LOOKING FOR DAYS!
BUT LARGE MARVIN ALWAYS FINDS FOOD! I HAVE TO SET TRAPS EVERY NIGHT JUST TO KEEP HIM OUT OF MY PANTRY.
WELL, WE ONLY FOUND ONE TINY DOOZER CONSTRUCTION. THESE LITTLE GUYS MIGHT BE THE LAST DOOZER STICKS IN FRAGGLE ROCK. I FEEL KINDA BAD EATING THEM.
WHO CARES?! I'M STARVIN' LIKE MARVIN.
HMMM...THESE DOOZER STICKS TASTE FUNNY TO ME.
YEAH, THEY TASTE SORT OF... STALE.
THE CONSTRUCTION HAD A LOT OF DUST ON IT. IT LOOKED PRETTY OLD.
SAY, HAS ANYONE SEEN ANY DOOZERS AT ALL LATELY?
COME TO THINK OF IT, NOT FOR A FEW DAYS NOW.
WHAT?! WHERE HAVE ALL THE DOOZERS GONE?!
THEY'VE DISAPPEARED! OH, SOMETHING AWFUL MUST'VE HAPPENED. THOSE LITTLE HARDHATS CAN ONLY PROTECT THEM FROM SO MUCH!

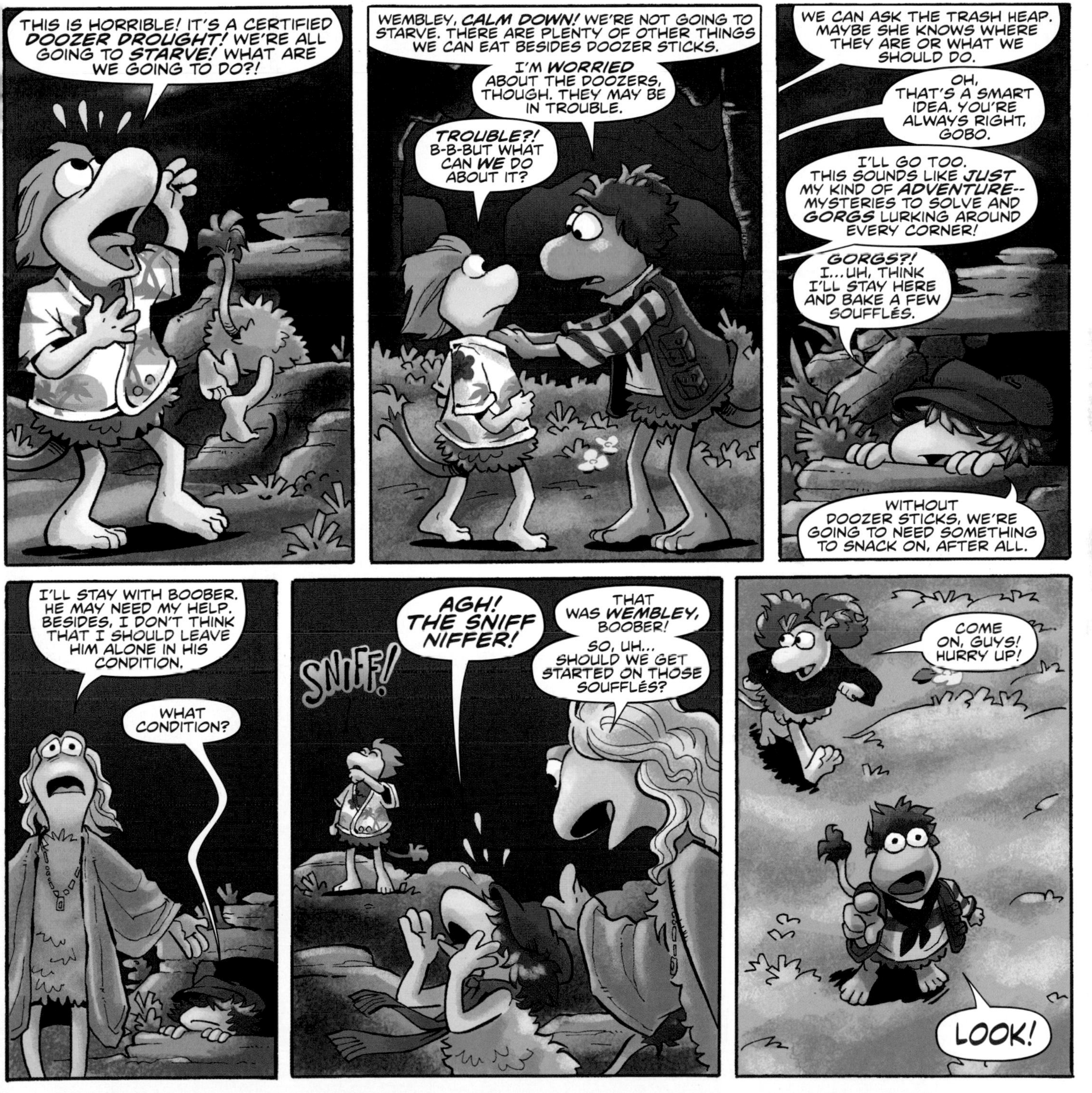
THIS IS HORRIBLE! IT'S A CERTIFIED DOOZER DROUGHT! WE'RE ALL GOING TO STARVE! WHAT ARE WE GOING TO DO?!
WEMBLEY, CALM DOWN! WE'RE NOT GOING TO STARVE. THERE ARE PLENTY OF OTHER THINGS WE CAN EAT BESIDES DOOZER STICKS.
I'M WORRIED ABOUT THE DOOZERS, THOUGH. THEY MAY BE IN TROUBLE.
TROUBLE?! B-B-BUT WHAT CAN WE DO ABOUT IT?
WE CAN ASK THE TRASH HEAP. MAYBE SHE KNOWS WHERE THEY ARE OR WHAT WE SHOULD DO.
OH, THAT'S A SMART IDEA. YOU'RE ALWAYS RIGHT, GOBO.
I'LL GO TOO. THIS SOUNDS LIKE JUST MY KIND OF ADVENTURE-- MYSTERIES TO SOLVE AND GORGS LURKING AROUND EVERY CORNER!
GORGS?! I...UH, THINK I'LL STAY HERE AND BAKE A FEW SOUFFLÉS.
WITHOUT DOOZER STICKS, WE'RE GOING TO NEED SOMETHING TO SNACK ON, AFTER ALL.
I'LL STAY WITH BOOBER. HE MAY NEED MY HELP. BESIDES, I DON'T THINK THAT I SHOULD LEAVE HIM ALONE IN HIS CONDITION.
WHAT CONDITION?
SNIFF!
AGH! THE SNIFF NIFFER!
THAT WAS WEMBLEY, BOOBER!
SO, UH... SHOULD WE GET STARTED ON THOSE SOUFFLÉS?
COME ON, GUYS! HURRY UP!
LOOK!

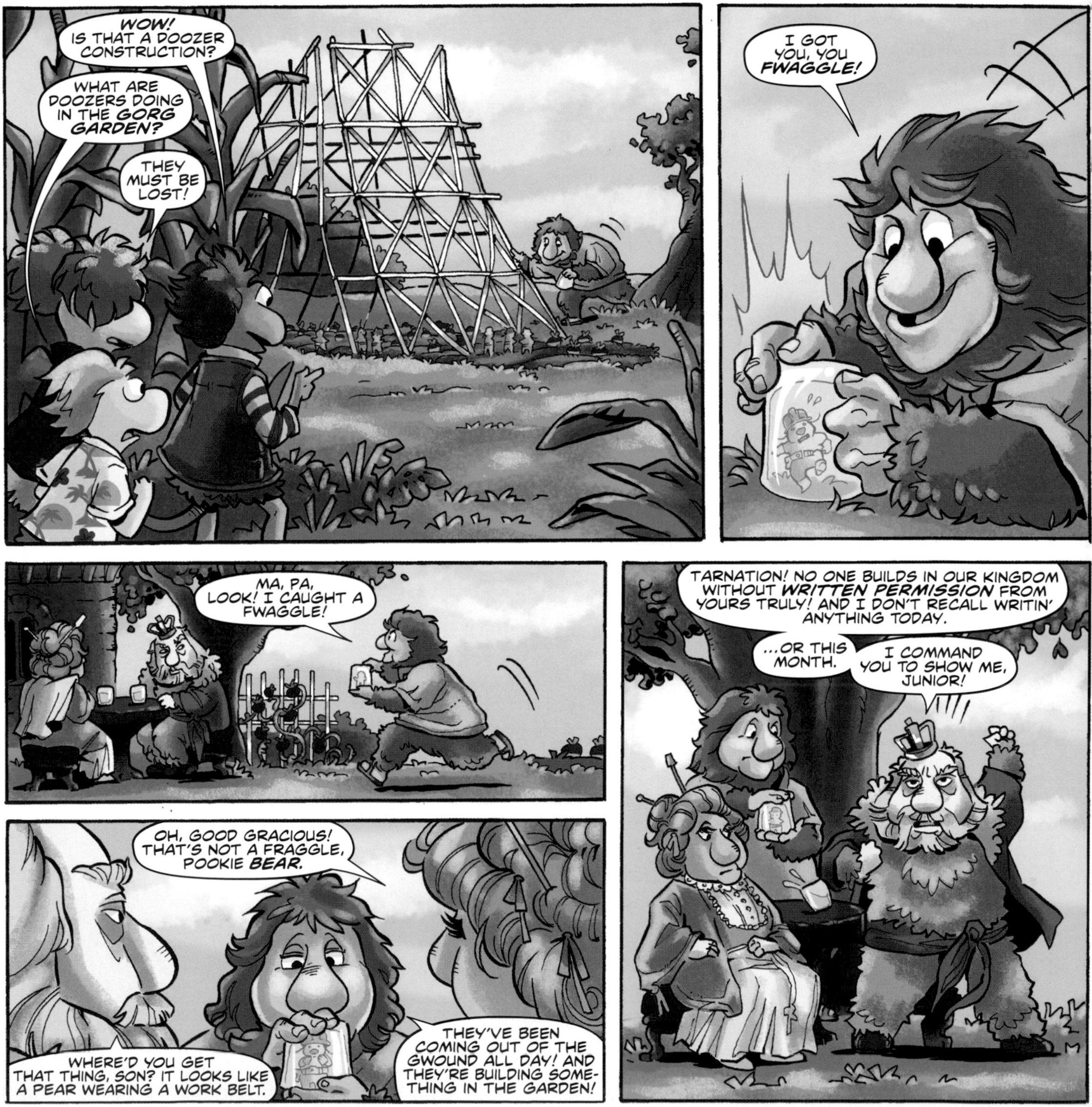
WOW! IS THAT A DOOZER CONSTRUCTION?
WHAT ARE DOOZERS DOING IN THE GORG GARDEN?
THEY MUST BE LOST!
I GOT YOU, YOU FWAGGLE!
MA, PA, LOOK! I CAUGHT A FWAGGLE!
OH, GOOD GRACIOUS! THAT'S NOT A FRAGGLE, POOKIE BEAR.
WHERE'D YOU GET THAT THING, SON? IT LOOKS LIKE A PEAR WEARING A WORK BELT.
THEY'VE BEEN COMING OUT OF THE GWOUND ALL DAY! AND THEY'RE BUILDING SOME-THING IN THE GARDEN!
TARNATION! NO ONE BUILDS IN OUR KINGDOM WITHOUT WRITTEN PERMISSION FROM YOURS TRULY! AND I DON'T RECALL WRITIN' ANYTHING TODAY.
...OR THIS MONTH.
I COMMAND YOU TO SHOW ME, JUNIOR!

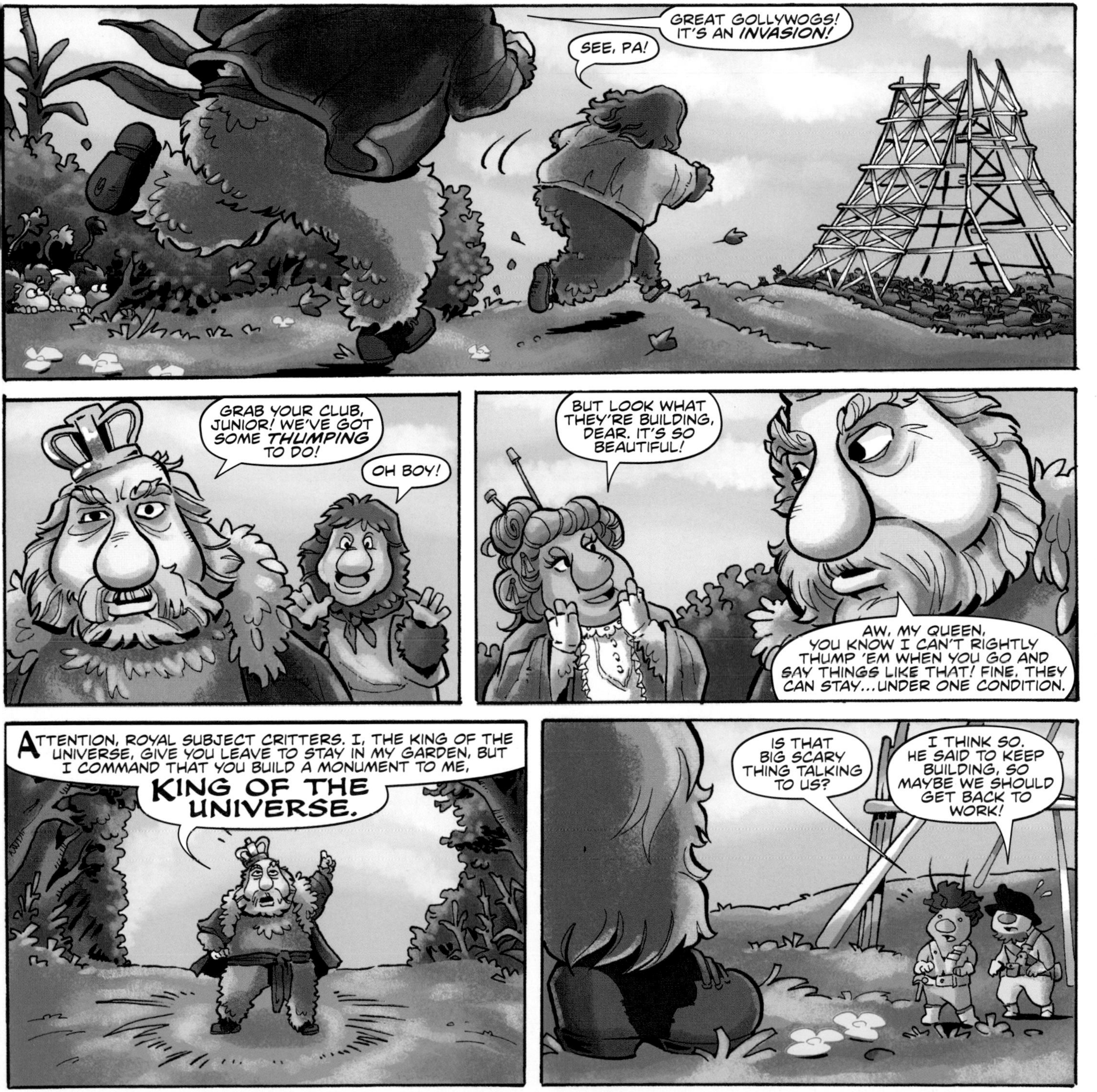
GREAT GOLLYWOGS! IT'S AN INVASION!
SEE, PA!
GRAB YOUR CLUB, JUNIOR! WE'VE GOT SOME THUMPING TO DO!
OH BOY!
BUT LOOK WHAT THEY'RE BUILDING, DEAR. IT'S SO BEAUTIFUL!
AW, MY QUEEN, YOU KNOW I CAN'T RIGHTLY THUMP 'EM WHEN YOU GO AND SAY THINGS LIKE THAT! FINE, THEY CAN STAY...UNDER ONE CONDITION.
ATTENTION, ROYAL SUBJECT CRITTERS. I, THE KING OF THE UNIVERSE, GIVE YOU LEAVE TO STAY IN MY GARDEN, BUT I COMMAND THAT YOU BUILD A MONUMENT TO ME, KING OF THE UNIVERSE.
IS THAT BIG SCARY THING TALKING TO US?
I THINK SO. HE SAID TO KEEP BUILDING, SO MAYBE WE SHOULD GET BACK TO WORK!

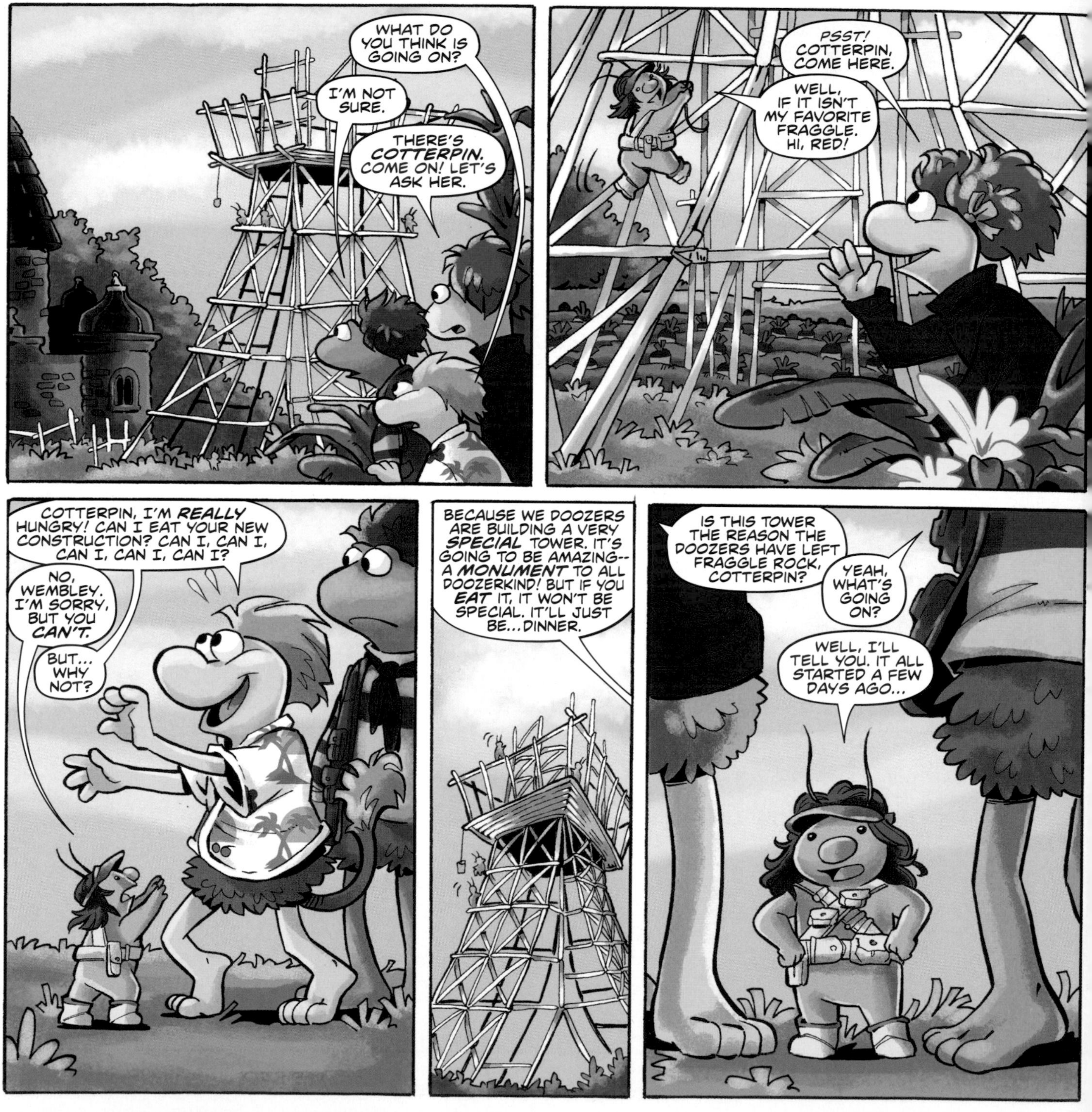
WHAT DO YOU THINK IS GOING ON?
I'M NOT SURE.
THERE'S COTTERPIN. COME ON! LET'S ASK HER.
PSST! COTTERPIN, COME HERE.
WELL, IF IT ISN'T MY FAVORITE FRAGGLE. HI, RED!
COTTERPIN, I'M REALLY HUNGRY! CAN I EAT YOUR NEW CONSTRUCTION? CAN I, CAN I, CAN I, CAN I, CAN I?
NO, WEMBLEY. I'M SORRY, BUT YOU CAN'T.
BUT... WHY NOT?
BECAUSE WE DOOZERS ARE BUILDING A VERY SPECIAL TOWER. IT'S GOING TO BE AMAZING-- A MONUMENT TO ALL DOOZERKIND! BUT IF YOU EAT IT, IT WON'T BE SPECIAL. IT'LL JUST BE... DINNER.
IS THIS TOWER THE REASON THE DOOZERS HAVE LEFT FRAGGLE ROCK, COTTERPIN?
YEAH, WHAT'S GOING ON?
WELL, I'LL TELL YOU. IT ALL STARTED A FEW DAYS AGO...

TOMORROW, WE'LL START WORK ON A NEW TOWER.

ANOTHER ONE? GEE, THAT'LL BE THE *THIRD* TOWER THIS WEEK. CAN'T WE EVER DO ANYTHING *NEW*?

BUILDING TOWERS IS A MIGHTY FINE THING, AND THIS ONE WILL BE PARTICULARLY FINE.

WHY? WHAT MAKES THIS ONE SO SPECIAL?

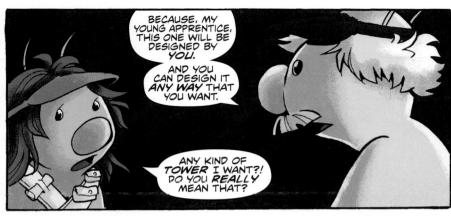

BECAUSE, MY YOUNG APPRENTICE, THIS ONE WILL BE DESIGNED BY *YOU*. AND YOU CAN DESIGN IT *ANY WAY* THAT YOU WANT.

ANY KIND OF *TOWER* I WANT?! DO YOU *REALLY* MEAN THAT?

WELL, THEN I'M GOING TO DESIGN THE *BIGGEST, TALLEST* TOWER FRAGGLE ROCK HAS *EVER* SEEN! I WANT TO SHOW THE WORLD HOW *SPECTACULAR* OUR CONSTRUCTIONS CAN BE WHEN WE LET OUR *IMAGINATIONS* RUN WILD! AND I WANT--

SLOW DOWN, COTTERPIN. YOU KNOW THAT AS *SOON* AS THAT TOWER GETS MORE THAN A *FEW STORIES* TALL, THE FRAGGLES ARE GOING TO EAT IT.

WELL, WE WON'T LET THEM! NOT THIS TOWER!

HEH HEH... IF ANYONE COULD KEEP THEM FROM DINING ON OUR WORK, I HAVE *NO* DOUBT IT WOULD BE *YOU*. BUT WHY WOULD WE DO THAT?

THE FRAGGLES ENJOY EATING OUR CONSTRUC-TIONS, AND WE ENJOY BUILDING FOR THEM. IT'S A GOOD ARRANGEMENT! WITHOUT IT, WE WOULD HAVE RUN OUT OF *ROOM* TO BUILD AGES AGO.

I KNOW, BUT FOR ONCE I'D LIKE TO SEE WHAT WE CAN CREATE WHEN WE'RE BUILDING SOMETHING ENTIRELY FOR OURSELVES. HAVEN'T YOU EVER WONDERED ABOUT THAT?

MAYBE WHEN I WAS A BIT YOUNGER... BACK WHEN I HAD TIME FOR THINKING SUCH THINGS.

=SIGH=...WELL, I'M SURE THE FRAGGLES WON'T MIND LEAVING ONE OF OUR TOWERS ALONE IF WE ASKED THEM TO.

BUT THERE'S ONLY SO MUCH ROOM IN FRAGGLE ROCK. WHERE DO YOU INTEND TO BUILD IT?

I DON'T KNOW, BUT I'M GOING TO START LOOKING *RIGHT NOW*!

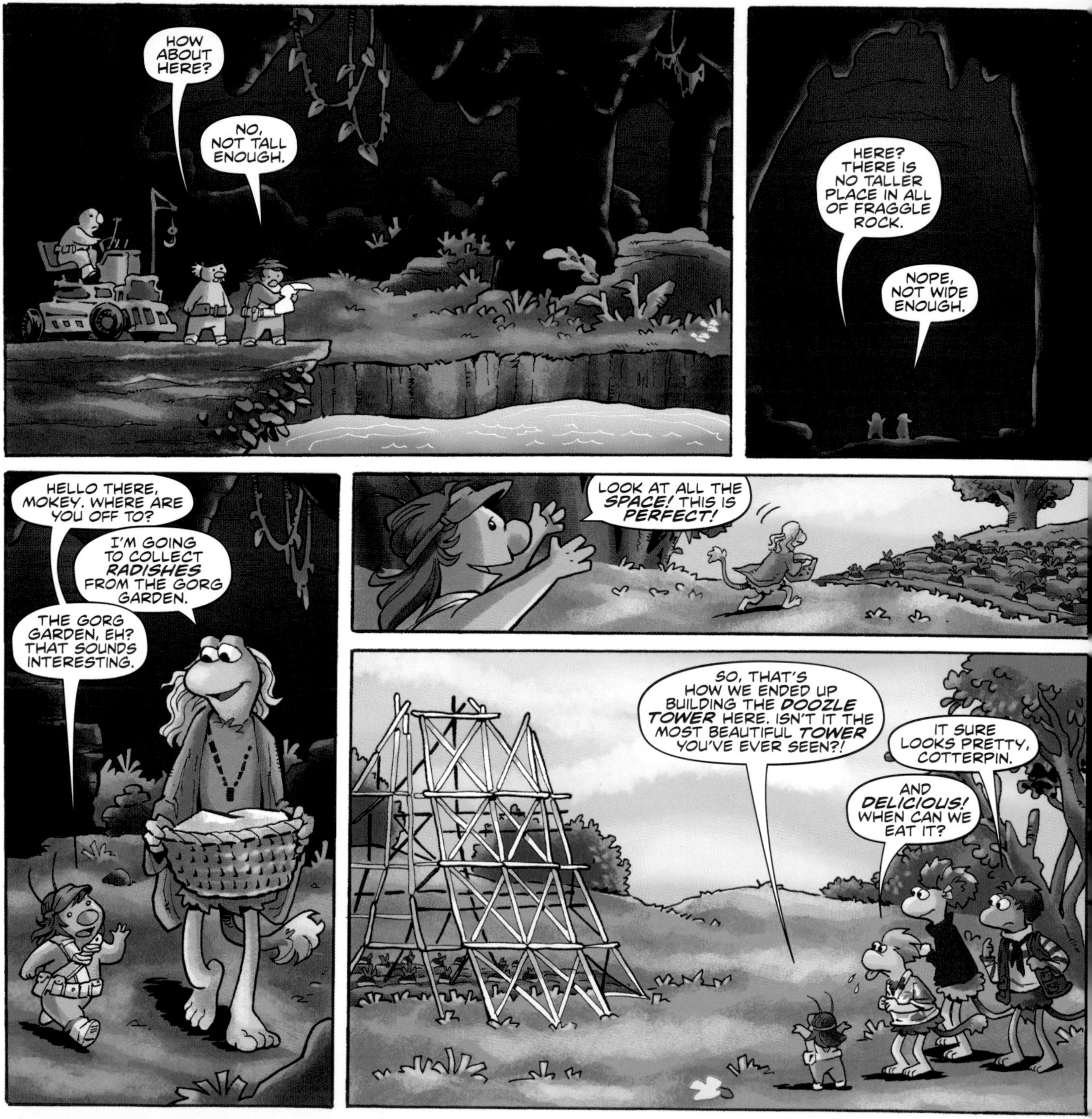
HOW ABOUT HERE?
NO, NOT TALL ENOUGH.
HERE? THERE IS NO TALLER PLACE IN ALL OF FRAGGLE ROCK.
NOPE, NOT WIDE ENOUGH.
HELLO THERE, MOKEY. WHERE ARE YOU OFF TO?
I'M GOING TO COLLECT RADISHES FROM THE GORG GARDEN.
THE GORG GARDEN, EH? THAT SOUNDS INTERESTING.
LOOK AT ALL THE SPACE! THIS IS PERFECT!
SO, THAT'S HOW WE ENDED UP BUILDING THE DOOZLE TOWER HERE. ISN'T IT THE MOST BEAUTIFUL TOWER YOU'VE EVER SEEN?!
IT SURE LOOKS PRETTY, COTTERPIN.
AND DELICIOUS! WHEN CAN WE EAT IT?

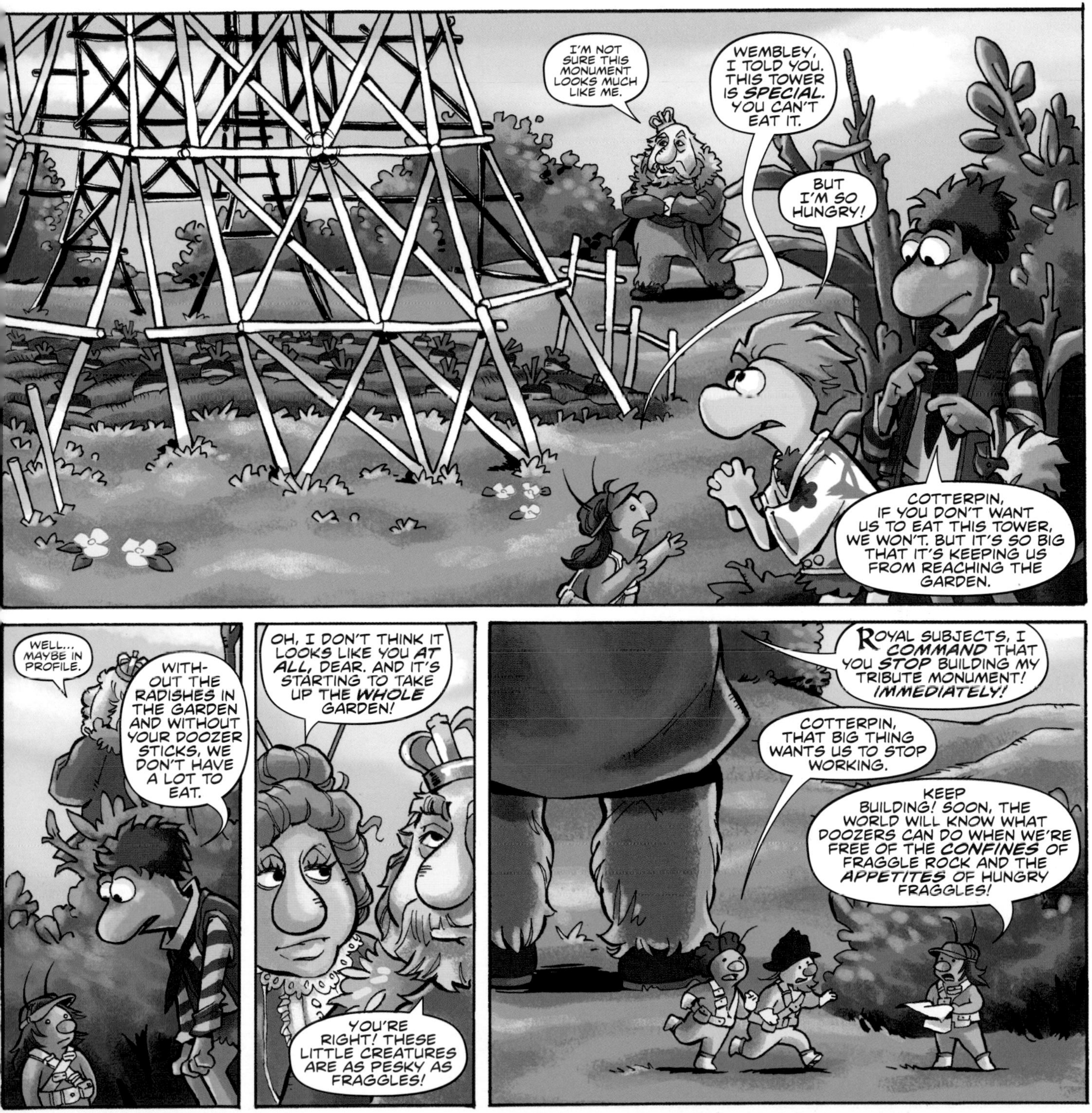

I'M NOT SURE THIS MONUMENT LOOKS MUCH LIKE ME.
WEMBLEY, I TOLD YOU. THIS TOWER IS SPECIAL. YOU CAN'T EAT IT.
BUT I'M SO HUNGRY!
COTTERPIN, IF YOU DON'T WANT US TO EAT THIS TOWER, WE WON'T. BUT IT'S SO BIG THAT IT'S KEEPING US FROM REACHING THE GARDEN.
WELL... MAYBE IN PROFILE.
WITH-OUT THE RADISHES IN THE GARDEN AND WITHOUT YOUR DOOZER STICKS, WE DON'T HAVE A LOT TO EAT.
OH, I DON'T THINK IT LOOKS LIKE YOU AT ALL, DEAR. AND IT'S STARTING TO TAKE UP THE WHOLE GARDEN!
YOU'RE RIGHT! THESE LITTLE CREATURES ARE AS PESKY AS FRAGGLES!
ROYAL SUBJECTS, I COMMAND THAT YOU STOP BUILDING MY TRIBUTE MONUMENT! IMMEDIATELY!
COTTERPIN, THAT BIG THING WANTS US TO STOP WORKING.
KEEP BUILDING! SOON, THE WORLD WILL KNOW WHAT DOOZERS CAN DO WHEN WE'RE FREE OF THE CONFINES OF FRAGGLE ROCK AND THE APPETITES OF HUNGRY FRAGGLES!

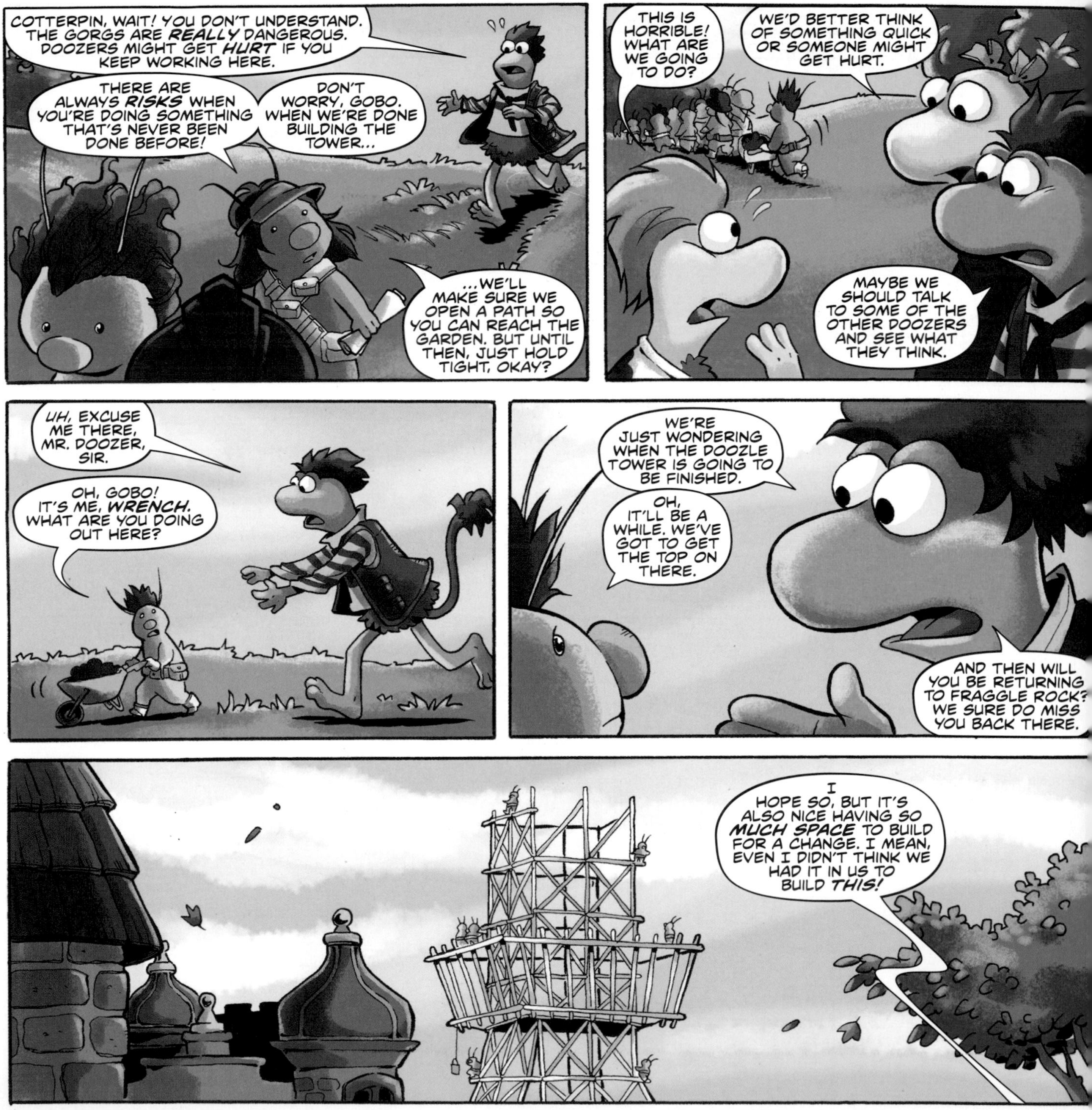

COTTERPIN, WAIT! YOU DON'T UNDERSTAND. THE GORGS ARE *REALLY* DANGEROUS. DOOZERS MIGHT GET *HURT* IF YOU KEEP WORKING HERE.
THERE ARE ALWAYS *RISKS* WHEN YOU'RE DOING SOMETHING THAT'S NEVER BEEN DONE BEFORE!
DON'T WORRY, GOBO. WHEN WE'RE DONE BUILDING THE TOWER...
...WE'LL MAKE SURE WE OPEN A PATH SO YOU CAN REACH THE GARDEN. BUT UNTIL THEN, JUST HOLD TIGHT, OKAY?
THIS IS HORRIBLE! WHAT ARE WE GOING TO DO?
WE'D BETTER THINK OF SOMETHING QUICK OR SOMEONE MIGHT GET HURT.
MAYBE WE SHOULD TALK TO SOME OF THE OTHER DOOZERS AND SEE WHAT THEY THINK.
UH, EXCUSE ME THERE, MR. DOOZER, SIR.
OH, GOBO! IT'S ME, *WRENCH*. WHAT ARE YOU DOING OUT HERE?
WE'RE JUST WONDERING WHEN THE DOOZLE TOWER IS GOING TO BE FINISHED.
OH, IT'LL BE A WHILE. WE'VE GOT TO GET THE TOP ON THERE.
AND THEN WILL YOU BE RETURNING TO FRAGGLE ROCK? WE SURE DO MISS YOU BACK THERE.
I HOPE SO, BUT IT'S ALSO NICE HAVING SO *MUCH SPACE* TO BUILD FOR A CHANGE. I MEAN, EVEN I DIDN'T THINK WE HAD IT IN US TO BUILD *THIS!*

KEEP BUILDING! WE'RE SO CLOSE TO FINISHING, I CAN ALMOST *TASTE* IT!

I THINK WE USED MORE DOOZER STICKS IN THIS SINGLE WALL THAN WE DID IN OUR ENTIRE LAST CONSTRUCTION.

YEAH, BUT WHO'S COUNTING?

UH... YOU *HAVEN'T* BEEN COUNTING, RIGHT?

WHOA! FROM DOWN HERE IT LOOKS LIKE IT GOES ON FOREVER!

IT'S IMPRESSIVE, BUT I HAVE TO SAY, I WISH THERE WERE MORE FRAGGLES HERE TO APPRECIATE IT.

OH... I'M SO HUNGRY. ARE YOU *SURE* WE CAN'T EAT THE TOWER?

COTTERPIN ASKED US NOT TO, WEMBLEY, AND WE DON'T EAT DOOZER CONSTRUCTIONS WITHOUT THEIR PERMISSION.

YOU SOUND LIKE MOKEY.

RUMBLE RUMBLE

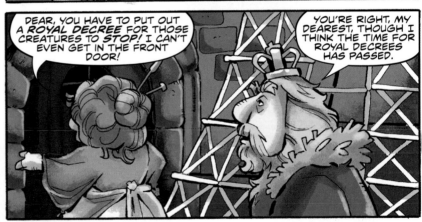

DEAR, YOU HAVE TO PUT OUT A *ROYAL DECREE* FOR THOSE CREATURES TO *STOP!* I CAN'T EVEN GET IN THE FRONT DOOR!

YOU'RE RIGHT, MY DEAREST, THOUGH I THINK THE TIME FOR ROYAL DECREES HAS PASSED.

JUNIOR! IT'S *THUMPING* TIME!

THUMPING TIME, NOT THUMPING TIME, NOW IT'S THUMPING TIME AGAIN. *SHEESH!* KING DADDY SURE CAN BE INDECISIVE.

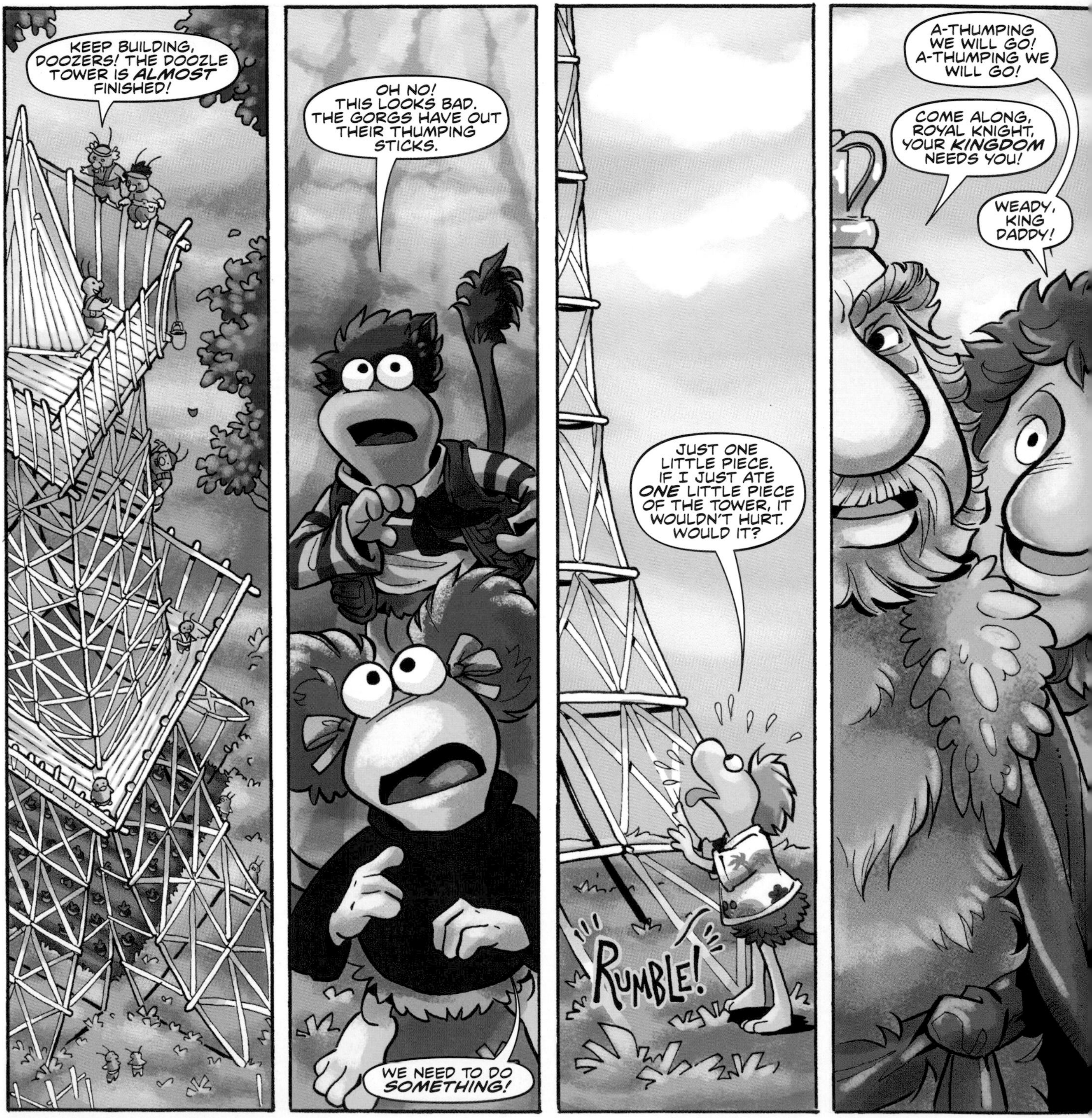
KEEP BUILDING, DOOZERS! THE DOOZLE TOWER IS ALMOST FINISHED!
OH NO! THIS LOOKS BAD. THE GORGS HAVE OUT THEIR THUMPING STICKS.
WE NEED TO DO SOMETHING!
JUST ONE LITTLE PIECE. IF I JUST ATE ONE LITTLE PIECE OF THE TOWER, IT WOULDN'T HURT. WOULD IT?
RUMBLE!
A-THUMPING WE WILL GO! A-THUMPING WE WILL GO!
COME ALONG, ROYAL KNIGHT, YOUR KINGDOM NEEDS YOU!
WEADY, KING DADDY!

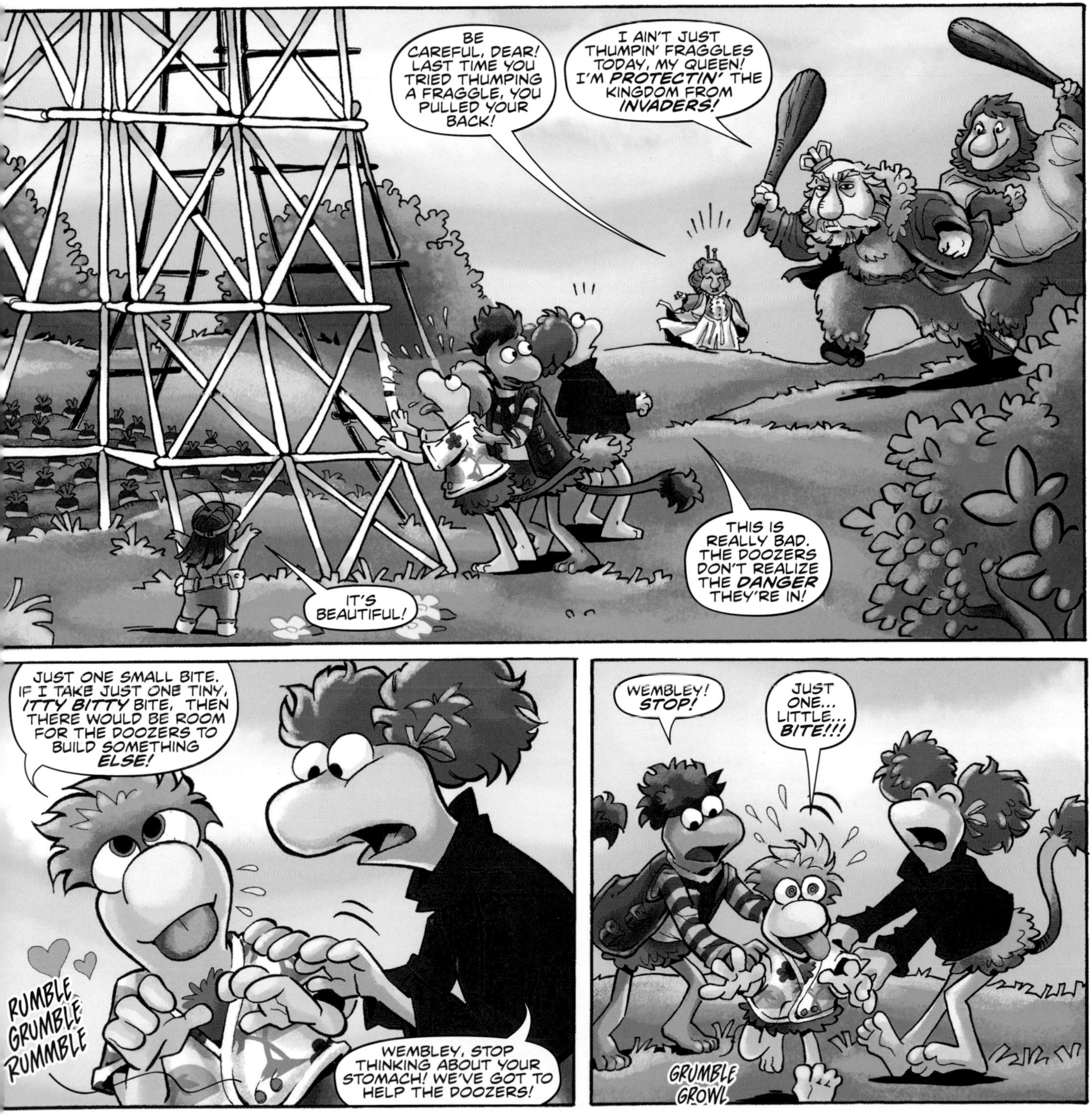
BE CAREFUL, DEAR! LAST TIME YOU TRIED THUMPING A FRAGGLE, YOU PULLED YOUR BACK!
I AIN'T JUST THUMPIN' FRAGGLES TODAY, MY QUEEN! I'M PROTECTIN' THE KINGDOM FROM INVADERS!
IT'S BEAUTIFUL!
THIS IS REALLY BAD. THE DOOZERS DON'T REALIZE THE DANGER THEY'RE IN!
JUST ONE SMALL BITE. IF I TAKE JUST ONE TINY, ITTY BITTY BITE, THEN THERE WOULD BE ROOM FOR THE DOOZERS TO BUILD SOMETHING ELSE!
RUMBLE GRUMBLE RUMMBLE
WEMBLEY, STOP THINKING ABOUT YOUR STOMACH! WE'VE GOT TO HELP THE DOOZERS!
WEMBLEY! STOP!
JUST ONE... LITTLE... BITE!!!
GRUMBLE GROWL

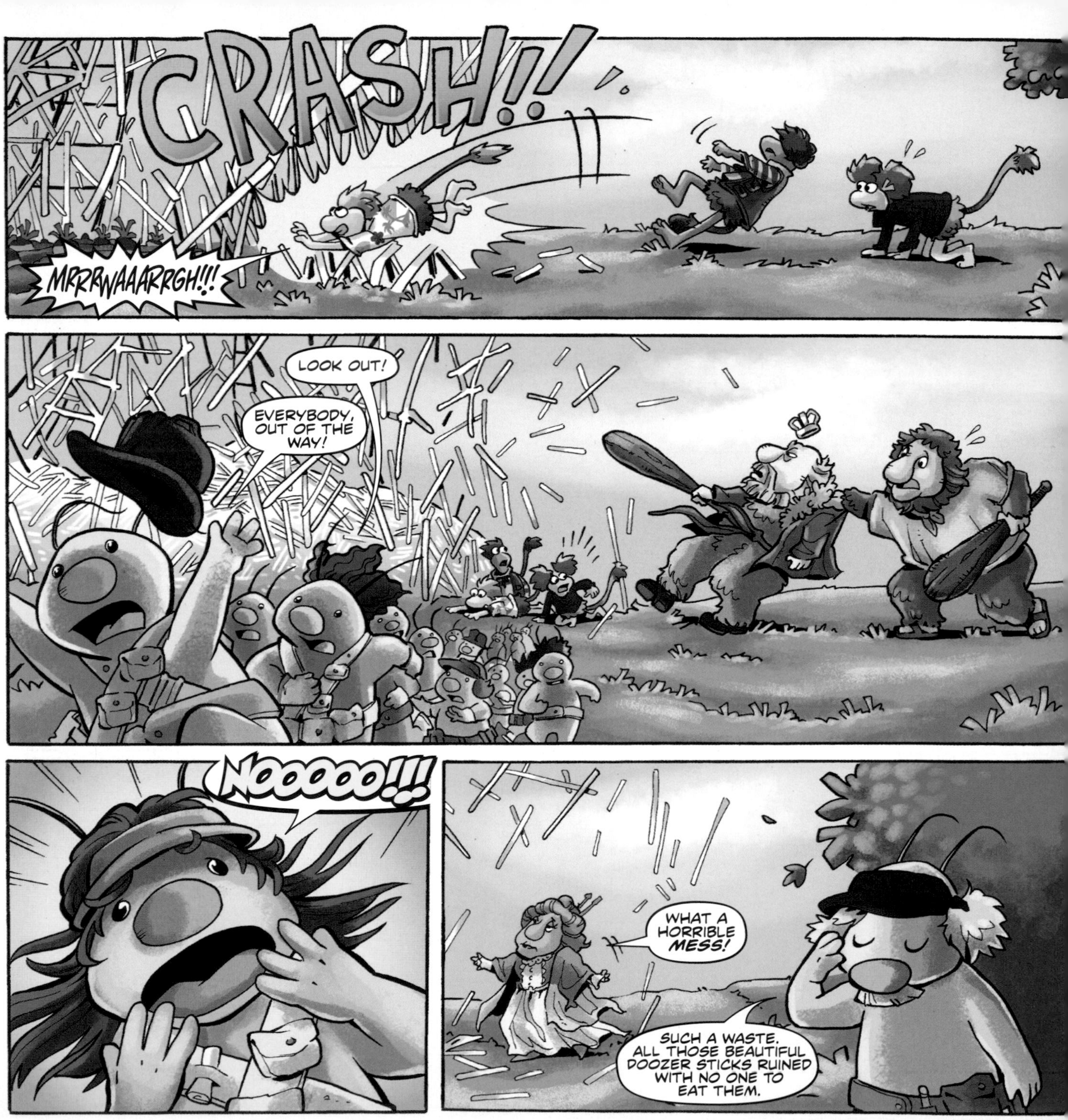
CRASH!!
MRRRWAAARRGH!!!
LOOK OUT!
EVERYBODY, OUT OF THE WAY!
NOOOOO!!!
WHAT A HORRIBLE MESS!
SUCH A WASTE. ALL THOSE BEAUTIFUL DOOZER STICKS RUINED WITH NO ONE TO EAT THEM.

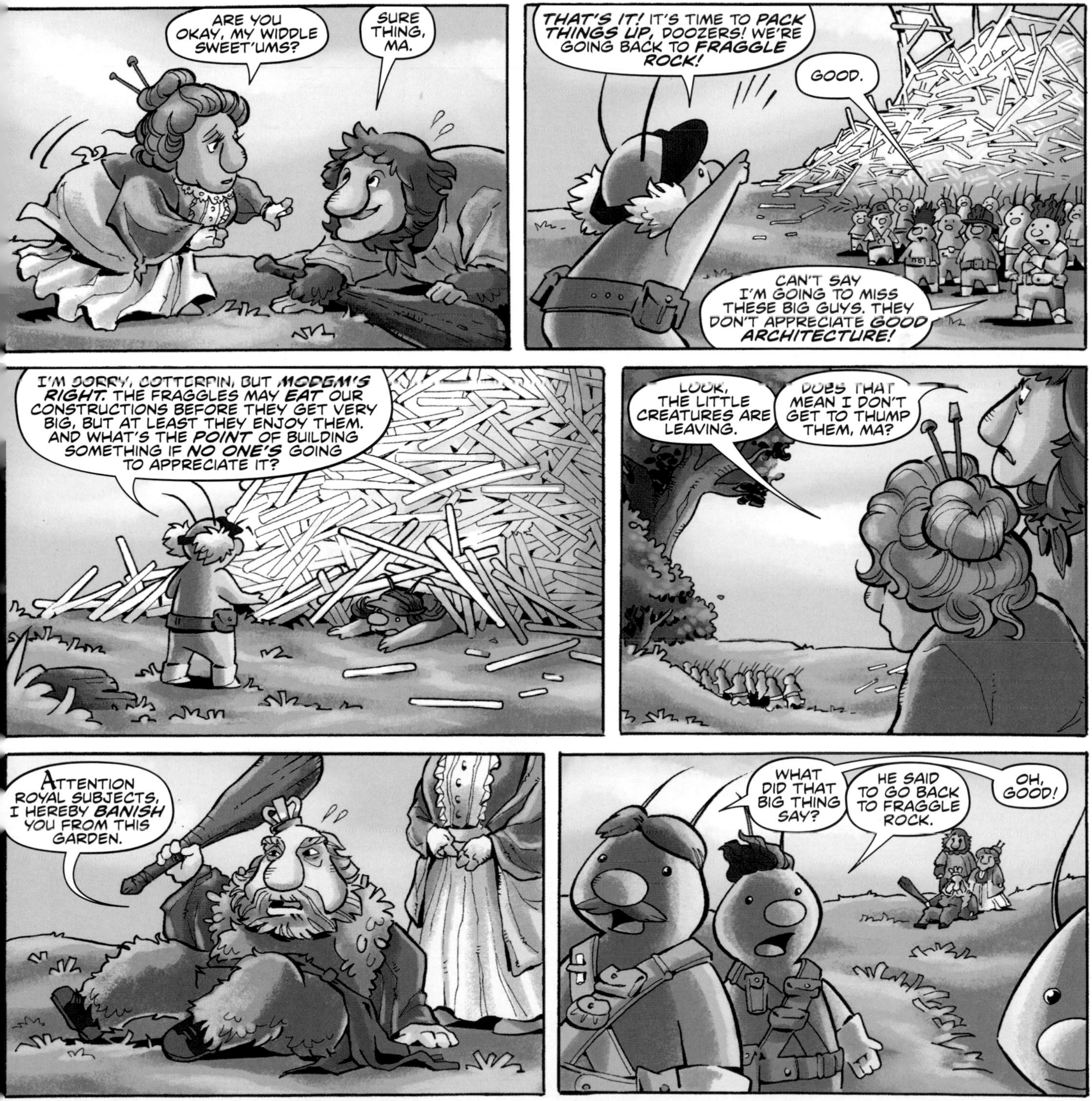
ARE YOU OKAY, MY WIDDLE SWEET'UMS?
SURE THING, MA.
THAT'S IT! IT'S TIME TO PACK THINGS UP, DOOZERS! WE'RE GOING BACK TO FRAGGLE ROCK!
GOOD.
CAN'T SAY I'M GOING TO MISS THESE BIG GUYS. THEY DON'T APPRECIATE GOOD ARCHITECTURE!
I'M SORRY, COTTERPIN, BUT MODEM'S RIGHT. THE FRAGGLES MAY EAT OUR CONSTRUCTIONS BEFORE THEY GET VERY BIG, BUT AT LEAST THEY ENJOY THEM. AND WHAT'S THE POINT OF BUILDING SOMETHING IF NO ONE'S GOING TO APPRECIATE IT?
LOOK, THE LITTLE CREATURES ARE LEAVING.
DOES THAT MEAN I DON'T GET TO THUMP THEM, MA?
ATTENTION ROYAL SUBJECTS, I HEREBY BANISH YOU FROM THIS GARDEN.
WHAT DID THAT BIG THING SAY?
HE SAID TO GO BACK TO FRAGGLE ROCK.
OH, GOOD!

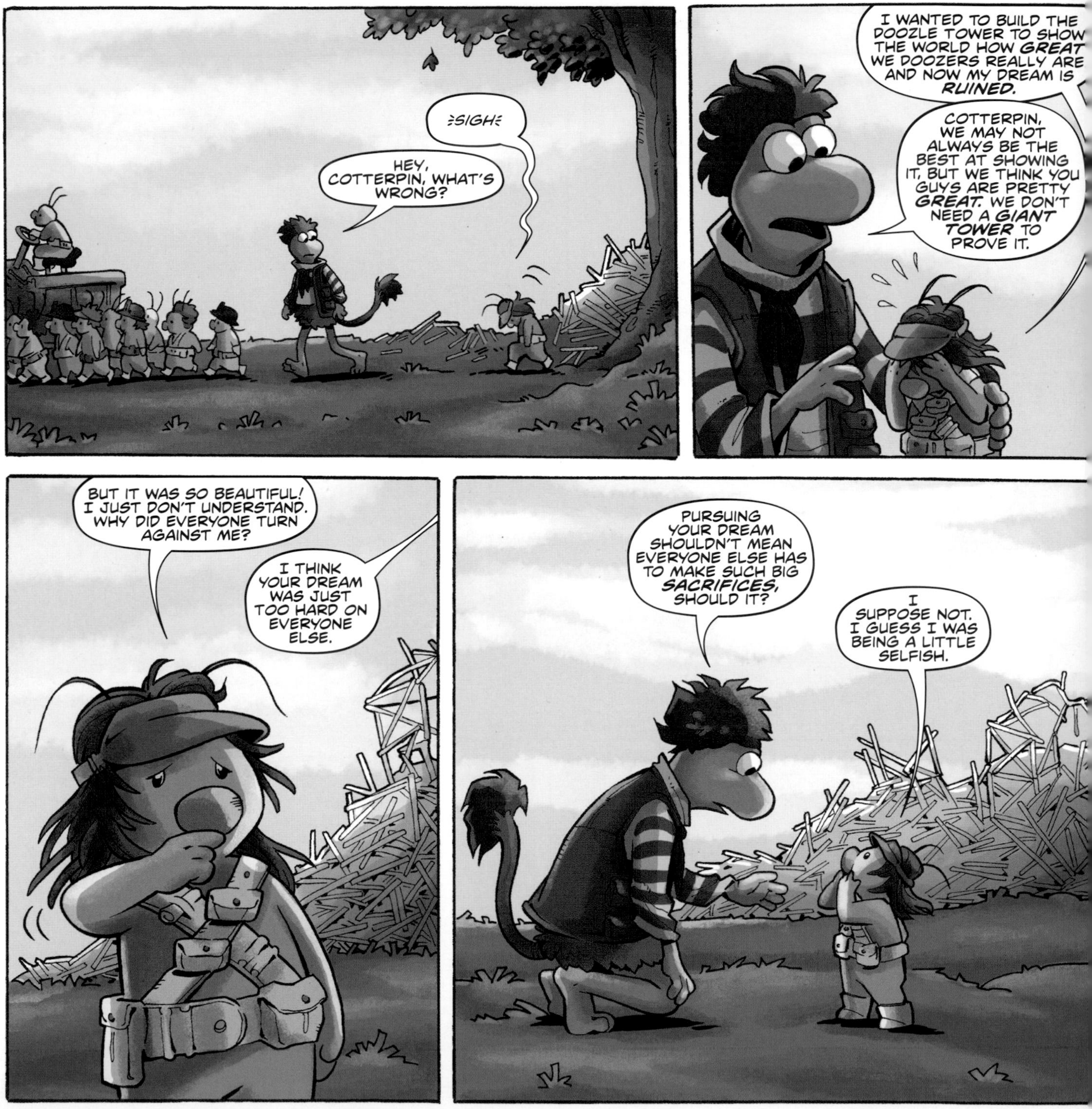

HEY, COTTERPIN, WHAT'S WRONG?
SIGH
I WANTED TO BUILD THE DOOZLE TOWER TO SHOW THE WORLD HOW GREAT WE DOOZERS REALLY ARE AND NOW MY DREAM IS RUINED.
COTTERPIN, WE MAY NOT ALWAYS BE THE BEST AT SHOWING IT, BUT WE THINK YOU GUYS ARE PRETTY GREAT. WE DON'T NEED A GIANT TOWER TO PROVE IT.
BUT IT WAS SO BEAUTIFUL! I JUST DON'T UNDERSTAND. WHY DID EVERYONE TURN AGAINST ME?
I THINK YOUR DREAM WAS JUST TOO HARD ON EVERYONE ELSE.
PURSUING YOUR DREAM SHOULDN'T MEAN EVERYONE ELSE HAS TO MAKE SUCH BIG SACRIFICES, SHOULD IT?
I SUPPOSE NOT. I GUESS I WAS BEING A LITTLE SELFISH.

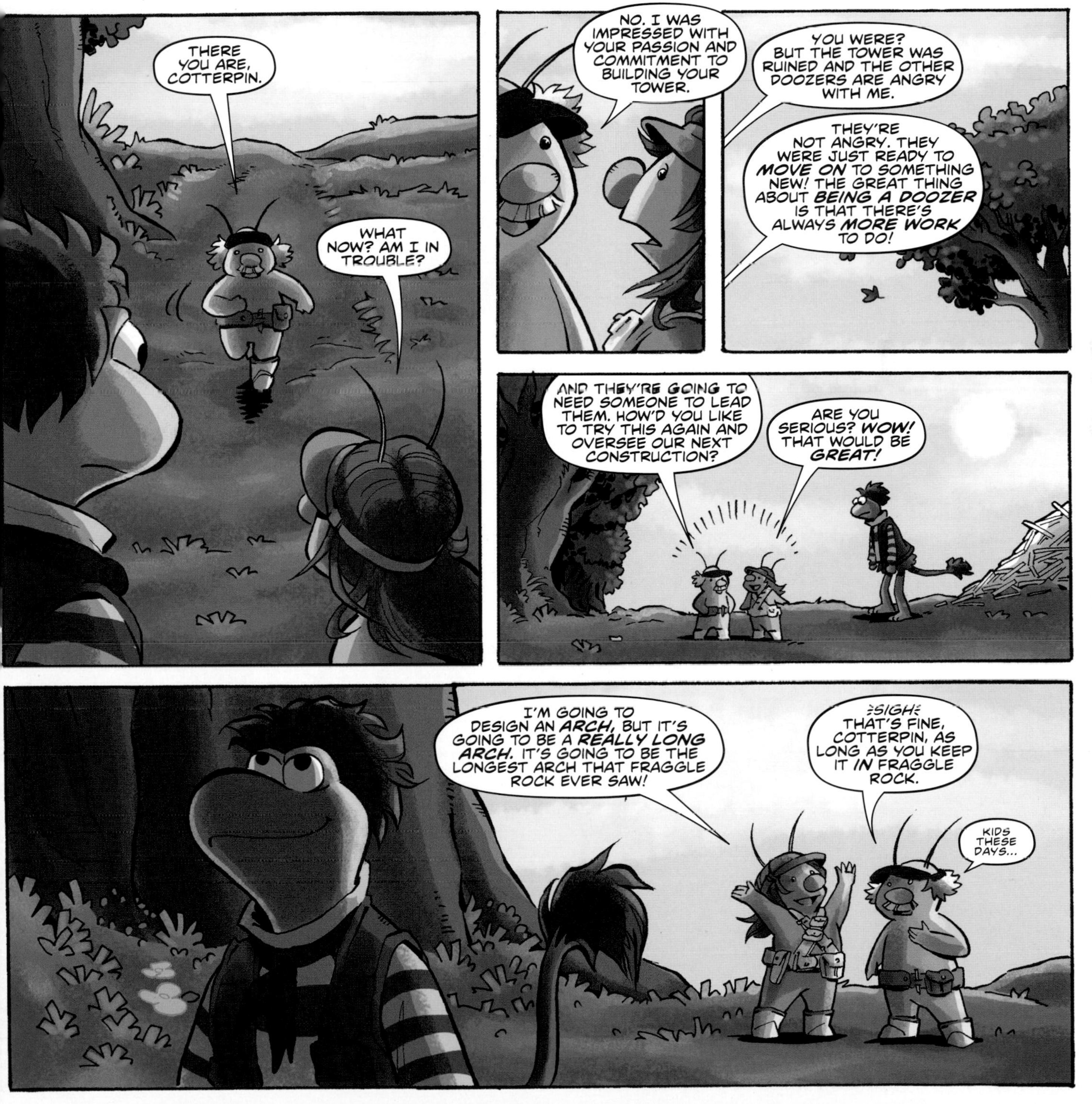
THERE YOU ARE, COTTERPIN.
WHAT NOW? AM I IN TROUBLE?
NO. I WAS IMPRESSED WITH YOUR PASSION AND COMMITMENT TO BUILDING YOUR TOWER.
YOU WERE? BUT THE TOWER WAS RUINED AND THE OTHER DOOZERS ARE ANGRY WITH ME.
THEY'RE NOT ANGRY. THEY WERE JUST READY TO MOVE ON TO SOMETHING NEW! THE GREAT THING ABOUT BEING A DOOZER IS THAT THERE'S ALWAYS MORE WORK TO DO!
AND THEY'RE GOING TO NEED SOMEONE TO LEAD THEM. HOW'D YOU LIKE TO TRY THIS AGAIN AND OVERSEE OUR NEXT CONSTRUCTION?
ARE YOU SERIOUS? WOW! THAT WOULD BE GREAT!
I'M GOING TO DESIGN AN ARCH, BUT IT'S GOING TO BE A REALLY LONG ARCH. IT'S GOING TO BE THE LONGEST ARCH THAT FRAGGLE ROCK EVER SAW!
SIGH THAT'S FINE, COTTERPIN, AS LONG AS YOU KEEP IT IN FRAGGLE ROCK.
KIDS THESE DAYS...

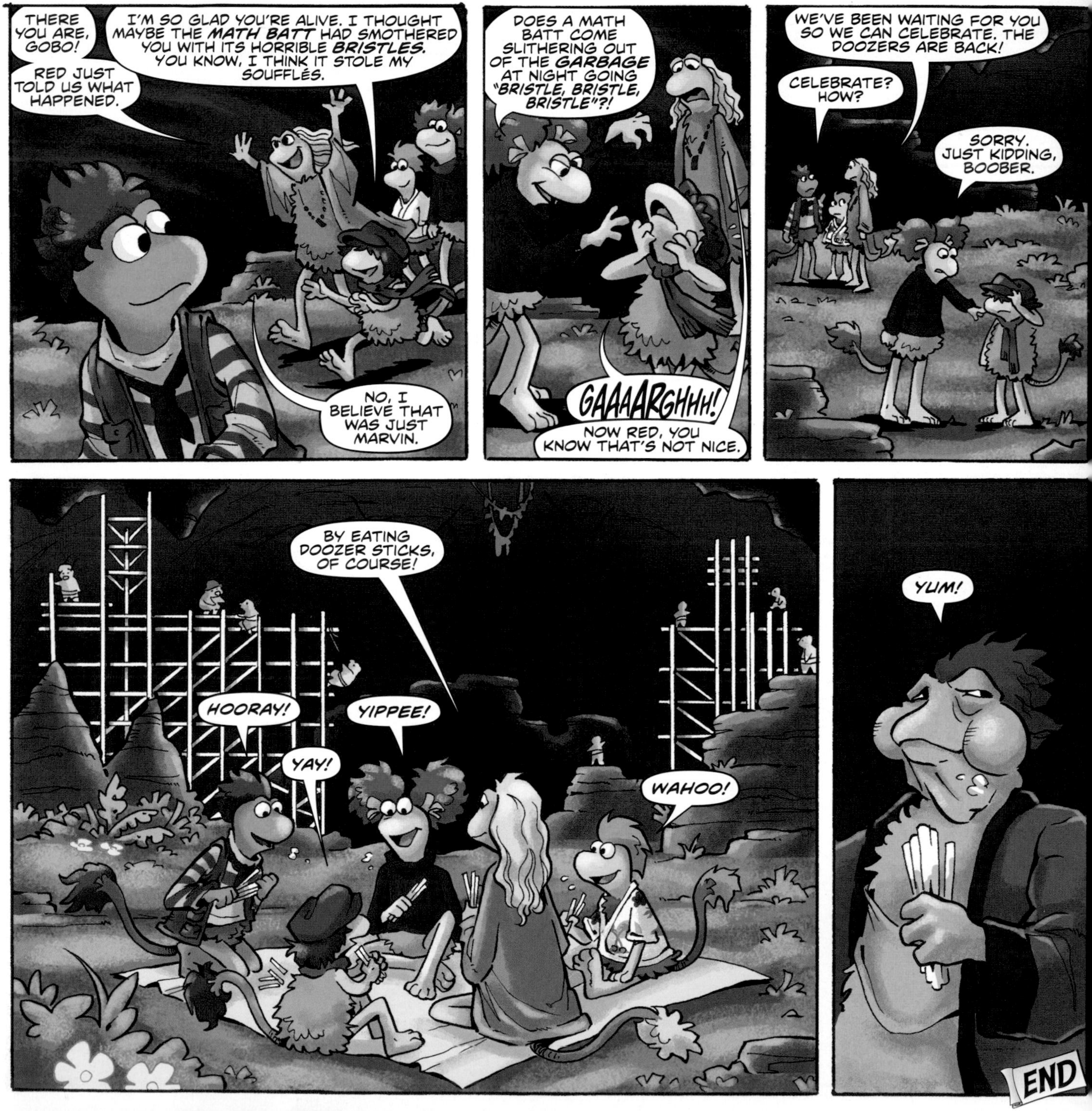
THERE YOU ARE, GOBO!
RED JUST TOLD US WHAT HAPPENED.
I'M SO GLAD YOU'RE ALIVE. I THOUGHT MAYBE THE MATH BATT HAD SMOTHERED YOU WITH ITS HORRIBLE BRISTLES. YOU KNOW, I THINK IT STOLE MY SOUFFLÉS.
NO, I BELIEVE THAT WAS JUST MARVIN.
DOES A MATH BATT COME SLITHERING OUT OF THE GARBAGE AT NIGHT GOING "BRISTLE, BRISTLE, BRISTLE"?!
GAAAARGHHH!
NOW RED, YOU KNOW THAT'S NOT NICE.
WE'VE BEEN WAITING FOR YOU SO WE CAN CELEBRATE. THE DOOZERS ARE BACK!
CELEBRATE? HOW?
SORRY. JUST KIDDING, BOOBER.
BY EATING DOOZER STICKS, OF COURSE!
HOORAY!
YIPPEE!
YAY!
WAHOO!
YUM!
END

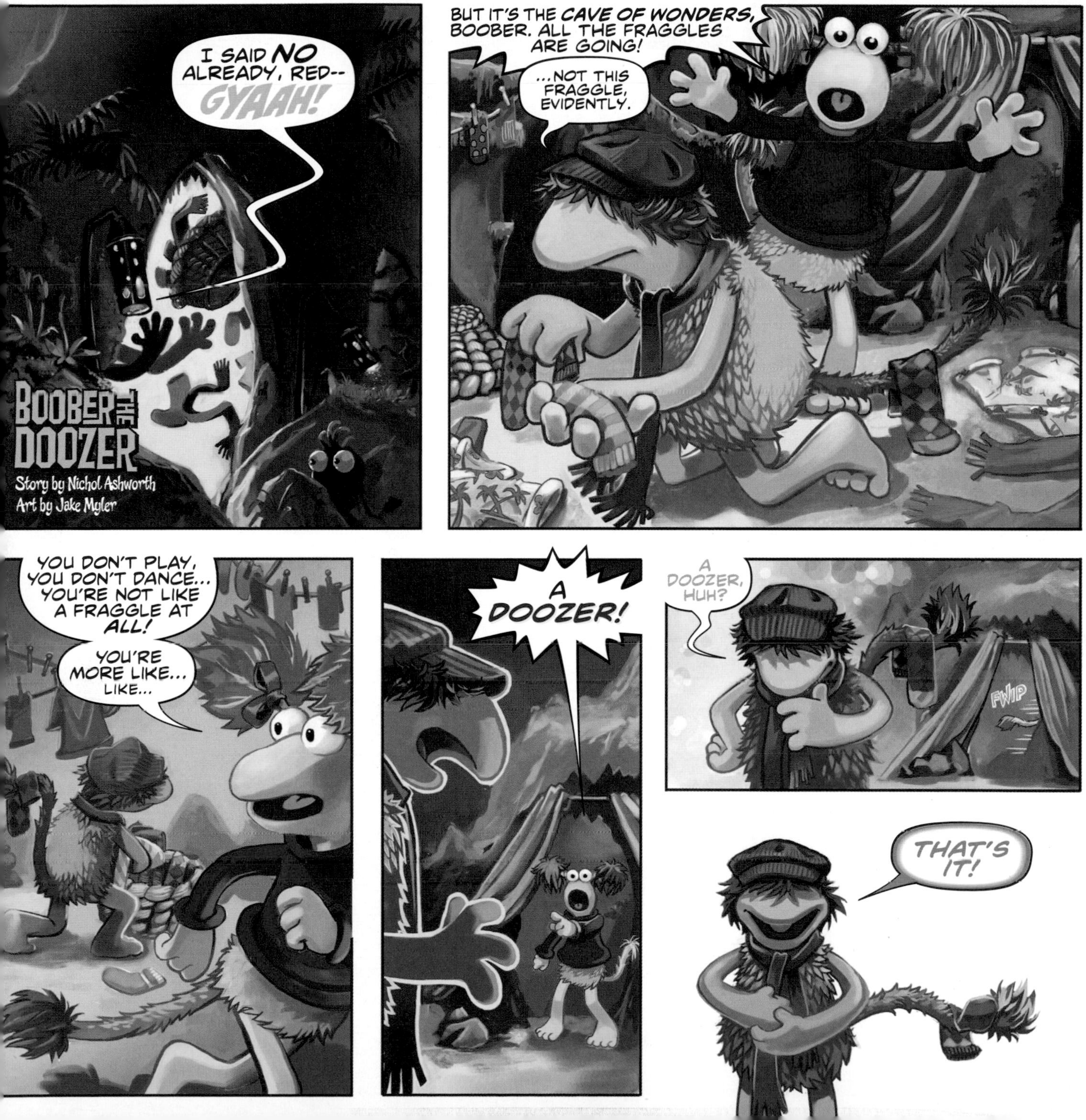
I SAID NO ALREADY, RED-- GYAAH!
BOOBER THE DOOZER
Story by Nichol Ashworth
Art by Jake Myler
BUT IT'S THE CAVE OF WONDERS, BOOBER. ALL THE FRAGGLES ARE GOING!
...NOT THIS FRAGGLE, EVIDENTLY.
YOU DON'T PLAY, YOU DON'T DANCE... YOU'RE NOT LIKE A FRAGGLE AT ALL!
YOU'RE MORE LIKE... LIKE...
A DOOZER!
A DOOZER, HUH?
FWIP
THAT'S IT!

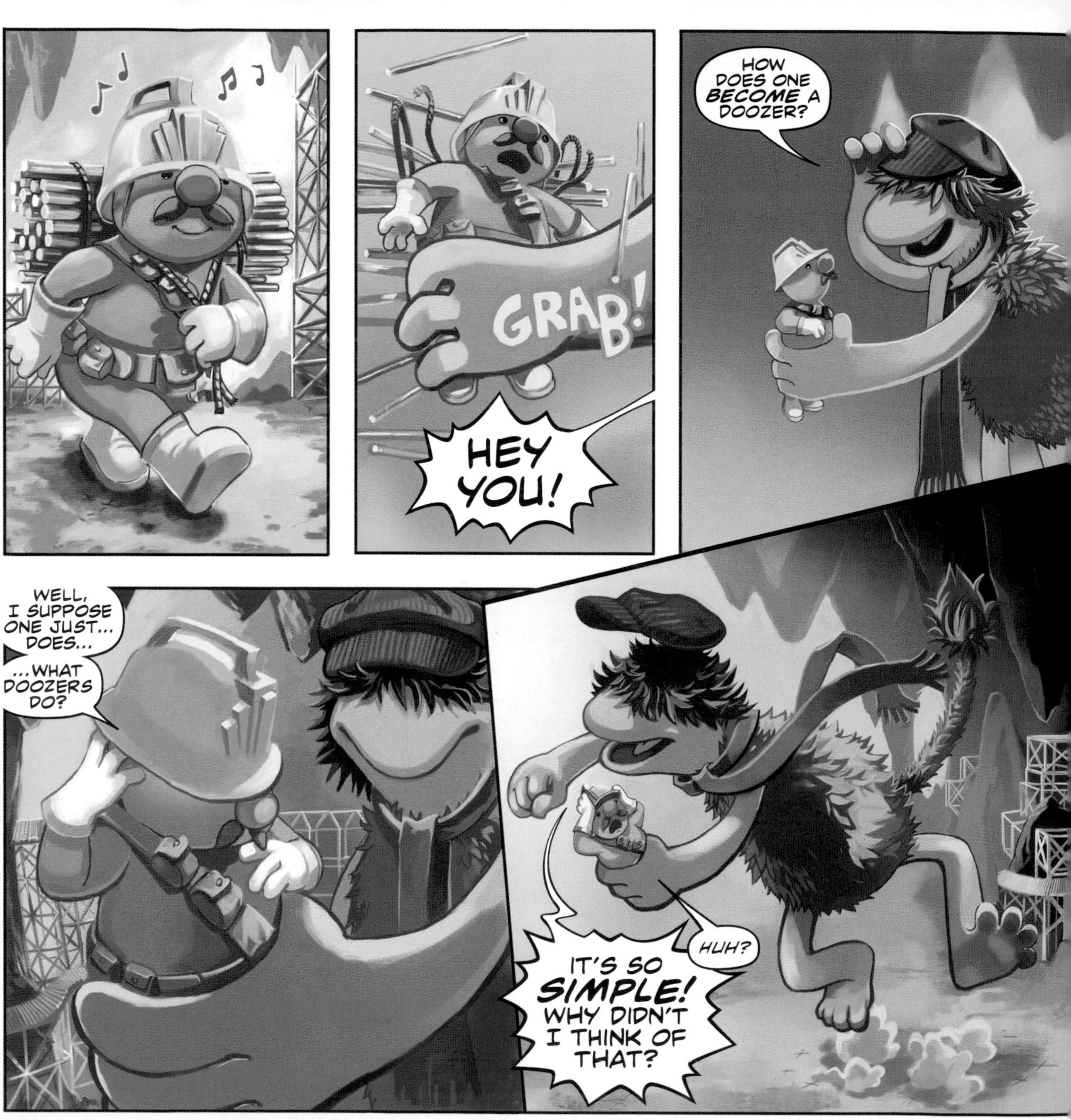
GRAB!
HEY YOU!
HOW DOES ONE BECOME A DOOZER?
WELL, I SUPPOSE ONE JUST... DOES...
...WHAT DOOZERS DO?
HUH?
IT'S SO SIMPLE! WHY DIDN'T I THINK OF THAT?

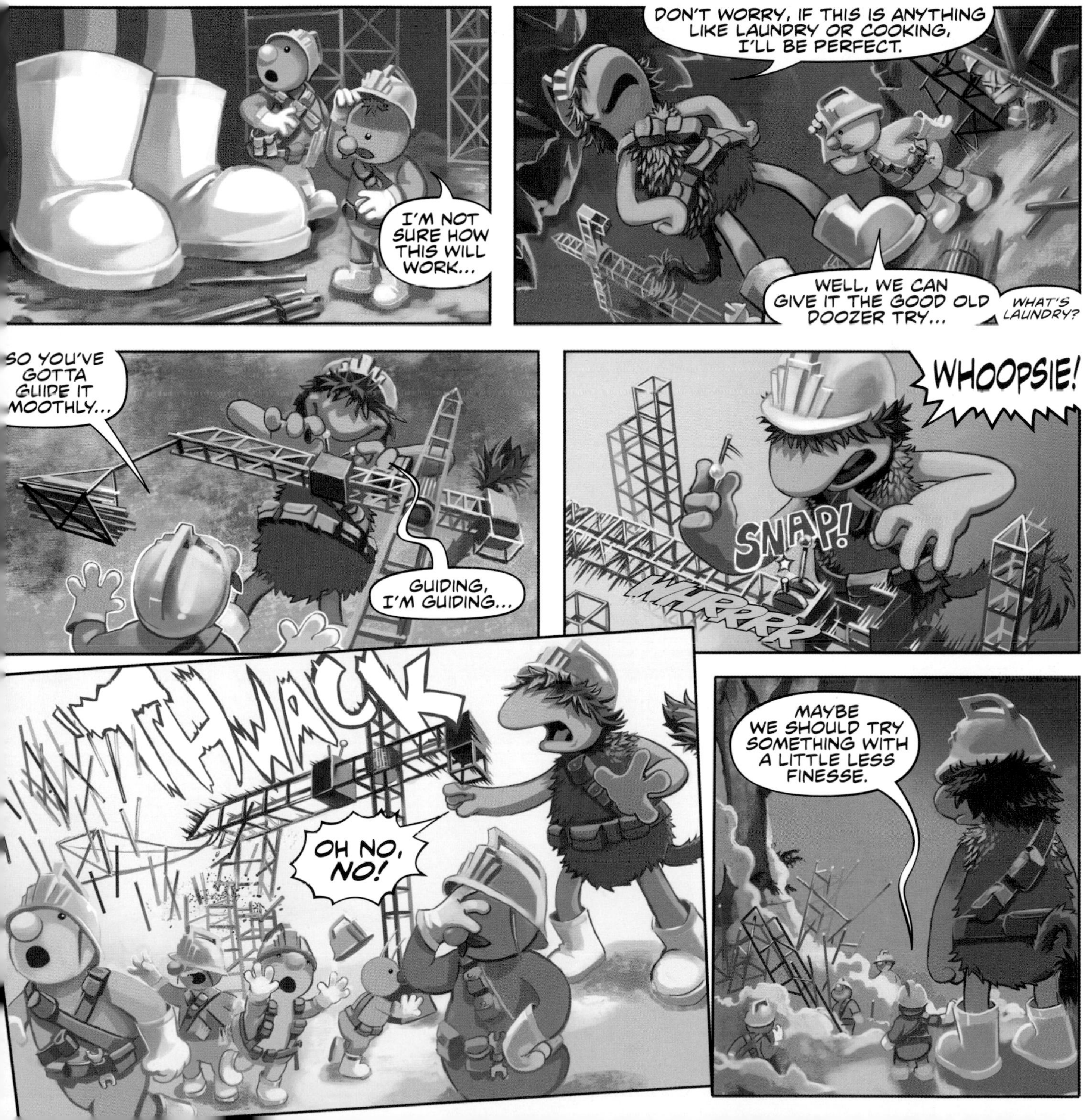
I'M NOT SURE HOW THIS WILL WORK...
DON'T WORRY, IF THIS IS ANYTHING LIKE LAUNDRY OR COOKING, I'LL BE PERFECT.
WELL, WE CAN GIVE IT THE GOOD OLD DOOZER TRY...
WHAT'S LAUNDRY?
SO YOU'VE GOTTA GUIDE IT MOOTHLY...
GUIDING, I'M GUIDING...
WHOOPSIE!
SNAP!
WHRRRR
THWACK
OH NO, NO!
MAYBE WE SHOULD TRY SOMETHING WITH A LITTLE LESS FINESSE.

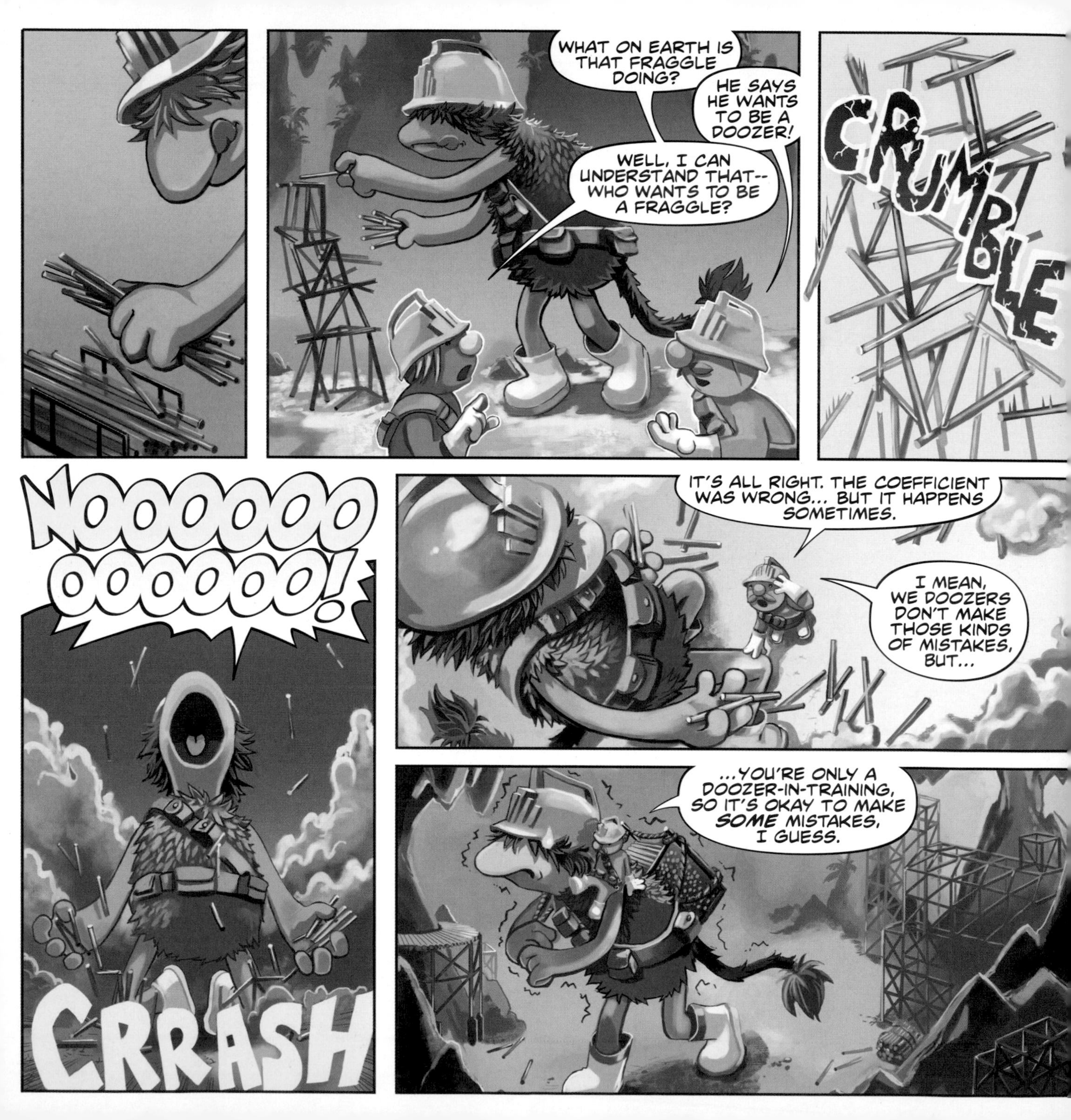
WHAT ON EARTH IS THAT FRAGGLE DOING?
HE SAYS HE WANTS TO BE A DOOZER!
WELL, I CAN UNDERSTAND THAT-- WHO WANTS TO BE A FRAGGLE?
CRUMBLE
NOOOOOOOOOOOOO!
CRRASH
IT'S ALL RIGHT. THE COEFFICIENT WAS WRONG... BUT IT HAPPENS SOMETIMES.
I MEAN, WE DOOZERS DON'T MAKE THOSE KINDS OF MISTAKES, BUT...
...YOU'RE ONLY A DOOZER-IN-TRAINING, SO IT'S OKAY TO MAKE *SOME* MISTAKES, I GUESS.

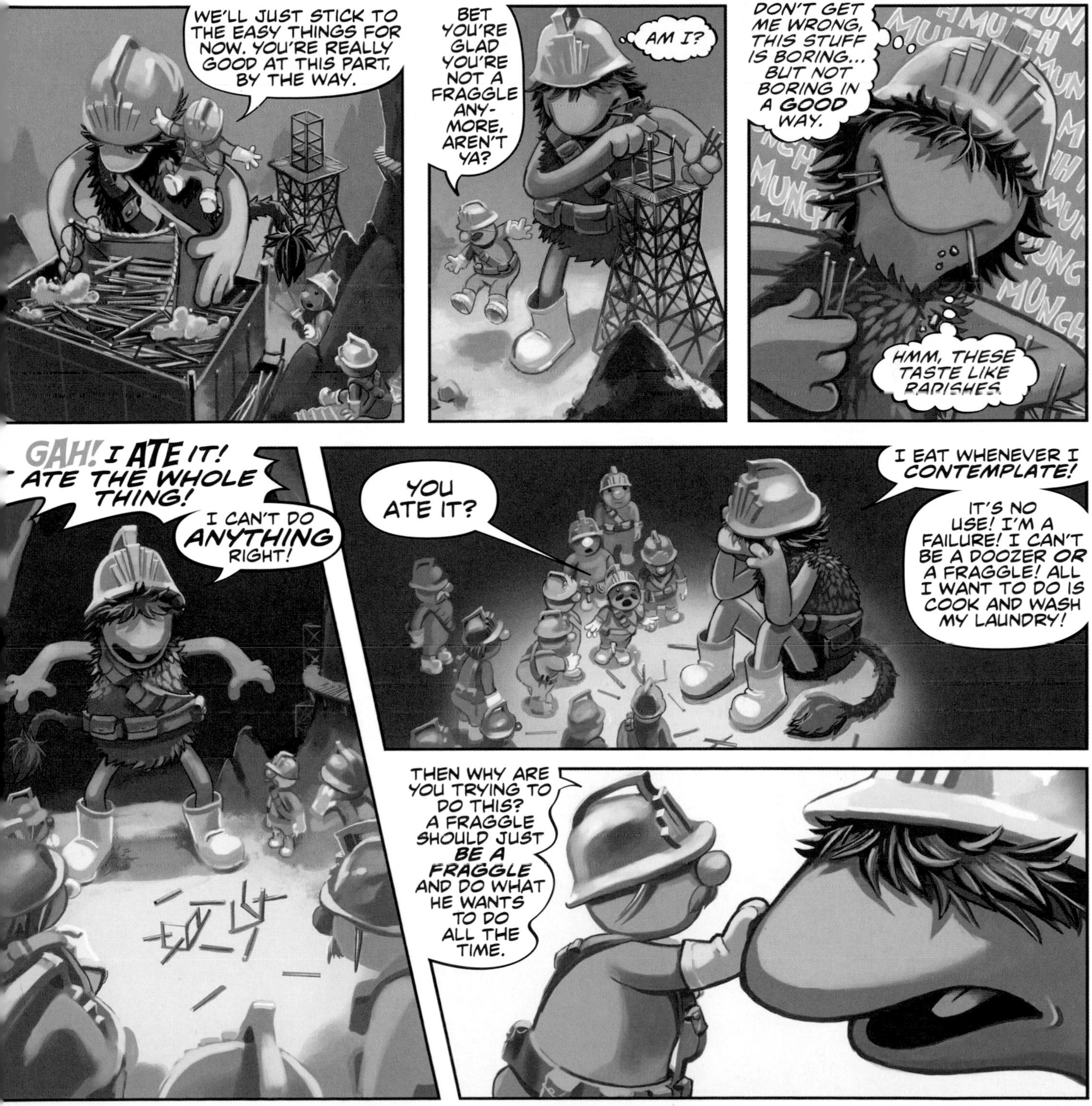
WE'LL JUST STICK TO THE EASY THINGS FOR NOW. YOU'RE REALLY GOOD AT THIS PART, BY THE WAY.
BET YOU'RE GLAD YOU'RE NOT A FRAGGLE ANY-MORE, AREN'T YA?
AM I?
DON'T GET ME WRONG, THIS STUFF IS BORING... BUT NOT BORING IN A GOOD WAY.
MUNCH MUNCH MUNCH
HMM, THESE TASTE LIKE RADISHES.
GAH! I ATE IT! ATE THE WHOLE THING!
I CAN'T DO ANYTHING RIGHT!
YOU ATE IT?
I EAT WHENEVER I CONTEMPLATE!
IT'S NO USE! I'M A FAILURE! I CAN'T BE A DOOZER OR A FRAGGLE! ALL I WANT TO DO IS COOK AND WASH MY LAUNDRY!
THEN WHY ARE YOU TRYING TO DO THIS? A FRAGGLE SHOULD JUST BE A FRAGGLE AND DO WHAT HE WANTS TO DO ALL THE TIME.

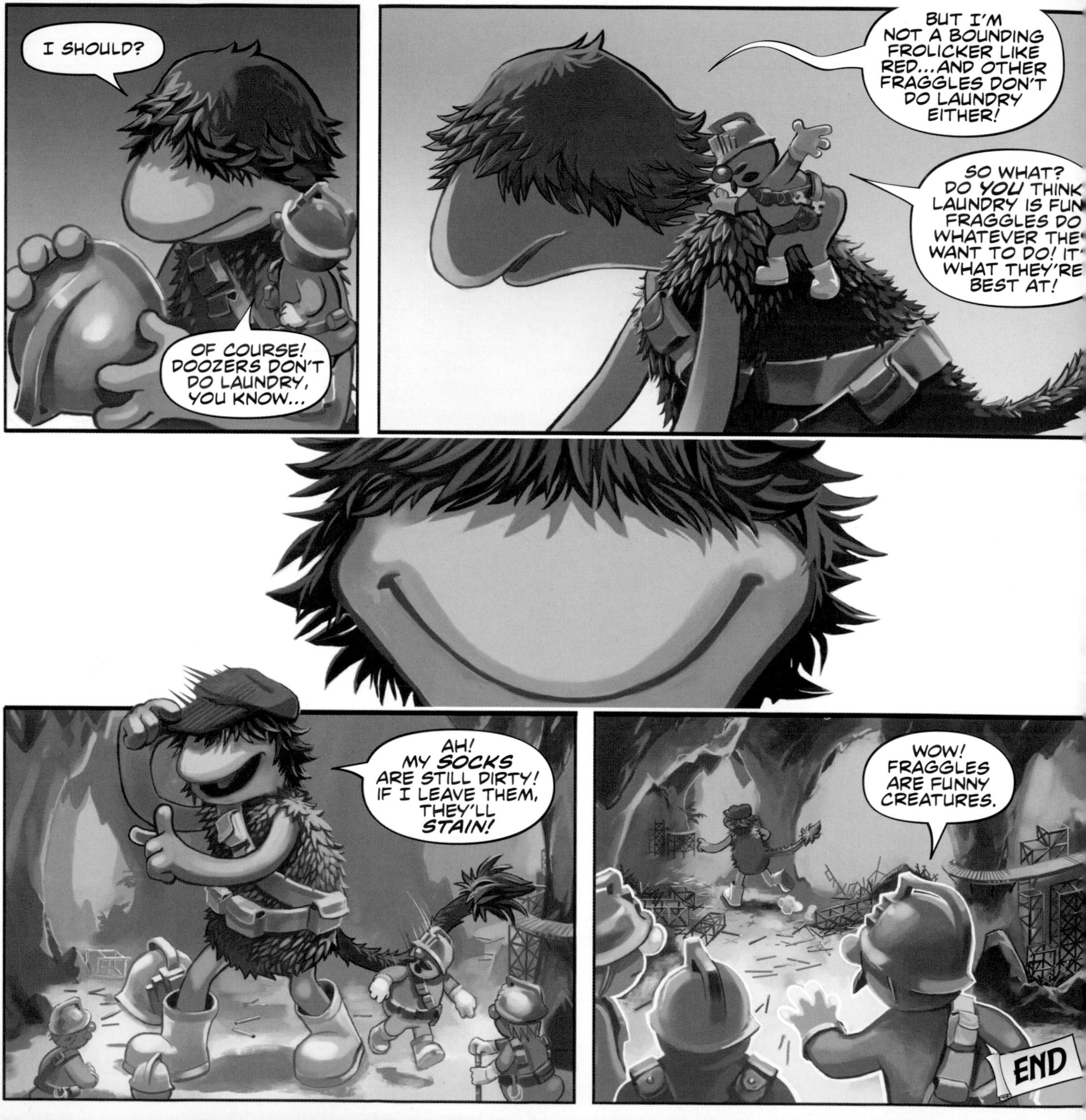
I SHOULD?
OF COURSE! DOOZERS DON'T DO LAUNDRY, YOU KNOW...
BUT I'M NOT A BOUNDING FROLICKER LIKE RED...AND OTHER FRAGGLES DON'T DO LAUNDRY EITHER!
SO WHAT? DO YOU THINK LAUNDRY IS FUN FRAGGLES DO WHATEVER THE WANT TO DO! IT WHAT THEY'RE BEST AT!
AH! MY SOCKS ARE STILL DIRTY! IF I LEAVE THEM, THEY'LL STAIN!
WOW! FRAGGLES ARE FUNNY CREATURES.
END

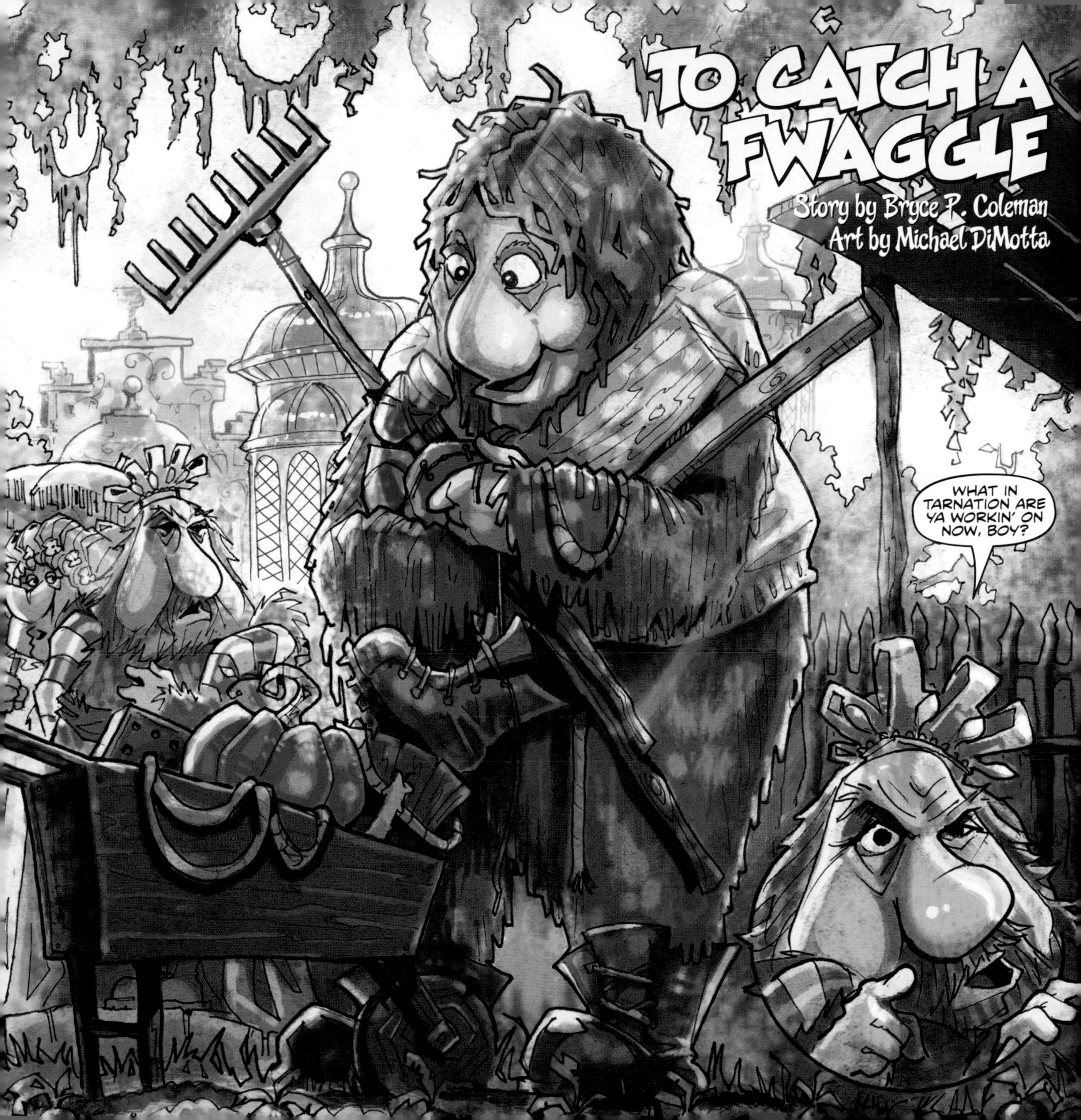
TO CATCH A FWAGGLE
Story by Bryce P. Coleman
Art by Michael DiMotta
WHAT IN TARNATION ARE YA WORKIN' ON NOW, BOY?

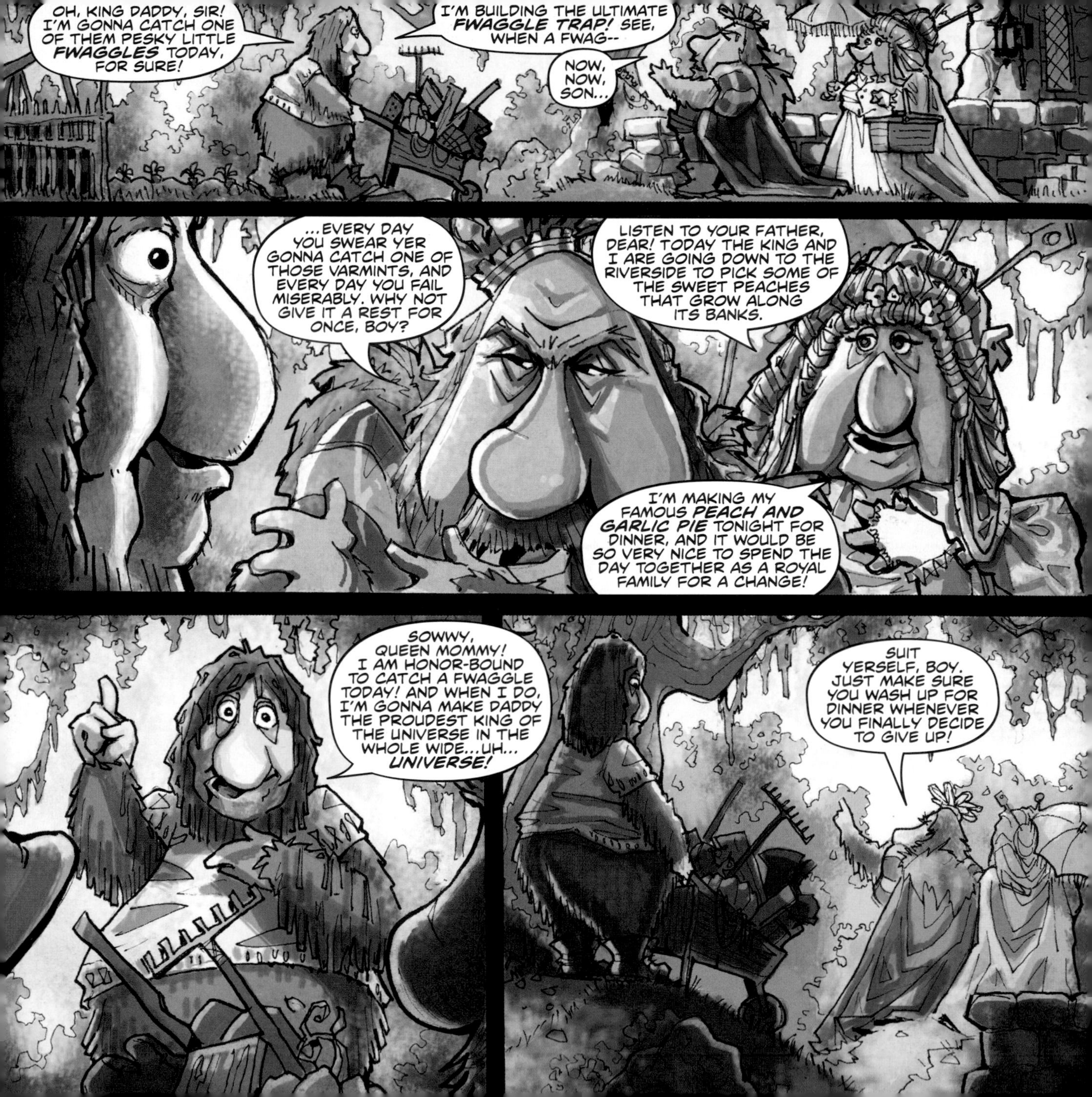
OH, KING DADDY, SIR! I'M GONNA CATCH ONE OF THEM PESKY LITTLE FWAGGLES TODAY, FOR SURE!
I'M BUILDING THE ULTIMATE FWAGGLE TRAP! SEE, WHEN A FWAG--
NOW, NOW, SON...
...EVERY DAY YOU SWEAR YER GONNA CATCH ONE OF THOSE VARMINTS, AND EVERY DAY YOU FAIL MISERABLY. WHY NOT GIVE IT A REST FOR ONCE, BOY?
LISTEN TO YOUR FATHER, DEAR! TODAY THE KING AND I ARE GOING DOWN TO THE RIVERSIDE TO PICK SOME OF THE SWEET PEACHES THAT GROW ALONG ITS BANKS.
I'M MAKING MY FAMOUS PEACH AND GARLIC PIE TONIGHT FOR DINNER, AND IT WOULD BE SO VERY NICE TO SPEND THE DAY TOGETHER AS A ROYAL FAMILY FOR A CHANGE!
SOWWY, QUEEN MOMMY! I AM HONOR-BOUND TO CATCH A FWAGGLE TODAY! AND WHEN I DO, I'M GONNA MAKE DADDY THE PROUDEST KING OF THE UNIVERSE IN THE WHOLE WIDE...UH... UNIVERSE!
SUIT YERSELF, BOY. JUST MAKE SURE YOU WASH UP FOR DINNER WHENEVER YOU FINALLY DECIDE TO GIVE UP!

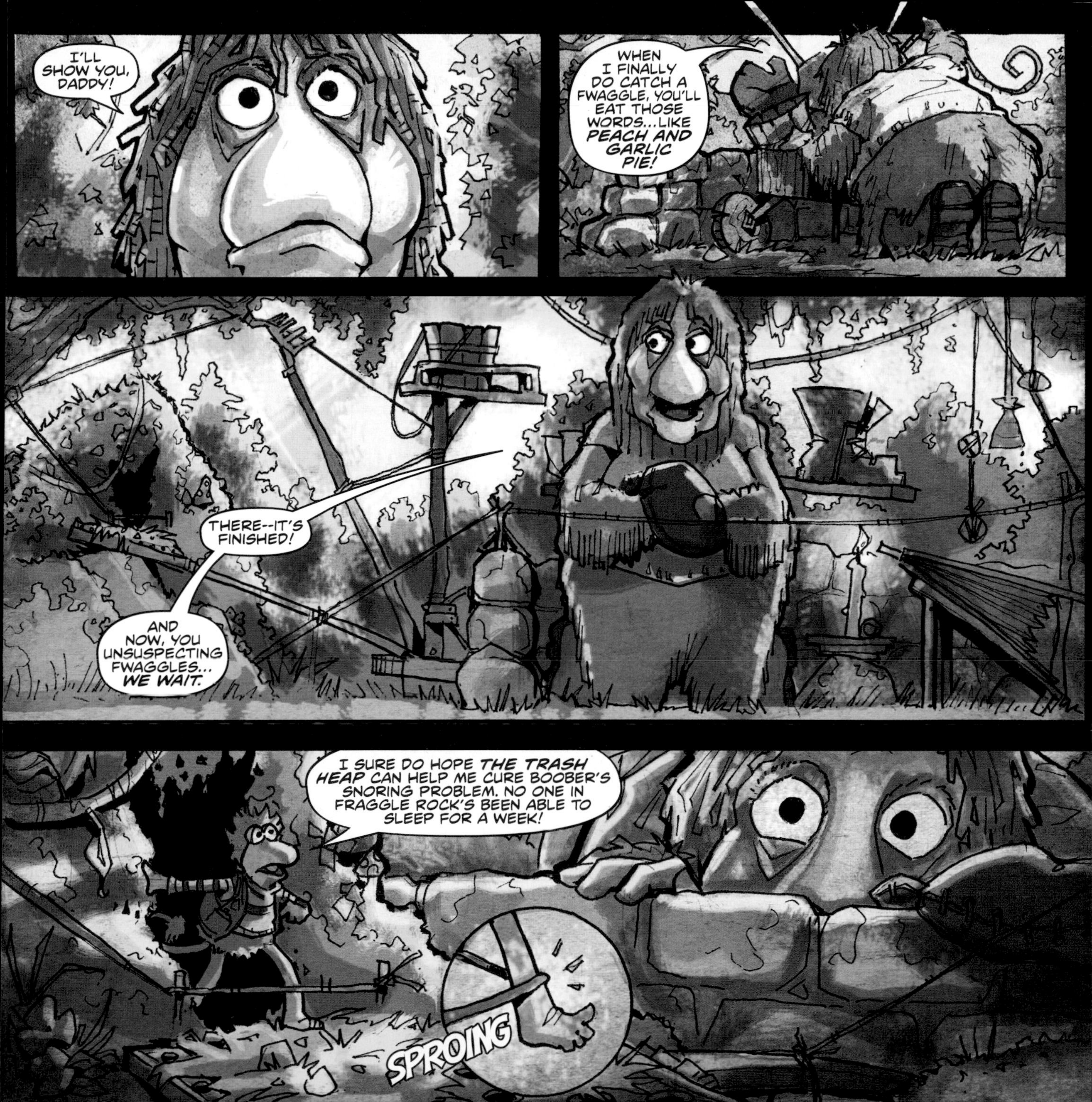
I'LL SHOW YOU, DADDY!
WHEN I FINALLY DO CATCH A FWAGGLE, YOU'LL EAT THOSE WORDS...LIKE PEACH AND GARLIC PIE!
THERE--IT'S FINISHED!
AND NOW, YOU UNSUSPECTING FWAGGLES... WE WAIT.
I SURE DO HOPE THE TRASH HEAP CAN HELP ME CURE BOOBER'S SNORING PROBLEM. NO ONE IN FRAGGLE ROCK'S BEEN ABLE TO SLEEP FOR A WEEK!
SPROING

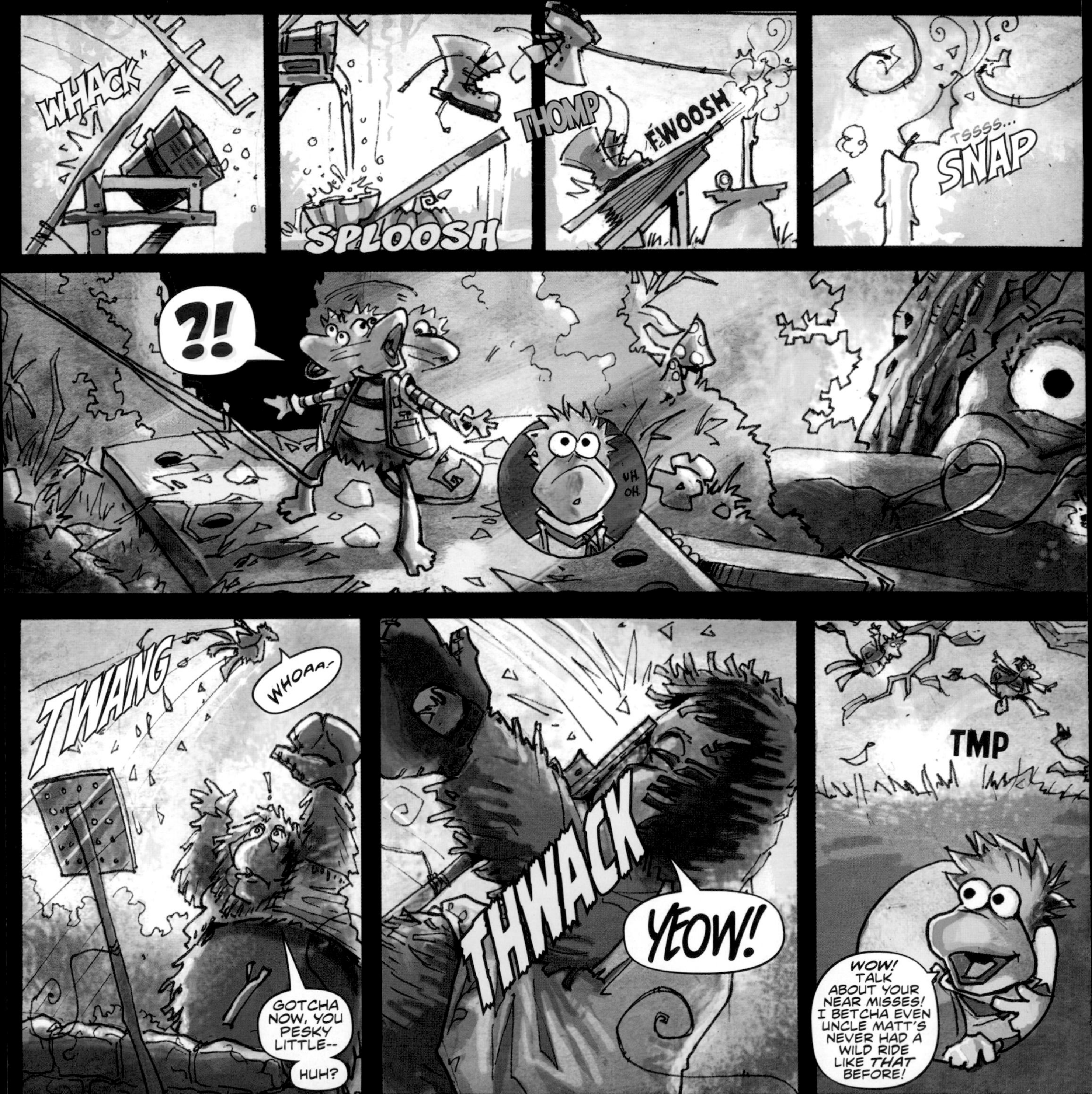
WHACK
SPLOOSH
THOMP
FWOOSH
TSSSS...
SNAP
?!
UH OH.
TWANG
WHOAA!
GOTCHA NOW, YOU PESKY LITTLE--
HUH?
THWACK
YEOW!
TMP
WOW! TALK ABOUT YOUR NEAR MISSES! I BETCHA EVEN UNCLE MATT'S NEVER HAD A WILD RIDE LIKE THAT BEFORE!

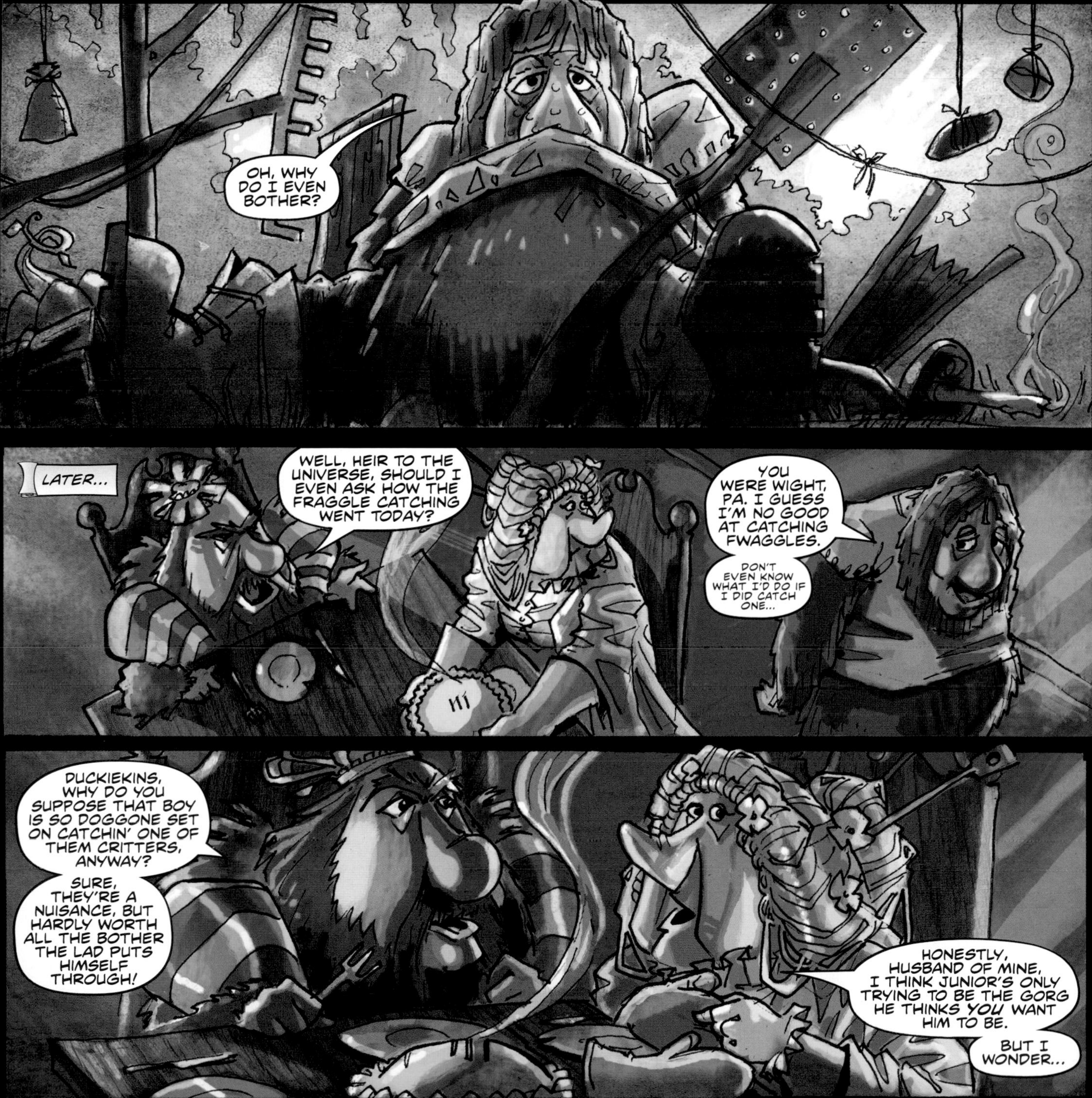
OH, WHY DO I EVEN BOTHER?
LATER...
WELL, HEIR TO THE UNIVERSE, SHOULD I EVEN ASK HOW THE FRAGGLE CATCHING WENT TODAY?
YOU WERE WIGHT, PA. I GUESS I'M NO GOOD AT CATCHING FWAGGLES.
DON'T EVEN KNOW WHAT I'D DO IF I DID CATCH ONE...
DUCKIEKINS, WHY DO YOU SUPPOSE THAT BOY IS SO DOGGONE SET ON CATCHIN' ONE OF THEM CRITTERS, ANYWAY?
SURE, THEY'RE A NUISANCE, BUT HARDLY WORTH ALL THE BOTHER THE LAD PUTS HIMSELF THROUGH!
HONESTLY, HUSBAND OF MINE, I THINK JUNIOR'S ONLY TRYING TO BE THE GORG HE THINKS *YOU* WANT HIM TO BE.
BUT I WONDER...

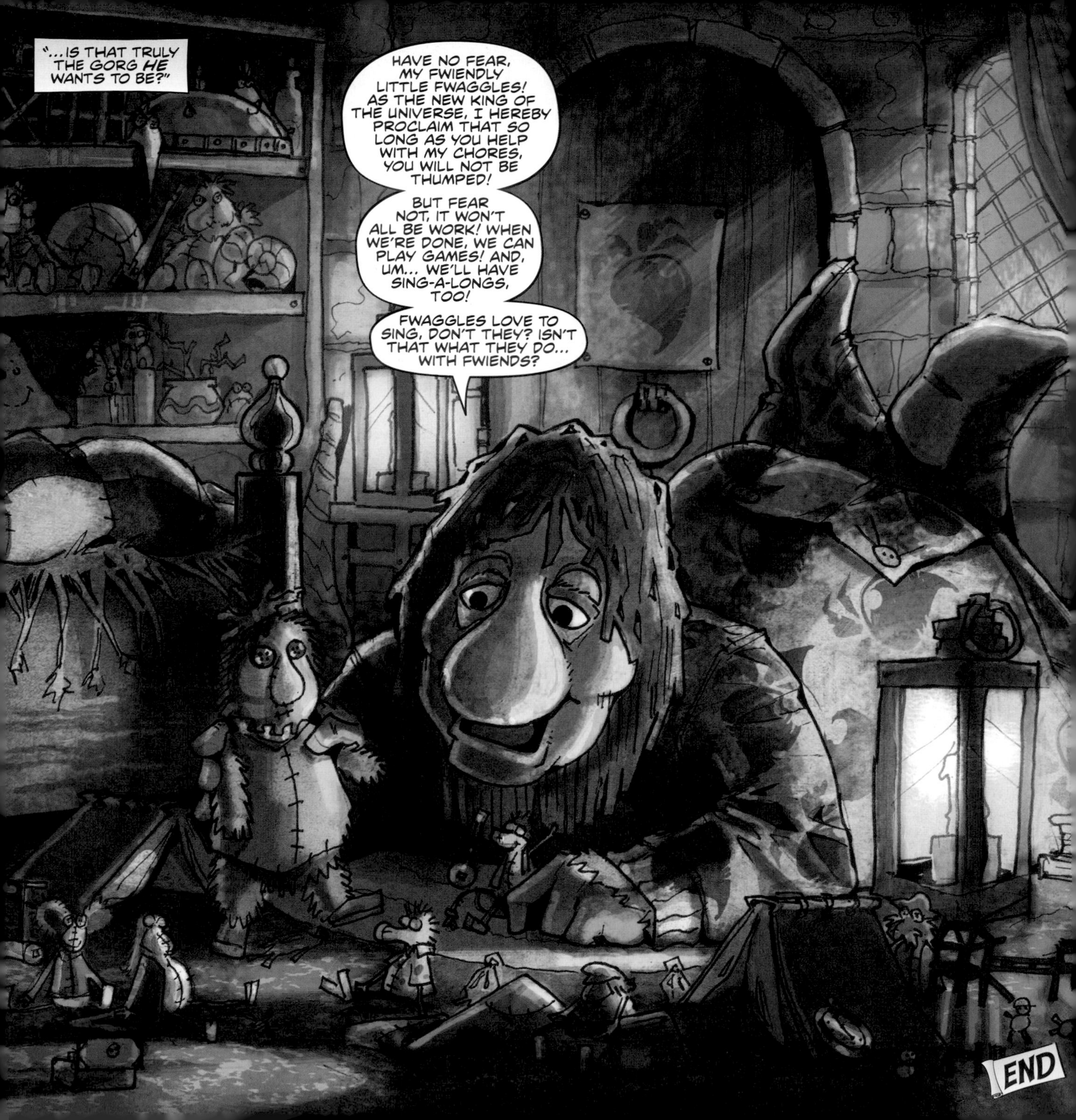
"...IS THAT TRULY THE GORG *HE* WANTS TO BE?"
HAVE NO FEAR, MY FWIENDLY LITTLE FWAGGLES! AS THE NEW KING OF THE UNIVERSE, I HEREBY PROCLAIM THAT SO LONG AS YOU HELP WITH MY CHORES, YOU WILL NOT BE THUMPED!
BUT FEAR NOT, IT WON'T ALL BE WORK! WHEN WE'RE DONE, WE CAN PLAY GAMES! AND, UM... WE'LL HAVE SING-A-LONGS, TOO!
FWAGGLES LOVE TO SING, DON'T THEY? ISN'T THAT WHAT THEY DO... WITH FWIENDS?
END

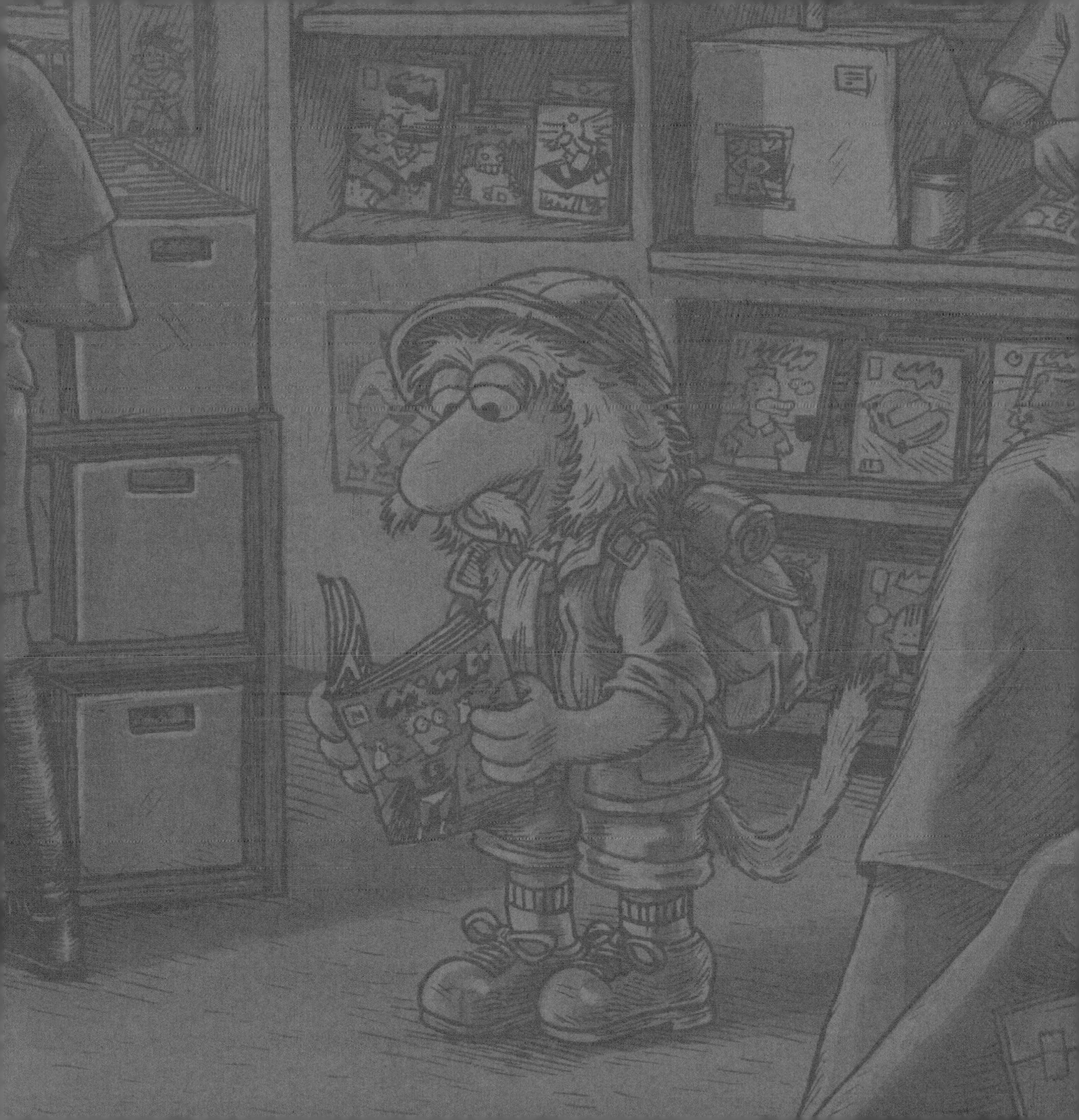

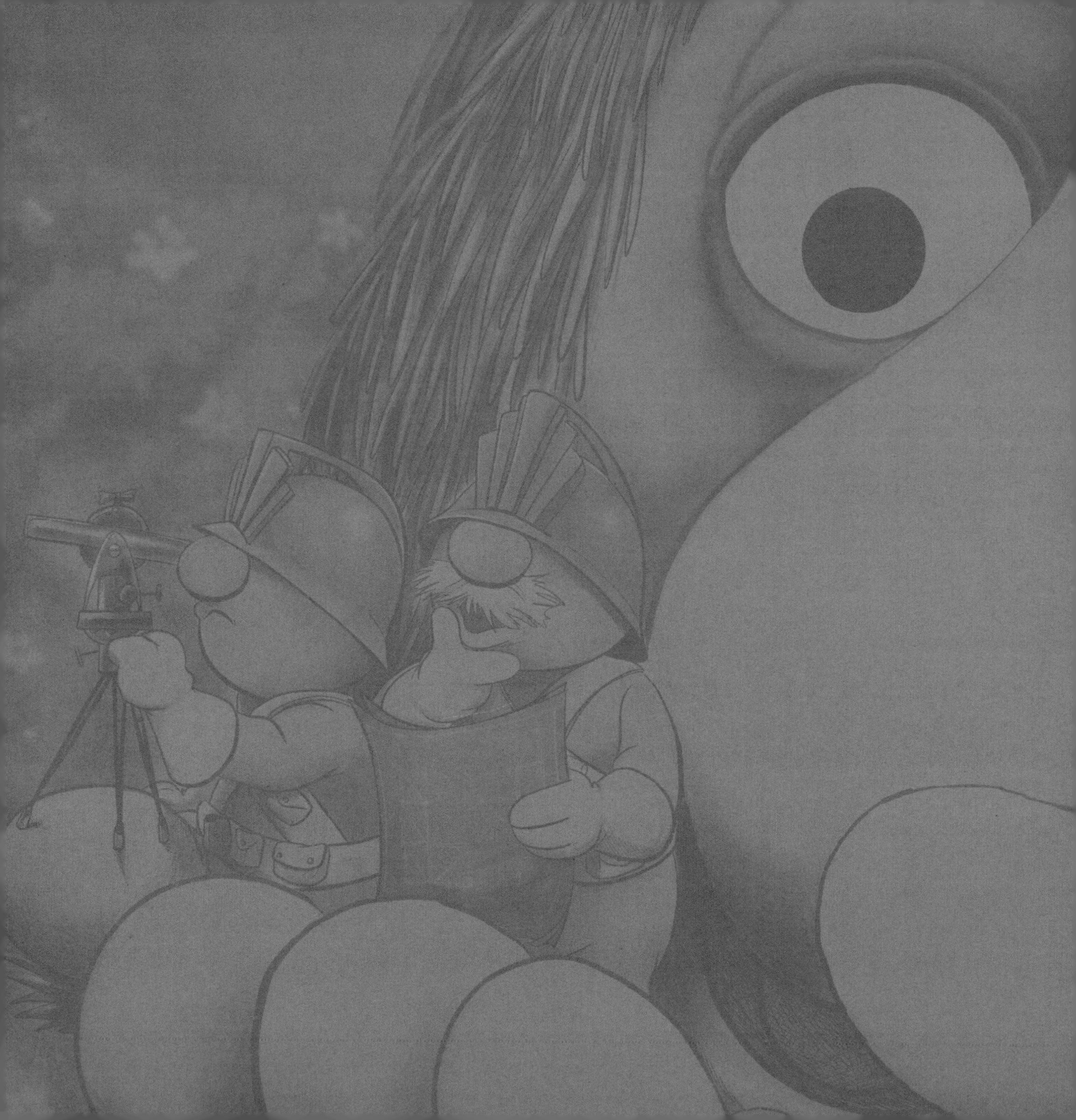

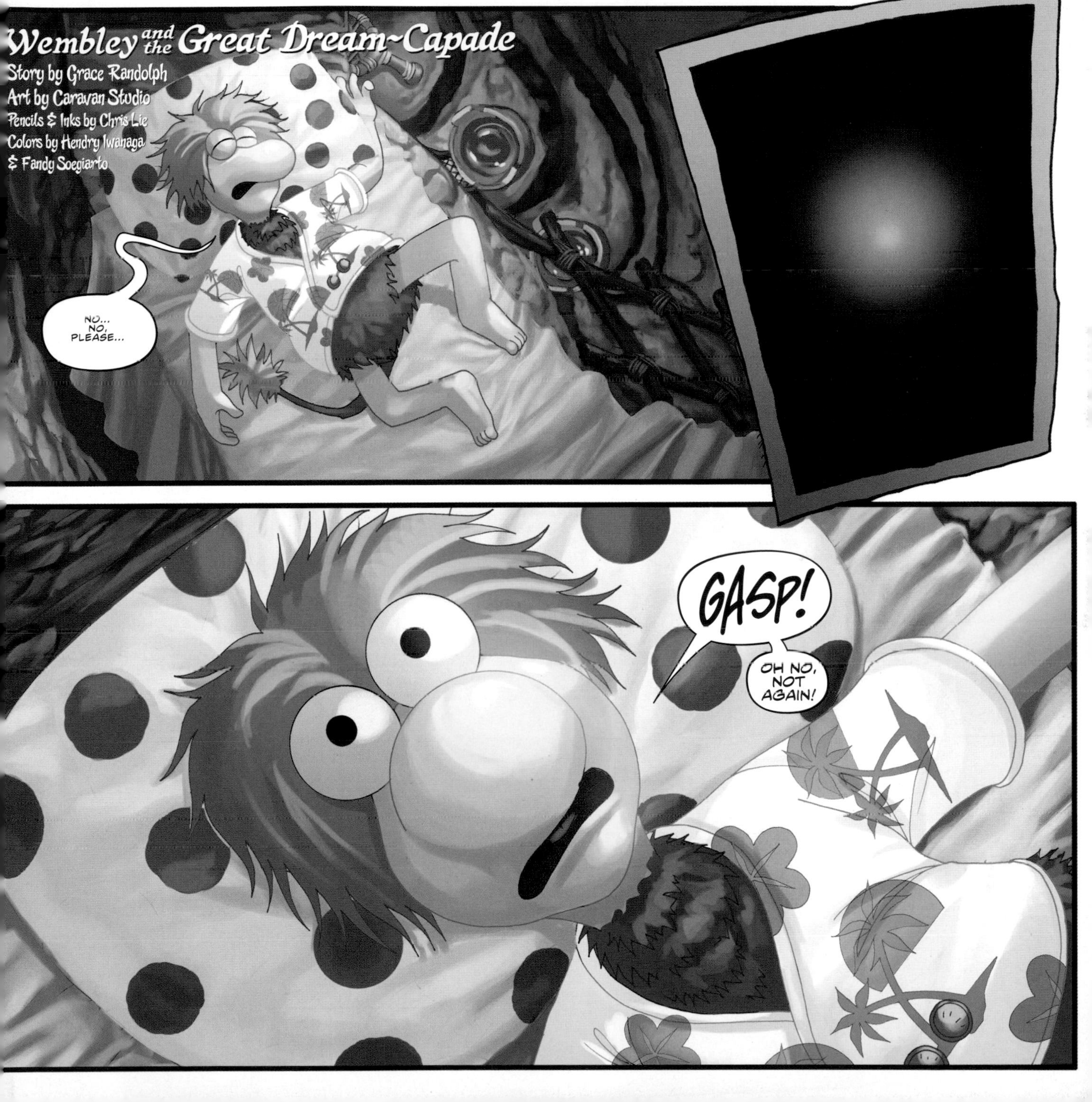
Wembley and the Great Dream~Capade
Story by Grace Randolph
Art by Caravan Studio
Pencils & Inks by Chris Lie
Colors by Hendry Iwanaga
& Fandy Soegiarto
NO... NO, PLEASE...
GASP!
OH NO, NOT AGAIN!

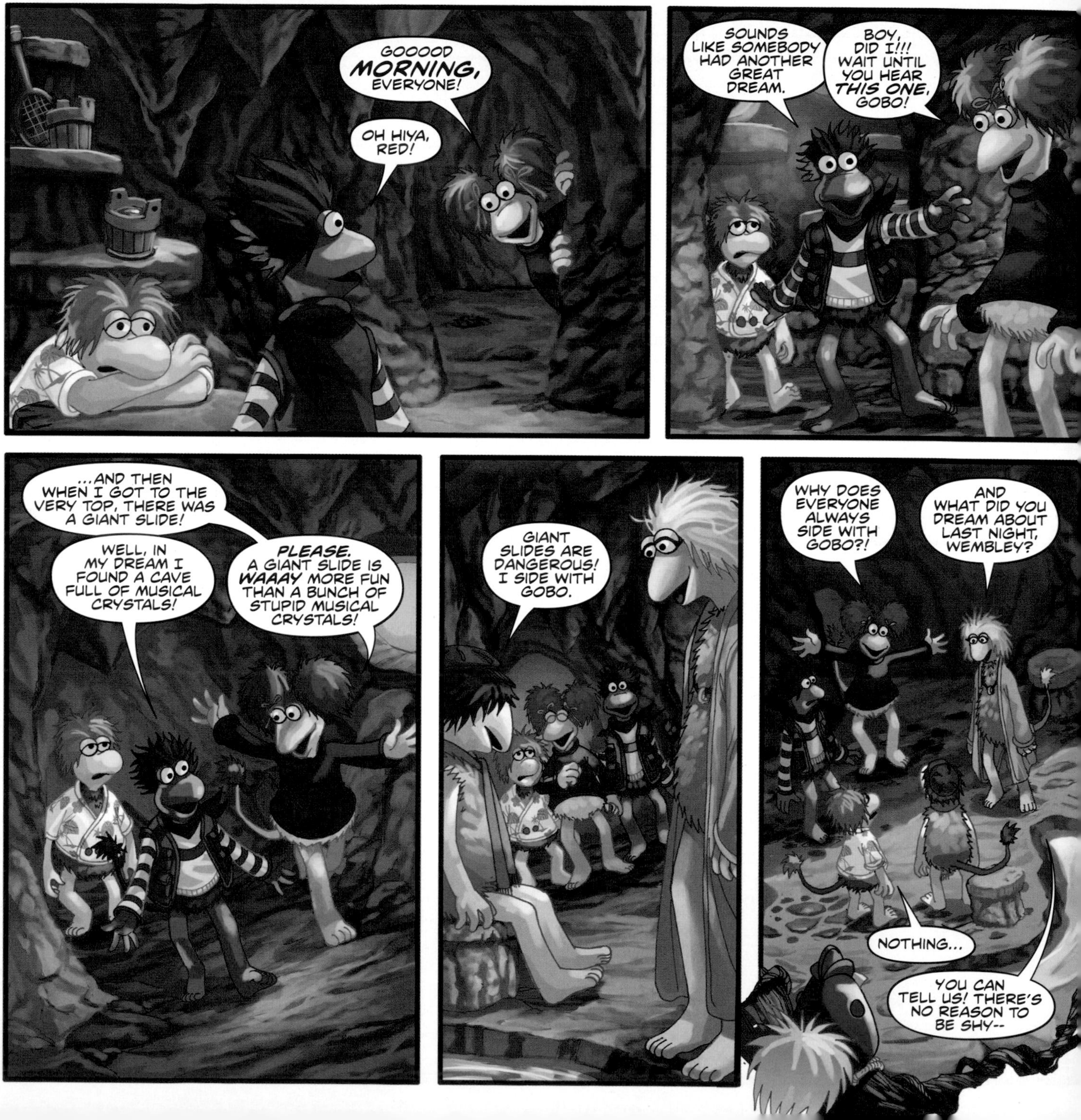
GOOOOD MORNING, EVERYONE!
OH HIYA, RED!
SOUNDS LIKE SOMEBODY HAD ANOTHER GREAT DREAM.
BOY, DID I!!! WAIT UNTIL YOU HEAR THIS ONE, GOBO!
...AND THEN WHEN I GOT TO THE VERY TOP, THERE WAS A GIANT SLIDE!
WELL, IN MY DREAM I FOUND A CAVE FULL OF MUSICAL CRYSTALS!
PLEASE. A GIANT SLIDE IS WAAAY MORE FUN THAN A BUNCH OF STUPID MUSICAL CRYSTALS!
GIANT SLIDES ARE DANGEROUS! I SIDE WITH GOBO.
WHY DOES EVERYONE ALWAYS SIDE WITH GOBO?!
AND WHAT DID YOU DREAM ABOUT LAST NIGHT, WEMBLEY?
NOTHING...
YOU CAN TELL US! THERE'S NO REASON TO BE SHY--

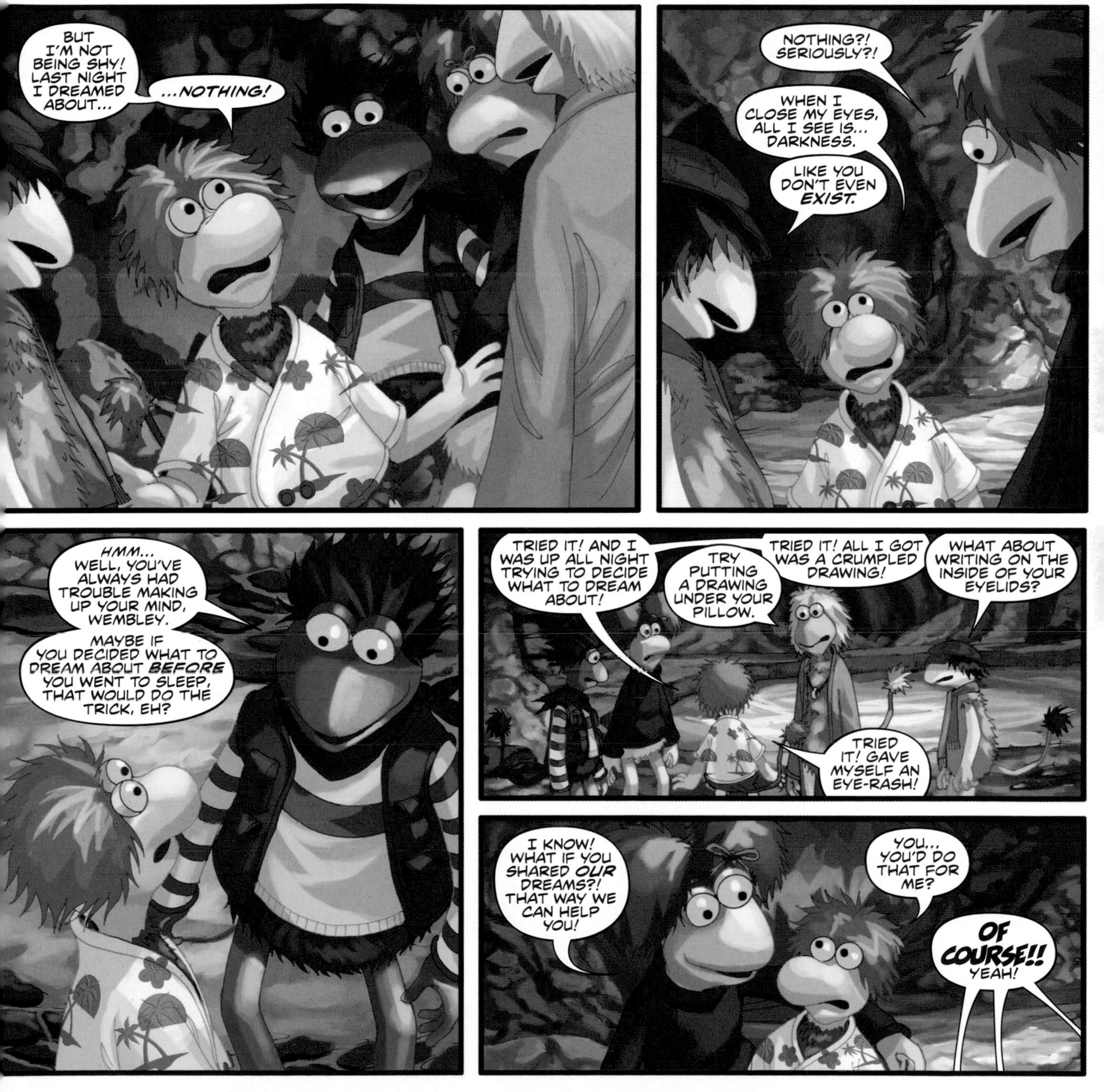
BUT I'M NOT BEING SHY! LAST NIGHT I DREAMED ABOUT...
...NOTHING!
NOTHING?! SERIOUSLY?!
WHEN I CLOSE MY EYES, ALL I SEE IS... DARKNESS.
LIKE YOU DON'T EVEN EXIST.
HMM... WELL, YOU'VE ALWAYS HAD TROUBLE MAKING UP YOUR MIND, WEMBLEY.
MAYBE IF YOU DECIDED WHAT TO DREAM ABOUT BEFORE YOU WENT TO SLEEP, THAT WOULD DO THE TRICK, EH?
TRIED IT! AND I WAS UP ALL NIGHT TRYING TO DECIDE WHAT TO DREAM ABOUT!
TRY PUTTING A DRAWING UNDER YOUR PILLOW.
TRIED IT! ALL I GOT WAS A CRUMPLED DRAWING!
WHAT ABOUT WRITING ON THE INSIDE OF YOUR EYELIDS?
TRIED IT! GAVE MYSELF AN EYE-RASH!
I KNOW! WHAT IF YOU SHARED OUR DREAMS?! THAT WAY WE CAN HELP YOU!
YOU... YOU'D DO THAT FOR ME?
OF COURSE!! YEAH!

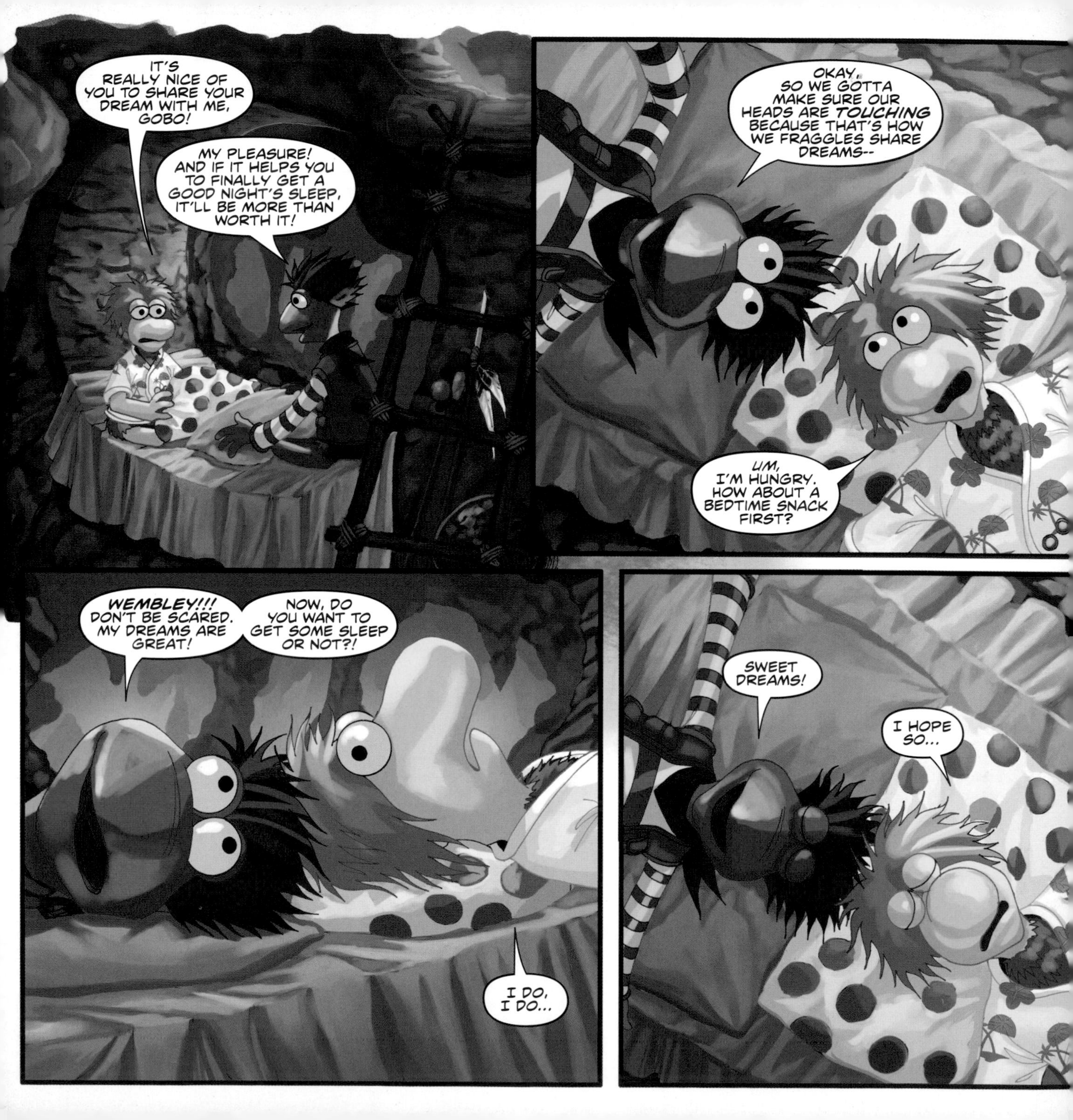
IT'S REALLY NICE OF YOU TO SHARE YOUR DREAM WITH ME, GOBO!
MY PLEASURE! AND IF IT HELPS YOU TO FINALLY GET A GOOD NIGHT'S SLEEP, IT'LL BE MORE THAN WORTH IT!
OKAY, SO WE GOTTA MAKE SURE OUR HEADS ARE *TOUCHING* BECAUSE THAT'S HOW WE FRAGGLES SHARE DREAMS--
UM, I'M HUNGRY. HOW ABOUT A BEDTIME SNACK FIRST?
WEMBLEY!!! DON'T BE SCARED. MY DREAMS ARE GREAT!
NOW, DO YOU WANT TO GET SOME SLEEP OR NOT?!
I DO, I DO...
SWEET DREAMS!
I HOPE SO...

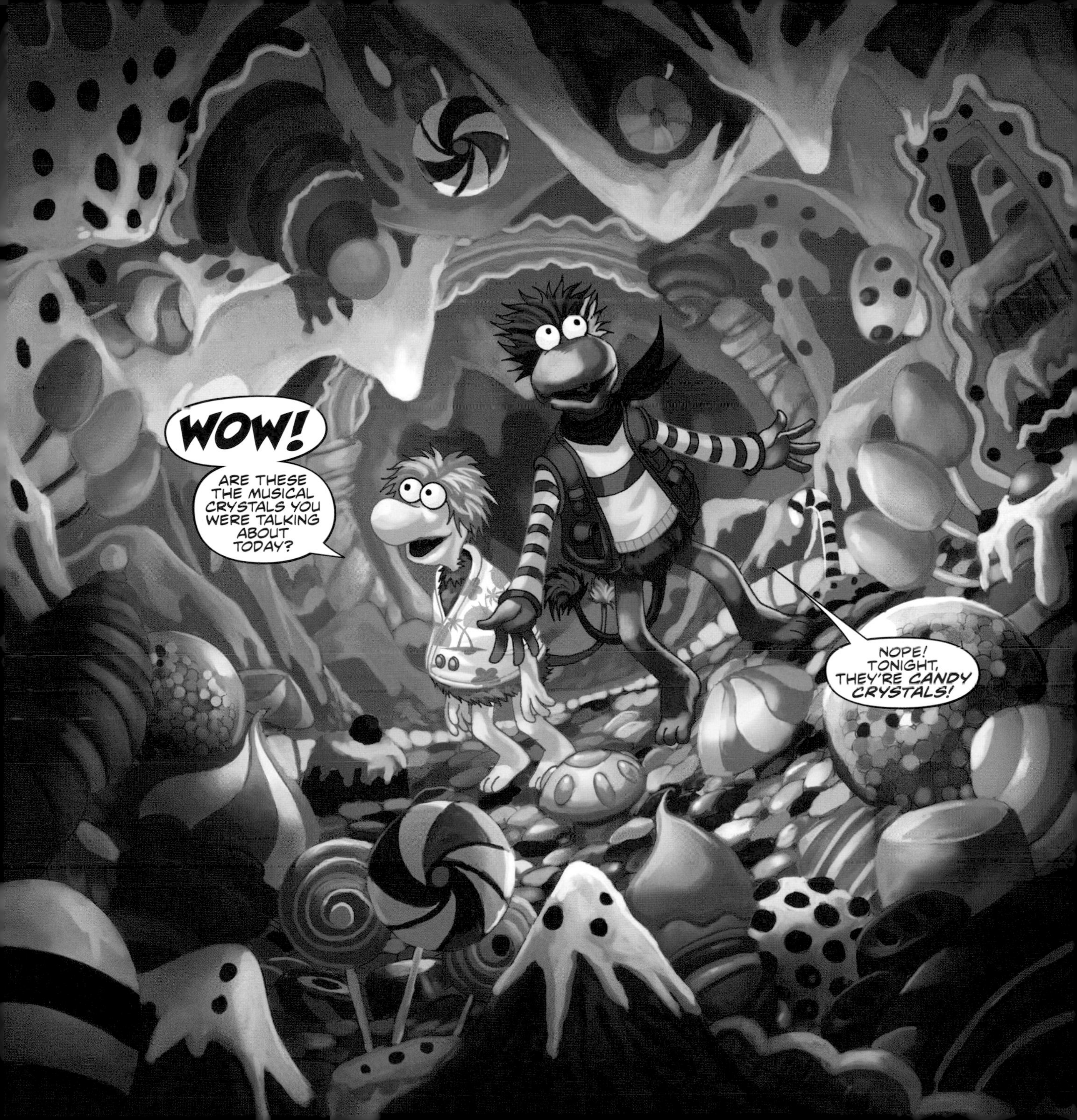
WOW!
ARE THESE THE MUSICAL CRYSTALS YOU WERE TALKING ABOUT TODAY?
NOPE! TONIGHT, THEY'RE CANDY CRYSTALS!

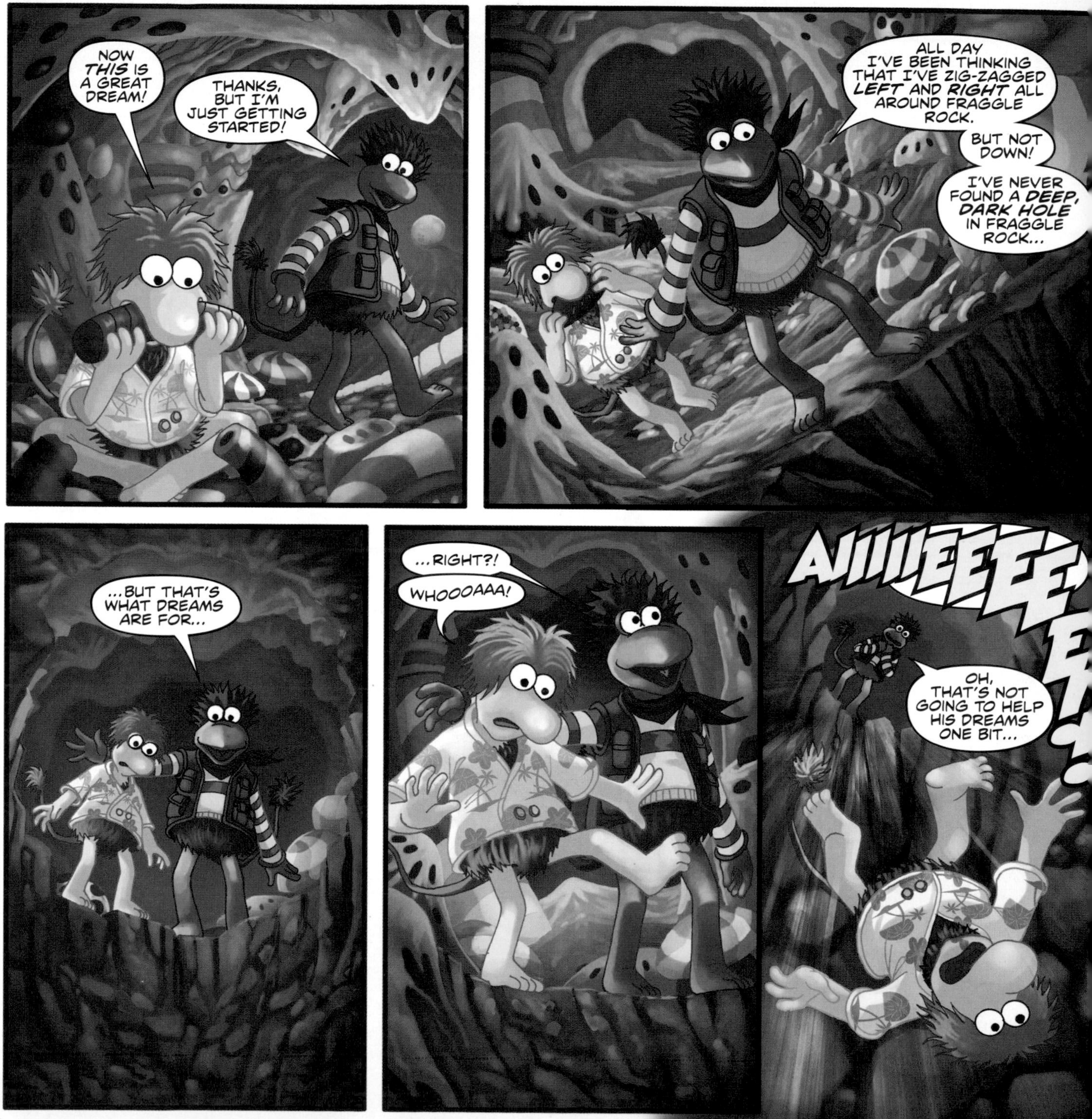
NOW *THIS* IS A GREAT DREAM!
THANKS, BUT I'M JUST GETTING STARTED!
ALL DAY I'VE BEEN THINKING THAT I'VE ZIG-ZAGGED *LEFT* AND *RIGHT* ALL AROUND FRAGGLE ROCK.
BUT NOT DOWN!
I'VE NEVER FOUND A *DEEP, DARK HOLE* IN FRAGGLE ROCK...
...BUT THAT'S WHAT DREAMS ARE FOR...
...RIGHT?!
WHOOOAAA!
AIIIIEEEE
OH, THAT'S NOT GOING TO HELP HIS DREAMS ONE BIT...

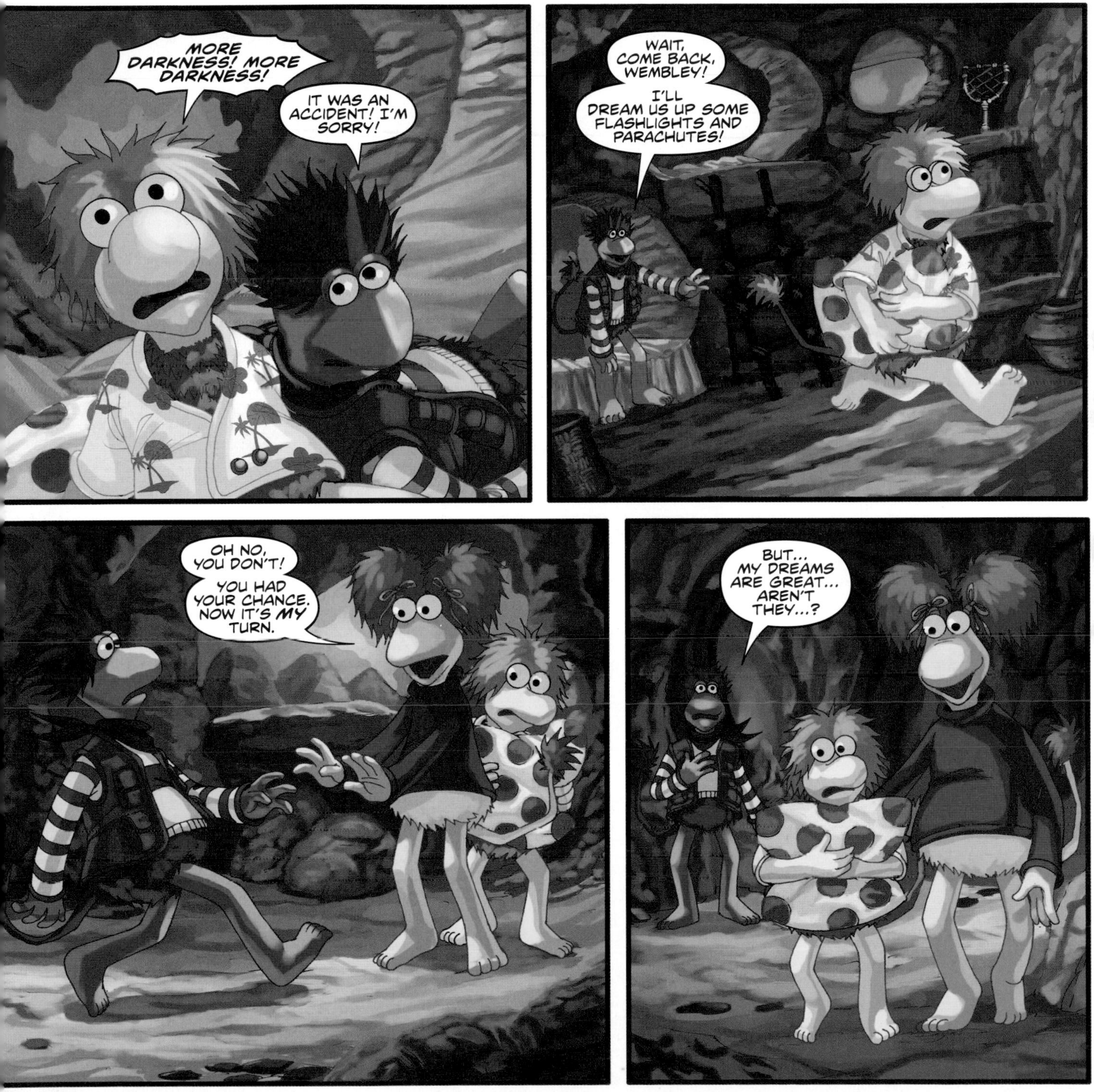
MORE DARKNESS! MORE DARKNESS!
IT WAS AN ACCIDENT! I'M SORRY!
WAIT, COME BACK, WEMBLEY!
I'LL DREAM US UP SOME FLASHLIGHTS AND PARACHUTES!
OH NO, YOU DON'T!
YOU HAD YOUR CHANCE. NOW IT'S *MY* TURN.
BUT... MY DREAMS ARE GREAT... AREN'T THEY...?

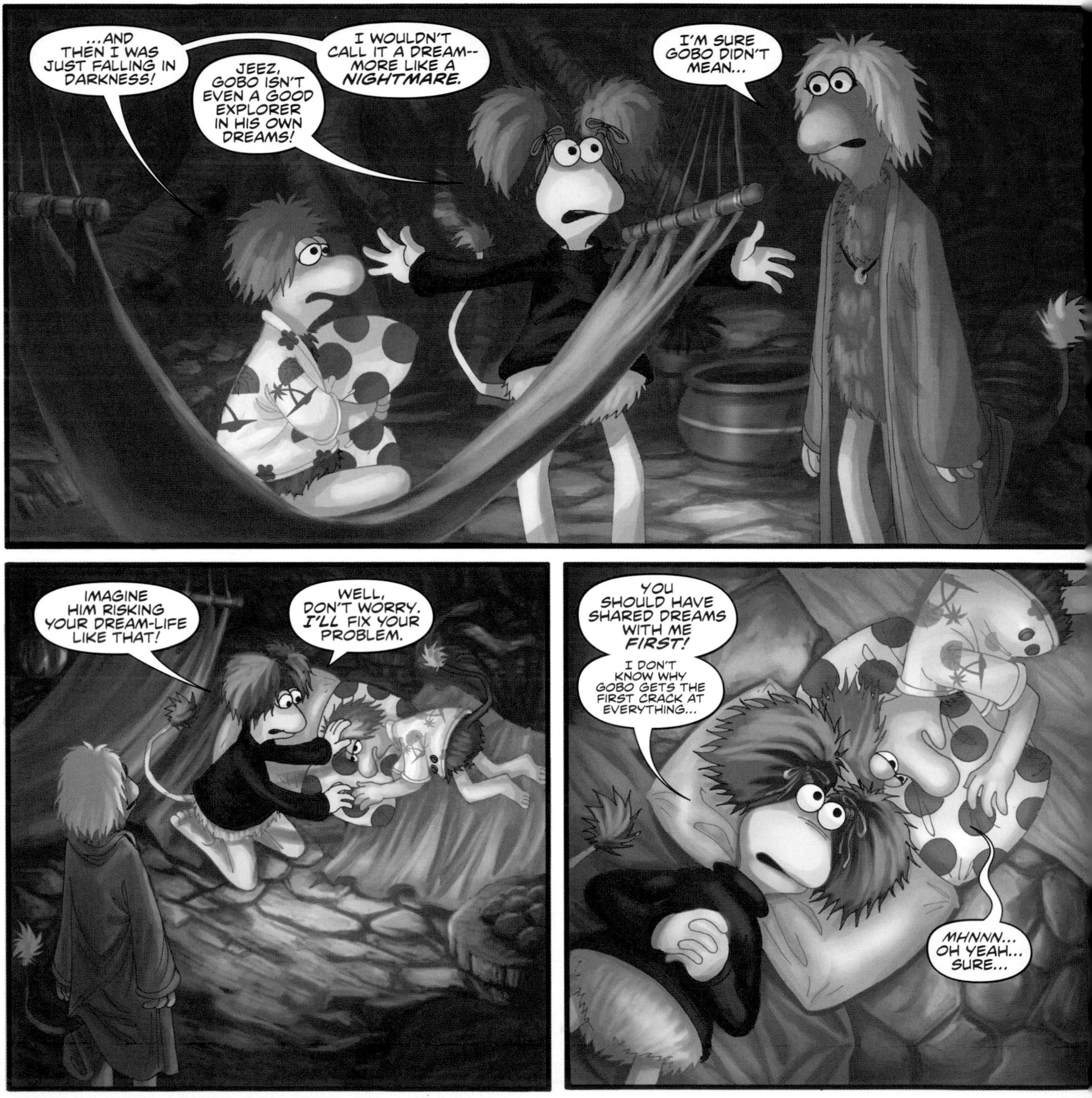
...AND THEN I WAS JUST FALLING IN DARKNESS!
I WOULDN'T CALL IT A DREAM-- MORE LIKE A NIGHTMARE.
JEEZ, GOBO ISN'T EVEN A GOOD EXPLORER IN HIS OWN DREAMS!
I'M SURE GOBO DIDN'T MEAN...
IMAGINE HIM RISKING YOUR DREAM-LIFE LIKE THAT!
WELL, DON'T WORRY. I'LL FIX YOUR PROBLEM.
YOU SHOULD HAVE SHARED DREAMS WITH ME FIRST!
I DON'T KNOW WHY GOBO GETS THE FIRST CRACK AT EVERYTHING...
MHNNN... OH YEAH... SURE...

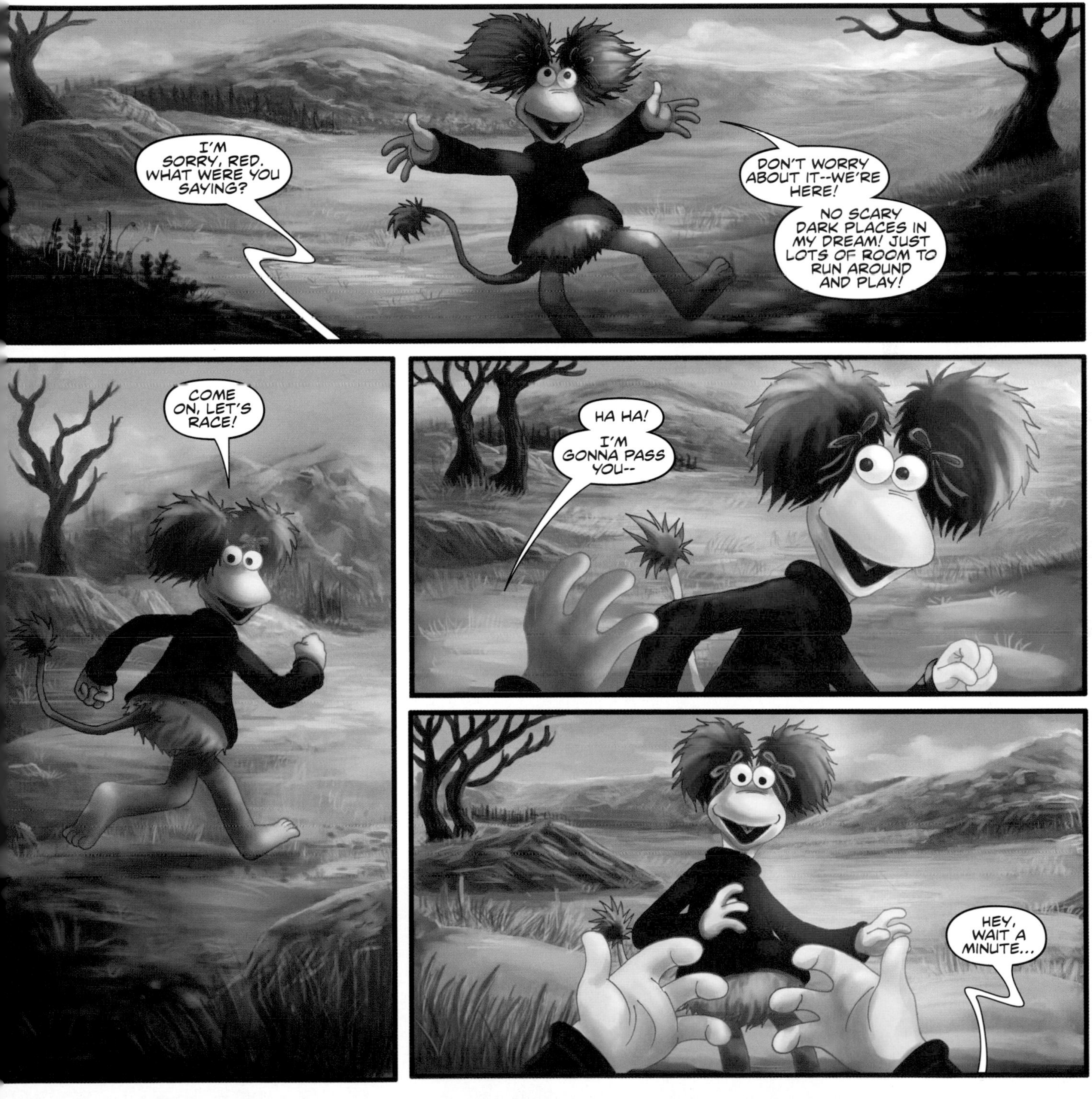
I'M SORRY, RED. WHAT WERE YOU SAYING?
DON'T WORRY ABOUT IT--WE'RE HERE!
NO SCARY DARK PLACES IN MY DREAM! JUST LOTS OF ROOM TO RUN AROUND AND PLAY!
COME ON, LET'S RACE!
HA HA!
I'M GONNA PASS YOU--
HEY, WAIT A MINUTE...

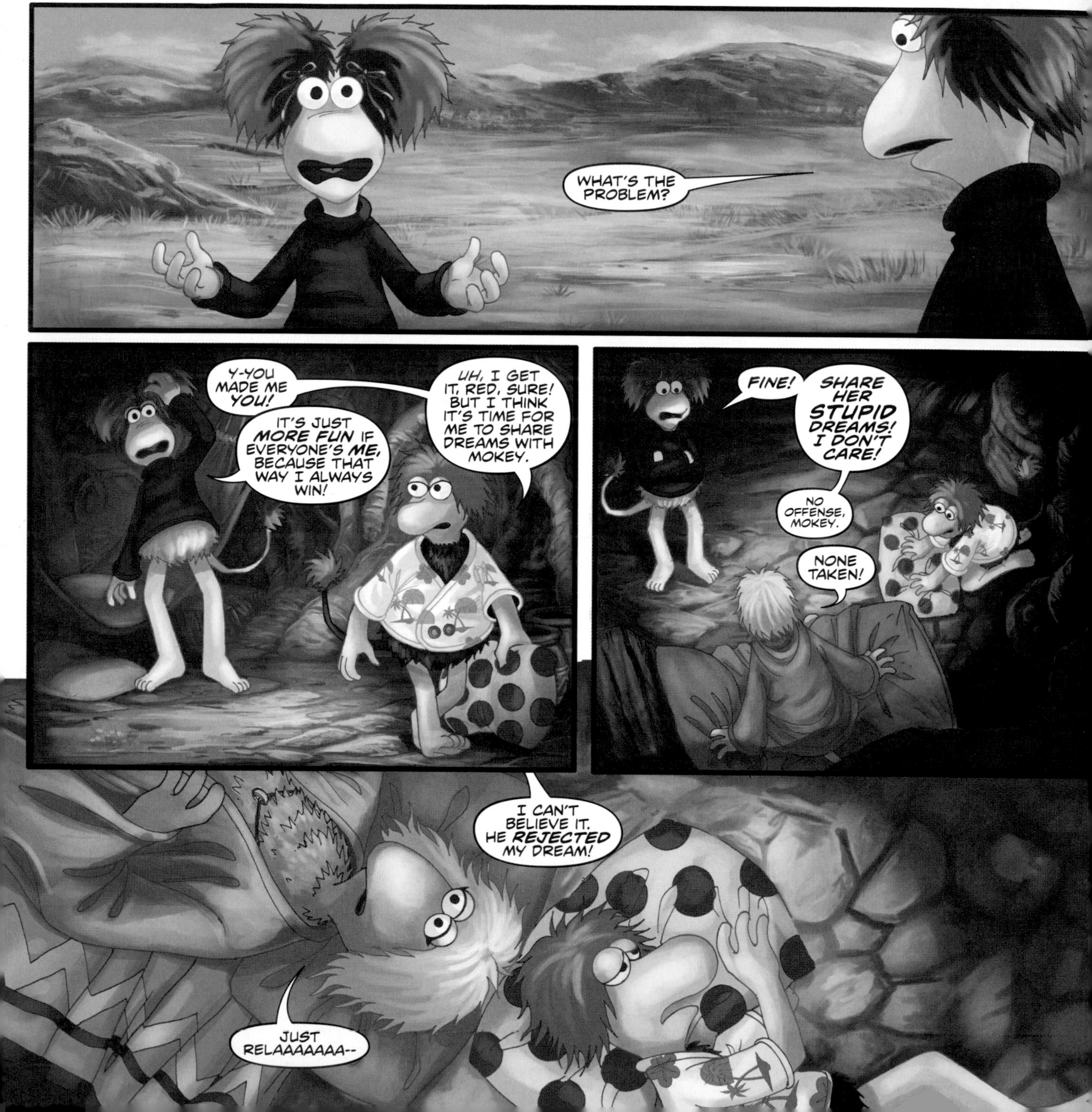
WHAT'S THE PROBLEM?
Y-YOU MADE ME YOU!
IT'S JUST MORE FUN IF EVERYONE'S ME, BECAUSE THAT WAY I ALWAYS WIN!
UH, I GET IT, RED, SURE! BUT I THINK IT'S TIME FOR ME TO SHARE DREAMS WITH MOKEY.
FINE!
SHARE HER STUPID DREAMS! I DON'T CARE!
NO OFFENSE, MOKEY.
NONE TAKEN!
I CAN'T BELIEVE IT. HE REJECTED MY DREAM!
JUST RELAAAAAAA--

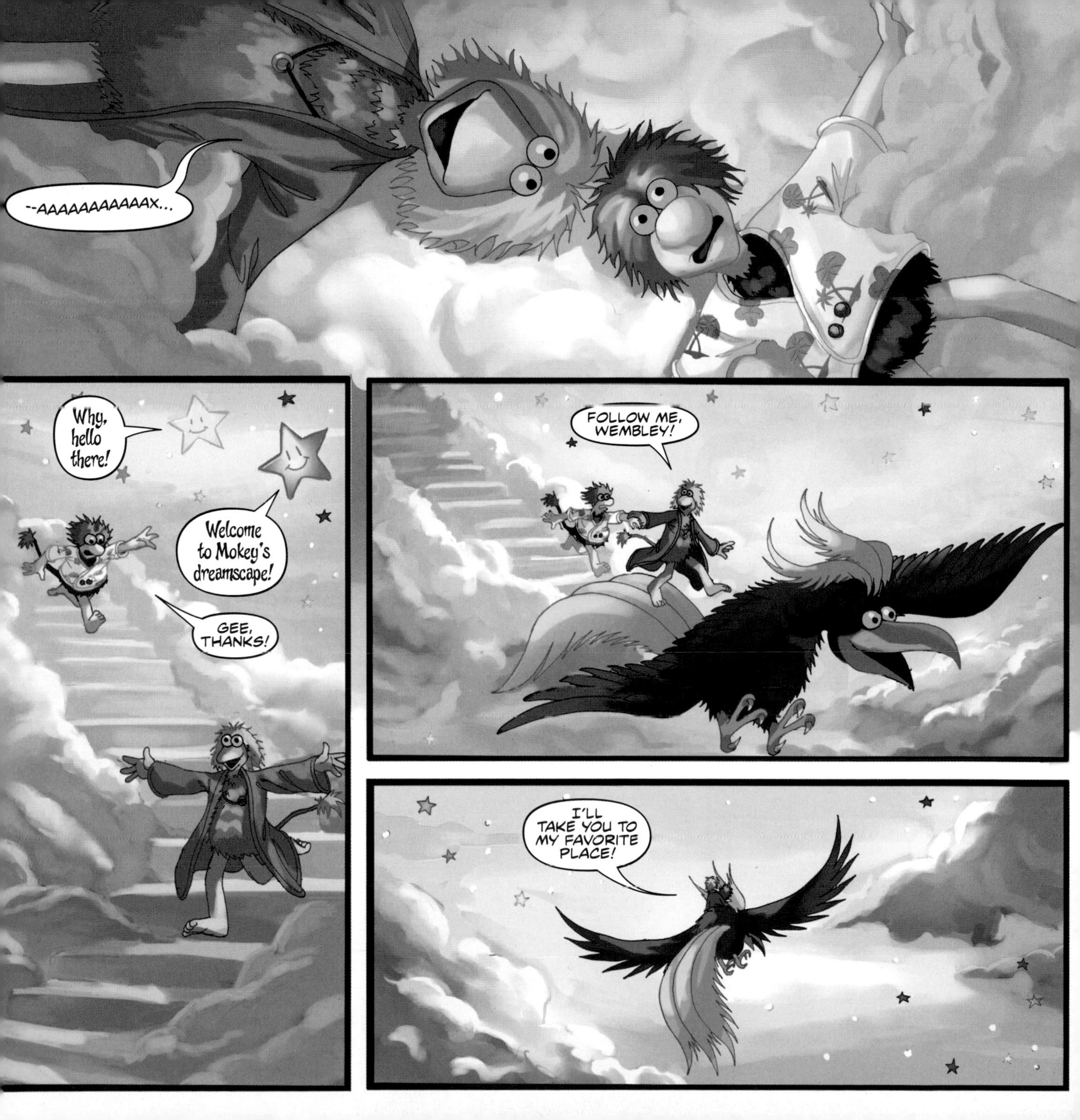
--AAAAAAAAAAAX...
Why, hello there!
Welcome to Mokey's dreamscape!
GEE, THANKS!
FOLLOW ME, WEMBLEY!
I'LL TAKE YOU TO MY FAVORITE PLACE!

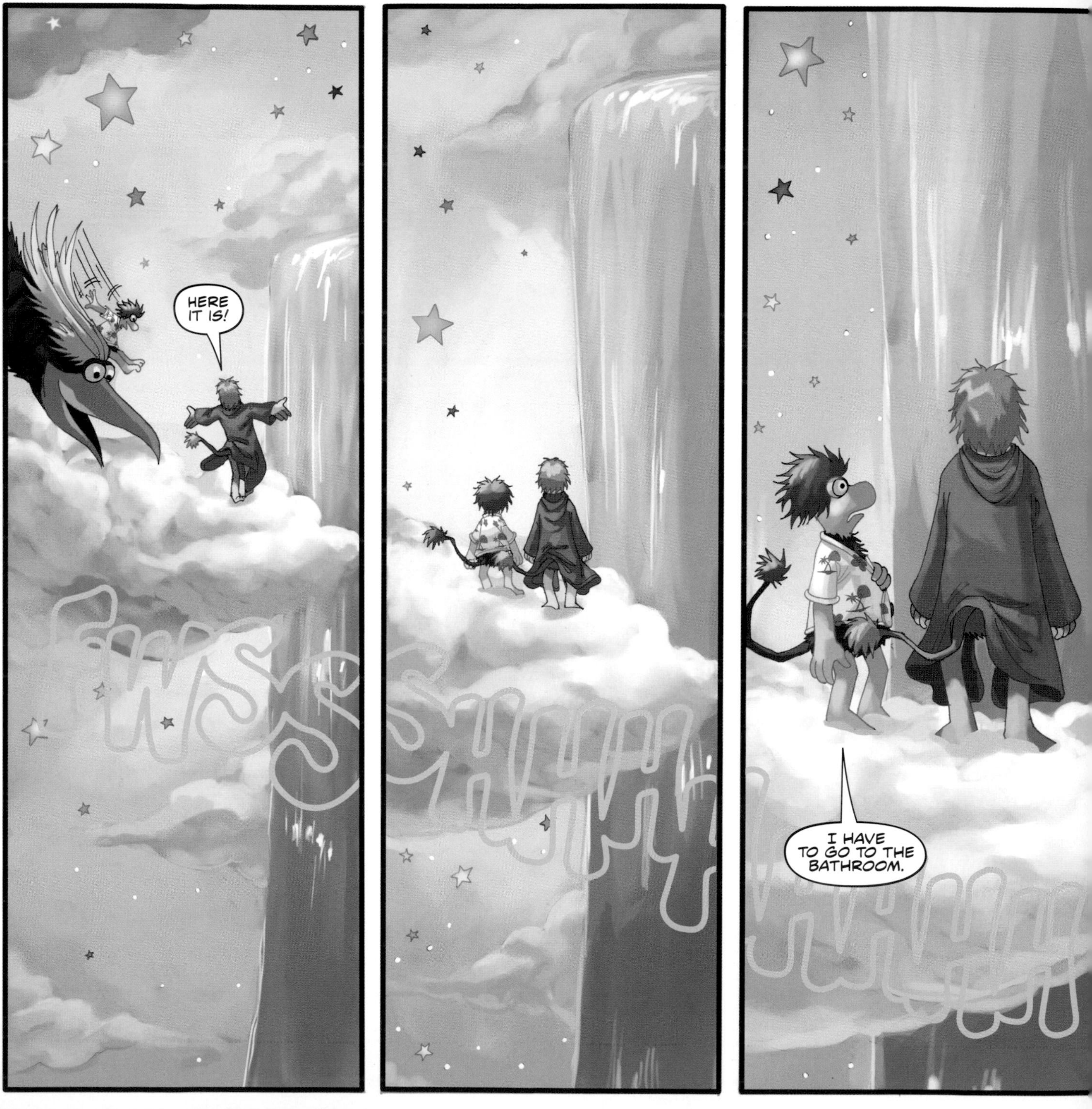
HERE IT IS!
I HAVE TO GO TO THE BATHROOM.

ME?! WOW, YOU GUYS MUST BE DESPERATE.

YOU'RE HIS LAST HOPE, BOOBER!

I'M AFRAID HE DIDN'T CARE FOR MY DREAM AT ALL...

IS HIS DREAM DARKNESS CONTAGIOUS?

I DON'T THINK SO. GOBO AND RED HAVEN'T SAID ANYTHING, AND I'M OKAY.

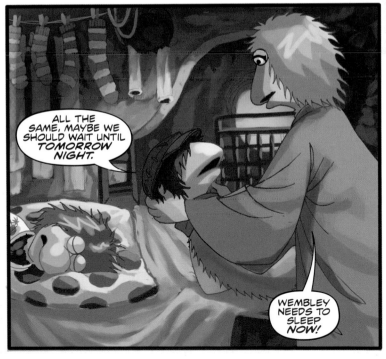

ALL THE SAME, MAYBE WE SHOULD WAIT UNTIL TOMORROW NIGHT.

WEMBLEY NEEDS TO SLEEP NOW!

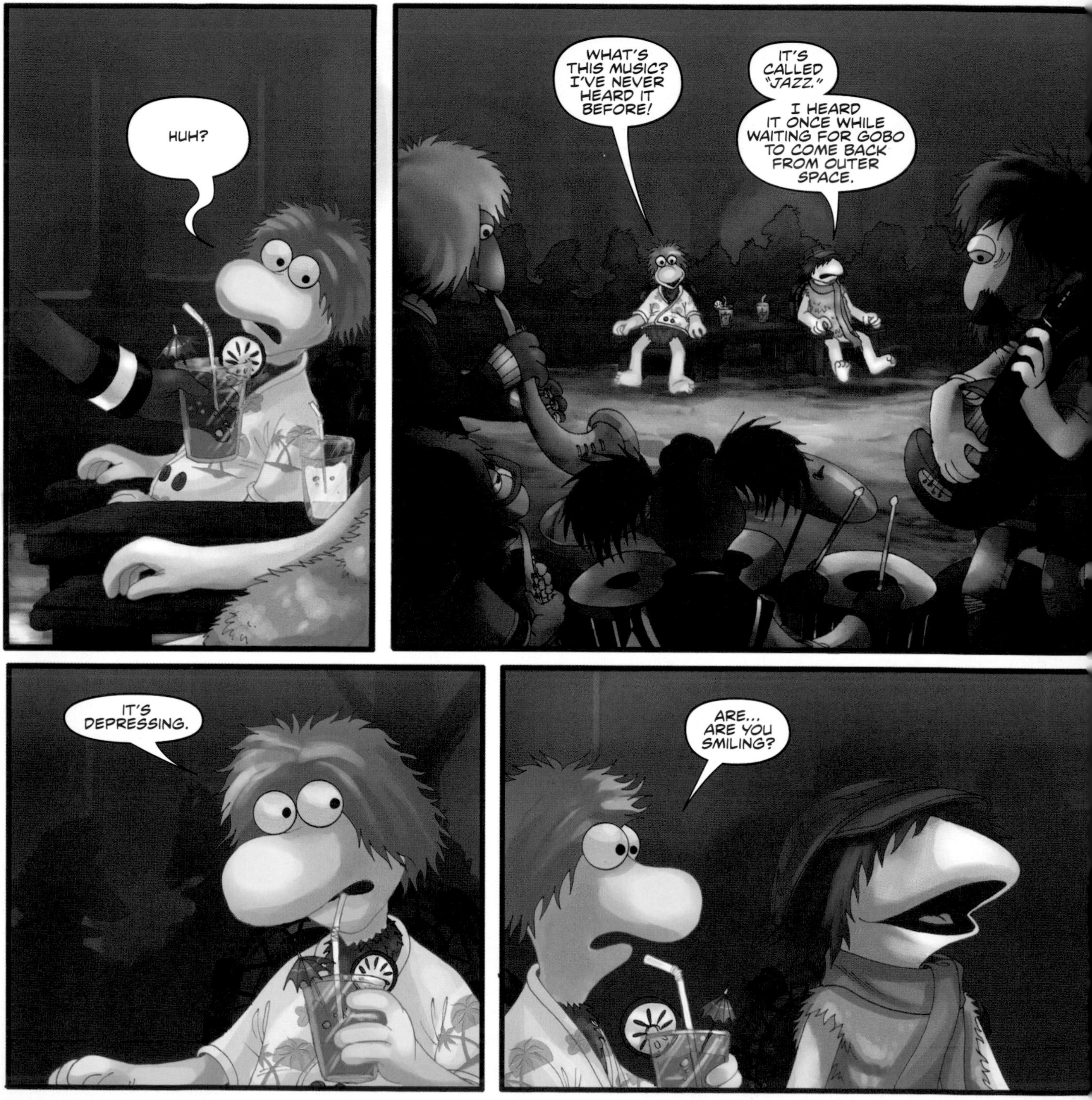
HUH?
WHAT'S THIS MUSIC? I'VE NEVER HEARD IT BEFORE!
IT'S CALLED "JAZZ."
I HEARD IT ONCE WHILE WAITING FOR GOBO TO COME BACK FROM OUTER SPACE.
IT'S DEPRESSING.
ARE... ARE YOU SMILING?

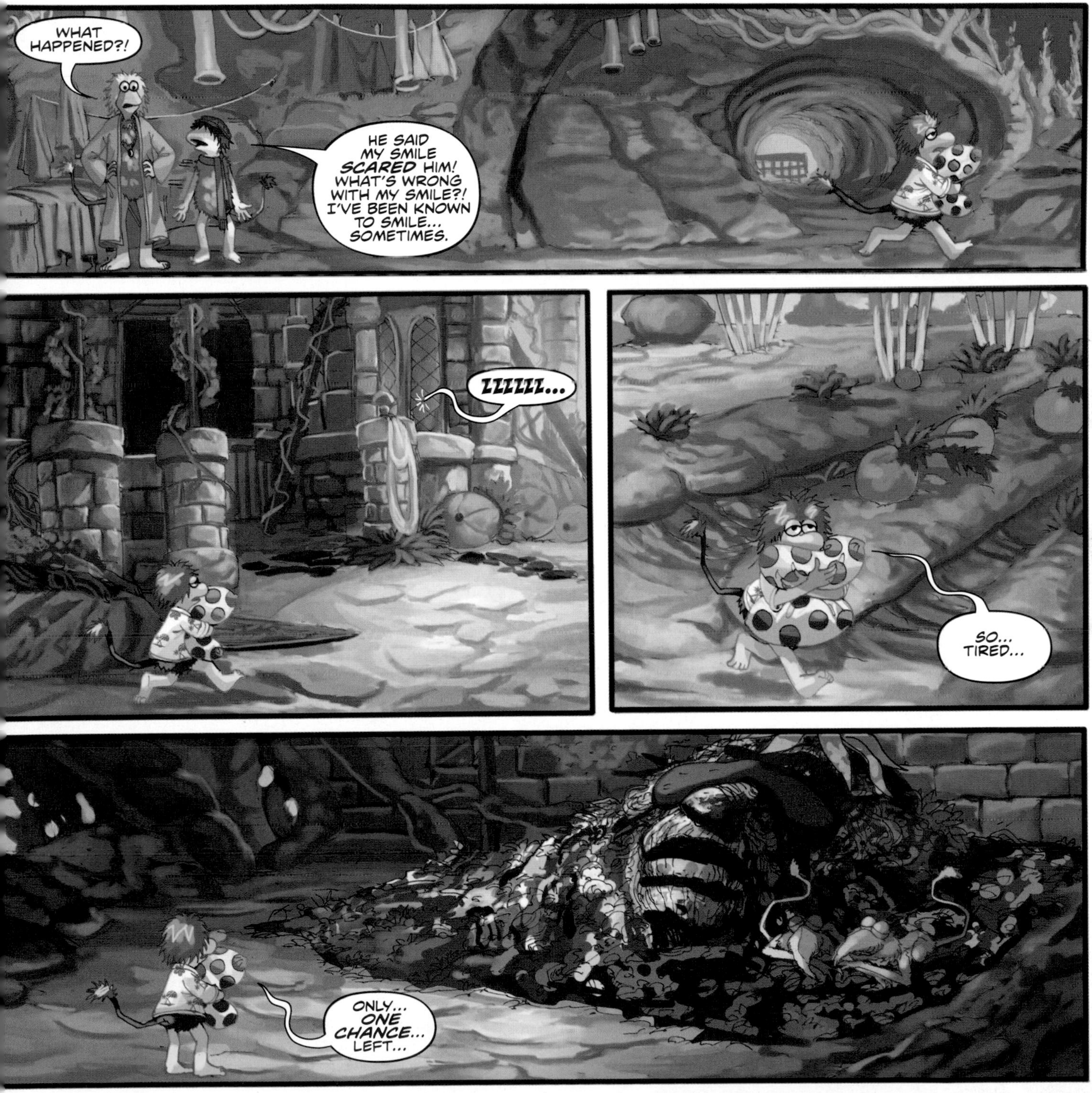
WHAT HAPPENED?!
HE SAID MY SMILE SCARED HIM! WHAT'S WRONG WITH MY SMILE?! I'VE BEEN KNOWN TO SMILE... SOMETIMES.
ZZZZZZ...
SO... TIRED...
ONLY... ONE CHANCE... LEFT...

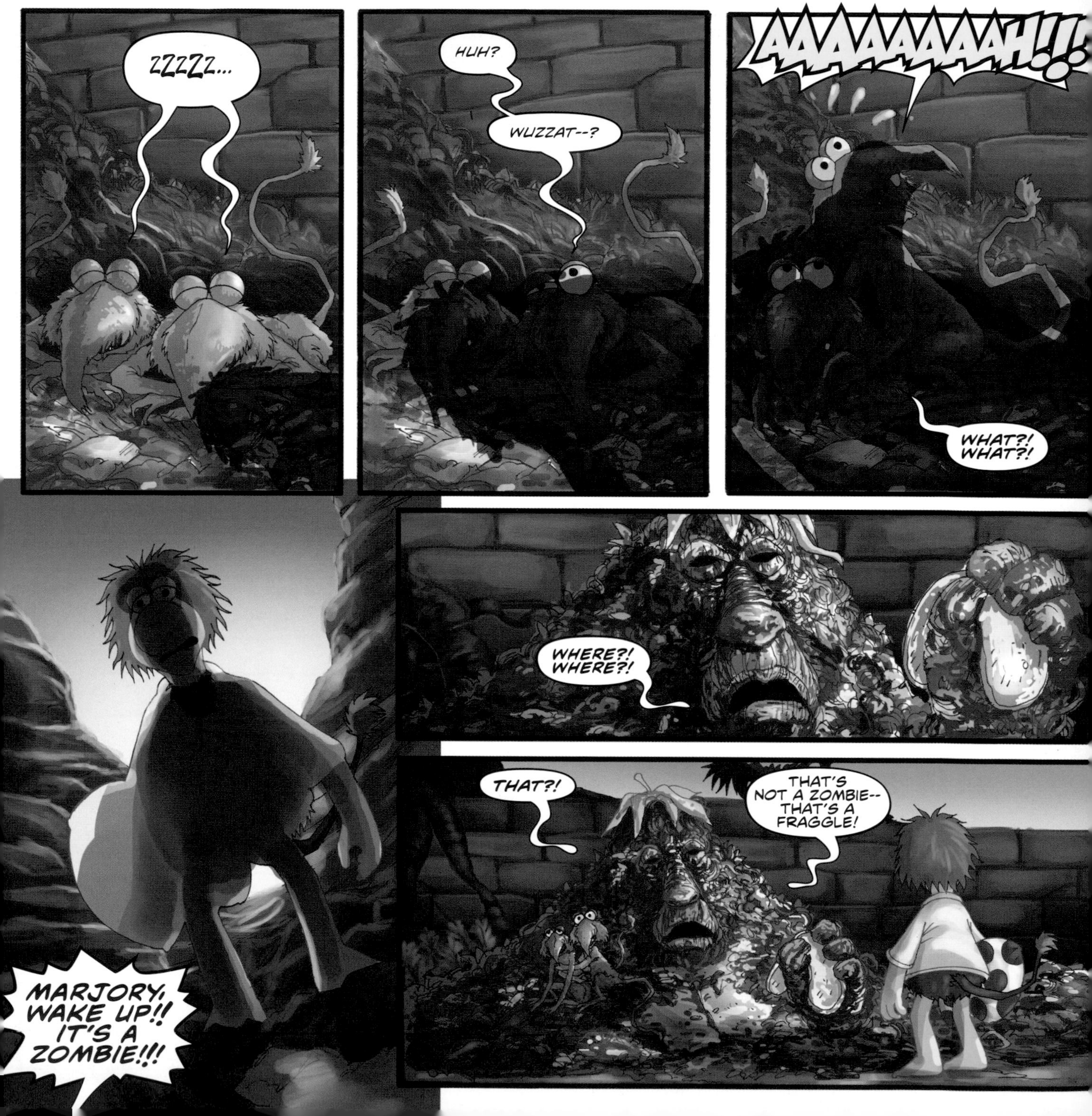
ZZZZZ...
HUH?
WUZZAT--?
AAAAAAAAAH!!!
WHAT?! WHAT?!
MARJORY, WAKE UP!! IT'S A ZOMBIE!!!
WHERE?! WHERE?!
THAT?!
THAT'S NOT A ZOMBIE-- THAT'S A FRAGGLE!

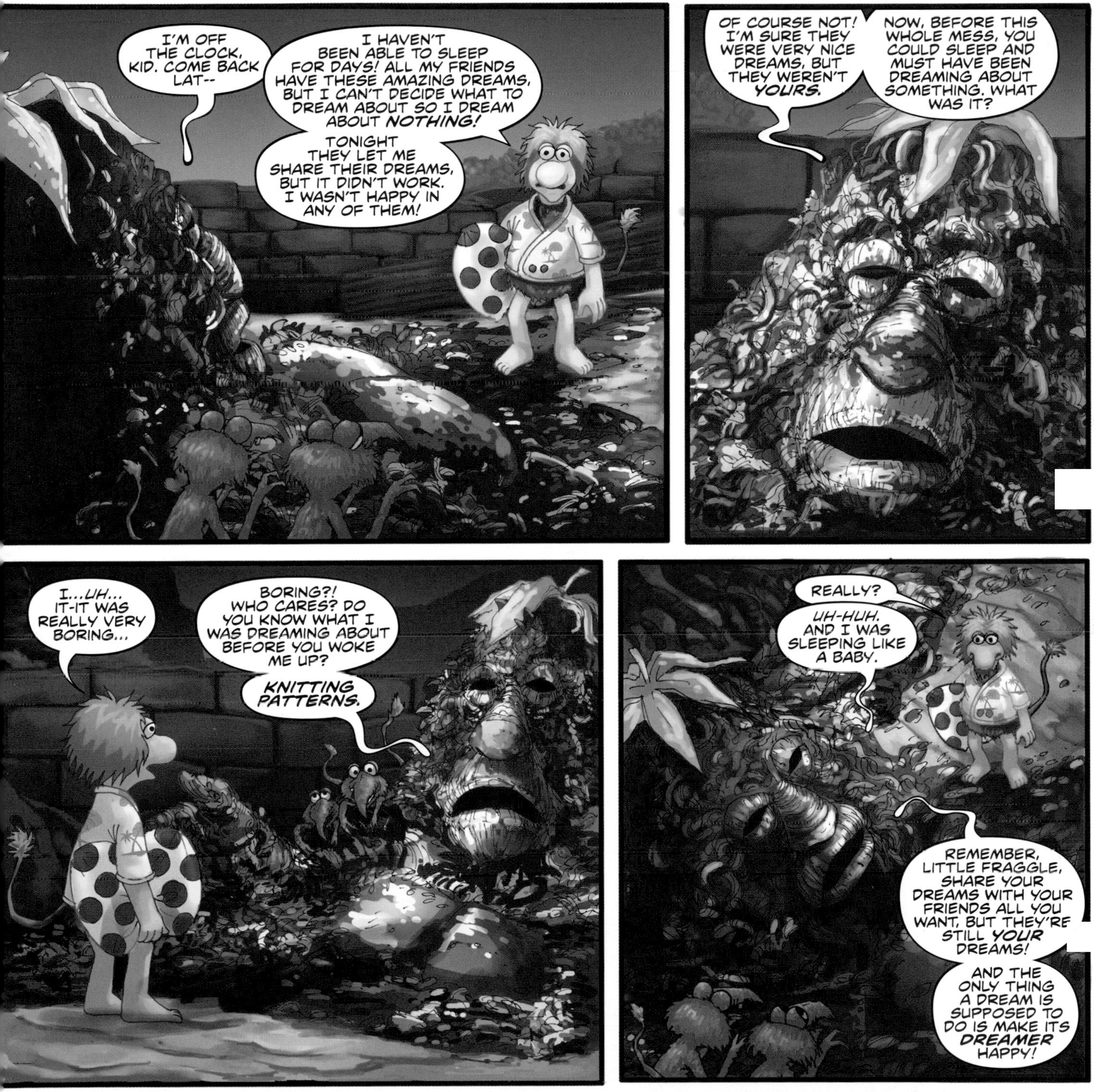
I'M OFF THE CLOCK, KID. COME BACK LAT--
I HAVEN'T BEEN ABLE TO SLEEP FOR DAYS! ALL MY FRIENDS HAVE THESE AMAZING DREAMS, BUT I CAN'T DECIDE WHAT TO DREAM ABOUT SO I DREAM ABOUT NOTHING!
TONIGHT THEY LET ME SHARE THEIR DREAMS, BUT IT DIDN'T WORK. I WASN'T HAPPY IN ANY OF THEM!
OF COURSE NOT! I'M SURE THEY WERE VERY NICE DREAMS, BUT THEY WEREN'T YOURS.
NOW, BEFORE THIS WHOLE MESS, YOU COULD SLEEP AND MUST HAVE BEEN DREAMING ABOUT SOMETHING. WHAT WAS IT?
I...UH... IT-IT WAS REALLY VERY BORING...
BORING?! WHO CARES? DO YOU KNOW WHAT I WAS DREAMING ABOUT BEFORE YOU WOKE ME UP?
KNITTING PATTERNS.
REALLY?
UH-HUH. AND I WAS SLEEPING LIKE A BABY.
REMEMBER, LITTLE FRAGGLE, SHARE YOUR DREAMS WITH YOUR FRIENDS ALL YOU WANT, BUT THEY'RE STILL YOUR DREAMS!
AND THE ONLY THING A DREAM IS SUPPOSED TO DO IS MAKE ITS DREAMER HAPPY!

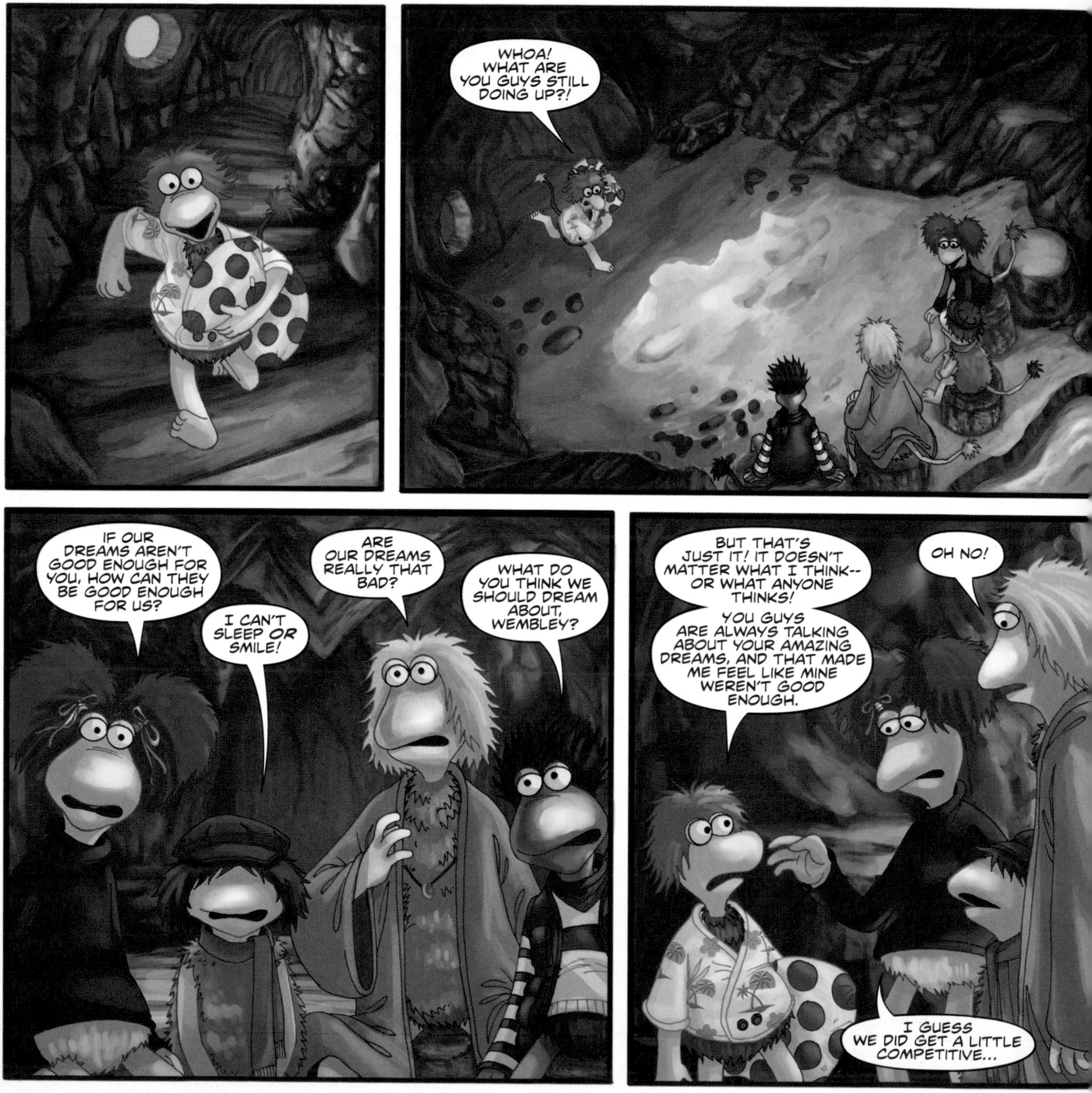
WHOA! WHAT ARE YOU GUYS STILL DOING UP?!
IF OUR DREAMS AREN'T GOOD ENOUGH FOR YOU, HOW CAN THEY BE GOOD ENOUGH FOR US?
I CAN'T SLEEP OR SMILE!
ARE OUR DREAMS REALLY THAT BAD?
WHAT DO YOU THINK WE SHOULD DREAM ABOUT, WEMBLEY?
BUT THAT'S JUST IT! IT DOESN'T MATTER WHAT I THINK-- OR WHAT ANYONE THINKS!
YOU GUYS ARE ALWAYS TALKING ABOUT YOUR AMAZING DREAMS, AND THAT MADE ME FEEL LIKE MINE WEREN'T GOOD ENOUGH.
OH NO!
I GUESS WE DID GET A LITTLE COMPETITIVE...

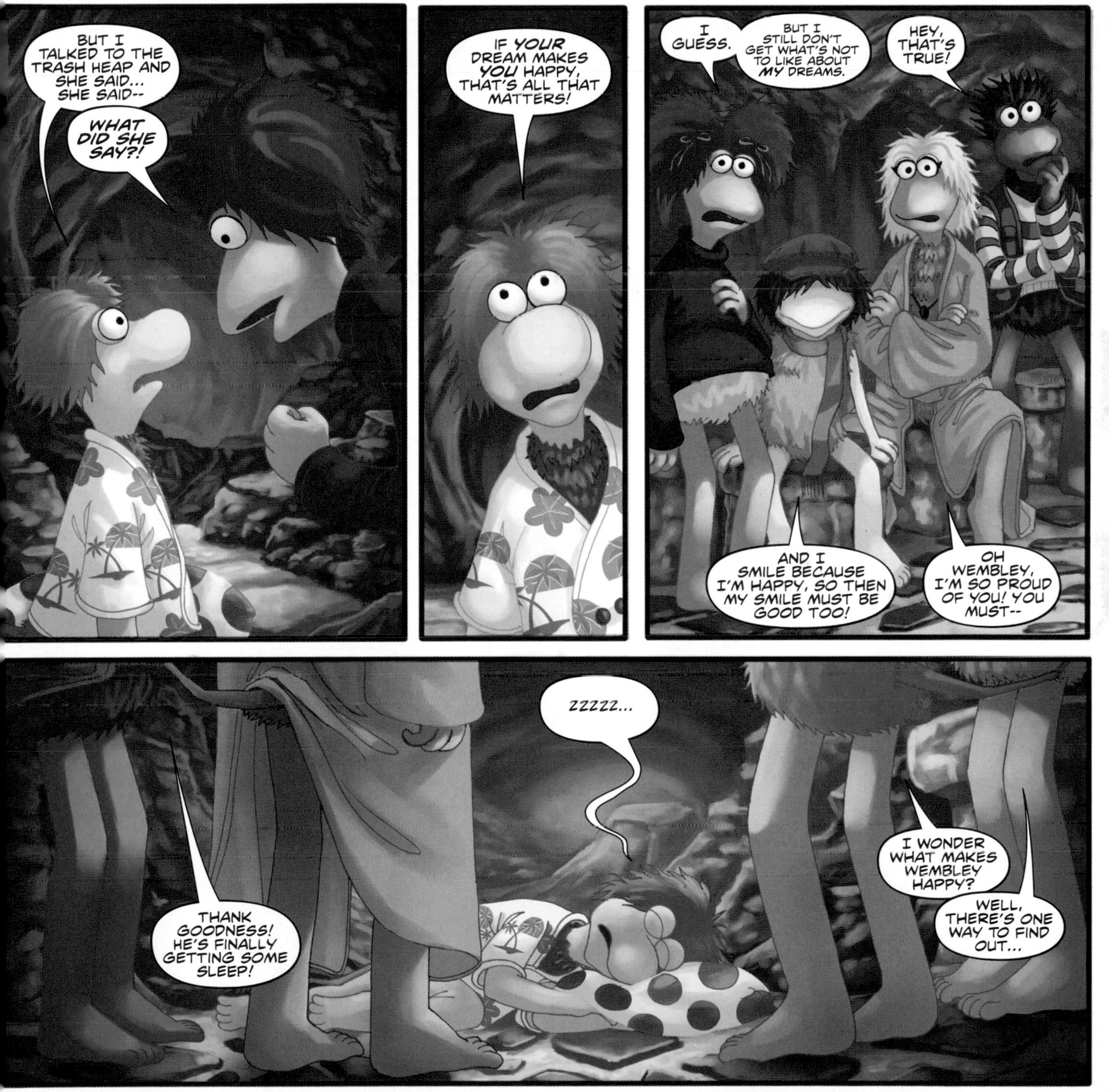
BUT I TALKED TO THE TRASH HEAP AND SHE SAID... SHE SAID--
WHAT DID SHE SAY?!
IF YOUR DREAM MAKES YOU HAPPY, THAT'S ALL THAT MATTERS!
I GUESS.
BUT I STILL DON'T GET WHAT'S NOT TO LIKE ABOUT MY DREAMS.
HEY, THAT'S TRUE!
AND I SMILE BECAUSE I'M HAPPY, SO THEN MY SMILE MUST BE GOOD TOO!
OH WEMBLEY, I'M SO PROUD OF YOU! YOU MUST--
ZZZZZ...
THANK GOODNESS! HE'S FINALLY GETTING SOME SLEEP!
I WONDER WHAT MAKES WEMBLEY HAPPY?
WELL, THERE'S ONE WAY TO FIND OUT...

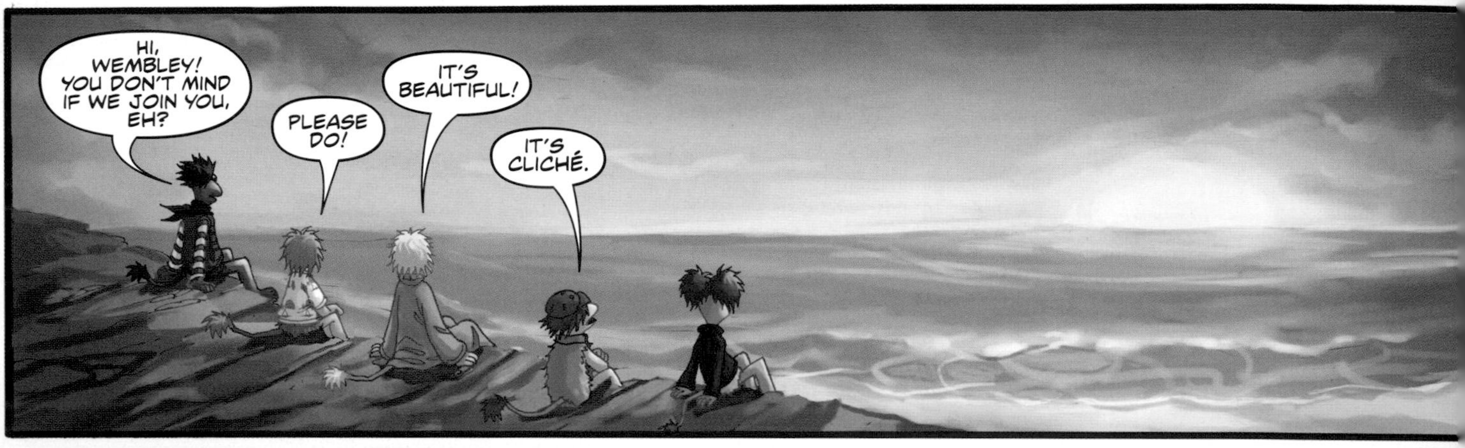
HI, WEMBLEY! YOU DON'T MIND IF WE JOIN YOU, EH?
PLEASE DO!
IT'S BEAUTIFUL!
IT'S CLICHÉ.

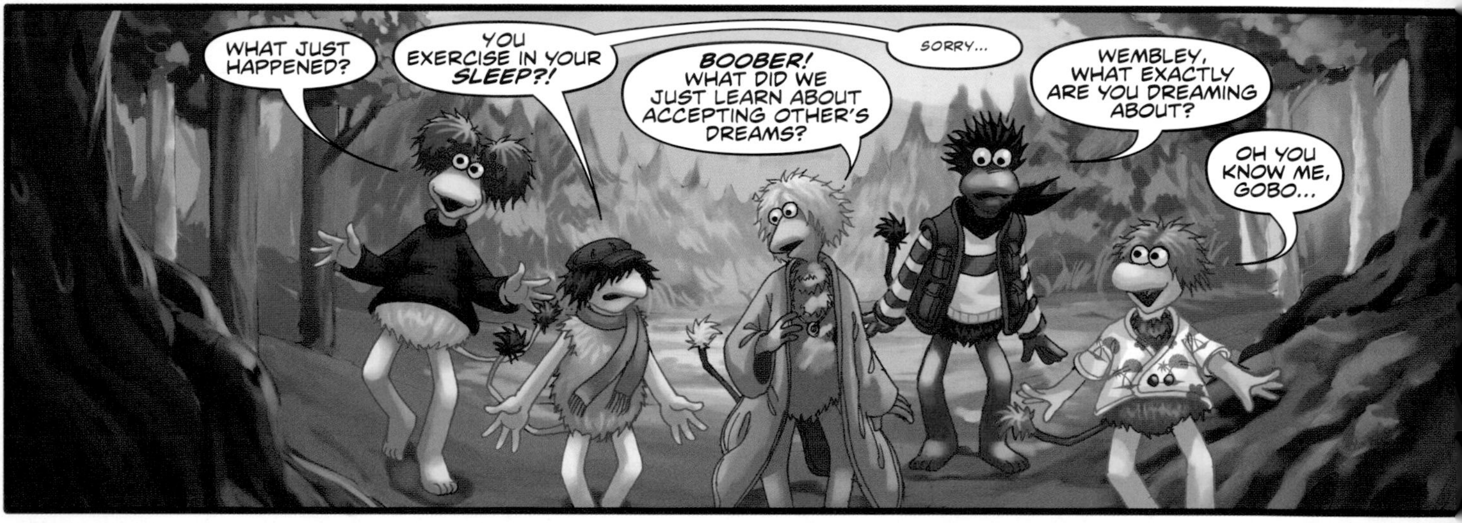
WHAT JUST HAPPENED?
YOU EXERCISE IN YOUR *SLEEP?!*
SORRY...
BOOBER! WHAT DID WE JUST LEARN ABOUT ACCEPTING OTHER'S DREAMS?
WEMBLEY, WHAT EXACTLY ARE YOU DREAMING ABOUT?
OH YOU KNOW ME, GOBO...

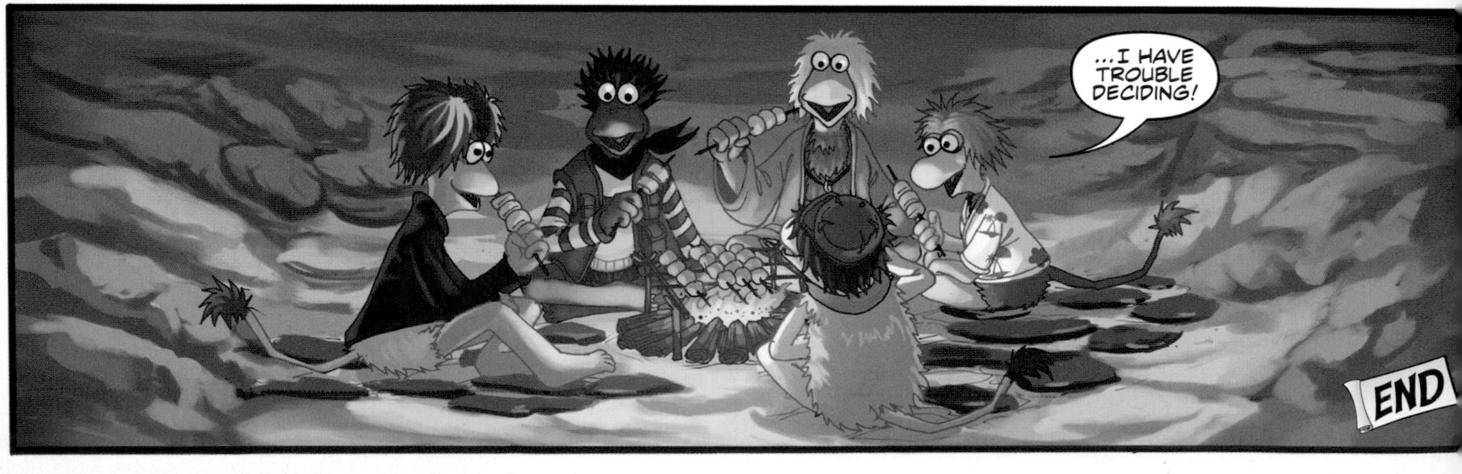
...I HAVE TROUBLE DECIDING!
END

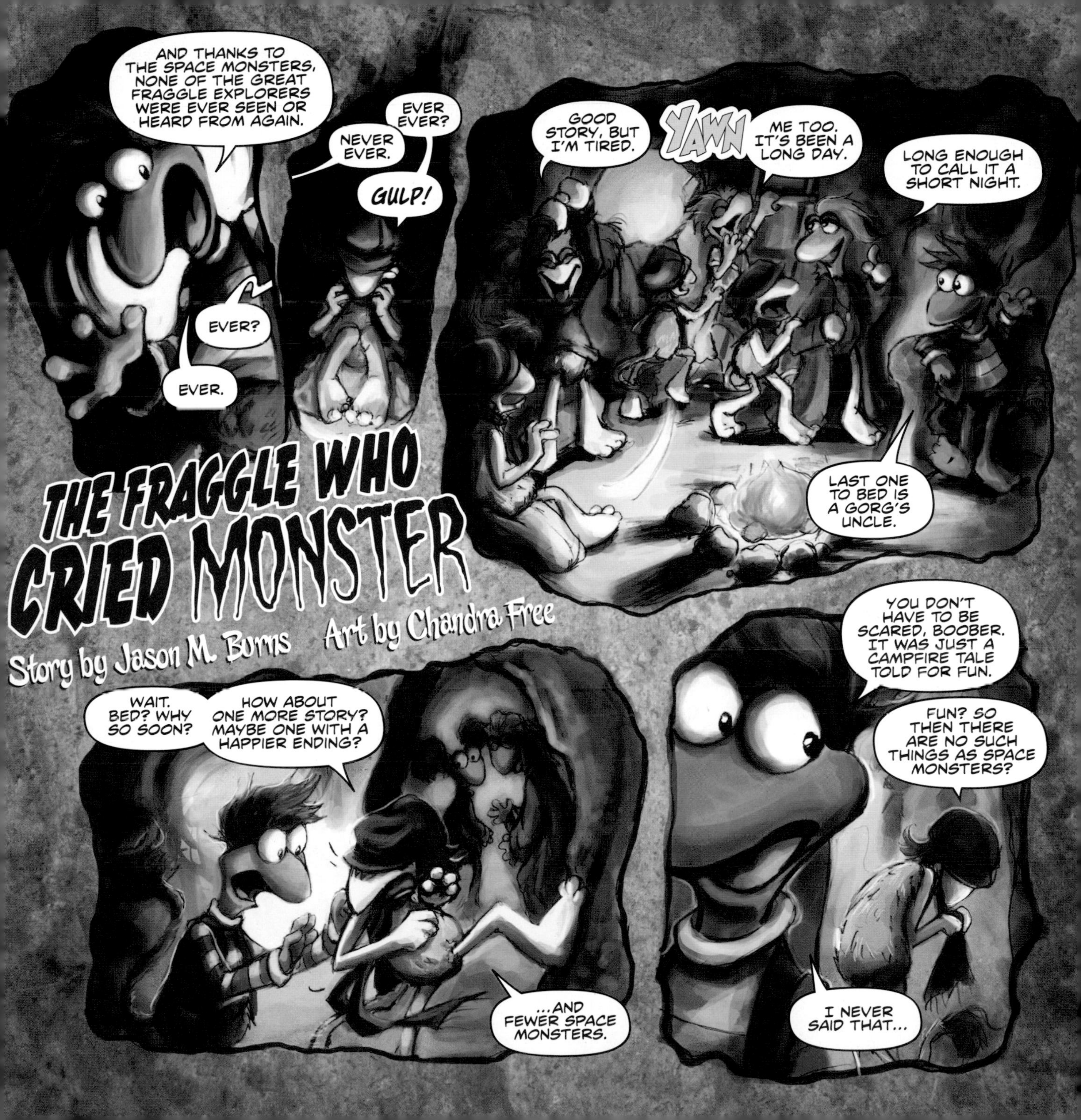
AND THANKS TO THE SPACE MONSTERS, NONE OF THE GREAT FRAGGLE EXPLORERS WERE EVER SEEN OR HEARD FROM AGAIN.
NEVER EVER.
EVER EVER?
GULP!
EVER?
EVER.
GOOD STORY, BUT I'M TIRED.
YAWN
ME TOO. IT'S BEEN A LONG DAY.
LONG ENOUGH TO CALL IT A SHORT NIGHT.
LAST ONE TO BED IS A GORG'S UNCLE.
THE FRAGGLE WHO CRIED MONSTER
Story by Jason M. Burns
Art by Chandra Free
WAIT. BED? WHY SO SOON?
HOW ABOUT ONE MORE STORY? MAYBE ONE WITH A HAPPIER ENDING?
...AND FEWER SPACE MONSTERS.
YOU DON'T HAVE TO BE SCARED, BOOBER. IT WAS JUST A CAMPFIRE TALE TOLD FOR FUN.
FUN? SO THEN THERE ARE NO SUCH THINGS AS SPACE MONSTERS?
I NEVER SAID THAT...

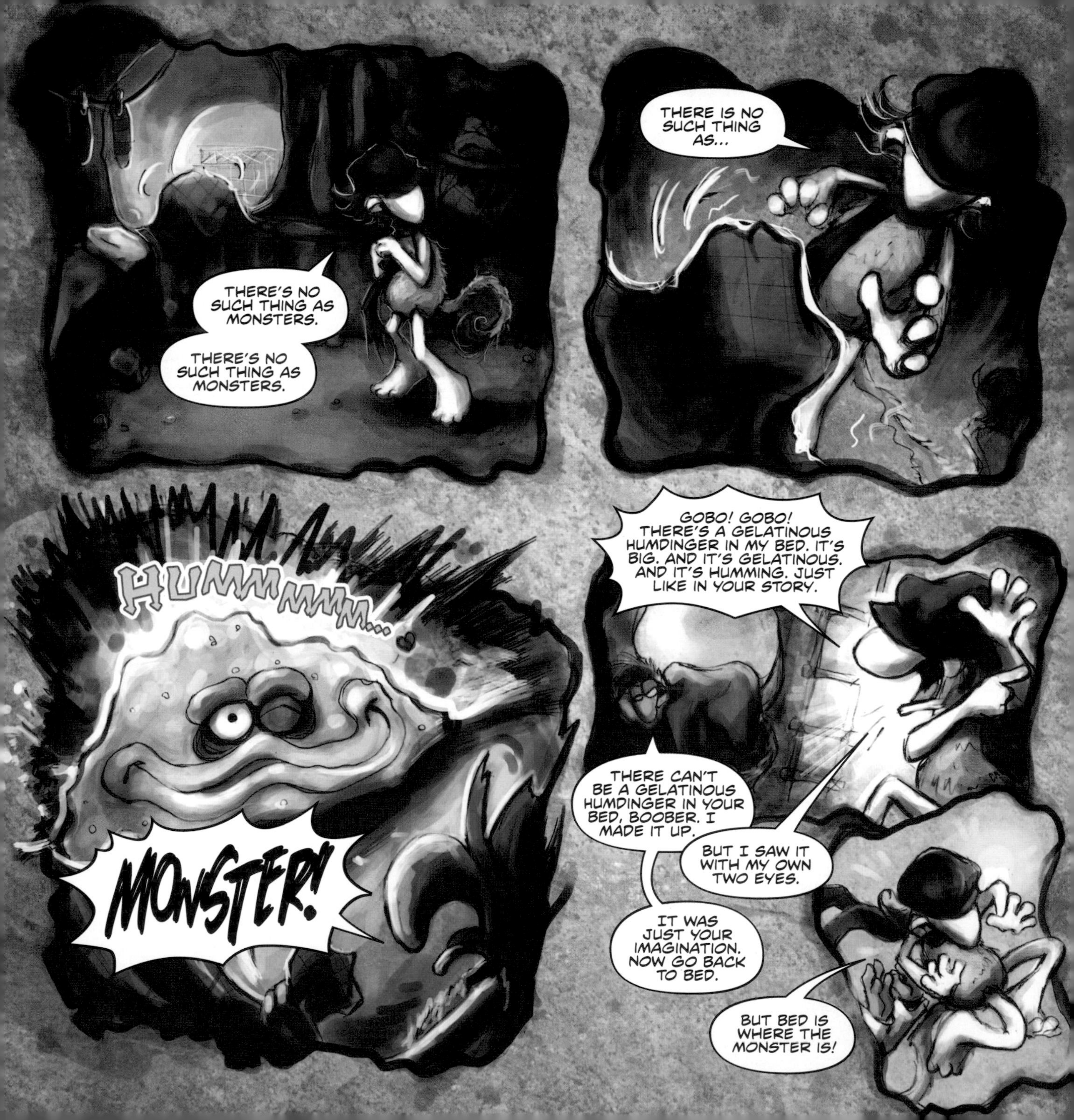
THERE'S NO SUCH THING AS MONSTERS.
THERE'S NO SUCH THING AS MONSTERS.
THERE IS NO SUCH THING AS...
HUMMMMMM...
MONSTER!
GOBO! GOBO! THERE'S A GELATINOUS HUMDINGER IN MY BED. IT'S BIG. AND IT'S GELATINOUS. AND IT'S HUMMING. JUST LIKE IN YOUR STORY.
THERE CAN'T BE A GELATINOUS HUMDINGER IN YOUR BED, BOOBER. I MADE IT UP.
BUT I SAW IT WITH MY OWN TWO EYES.
IT WAS JUST YOUR IMAGINATION. NOW GO BACK TO BED.
BUT BED IS WHERE THE MONSTER IS!

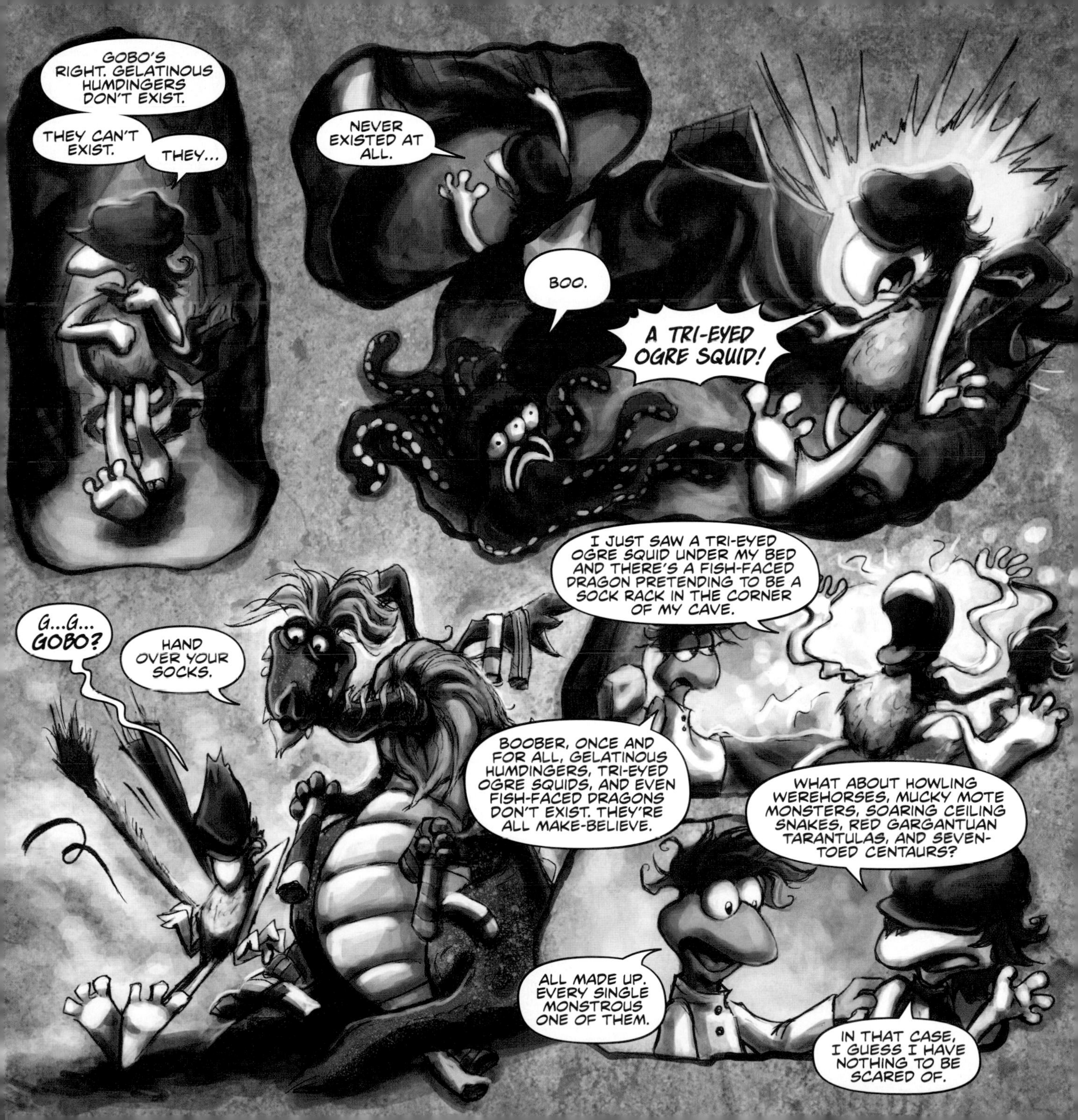
GOBO'S RIGHT. GELATINOUS HUMDINGERS DON'T EXIST.
THEY CAN'T EXIST.
THEY...
NEVER EXISTED AT ALL.
BOO.
A TRI-EYED OGRE SQUID!
G...G... GOBO?
HAND OVER YOUR SOCKS.
I JUST SAW A TRI-EYED OGRE SQUID UNDER MY BED AND THERE'S A FISH-FACED DRAGON PRETENDING TO BE A SOCK RACK IN THE CORNER OF MY CAVE.
BOOBER, ONCE AND FOR ALL, GELATINOUS HUMDINGERS, TRI-EYED OGRE SQUIDS, AND EVEN FISH-FACED DRAGONS DON'T EXIST. THEY'RE ALL MAKE-BELIEVE.
WHAT ABOUT HOWLING WEREHORSES, MUCKY MOTE MONSTERS, SOARING CEILING SNAKES, RED GARGANTUAN TARANTULAS, AND SEVEN-TOED CENTAURS?
ALL MADE UP. EVERY SINGLE MONSTROUS ONE OF THEM.
IN THAT CASE, I GUESS I HAVE NOTHING TO BE SCARED OF.

NOTHING TO BE AFRAID OF. NOTHING TO BE AFRAID OF.
GOBO!!!
AAAAAAH!
BWAAAAH!
GOBOOOO!!!
SO...MANY... MONSTERS. ALL OF THEM... REAL.
THAT'S IT! I CAN'T TAKE IT ANYMORE, BOOBER! YOU'RE NOT WELCOME IN MY CAVE UNTIL TOMORROW MORNING, SO FOR THE LAST TIME... GOOD NIGHT!

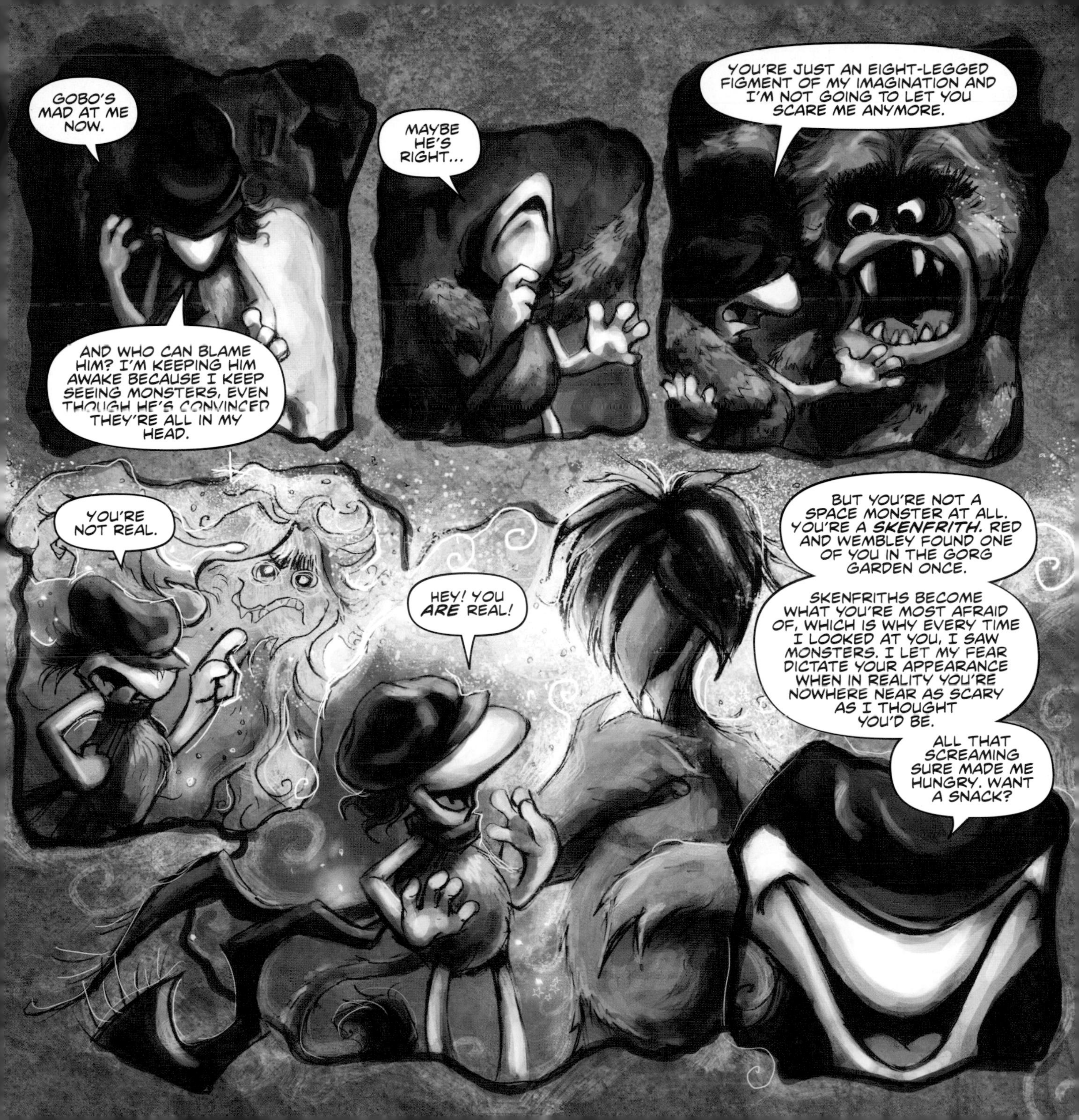
GOBO'S MAD AT ME NOW.
AND WHO CAN BLAME HIM? I'M KEEPING HIM AWAKE BECAUSE I KEEP SEEING MONSTERS, EVEN THOUGH HE'S CONVINCED THEY'RE ALL IN MY HEAD.
MAYBE HE'S RIGHT...
YOU'RE JUST AN EIGHT-LEGGED FIGMENT OF MY IMAGINATION AND I'M NOT GOING TO LET YOU SCARE ME ANYMORE.
YOU'RE NOT REAL.
HEY! YOU *ARE* REAL!
BUT YOU'RE NOT A SPACE MONSTER AT ALL. YOU'RE A *SKENFRITH.* RED AND WEMBLEY FOUND ONE OF YOU IN THE GORG GARDEN ONCE.
SKENFRITHS BECOME WHAT YOU'RE MOST AFRAID OF, WHICH IS WHY EVERY TIME I LOOKED AT YOU, I SAW MONSTERS. I LET MY FEAR DICTATE YOUR APPEARANCE WHEN IN REALITY YOU'RE NOWHERE NEAR AS SCARY AS I THOUGHT YOU'D BE.
ALL THAT SCREAMING SURE MADE ME HUNGRY. WANT A SNACK?

A SHORT TIME LATER...
ARE YOU STILL AWAKE, BOOBER? I FEEL BAD THAT I YELLED AT YOU AND SCARED YOU WITH MY STORY. I WANT TO APOLOGIZE.
BOOBER?
HUNGRY.
M... M...M...
MONSTER!
SOME PEOPLE HAVE SUCH OVERACTIVE IMAGINATIONS.
END

SHOPPING WITH SILLY CREATURES

Story by Katie Strickland
Art by Lindsay Cibos

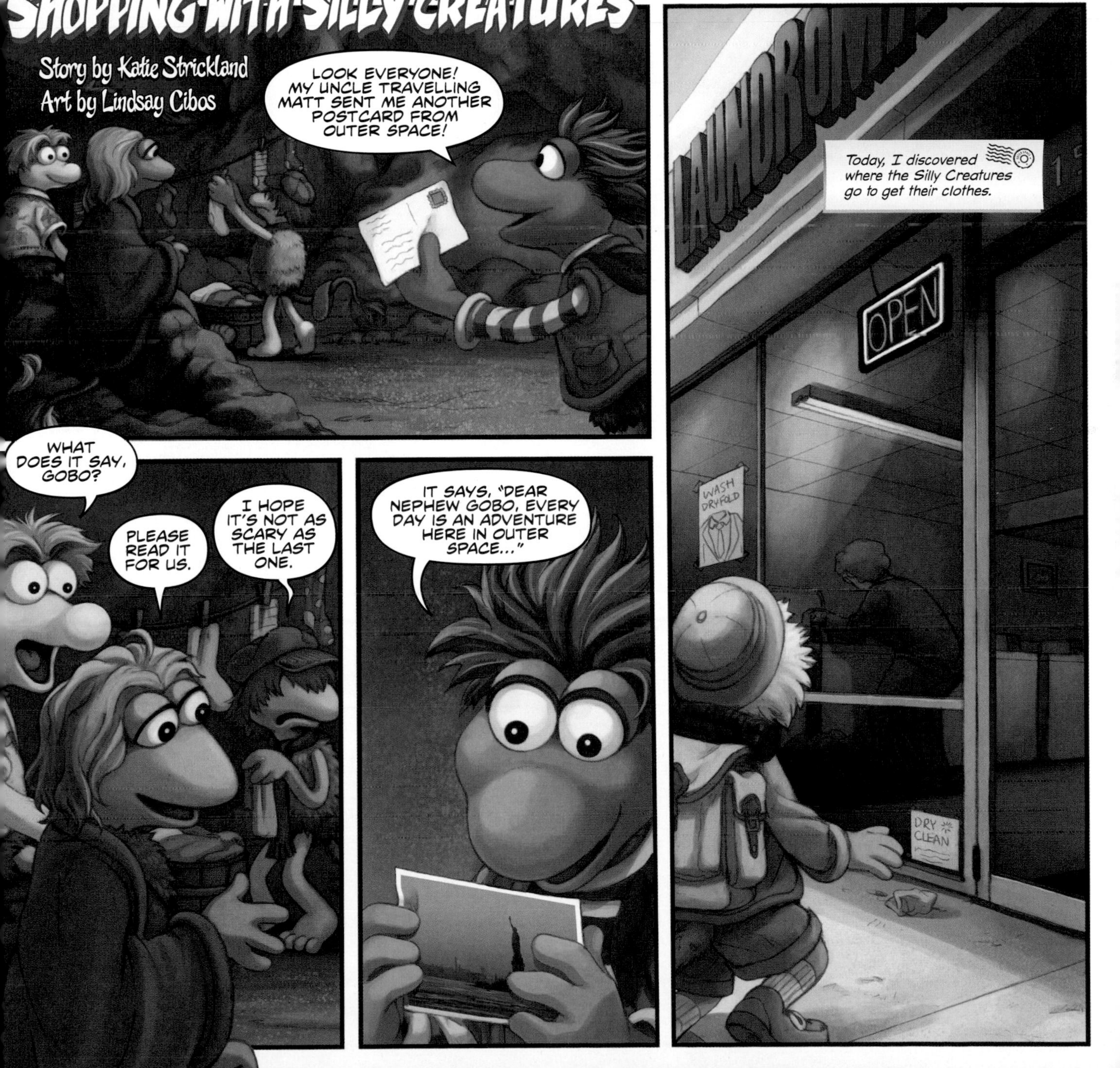
LOOK EVERYONE! MY UNCLE TRAVELLING MATT SENT ME ANOTHER POSTCARD FROM OUTER SPACE!
WHAT DOES IT SAY, GOBO?
PLEASE READ IT FOR US.
I HOPE IT'S NOT AS SCARY AS THE LAST ONE.
IT SAYS, "DEAR NEPHEW GOBO, EVERY DAY IS AN ADVENTURE HERE IN OUTER SPACE..."
Today, I discovered where the Silly Creatures go to get their clothes.
LAUNDROM
OPEN
WASH DRY FOLD
DRY CLEAN

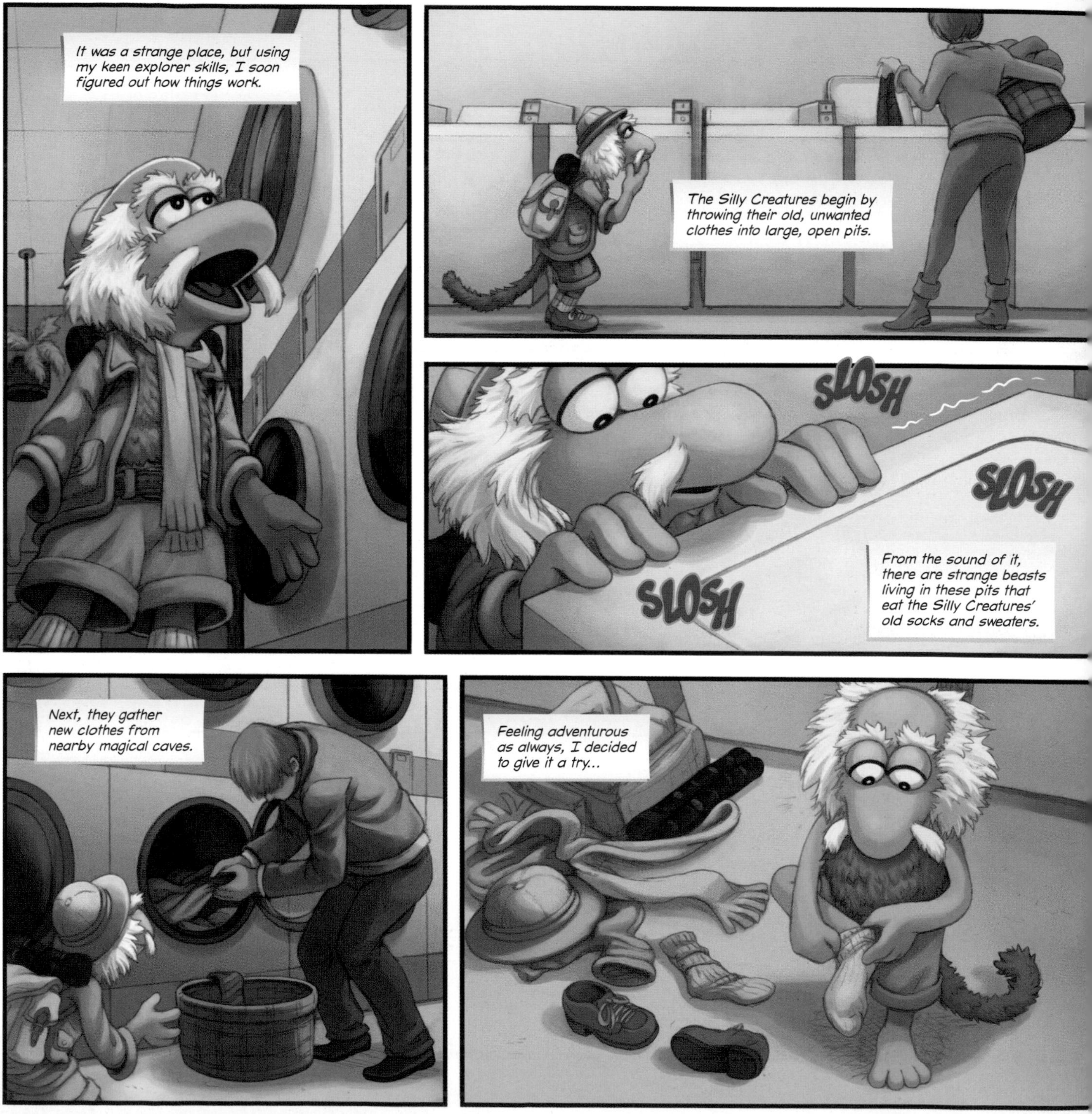
It was a strange place, but using my keen explorer skills, I soon figured out how things work.
The Silly Creatures begin by throwing their old, unwanted clothes into large, open pits.
SLOSH
SLOSH
SLOSH
From the sound of it, there are strange beasts living in these pits that eat the Silly Creatures' old socks and sweaters.
Next, they gather new clothes from nearby magical caves.
Feeling adventurous as always, I decided to give it a try...

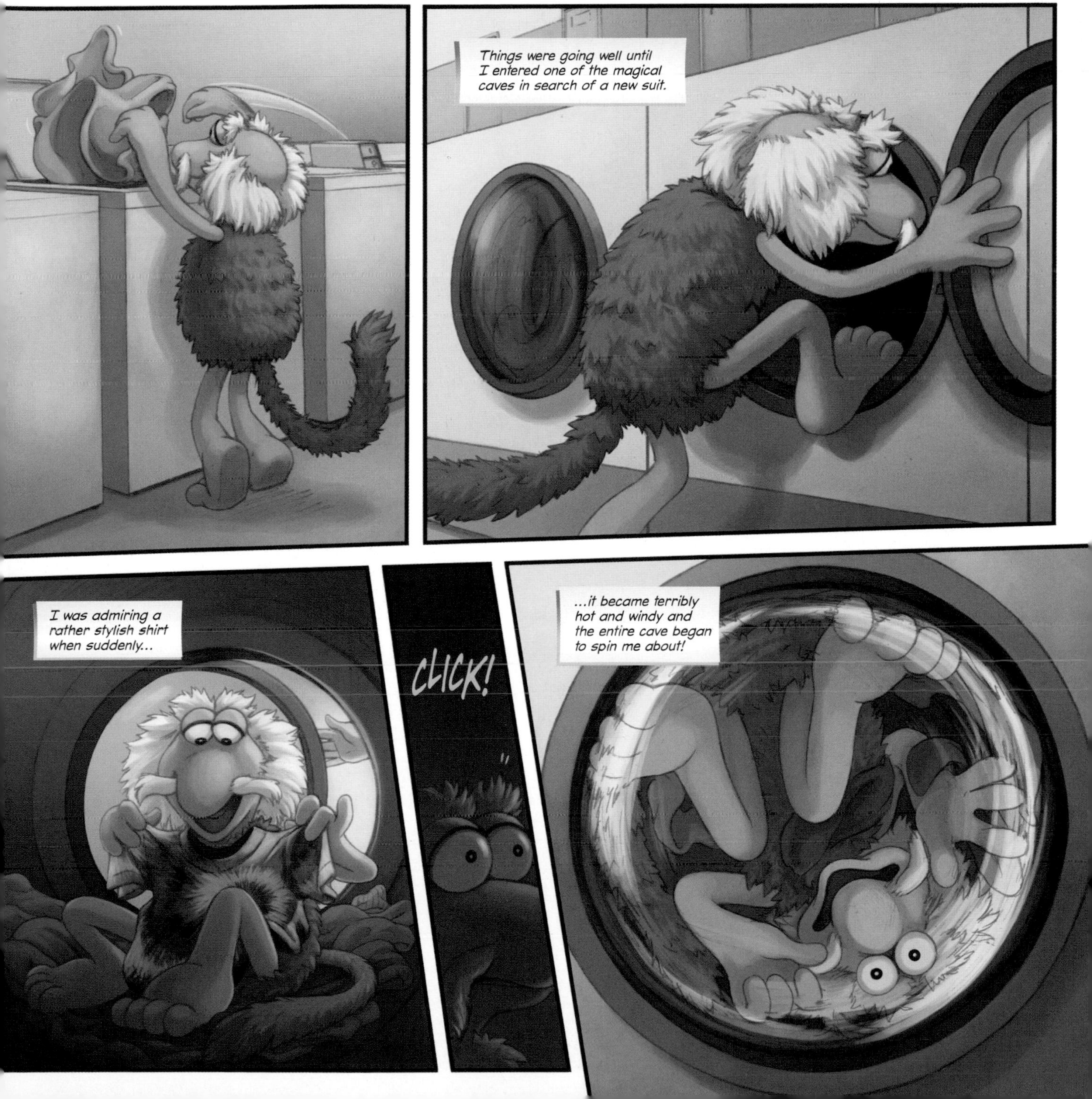
Things were going well until I entered one of the magical caves in search of a new suit.
I was admiring a rather stylish shirt when suddenly...
CLICK!
...it became terribly hot and windy and the entire cave began to spin me about!

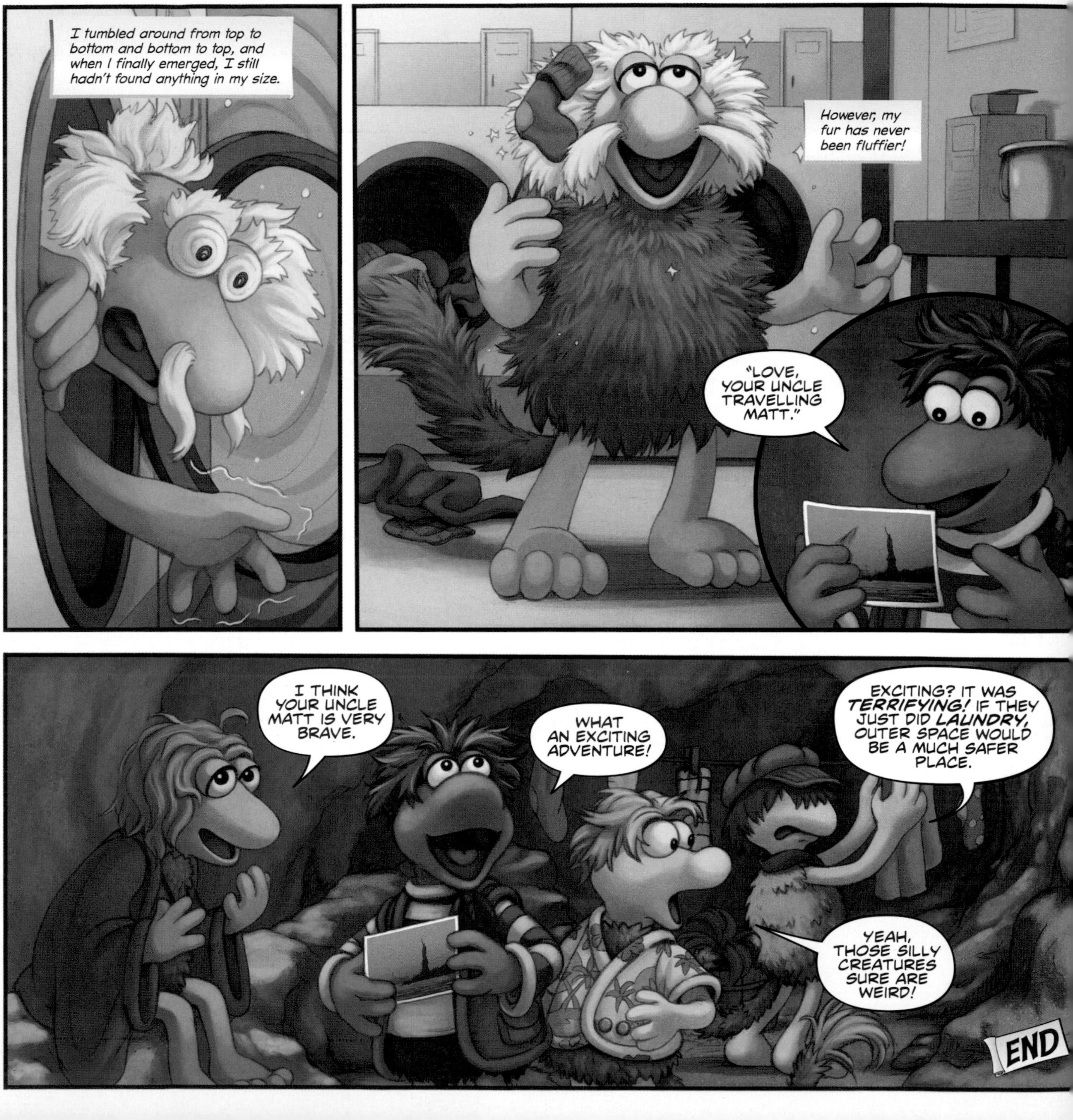

I tumbled around from top to bottom and bottom to top, and when I finally emerged, I still hadn't found anything in my size.
However, my fur has never been fluffier!
"LOVE, YOUR UNCLE TRAVELLING MATT."
I THINK YOUR UNCLE MATT IS VERY BRAVE.
WHAT AN EXCITING ADVENTURE!
EXCITING? IT WAS TERRIFYING! IF THEY JUST DID LAUNDRY, OUTER SPACE WOULD BE A MUCH SAFER PLACE.
YEAH, THOSE SILLY CREATURES SURE ARE WEIRD!
END

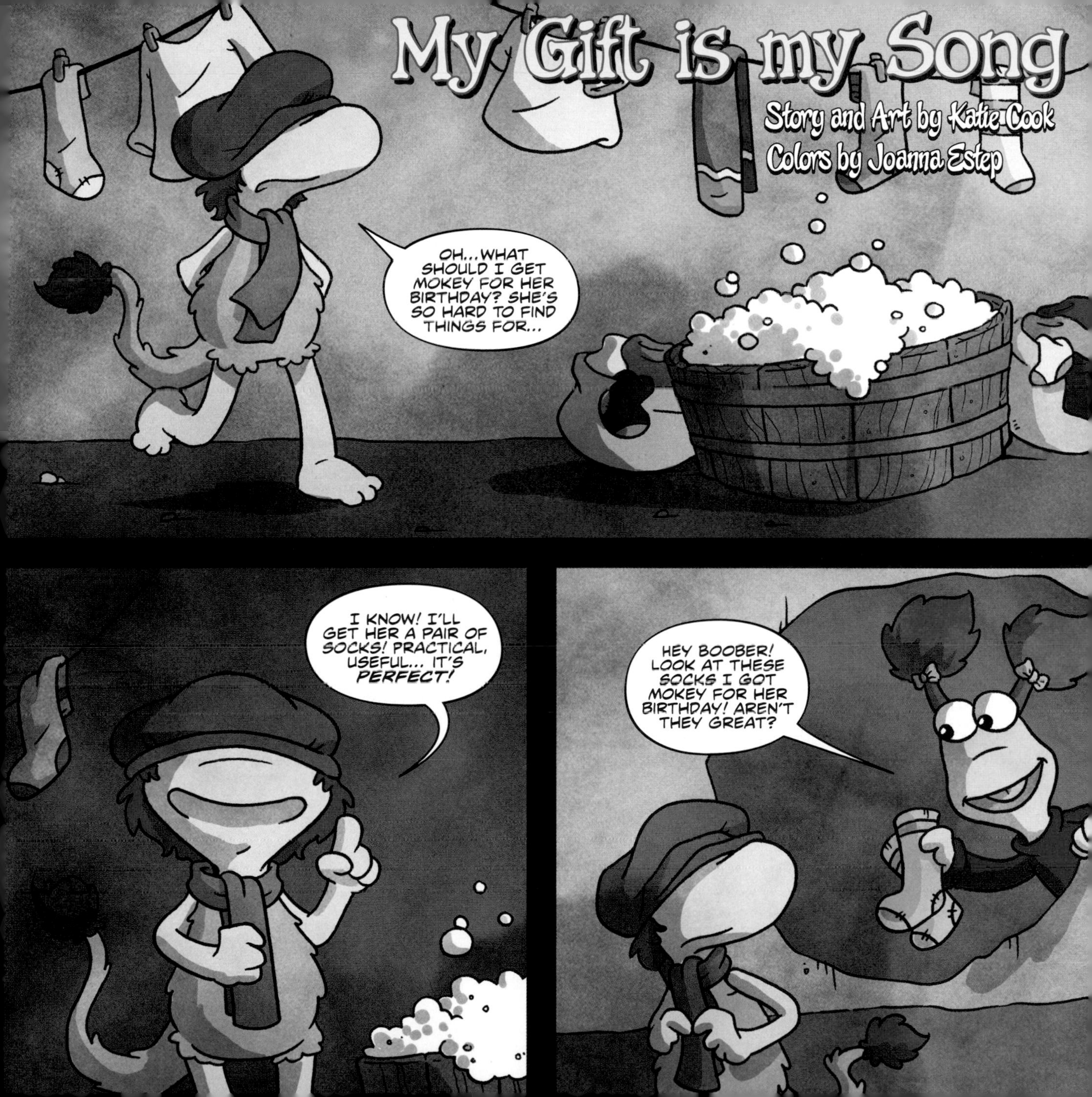

My Gift is my Song
Story and Art by Katie Cook
Colors by Joanna Estep
OH...WHAT SHOULD I GET MOKEY FOR HER BIRTHDAY? SHE'S SO HARD TO FIND THINGS FOR...
I KNOW! I'LL GET HER A PAIR OF SOCKS! PRACTICAL, USEFUL... IT'S *PERFECT!*
HEY BOOBER! LOOK AT THESE SOCKS I GOT MOKEY FOR HER BIRTHDAY! AREN'T THEY GREAT?

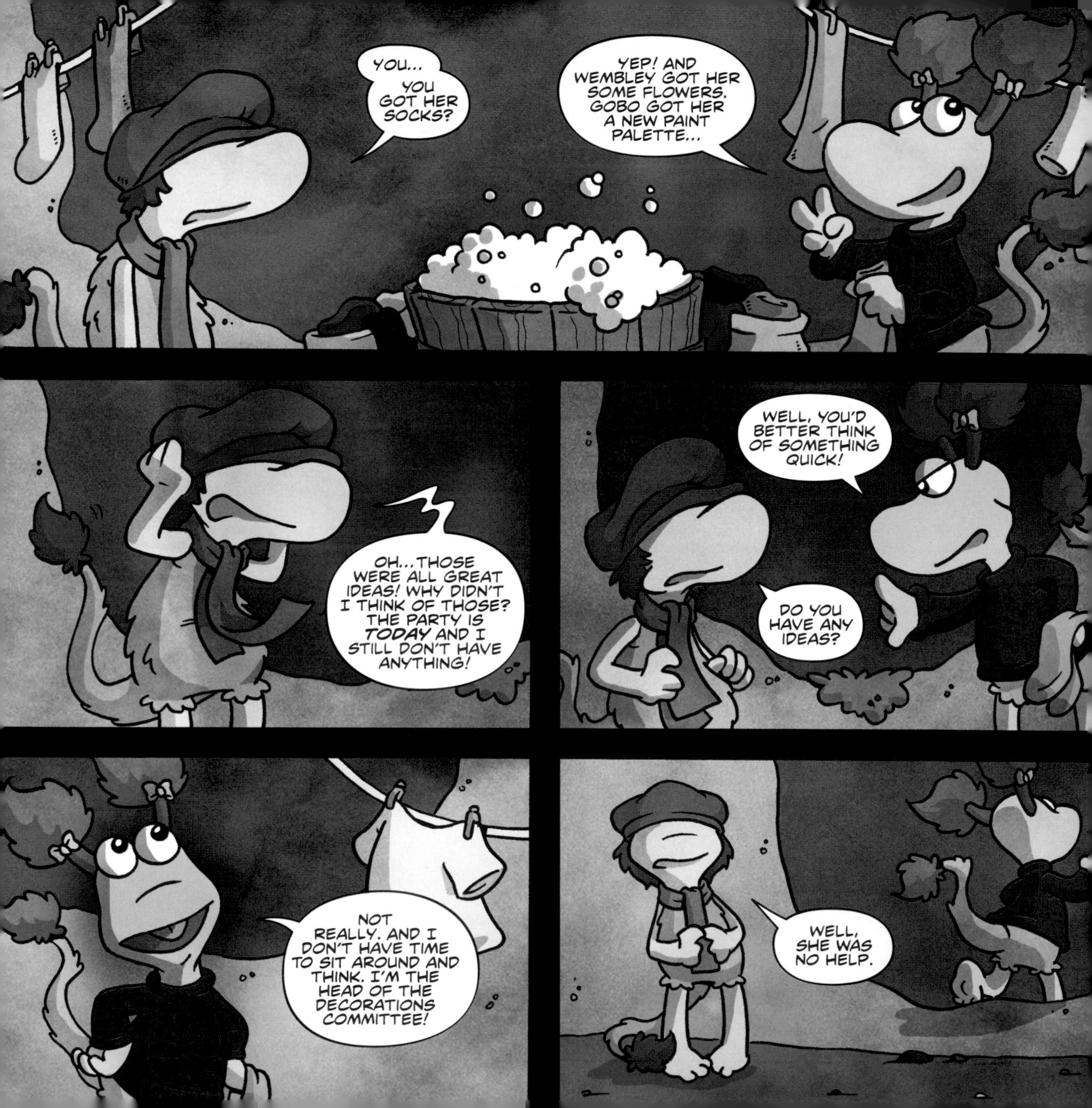
YOU... YOU GOT HER SOCKS?
YEP! AND WEMBLEY GOT HER SOME FLOWERS. GOBO GOT HER A NEW PAINT PALETTE...
OH...THOSE WERE ALL GREAT IDEAS! WHY DIDN'T I THINK OF THOSE? THE PARTY IS *TODAY* AND I STILL DON'T HAVE ANYTHING!
WELL, YOU'D BETTER THINK OF SOMETHING QUICK!
DO YOU HAVE ANY IDEAS?
NOT REALLY. AND I DON'T HAVE TIME TO SIT AROUND AND THINK. I'M THE HEAD OF THE DECORATIONS COMMITTEE!
WELL, SHE WAS NO HELP.

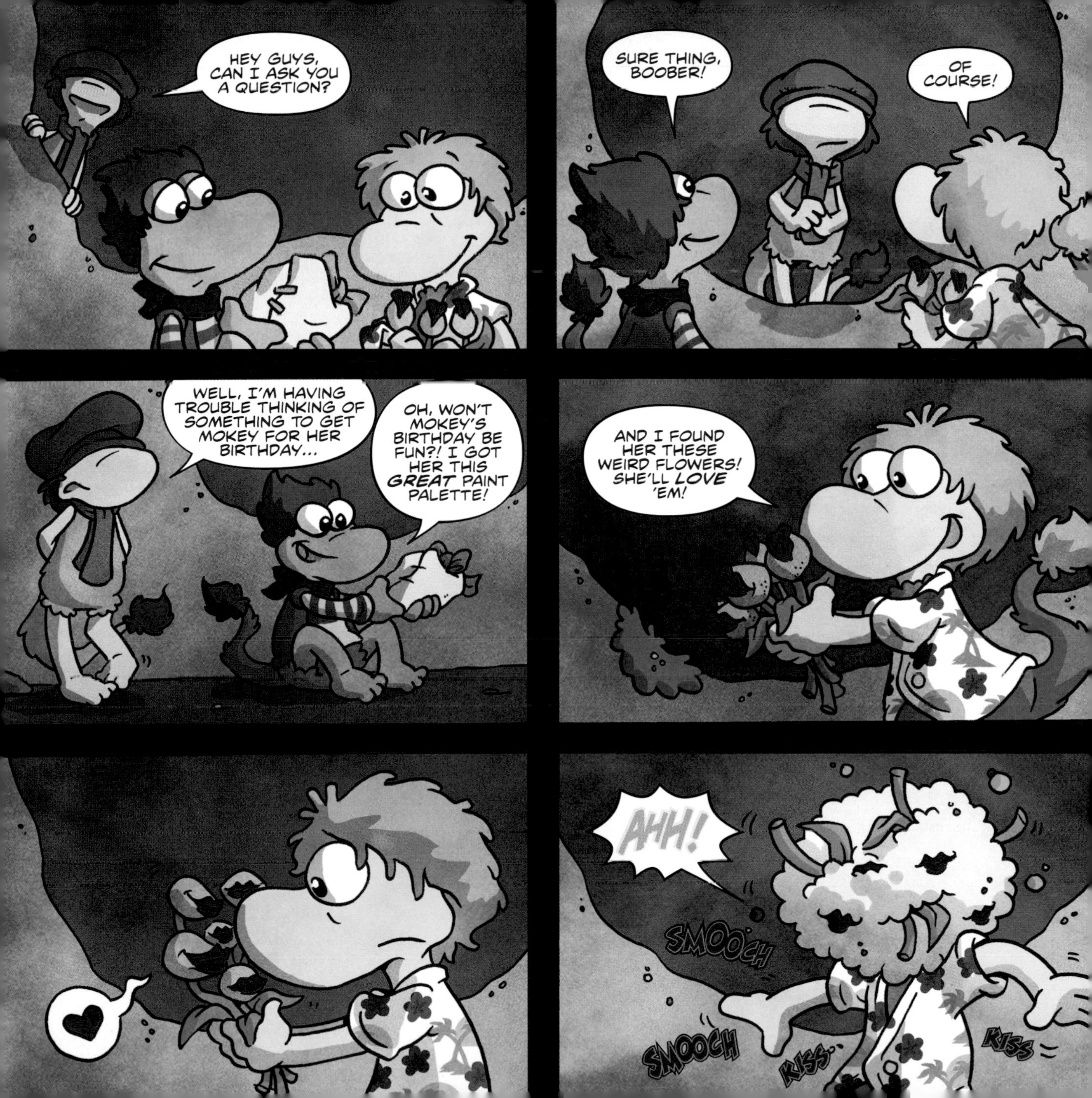
HEY GUYS, CAN I ASK YOU A QUESTION?
SURE THING, BOOBER!
OF COURSE!
WELL, I'M HAVING TROUBLE THINKING OF SOMETHING TO GET MOKEY FOR HER BIRTHDAY...
OH, WON'T MOKEY'S BIRTHDAY BE FUN?! I GOT HER THIS GREAT PAINT PALETTE!
AND I FOUND HER THESE WEIRD FLOWERS! SHE'LL LOVE 'EM!
AHH!
SMOOCH
SMOOCH
KISS
KISS

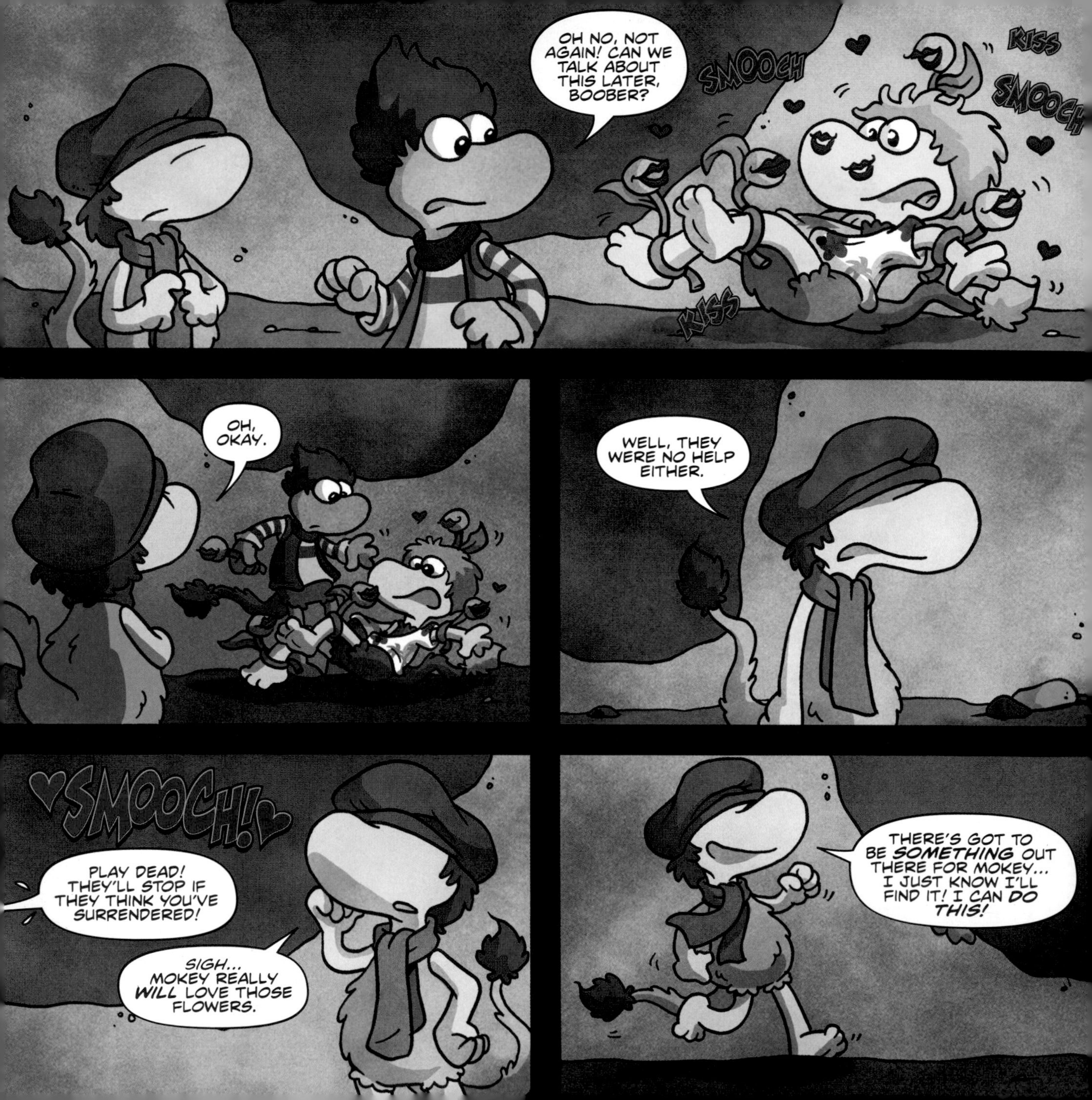
OH NO, NOT AGAIN! CAN WE TALK ABOUT THIS LATER, BOOBER?
SMOOCH
KISS
SMOOCH
KISS
OH, OKAY.
WELL, THEY WERE NO HELP EITHER.
SMOOCH!
PLAY DEAD! THEY'LL STOP IF THEY THINK YOU'VE SURRENDERED!
SIGH... MOKEY REALLY WILL LOVE THOSE FLOWERS.
THERE'S GOT TO BE SOMETHING OUT THERE FOR MOKEY... I JUST KNOW I'LL FIND IT! I CAN DO THIS!

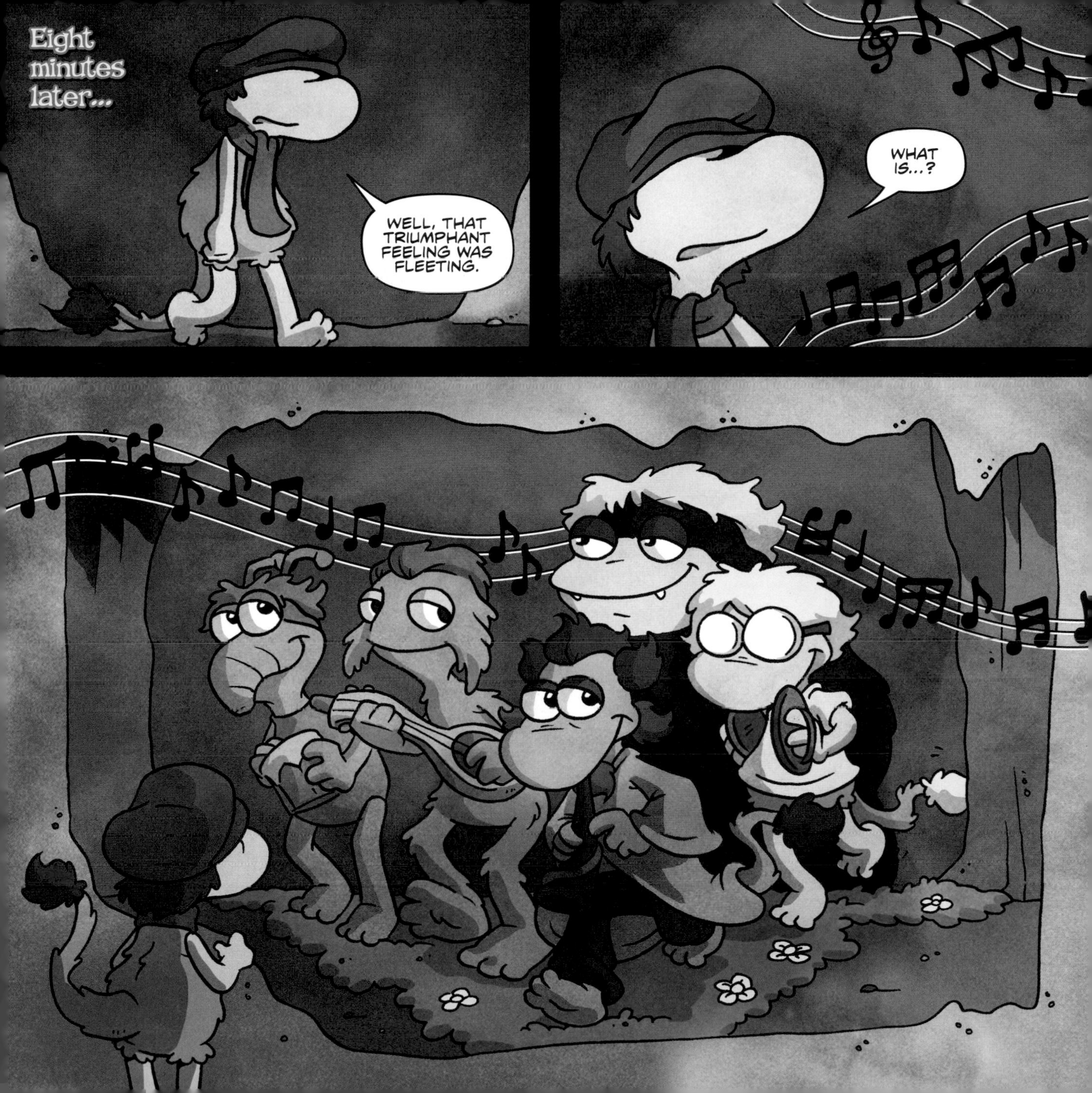
Eight minutes later...
WELL, THAT TRIUMPHANT FEELING WAS FLEETING.
WHAT IS...?

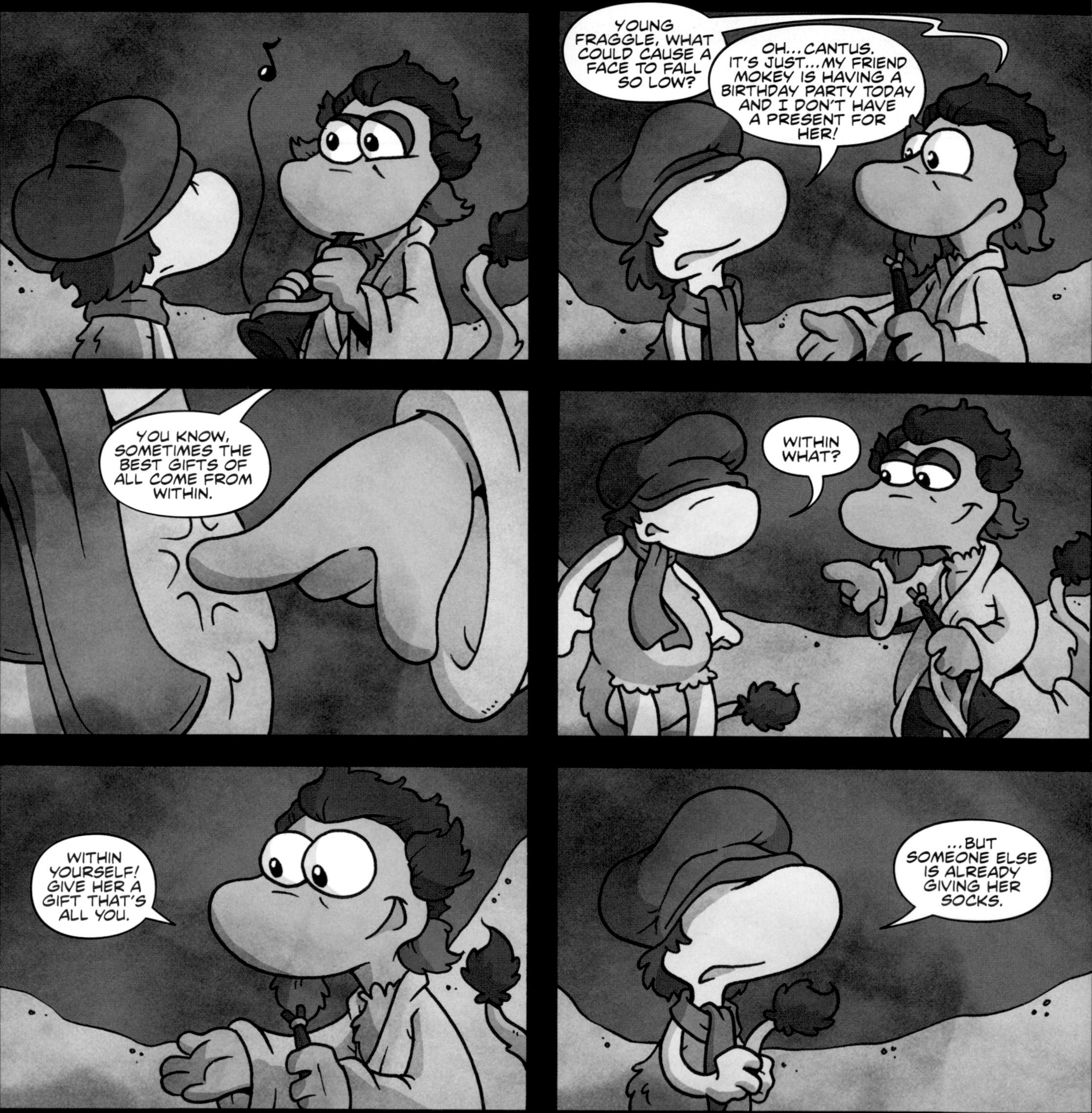
YOUNG FRAGGLE, WHAT COULD CAUSE A FACE TO FALL SO LOW?
OH...CANTUS. IT'S JUST...MY FRIEND MOKEY IS HAVING A BIRTHDAY PARTY TODAY AND I DON'T HAVE A PRESENT FOR HER!
YOU KNOW, SOMETIMES THE BEST GIFTS OF ALL COME FROM WITHIN.
WITHIN WHAT?
WITHIN YOURSELF! GIVE HER A GIFT THAT'S ALL YOU.
...BUT SOMEONE ELSE IS ALREADY GIVING HER SOCKS.

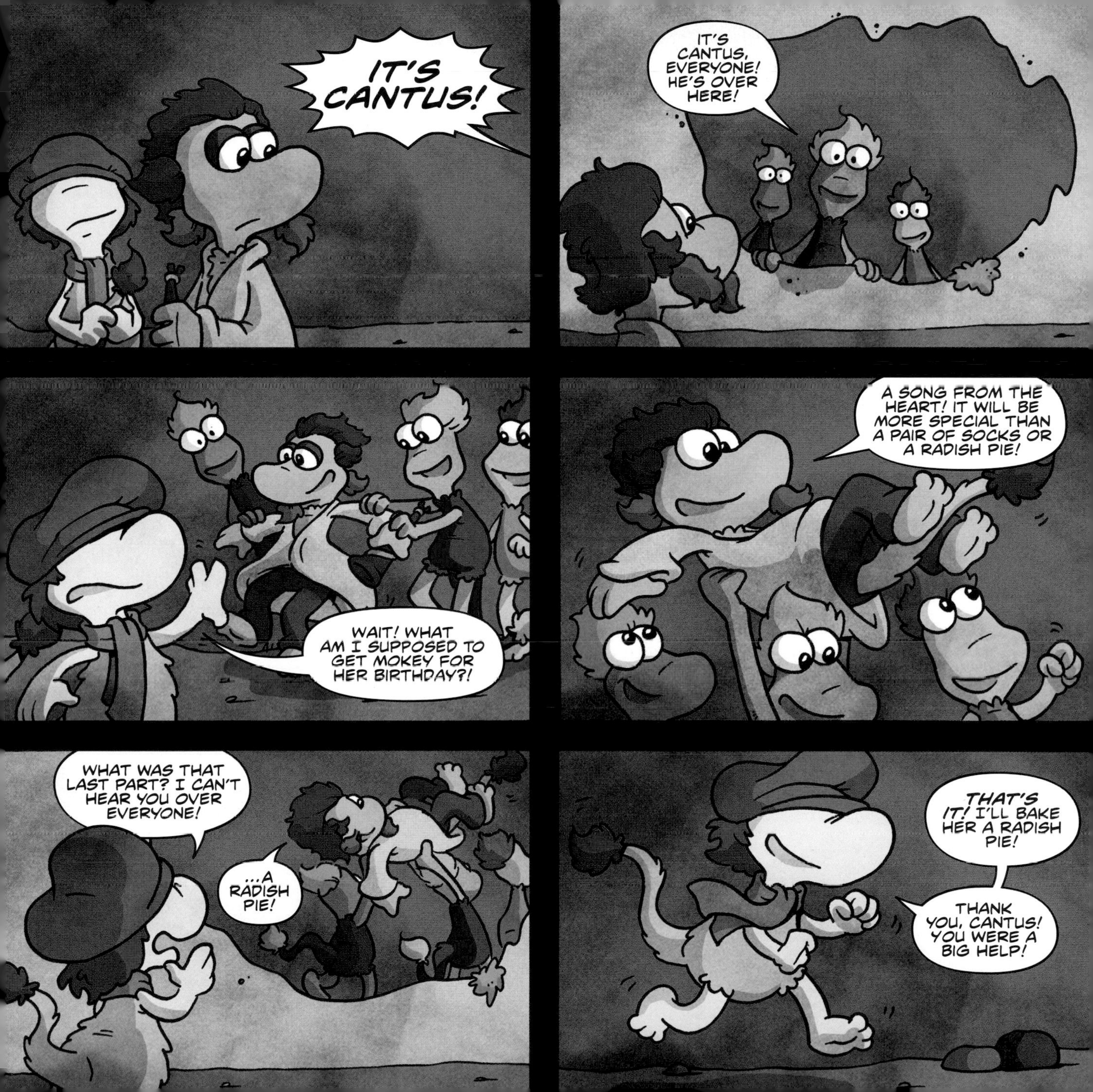
IT'S CANTUS!
IT'S CANTUS, EVERYONE! HE'S OVER HERE!
WAIT! WHAT AM I SUPPOSED TO GET MOKEY FOR HER BIRTHDAY?!
A SONG FROM THE HEART! IT WILL BE MORE SPECIAL THAN A PAIR OF SOCKS OR A RADISH PIE!
WHAT WAS THAT LAST PART? I CAN'T HEAR YOU OVER EVERYONE!
...A RADISH PIE!
THAT'S IT! I'LL BAKE HER A RADISH PIE!
THANK YOU, CANTUS! YOU WERE A BIG HELP!

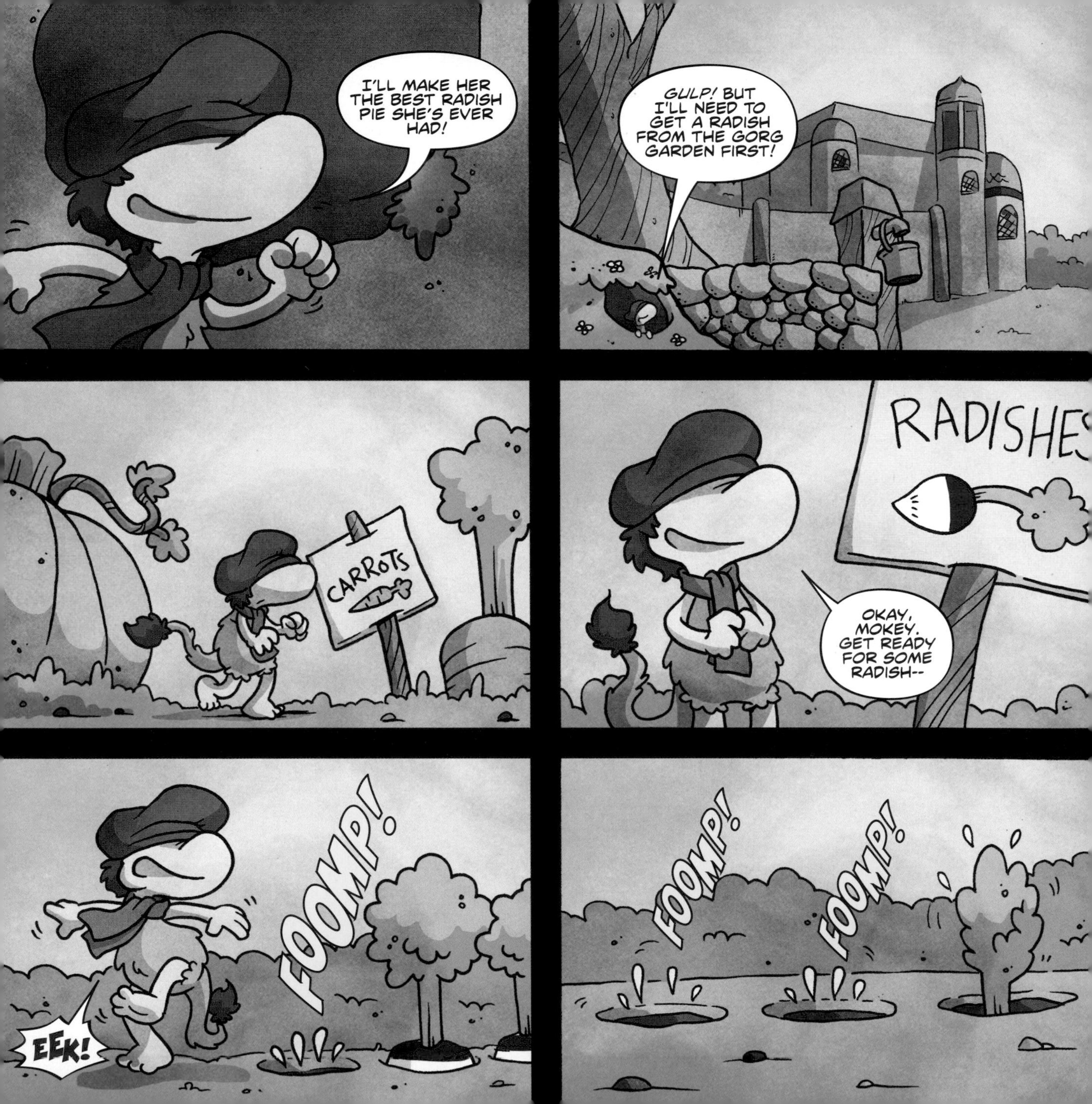
I'LL MAKE HER THE BEST RADISH PIE SHE'S EVER HAD!
GULP! BUT I'LL NEED TO GET A RADISH FROM THE GORG GARDEN FIRST!
CARROTS
RADISHES
OKAY, MOKEY. GET READY FOR SOME RADISH--
FOOMP!
EEK!
FOOMP!
FOOMP!

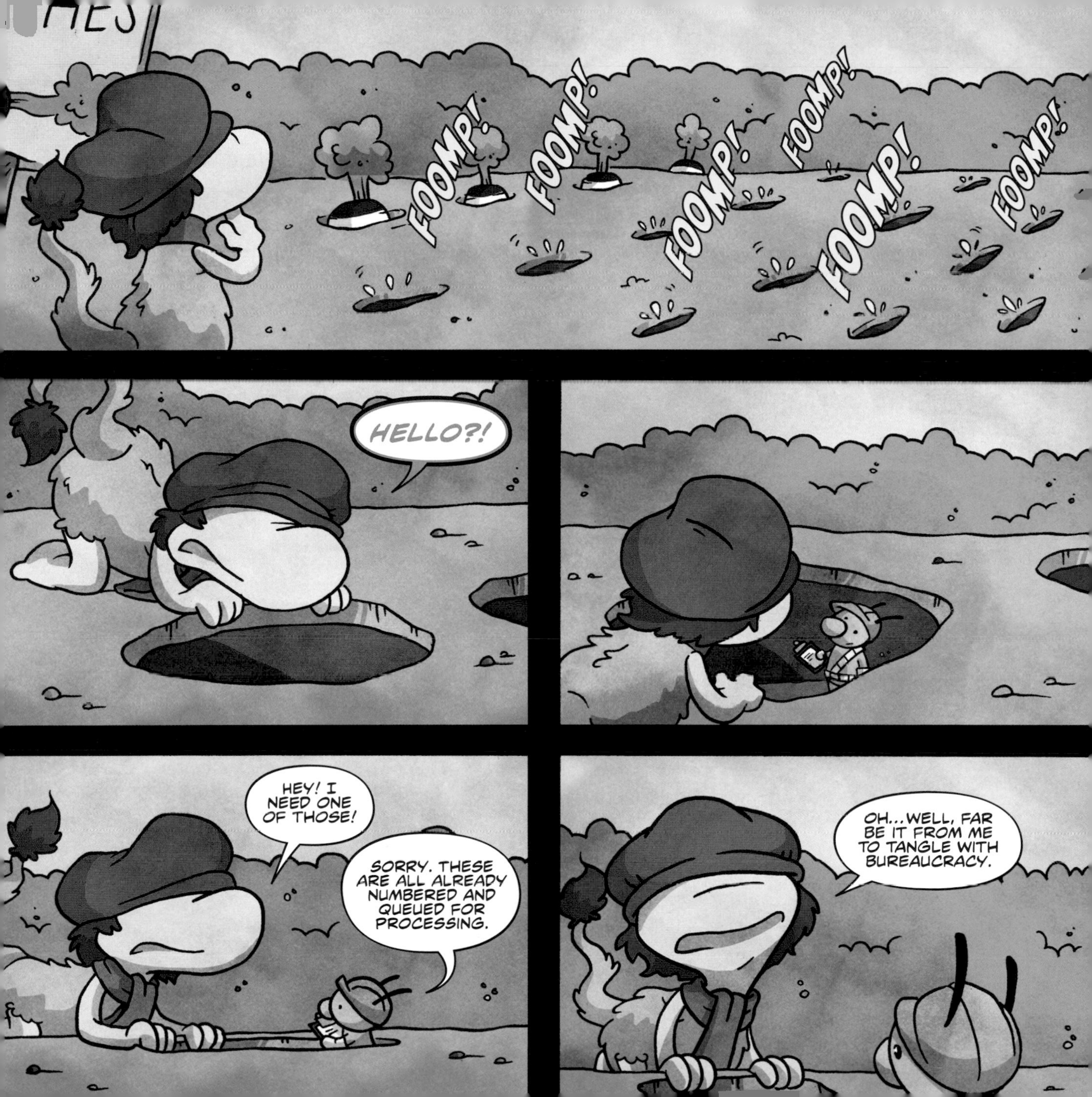

FOOMP!
FOOMP!
FOOMP!
FOOMP!
FOOMP!
FOOMP!
HELLO?!
HEY! I NEED ONE OF THOSE!
SORRY. THESE ARE ALL ALREADY NUMBERED AND QUEUED FOR PROCESSING.
OH...WELL, FAR BE IT FROM ME TO TANGLE WITH BUREAUCRACY.

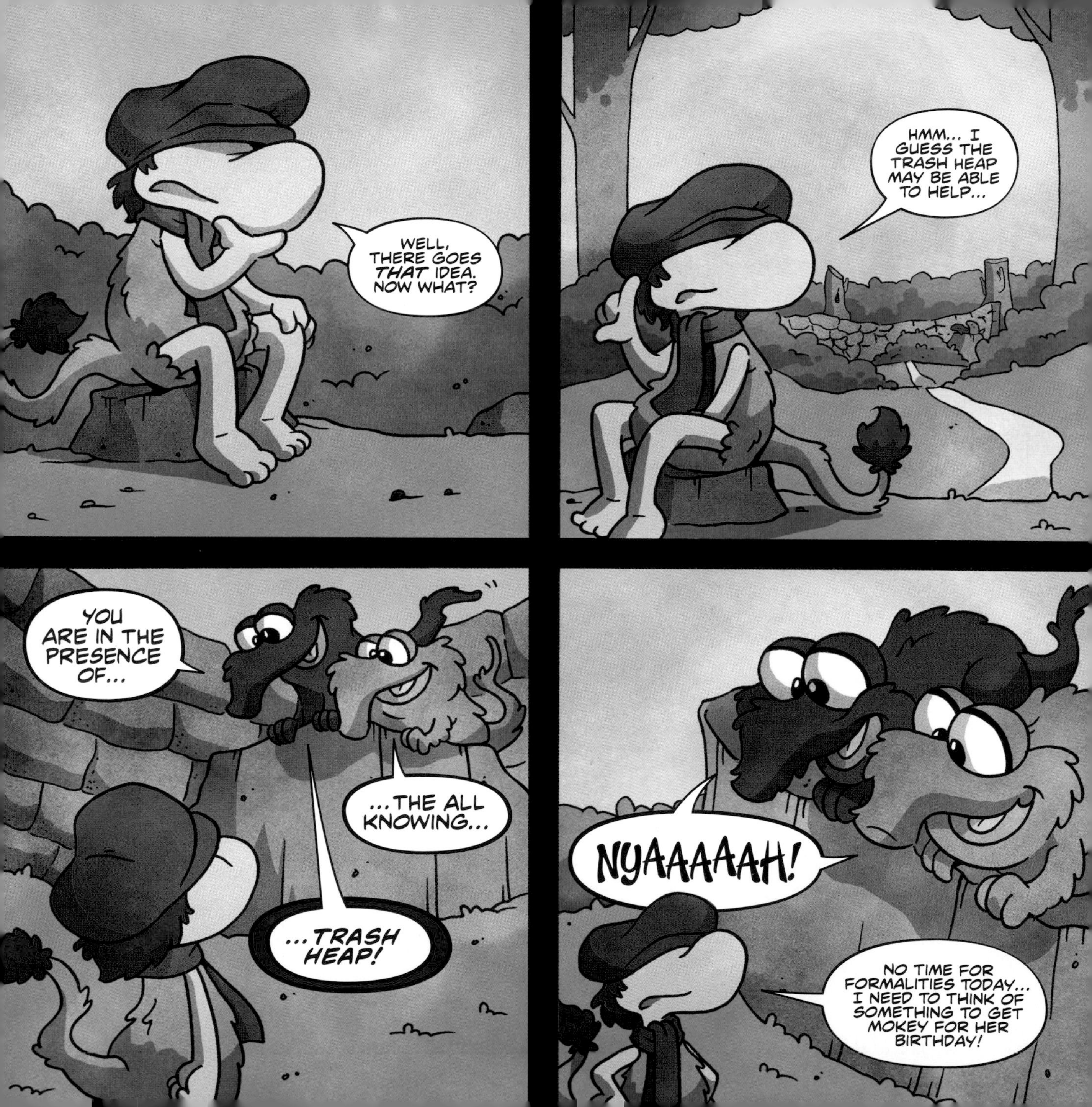
WELL, THERE GOES *THAT* IDEA. NOW WHAT?
HMM... I GUESS THE TRASH HEAP MAY BE ABLE TO HELP...
YOU ARE IN THE PRESENCE OF...
...THE ALL KNOWING...
...TRASH HEAP!
NYAAAAAH!
NO TIME FOR FORMALITIES TODAY... I NEED TO THINK OF SOMETHING TO GET MOKEY FOR HER BIRTHDAY!

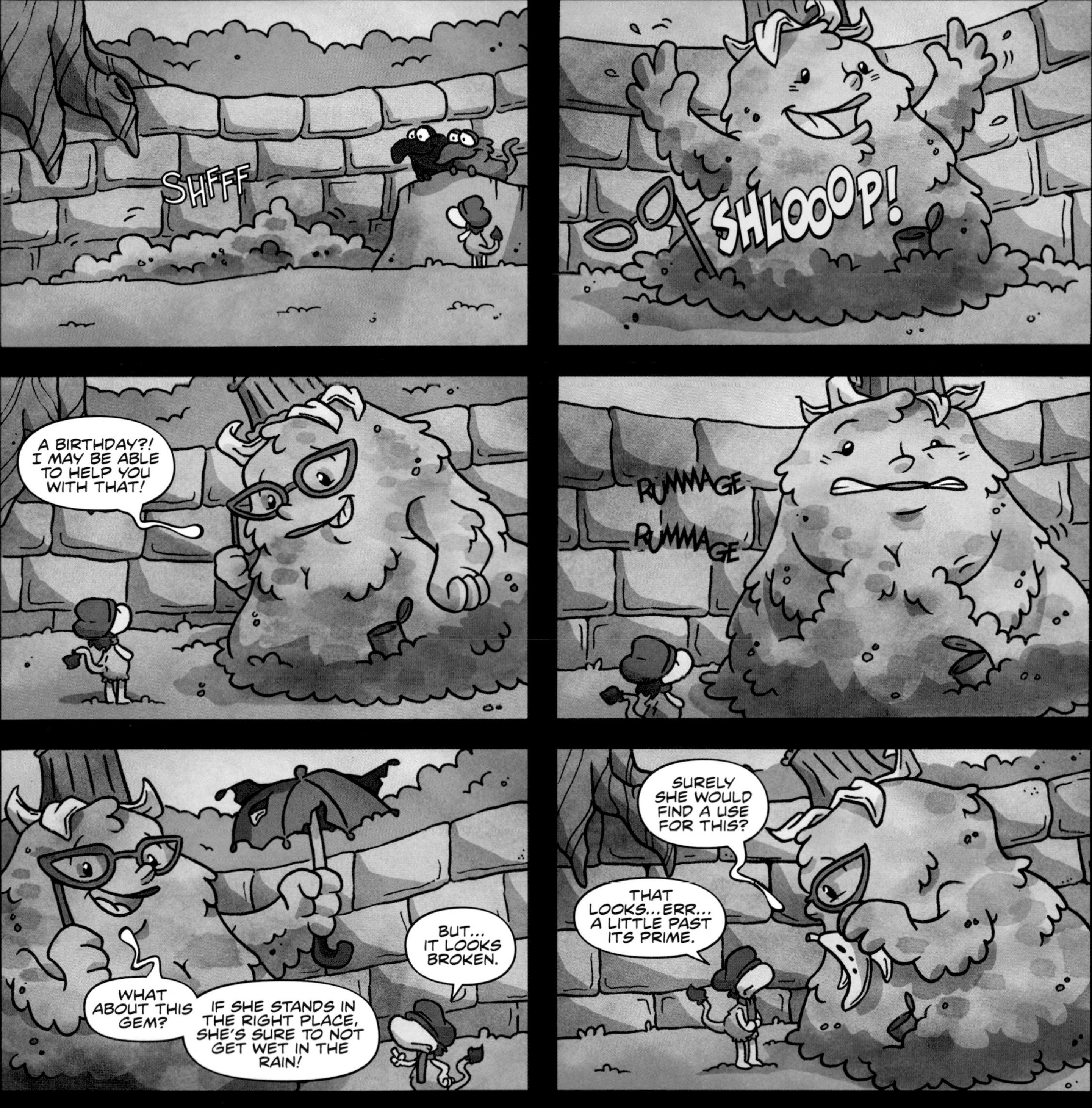
SHFFF
SHLOOOP!
A BIRTHDAY?! I MAY BE ABLE TO HELP YOU WITH THAT!
RUMMAGE
RUMMAGE
WHAT ABOUT THIS GEM?
IF SHE STANDS IN THE RIGHT PLACE, SHE'S SURE TO NOT GET WET IN THE RAIN!
BUT... IT LOOKS BROKEN.
SURELY SHE WOULD FIND A USE FOR THIS?
THAT LOOKS...ERR... A LITTLE PAST ITS PRIME.

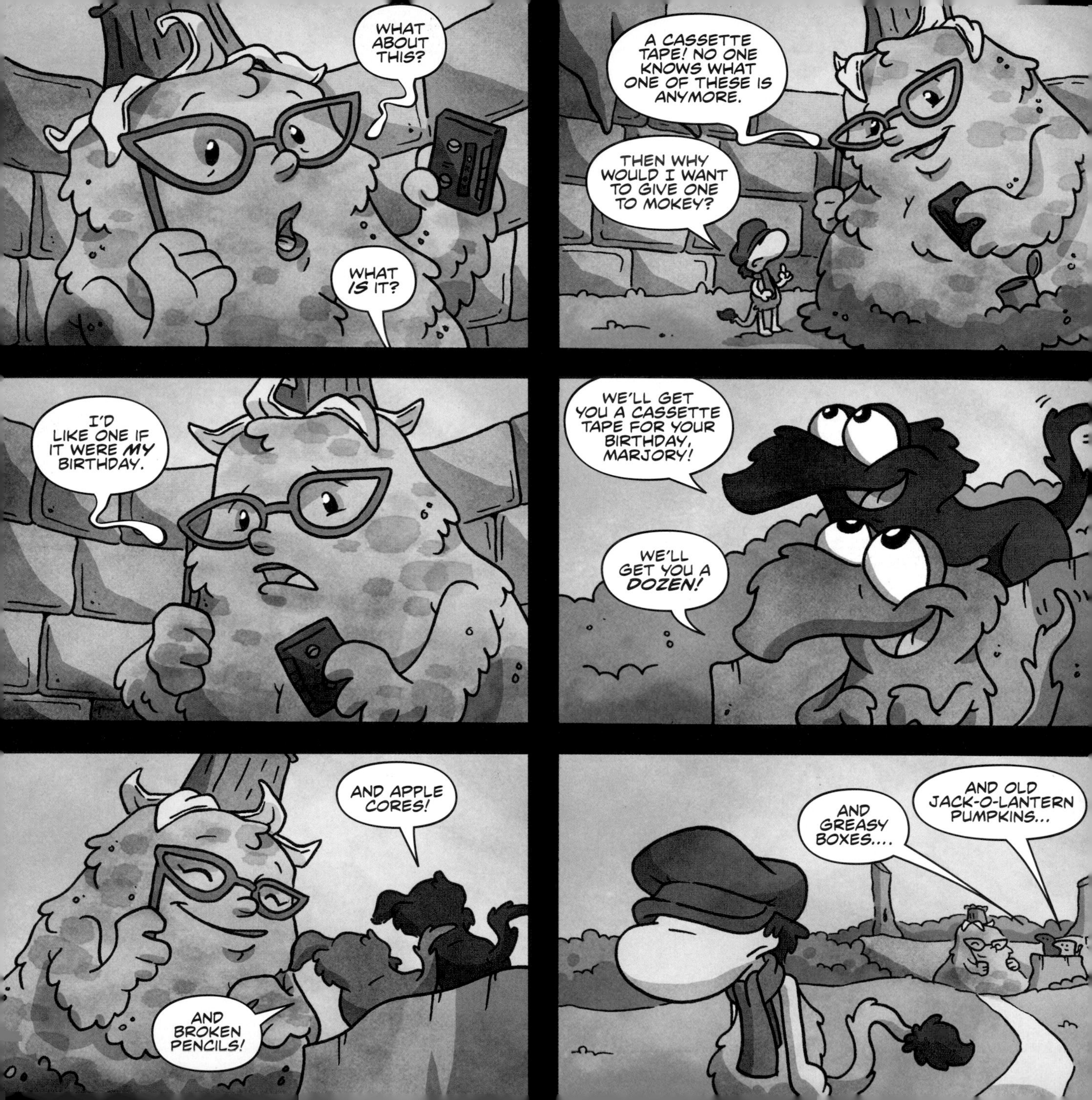
WHAT ABOUT THIS?
WHAT IS IT?
A CASSETTE TAPE! NO ONE KNOWS WHAT ONE OF THESE IS ANYMORE.
THEN WHY WOULD I WANT TO GIVE ONE TO MOKEY?
I'D LIKE ONE IF IT WERE MY BIRTHDAY.
WE'LL GET YOU A CASSETTE TAPE FOR YOUR BIRTHDAY, MARJORY!
WE'LL GET YOU A DOZEN!
AND APPLE CORES!
AND BROKEN PENCILS!
AND GREASY BOXES....
AND OLD JACK-O-LANTERN PUMPKINS...

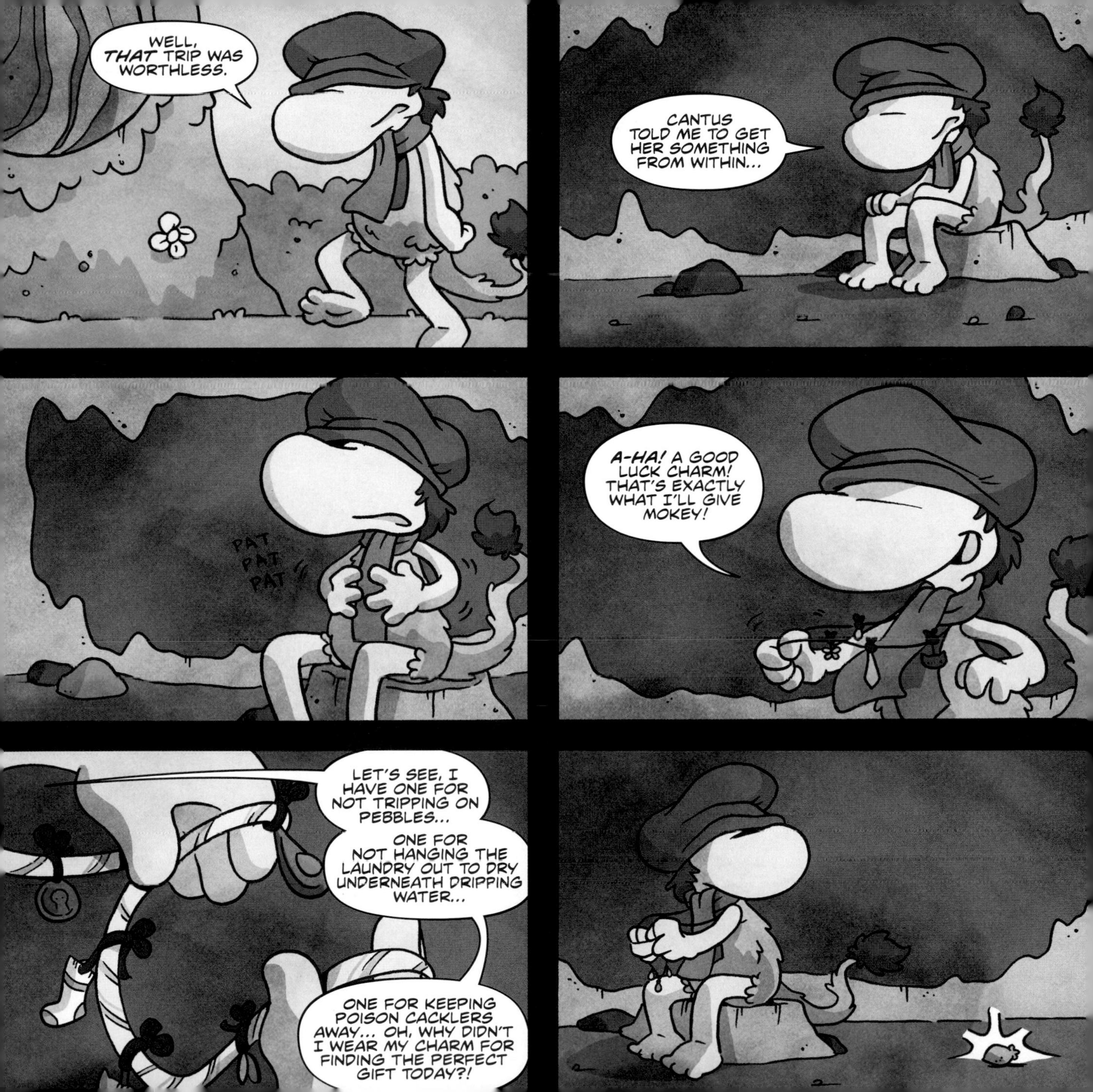
WELL, *THAT* TRIP WAS WORTHLESS.
CANTUS TOLD ME TO GET HER SOMETHING FROM WITHIN...
PAT PAT PAT
A-HA! A GOOD LUCK CHARM! THAT'S EXACTLY WHAT I'LL GIVE MOKEY!
LET'S SEE, I HAVE ONE FOR NOT TRIPPING ON PEBBLES...
ONE FOR NOT HANGING THE LAUNDRY OUT TO DRY UNDERNEATH DRIPPING WATER...
ONE FOR KEEPING POISON CACKLERS AWAY... OH, WHY DIDN'T I WEAR MY CHARM FOR FINDING THE PERFECT GIFT TODAY?!

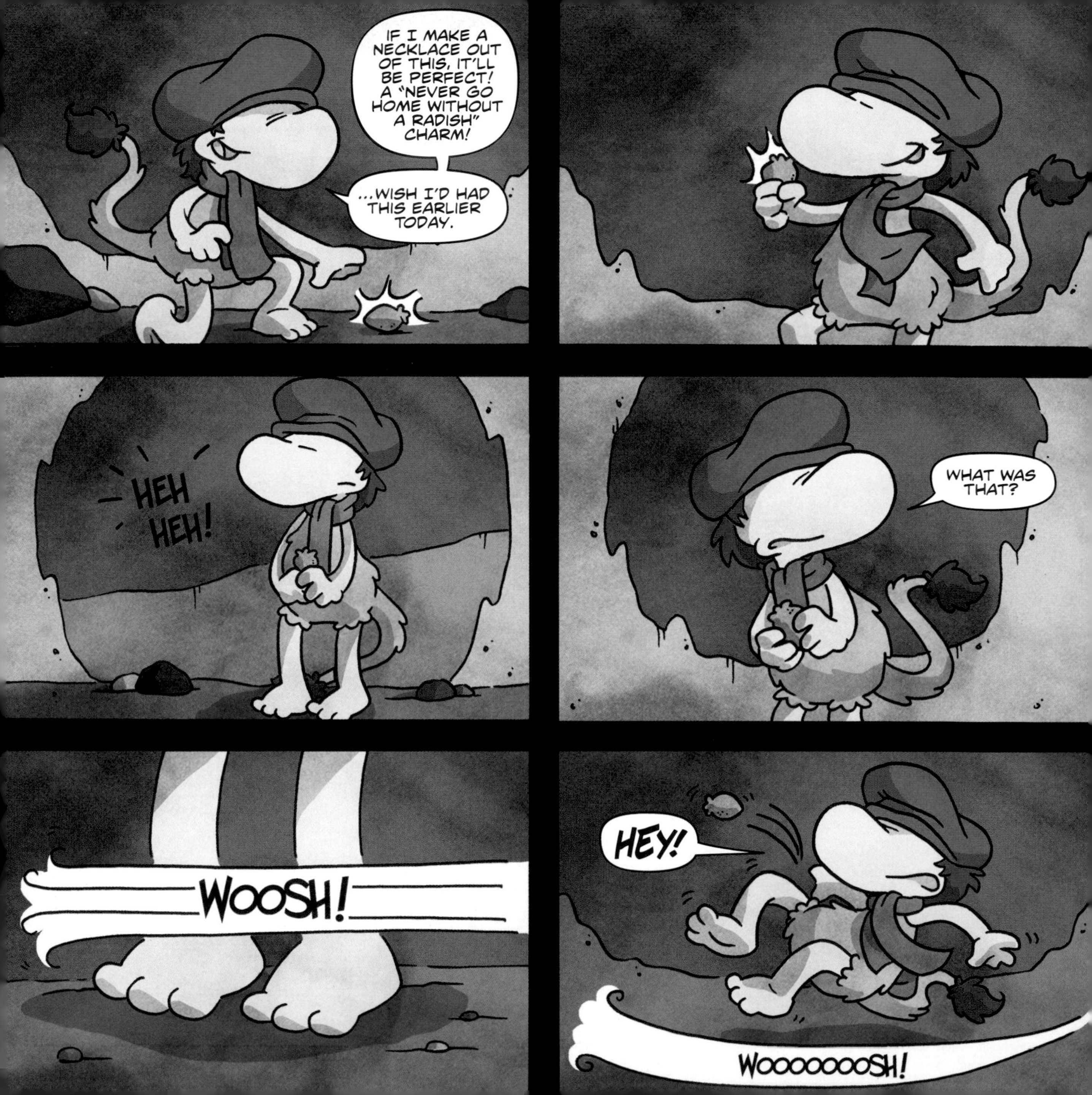
IF I MAKE A NECKLACE OUT OF THIS, IT'LL BE PERFECT! A "NEVER GO HOME WITHOUT A RADISH" CHARM!
...WISH I'D HAD THIS EARLIER TODAY.
HEH HEH!
WHAT WAS THAT?
WOOSH!
HEY!
WOOOOOOOOSH!

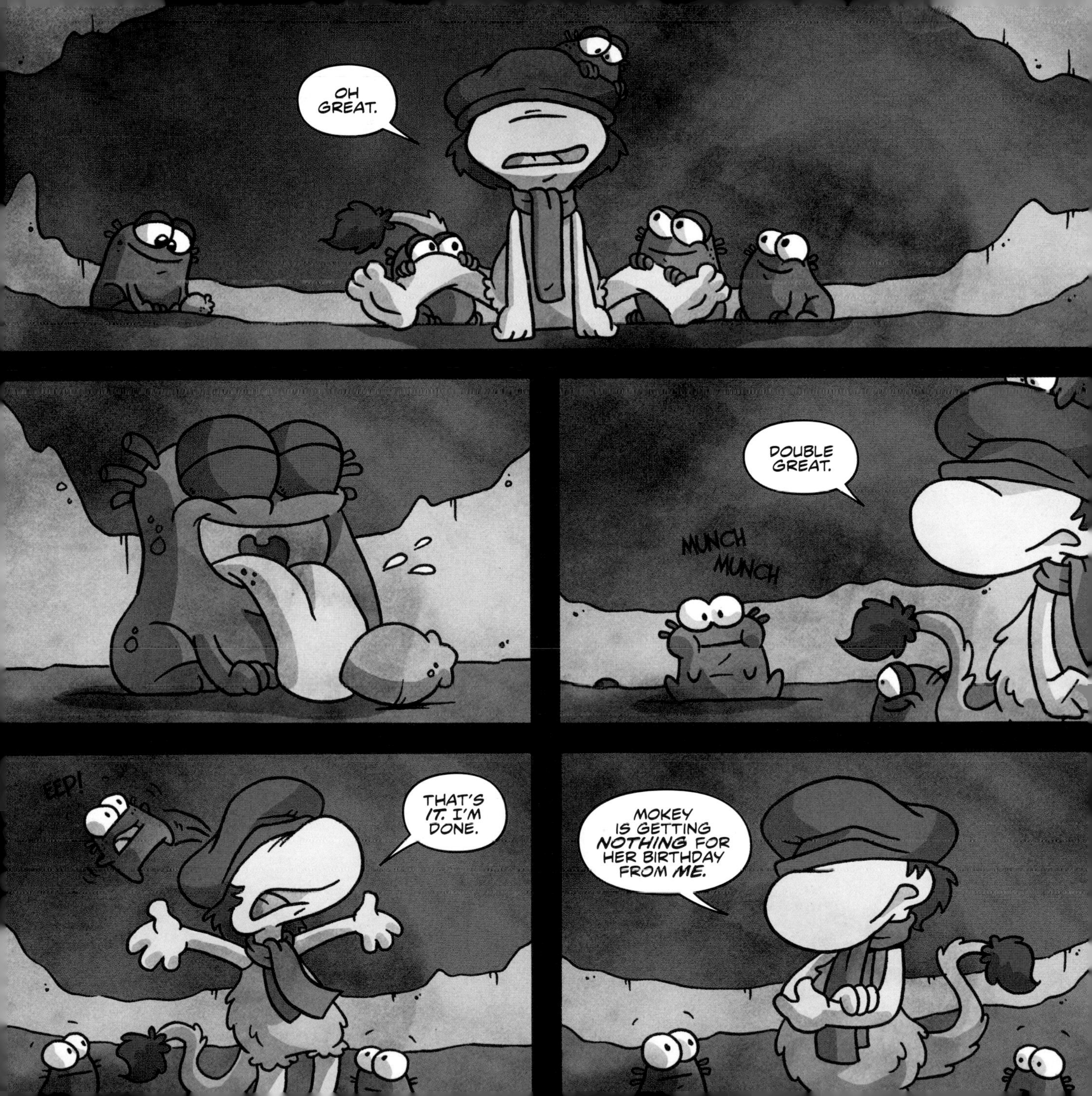
OH GREAT.
DOUBLE GREAT.
MUNCH MUNCH
EEP!
THAT'S *IT.* I'M DONE.
MOKEY IS GETTING ***NOTHING*** FOR HER BIRTHDAY FROM ***ME.***

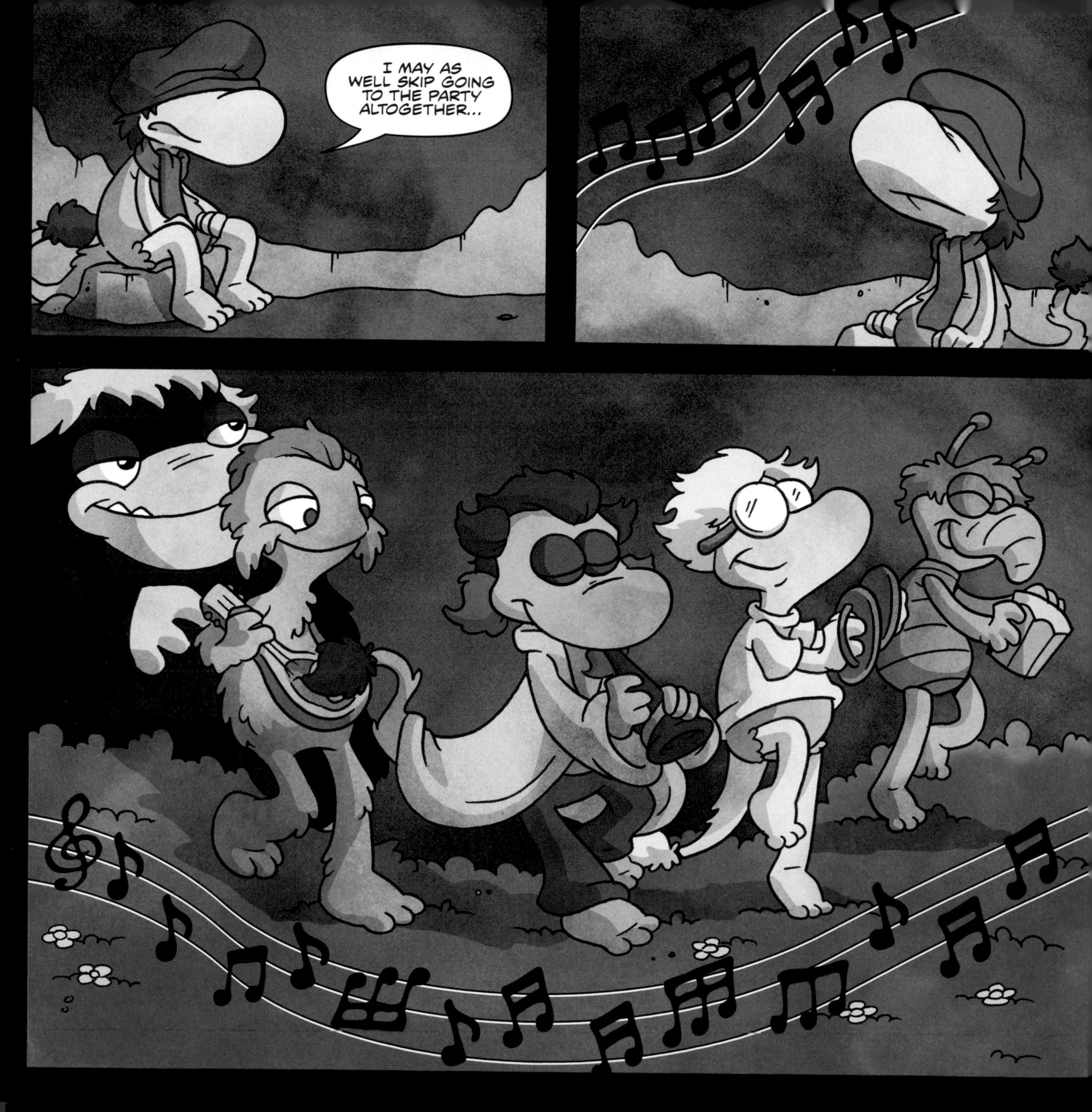
I MAY AS WELL SKIP GOING TO THE PARTY ALTOGETHER...

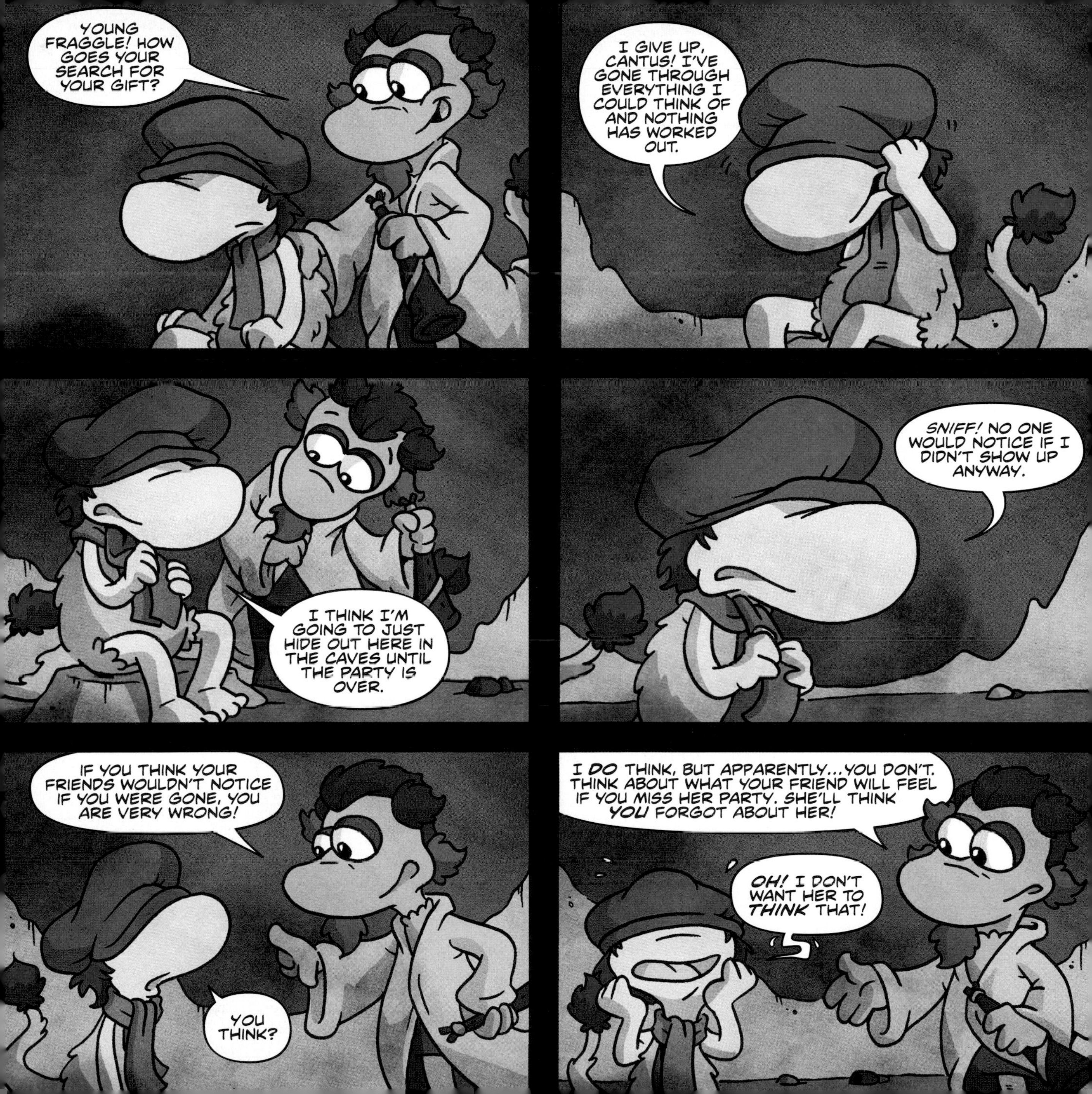
YOUNG FRAGGLE! HOW GOES YOUR SEARCH FOR YOUR GIFT?
I GIVE UP, CANTUS! I'VE GONE THROUGH EVERYTHING I COULD THINK OF AND NOTHING HAS WORKED OUT.
I THINK I'M GOING TO JUST HIDE OUT HERE IN THE CAVES UNTIL THE PARTY IS OVER.
SNIFF! NO ONE WOULD NOTICE IF I DIDN'T SHOW UP ANYWAY.
IF YOU THINK YOUR FRIENDS WOULDN'T NOTICE IF YOU WERE GONE, YOU ARE VERY WRONG!
YOU THINK?
I DO THINK, BUT APPARENTLY...YOU DON'T. THINK ABOUT WHAT YOUR FRIEND WILL FEEL IF YOU MISS HER PARTY. SHE'LL THINK YOU FORGOT ABOUT HER!
OH! I DON'T WANT HER TO THINK THAT!

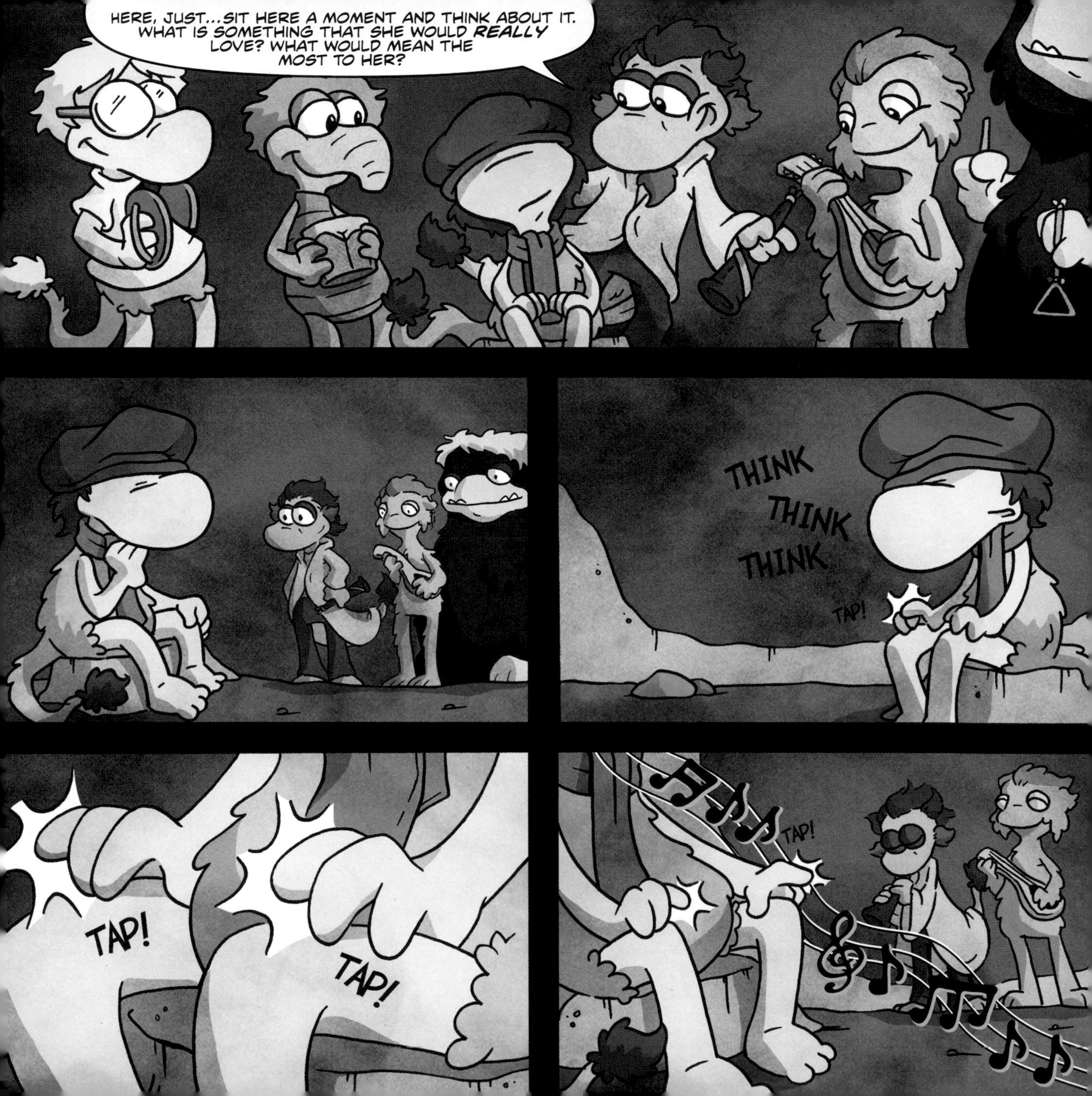
HERE, JUST...SIT HERE A MOMENT AND THINK ABOUT IT. WHAT IS SOMETHING THAT SHE WOULD *REALLY* LOVE? WHAT WOULD MEAN THE MOST TO HER?
THINK
THINK
THINK
TAP!
TAP!
TAP!
TAP!

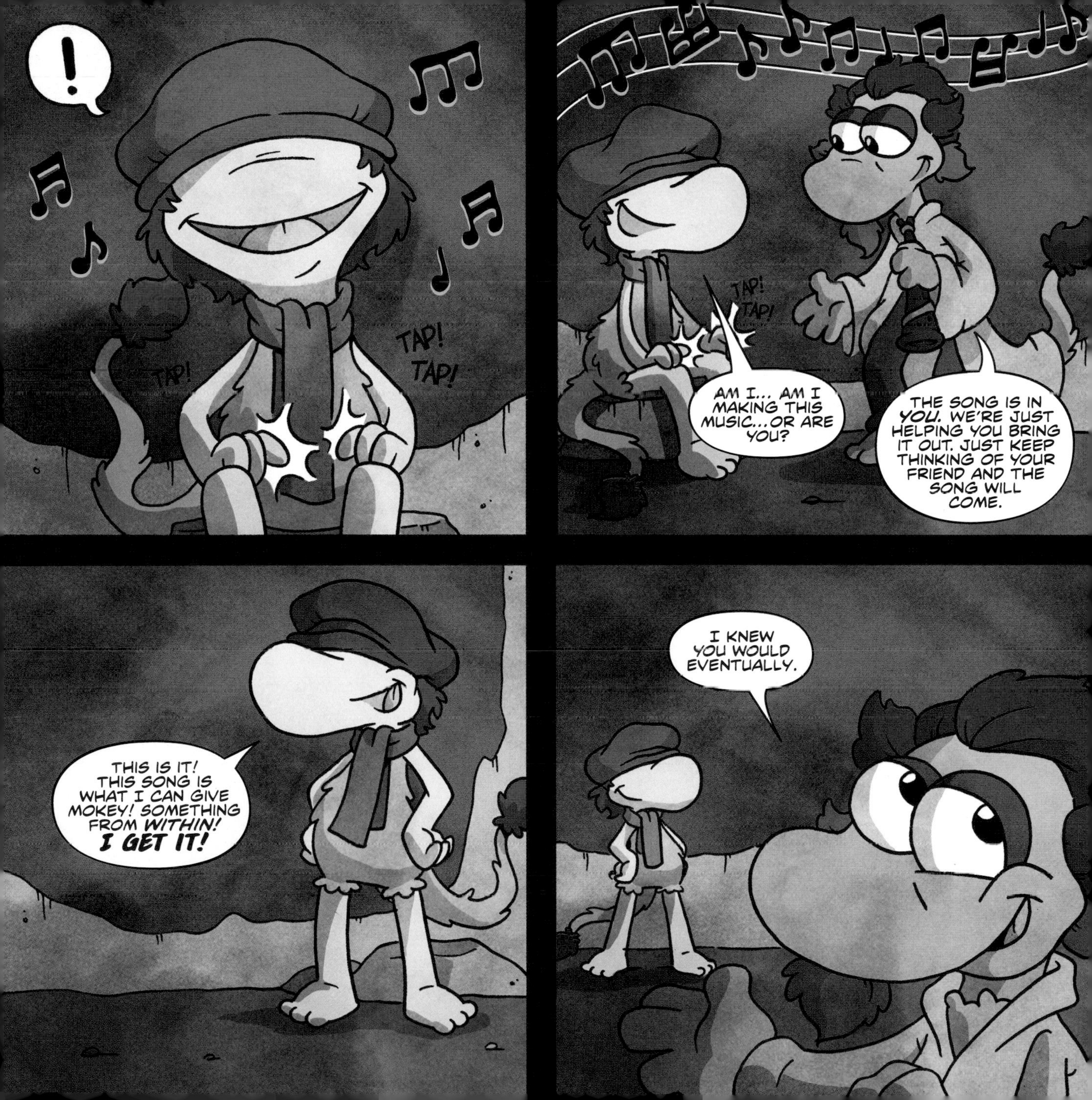
!
TAP!
TAP! TAP!
TAP! TAP!
AM I... AM I MAKING THIS MUSIC...OR ARE YOU?
THE SONG IS IN YOU. WE'RE JUST HELPING YOU BRING IT OUT. JUST KEEP THINKING OF YOUR FRIEND AND THE SONG WILL COME.
THIS IS IT! THIS SONG IS WHAT I CAN GIVE MOKEY! SOMETHING FROM WITHIN! I GET IT!
I KNEW YOU WOULD EVENTUALLY.

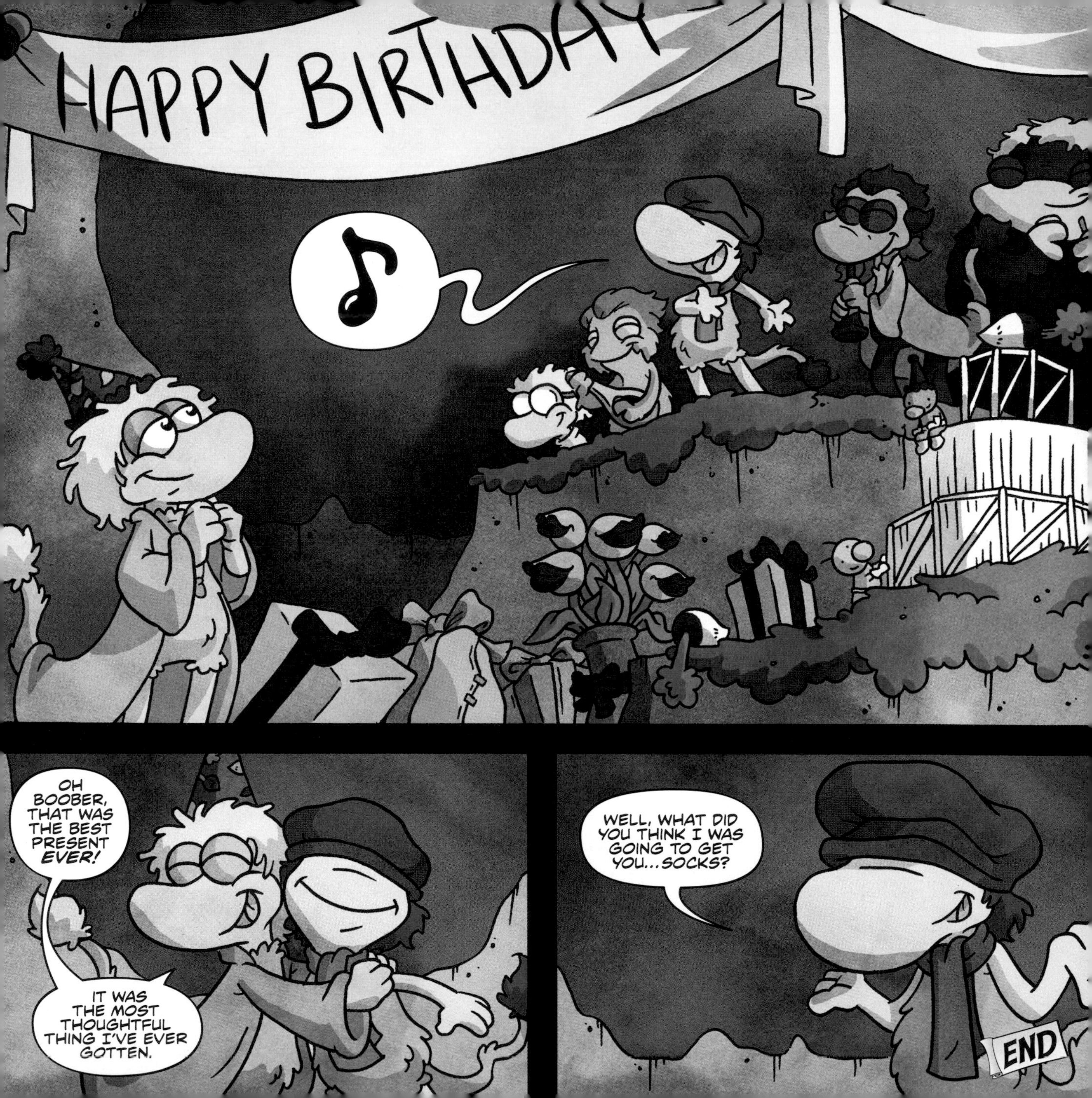

HAPPY BIRTHDAY
OH BOOBER, THAT WAS THE BEST PRESENT EVER!
IT WAS THE MOST THOUGHTFUL THING I'VE EVER GOTTEN.
WELL, WHAT DID YOU THINK I WAS GOING TO GET YOU...SOCKS?
END

IT'S SURE NICE OF YOU TO COME ALONG, BOOBER.
I FIGURED THAT IF YOU WERE GOING TO DIE, SOMEONE SHOULD KNOW THE DETAILS OF YOUR TRAGIC END. IT'S NEVER GOOD TO LEAVE THESE THINGS TO QUESTION.
BOOBER, GOBO NEEDS ME, AND FRIENDS HELP FRIENDS NO MATTER WHAT.
BESIDES, GOBO DOES THIS ALL THE TIME. WHAT'S THE WORST THAT COULD HAPPEN?
OH, I COULD THINK OF LOTS OF THINGS.
FOR INSTANCE, WHAT IF THAT HORRIBLE, SLOBBERY BEAST IS AWAKE?
HE COULD CHASE YOU AND CATCH YOU AND EAT YOU OVER DAYS AND DAYS.
OH, HE'S NOT SO BAD. GOBO ALWAYS SEEMS TO GET AWAY.
YES, BUT GOBO'S REALLY FAST. ARE YOU THAT FAST?
WELL, NO. NOT REALLY, BUT--

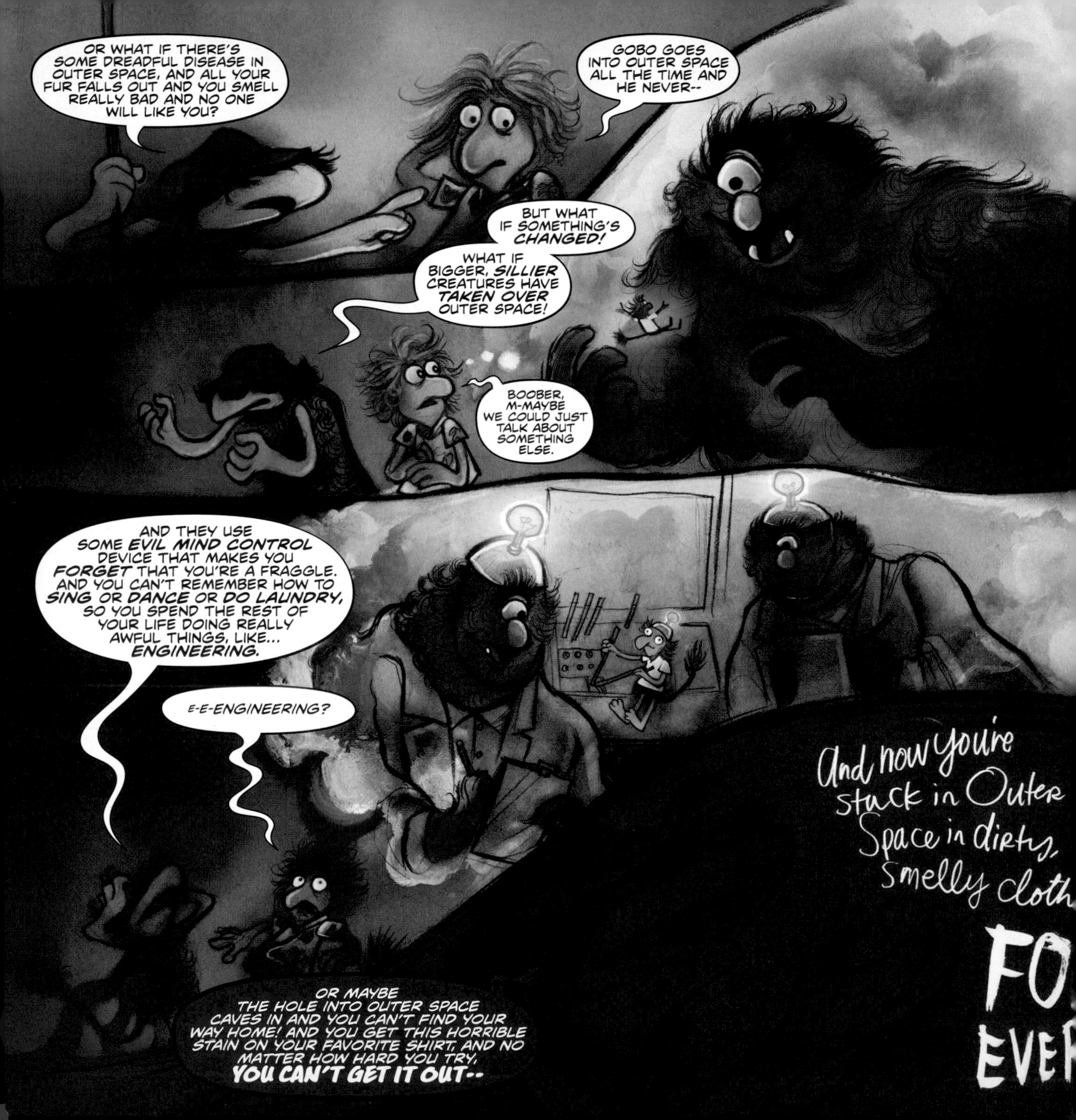
OR WHAT IF THERE'S SOME DREADFUL DISEASE IN OUTER SPACE, AND ALL YOUR FUR FALLS OUT AND YOU SMELL REALLY BAD AND NO ONE WILL LIKE YOU?
GOBO GOES INTO OUTER SPACE ALL THE TIME AND HE NEVER--
BUT WHAT IF SOMETHING'S CHANGED!
WHAT IF BIGGER, SILLIER CREATURES HAVE TAKEN OVER OUTER SPACE!
BOOBER, M-MAYBE WE COULD JUST TALK ABOUT SOMETHING ELSE.
AND THEY USE SOME EVIL MIND CONTROL DEVICE THAT MAKES YOU FORGET THAT YOU'RE A FRAGGLE. AND YOU CAN'T REMEMBER HOW TO SING OR DANCE OR DO LAUNDRY, SO YOU SPEND THE REST OF YOUR LIFE DOING REALLY AWFUL THINGS, LIKE... ENGINEERING.
E-E-ENGINEERING?
OR MAYBE THE HOLE INTO OUTER SPACE CAVES IN AND YOU CAN'T FIND YOUR WAY HOME! AND YOU GET THIS HORRIBLE STAIN ON YOUR FAVORITE SHIRT, AND NO MATTER HOW HARD YOU TRY, YOU CAN'T GET IT OUT--
And now you're stuck in Outer Space in dirty, smelly cloth
FO
EVER

OH, HERE WE ARE! WELL, GO GET THAT POSTCARD, BRAVE WEMBLEY, AND LET'S GET BACK TO THE...
...PARTY?
WEMBLEY, ARE YOU OKAY? WHAT'S WRONG?
COME ON, WEMBLEY! GOBO IS COUNTING ON US TO GET THAT POSTCARD!!!
SNAP OUT OF IT!
OH NO, BOOBER. DON'T EVEN THINK ABOUT IT.

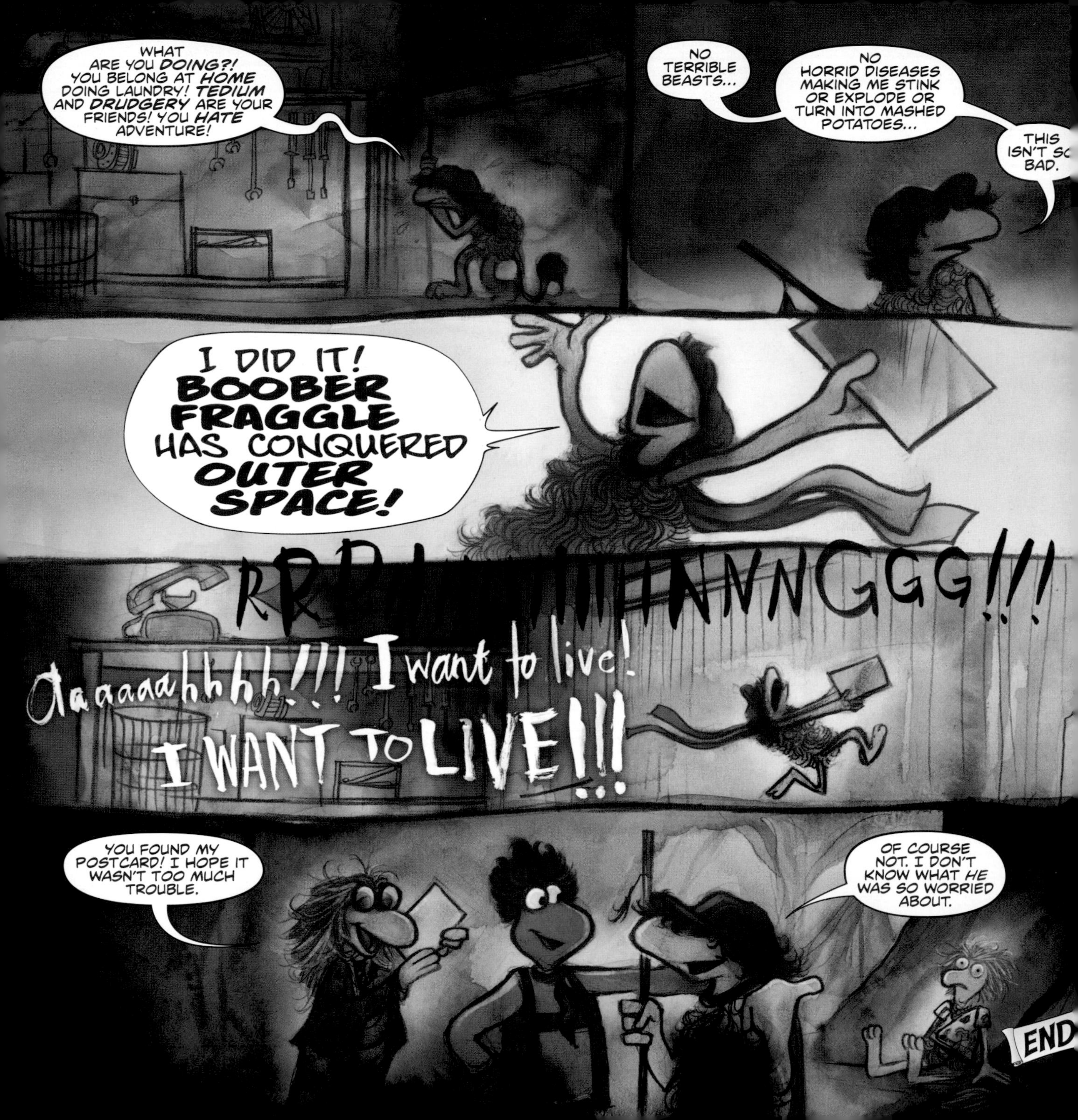
WHAT ARE YOU DOING?! YOU BELONG AT HOME DOING LAUNDRY! TEDIUM AND DRUDGERY ARE YOUR FRIENDS! YOU HATE ADVENTURE!
NO TERRIBLE BEASTS...
NO HORRID DISEASES MAKING ME STINK OR EXPLODE OR TURN INTO MASHED POTATOES...
THIS ISN'T SO BAD.
I DID IT! BOOBER FRAGGLE HAS CONQUERED OUTER SPACE!
RRRIIIIIIIIINNNNGGG!!!
Aaaaaahhhh!!! I want to live!
I WANT TO LIVE!!!
YOU FOUND MY POSTCARD! I HOPE IT WASN'T TOO MUCH TROUBLE.
OF COURSE NOT. I DON'T KNOW WHAT HE WAS SO WORRIED ABOUT.
END

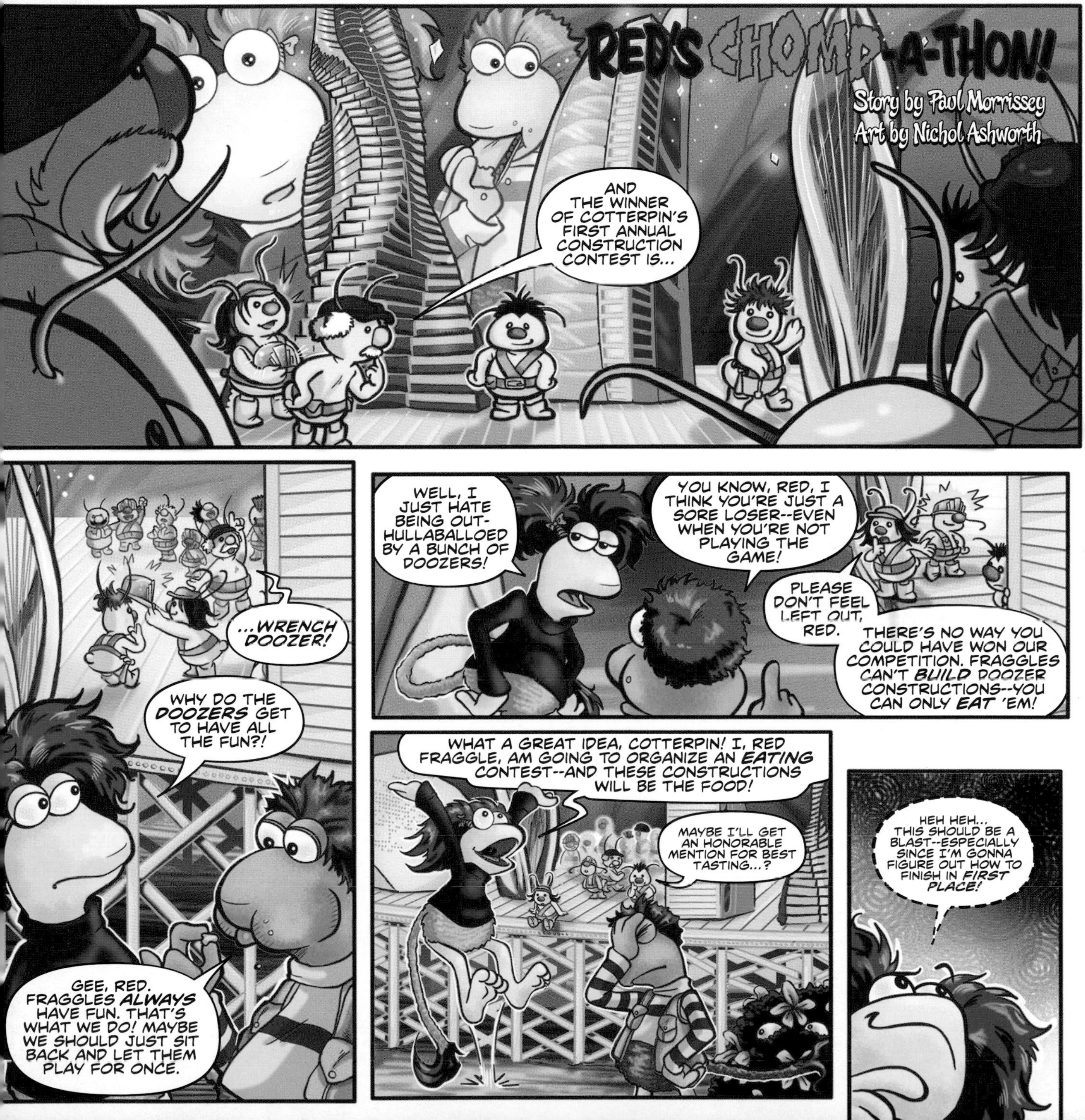
RED'S CHOMP-A-THON!
Story by Paul Morrissey
Art by Nichol Ashworth
AND THE WINNER OF COTTERPIN'S FIRST ANNUAL CONSTRUCTION CONTEST IS...
...WRENCH DOOZER!
WHY DO THE DOOZERS GET TO HAVE ALL THE FUN?!
GEE, RED. FRAGGLES ALWAYS HAVE FUN. THAT'S WHAT WE DO! MAYBE WE SHOULD JUST SIT BACK AND LET THEM PLAY FOR ONCE.
WELL, I JUST HATE BEING OUT-HULLABALLOOED BY A BUNCH OF DOOZERS!
YOU KNOW, RED, I THINK YOU'RE JUST A SORE LOSER--EVEN WHEN YOU'RE NOT PLAYING THE GAME!
PLEASE DON'T FEEL LEFT OUT, RED.
THERE'S NO WAY YOU COULD HAVE WON OUR COMPETITION. FRAGGLES CAN'T BUILD DOOZER CONSTRUCTIONS--YOU CAN ONLY EAT 'EM!
WHAT A GREAT IDEA, COTTERPIN! I, RED FRAGGLE, AM GOING TO ORGANIZE AN EATING CONTEST--AND THESE CONSTRUCTIONS WILL BE THE FOOD!
MAYBE I'LL GET AN HONORABLE MENTION FOR BEST TASTING...?
HEH HEH... THIS SHOULD BE A BLAST--ESPECIALLY SINCE I'M GONNA FIGURE OUT HOW TO FINISH IN FIRST PLACE!

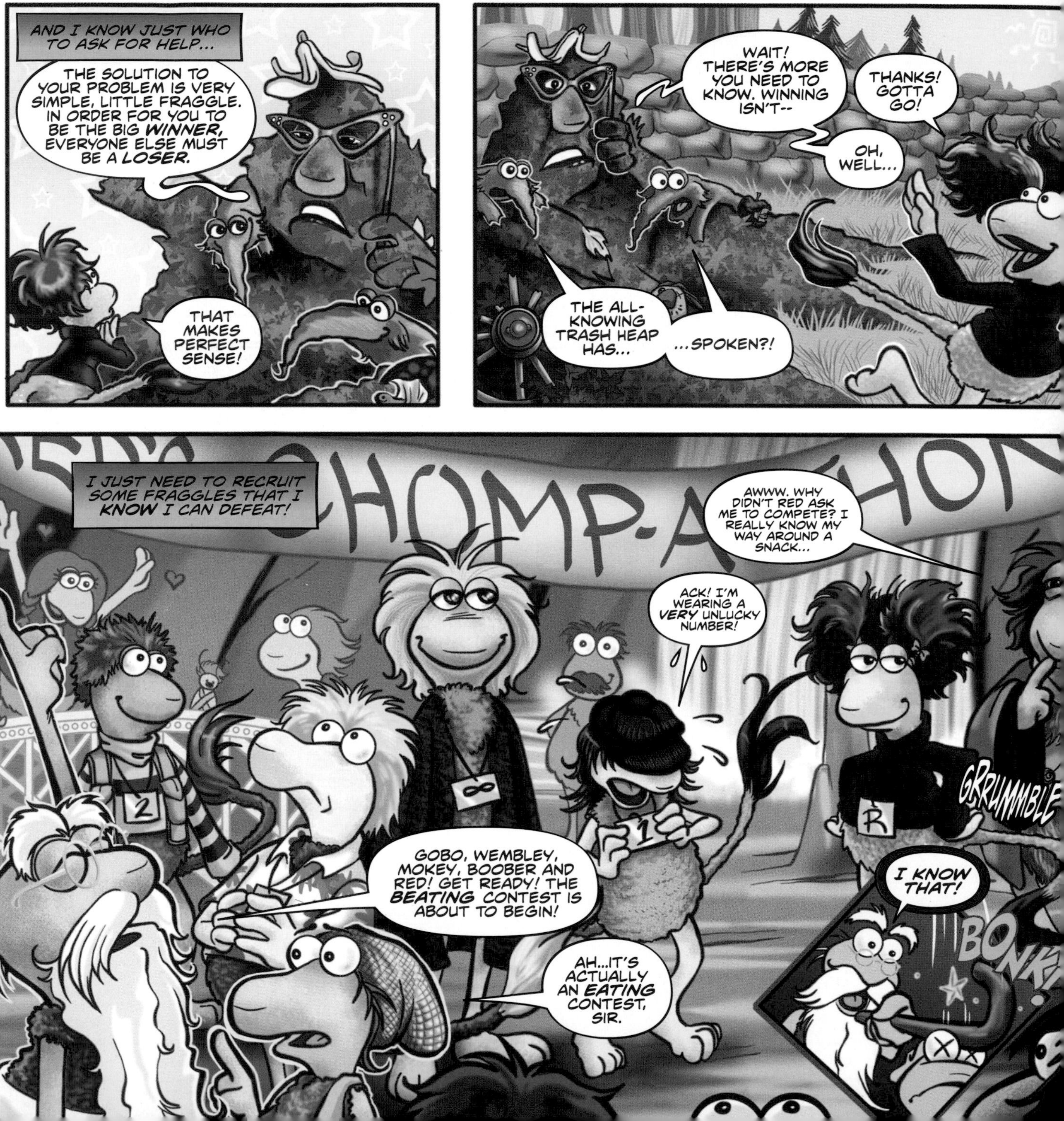
AND I KNOW JUST WHO TO ASK FOR HELP...
THE SOLUTION TO YOUR PROBLEM IS VERY SIMPLE, LITTLE FRAGGLE. IN ORDER FOR YOU TO BE THE BIG WINNER, EVERYONE ELSE MUST BE A LOSER.
THAT MAKES PERFECT SENSE!
WAIT! THERE'S MORE YOU NEED TO KNOW. WINNING ISN'T--
THANKS! GOTTA GO!
OH, WELL...
THE ALL-KNOWING TRASH HEAP HAS...
...SPOKEN?!
I JUST NEED TO RECRUIT SOME FRAGGLES THAT I KNOW I CAN DEFEAT!
CHOMP-A
AWWW. WHY DIDN'T RED ASK ME TO COMPETE? I REALLY KNOW MY WAY AROUND A SNACK...
ACK! I'M WEARING A VERY UNLUCKY NUMBER!
2
1
R
GRRUMMBLE
GOBO, WEMBLEY, MOKEY, BOOBER AND RED! GET READY! THE BEATING CONTEST IS ABOUT TO BEGIN!
I KNOW THAT!
AH...IT'S ACTUALLY AN EATING CONTEST, SIR.

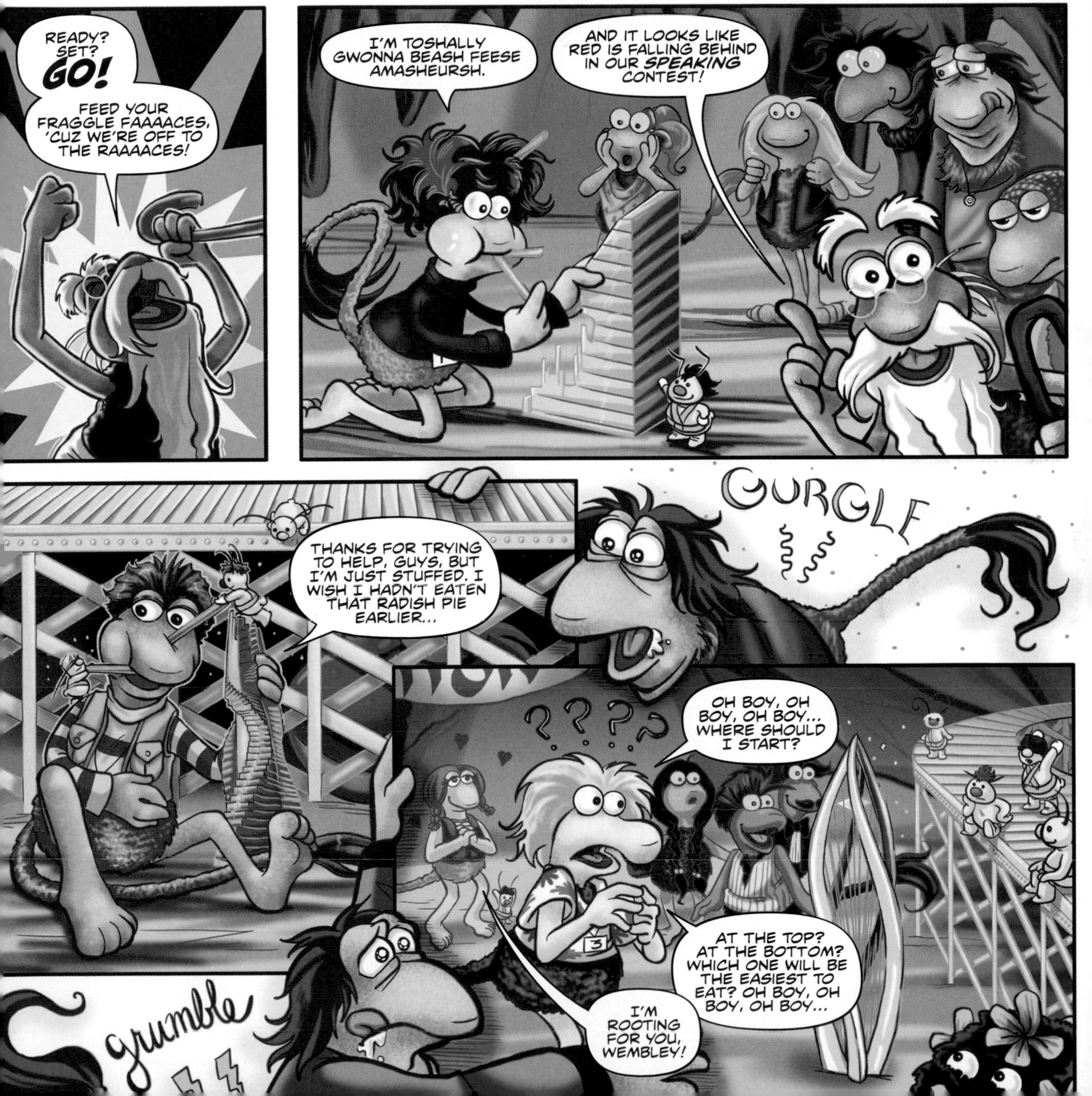
READY? SET? GO!
FEED YOUR FRAGGLE FAAAACES, 'CUZ WE'RE OFF TO THE RAAAACES!
I'M TOSHALLY GWONNA BEASH FEESE AMASHEURSH.
AND IT LOOKS LIKE RED IS FALLING BEHIND IN OUR SPEAKING CONTEST!
GURGLE
THANKS FOR TRYING TO HELP, GUYS, BUT I'M JUST STUFFED. I WISH I HADN'T EATEN THAT RADISH PIE EARLIER...
OH BOY, OH BOY, OH BOY... WHERE SHOULD I START?
AT THE TOP? AT THE BOTTOM? WHICH ONE WILL BE THE EASIEST TO EAT? OH BOY, OH BOY, OH BOY...
I'M ROOTING FOR YOU, WEMBLEY!
grumble

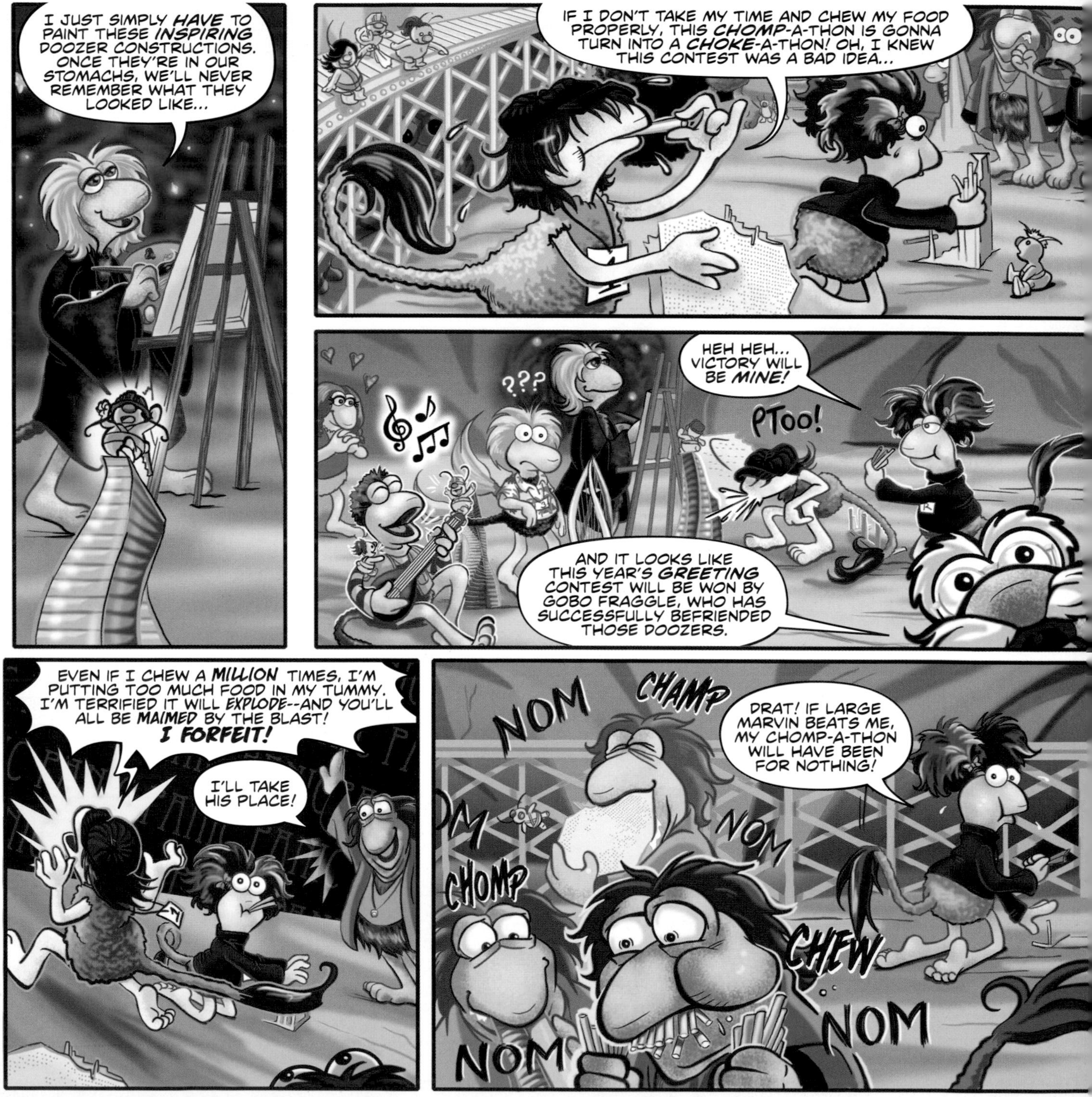
I JUST SIMPLY *HAVE* TO PAINT THESE *INSPIRING* DOOZER CONSTRUCTIONS. ONCE THEY'RE IN OUR STOMACHS, WE'LL NEVER REMEMBER WHAT THEY LOOKED LIKE...
IF I DON'T TAKE MY TIME AND CHEW MY FOOD PROPERLY, THIS *CHOMP*-A-THON IS GONNA TURN INTO A *CHOKE*-A-THON! OH, I KNEW THIS CONTEST WAS A BAD IDEA...
???
HEH HEH... VICTORY WILL BE *MINE!*
PTOO!
AND IT LOOKS LIKE THIS YEAR'S *GREETING* CONTEST WILL BE WON BY GOBO FRAGGLE, WHO HAS SUCCESSFULLY BEFRIENDED THOSE DOOZERS.
EVEN IF I CHEW A *MILLION* TIMES, I'M PUTTING TOO MUCH FOOD IN MY TUMMY. I'M TERRIFIED IT WILL *EXPLODE*--AND YOU'LL ALL BE *MAIMED* BY THE BLAST! **I FORFEIT!**
I'LL TAKE HIS PLACE!
NOM
CHAMP
DRAT! IF LARGE MARVIN BEATS ME, MY CHOMP-A-THON WILL HAVE BEEN FOR NOTHING!
NOM
CHOMP
CHEW
NOM
NOM

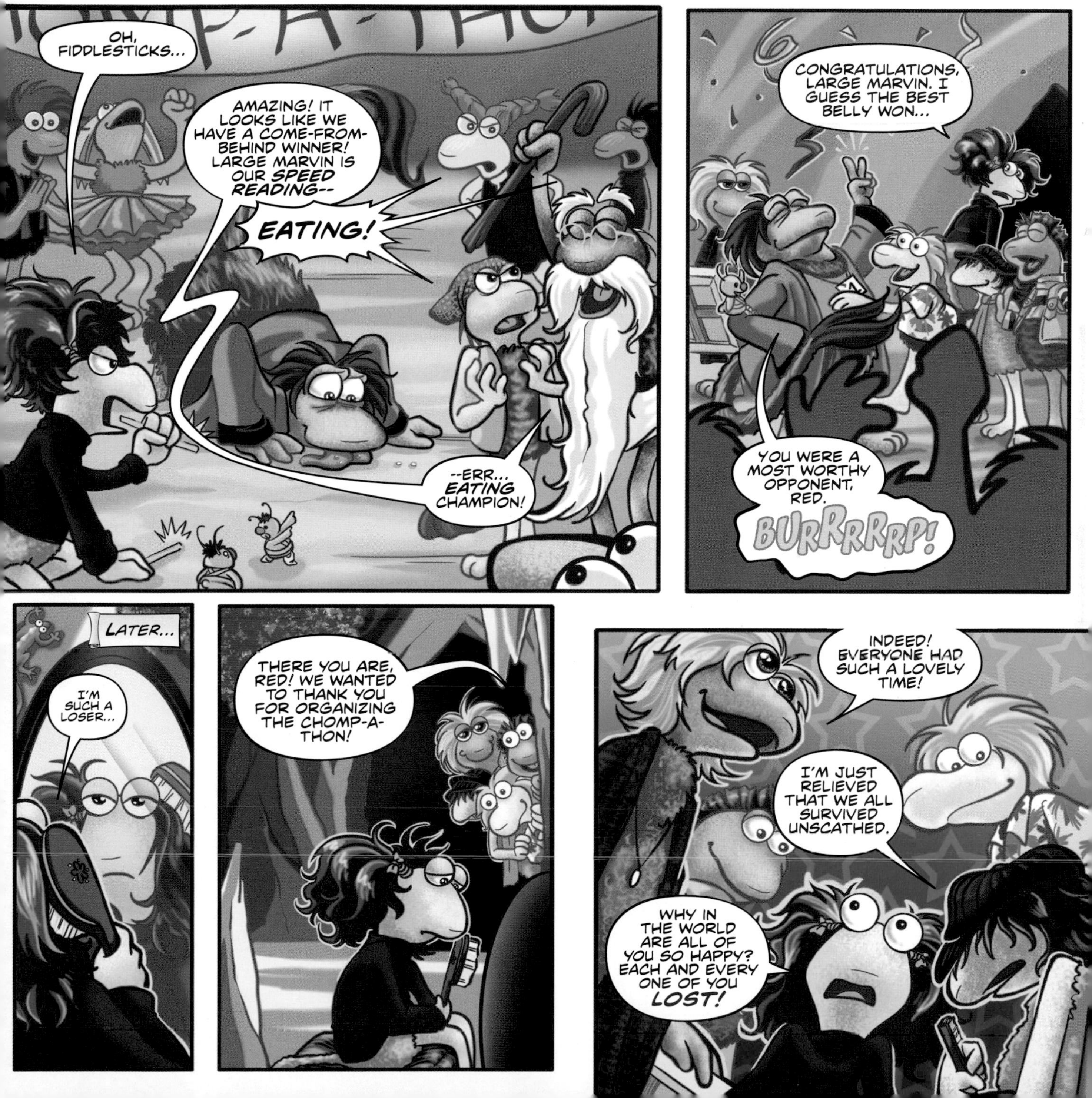
OH, FIDDLESTICKS...
AMAZING! IT LOOKS LIKE WE HAVE A COME-FROM-BEHIND WINNER! LARGE MARVIN IS OUR SPEED READING--
EATING!
--ERR... EATING CHAMPION!
CONGRATULATIONS, LARGE MARVIN. I GUESS THE BEST BELLY WON...
YOU WERE A MOST WORTHY OPPONENT, RED.
BURRRRRP!
LATER...
I'M SUCH A LOSER...
THERE YOU ARE, RED! WE WANTED TO THANK YOU FOR ORGANIZING THE CHOMP-A-THON!
INDEED! EVERYONE HAD SUCH A LOVELY TIME!
I'M JUST RELIEVED THAT WE ALL SURVIVED UNSCATHED.
WHY IN THE WORLD ARE ALL OF YOU SO HAPPY? EACH AND EVERY ONE OF YOU LOST!

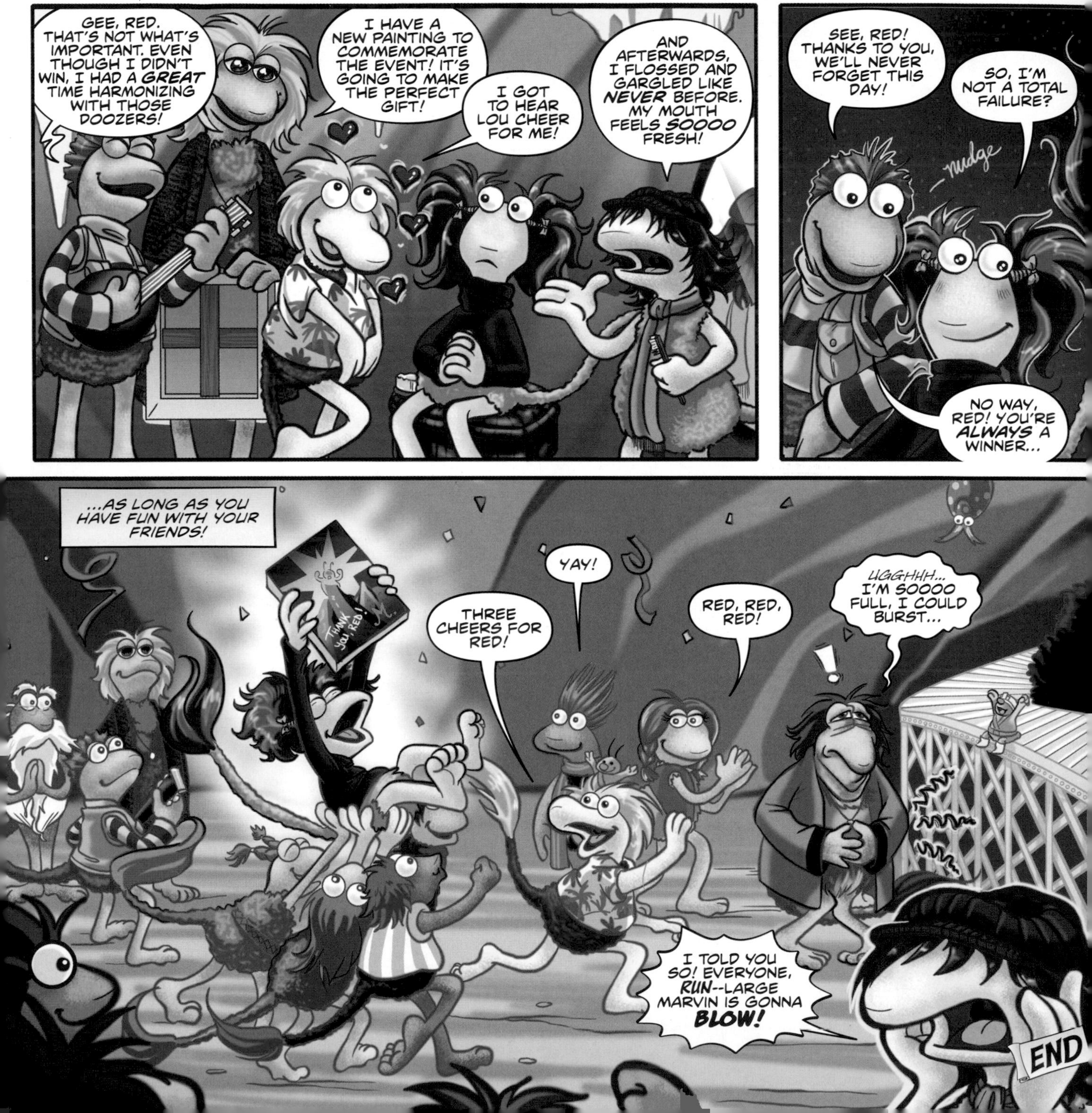
GEE, RED. THAT'S NOT WHAT'S IMPORTANT. EVEN THOUGH I DIDN'T WIN, I HAD A GREAT TIME HARMONIZING WITH THOSE DOOZERS!
I HAVE A NEW PAINTING TO COMMEMORATE THE EVENT! IT'S GOING TO MAKE THE PERFECT GIFT!
I GOT TO HEAR LOU CHEER FOR ME!
AND AFTERWARDS, I FLOSSED AND GARGLED LIKE NEVER BEFORE. MY MOUTH FEELS SOOOO FRESH!
SEE, RED! THANKS TO YOU, WE'LL NEVER FORGET THIS DAY!
SO, I'M NOT A TOTAL FAILURE?
—nudge
NO WAY, RED! YOU'RE ALWAYS A WINNER...
...AS LONG AS YOU HAVE FUN WITH YOUR FRIENDS!
THANK YOU, RED!
THREE CHEERS FOR RED!
YAY!
RED, RED, RED!
UGGHHH... I'M SOOOO FULL, I COULD BURST...
!
I TOLD YOU SO! EVERYONE, RUN--LARGE MARVIN IS GONNA BLOW!
END

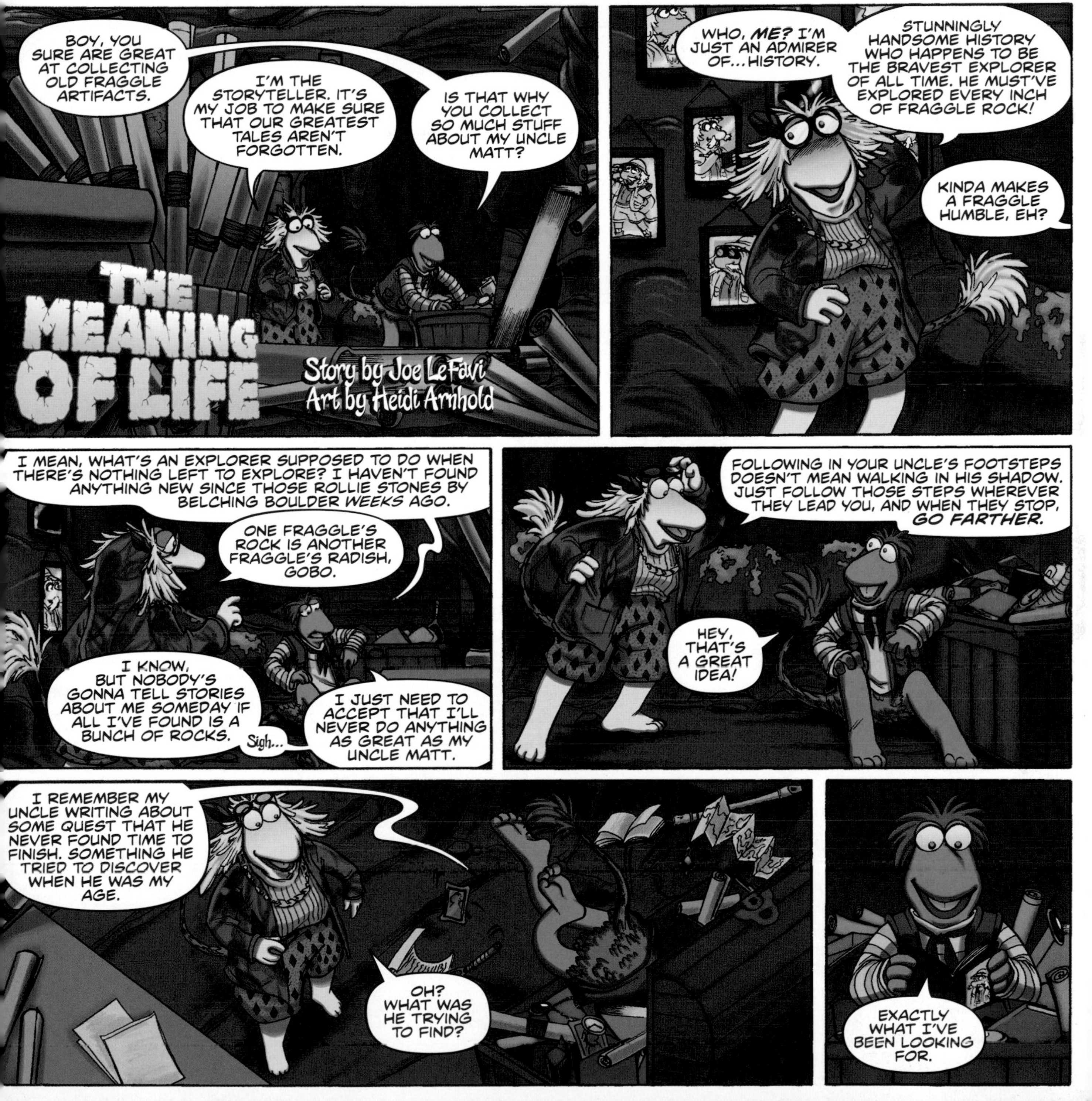
BOY, YOU SURE ARE GREAT AT COLLECTING OLD FRAGGLE ARTIFACTS.
I'M THE STORYTELLER. IT'S MY JOB TO MAKE SURE THAT OUR GREATEST TALES AREN'T FORGOTTEN.
IS THAT WHY YOU COLLECT SO MUCH STUFF ABOUT MY UNCLE MATT?
THE MEANING OF LIFE
Story by Joe LeFavi
Art by Heidi Arnhold
WHO, ME? I'M JUST AN ADMIRER OF... HISTORY.
STUNNINGLY HANDSOME HISTORY WHO HAPPENS TO BE THE BRAVEST EXPLORER OF ALL TIME. HE MUST'VE EXPLORED EVERY INCH OF FRAGGLE ROCK!
KINDA MAKES A FRAGGLE HUMBLE, EH?
I MEAN, WHAT'S AN EXPLORER SUPPOSED TO DO WHEN THERE'S NOTHING LEFT TO EXPLORE? I HAVEN'T FOUND ANYTHING NEW SINCE THOSE ROLLIE STONES BY BELCHING BOULDER WEEKS AGO.
ONE FRAGGLE'S ROCK IS ANOTHER FRAGGLE'S RADISH, GOBO.
I KNOW, BUT NOBODY'S GONNA TELL STORIES ABOUT ME SOMEDAY IF ALL I'VE FOUND IS A BUNCH OF ROCKS.
Sigh...
I JUST NEED TO ACCEPT THAT I'LL NEVER DO ANYTHING AS GREAT AS MY UNCLE MATT.
FOLLOWING IN YOUR UNCLE'S FOOTSTEPS DOESN'T MEAN WALKING IN HIS SHADOW. JUST FOLLOW THOSE STEPS WHEREVER THEY LEAD YOU, AND WHEN THEY STOP, GO FARTHER.
HEY, THAT'S A GREAT IDEA!
I REMEMBER MY UNCLE WRITING ABOUT SOME QUEST THAT HE NEVER FOUND TIME TO FINISH. SOMETHING HE TRIED TO DISCOVER WHEN HE WAS MY AGE.
OH? WHAT WAS HE TRYING TO FIND?
EXACTLY WHAT I'VE BEEN LOOKING FOR.

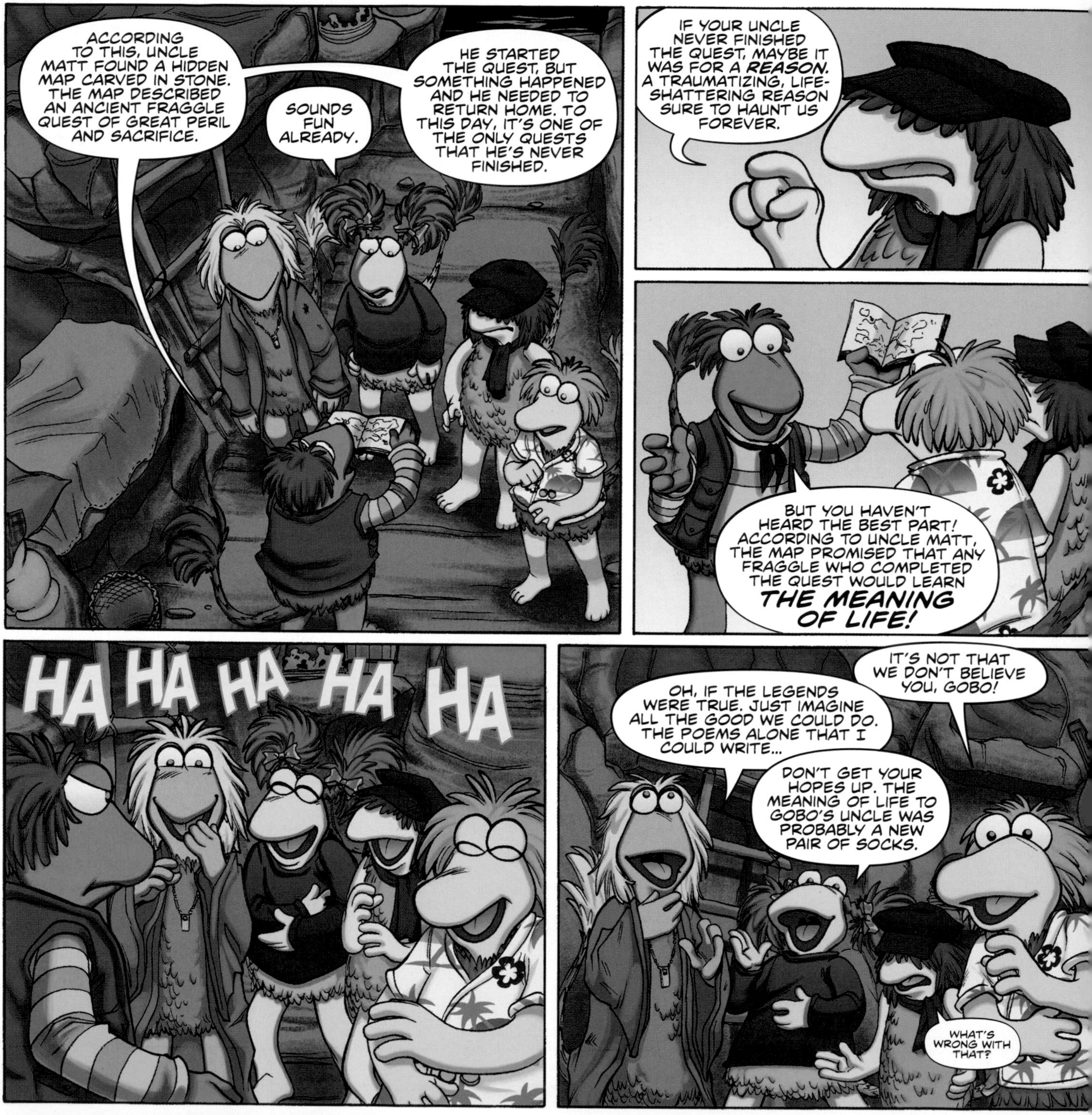

ACCORDING TO THIS, UNCLE MATT FOUND A HIDDEN MAP CARVED IN STONE. THE MAP DESCRIBED AN ANCIENT FRAGGLE QUEST OF GREAT PERIL AND SACRIFICE.
SOUNDS FUN ALREADY.
HE STARTED THE QUEST, BUT SOMETHING HAPPENED AND HE NEEDED TO RETURN HOME. TO THIS DAY, IT'S ONE OF THE ONLY QUESTS THAT HE'S NEVER FINISHED.
IF YOUR UNCLE NEVER FINISHED THE QUEST, MAYBE IT WAS FOR A *REASON.* A TRAUMATIZING, LIFE-SHATTERING REASON SURE TO HAUNT US FOREVER.
BUT YOU HAVEN'T HEARD THE BEST PART! ACCORDING TO UNCLE MATT, THE MAP PROMISED THAT ANY FRAGGLE WHO COMPLETED THE QUEST WOULD LEARN ***THE MEANING OF LIFE!***
HA HA HA HA HA HA
IT'S NOT THAT WE DON'T BELIEVE YOU, GOBO!
OH, IF THE LEGENDS WERE TRUE. JUST IMAGINE ALL THE GOOD WE COULD DO. THE POEMS ALONE THAT I COULD WRITE...
DON'T GET YOUR HOPES UP. THE MEANING OF LIFE TO GOBO'S UNCLE WAS PROBABLY A NEW PAIR OF SOCKS.
WHAT'S WRONG WITH THAT?

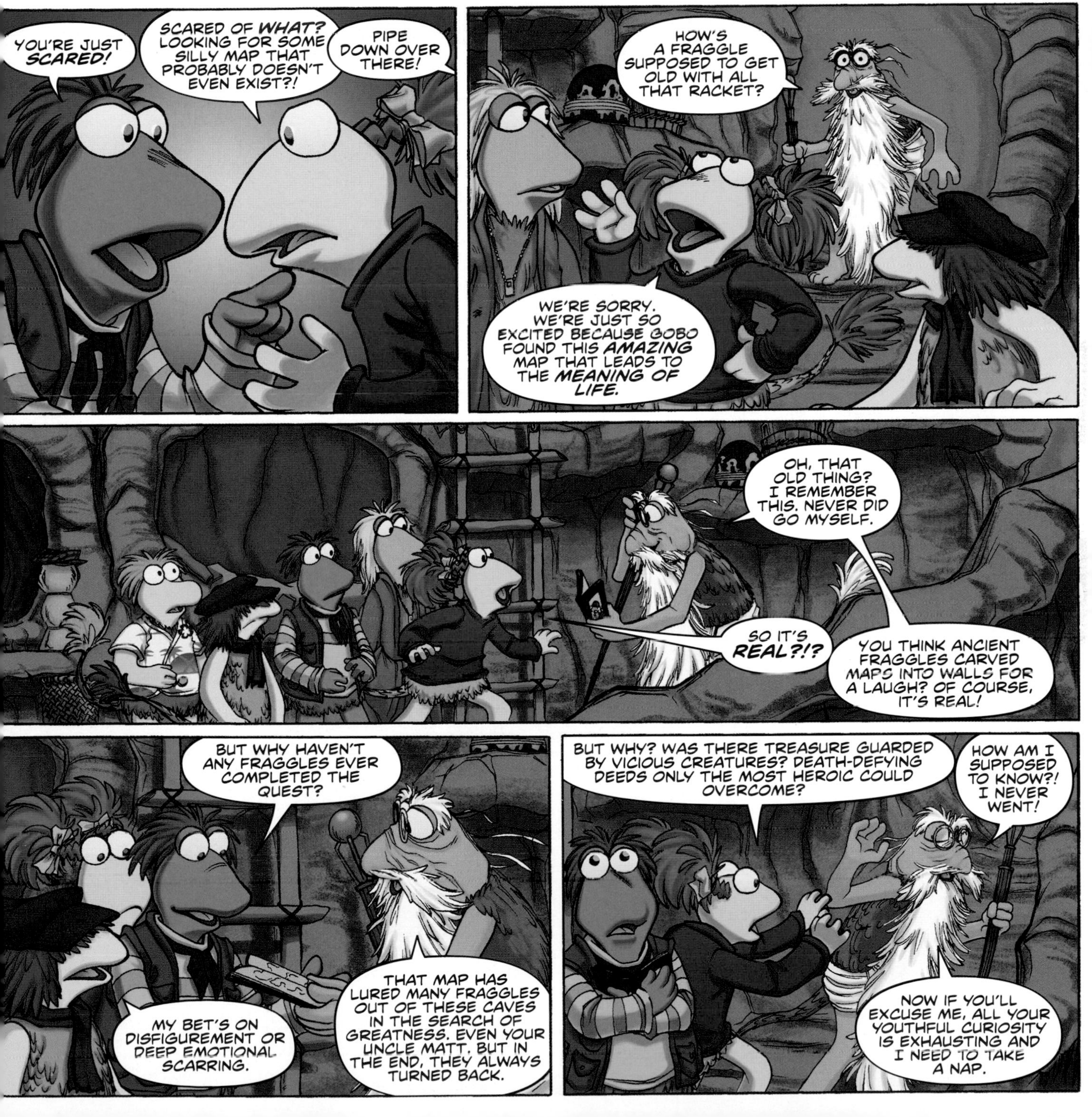
YOU'RE JUST SCARED!
SCARED OF WHAT? LOOKING FOR SOME SILLY MAP THAT PROBABLY DOESN'T EVEN EXIST?!
PIPE DOWN OVER THERE!
HOW'S A FRAGGLE SUPPOSED TO GET OLD WITH ALL THAT RACKET?
WE'RE SORRY. WE'RE JUST SO EXCITED BECAUSE GOBO FOUND THIS AMAZING MAP THAT LEADS TO THE MEANING OF LIFE.
OH, THAT OLD THING? I REMEMBER THIS. NEVER DID GO MYSELF.
SO IT'S REAL?!?
YOU THINK ANCIENT FRAGGLES CARVED MAPS INTO WALLS FOR A LAUGH? OF COURSE, IT'S REAL!
BUT WHY HAVEN'T ANY FRAGGLES EVER COMPLETED THE QUEST?
THAT MAP HAS LURED MANY FRAGGLES OUT OF THESE CAVES IN THE SEARCH OF GREATNESS. EVEN YOUR UNCLE MATT. BUT IN THE END, THEY ALWAYS TURNED BACK.
MY BET'S ON DISFIGUREMENT OR DEEP EMOTIONAL SCARRING.
BUT WHY? WAS THERE TREASURE GUARDED BY VICIOUS CREATURES? DEATH-DEFYING DEEDS ONLY THE MOST HEROIC COULD OVERCOME?
HOW AM I SUPPOSED TO KNOW?! I NEVER WENT!
NOW IF YOU'LL EXCUSE ME, ALL YOUR YOUTHFUL CURIOSITY IS EXHAUSTING AND I NEED TO TAKE A NAP.

SO YOU'RE REALLY GOING ON THAT QUEST?

I'M AN EXPLORER, BOOBER. AND IF YOU GOT WHAT IT TAKES, THEN YOU TAKE WHAT YOU GOT AND GET GOING. THAT'S THE EXPLORER'S CODE.

BUT WHY ARE YOU GOING, WEMBLEY?

GOBO'S MY BEST FRIEND, AND IF THIS MEANS A LOT TO HIM, THEN IT MEANS A LOT TO ME, TOO.

WELL I'M GOING FOR THE GLORY! YOU THINK I'M LETTING YOU HOG ALL THE FAME?

YOU SURE YOU WANT TO COME?

IF THE MEANING OF LIFE IS OUT THERE, THEN WE MUST FIND IT FOR THE SAKE OF ALL FRAGGLES.

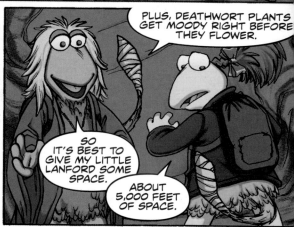

PLUS, DEATHWORT PLANTS GET MOODY RIGHT BEFORE THEY FLOWER.

SO IT'S BEST TO GIVE MY LITTLE LANFORD SOME SPACE.

ABOUT 5,000 FEET OF SPACE.

WHAT DO YOU SAY, BOOBER? IF YOU STAY, YOU REALIZE THAT YOU'LL NEVER HEAR THE END OF IT.

I CAN LIVE WITH THAT.

YES, BUT WHEN WE RETURN WITH PERMANENT STAINS ALL OVER OUR CLOTHES, CAN YOU LIVE WITH THE GUILT?

I'LL GET MY THINGS.

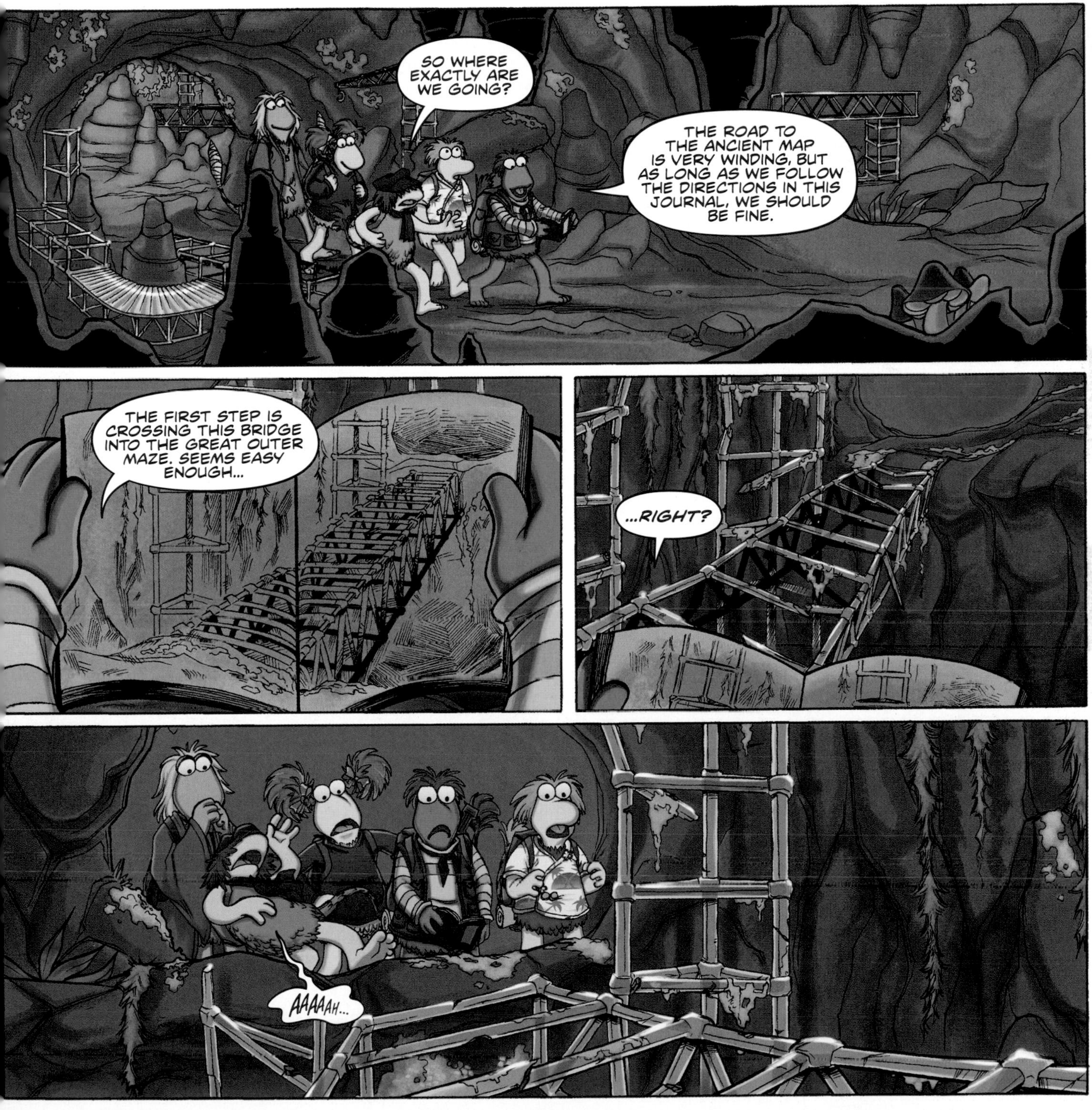
SO WHERE EXACTLY ARE WE GOING?
THE ROAD TO THE ANCIENT MAP IS VERY WINDING, BUT AS LONG AS WE FOLLOW THE DIRECTIONS IN THIS JOURNAL, WE SHOULD BE FINE.
THE FIRST STEP IS CROSSING THIS BRIDGE INTO THE GREAT OUTER MAZE. SEEMS EASY ENOUGH...
...RIGHT?
AAAAAH...

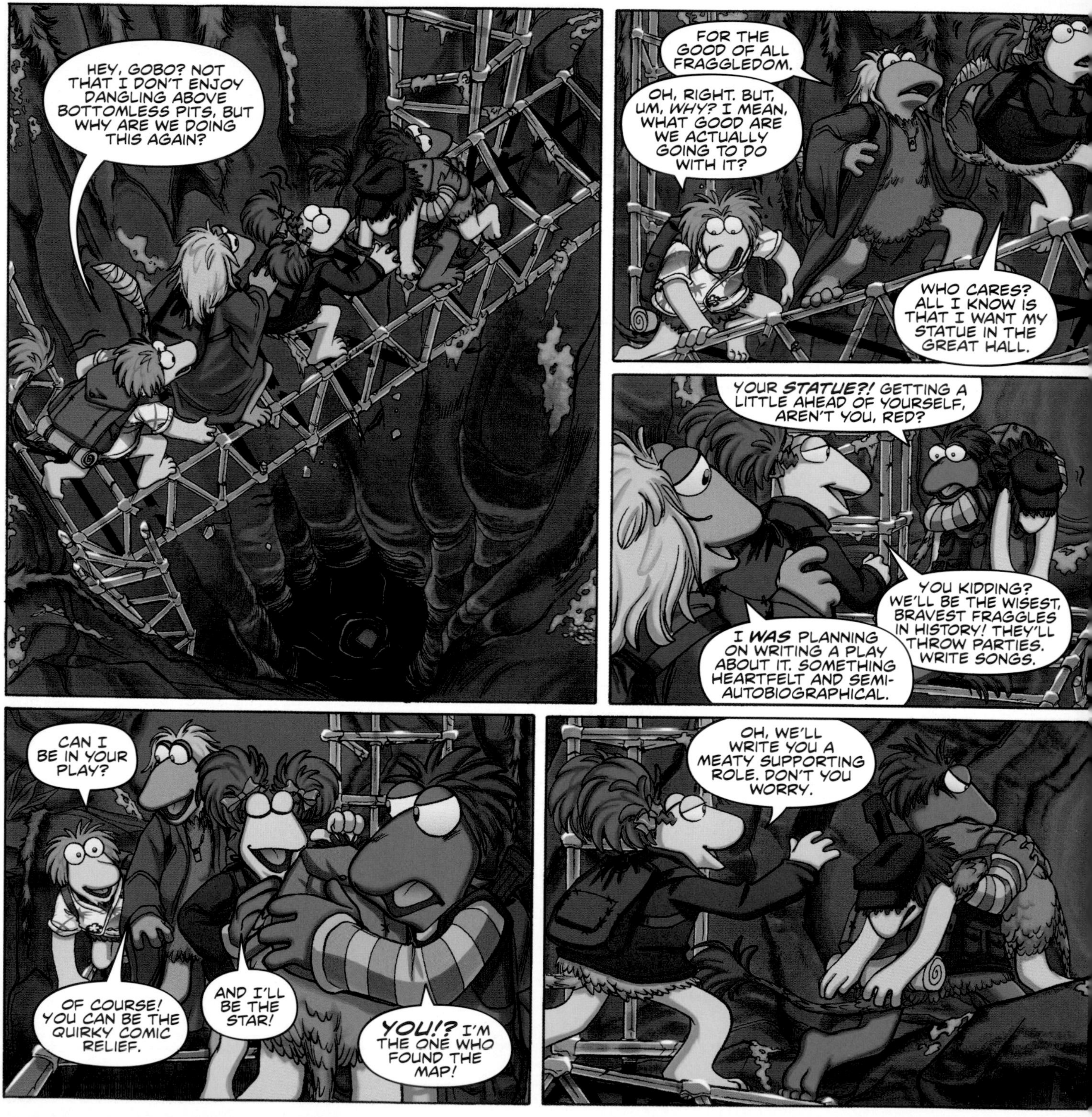
HEY, GOBO? NOT THAT I DON'T ENJOY DANGLING ABOVE BOTTOMLESS PITS, BUT WHY ARE WE DOING THIS AGAIN?
FOR THE GOOD OF ALL FRAGGLEDOM.
OH, RIGHT. BUT, UM, WHY? I MEAN, WHAT GOOD ARE WE ACTUALLY GOING TO DO WITH IT?
WHO CARES? ALL I KNOW IS THAT I WANT MY STATUE IN THE GREAT HALL.
YOUR STATUE?! GETTING A LITTLE AHEAD OF YOURSELF, AREN'T YOU, RED?
YOU KIDDING? WE'LL BE THE WISEST, BRAVEST FRAGGLES IN HISTORY! THEY'LL THROW PARTIES. WRITE SONGS.
I WAS PLANNING ON WRITING A PLAY ABOUT IT. SOMETHING HEARTFELT AND SEMI-AUTOBIOGRAPHICAL.
CAN I BE IN YOUR PLAY?
OF COURSE! YOU CAN BE THE QUIRKY COMIC RELIEF.
AND I'LL BE THE STAR!
YOU!? I'M THE ONE WHO FOUND THE MAP!
OH, WE'LL WRITE YOU A MEATY SUPPORTING ROLE. DON'T YOU WORRY.

I FORGOT HOW BEAUTIFUL THE SINGING CAVE IS.

BEAUTIFUL IS ONE WORD FOR IT. THE WORDS DARK, CREEPY, AND RUN-FOR-YOUR-LIFE ALSO COME TO MIND.

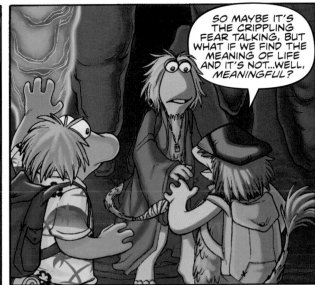

SO MAYBE IT'S THE CRIPPLING FEAR TALKING, BUT WHAT IF WE FIND THE MEANING OF LIFE AND IT'S NOT...WELL, MEANINGFUL?

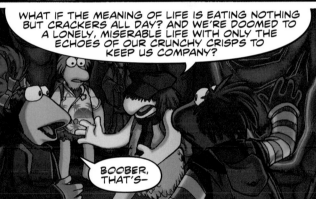

WHAT IF THE MEANING OF LIFE IS EATING NOTHING BUT CRACKERS ALL DAY? AND WE'RE DOOMED TO A LONELY, MISERABLE LIFE WITH ONLY THE ECHOES OF OUR CRUNCHY CRISPS TO KEEP US COMPANY?

BOOBER, THAT'S—

OR WHAT IF IT'S **TOO** MEANINGFUL! WHAT IF THE SECRET IS A NOTION SO IMPOSSIBLY VAST THAT OUR LITTLE MINDS SNAP AND OUR HEADS EXPLODE!

GOBO, I DON'T WANT TO EXPLODE!

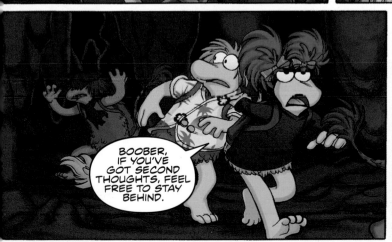

BOOBER, IF YOU'VE GOT SECOND THOUGHTS, FEEL FREE TO STAY BEHIND.

NO, I'M GOOD.

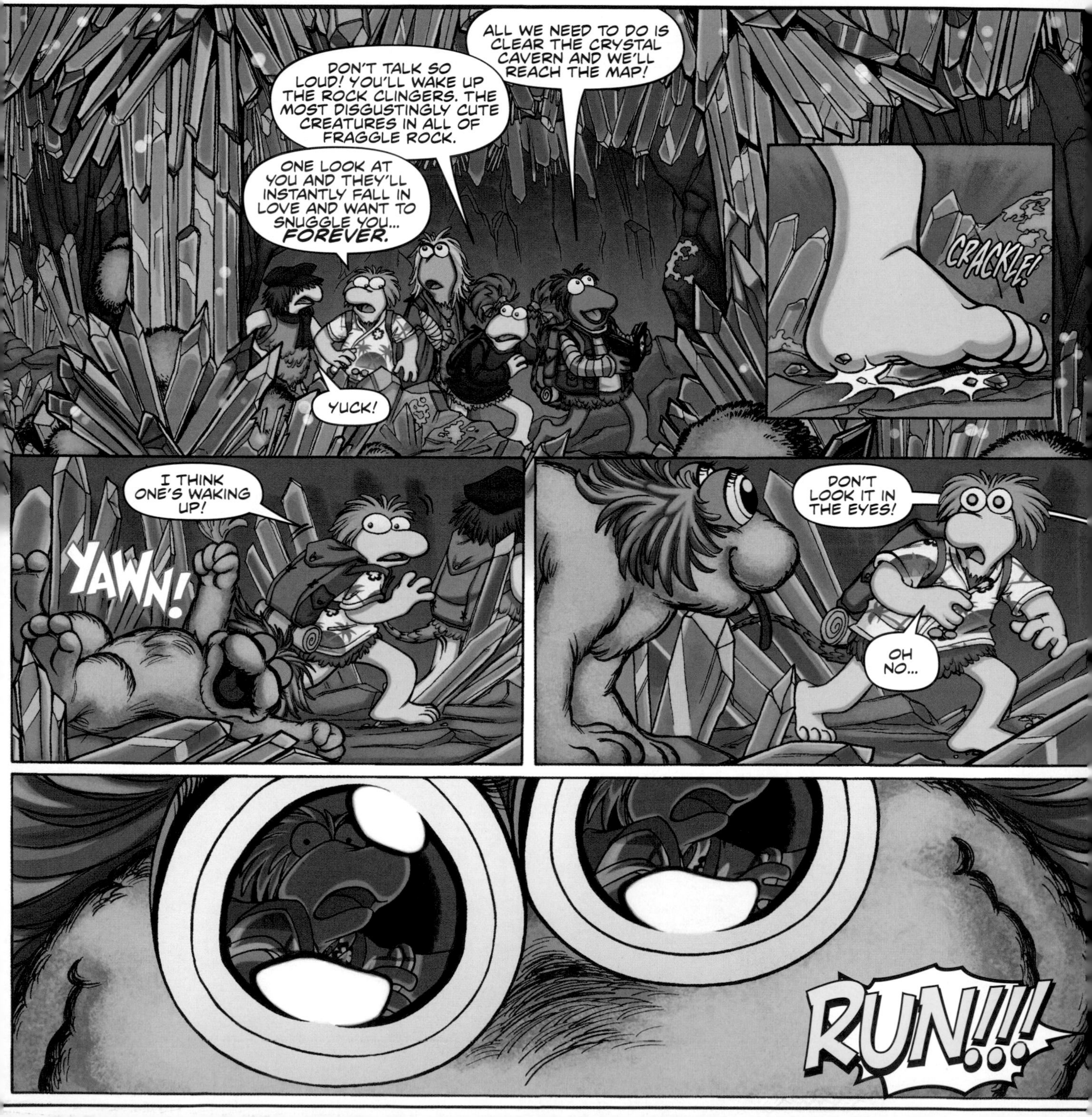
DON'T TALK SO LOUD! YOU'LL WAKE UP THE ROCK CLINGERS. THE MOST DISGUSTINGLY CUTE CREATURES IN ALL OF FRAGGLE ROCK.
ONE LOOK AT YOU AND THEY'LL INSTANTLY FALL IN LOVE AND WANT TO SNUGGLE YOU... FOREVER.
ALL WE NEED TO DO IS CLEAR THE CRYSTAL CAVERN AND WE'LL REACH THE MAP!
YUCK!
CRACKLE!
I THINK ONE'S WAKING UP!
YAWN!
DON'T LOOK IT IN THE EYES!
OH NO...
RUN!!!

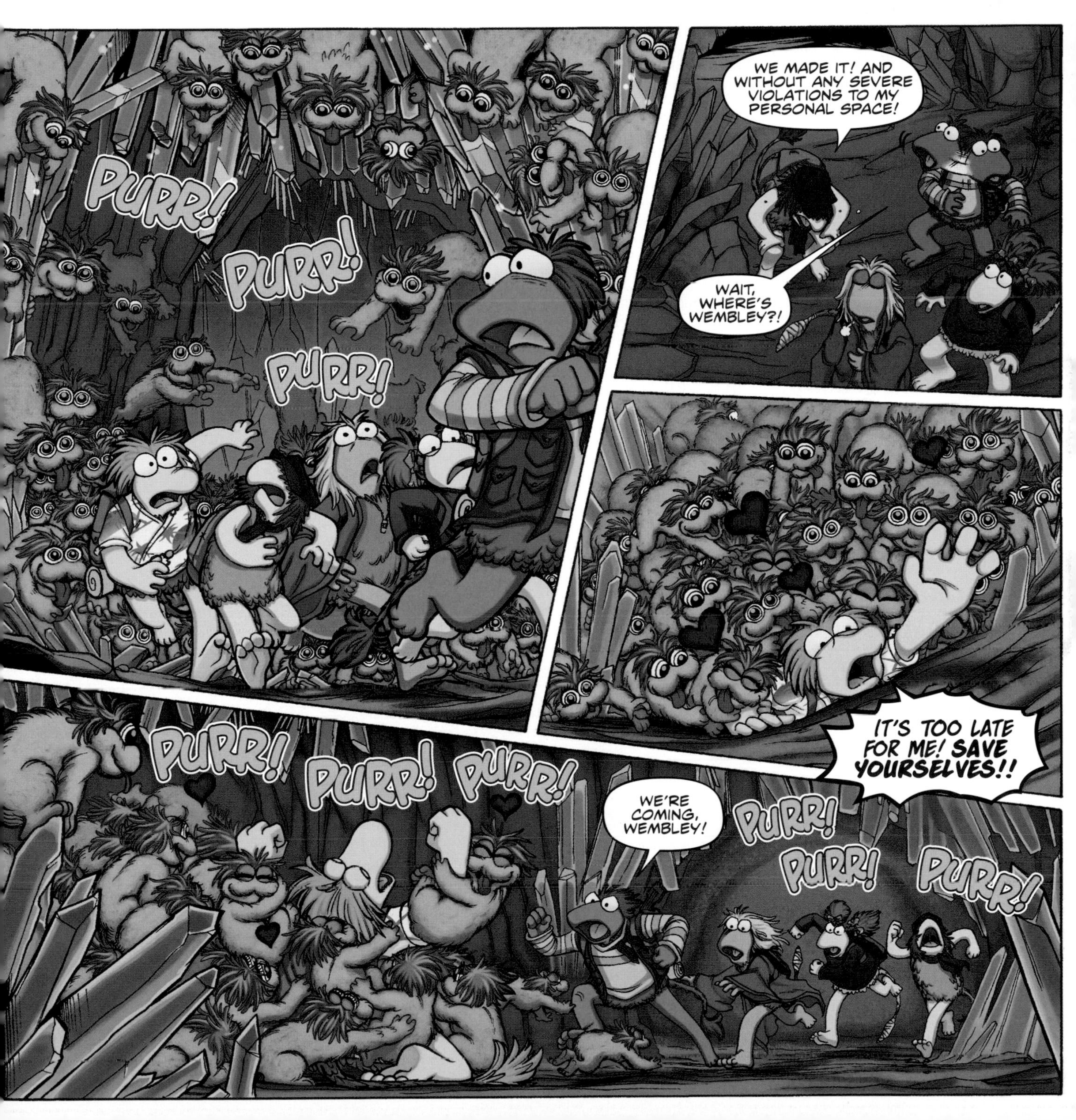
PURR!
PURR!
PURR!
WE MADE IT! AND WITHOUT ANY SEVERE VIOLATIONS TO MY PERSONAL SPACE!
WAIT, WHERE'S WEMBLEY?!
IT'S TOO LATE FOR ME! SAVE YOURSELVES!!
PURR!
PURR!
PURR!
WE'RE COMING, WEMBLEY!
PURR!
PURR!
PURR!

Sigh... THIS HAD BETTER BE WORTH IT.

WE'RE SEEKING THE MEANING OF LIFE, RED. WHAT MORE CAN YOU ASK FOR?

A MONTH NAMED AFTER ME. PREFERABLY IN LATE SPRING OR SUMMER AROUND MY BIRTHDAY.

HOW MUCH LONGER, GOBO? MY EVERYTHING HURTS.

THIS SHOULD BE IT. THE ANCIENT MAP SHOULD BE CARVED INTO THAT FAR WALL.

I CAN'T BELIEVE IT! WE ACTUALLY FOUND IT!

WHAT DOES IT SAY?

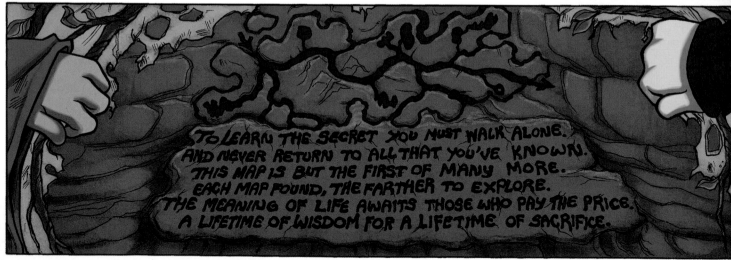

TO LEARN THE SECRET YOU MUST WALK ALONE.
AND NEVER RETURN TO ALL THAT YOU'VE KNOWN.
THIS MAP IS BUT THE FIRST OF MANY MORE.
EACH MAP FOUND, THE FARTHER TO EXPLORE.
THE MEANING OF LIFE AWAITS THOSE WHO PAY THE PRICE.
A LIFETIME OF WISDOM FOR A LIFETIME OF SACRIFICE.

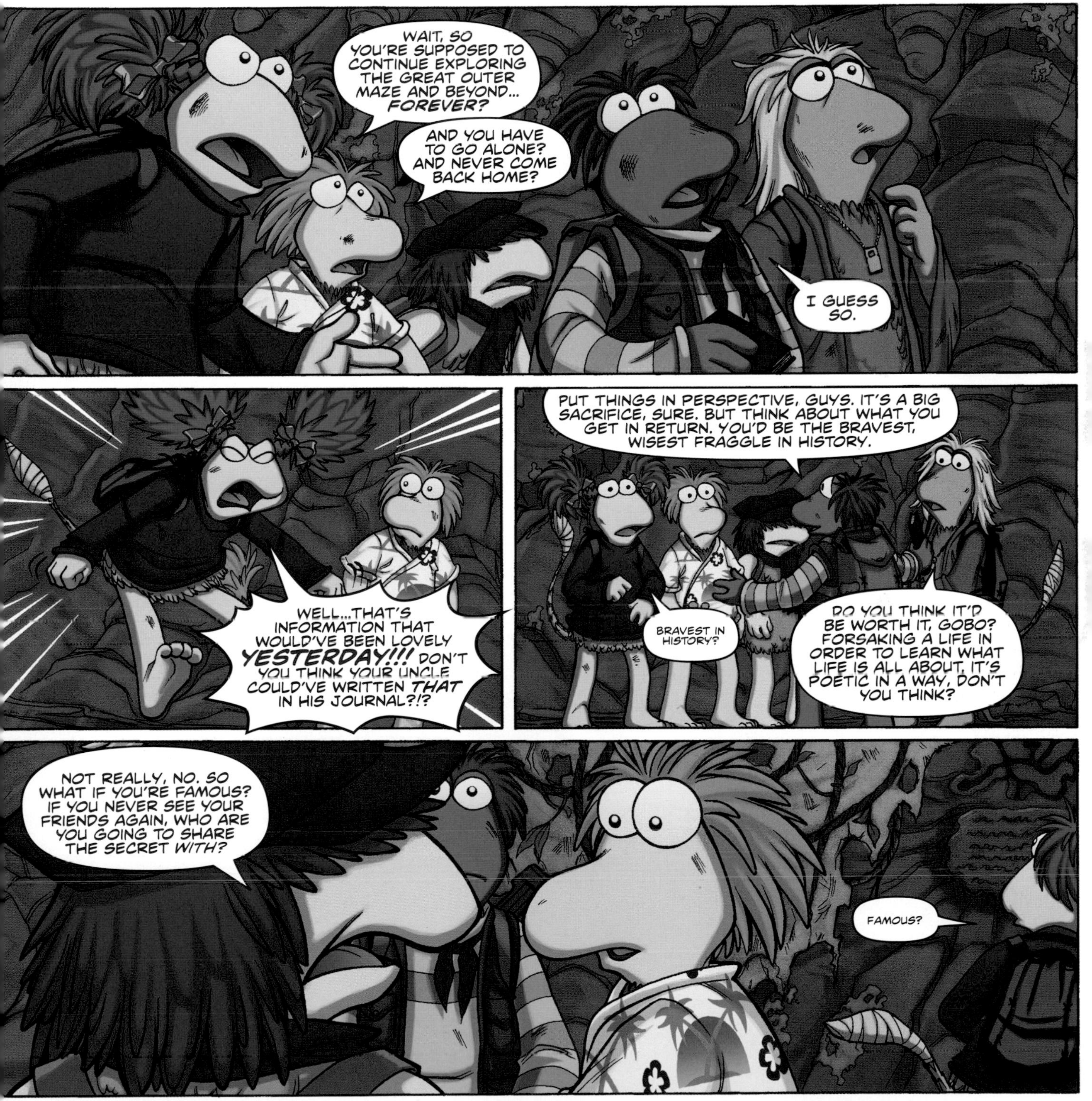
WAIT, SO YOU'RE SUPPOSED TO CONTINUE EXPLORING THE GREAT OUTER MAZE AND BEYOND... FOREVER?
AND YOU HAVE TO GO ALONE? AND NEVER COME BACK HOME?
I GUESS SO.
WELL...THAT'S INFORMATION THAT WOULD'VE BEEN LOVELY YESTERDAY!!! DON'T YOU THINK YOUR UNCLE COULD'VE WRITTEN THAT IN HIS JOURNAL?!?
PUT THINGS IN PERSPECTIVE, GUYS. IT'S A BIG SACRIFICE, SURE. BUT THINK ABOUT WHAT YOU GET IN RETURN. YOU'D BE THE BRAVEST, WISEST FRAGGLE IN HISTORY.
BRAVEST IN HISTORY?
DO YOU THINK IT'D BE WORTH IT, GOBO? FORSAKING A LIFE IN ORDER TO LEARN WHAT LIFE IS ALL ABOUT. IT'S POETIC IN A WAY, DON'T YOU THINK?
NOT REALLY, NO. SO WHAT IF YOU'RE FAMOUS? IF YOU NEVER SEE YOUR FRIENDS AGAIN, WHO ARE YOU GOING TO SHARE THE SECRET WITH?
FAMOUS?

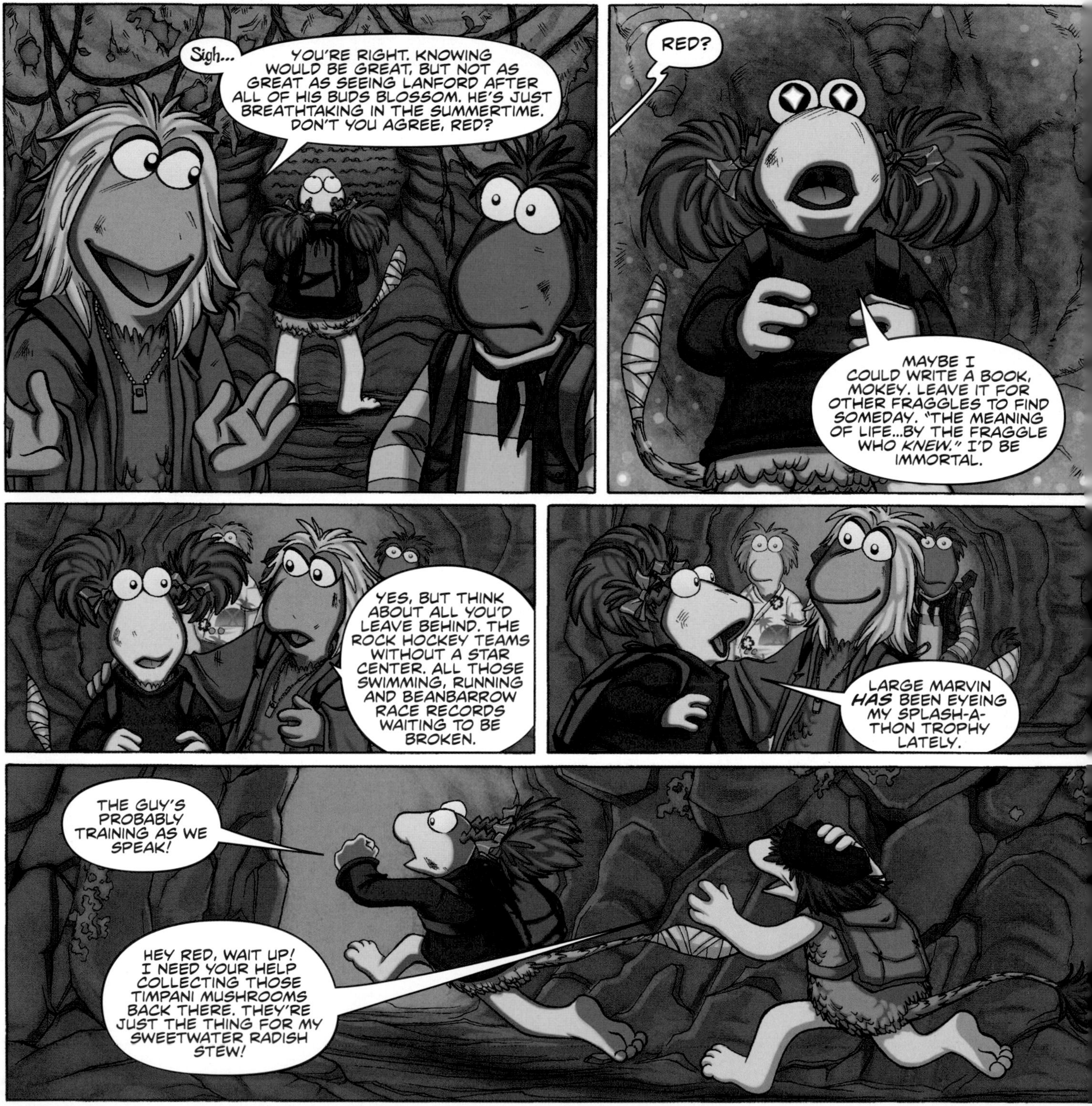

Sigh...
YOU'RE RIGHT. KNOWING WOULD BE GREAT, BUT NOT AS GREAT AS SEEING LANFORD AFTER ALL OF HIS BUDS BLOSSOM. HE'S JUST BREATHTAKING IN THE SUMMERTIME. DON'T YOU AGREE, RED?
RED?
MAYBE I COULD WRITE A BOOK, MOKEY. LEAVE IT FOR OTHER FRAGGLES TO FIND SOMEDAY. "THE MEANING OF LIFE...BY THE FRAGGLE WHO *KNEW*." I'D BE IMMORTAL.
YES, BUT THINK ABOUT ALL YOU'D LEAVE BEHIND. THE ROCK HOCKEY TEAMS WITHOUT A STAR CENTER. ALL THOSE SWIMMING, RUNNING AND BEANBARROW RACE RECORDS WAITING TO BE BROKEN.
LARGE MARVIN ***HAS*** BEEN EYEING MY SPLASH-A-THON TROPHY LATELY.
THE GUY'S PROBABLY TRAINING AS WE SPEAK!
HEY RED, WAIT UP! I NEED YOUR HELP COLLECTING THOSE TIMPANI MUSHROOMS BACK THERE. THEY'RE JUST THE THING FOR MY SWEETWATER RADISH STEW!

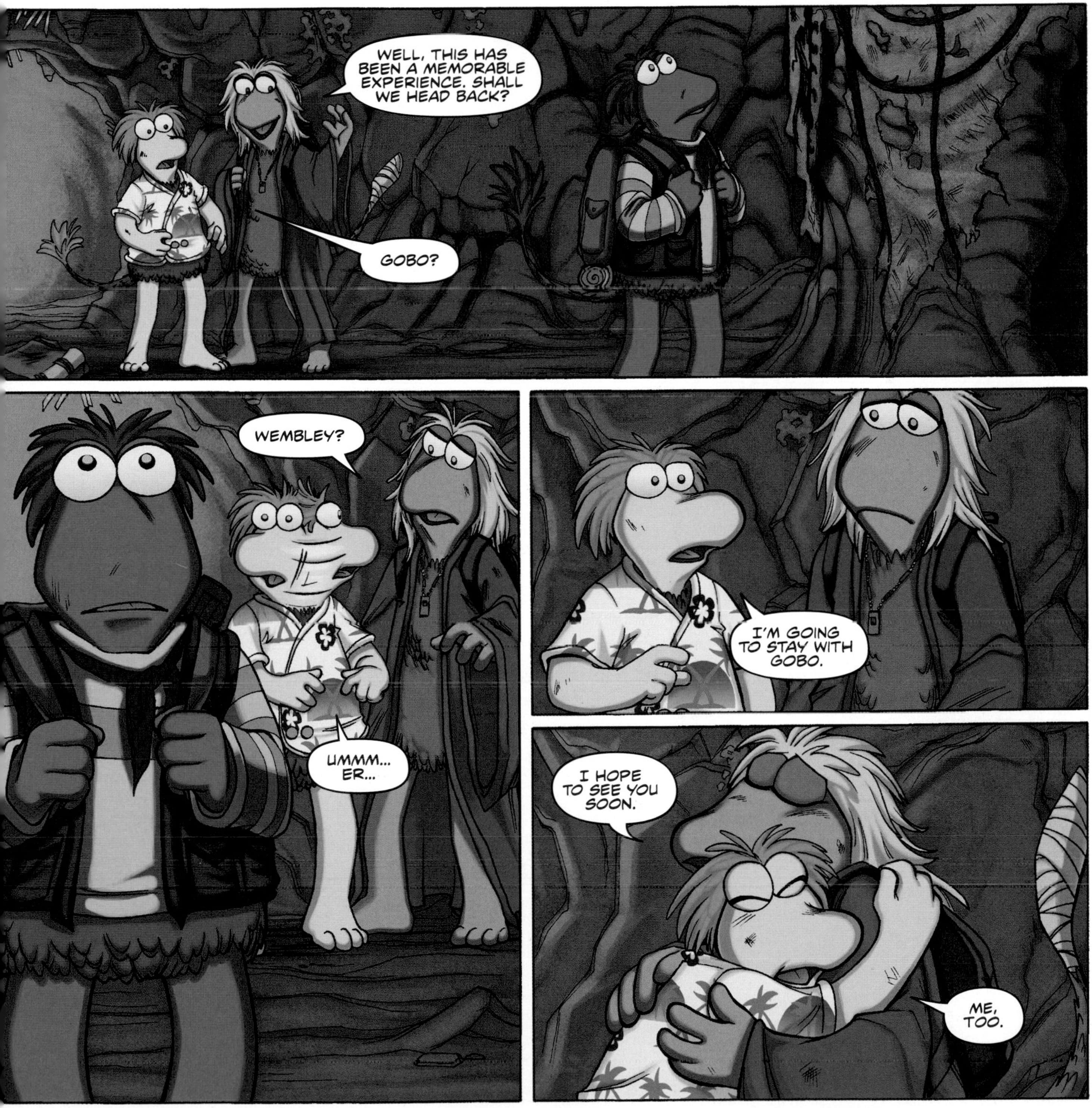
WELL, THIS HAS BEEN A MEMORABLE EXPERIENCE. SHALL WE HEAD BACK?
GOBO?
WEMBLEY?
UMMM... ER...
I'M GOING TO STAY WITH GOBO.
I HOPE TO SEE YOU SOON.
ME, TOO.

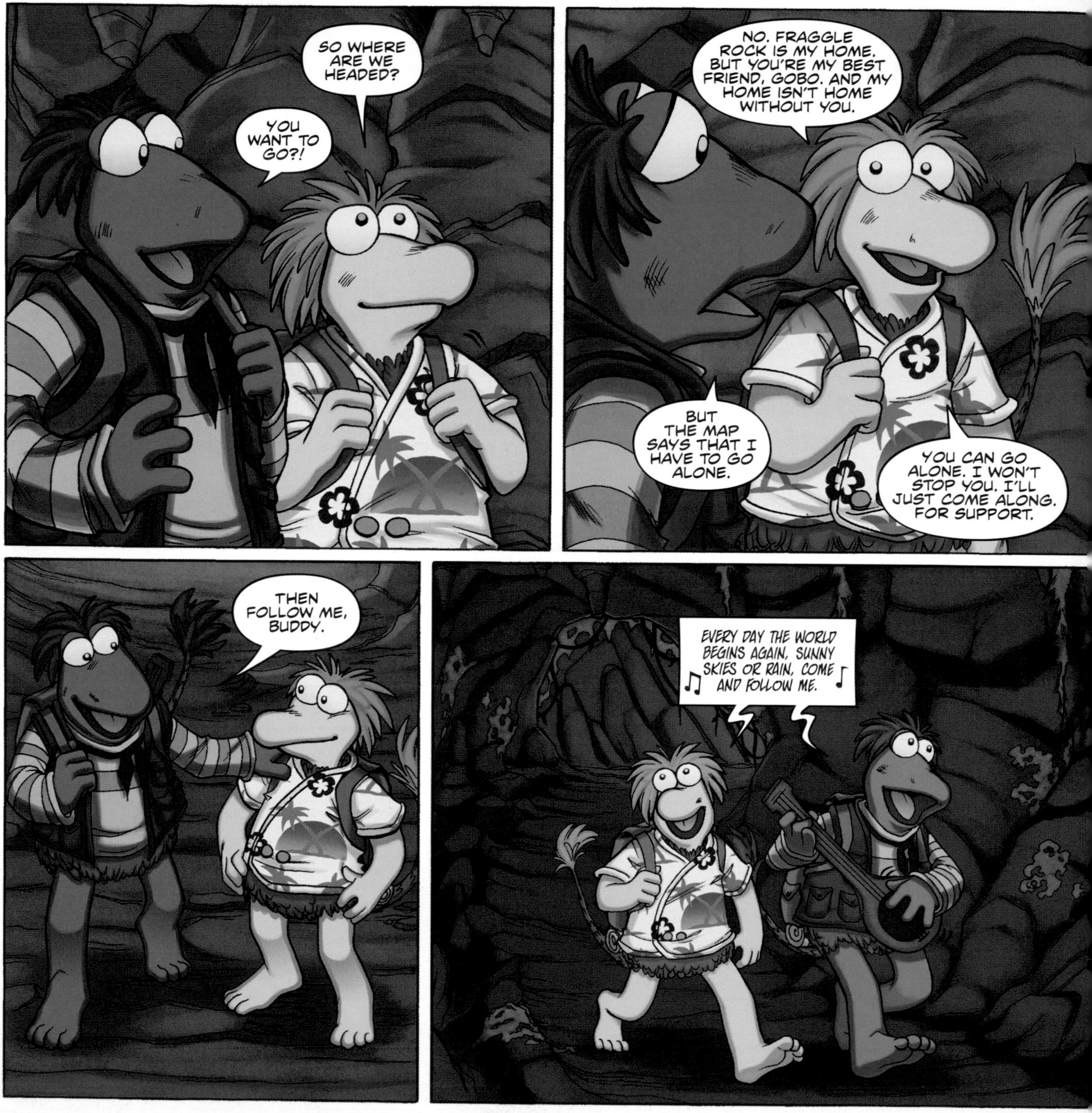
SO WHERE ARE WE HEADED?
YOU WANT TO GO?!
NO. FRAGGLE ROCK IS MY HOME. BUT YOU'RE MY BEST FRIEND, GOBO. AND MY HOME ISN'T HOME WITHOUT YOU.
BUT THE MAP SAYS THAT I HAVE TO GO ALONE.
YOU CAN GO ALONE. I WON'T STOP YOU. I'LL JUST COME ALONG. FOR SUPPORT.
THEN FOLLOW ME, BUDDY.
EVERY DAY THE WORLD BEGINS AGAIN, SUNNY SKIES OR RAIN, COME AND FOLLOW ME.

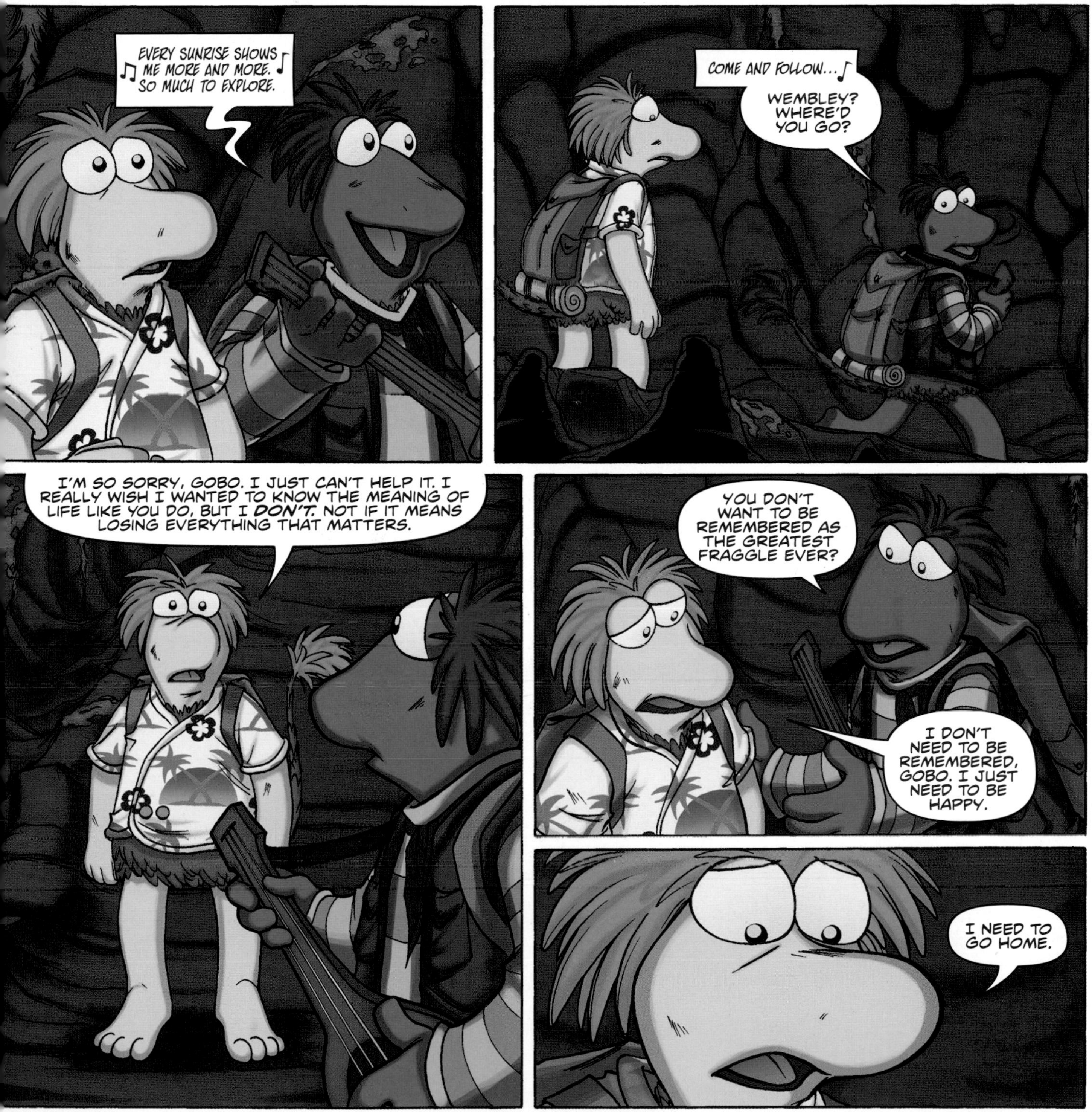
EVERY SUNRISE SHOWS ME MORE AND MORE. SO MUCH TO EXPLORE.
COME AND FOLLOW...
WEMBLEY? WHERE'D YOU GO?
I'M SO SORRY, GOBO. I JUST CAN'T HELP IT. I REALLY WISH I WANTED TO KNOW THE MEANING OF LIFE LIKE YOU DO, BUT I *DON'T.* NOT IF IT MEANS LOSING EVERYTHING THAT MATTERS.
YOU DON'T WANT TO BE REMEMBERED AS THE GREATEST FRAGGLE EVER?
I DON'T NEED TO BE REMEMBERED, GOBO. I JUST NEED TO BE HAPPY.
I NEED TO GO HOME.

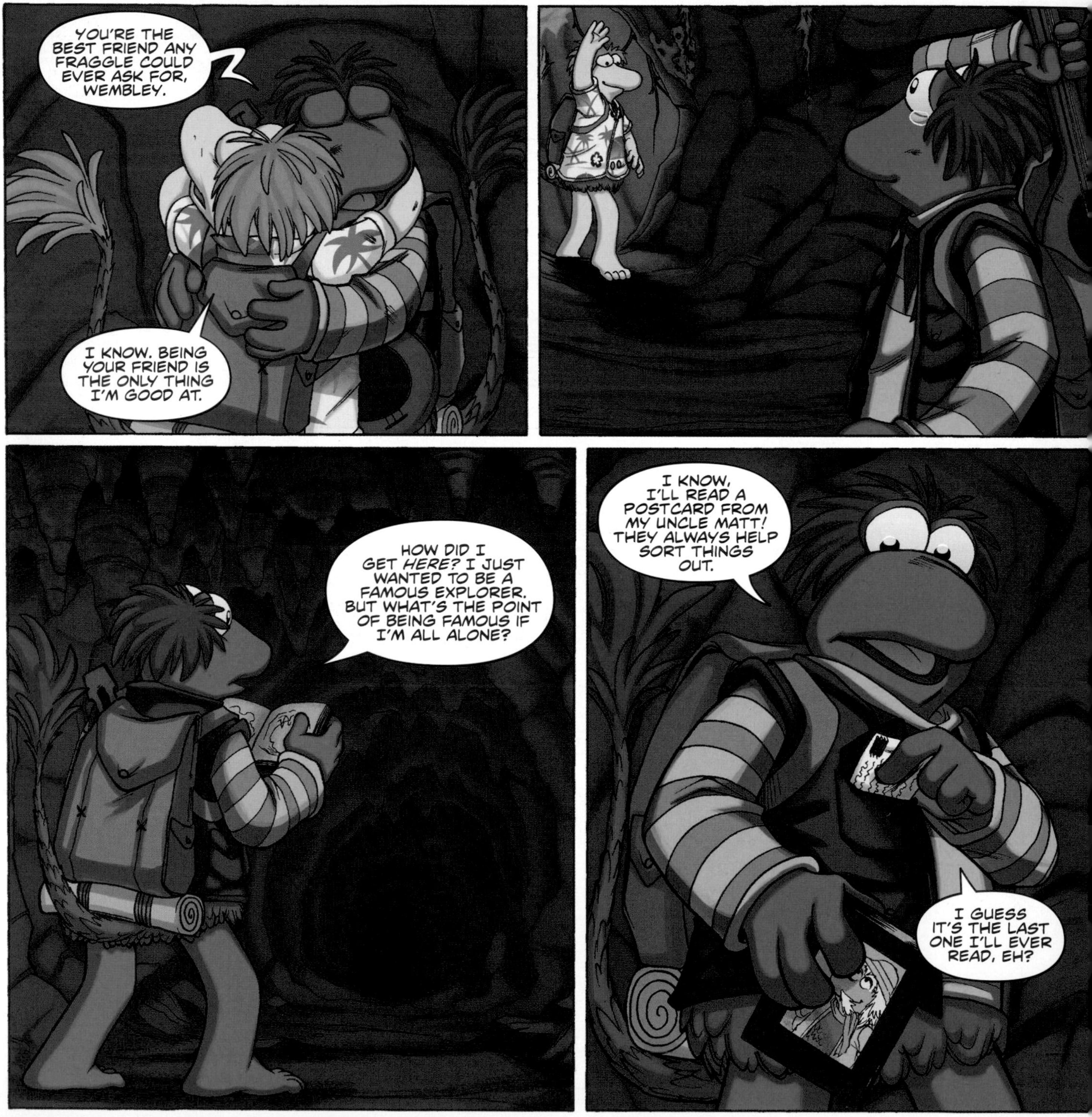
YOU'RE THE BEST FRIEND ANY FRAGGLE COULD EVER ASK FOR, WEMBLEY.
I KNOW. BEING YOUR FRIEND IS THE ONLY THING I'M GOOD AT.
HOW DID I GET *HERE?* I JUST WANTED TO BE A FAMOUS EXPLORER. BUT WHAT'S THE POINT OF BEING FAMOUS IF I'M ALL ALONE?
I KNOW, I'LL READ A POSTCARD FROM MY UNCLE MATT! THEY ALWAYS HELP SORT THINGS OUT.
I GUESS IT'S THE LAST ONE I'LL EVER READ, EH?

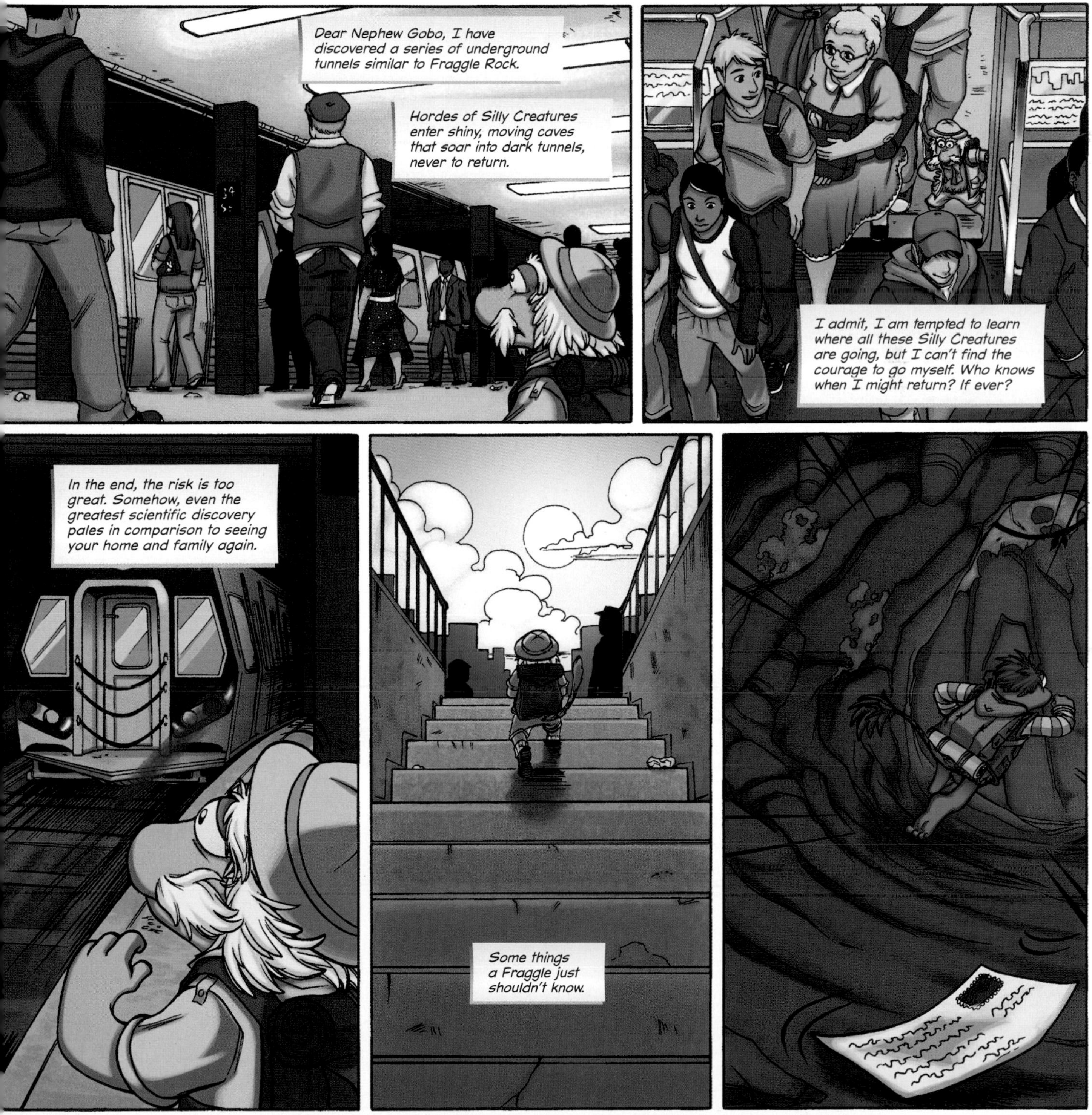

Dear Nephew Gobo, I have discovered a series of underground tunnels similar to Fraggle Rock.
Hordes of Silly Creatures enter shiny, moving caves that soar into dark tunnels, never to return.
I admit, I am tempted to learn where all these Silly Creatures are going, but I can't find the courage to go myself. Who knows when I might return? If ever?
In the end, the risk is too great. Somehow, even the greatest scientific discovery pales in comparison to seeing your home and family again.
Some things a Fraggle just shouldn't know.

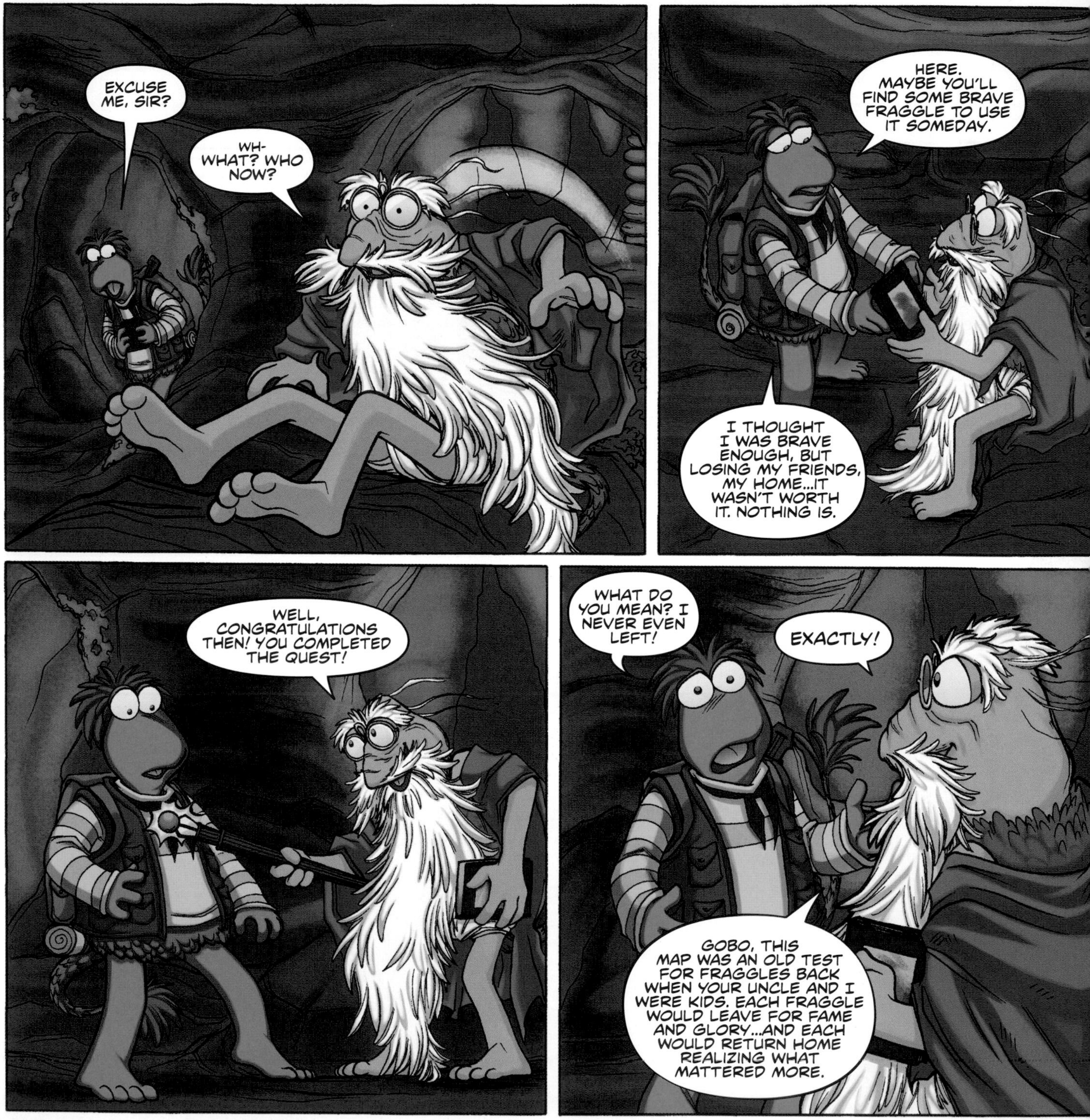
EXCUSE ME, SIR?
WH- WHAT? WHO NOW?
HERE. MAYBE YOU'LL FIND SOME BRAVE FRAGGLE TO USE IT SOMEDAY.
I THOUGHT I WAS BRAVE ENOUGH, BUT LOSING MY FRIENDS, MY HOME...IT WASN'T WORTH IT. NOTHING IS.
WELL, CONGRATULATIONS THEN! YOU COMPLETED THE QUEST!
WHAT DO YOU MEAN? I NEVER EVEN LEFT!
EXACTLY!
GOBO, THIS MAP WAS AN OLD TEST FOR FRAGGLES BACK WHEN YOUR UNCLE AND I WERE KIDS. EACH FRAGGLE WOULD LEAVE FOR FAME AND GLORY...AND EACH WOULD RETURN HOME REALIZING WHAT MATTERED MORE.

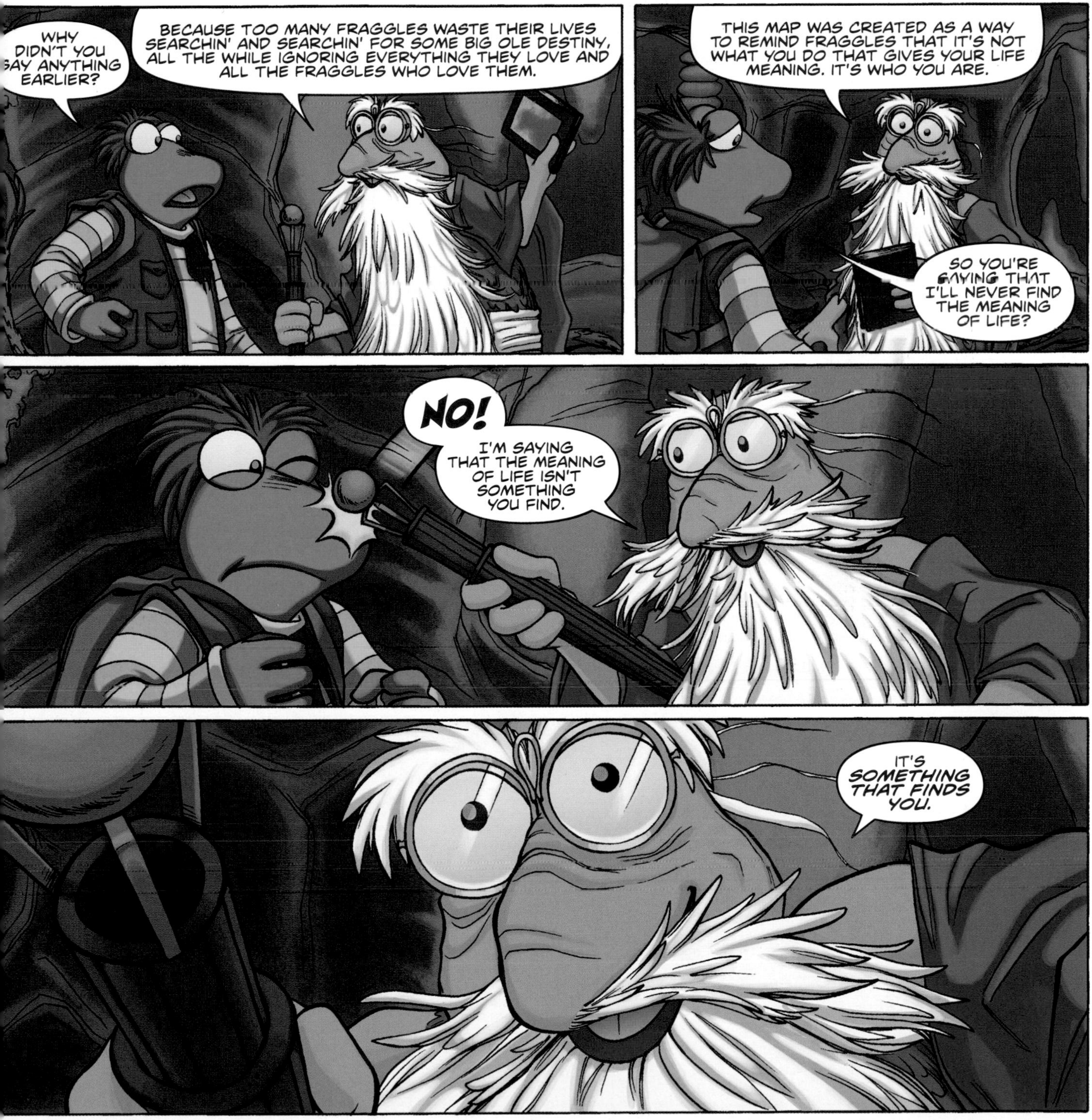
WHY DIDN'T YOU SAY ANYTHING EARLIER?
BECAUSE TOO MANY FRAGGLES WASTE THEIR LIVES SEARCHIN' AND SEARCHIN' FOR SOME BIG OLE DESTINY, ALL THE WHILE IGNORING EVERYTHING THEY LOVE AND ALL THE FRAGGLES WHO LOVE THEM.
THIS MAP WAS CREATED AS A WAY TO REMIND FRAGGLES THAT IT'S NOT WHAT YOU DO THAT GIVES YOUR LIFE MEANING. IT'S WHO YOU ARE.
SO YOU'RE SAYING THAT I'LL NEVER FIND THE MEANING OF LIFE?
NO!
I'M SAYING THAT THE MEANING OF LIFE ISN'T SOMETHING YOU FIND.
IT'S SOMETHING THAT FINDS YOU.

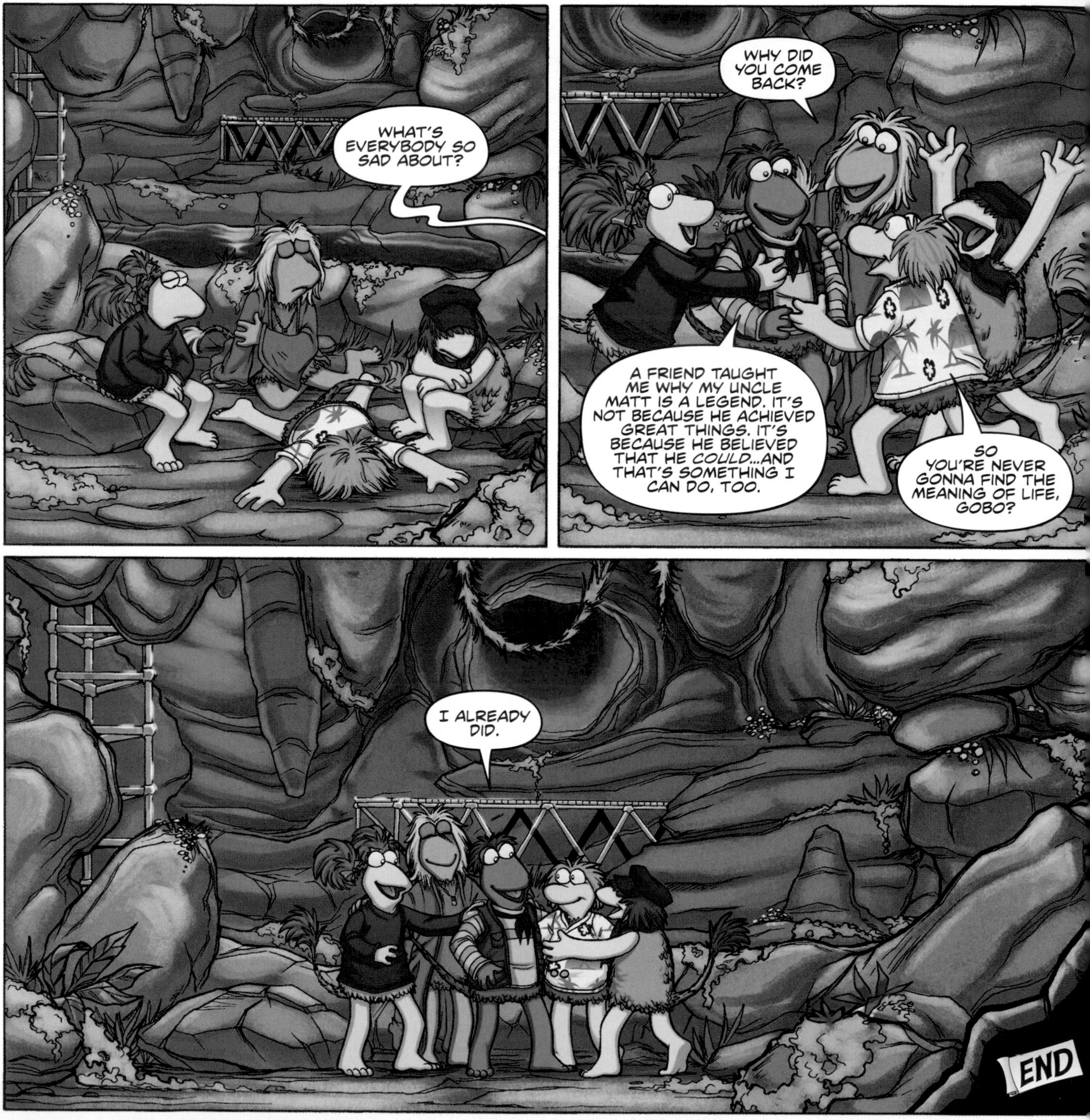
WHAT'S EVERYBODY SO SAD ABOUT?
WHY DID YOU COME BACK?
A FRIEND TAUGHT ME WHY MY UNCLE MATT IS A LEGEND. IT'S NOT BECAUSE HE ACHIEVED GREAT THINGS. IT'S BECAUSE HE BELIEVED THAT HE *COULD*...AND THAT'S SOMETHING I CAN DO, TOO.
SO YOU'RE NEVER GONNA FIND THE MEANING OF LIFE, GOBO?
I ALREADY DID.
END

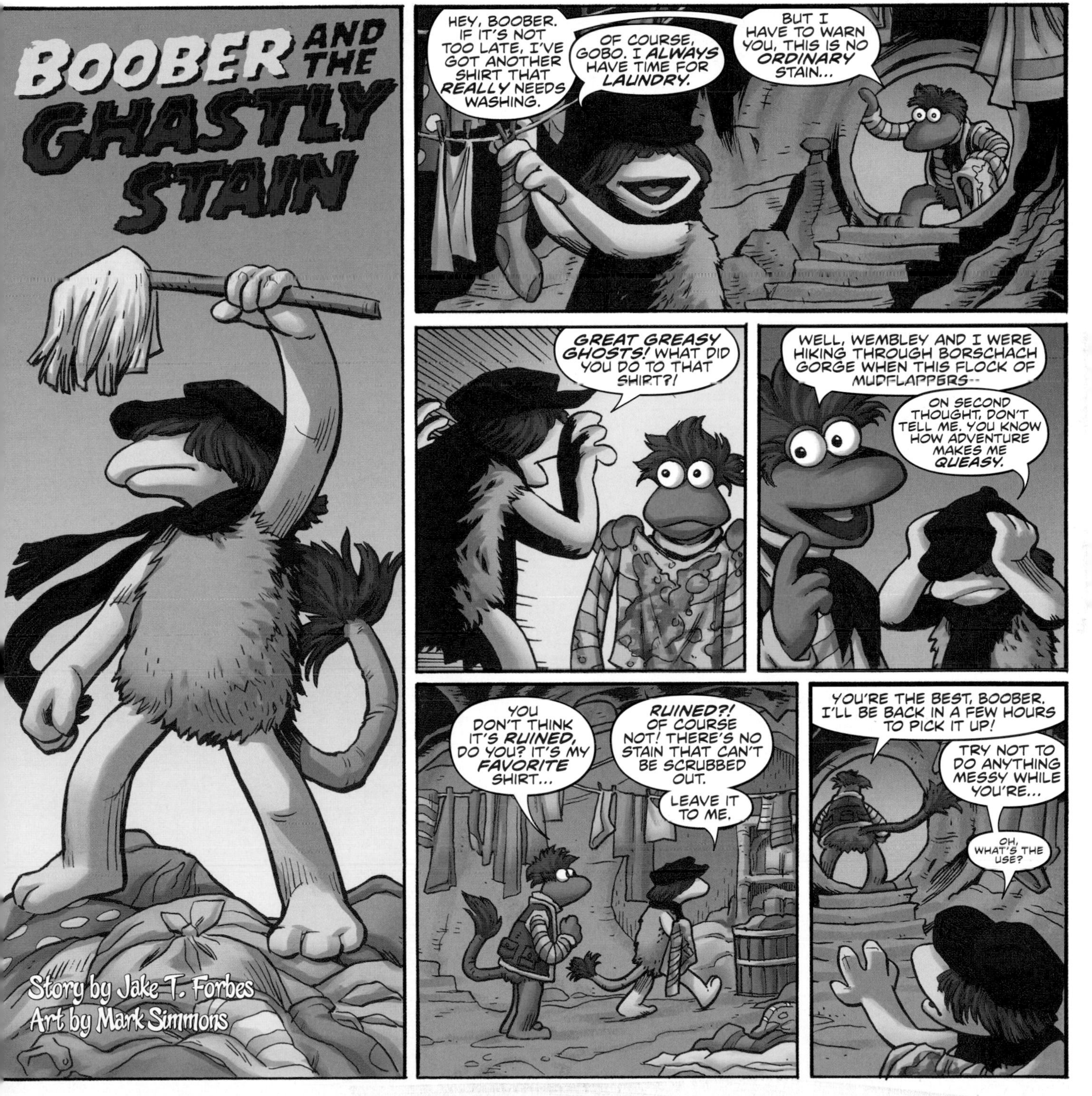
BOOBER AND THE GHASTLY STAIN
Story by Jake T. Forbes
Art by Mark Simmons
HEY, BOOBER. IF IT'S NOT TOO LATE, I'VE GOT ANOTHER SHIRT THAT REALLY NEEDS WASHING.
OF COURSE, GOBO. I ALWAYS HAVE TIME FOR LAUNDRY.
BUT I HAVE TO WARN YOU, THIS IS NO ORDINARY STAIN...
GREAT GREASY GHOSTS! WHAT DID YOU DO TO THAT SHIRT?!
WELL, WEMBLEY AND I WERE HIKING THROUGH BORSCHACH GORGE WHEN THIS FLOCK OF MUDFLAPPERS--
ON SECOND THOUGHT, DON'T TELL ME. YOU KNOW HOW ADVENTURE MAKES ME QUEASY.
YOU DON'T THINK IT'S RUINED, DO YOU? IT'S MY FAVORITE SHIRT...
RUINED?! OF COURSE NOT! THERE'S NO STAIN THAT CAN'T BE SCRUBBED OUT.
LEAVE IT TO ME.
YOU'RE THE BEST, BOOBER. I'LL BE BACK IN A FEW HOURS TO PICK IT UP!
TRY NOT TO DO ANYTHING MESSY WHILE YOU'RE...
OH, WHAT'S THE USE?

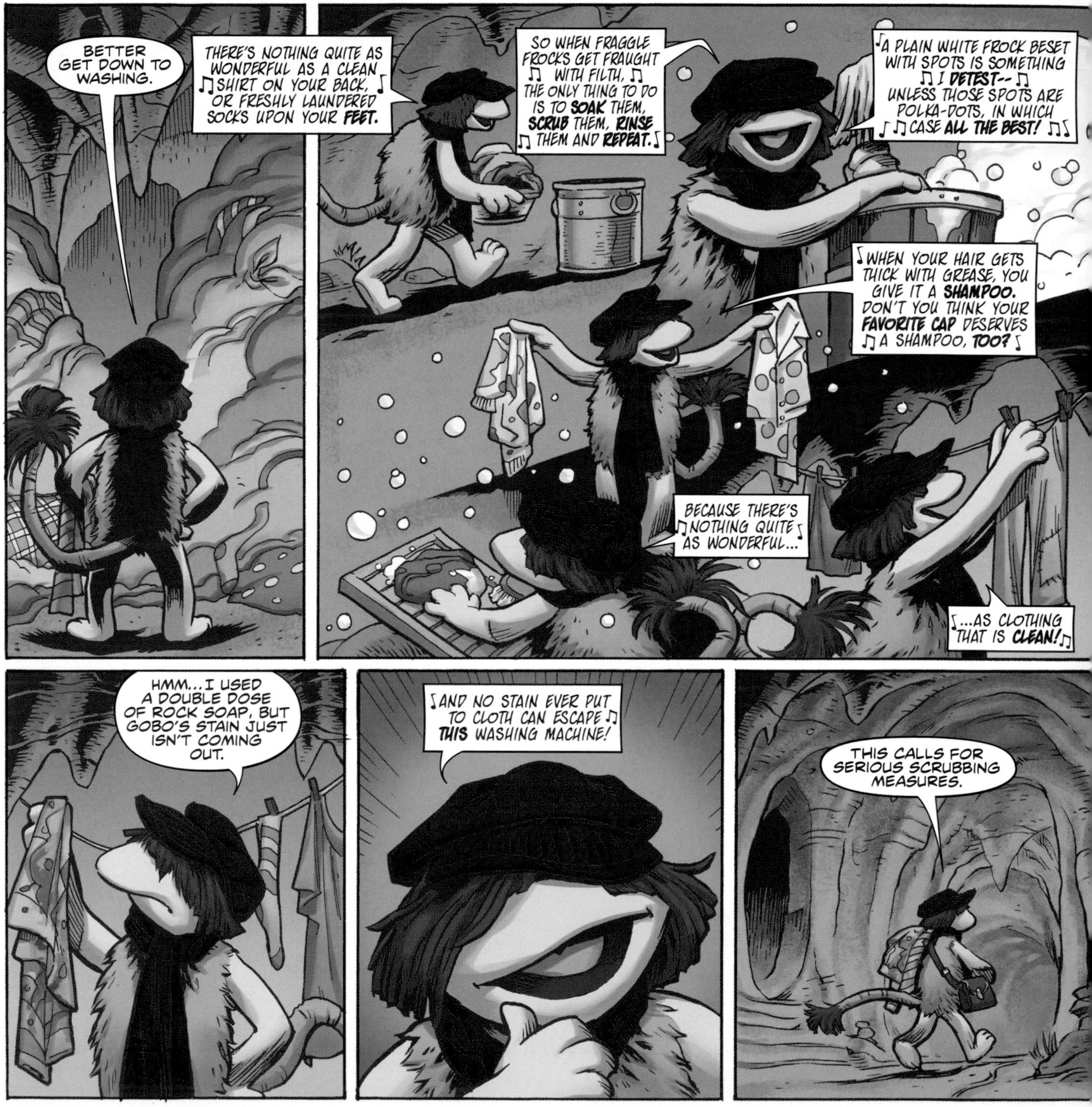
BETTER GET DOWN TO WASHING.
THERE'S NOTHING QUITE AS WONDERFUL AS A CLEAN ♫ SHIRT ON YOUR BACK, ♪ OR FRESHLY LAUNDERED SOCKS UPON YOUR **FEET.**
SO WHEN FRAGGLE FROCKS GET FRAUGHT ♫ WITH FILTH, ♫ THE ONLY THING TO DO IS TO **SOAK** THEM, **SCRUB** THEM, **RINSE** ♫ THEM AND **REPEAT.** ♪
♪ A PLAIN WHITE FROCK BESET WITH SPOTS IS SOMETHING ♫ I **DETEST--** ♫ UNLESS THOSE SPOTS ARE POLKA-DOTS, IN WHICH ♪ ♫ CASE **ALL THE BEST!** ♫♪
♪ WHEN YOUR HAIR GETS THICK WITH GREASE, YOU GIVE IT A **SHAMPOO.** DON'T YOU THINK YOUR **FAVORITE CAP** DESERVES ♫ A SHAMPOO, **TOO?** ♪
BECAUSE THERE'S ♫ NOTHING QUITE ♪ AS WONDERFUL...
♪ ...AS CLOTHING THAT IS **CLEAN!** ♫
HMM... I USED A DOUBLE DOSE OF ROCK SOAP, BUT GOBO'S STAIN JUST ISN'T COMING OUT.
♪ AND NO STAIN EVER PUT TO CLOTH CAN ESCAPE ♫ **THIS** WASHING MACHINE!
THIS CALLS FOR SERIOUS SCRUBBING MEASURES.

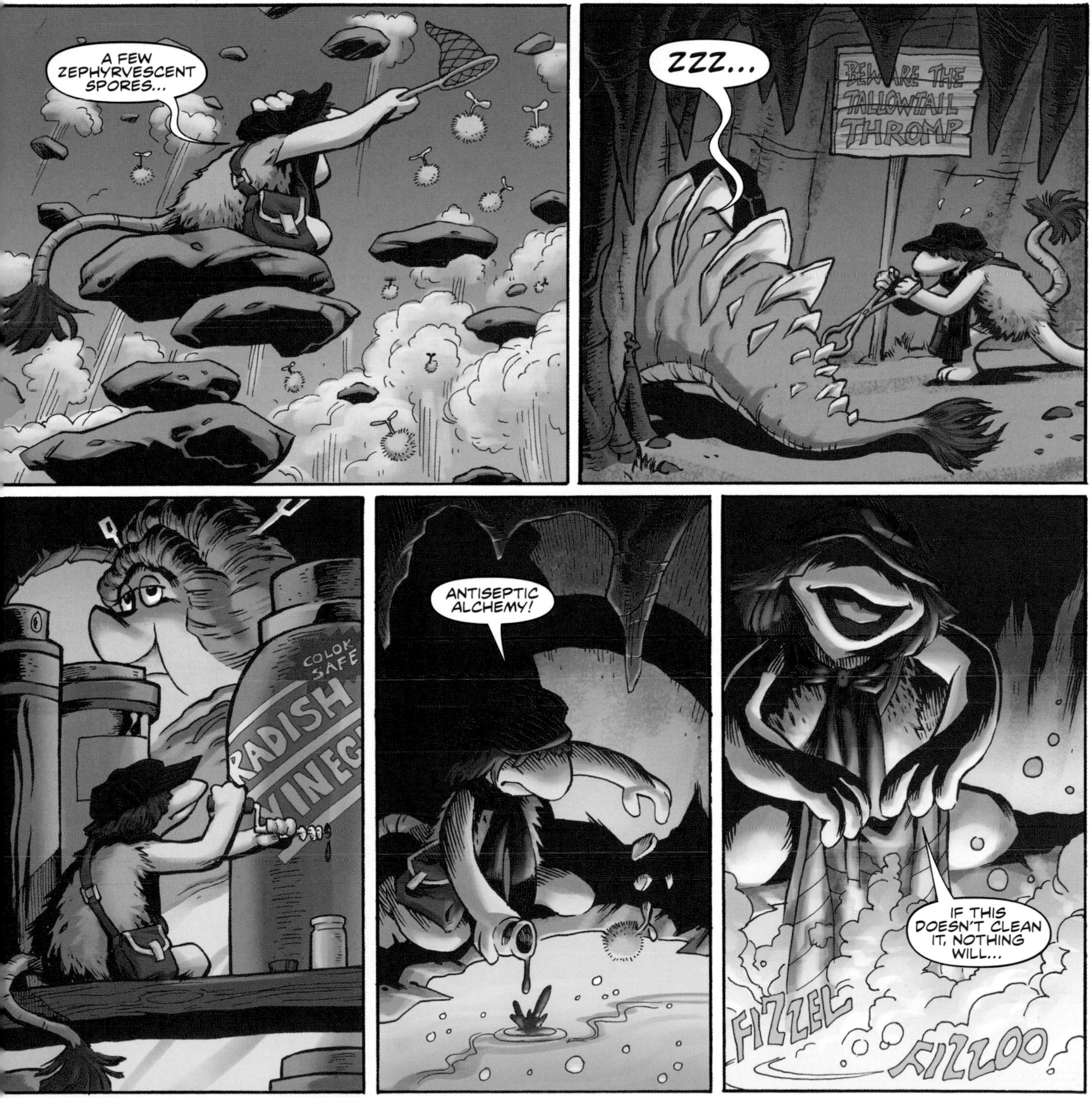
A FEW ZEPHYRVESCENT SPORES...
ZZZ...
BEWARE THE TALLOWTAIL THROMP
COLOR SAFE
RADISH
VINEG
ANTISEPTIC ALCHEMY!
IF THIS DOESN'T CLEAN IT, NOTHING WILL...
FIZZEL
KIZZOO

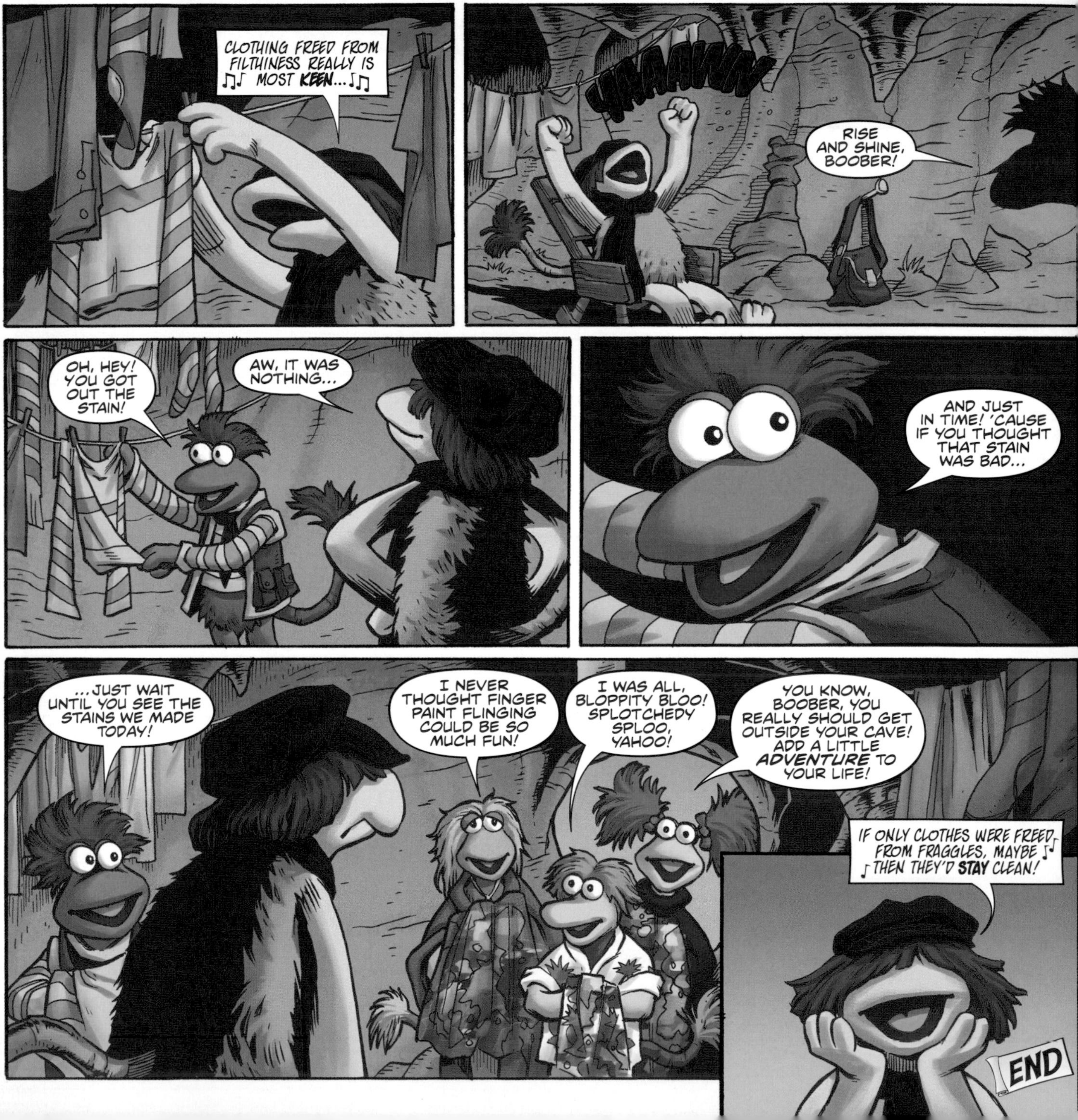
CLOTHING FREED FROM FILTHINESS REALLY IS ♫♩ MOST KEEN... ♩♫
YAAAAWN
RISE AND SHINE, BOOBER!
OH, HEY! YOU GOT OUT THE STAIN!
AW, IT WAS NOTHING...
AND JUST IN TIME! 'CAUSE IF YOU THOUGHT THAT STAIN WAS BAD...
...JUST WAIT UNTIL YOU SEE THE STAINS WE MADE TODAY!
I NEVER THOUGHT FINGER PAINT FLINGING COULD BE SO MUCH FUN!
I WAS ALL, BLOPPITY BLOO! SPLOTCHEDY SPLOO, YAHOO!
YOU KNOW, BOOBER, YOU REALLY SHOULD GET OUTSIDE YOUR CAVE! ADD A LITTLE ADVENTURE TO YOUR LIFE!
IF ONLY CLOTHES WERE FREED FROM FRAGGLES, MAYBE ♩ THEN THEY'D STAY CLEAN!
END

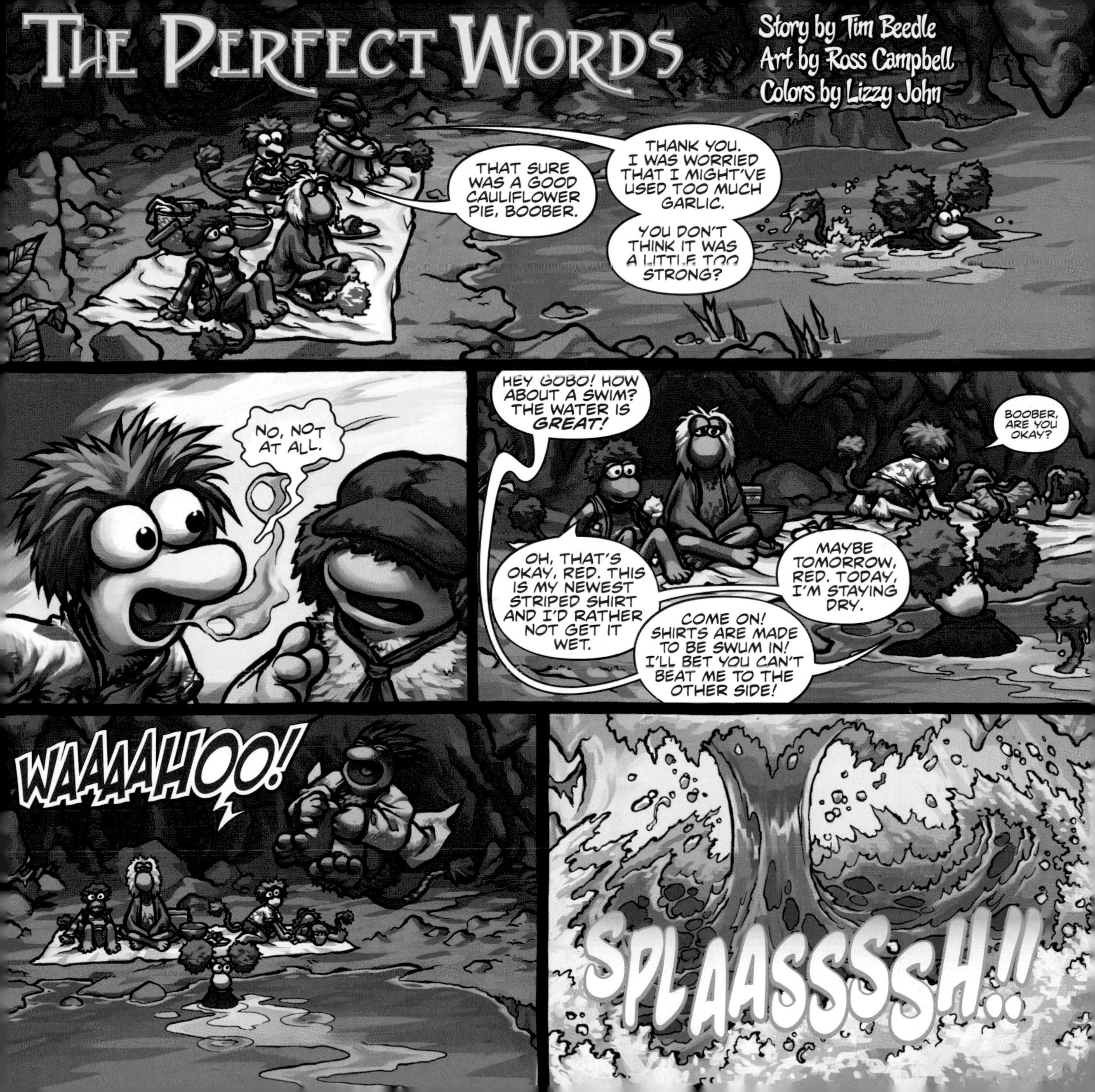
THE PERFECT WORDS
Story by Tim Beedle
Art by Ross Campbell
Colors by Lizzy John
THAT SURE WAS A GOOD CAULIFLOWER PIE, BOOBER.
THANK YOU. I WAS WORRIED THAT I MIGHT'VE USED TOO MUCH GARLIC.
YOU DON'T THINK IT WAS A LITTLE TOO STRONG?
NO, NOT AT ALL.
HEY GOBO! HOW ABOUT A SWIM? THE WATER IS GREAT!
BOOBER, ARE YOU OKAY?
OH, THAT'S OKAY, RED. THIS IS MY NEWEST STRIPED SHIRT AND I'D RATHER NOT GET IT WET.
MAYBE TOMORROW, RED. TODAY, I'M STAYING DRY.
COME ON! SHIRTS ARE MADE TO BE SWUM IN! I'LL BET YOU CAN'T BEAT ME TO THE OTHER SIDE!
WAAAAHOO!
SPLAASSSSH!!

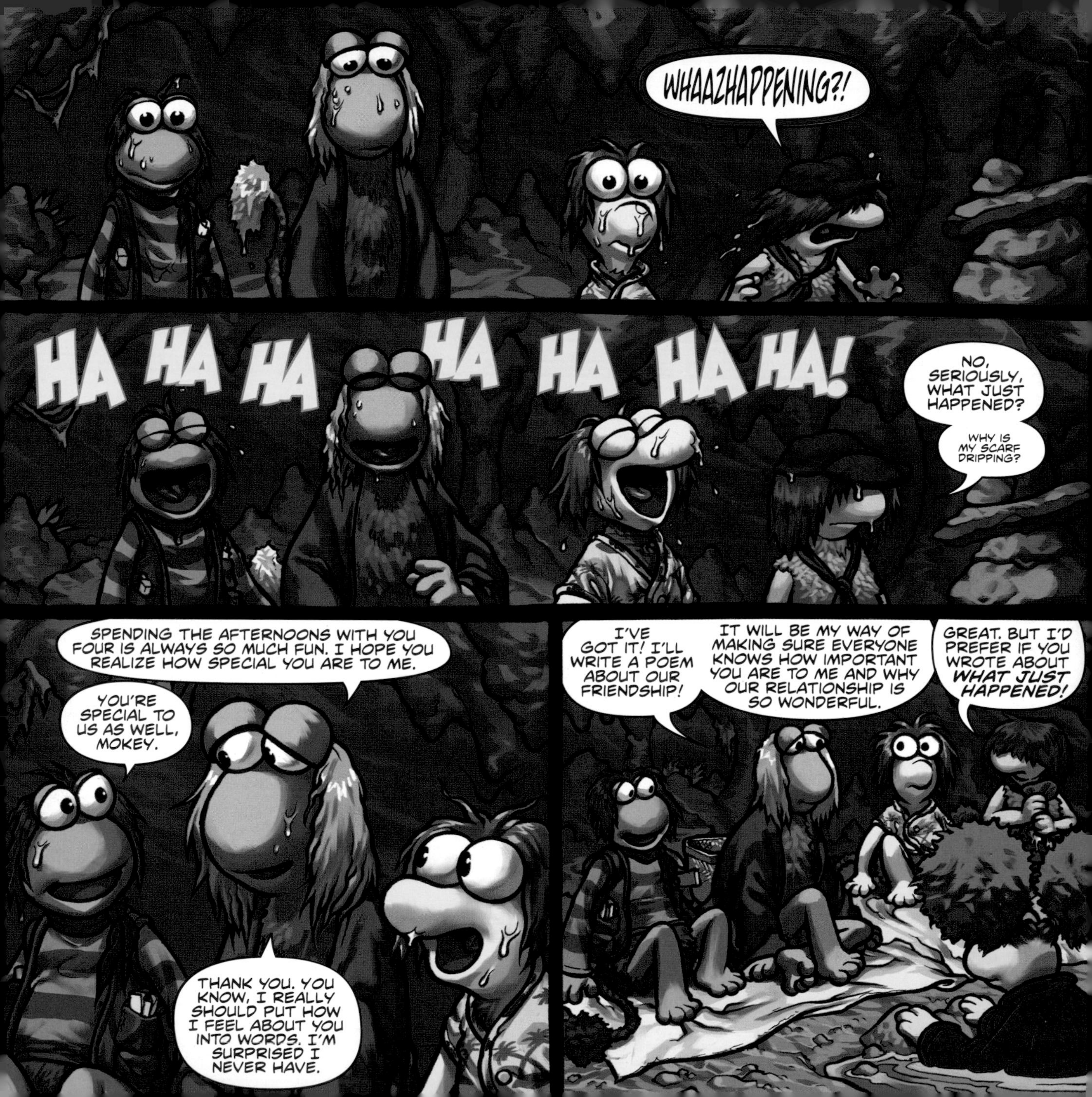
WHAAZHAPPENING?!
HA HA HA HA HA HA HA!
NO, SERIOUSLY, WHAT JUST HAPPENED?
WHY IS MY SCARF DRIPPING?
SPENDING THE AFTERNOONS WITH YOU FOUR IS ALWAYS SO MUCH FUN. I HOPE YOU REALIZE HOW SPECIAL YOU ARE TO ME.
YOU'RE SPECIAL TO US AS WELL, MOKEY.
THANK YOU. YOU KNOW, I REALLY SHOULD PUT HOW I FEEL ABOUT YOU INTO WORDS. I'M SURPRISED I NEVER HAVE.
I'VE GOT IT! I'LL WRITE A POEM ABOUT OUR FRIENDSHIP!
IT WILL BE MY WAY OF MAKING SURE EVERYONE KNOWS HOW IMPORTANT YOU ARE TO ME AND WHY OUR RELATIONSHIP IS SO WONDERFUL.
GREAT. BUT I'D PREFER IF YOU WROTE ABOUT ***WHAT JUST HAPPENED!***

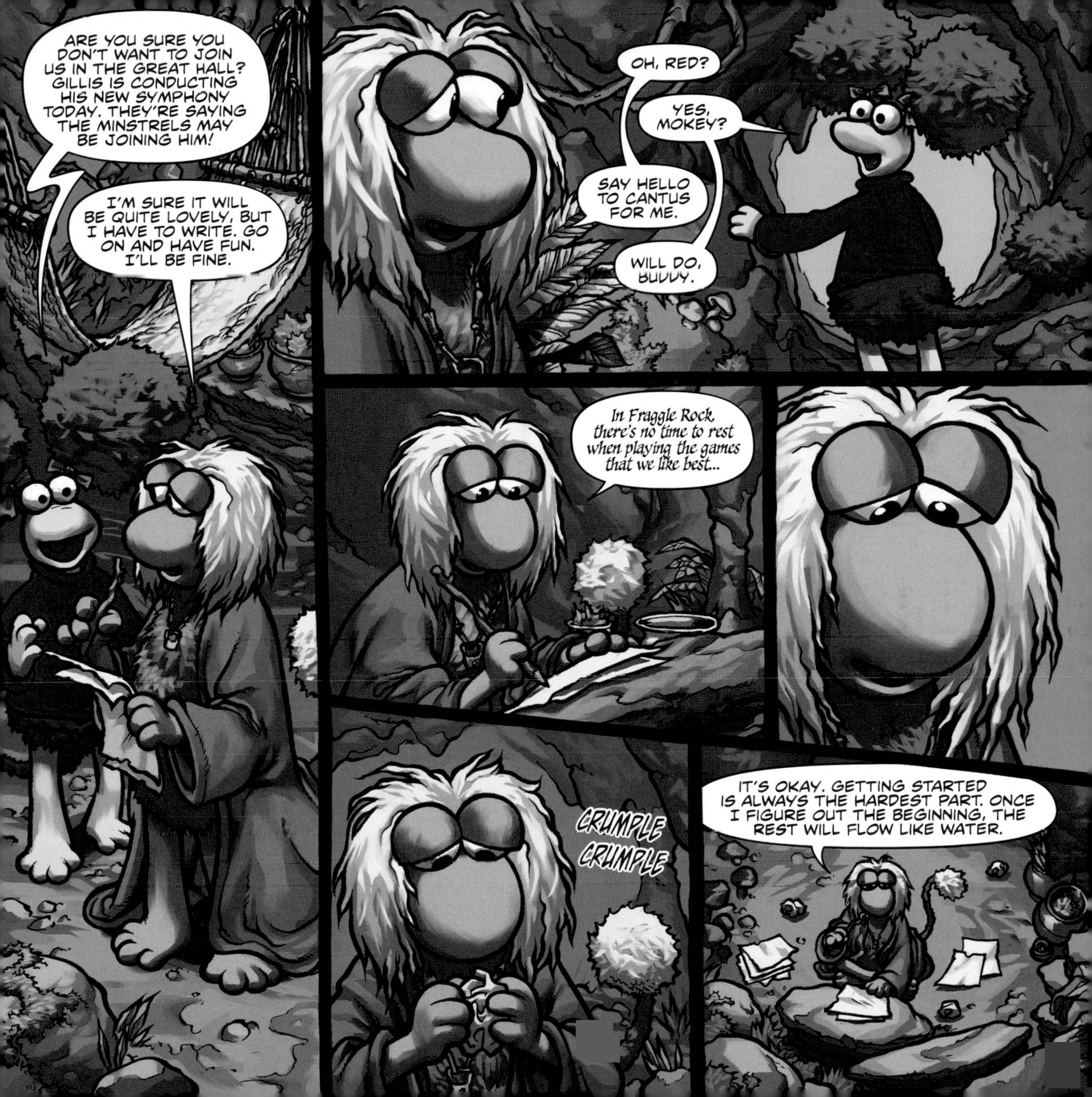
ARE YOU SURE YOU DON'T WANT TO JOIN US IN THE GREAT HALL? GILLIS IS CONDUCTING HIS NEW SYMPHONY TODAY. THEY'RE SAYING THE MINSTRELS MAY BE JOINING HIM!
I'M SURE IT WILL BE QUITE LOVELY, BUT I HAVE TO WRITE. GO ON AND HAVE FUN. I'LL BE FINE.
OH, RED?
YES, MOKEY?
SAY HELLO TO CANTUS FOR ME.
WILL DO, BUDDY.
In Fraggle Rock, there's no time to rest when playing the games that we like best...
CRUMPLE CRUMPLE
IT'S OKAY. GETTING STARTED IS ALWAYS THE HARDEST PART. ONCE I FIGURE OUT THE BEGINNING, THE REST WILL FLOW LIKE WATER.

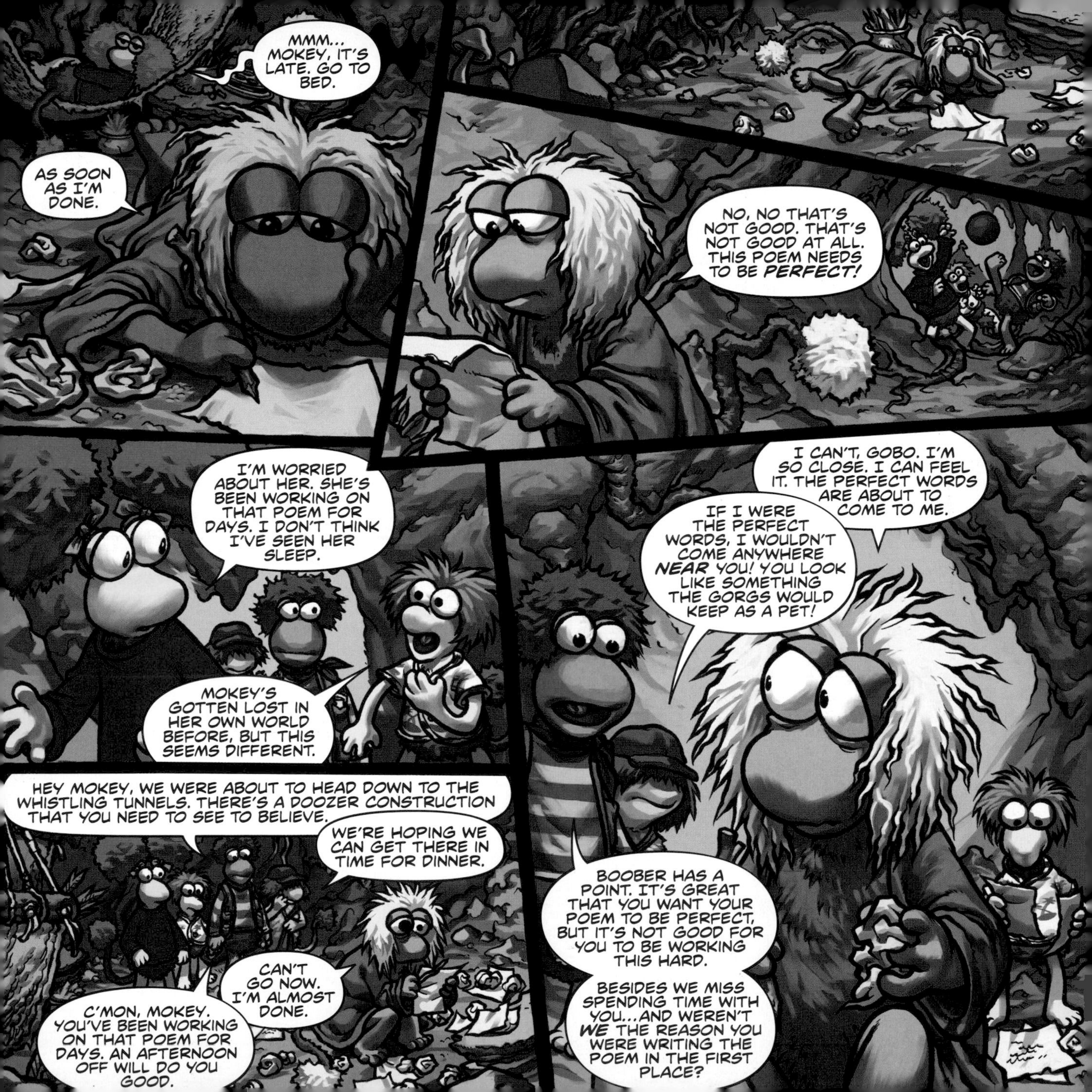
MMM... MOKEY, IT'S LATE. GO TO BED.
AS SOON AS I'M DONE.
NO, NO THAT'S NOT GOOD. THAT'S NOT GOOD AT ALL. THIS POEM NEEDS TO BE *PERFECT*!
I'M WORRIED ABOUT HER. SHE'S BEEN WORKING ON THAT POEM FOR DAYS. I DON'T THINK I'VE SEEN HER SLEEP.
MOKEY'S GOTTEN LOST IN HER OWN WORLD BEFORE, BUT THIS SEEMS DIFFERENT.
HEY MOKEY, WE WERE ABOUT TO HEAD DOWN TO THE WHISTLING TUNNELS. THERE'S A DOOZER CONSTRUCTION THAT YOU NEED TO SEE TO BELIEVE.
WE'RE HOPING WE CAN GET THERE IN TIME FOR DINNER.
CAN'T GO NOW. I'M ALMOST DONE.
C'MON, MOKEY. YOU'VE BEEN WORKING ON THAT POEM FOR DAYS. AN AFTERNOON OFF WILL DO YOU GOOD.
I CAN'T, GOBO. I'M SO CLOSE. I CAN FEEL IT. THE PERFECT WORDS ARE ABOUT TO COME TO ME.
IF I WERE THE PERFECT WORDS, I WOULDN'T COME ANYWHERE *NEAR* YOU! YOU LOOK LIKE SOMETHING THE GORGS WOULD KEEP AS A PET!
BOOBER HAS A POINT. IT'S GREAT THAT YOU WANT YOUR POEM TO BE PERFECT, BUT IT'S NOT GOOD FOR YOU TO BE WORKING THIS HARD.
BESIDES WE MISS SPENDING TIME WITH YOU...AND WEREN'T *WE* THE REASON YOU WERE WRITING THE POEM IN THE FIRST PLACE?

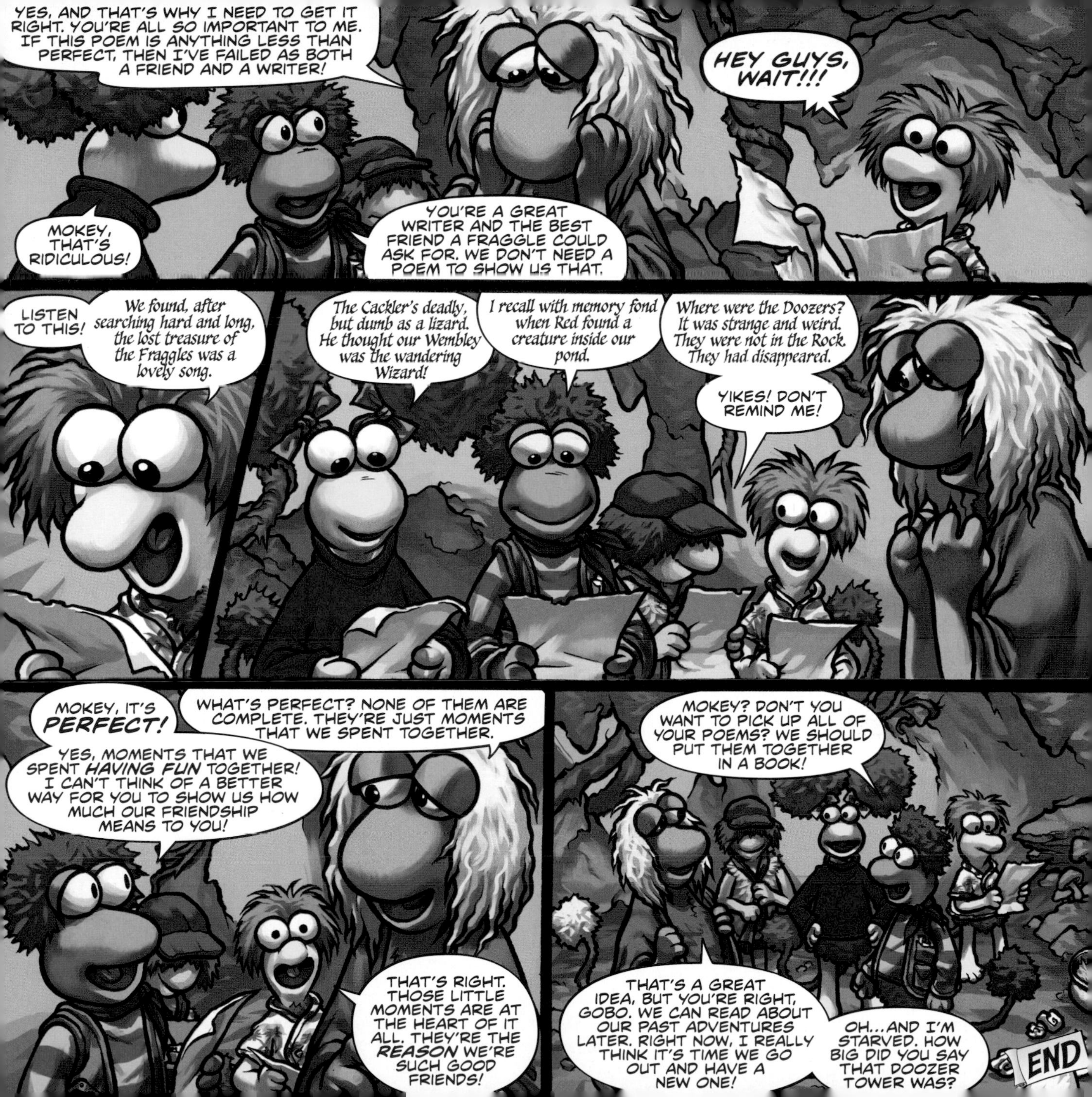
YES, AND THAT'S WHY I NEED TO GET IT RIGHT. YOU'RE ALL SO IMPORTANT TO ME. IF THIS POEM IS ANYTHING LESS THAN PERFECT, THEN I'VE FAILED AS BOTH A FRIEND AND A WRITER!
HEY GUYS, WAIT!!!
MOKEY, THAT'S RIDICULOUS!
YOU'RE A GREAT WRITER AND THE BEST FRIEND A FRAGGLE COULD ASK FOR. WE DON'T NEED A POEM TO SHOW US THAT.
LISTEN TO THIS!
We found, after searching hard and long, the lost treasure of the Fraggles was a lovely song.
The Cackler's deadly, but dumb as a lizard. He thought our Wembley was the wandering Wizard!
I recall with memory fond when Red found a creature inside our pond.
Where were the Doozers? It was strange and weird. They were not in the Rock. They had disappeared.
YIKES! DON'T REMIND ME!
MOKEY, IT'S PERFECT!
WHAT'S PERFECT? NONE OF THEM ARE COMPLETE. THEY'RE JUST MOMENTS THAT WE SPENT TOGETHER.
YES, MOMENTS THAT WE SPENT HAVING FUN TOGETHER! I CAN'T THINK OF A BETTER WAY FOR YOU TO SHOW US HOW MUCH OUR FRIENDSHIP MEANS TO YOU!
THAT'S RIGHT. THOSE LITTLE MOMENTS ARE AT THE HEART OF IT ALL. THEY'RE THE REASON WE'RE SUCH GOOD FRIENDS!
MOKEY? DON'T YOU WANT TO PICK UP ALL OF YOUR POEMS? WE SHOULD PUT THEM TOGETHER IN A BOOK!
THAT'S A GREAT IDEA, BUT YOU'RE RIGHT, GOBO. WE CAN READ ABOUT OUR PAST ADVENTURES LATER. RIGHT NOW, I REALLY THINK IT'S TIME WE GO OUT AND HAVE A NEW ONE!
OH... AND I'M STARVED. HOW BIG DID YOU SAY THAT DOOZER TOWER WAS?
END

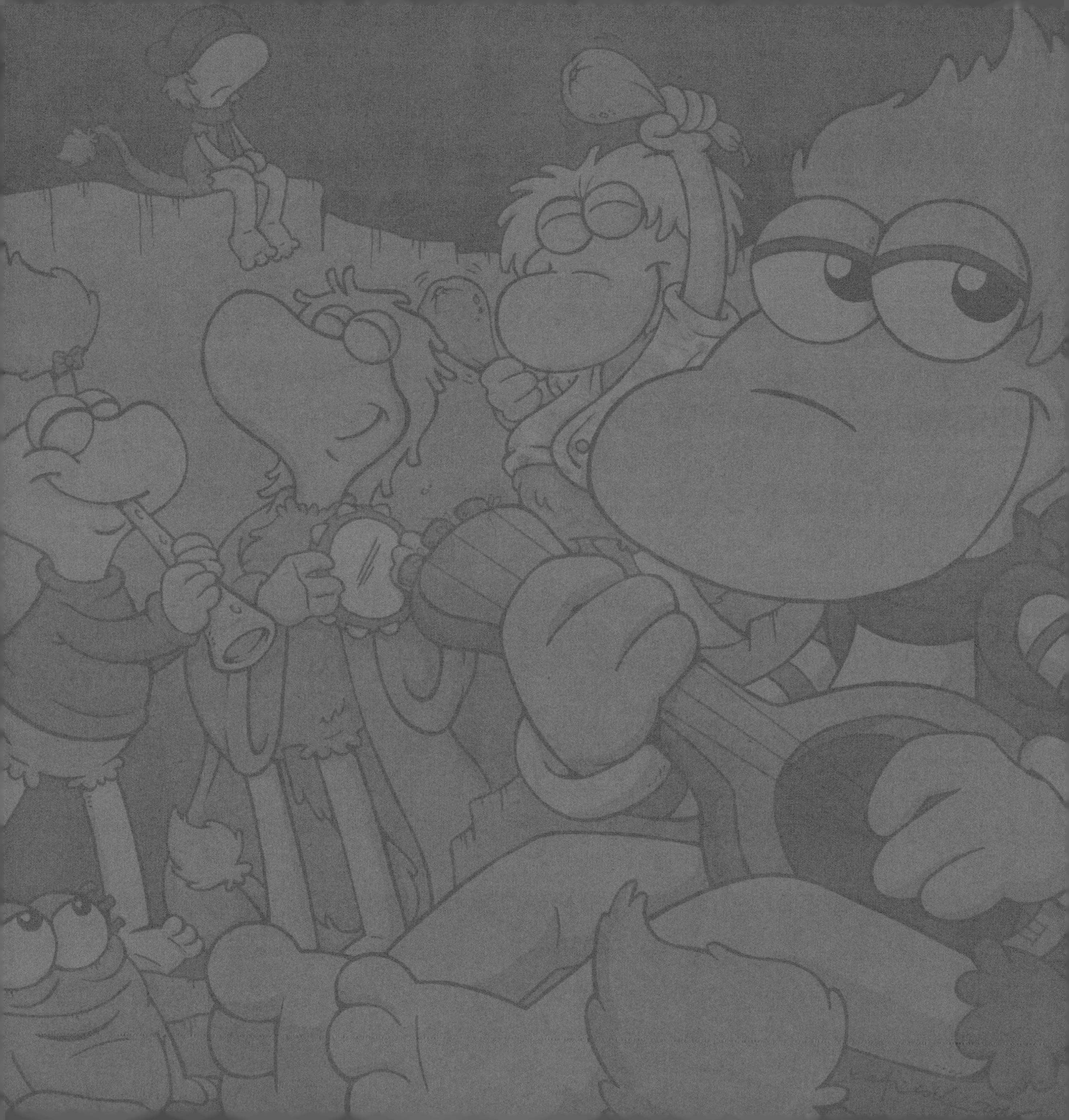

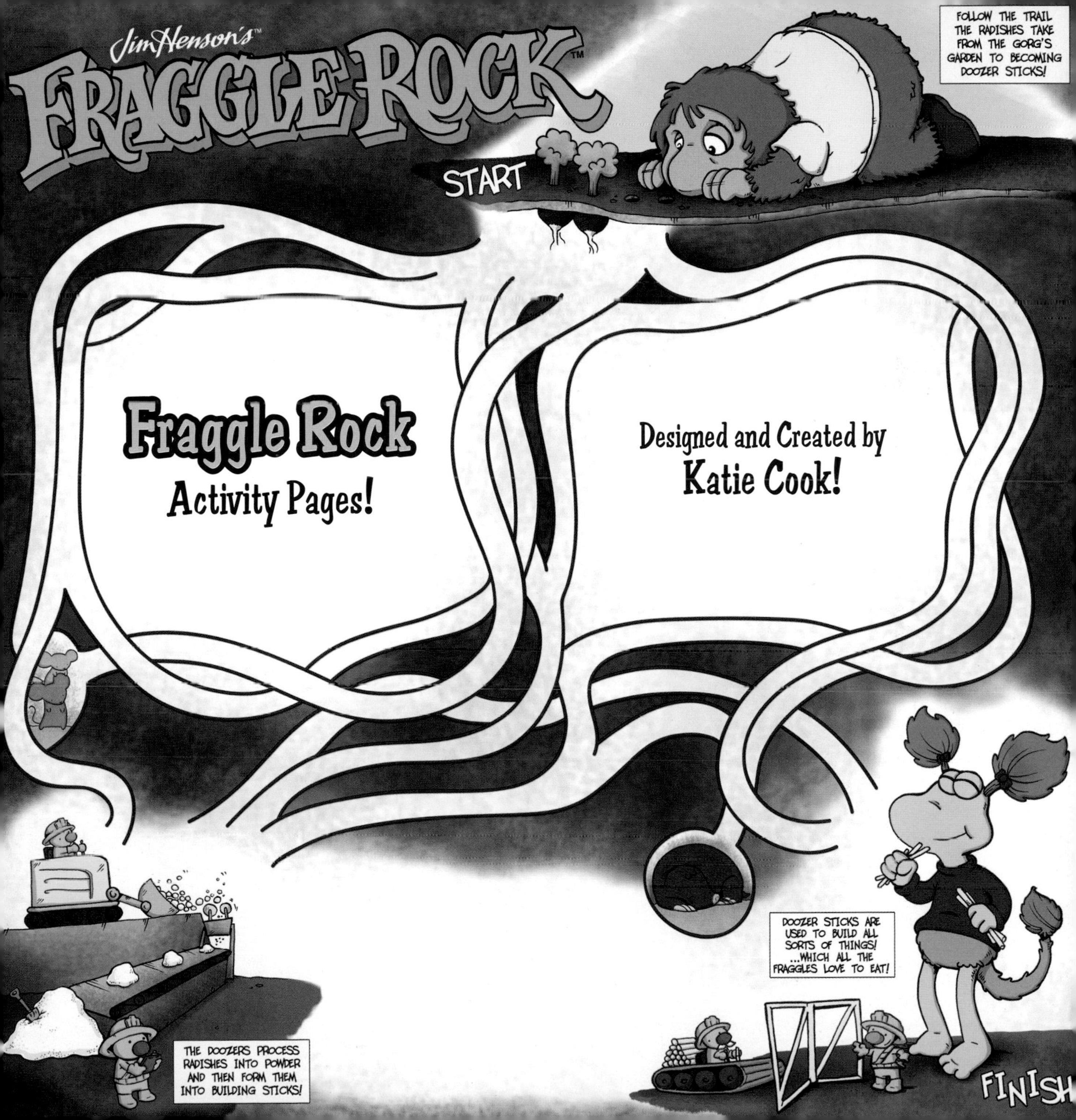
Jim Henson's
FRAGGLE ROCK™
FOLLOW THE TRAIL THE RADISHES TAKE FROM THE GORG'S GARDEN TO BECOMING DOOZER STICKS!
START
Fraggle Rock
Activity Pages!
Designed and Created by
Katie Cook!
THE DOOZERS PROCESS RADISHES INTO POWDER AND THEN FORM THEM INTO BUILDING STICKS!
DOOZER STICKS ARE USED TO BUILD ALL SORTS OF THINGS! ...WHICH ALL THE FRAGGLES LOVE TO EAT!
FINISH

"how to draw a doozer"
a lesson in artistic interpretation by
MOKEY FRAGGLE

Step 1:
First, in PENCIL, lightly rough in the basic shape of the head and the body of our little Doozer friend!

Step 2:
Next, still in pencil, we can add the details of his arms and legs... He's starting to take shape!

Step 3:
On to some more details. Pencil in his facial features and the shape of his boots, gloves and belts.

Step 4:
Details, details! More details! Now it's time to pencil in the pockets on his belts, his tools and his antennae!

Step 5:
Now, with a black pen or marker, trace over your pencil drawing. Erase your pencil lines and you're done!

"how to build a doozer structure"

a lesson in artistic interpretation by
MOKEY FRAGGLE

Things you will need:
- 1/2 cup salt
- 1/2 cup water
- 1 cup flour
- mixing bowl
- toothpicks
- newspaper

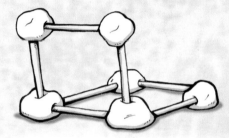

Step 3:
Shape the dough into 1/2" inch round balls. Use them to hold the toothpicks in place so you can create cube structures.

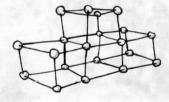

Step 1:
Making homemade play dough! Mix the flour, salt and water in a bowl. When the dough stiffens, knead it with your hands. (Add food coloring if you want to make it colorful!)

Step 2:
Lay down newspaper to protect the surface of the tabletop you'll be working on.

Step 4:
Create your masterpiece! (How tall can you make it without it toppling? How many shapes can you use to make your building unique?)

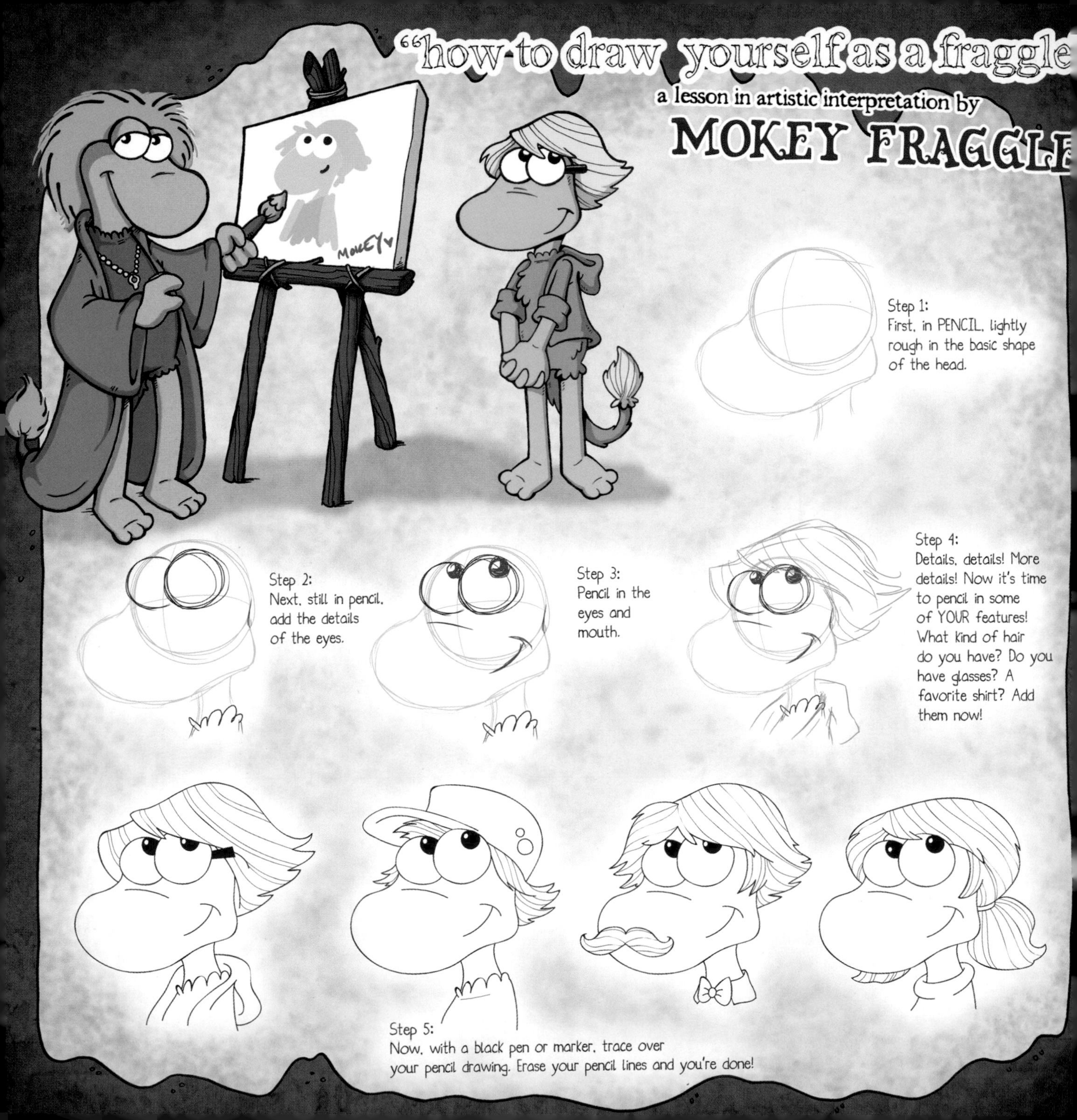
"how to draw yourself as a fraggle"
a lesson in artistic interpretation by
MOKEY FRAGGLE
MOKEY
Step 1:
First, in PENCIL, lightly rough in the basic shape of the head.
Step 2:
Next, still in pencil, add the details of the eyes.
Step 3:
Pencil in the eyes and mouth.
Step 4:
Details, details! More details! Now it's time to pencil in some of YOUR features! What kind of hair do you have? Do you have glasses? A favorite shirt? Add them now!
Step 5:
Now, with a black pen or marker, trace over your pencil drawing. Erase your pencil lines and you're done!

"how to make a radish stamp"
with GOBO FRAGGLE

you will need:
- a radish or apple
- blank paper
- paint
- a knife
- markers

Step 1:
First, get an adult to help. Then cut the radish (or apple!) in half.

Step 2:
On a piece of scrap paper, squeeze out a healthy portion of paint.

Step 3:
Next, dip one half of the radish or apple into the paint, making sure to coat the whole surface.

Step 4:
Use the radish or apple to stamp onto your blank sheet of paper.

TO RYAN
FROM OSCAR

YOU'RE THE
APPLE OF MY EYE

Step 5:
Decorate around the stamped art using markers, paint and glitter. You can make someone a card or create a fun piece of artwork... What else can you make? What else can you use as a stamp?

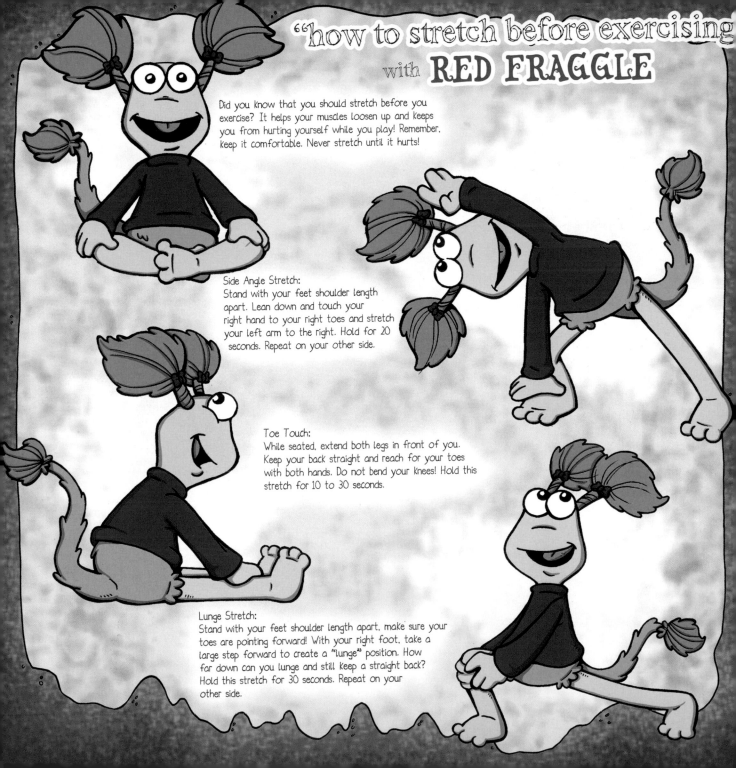

"how to stretch before exercising" with RED FRAGGLE

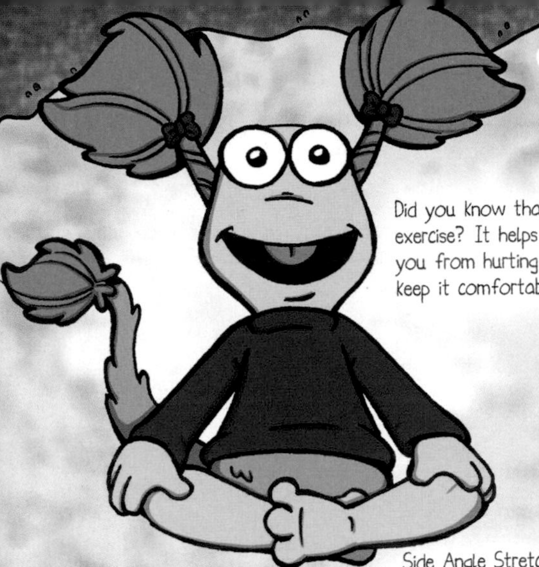

Did you know that you should stretch before you exercise? It helps your muscles loosen up and keeps you from hurting yourself while you play! Remember, keep it comfortable. Never stretch until it hurts!

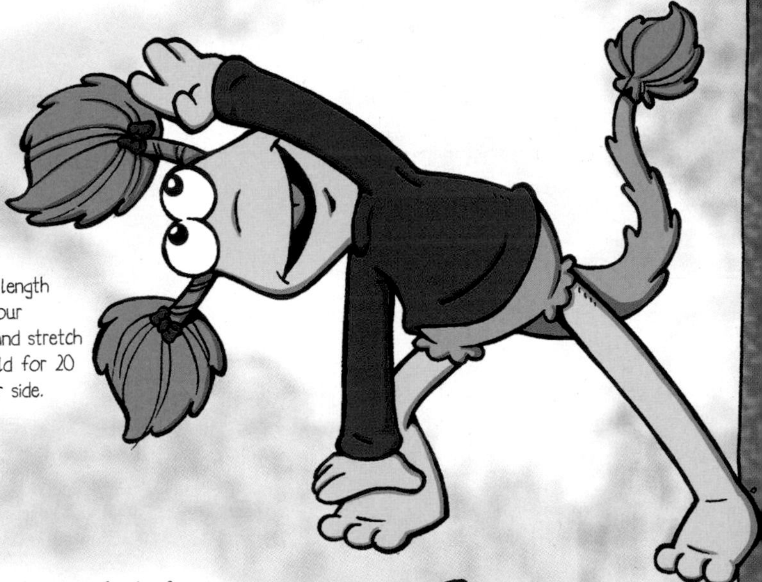

Side Angle Stretch:
Stand with your feet shoulder length apart. Lean down and touch your right hand to your right toes and stretch your left arm to the right. Hold for 20 seconds. Repeat on your other side.

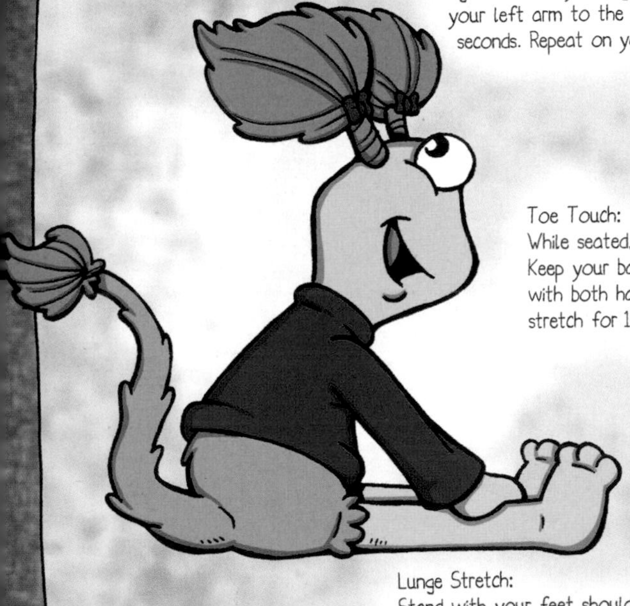

Toe Touch:
While seated, extend both legs in front of you. Keep your back straight and reach for your toes with both hands. Do not bend your knees! Hold this stretch for 10 to 30 seconds.

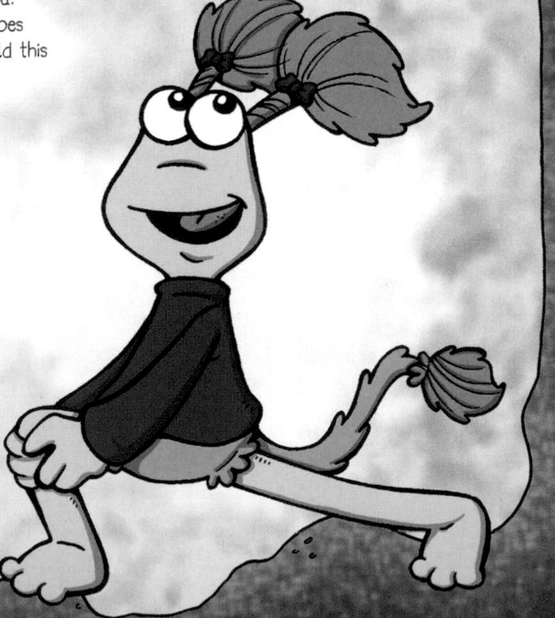

Lunge Stretch:
Stand with your feet shoulder length apart, make sure your toes are pointing forward! With your right foot, take a large step forward to create a "lunge" position. How far down can you lunge and still keep a straight back? Hold this stretch for 30 seconds. Repeat on your other side.

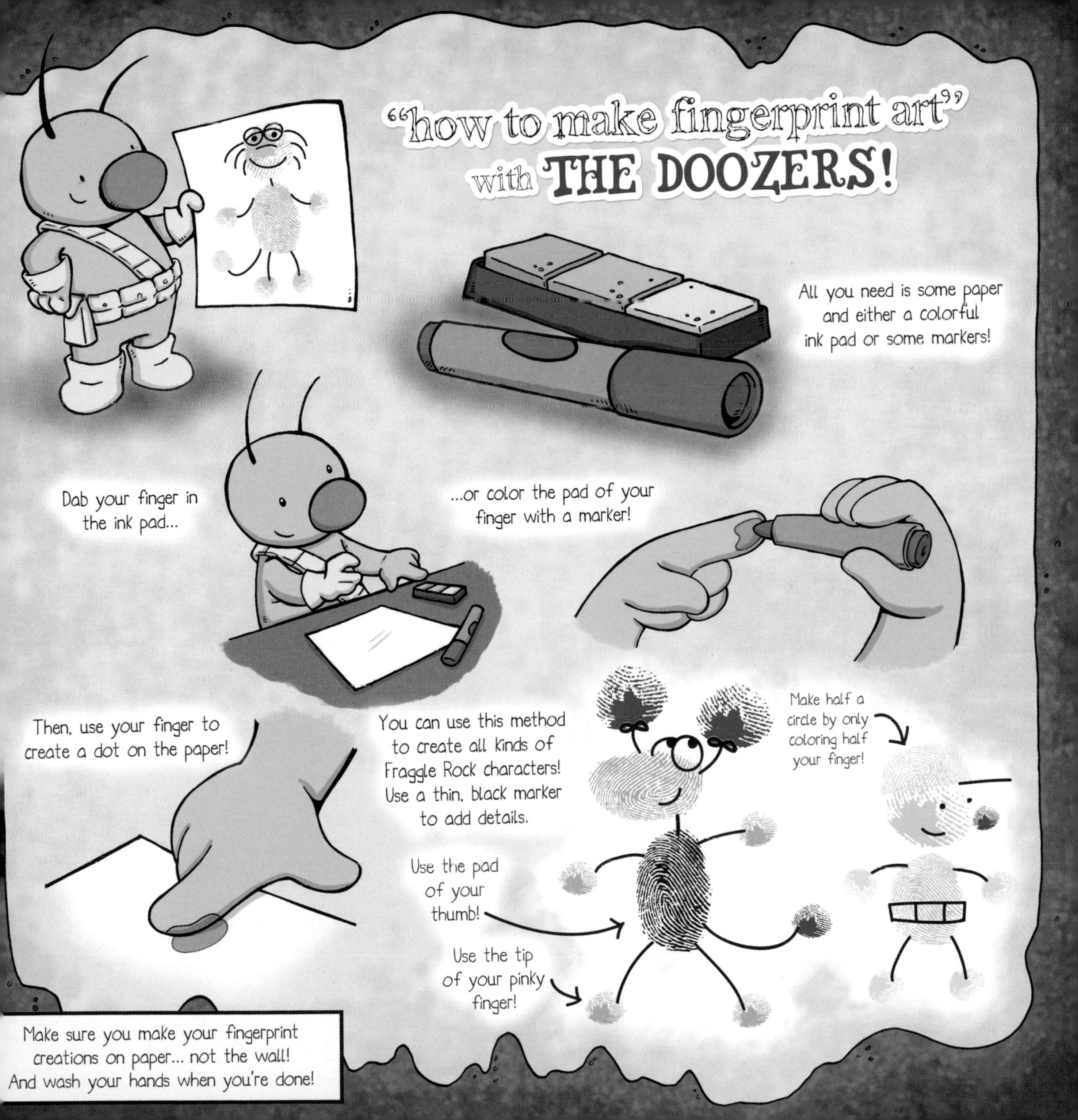
"how to make fingerprint art" with THE DOOZERS!
All you need is some paper and either a colorful ink pad or some markers!
Dab your finger in the ink pad...
...or color the pad of your finger with a marker!
Then, use your finger to create a dot on the paper!
You can use this method to create all kinds of Fraggle Rock characters! Use a thin, black marker to add details.
Make half a circle by only coloring half your finger!
Use the pad of your thumb!
Use the tip of your pinky finger!
Make sure you make your fingerprint creations on paper... not the wall! And wash your hands when you're done!

"how to draw a gorg"

a lesson in artistic interpretation by

MOKEY FRAGGLE

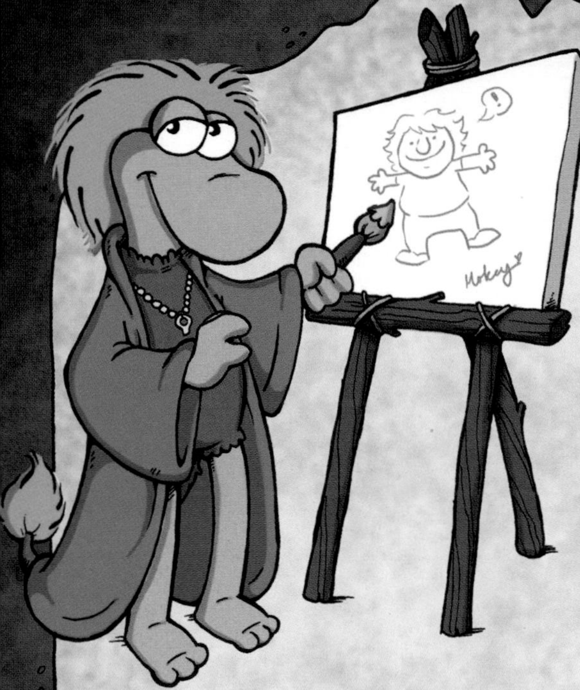

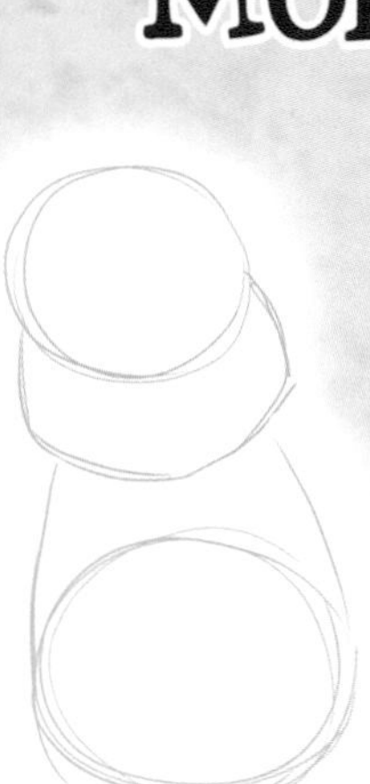

Step 1:
First, in PENCIL, lightly rough in the basic shape of the head and body.

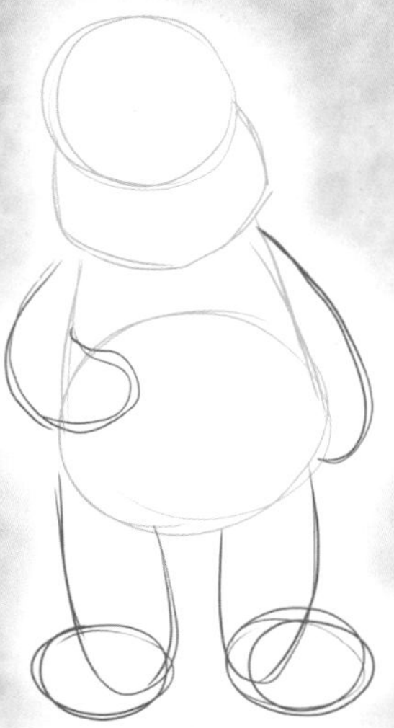

Step 2:
Next, still in pencil, add the details of the arms and legs.

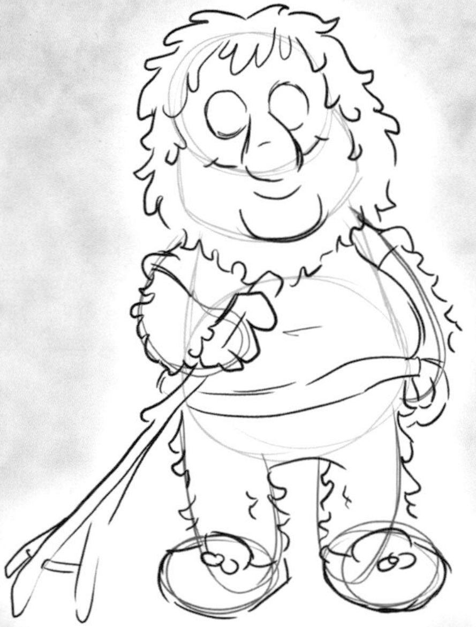

Step 3:
Details, details! More details! Now it's time to pencil in some of Junior's features!

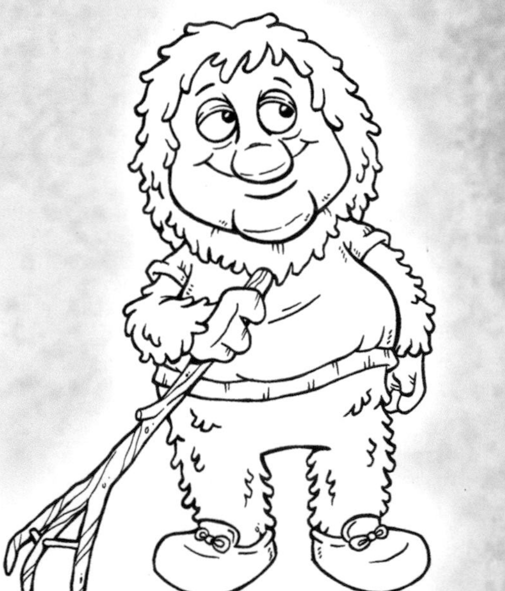

Step 4:
Now, with a black pen or marker, trace over your pencil drawing. Erase your pencil lines and you're done!

"how to make a radish flower" with BOOBER FRAGGLE

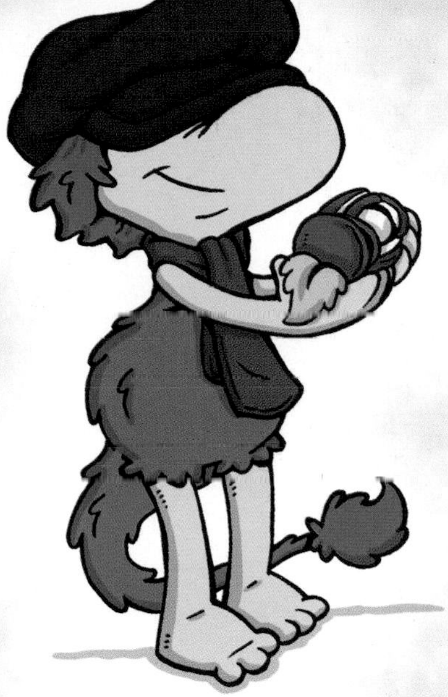

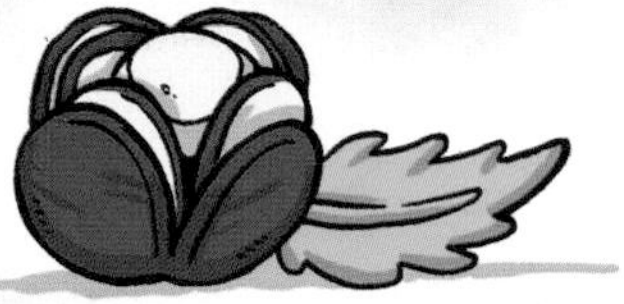

You will need:
- radishes
- a small paring knife
- a cutting board
- adult supervision (Knives are sharp!)

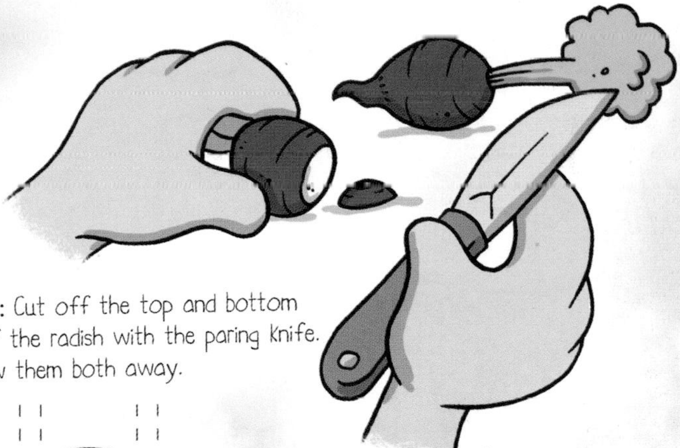

Step 1: Cut off the top and bottom tip of the radish with the paring knife. Throw them both away.

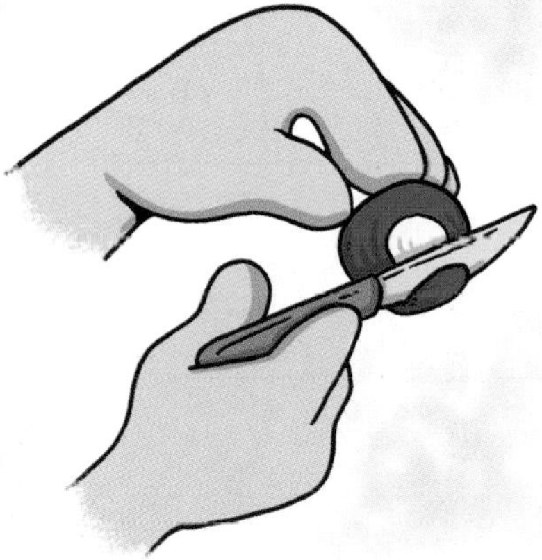

Step 2: Set the radish upright on the cutting board. Cut a thin, vertical slice down one side of the radish with the knife. You want to cut about 3/4ths of the way into it.

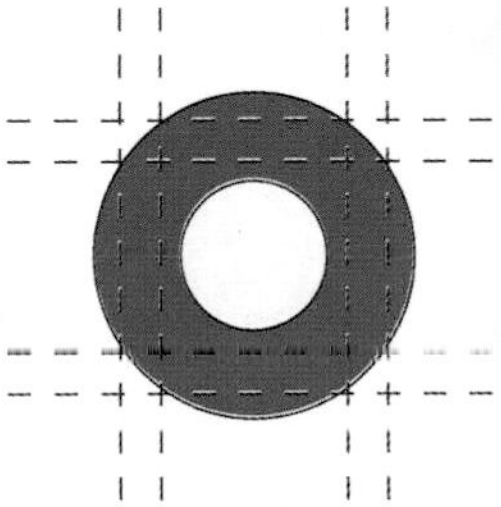

Step 3: Make one or two additional slices down all sides of the radish, spacing the slices evenly around. DO NOT CUT ALL THE WAY THROUGH!!!

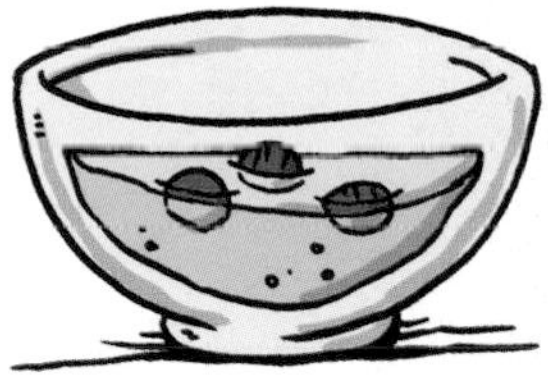

Step 4: Place the radish in ice water until it opens slightly. Remove it from the water and drain it well.

Step 5: Garnish your radish flower with a leaf and you're done!

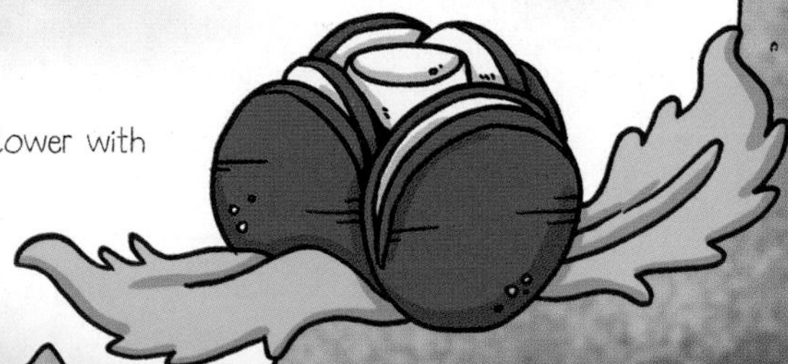

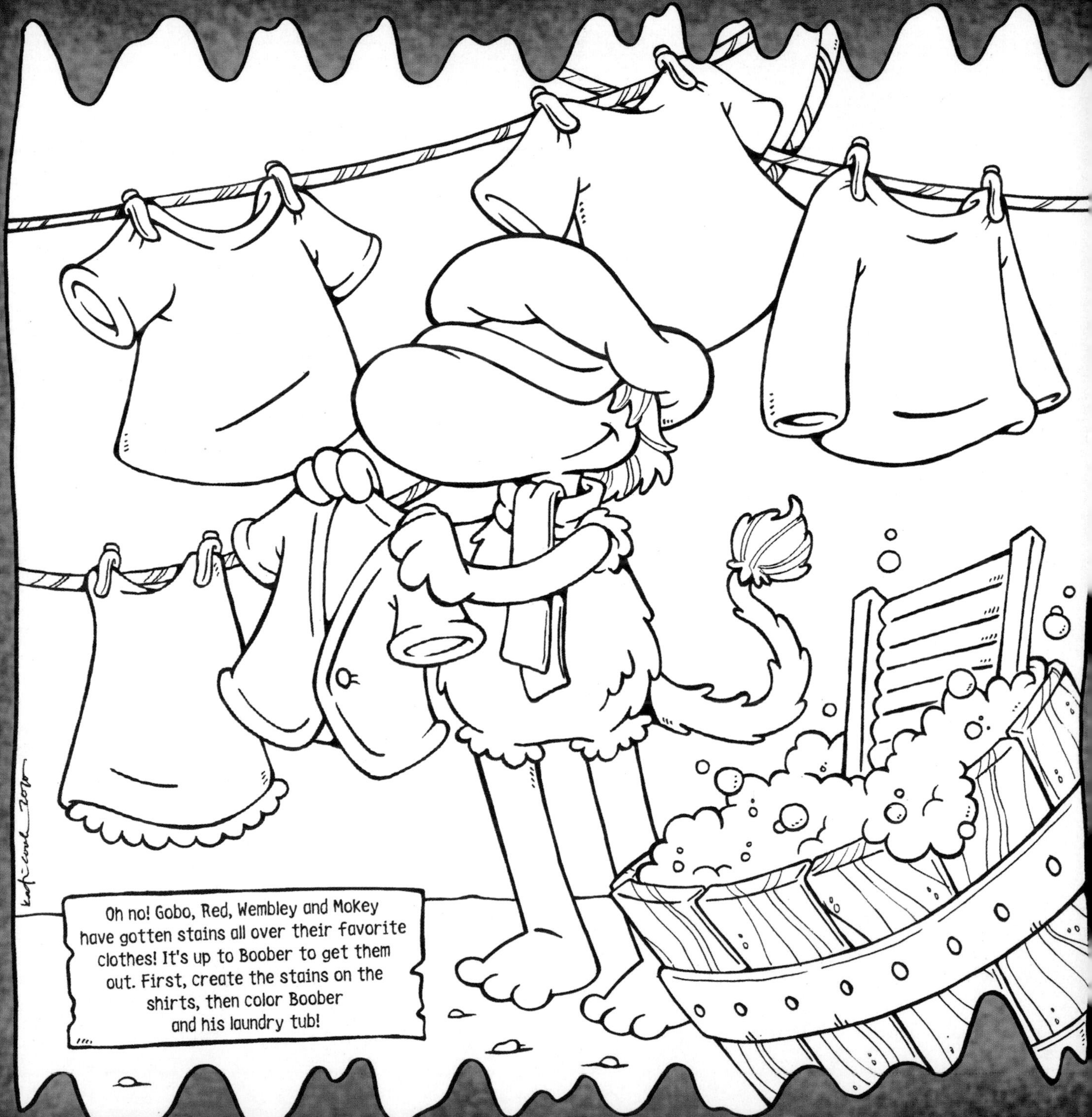
Oh no! Gobo, Red, Wembley and Mokey have gotten stains all over their favorite clothes! It's up to Boober to get them out. First, create the stains on the shirts, then color Boober and his laundry tub!

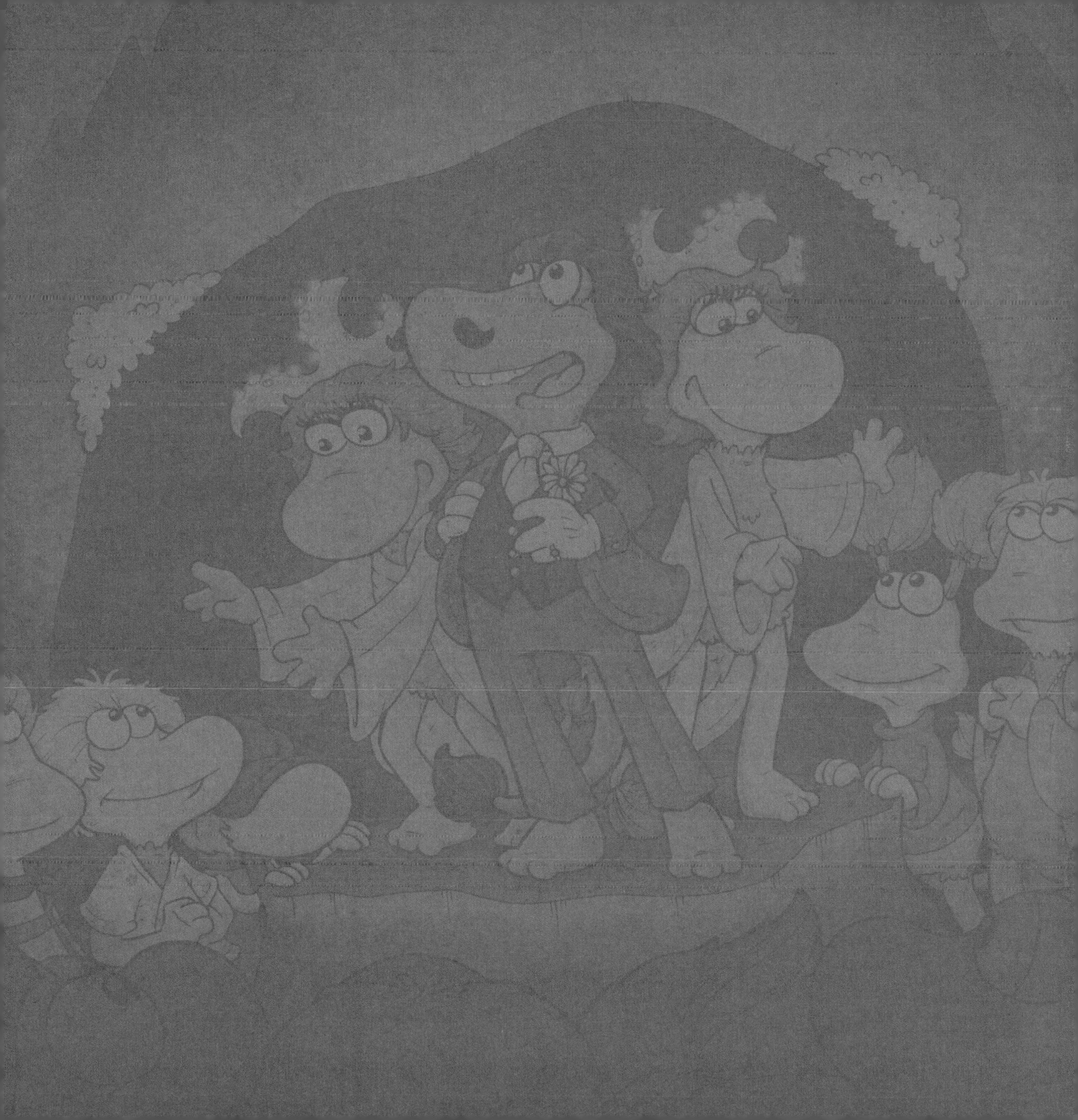

COVER GALLERY

Jeff Stokely and **Lizzy John**
Jeffrey Brown and **Michael DiMotta**
Jeremy Love
Jake Myler
Katie Cook
Joanna Estep
Amy Mebberson
Chris Lie
David Petersen
Heidi Arnhold
Sophie Campbell
Katie Cook
Lindsay Cibos

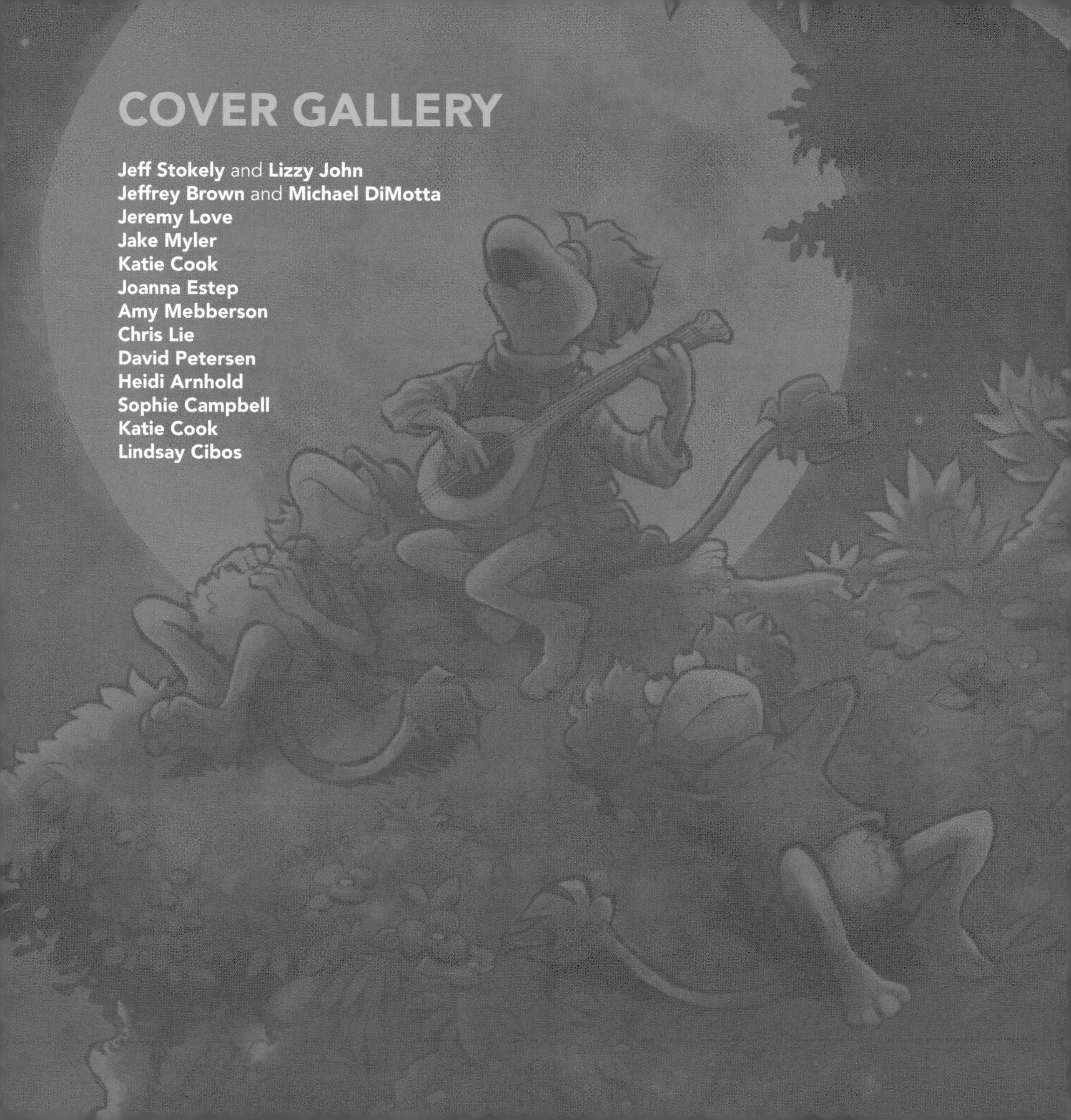

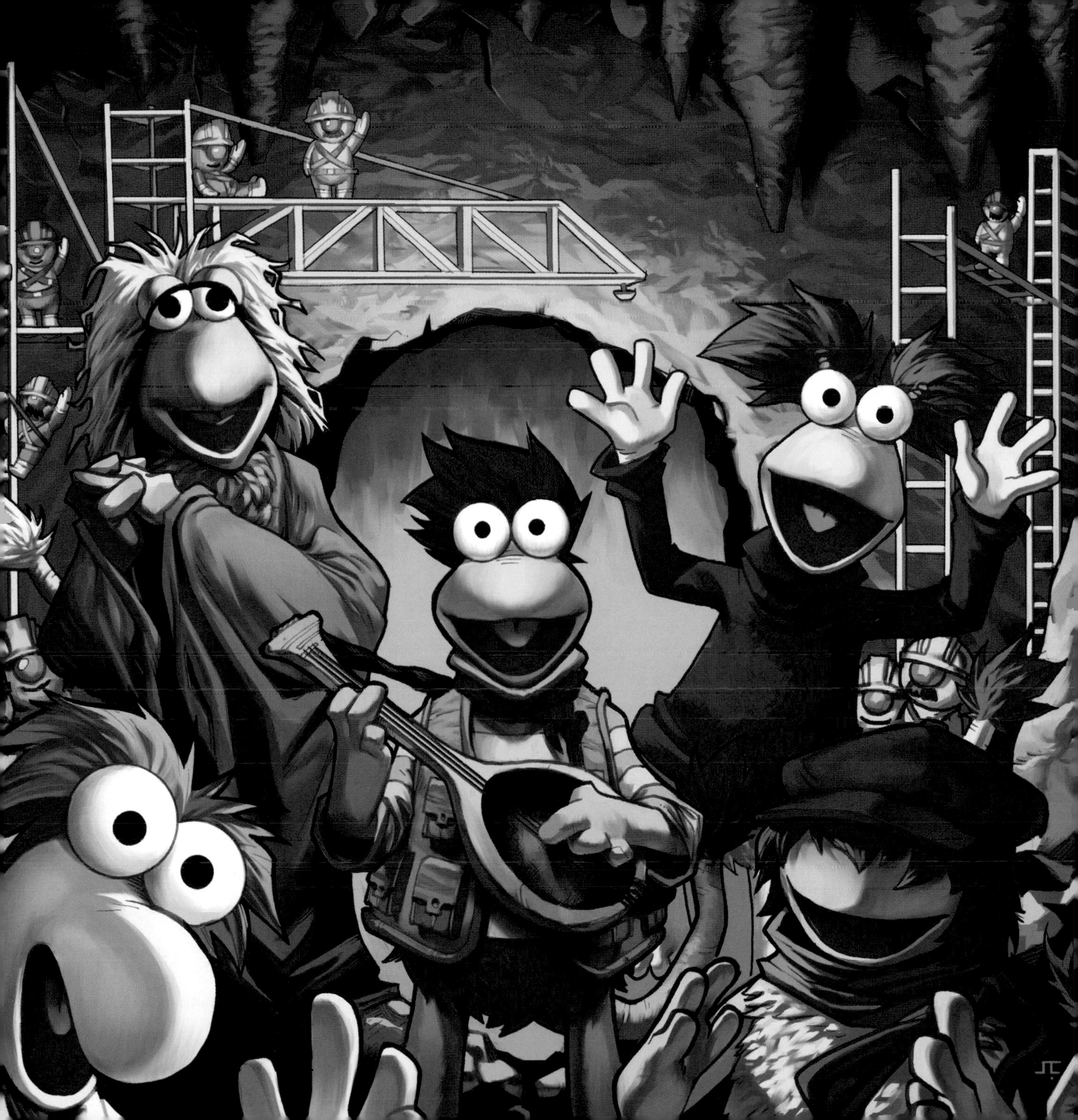

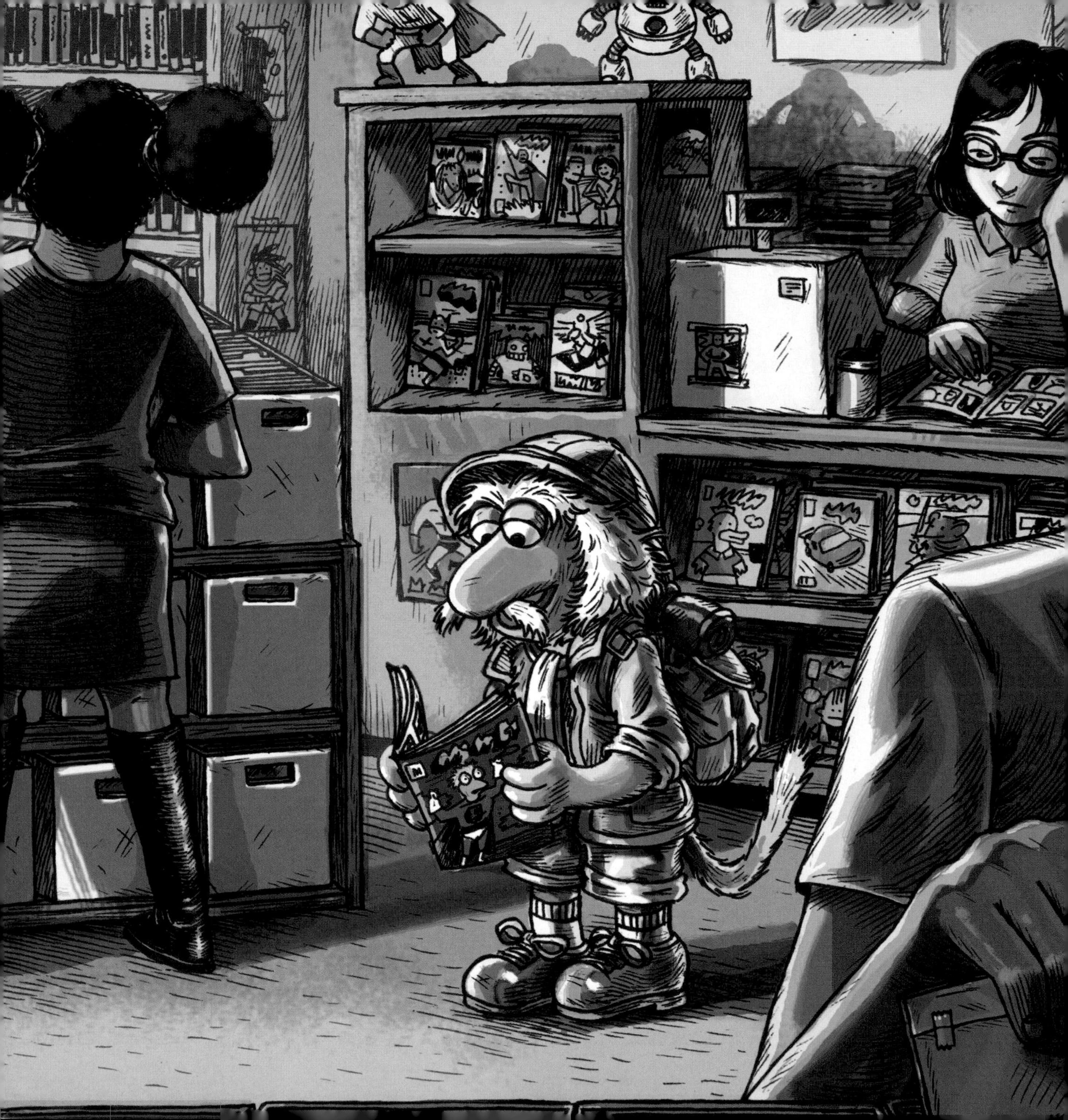

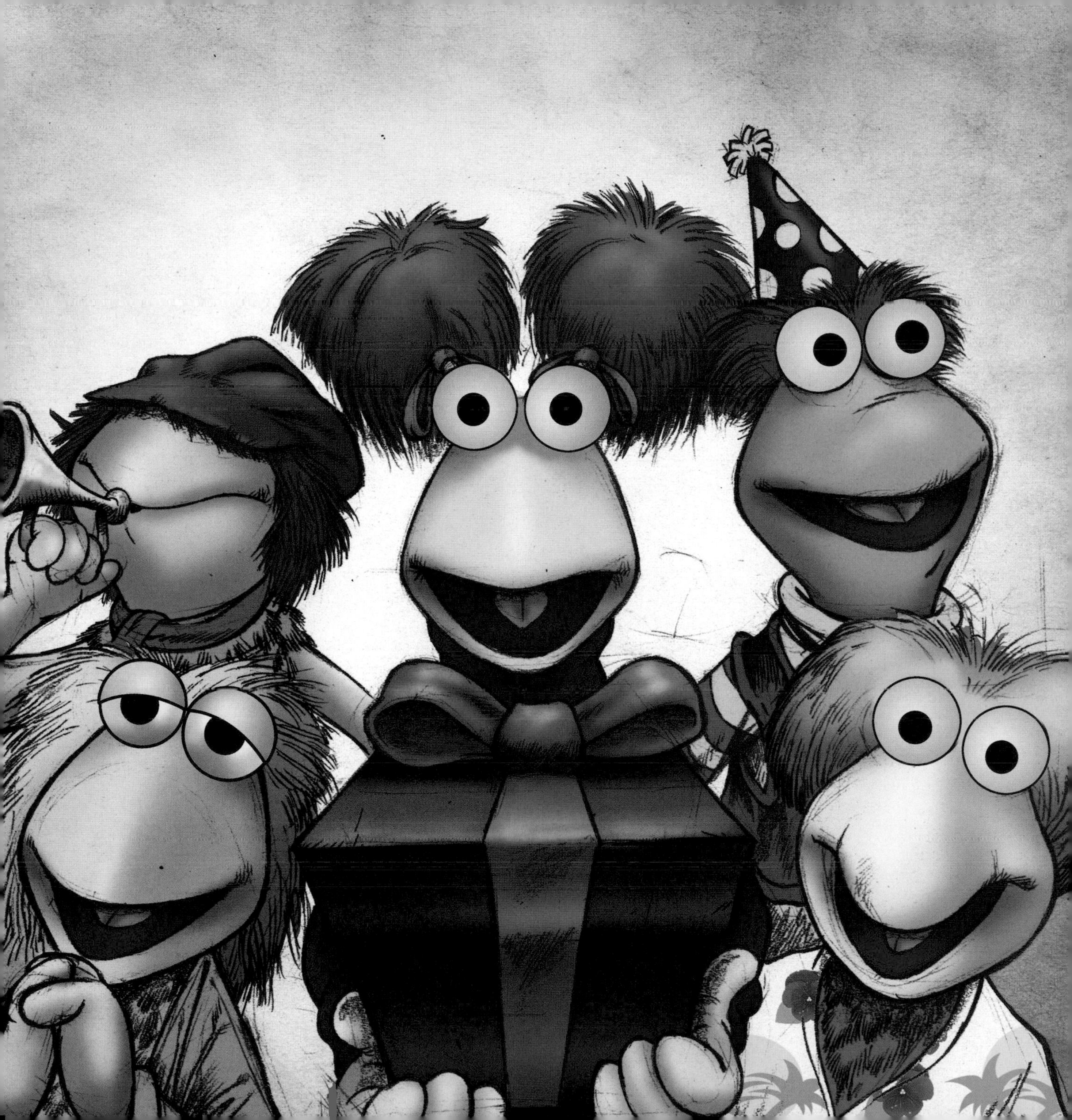

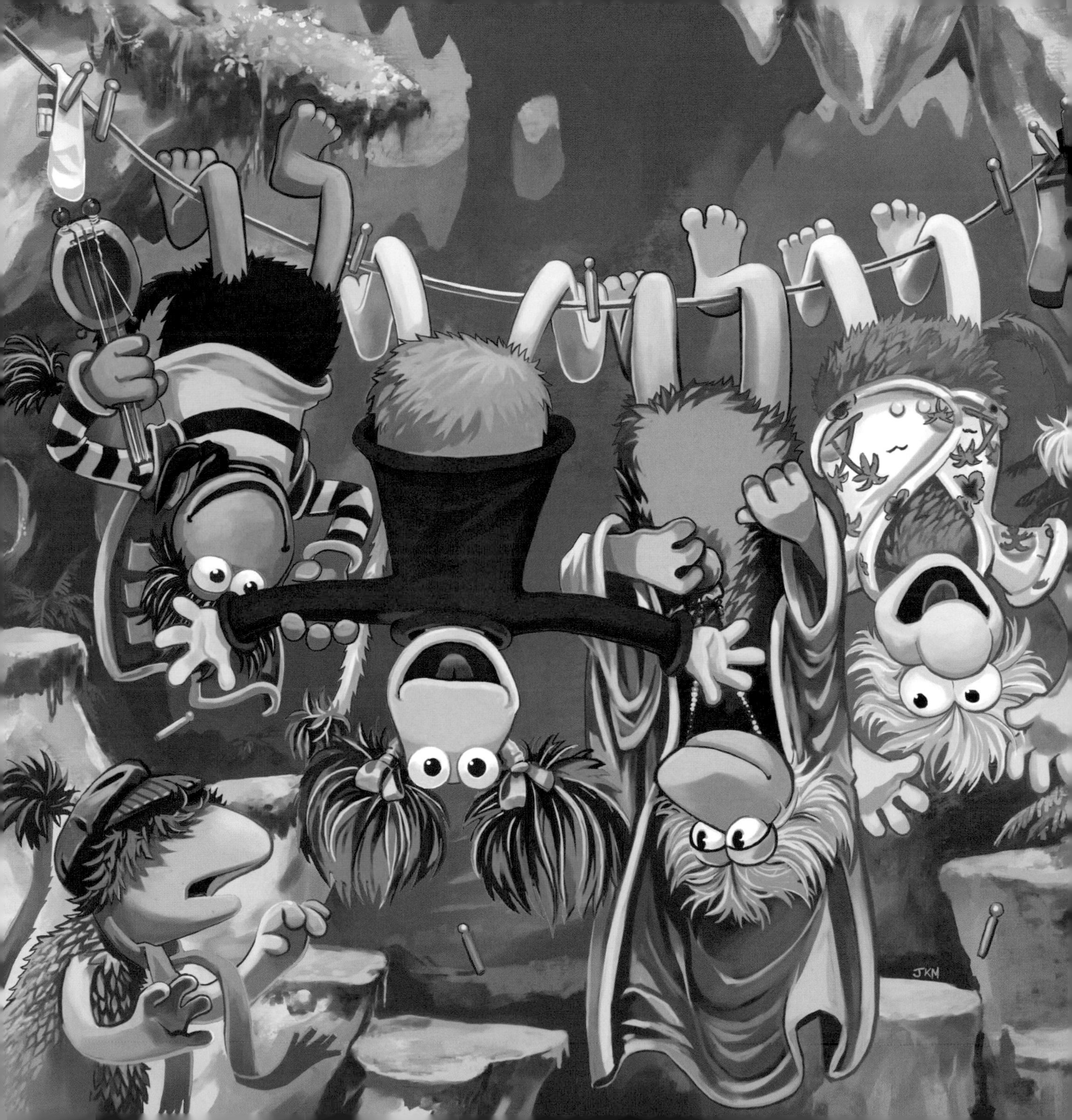
JKM

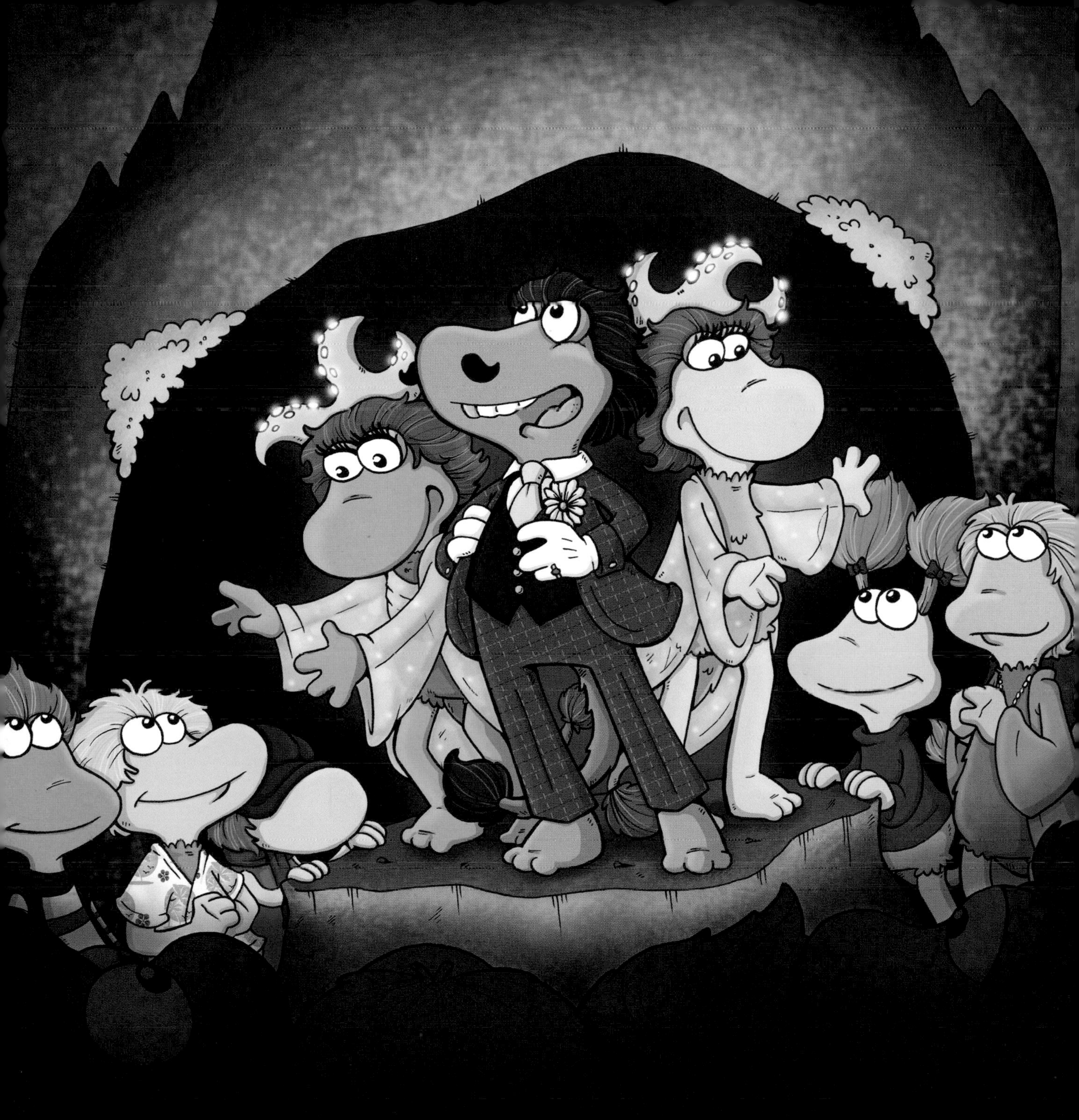

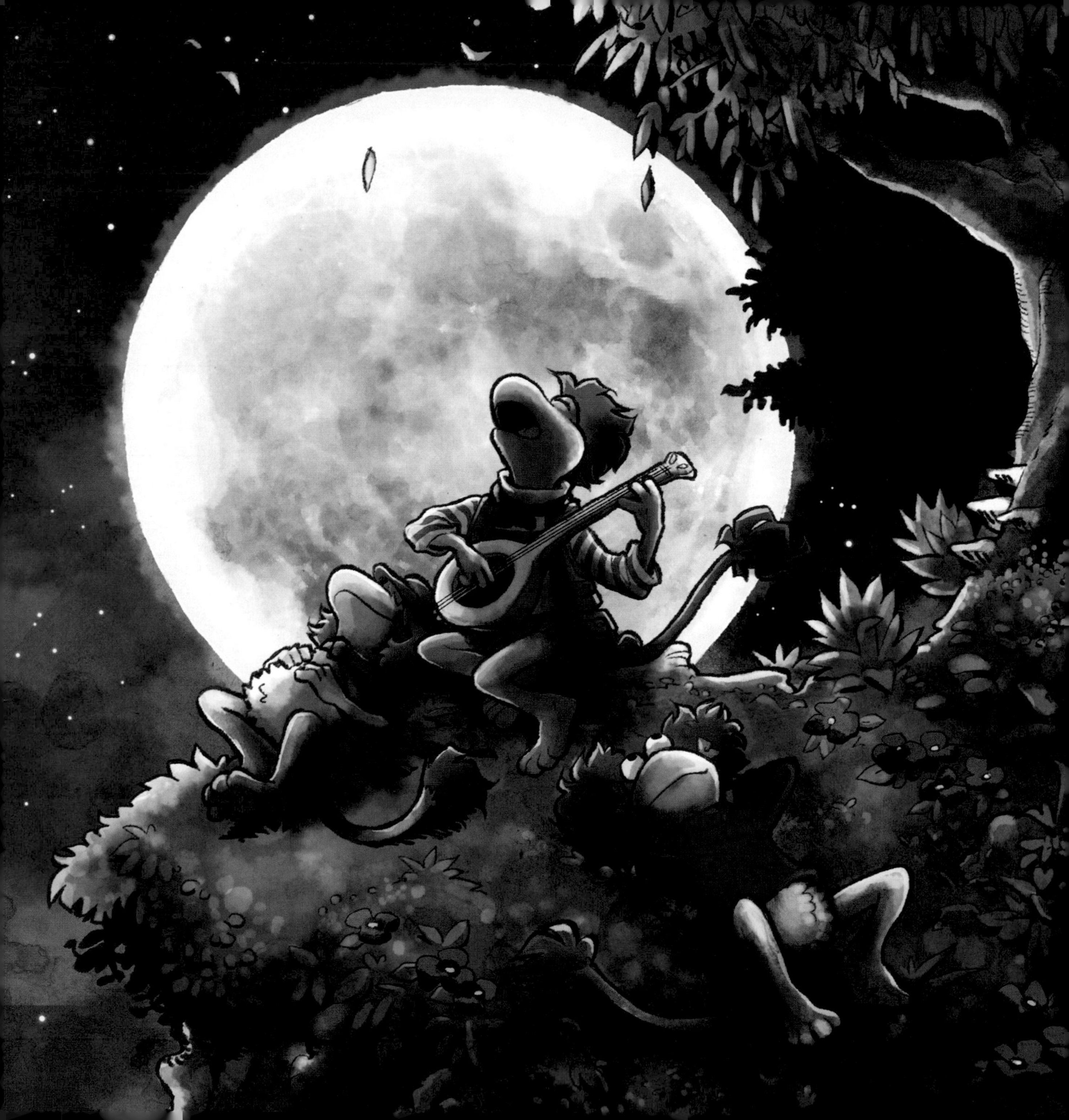

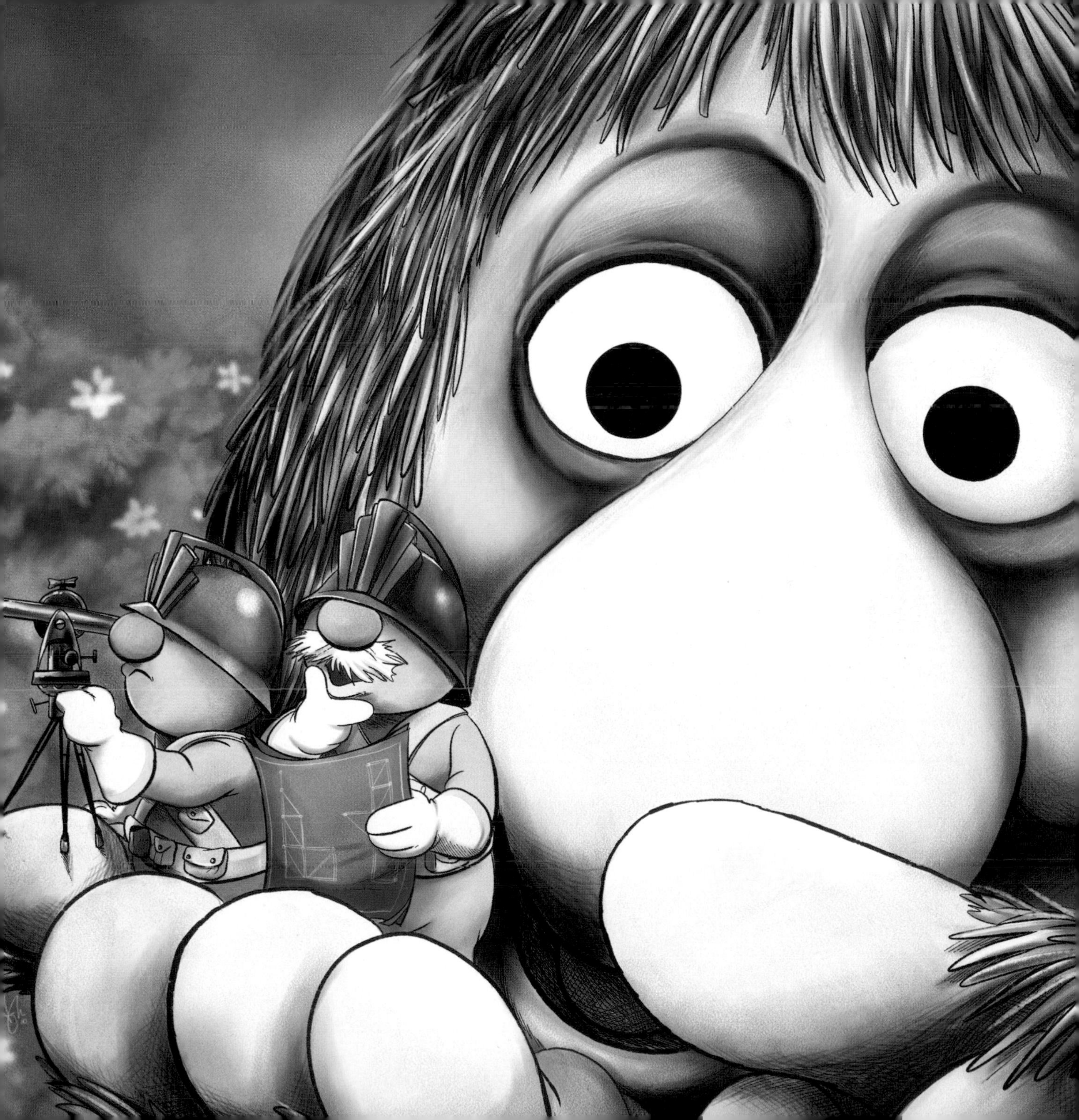

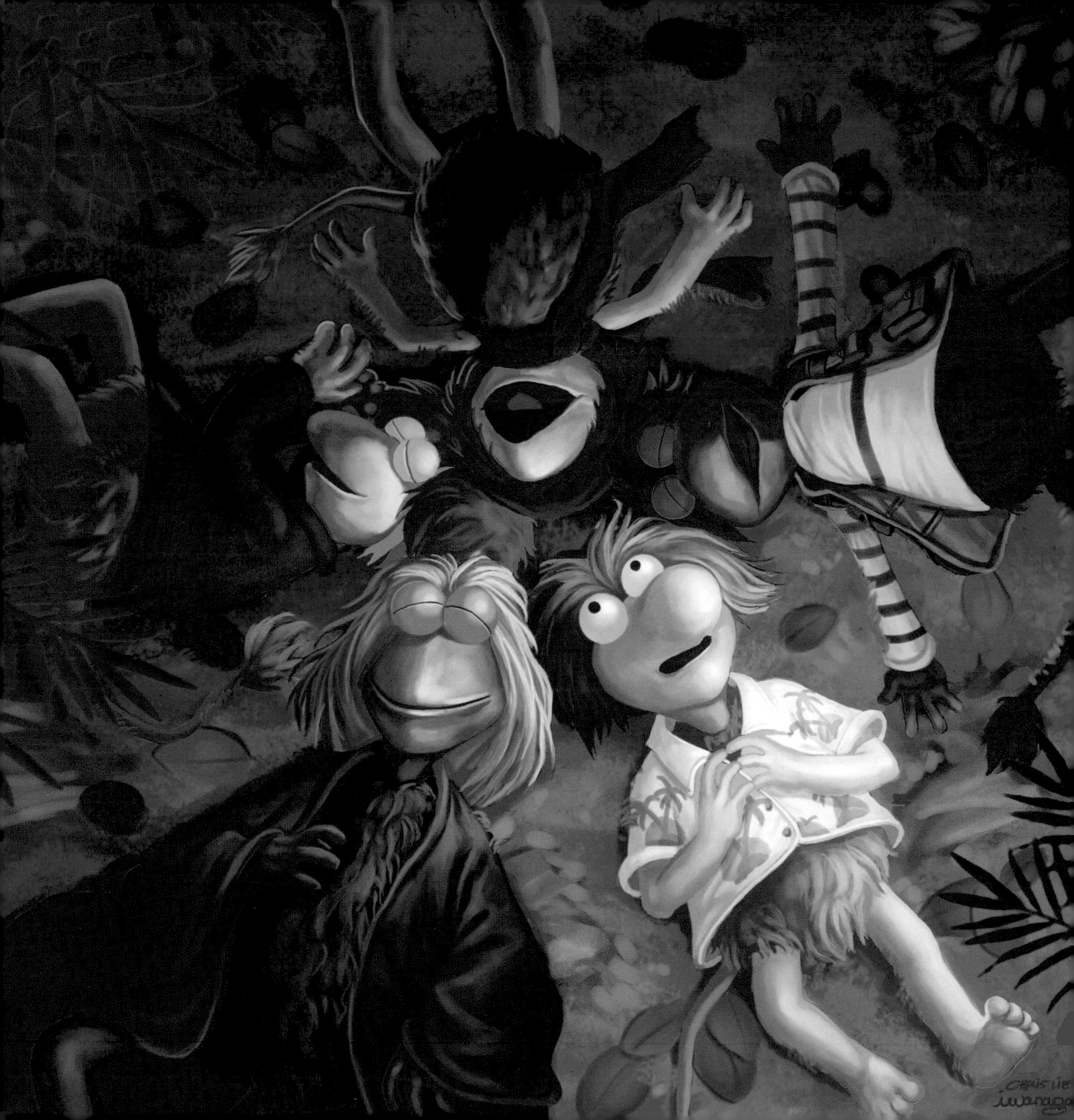

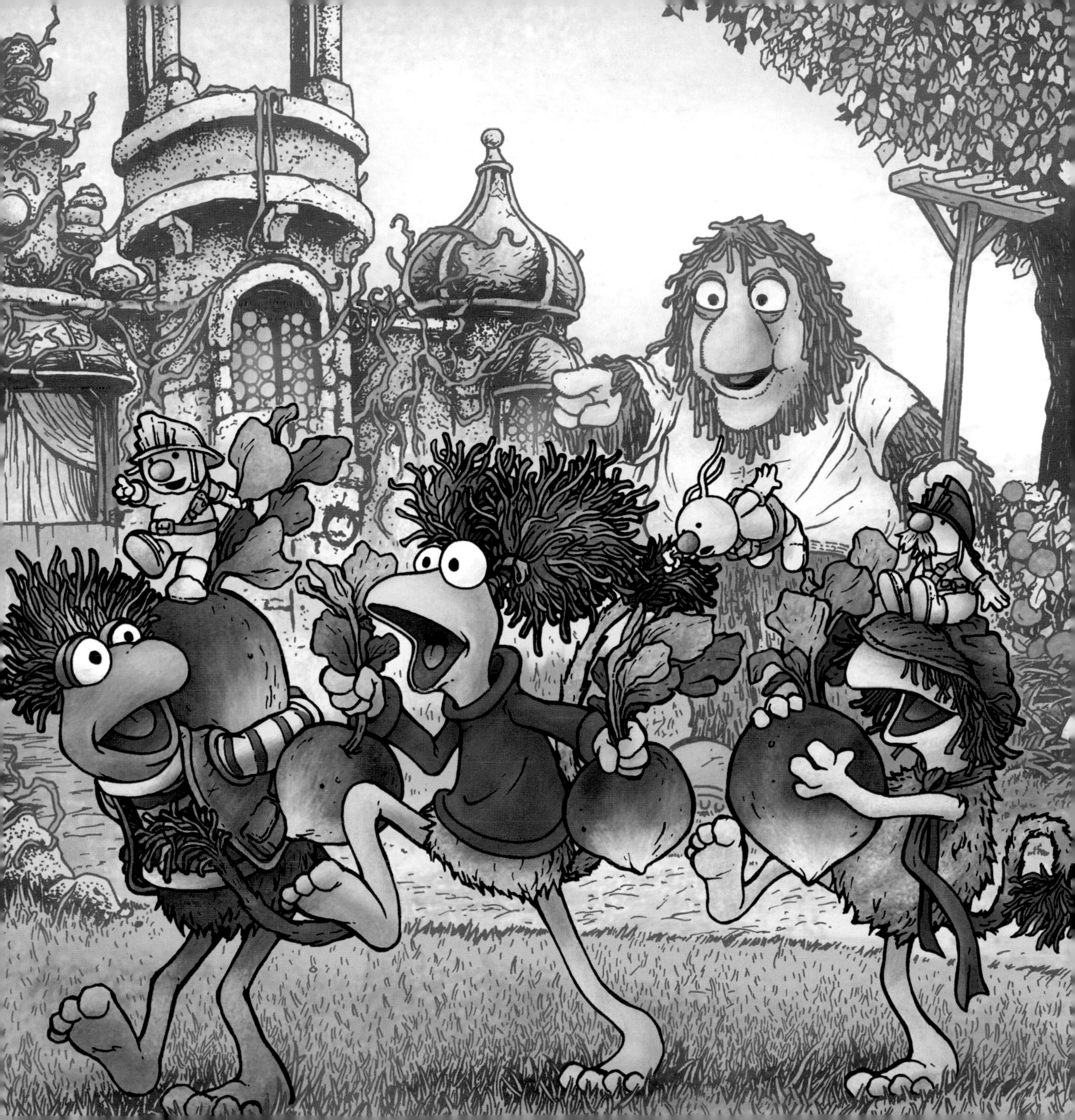

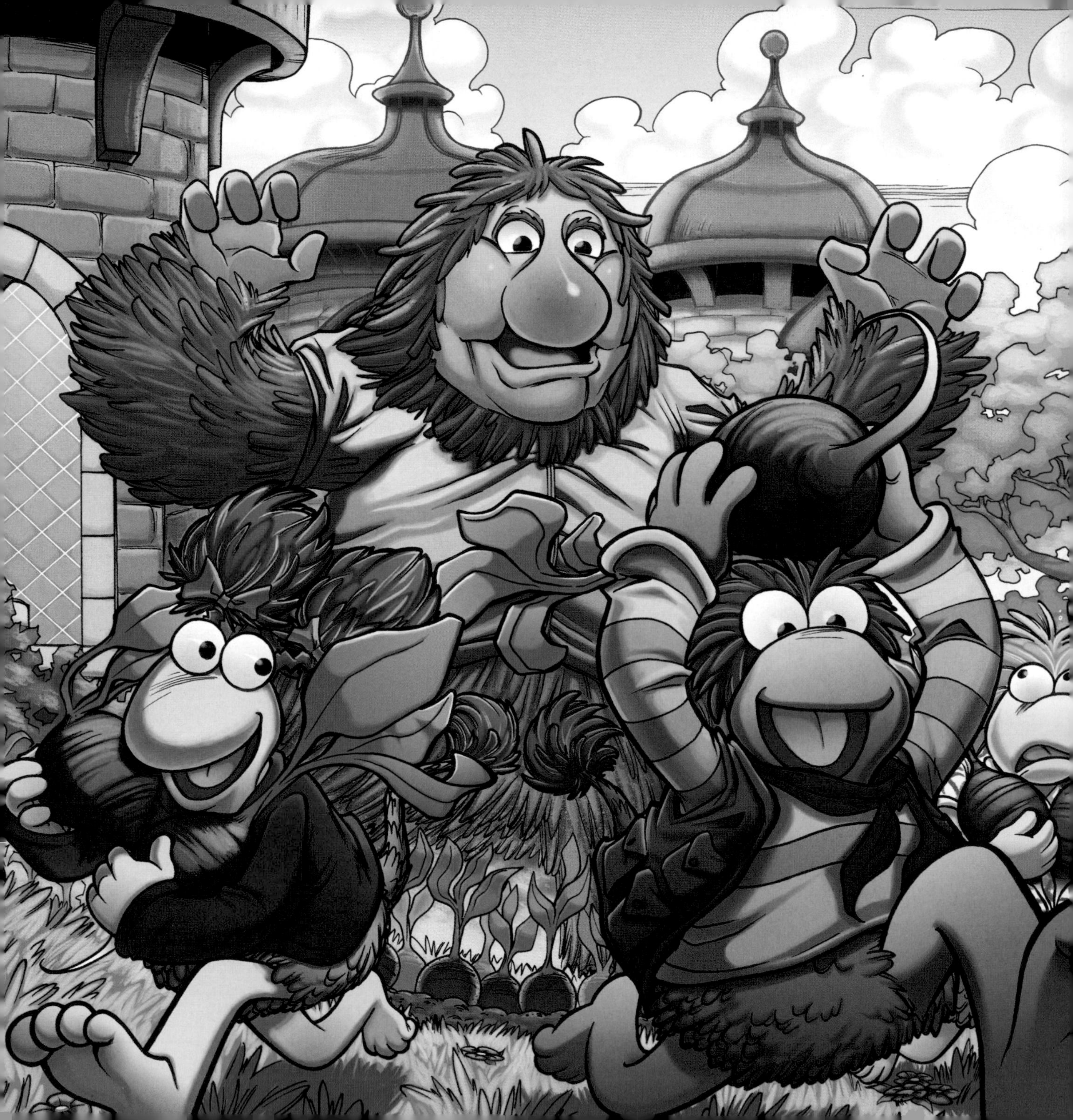

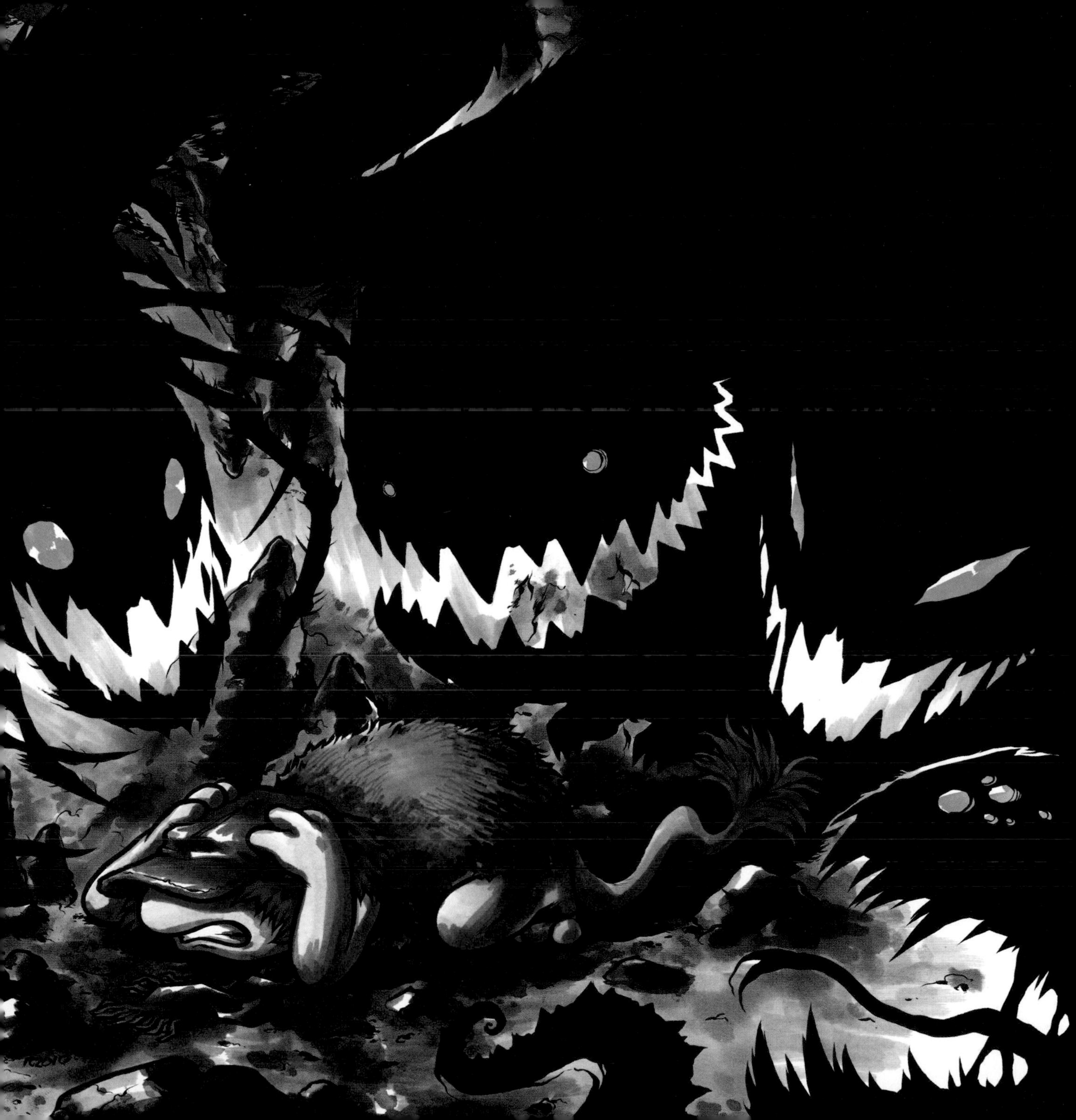

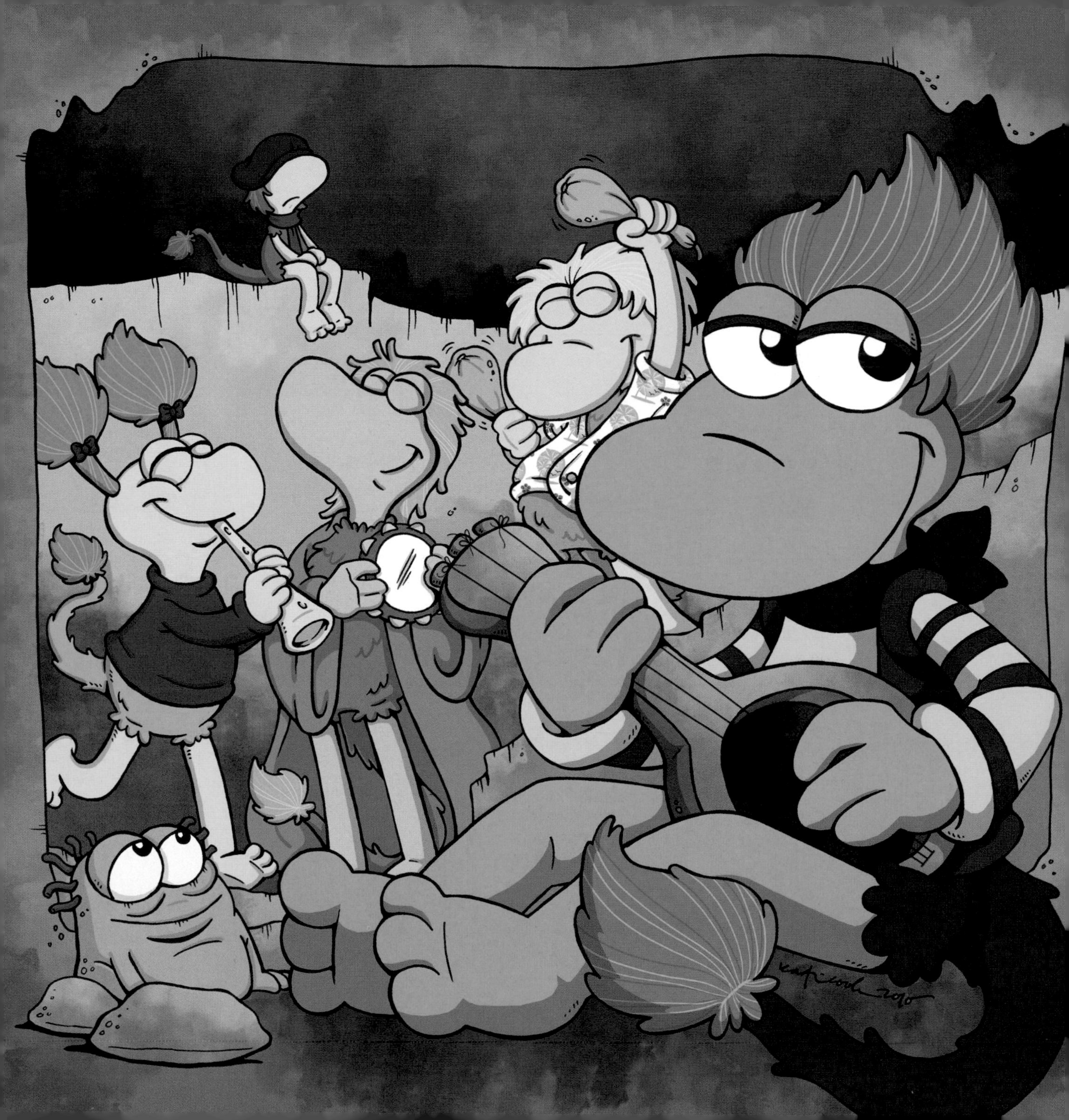

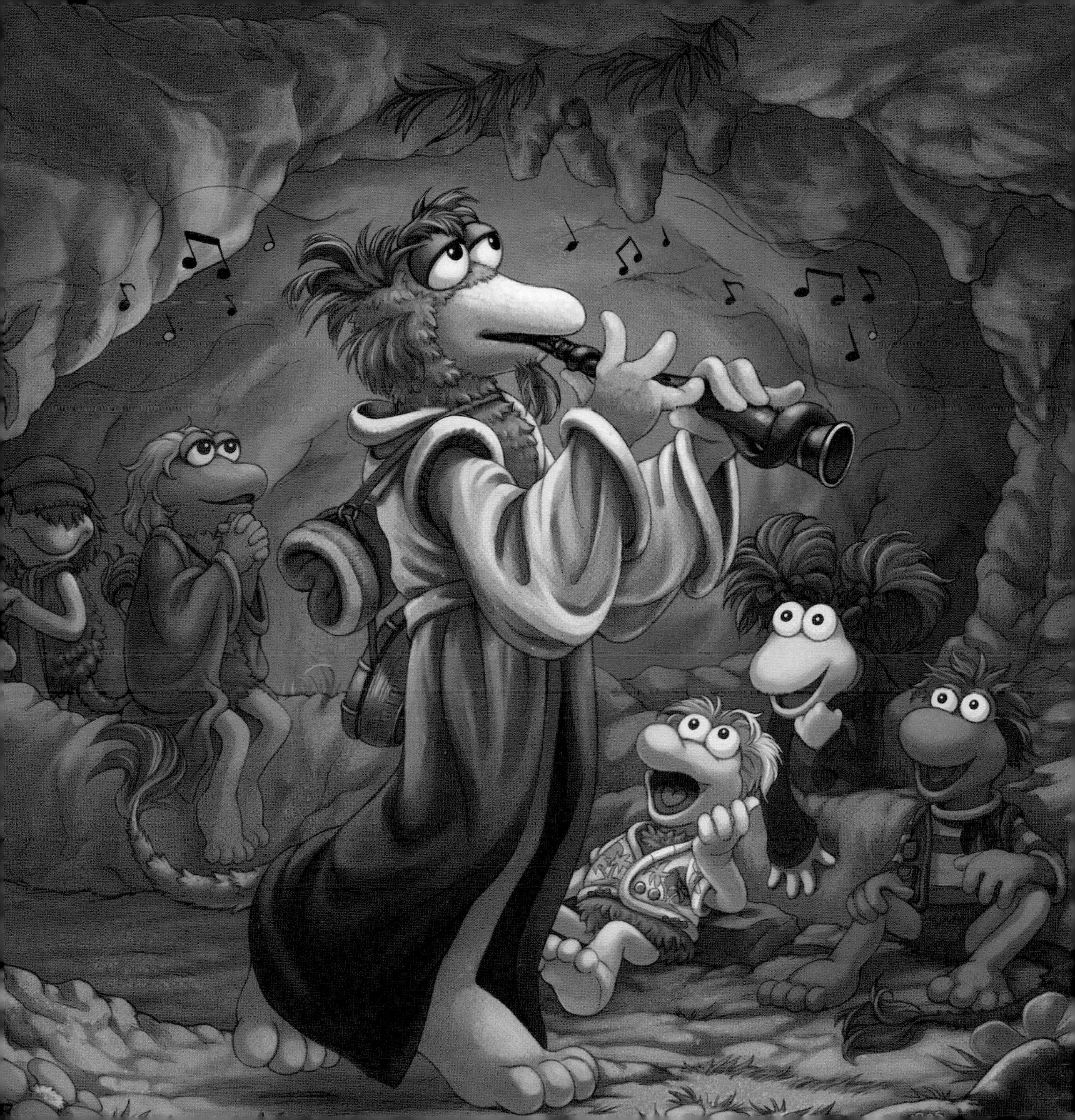

FRAGGLE ROCK SKETCHBOOK

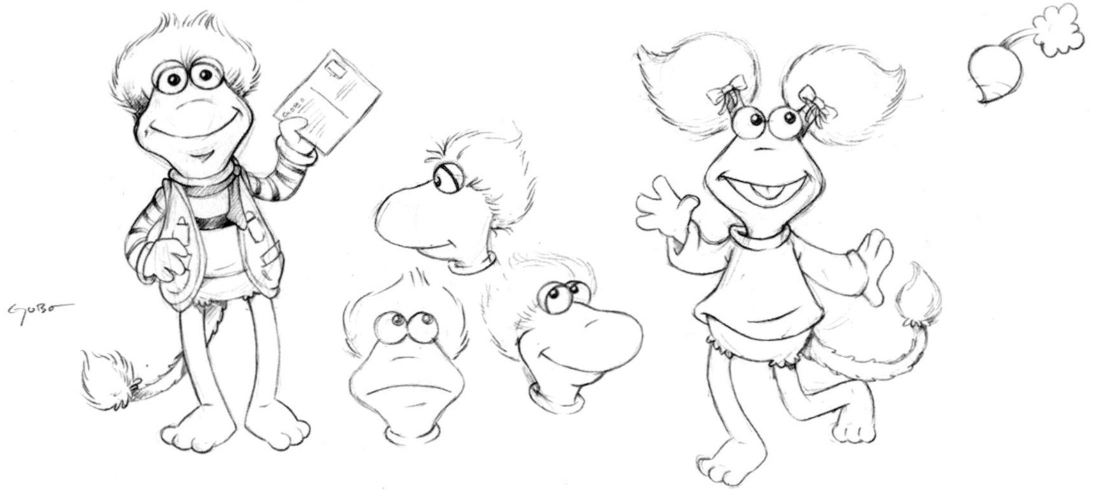
GOBO

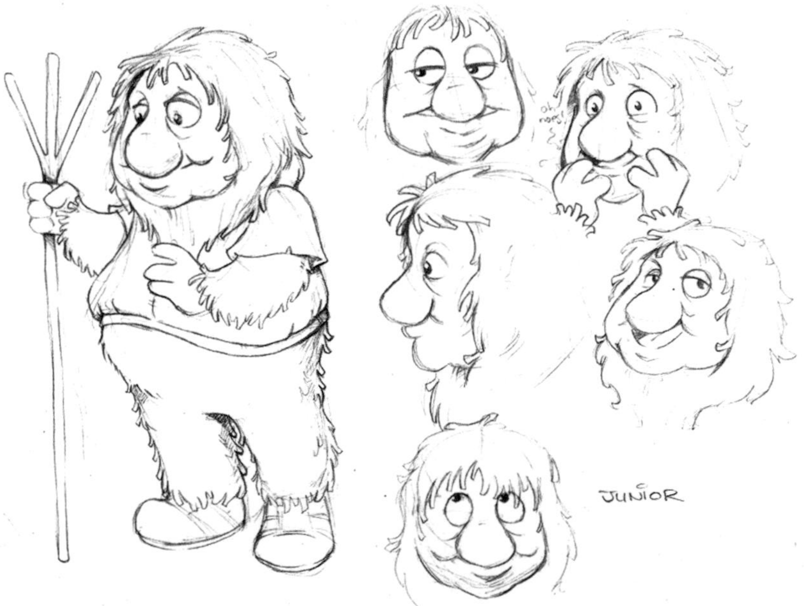
Oh, noes!
JUNIOR

Art by **Katie Cook**

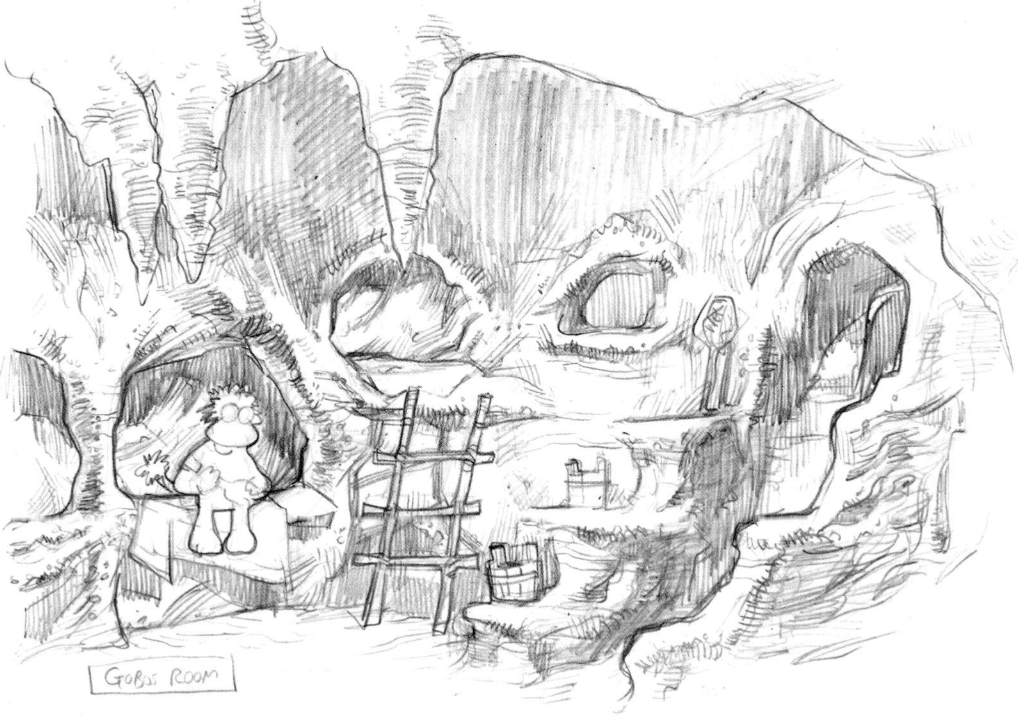
GOBO'S ROOM

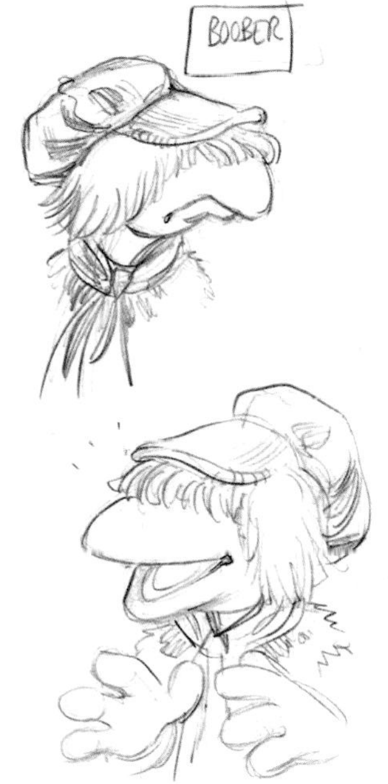
BOOBER

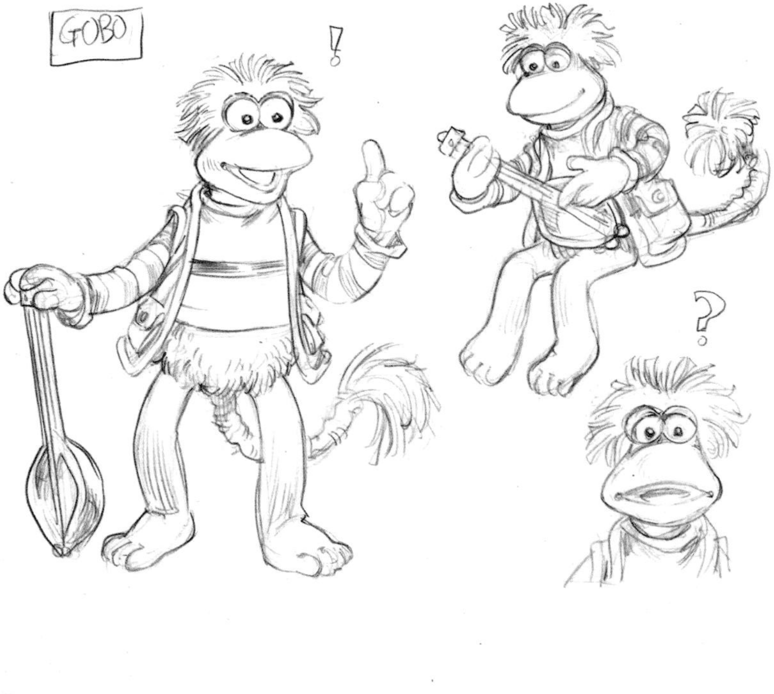
GOBO
!
?

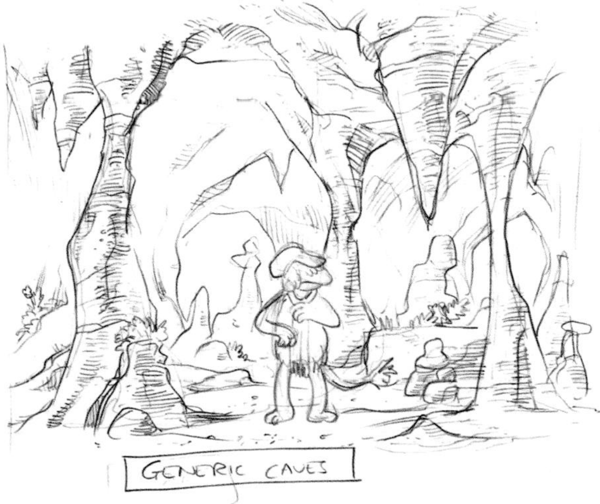
GENERIC CAVES

Art by **Mark Simmons**

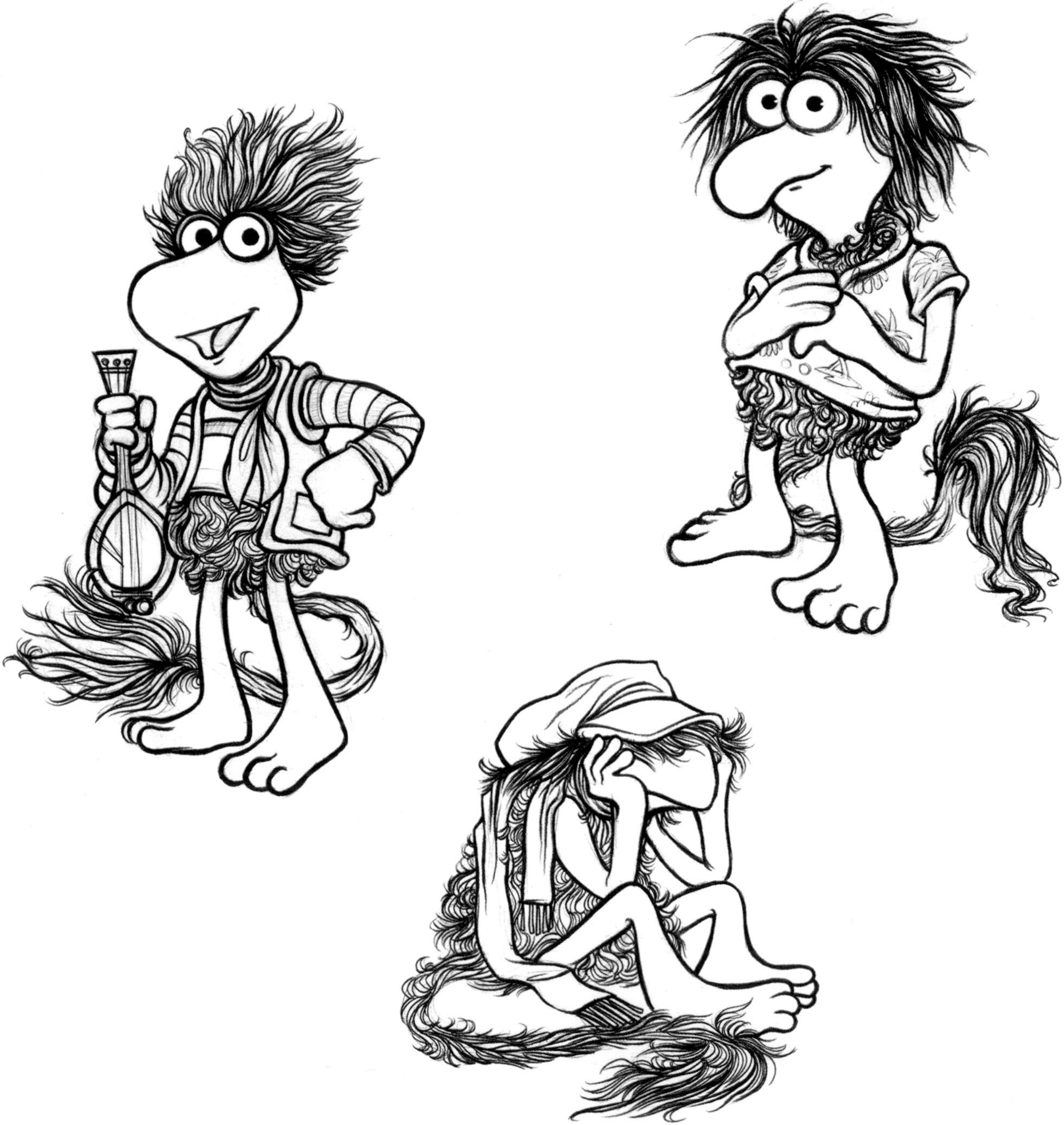

Art by **Cory Godbey**

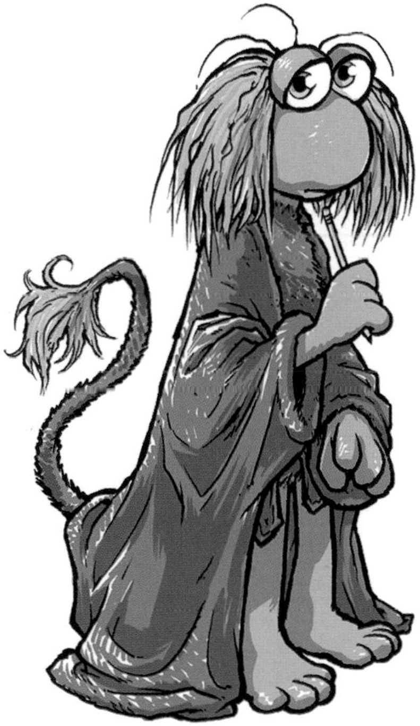

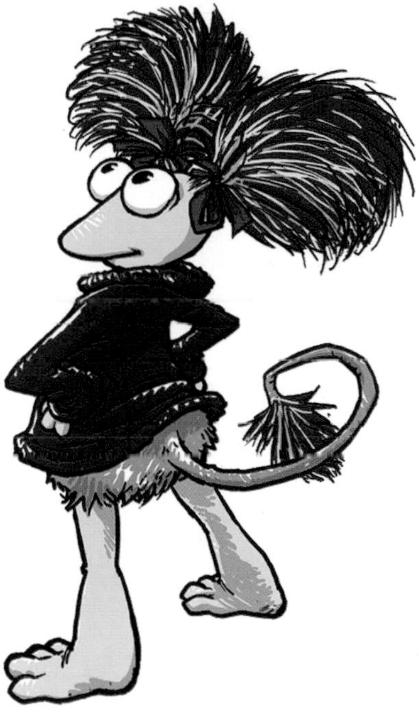

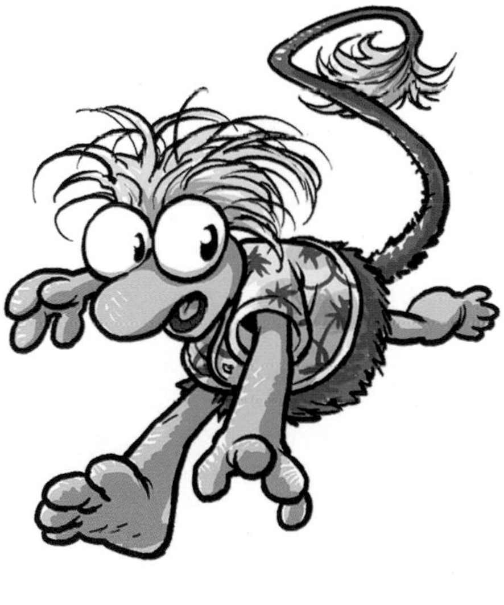

Art by **Sophie Campbell**

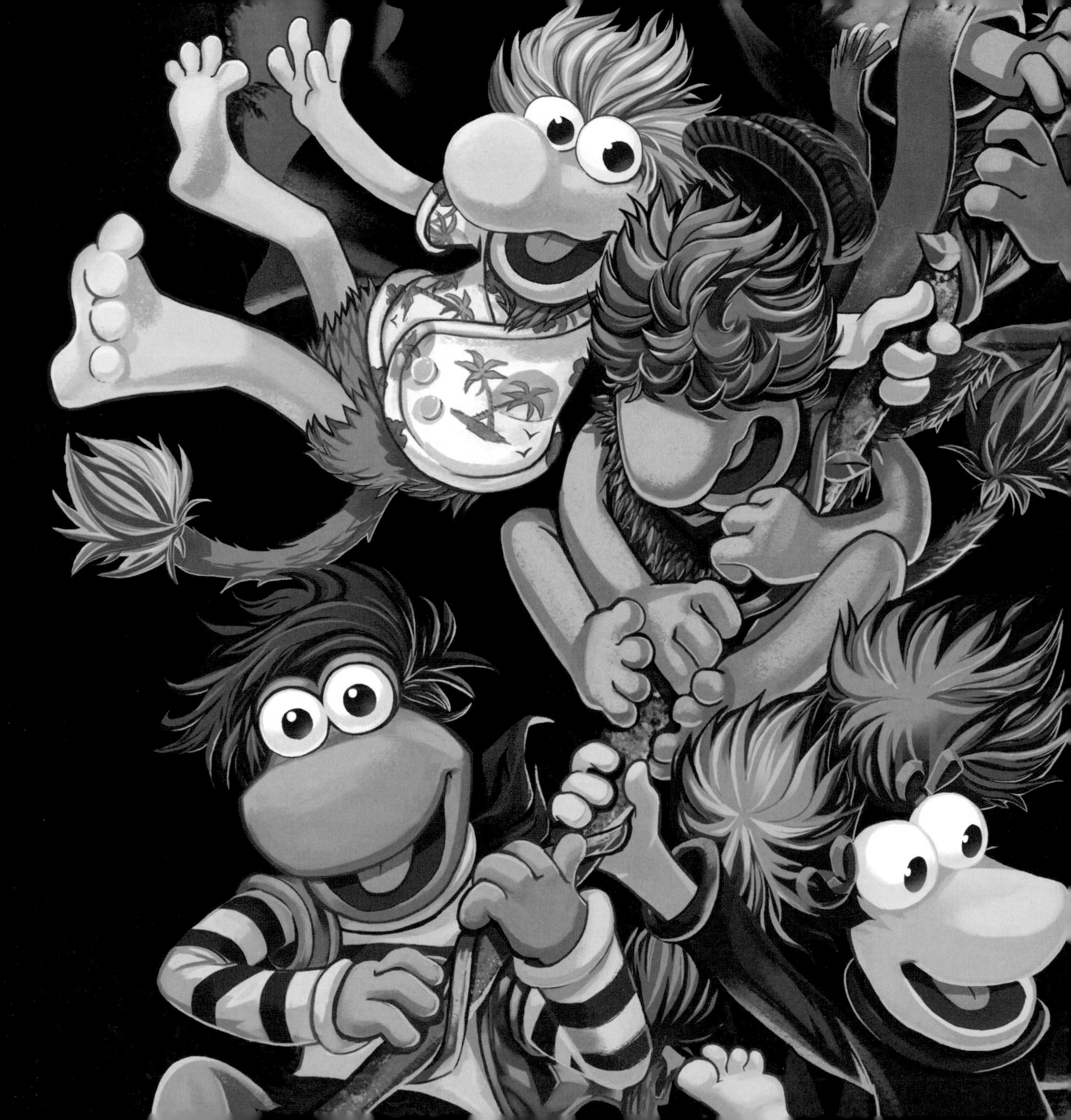

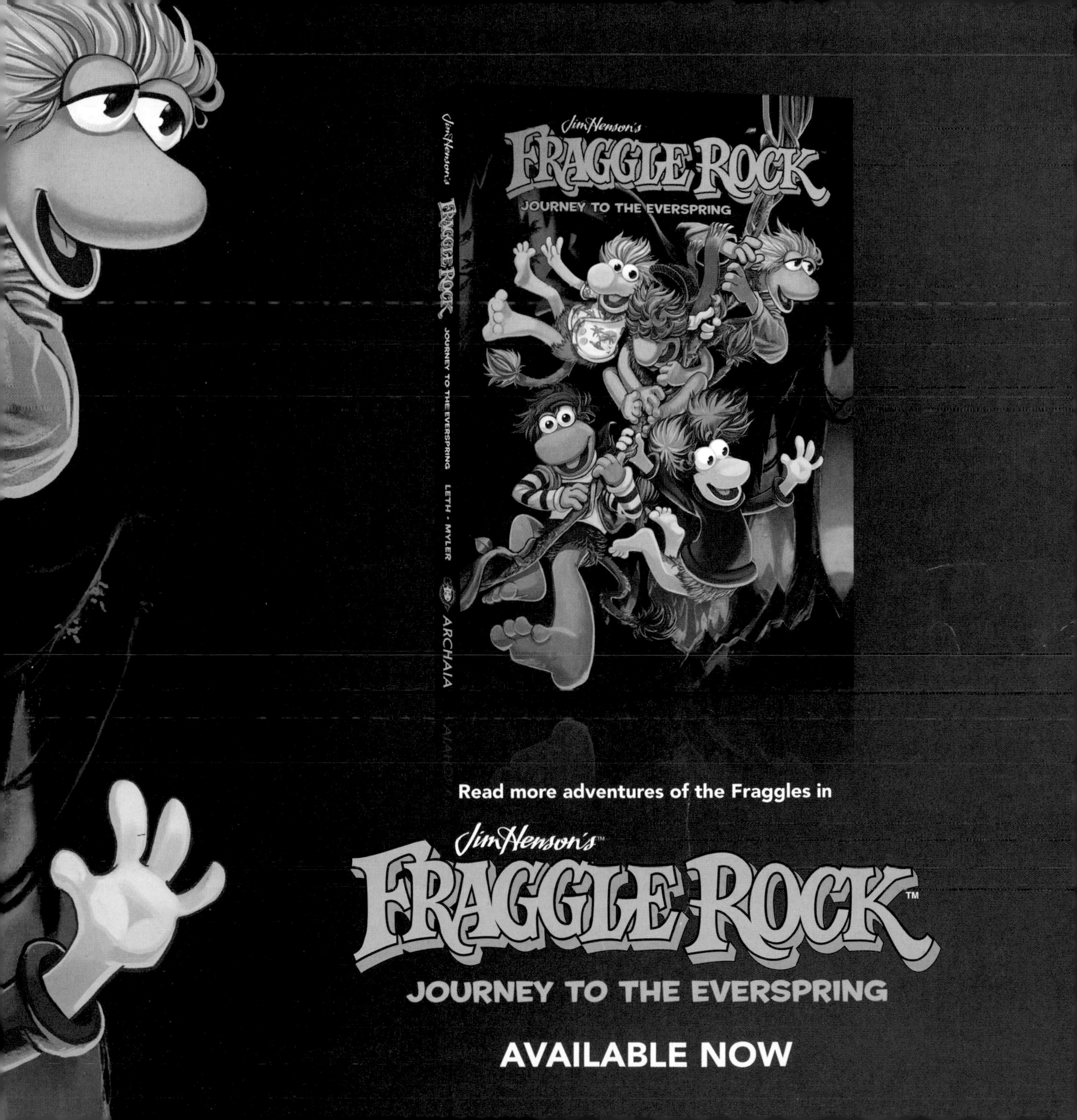
Jim Henson's
FRAGGLE ROCK
JOURNEY TO THE EVERSPRING
Jim Henson's FRAGGLE ROCK JOURNEY TO THE EVERSPRING LETH · MYLER ARCHAIA
Read more adventures of the Fraggles in
Jim Henson's
FRAGGLE ROCK™
JOURNEY TO THE EVERSPRING
AVAILABLE NOW

DISCOVER
THE WORLD OF JIM HENSON

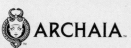
Jim Henson's Tale of Sand
Jim Henson, Jerry Juhl, Ramón K. Pérez
ISBN: 978-1-93639-309-1 | $29.95 US

Jim Henson's The Dark Crystal: Creation Myths
Brian Froud, Alex Sheikman, Joshua Dysart, and others
Volume 1
ISBN: 978-1-60886-704-2 | $14.99 US
Volume 2
ISBN: 978-1-60886-887-2 | $14.99 US
Volume 3
ISBN: 978-1-60886-906-0 | $14.99 US

Jim Henson's The Power of the Dark Crystal
Simon Spurrier, Kelly and Nichole Matthews
Volume 1
ISBN: 978-1-60886-992-3 | $24.99 US

Jim Henson's The Dark Crystal Tales
Cory Godbey
ISBN: 978-1-60886-845-2 | $16.99 US

Jim Henson's Labyrinth Artist Tribute
Michael Allred, Dave McKean, Faith Erin Hicks, and others
ISBN: 978-1-60886-897-1 | $24.99 US

Jim Henson's Labyrinth Adult Coloring Book
Jorge Corona, Jay Fosgitt, Phil Murphy
ISBN: 978-1-68415-111-0 | $16.99 US

Jim's Henson's The Musical Monsters of Turkey Hollow
Jim Henson, Jerry Juhl, Roger Langridge
ISBN: 978-1-60886-434-8 | $24.99 US

Jim Henson's The Storyteller: Witches
S.M. Vidaurri, Kyla Vanderklugt, Matthew Dow Smith, Jeff Stokely
ISBN: 978-1-60886-747-9 | $24.99 US

Jim Henson's The Storyteller: Dragons
Daniel Bayliss, Jorge Corona, Hannah Christensen, Nathan Pride
ISBN: 978-1-60886-874-2 | $24.99 US